THE
PRINCE'S
DOOM

THE
PRINCE'S
DOOM

DAVID BLIXT

Published by
Sordelet Ink

The Prince's Doom

In Loving Memory

Molly Glynn
(1968 – 2014)

A star so bright, she now
lights us from above.

For Janice —

I would be lost without you

CONTENTS

Dramatis Personae

♦ a character recorded by history   ◊ a character from Shakespeare

Della Scala Family of Verona

♦   FRANCESCO 'CANGRANDE' DELLA SCALA – Prince of Verona

♦   GIOVANNA DA SVEVIA – Cangrande's wife, Paride's aunt

♦   ALBERTO II DELLA SCALA – Cangrande's eldest nephew

♦/◊   MASTINO II DELLA SCALA – Cangrande's youngest nephew

♦   VERDE DELLA SCALA – Cangrande's eldest niece

♦   CATERINA DELLA SCALA – Cangrande's middle niece

♦   ALBUINA DELLA SCALA – Cangrande's youngest niece

♦/◊   FRANCESCO 'CESCO' DELLA SCALA – Cangrande's heir

◊   PARIDE DELLA SCALA – Cangrande's great-nephew, son of the late Cecchino della Scala

Nogarola Family of Vicenza

- **ANTONIO NOGAROLA** – Vicentine nobleman, elder brother to Bailardino

- **BAILARDINO NOGAROLA** – Lord of Vicenza, husband to Cangrande's sister, Katerina

- **KATERINA DELLA SCALA** – sister to Cangrande, wife of Bailardino

  BAILARDETTO 'DETTO' NOGAROLA – elder son of Bailardino and Katerina

◊ **VALENTINO NOGAROLA** – younger son of Bailardino and Katerina

Alaghieri Family of Florence

- **PIETRO ALAGHIERI** – Dante's heir, lawyer, knight of Verona

- **JACOPO 'POCO' ALAGHIERI** – Dante's youngest son

- **ANTONIA ALAGHIERI** – Dante's daughter, taking holy vows as Suor Beatrice

Carrara Family of Padua

- **MARSILIO DA CARRARA** – Lord of Padua, cousin of Gianozza Montecchio

- **NICCOLO DA CARRARA** – cousin of Marsilio, brother to Ubertino

- **UBERTINO DA CARRARA** – cousin of Marsilio, brother to Niccolo

- **CUNIZZA DA CARRARA** – sister of Marsilio

- **TADDEA DA CARRARA** – daughter of the late Il Grande da Carrara, cousin to Marsilio

Montecchio Family of Verona

◊ ROMEO MARIOTTO 'MARI' MONTECCHIO – Lord of the Montecchio family

◊ GIANOZZA DELLA BELLA – Mari's wife, cousin to Marsilio da Carrara

◊ ROMEO MARIOTTO MONTECCHIO II – son of Mari and Gianozza

AURELIA MONTECCHIO – sister to Mari, wife of Benvenito Lenoti

BENVENITO LENOTI – knight of Verona, husband to Aurelia Montecchio

◊ BENVOLIO LENOTI – son of Benvenito and Aurelia

Capulletto Family of Verona

◊ ANTONIO 'ANTONY' CAPULLETTO – Lord of the Capulletto family

◊ ARNALDO CAPULLETTO – uncle of Antony

◊ TESSA GUARINI – wife of Antony

◊ THEOBALDO 'THIBAULT' CAPULLETTO – nephew of Antony

◊ GIULIETTA CAPULLETTO – daughter of Antony and Tessa

Rienzi Family of Verona

GASPARDO RIENZI – Lord of the Rienzi family, cuckolded by Cangrande

ADAMO RIENZI – Gaspardo's son

ROSALIA 'LIA' RIENZI – Cangrande's natural daughter by Gaspardo's wife

SUPPORTING CHARACTERS

ABBESS VERDIANA – Benedictine abbess in charge of Santa Maria in Organo

◊ ABRAMO TIBERIO – gruff Veronese noble, friend to Rienzi

◆ ALBERTINO MUSSATO – Paduan historian-poet

◊ ANDRIOLO DA VERONA – Capulletto's chief groom, husband to Angelica

◊ ANGELICA DA VERONA –Giulietta's Nurse, wife to Andriolo

AVENTINO FRACASTORO – Personal physician to Cangrande

◊ BAPTISTA MINOLA – Paduan noble, father of Katerina and Bianca

◆ BERNARDO ERVARI – knight of Verona, member of the Anziani

◆ BISHOP FRANCIS – Franciscan Bishop, leader of Veronese spiritual growth

◊ FRA LORENZO – Franciscan friar with family in France

◆ FRANCESCO DANDOLO – Venetian nobleman

◆ FRANCESCO 'PETRARCH' PETRARCHA – Florentine exile, aspiring poet, studied at Bologna

◆ GHERARDO PETRARCHA – younger brother to Petrarch

◆ GUGLIELMO CASTELBARCO – Veronese nobleman, Cangrande's Armourer

◆ GUGLIELMO CASTELBARCO II – Castelbarco's son

GUISEPPE MORSICATO – Nogarola family doctor

◊ HORTENSO & PETRUCHIO II BONAVENTURA – twin sons of Katerina and Petruchio

◊ KATERINA BONAVENTURA – Paduan-born heiress, daughter of Baptista Minola

♦ MANOELLO GIUDEO – Cangrande's Master of Revels

MASSIMILIANO DA VILLAFRANCA – Constable of Cangrande's palace

♦ NICCOLO DA LOZZO – Paduan-born knight, changed sides to join Cangrande

◊ PETRUCHIO BONAVENTURA – Veronese noble, married to Katerina

◊ SHALAKH – Jewish Venetian money-lender, father of Jessica

THARWAT AL-DHAAMIN – Moorish master astrologer, called the Arūs

TULLIO D'ISOLA – aged steward, Grand Butler to Cangrande

♦ WILLIAM MONTAGU – English knight, distant relative of the Montecchi

♦ ZILIBERTO DELL'ANGELO – Cangrande's Master of the Hunt

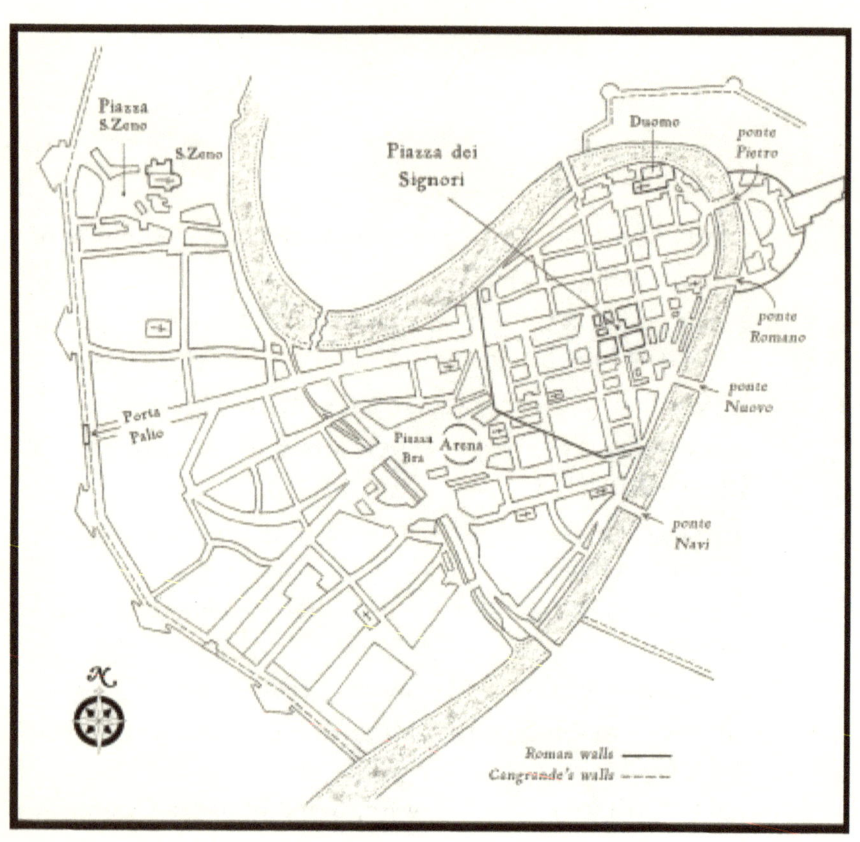

The City of Verona

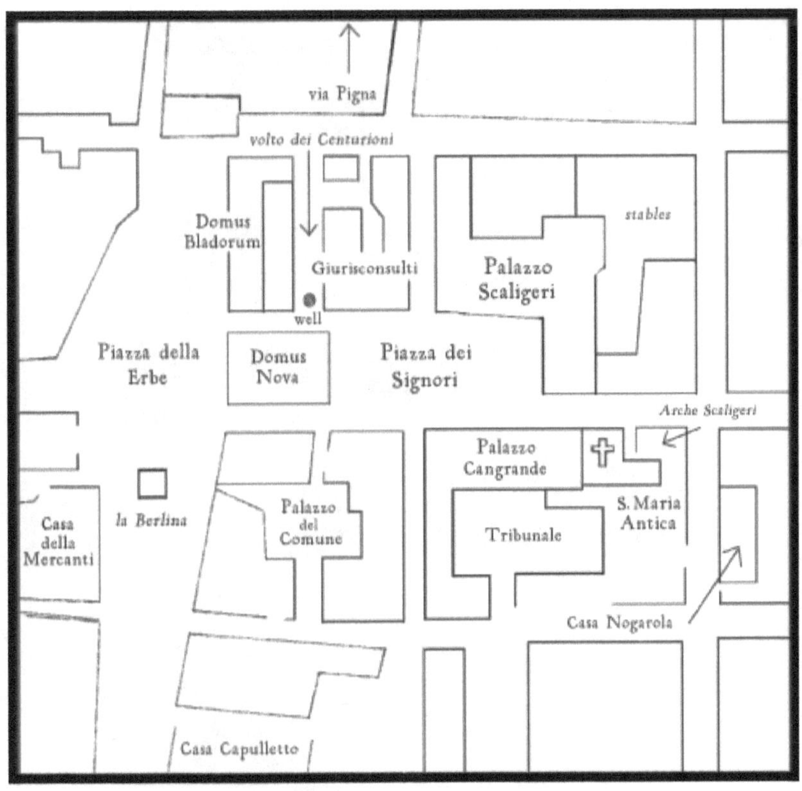

Piazza dei Signori

Northern Italy
Adige
Lago di Garda
Rivole
Treviso
Vicenza
Illasi
Montecchio
Venice
Verona
San Bonifacio
Padua
Cremona
Adige River
Calvatone
Mantua
Po River
Bologna
Ravenna
40 Miles
Lucca
Florence
Pisa
Arno River

ROMEO

Father, what news? what is the prince's doom?
What sorrow craves acquaintance at my hand,
That I yet know not?

FRIAR LAURENCE

                    Too familiar
Is my dear son with such sour company:
I bring thee tidings of the prince's doom.

~ Romeo & Juliet
Act Three, Scene Three

PROLOGUE

Verona, Italy
Saturday, 26 November 1328

"Show me 'yes'."

Dark as an angry sky, the polished marble teardrop twitched, then began to describe a sinister circle.

"Show me 'no'."

The stone at the end of the chain adroitly changed direction. Watching, Elisabetta Contarini gasped and clutched the medal of her namesake, Santa Elizabetta of Portugal. "You're doing that."

"No, Madonna. Ask your questions and you will hear the truth."

It took her a moment to parse his accent before she obeyed. "Tell me – will Soranzo survive the year?"

The question was repeated. The chain at the end of the diviner's finger continued in the same direction. *No.*

Elisabetta glanced anxiously to her husband, sitting in bored submission.

"Will my husband become Doge?"

Reversing, the teardrop spun leftwards with some force. A resounding *Yes*.

Watching from across the room, Francesco Dandolo was annoyed with himself for feeling pleased. Everyone knew he would be the next Doge. At seventy years of age, he had certainly showed patience, serving Venice with able devotion. He had endured many hardships and perjured his soul to rise to the top of the Signoria. Barring any drastic change in Fortune's wheel, Dandolo would be elected the moment Soranzo released the last bonds of life.

Which would happen soon, according to this man. But Dandolo refused to be drawn in by such a grotesque mountebank. He had not wanted to admit the man at all, but Zanino had been favourably impressed. As guests in an enemy city, and without invitation to the revels this night, they required amusement. If Elisabetta found the man's trade entrancing, it did not hurt to indulge her, even if it was utter nonsense. Astrology, phrenology, numerology, palmistry, divination – fashionable pastimes. Though Doge Soranzo certainly put stock in such arts.

Not that the Doge would appreciate tonight's prediction. While Elisabetta pressed on to more mundane matters – when the next shipment of silk would arrive, the birthdate of their latest grandchild – Dandolo tried to divine the man himself. Perhaps a soldier, crippled on some battlefield. For there had been an injury, a dreadful one. The right shoulder was badly bunched, and there was a crimp in the diviner's left hip that forced him to rely on a heavy crutch. Worst of all was his visage. Whatever his other wounds, the left side of his face had received a devastating blow, causing his eye-socket to collapse inwards. Little wonder he kept his cowl forward. His was a face to turn the stoutest stomach.

But his voice was strong and clear, if marred by the unintelligible accent of Bergamo. His pendulum answered each question in turn. Wisely, not every answer was satisfying. Nothing makes an audience more suspicious than convenient truths.

There were clever wrinkles to the business, too. He carried a calendar, and let the pendulum hover over this date or that. He also carried a map of Italy, crudely drawn. Naples was in the wrong place. But it allowed him to answer more than simple binary questions.

After twenty minutes, Elisabetta turned to her husband. "Ask it something."

Dandolo smiled thinly. "Why is the sky blue?"

Elisabetta pouted. "Ask it something only you would know."

Loving his wife, he relented. "Did I eat pickled apricots yesterday?"

The man had a fifty-fifty chance, and guessed correctly. At his wife's urging, Dandolo posed several more queries of no consequence. Each time the answer was true.

Being lucky was better than being good. Time to trick the diviner. "Did I meet the Greyhound today?"

It was well known that he had dined at the Scaligeri palace

at noon, part of the many who had flooded into Verona for this momentous occasion. So when the dark pendulum tugged the chain to describe a negative, Elisabetta sighed in disappointment.

Dandolo frowned. "Has Venice bestowed its citizenship upon the Greyhound?"

Again, the answer was no. Elisabetta was distraught. Venice had certainly offered citizenship to Cangrande della Scala – it had happened months ago. Everyone knew.

Not by word or gesture did Dandolo betray his sudden interest. It was a truth known only to a few that the man commonly called *Il Veltro*, the Greyhound, was not the true owner of that mythic title. The name belonged to his natural child, whom Dandolo had not seen today, and who had not been granted the rare privilege of citizenship.

Several more questions, pointed now. All the answers were true. Either this crippled hulk was a genius of deception, or his gift was real.

Dandolo called for wine. "Put your tool down. If we go on, you'll flay the skin from your hand."

The man's finger and thumb were indeed raw, and he accepted the cup of mulled wine with surprise. He knew the pendulum had been wrong about those two questions. Yet clearly the Venetian lord's interest had been piqued.

Dandolo sipped his favoured beverage. "I can see why Zanino insisted you call upon us. You have a rare talent. Have you always been so blessed?"

"There are some would call it a curse, my lord."

"Of course. In Venice such things are tolerated. But many devout souls see it as witchcraft. Trading with the Devil. Is that how you came by your infirmities?"

"No, my lord. I took these many years ago, in Padua."

"It has been a long war," offered Dandolo. "You must be pleased to see the seal set on peace."

The man shrugged his good shoulder. "I'm here to ply my trade. This is where the people are."

"Where the people are indeed," said Dandolo after navigating the man's accent. "But you did not answer my question. Have you always been so talented?"

"No," admitted the diviner. "It came after my injuries."

Dandolo raised his brows. "Compensation, after a fashion."

"Yes, lord." Clearly uncomfortable, the cripple finished his drink, too quickly to be polite, then set it aside. "It grows late. Are there any last questions you'd like answered?"

Dandolo rose. "No, but thank you. It has been an illuminating evening."

Elisabetta said, "O, you're not leaving? Francesco, you should put him on retainer. Your own spy into the divine."

Dandolo paused. There *was* one question to which he would like an honest answer. How to phrase it? "Tell me this. I have been made an offer by someone here in Verona. My question is twofold. One, is the offer honest?"

The chain, the teardrop, the question. For the first time, the answer was equivocal, with the pendulum swinging in all directions. The diviner apologized, but Dandolo waved him off. "It was a poor question. Here is a better one. If I accept, will it benefit Venice?"

The bob on the chain spun leftwards so hard and so fast it might have pulled itself from the diviner's fingers.

Dandolo's mouth twitched. "Thank you. My mind is quite made up. Zanino will see you paid. One more thing. Should I seek your services again, where shall I find you?"

"I'm at the Duo Gentes, lord."

"And what was your name?"

"Girolamo of Bergamo, my lord."

"Thank you, Girolamo, for a most illuminating evening."

As an excited Elisabetta raced to her closet to pen letters to her daughters, Dandolo waited until Zanino returned. How distressing, to see the first streaks of grey in his own son's hair. The only son left to him, regrettably not by his wife. But it is a foolish man who places all hope of posterity in one womb.

"I hope your guest amused Donna Elisabetta, my lord."

"Mightily. Now, as to the other matter. Send word to our Veronese friend – we accept."

♦   ◊   ♦

London, England

"And where is the Earl of March today?" It was the middle of the night, and the king tapped his foot in annoyance.

"On the road, your highness," said Lord William Montagu, the king's longtime friend. "He's chased Lancaster out of Winchester, and is returning."

Edward III, King of England, grew momentarily still. "He did not catch Lancaster then?"

"The Earl had a lucky escape."

Lucky indeed. Lancaster was a danger. But more dangerous was what would happen once he was dead. The king grunted and resumed his troubled tapping.

Montagu reflected that it had been a year for narrow escapes. Edward himself had almost been captured by the Scots. Returning, the king had barely escaped falling into the power of one of his own subjects, the Earl of Lancaster.

Not that escape meant freedom. The sixteen year-old king was under the sway of Roger Mortimer, newly-made Earl of March and, as all knew, lover to the King's mother, Isabella of France. King Edward hated his mother's paramour, of that Montagu was sure. That he was obedient to Mortimer's wishes was equally certain. Montagu wished he understood why.

Mortimer had spearheaded the invasion two years ago, championing his lover's son as rightful ruler of England in place of that degenerate cuckold Edward II. Victorious, Mortimer discovered a taste for power, for riches, for rule. He was opposed by many, the most recent being Henry Crouchback, Third Earl of Lancaster, who sought to capture the young king and use him to rule in Mortimer's place.

Lions fighting over their prey. Having spent twenty-one of his twenty-seven years at court, Montagu knew that this new King Edward was not one to enjoy being thought of as prey.

Pent-up energy propelled the king from his chair. "Stuck here all winter! We should have gone abroad."

Freshly knighted, the king's brother John grinned. "I *told* you. We should have gone to Crecy."

"If I go to France, it will have to be with either gold or an army. Cousin Philippe is demanding tribute."

"An army, then." John was twelve years old.

"What army? All our soldiers are too busy fighting each other. They can't even hold Scotland...!"

Montagu knew that was the root of the king's ill-humour. While his growth was stunted under other men's shears, the rights his grandfather had squeezed from Scotland were all lost through the so-called Peace of Northampton. Now his French lands were threatened too, and there was nothing to be done. Not until the day when he was free to wield the power he held now only in name.

The king paced, biting back the worst of his thoughts, lest an incautious word be reported to Mortimer. They all knew they were being overheard by servants feed by the Earl of March.

The king saw Montagu yawn. "Do we bore you, Lord William?"

"No, your grace. I was kept awake last night by my son's bawling." In June, William's wife had given birth to a lusty boy with lungs of iron.

The king grunted. Montagu knew his sovereign was abstaining from the royal marriage bed, and for good cause. If he should produce an heir on his fourteen year-old bride, the Earl of March might see an opportunity to remove a second king and rule until the infant reached his majority. Best not to tempt Lord Mortimer to a second usurpation.

This shared thought sent Edward into a new tirade. When the king said, "…it makes me sick…", Montagu felt a flash of inspiration.

"If it truly makes your highness unwell, perhaps we should send to the Italian for a cure."

Edward frowned. "And what should Pancio do to cure a man sick at heart?" Pancio de Controne was the king's personal physician, a native of the city of Lucca who studied medicine at the University of Bologna.

"Tell you tales from Italy, of course. He still has many correspondents there. I know he is friendly with a doctor I met in Verona two years ago." The king was uninterested. There had to be some way to make his meaning heard. Snapping his fingers, Montagu pretended to think. "What is the date?"

With the king occupied in frustration, the Prince of Wales replied. "Four days until the Feast of Saint Andrew."

"Ah!" cried Lord Montagu. "The heirs of Verona are to wed tomorrow!"

Edward paused in his pacing. "Each other?"

The king's little brother howled with laughter while Montagu pressed doggedly on. "Forgive me, your highness, no. The two male cousins are each to marry young women from outside Verona."

"How old is the heir?"

"Fourteen or so."

"I sympathize," said the king.

Montagu pursed his lips. "Marriage has its challenges."

Edward grinned. "And rewards. I've seen Catherine. I hope she has recovered from being brought to bear."

"Fully recovered, my liege." Dismissing a frisson of unease, Montagu tried again to convey his message. "They are celebrating a peace as well. But in their case, they have won all their rights. I've told you of Verona's daring lord. As I understand, only one city holds out against him." Feeling the king's outraged eyes upon him, only too late did Montagu realize that his words were insulting. He quickly pressed on. "When your Grace gave me permission to joust there, I found Italy a most friendly land. Verona, especially." It was as far as he could go.

It was far enough. The King's eyes sharpened for a scant moment before glazing with feigned boredom. "I would like to see an Italian of the mold you describe. I've never met one yet worth a groat. Or a goat."

"Your highness, shall I buy you one?"

"A goat?" asked John with a grin.

The king smacked his brother's head playfully. "I have no need of goats, Sir John. William meant an Italian. Do, Lord Montagu, by all means. Find me an Italian to lighten my spirits. If you find one that is not too dear, perhaps we can make him dance."

A question asked, a question answered. Now, whom to send? Who could be trusted, and was yet expendable? Montagu only felt a small shame when the name came to him.

That name was Montagu.

◆　　◇　　◆

Bellamonte, Italy

Tail between his legs, Don Pedro, Prince of Aragon, tried not to gallop from the palace of the orphaned heiress. Never had he been so humiliated. He imagined the beautiful, cruel woman laughing at him, though she had not laughed to his face. Her cousin Nerissa had, though, and he'd heard their voices raised in the tiled chamber as he fled, dignity in tatters.

Still clutched in his hand was a mocking device, the source of his humiliation. A small head on a stick, painted as a foole, a jester, complete with bells and ribbons. From inside its head came the rattle of a single stone knocking about as proof of the cavernous emptiness it contained.

The only warm spot for him was the obvious sympathy conveyed by the lady's servant. Young Balthasar had not been bold enough to speak, but his eyes were free of contempt or, worse, pity. They had said, *You're well out of it, my lord.*

But Pedro was not out of it. He had taken a vow, one he had thought nothing of at the time, since he had not conceived he would fail. *Hubris. A meaningless word, until applied.*

The vow was in three parts. For the first, never to reveal the details of his failure, he was happy – nay, eager – to comply. Second, to depart at once and never trouble the woman more – well, Pedro was more than willing never to see the lady again in this life.

It was the last part of the oath that troubled him. His father would never have allowed him to swear it, for Pedro had just blunted his line. No more sons for the house of Aragon. *Legitimate sons,* Pedro corrected himself. *There is always Juan. He swore no vow. But he was always cleverer than I.*

After a considerable time sulking on the road, in the dark, Pedro had enough sense to order them to find a place for the night. He had not told his steward anything save that he had guessed wrong. The crimson in his cheek instructed Maurizio not to speak further. "Very good, my lord. And, so that I might prepare our train, where shall we be heading in the morning?"

After today, Pedro did not want to think of facing anyone. But at last he found an answer. "Verona. We shall arrive too late for the wedding, but I should like to meet this young prince."

It was not the wedding he had hoped to celebrate. Don Pedro hoped this other young prince proved wiser than he. For though chastened, there was not a mean bone in Don Pedro's body. Privilege had made him arrogant, this Prince of Aragon. But now, he hoped, he would amend his faults and live a better life in the future.

And, he did not say, *I should also like to speak again to this astrologer my father sets so much store by. If my future is not here, then I should like to know where it lies, and what my foolish vow means.* He looked down at the grinning rattle in his hand. *For I am a foole. And by my own doing, no one else's. I made a foole of myself.*

There was at least some comfort in that. If the foolishness was his, then it was within his power to mend. Even in the crimson surge of humiliation, he took comfort in that. It would be worse if he were powerless, unable to remove the taint of the foole from his person. He was in control of his destiny. This was a lesson. It was time to grow up. No more cut doublets and pearled hose. Practicality, that was the key. Be practical, and preserve what honour he retained. He could no longer be above anything, not even the most menial task...

Recalling, he realized there was something he could do to prove himself. A small deed, but one that just yesterday he would have found degrading. "We shall stop at Pisa along the way and retrieve Señor Leonato's niece. And from there, on to Verona to congratulate the Greyhound and his heir."

◆   ◊   ◆

Aden, Yemen

Abū 'Abd Allāh Muḥammad ibn 'Abd Allāh al-Lawātī al-Ṭanjī ibn Baṭūṭah, known to his few Latin acquaintances as Ibn Battuta, paused in his writing to gaze west. The setting sun sparkled across the water and cast long shadows on the land beyond.

Travel invigorated Ibn Battuta. Already he had twice completed the *hajj*, journeying from Alexandria to Cairo, then up the Nile to Aydhab, only to be turned back and forced to reach Mecca through Damascus and Medina. But that was not nearly enough. Bitten with wanderlust, he had gone on to Shiraz and Bagdad before returning to Mecca to study for almost a year. Now he was off again, exploring the area around the Red Sea, first on the dangerous waters, then overland to Taiz and now Aden.

His lone regret, occasional yet striking, was lacking the right person with whom to share this adventure. Not a woman — there were always women. Rather, a friend, a kindred soul, someone as interested in the heated baths of Bagdad as in the stars of a desert sky.

Thought of the stars brought one man to mind. The tutor, whom he had not seen but once in the last fifteen years, yet with whom he still corresponded when so many friends had fallen away. Ibn Battuta considered himself blessed to have been able to study at the knee of such a wise man even for that one year. It was precious in life to find a teacher like Tharwat al-Dhaamin.

Three years ago, al-Dhaamin had been Battuta's only choice for a companion. That letter had gone astray, taking nearly a year to find his mentor. Al-Dhaamin's reply found Battuta already in Medina, and spoke of obligations of iron.

Ibn Battuta continued to write, cajoling the elder man with all the wondrous sights of the East. Tharwat did not reply for a long time, and when he did he wrote of injuries. Severe ones, if mentioned at all by one so reticent. Indeed, the only subject al-Dhaamin waxed eloquently upon was his latest pupil, the young Prince of Verona. Nothing would please the old astrologer more than that his two disciples should meet and share their knowledge. But al-Dhaamin worried it might be too soon for such a meeting:

> His mind is ready, but his spirit is not. He is in a temper, and must be tempered by the hammer of age before he is ready. If that day comes, if I am still alive, if he is free, I shall bring him. We sail on a sea of uncertainty.

So eloquent in writing. Yet Battuta could not help imagining each word being conjured through that scarred and mistreated throat. He had never heard the tale of those scars. He worried he never would.

Ibn Battuta dipped the quill in ink and set it to the paper:

> I am troubled to hear of your infirmities. You are kind to remind me of my good fortune, for good health is truly a crown worn by the healthy that only the ill can see.
>
> As for your charge, the little prince who is almost a man, I say from this city, built in a volcano's shell, be careful of striking cold iron. A carpenter's door is loose. Do not be so free with your wisdom that there is none left for your worthy self.
>
> Still, if that day comes, if he is free, bring him to me, and I shall teach him how I ride the wind.

With that, Ibn Battuta washed the ink from his fingers and offered the packet of letters to the next ship sailing westwards. There was no telling when it would arrive. But at least the astrologer could now easily be found. His stars had placed him in Verona.

◆　　　◊　　　◆

Verona, Italy

The noise was annihilating. Berthold von Neifen, Count of Marstetten, Imperial Vicar of Italy, trusted right-hand to His Grace Ludwig, King of Germany, King of Italy, King of the Romans, and Holy Roman Emperor, closed the shutters, hoping to shutter the sound as well. Prince Rupert was out there, carousing and cavorting with the bridegrooms and the rest of the nobility. But Berthold wanted sleep. It would be an early morning, and while the intemperate Rupert was the emperor's nephew, it was the Count of Marstetten who stood as official imperial representative. For the second time in ten years, Berthold held the title of Imperial Vicar to this rich and richly contested country.

It was a duty Berthold both enjoyed and loathed. He liked Italy, but not Italians. He found them too susceptible to types. Heartless Florentines. Loud and lusty Romans. Those noble inebriates, the Venetians. Big-hearted but sly and lazy Napolitani. Puffed-up Milanese. Skinflint Genoese. Stuffy Padovani. Hedonistic Bolognese. Unintelligible Bergamaschi. Every one of them ready to smile and wrap you in their arms, leaving a knife in your back.

The country had so much promise – land, climate, sea, all full of prosperity. And prosperity led to achievement, both materially and philosophically. So much of culture had begun here.

Yet that culture had fled. The Holy Roman throne was now in Germany, while the papacy was in Avignon (despite Berthold's friend the anti-pope now in Rome). So busy squabbling over minutiae, these Italians could not hold on to what was their own. Woe betide the world if there ever came another Aeneas, another Romulus, another Caesar, to pull them together and unite them once more.

Which is why Verona gave the Emperor such unease. Other cities focused on excelling in one or two fields – war, trade, banking, religion, art. Verona threatened to exceed its neighbors in all. Tomorrow it would take another large stride towards ultimate excellence. After that, it was not a question of if Italy would challenge the Empire, but when. The Greyhound's ambition swelled so large, it stretched the sides of the world.

Despite the loss of an eye, the Count of Marstetten saw the world clearly. At thirty-eight years he was able to hold two opposing thoughts without qualm. In his heart he quite liked the heir of Verona, if not his sire. But in his mind he saw the danger in them both. If Rupert did not succeed, if this prince was not brought under the imperial yoke, there was only one alternative.

While it would pain Berthold to cause young Franz's destruction, pain would not stay his hand.

◆   ◇   ◆

Avignon, France

"Verona shows potential."

Cardinal Napoleone Orsini nearly choked on his bread. His host quickly offered water to wash it down. When he could speak, Orsini merely repeated the city's name, his tone conveying his incredulity.

"You've had letters, I trust. Tomorrow is the wedding. The Greyhound makes peace, not war. The Holy Father approves such Christian acts, yes?"

"I think his approval is tempered by the fact that Verona is thick with the Bavarian. Those runagates Occam and Bonagratia – they were welcomed by the Scaliger. And helped by your friend Alaghieri," added the Cardinal with heavy warning.

Francesco Petrarca ran a finger around the lip of his goblet.

"Ser Pietro knew them while he was here. No one can fault him for friendship to a pair of wayward souls."

"He helped introduce them to the Emperor. He and his master are lucky not to find themselves excommunicated once more."

Again Orsini's tone conveyed more than his words. This time it said his sympathies were not entirely aligned with Avignon's. Not that they had ever been. More than rooting the Church in a foreign land, this pope had changed the very nature of the papacy, in ways Orsini could barely stomach, loyal though he was sworn to be. And the cardinal liked Pietro Alaghieri very much.

Petrarch continued to trace the circle of his cup. "Still, I think you should suggest the Holy Father reach out to the Greyhound again."

"Whyever would he do that?"

"Because Pietro writes that the Scaliger and the Emperor are like two stags in a forest. The elder may have more bulk, but the young one is eager, and has more points on his rack. The Pope might be interested in taming the younger one. After all, which would the Scaliger prefer, an overlord close at hand, or one far away in Avignon?"

"That sounds rather more fanciful than I recall Pietro being."

Petrarch bowed his head. "I may have added the colour of simile."

"I had a feeling." Orsini was beginning to warm to the idea, which worked on many levels. There were obvious papal benefits in driving a wedge between Verona and Emperor Ludwig. Obvious, too, the accolades that would fall on Orsini should he suggest it and be proven correct.

Less obvious was why Petrarch was making the suggestion. Helping Verona would benefit his former client, Ser Alaghieri of Florence. Who, it was said, had topped Petrarca's sister and left her with child. Yet here was the girl's brother, acting in Alaghieri's interest. Far from aggrieved, it seemed almost as if he owed something to the Italian knight.

Perhaps it was solidarity, from one aspiring poet to the son of another. Perhaps Petrarch had even played Pander under his own roof. One never knew with poets, who were hardly better than actors.

Whatever the suggestion's origin, it was worth exploring. "I shall suggest it to His Holiness. But he does not often listen to me."

Petrarch raised his gaze from his cup and grinned. "Your Eminence, I'm amazed you're listening to *me*."

◆   ◊   ◆

Verona, Italy

Not being at all fanciful, Pietro Alaghieri was not prone to dreams. Yet through the years, one dream had plagued him. It came again tonight. He prayed this time would be different. But the end was never in doubt.

As always, it began with him climbing down a rocky slope towards a river very like the Adige, where the landslides from the mountains had left great stones lining the water's edge. He felt the bite of the stone on his fingers.

By his side was Pietro's ward and foster-son. The dream Cesco had once been only a child. Now he mirrored his age in the waking world. Curling chestnut hair reached his shoulders, partially obscuring the eyes that shifted between calm blue and wild green. Nearly a man, there was the first trace of stubble on his chin. The scar by his eye crinkled whenever he smiled.

The ferociously lean black hound by Cesco's side yelped as something crashed behind them. Pietro glanced back at the terrible monster hurling stones at them from high on the hill. Cesco merely laughed, wild and careless.

As always, the only hope of safety was the river. But this was not the Adige. It was the *Phlegethon*, the burning river of blood where those damned for violence were tortured for all eternity.

All at once their path was blocked by centaurs, an unending army of half-horse, half-men battling each other on the water's edge. They did not fight with bow and arrow, as centaurs should. Instead Pietro saw their curved swords arcing, slicing, casting flecks of blood and viscera into the air.

The ground beneath them shifted slightly. No longer upon a ruined hillside, Pietro and Cesco viewed the roiling river from the balcony of Verona's famous Arena. The stands were filled with cheering men and women, like at the gladiatorial games of old.

Pietro wanted the dream to be different. He wanted to flee, to hide, to survive. Above all, he wanted to keep quiet. He knew what speaking would bring. Still, he found himself saying, "We're safe now."

Fateful words. The centaurs all looked up, their leader shouting, "To what torment do you come, you two approaching down the slope! Tell us from there. If not, I draw my bow!"

A centaur with grey haunches pointed to Pietro. "Do you observe the one behind dislodges what he touches? That's not what the feet of dead men do!"

The bloody corpses on the Arena floor and the writhing figures in the river beyond all turned their heads, spying Pietro with accusing eyes.

Cesco held up his hands, palms forward. "It is true! He is not dead! I am his guide here, at the request of the Scaligeri!"

If this had been his father's poem, they would have climbed onto a centaur's back and been carried across the river. But Cesco's answer enraged the centaurs, who bucked and reared, clanging their swords together in dire applause. Cesco grasped the coin at his neck.

"Who are you?" asked Pietro.

Cesco's smile was wry. "Who were you expecting?"

"A god. Or a poet."

"Granted in both!" Screaming in joy, Cesco leapt from the balcony into the fray, the massive black hound charging after him.

Down among the centaurs, dancing across the backs of his foes, Cesco was slaughter personified, slicing horse and human flesh with wild swings of his sword. In French, Cesco sang out, *"Si Dieu ne me veut ayder, le Diable ne me peut manquer!"*

Pietro ran to the lip of the balcony, watching in desperate hope. Would Cesco make it this time? Would he reach the river? "Mercurio!" he called in encouragement. "Mercurio!"

"Close enough!" the warrior-child shouted in Arabic.

The dream was almost over, but Pietro fought wakefulness. This time Cesco would make it! He would reach the river, cross it, be free! This time—

Cesco disappeared beneath the centaurs, who turned to cats, pawing and ripping at something beneath them. Pietro screamed—

And woke. Sweating, pale, terrified, with the name of Mercury on his lips. Rolling out of bed, he rose and threw open a shutter to gaze out at the still November night. He had never really had nightmares – not like Cesco, who had suffered them all his life. But this one had pursued Pietro for fourteen years. The details altered. For a time, Pietro had worn silver armor. For a year and more, Cesco had worn a mask. Once in a while other faces appeared – the Moor, the doctor, Pietro's sister.

One face was notable for its absence. The *Capitano di Verona* had never once made an appearance. The omission felt significant.

Pietro had tried to make sense of the dream, of course. As portents were the Moor's business, he'd shared the details with Tharwat al-Dhaamin, but found no answers. The scene was from

L'Inferno. The Mercury references were likely due to the coin at the boy's throat, though somehow Pietro felt they pre-dated that ornament. The coin was real enough. Pietro had found it on the night he first met Cesco, and for a time it had hung about the neck of Pietro's own hound called Mercurio.

In daylight, Pietro could convince himself that this was just a dream born of his father's poetry. In moments like this, the dream was all too real. Cesco, fighting until his death. Pietro watching, helpless.

Knowing sleep would not return, Pietro started to dress. His page had laid out the clothes the night before. They were new, and remarkably fine, the best he had ever owned. Putting them on, he felt like he was donning a funeral shroud.

No need to wonder why the dream had bubbled up on this of all nights. For this was the eve of what promised to be the worst day of his life. Of all their lives.

Father knew, thought Pietro. *Father understood there are worse things than a river of blood, or death by a sword. Worse even than a lake of ice, where betrayers dwell. There is exile. Not exile from home. Exile from one's self.*

Bells began to ring, and with them came the first strains of music. Resting his head against the doorjamb, Pietro breathed deeply. Then, squaring his shoulders, he opened the door to face the trial ahead.

Just as in the dream, Pietro was doomed to watch helplessly as events swallowed the marvelous mischief-maker whole.

I

To Wive and Thrive

ONE

Verona, Italy
Saturday, 26 November 1328

VERONA'S ENDURING WAR with Padua ended not with a clash of steel or a charge of horse, but a peal of bells. Wedding bells. Today the leading families of the feuding cities were sealing the bond of peace in matrimonial bliss, binding the kindred of Cangrande della Scala, Capitano di Verona, to that of Marsilio da Carrara, Capitano da Padua.

Whatever talk there was of union and partnership, one family would clearly dominate. After fifteen years of war, Padua was vowing to love, honour, and obey.

The two months prior had been a frantic rush unparalleled in recent history. To start, Carrara surprised everyone by recalling all the Paduan exiles save two. Padua's internal strife had been far more destabilizing than the war itself, rising to such a crescendo of violence that it was preferable for Carrara to hand the city to his enemy than to trust his own family. Thus his cousin Niccolo did not receive a pardon.

Nor did the poet Albertino Mussato, who'd savaged Carrara's disastrous rule and even this recent salvation. Mussato's continued exile entirely suited Cangrande, who had never quite forgiven the poet for the savage literary tongue-lashing he'd received in Mussato's play *Ecerinis*.

Today's double wedding promised to be the grandest event in Veronese history – quite a statement! Cangrande had always been praised for his open-handed entertainments, but now florins and ducats flowed as if carried down the Alps along the Adige.

Not that he spent his own money. Verona's allies — Mantua, Bergamo, Cremona, and Vicenza — all sent presents of food, drink, and expensive wedding trinkets, while Lucca donated huge rolls of their famous cloth. As the bride, Padua was forced to offer a substantial dowry to defray the cost of these nuptial extravagances.

The most surprising gift came from the Venetians. In place of the traditional gold cup for the bride, they presented two heavy goblets of flawless blue glass, one for each couple. A credulous soul might even think they approved.

These signs of respect were evidence of Cangrande's growing pre-eminence. By conquering Padua, the Scaliger had arguably become the most powerful man in Italy, and the way it had been done — peacefully, reasonably — only enhanced his stature. At thirty-seven, Cangrande was now the undisputed leader of the Ghibelline party, controlling all of the Feltro.

Almost. There was no gift from Guecello Tempesta, ruler of Treviso, who was too occupied in fortifying his walls in anticipation of a summer siege to send his regards.

But the prospect of war with Treviso paled against the incredible goings-on inside Verona's own walls. Members of various guilds capered in the streets as if it were *Carnevale*, dressed in silks and linens of every shade the dyers' rainbow could offer. Entertainers of all stripes descended on the city in droves, all housed at the Scaliger's expense. Actors, musicians, painters, poets, magicians, dancers, riders, and jugglers were put to work at once for impromptu plays, shows, and concerts at all hours, in every square.

Verona owned a deserved reputation for contests. The hunts during the late Cecchino della Scala's wedding were fabled, the annual twin races known as the Palio legendary, and the tourney two years past had been as exciting as any contest in Rome's Colosseum. But the wedding celebrations promised to show them all up as cheap and tawdry masques.

After weeks of revels and sport, the promised day had arrived. The private stages of the marriage, *impalmamento* and *sponsalia*, had already been performed. Today was *matrimonium*, the ring-day, a ceremony that was particularly Italian. Germans and Frenchmen exchanged rings upon betrothal, but in Italy the ring set the seal on the marriage.

Verona was packed to bursting. Nobles from France, Germany, Brabant, Burgundy, Aragon, Sicily, Zeeland, Denmark and other nearby nations flocked for the event, only to find the city already teeming with citizens from all over the Italian peninsula. Even the Emperor had overlooked his festering discontent with the Scaliger to send his nephew along with many favoured knights and courtiers. After all, one of the bridegrooms had been the Emperor's own page for over a year.

The packed streets were ripe for low thieves and rascals who knew how to cut a purse, pluck a ring from a finger, or strip a man of his best knife without giving the slightest sign. City guards were conspicuous, resplendent in their bright yellow and blue garb. Their striped tabards bore the Scaligeri seal, the ladder topped by a two-headed eagle with a snarling hound at the base. Their halberds, bedecked in garlands, demonstrated the victory of peace over war that these marriages symbolized.

As dawn approached, excitement rippled through the air. Manuello Giudeo, Cangrande's aged Master of Revels, meant this to be his swan song, the pinnacle of his career.

It began, as all weddings should, with music. At first simply a select band of strings to greet the pre-dawn light. The musicians were placed on balconies and rooftops across the city, filling the air with sustained notes, long strings to fish for men's hearts.

The fifes joined in with the rising sun, livening the jostle and bustle below. More wind instruments followed and finally, scant minutes before the procession set out, drums. But these drums were placed below ground, in the excavated Roman ruins beneath the Piazza dei Signori and the Piazza delle Erbe. Their hammering pulse seemed to rise from the very earth itself.

The drums stopped as the air was shattered by a blaze of trumpets. The palace doors flung wide to hurl forth twenty angelic children strewing rose-petals in their wake, followed by acrobats and jugglers. Next came minor priests and monks, holy men without family to elevate them to notoriety. Solemn as the moment was, they could not help smiling, their joy mirroring their flock's.

The gentry came next, mounted knights and nobles riding in matched pairs, one Paduan beside one Veronese. This was no traditional parade, with the most important at the head, but more in the mode of an ancient Roman Triumph, building man after man to the most illustrious.

Yet they started strong. Leading the way were the Paduan Baptista Minola, whose son-in-law was Veronese, and Guglielmo del Castelbarco, Cangrande's most valued statesman. They were immediately followed by Nico da Lozzo, who had long ago traded Padua's colours for Cangrande's, and his cousin Schinelli, who had refused to change sides. Blood enemies for a score of years, they now smiled in perfect amity.

More Veronese faces paired with their Paduan opposites. Some of the loudest cheers were for Petruchio da Bonaventura, he of the mad Paduan wife, riding beside his lifelong friend, Hortensio Alvarotti, namesake of Petruchio's second son. The two laughed and waved, clearly well-pleased that they could now live in public concord.

Some pairs had no link, placed together only to honour their rank. Others were more awkward, such as the pairing of Antonio Capulletto with Ubertino da Carrara. Capulletto had once been betrothed to Ubertino's cousin, only to have her run off with his best friend. An eternally-festering sore. But Antony put on a brave face for the crowd.

Not far behind rode that same former friend. As Mariotto Montecchio was wed to a Paduan noblewoman, he was among the last duos to issue forth from the Scaligeri palace. His partner for the ride was a relation by marriage, Tiso da Camposampiero, though until last month the two men had never met outside a battlefield.

Nearing the ultimate set of riders, out came four of Scaligeri sympathy, bound by blood and marriage. Antonio and Bailardino da Nogarola, along with Bail's two sons Bailardetto and Valentino. They were paired with four of the Papafava clan, tied to the Carrarese much the same way the Nogarola family was to the Scaligeri.

Dressed in purple and gold, Detto's head should have been high. Yet he neither waved nor smiled, keeping his eyes fixed rigidly upon his father's back as though drawing strength from his sire's gregarious, warlike bulk.

Next came the only rider without a mate. The rumoured architect of this grand peace, Ser Pietro Alaghieri had been given the honour of riding in solitary prominence. Fitting, as he was neither Veronese nor Paduan. He was a Florentine, though still labouring under his father's decree of exile. Known as a knight of scrupulous honour, recently returned to the light of God, he was said to be the Scaliger's most trusted confidant. Hadn't he been given the chore of secretly raising Cangrande's heir? Hadn't he gone to Avignon to plead the Scaliger's reinstatement by the Pope? Hadn't he been wounded fighting the Paduans, and yet devised this new glorious peace? Moreover, was he not the son of the poet Dante, who had braved Hell in order to achieve Heaven?

Certainly the son looked as though he'd shared his father's journey, so grim and tired and sad all at once. Like Detto before him, he looked braced more for a funeral than a wedding.

Ah, but the next pair bore smiles that angels would have envied. Cangrande della Scala and Marsilio da Carrara rode side by side, dressed in the colours of their cities, but reversed – the Paduan wore Verona's gold and azure, while Cangrande was draped in the crimson and white of Padua.

At the prime of his life at thirty-five years, Carrara was dark of hair and eye, the flower of Paduan nobility. He waved his clasped hands above his head as though this were *his* triumph – as, in many ways, it was. No longer under siege, he was free to lead his people to the prosperity that had so long eluded Padua.

Yet Carrara's joy paled beside the Scaliger's. It was not years that gave Cangrande such a dominance, nor was it his position as the victor. There was something innate in the man, something grand and eternal. It did not hurt that his flawless smile was famous across the known world, or that his chestnut hair framed orbs of such unearthly blue that women had made spectacles of themselves just to be seen by those eyes. Having shed the weight gained in recent times, he appeared far younger than his modest thirty-eight years.

Decisive, cunning, foresighted, generous, forgiving, proud, able, and charming, Cangrande was such a man as to come along once in a generation, a dozen generations. With this victory, the world had begun to recognize that fact. And fear it.

Both lords were hung with so much gold as to dazzle the eye – even the stitching of their gloves was gold. Neither was armed in the slightest, not even knives on their belts, so secure were they in the peace they had made. A peace that would be forever signified by the mingling of their kindred's blood.

The ultimate pair appeared. Both bridegrooms were dressed in flawlessly matched embroidered farsettos and capes. Not gold but silver, head to spurs, with the deepest and most expensive black to accent their luster.

The elder by six years, Mastino della Scala was now twenty and had all the handsomeness youthful vigour could endow. Moreover, his dark hair was cut short, making him look quite martial, in a Roman way. One might have mistaken Mastino for the son of Carrara, not the nephew of Cangrande. Mastino was mounted on a pure white stallion that even the horse-loving Montecchio had been forced to admire.

Beside him, on an equally white steed, rode Francesco di Cangrande, the bastard heir of Verona. Cesco's curling chestnut hair was long enough to tie back. He had a more crooked smile than

Cangrande's, curling up on the left side and pressed tight on the right. It was a smile, not of joy, but of wry amusement, one that would have looked out of place on any other fourteen year-old. But Cesco already owned something of the Scaliger's immense presence, one that would only increase with time.

Since his dramatic reappearance three years earlier, Verona had watched this young man grow. Just last summer he had guided the city through the aftermath of a terrifying earthquake with remarkable ability and assurance. Better still, the running duel of wills between Cangrande and his bastard heir seemed to have ended. For the first time, Verona's future seemed not only bright, but replete with promise. There lacked only a victory over Treviso. Then, with the Feltro united, with the support of the Emperor and respect of the Pope, with control of the Alps, with an experienced and eager army, with Cangrande to lead and Cesco as the promised future, Verona's possibilities were limited only by imagination. The city so beloved of Charlemagne could easily become the new Paris, the new Rome, the new Athens. Verona would become the center of the world.

If no one that day recalled the words uttered by an oracle thirteen years before, could they be blamed? Indeed, was there ever blame for what the stars had ordained?

♦   ◊   ♦

"I really must thank you again, cos," said Mastino as he waved to his half of the crowd.

"I rather think you should practice forbearance, cos," replied Cesco, no chink in his armour of good cheer. "You have an expectant bride who will doubtless already be disappointed in her wedding night. Restraint might prevent you from ruining it entirely."

"But that's just what I must thank you for! Taddea is a lovely girl. Ripe, noble. Rich too. And of the purest lineage! One look and you know whose daughter she is. Pure Carrara from hair to heel. And it was you that brought us together. I will forever be in your debt."

Turning from the crowd, Cesco bent his crooked smile upon Mastino. "O no, cos! Trust me, it is I who am in your debt. And I plan to have an epitaph like the one of Sulla Felix. *Οὔτε τῶν φίλων τις αὐτὸν εὖ ποιῶν, οὔτε τῶν ἐχθρῶν κακῶς ὑπερεβάλετο.*"

Mastino felt the hairs on his neck rise. His Greek was lacking, but the quote was famous enough to be familiar. *'No friend ever served me, and no enemy ever wronged me, whom I have not repaid in full.'* A threat, no doubt. Yet Cesco's mirth did not seem feigned, nor did it force its way through gritted teeth, as it might from any normal man. No, Cesco's untethered laughter was far more menacing than the threat itself.

And why should the boy threaten him? Mastino had saved him, dragging what was hidden into light. That he'd meant to wield it as a weapon of his vengeance – for his dead friend Fuchs, for the usurpation of Mastino's rightful place as Verona's heir, for a hundred slights both public and private, for simply living at all – none of that meant anything. What did motives matter?

The brat needn't have gone through with this wedding. *That* was none of Mastino's doing. Why the Devil had Cesco forced himself to partake of this mad, laughable, shameful marriage? Cangrande would have been perfectly pleased to call it off. Mastino would certainly have preferred to have this wedding day all to himself. What had possessed the boy to go through with it?

That was the most fearful thing about the bastard. He could not be predicted. Mastino wondered what form Cesco's revenge might take. For revenge was coming, nothing surer. It was important, then, to be prepared.

♦   ◊   ♦

As the distance from the palace to the cathedral was not long enough for a proper spectacle, the triumphal procession took a round-about track, looping west to the Arena, then north to the river's edge. Here, cheered by crowds lining both banks of the river, they turned and followed the water until they reached Verona's Duomo, the Cathedral of Santa Maria Matricular.

Like the fabled entryway to San Zeno, Verona's Duomo was designed by the architect Nicholò. An austerely beautiful structure, the century and a half old cathedral had a *protiro* in front of the main entrance, its stubbed roof supported by pillars rising from the backs of two winged griffons. Above the door was a painted Madonna and child with the Magi and shepherds, as well as images of hunting scenes and prophets and three stone medallions bearing the virtues of Faith, Charity, and Hope.

Behind the pillars, blind arches cascaded out from the doors, separated by half-columns of rosy stone twisting heavenwards. Each arch bore its own prophet, ten in all, while the whole church was symbolically protected by two painted paladins, Roland and Oliver, plucked from the chivalric cycles of Charlemagne. Ten prophets and two paladins, making the holy number of twelve.

There were far more than twelve Franciscans present to officiate. Bishop Francis was beaming, and his Holiness Tebaldo III had taken the trouble to groom his hirsute face. Among the many other brothers was Fra Lorenzo, who looked with a fearful eye at the proceedings, wondering if he were in part to blame.

The Benedictine and Dominican orders were represented as well. Most prominently placed were the sisters of Santa Maria in Organo, who had among their number a lady dear to one of the grooms. Suor Beatrice stood beside Abbess Verdiana. Before beginning her cloistered life, she had been Antonia Alaghieri, daughter of Dante, sister to Pietro, and combination mother, aunt, and sister to Cangrande's heir.

The brisk air was sharp enough to bite Antonia in the throat and sting her eyes. A good excuse to let fall the tears welling behind them. Why should she not cry? Did not people cry at weddings?

These last weeks Cesco had avoided Antonia in all but the most public settings. Whenever she called, he contrived to be absent, asleep, or busy with a new hawk, or sword, or horse. She understood his reticence. Two years before, Antonia had been violently and repeatedly assaulted in an attempt to separate Cesco from those that cared for him. Whenever she had given the boy comfort, she'd been punished in the most violating way. Worse, she'd never known who had done it.

Antonia had chosen to suffer in silence, keeping that horrible knowledge from her brother and Cesco. She had thought that, through confessing to her Abbess and Fra Lorenzo, she had made peace with the event. Then Cesco's fiancée had passed along a brief message saying that the man responsible was dead. Fuchs, famous jouster and erstwhile companion to Mastino, had kidnapped Cesco and tried to sell the fourteen year-old into slavery. Cesco had escaped, but not before ending Fuchs' life.

Antonia's rage at the revelation of her assailant's identity was dwarfed by her failure to protect Cesco. She knew him well enough to fear he was claiming the responsibility, blaming himself for her plight. She wished they could agree to let the past lie, so that she could comfort his present. Her brother Pietro had confided the truth about what had happened in Padua, the disastrous secret about Cesco's love. Antonia wanted to hold the boy in her arms as she'd done when he was small, absorbing his pain and rage. But he was no more willing to share his pain than she had been to share hers. In the end, Fuchs had won – he'd driven her little boy away from her.

Not that he was so little anymore. As if adversity had thrown a lever within him, over the past two months he had grown a full two inches. He'd always lamented his lack of height. But now his

Scaligeri heritage, always present in his face, was beginning to show in his stature. It made him even thinner than his usual wiry frame. His face looked longer. Even the scar above his eye looked stretched. But thinness didn't make him look weak. Rather he seemed hard, strong. *Like a Greyhound*, thought Antonia with real sadness.

This was the prophecy at the heart of the strife in their lives. Attributed to the British wizard Merlin, it carried an awesome prediction:

> *To Italy there will come The Greyhound.*
> *The Leopard and the Lion, who feast on our Fear,*
> *He will vanquish with cunning and strength.*
> *The She-Wolf, who triumphs in our Fragility,*
> *He will chase through all the great Cities*
> *And slay Her in Her Lair, and thus to Hell.*
> *He will unite the land with Wit, Wisdom, and Courage,*
> *And bring to Italy, the home of men,*
> *A Power unknown since before the Fall of Man.*

These lines had inspired Antonia's father when creating the opening scene of his *Commedia*. In it, the character of Dante starts his journey through Hell because he is frightened by the leopard, the lion, and the she-wolf, the last of whom is said to mate with men *'until the Greyhound shall come, who'll make her die in pain.'*

But there was a coda to the prophecy her father had never known:

> *He will evanesce at the zenith of his glory.*
> *By the setting of three suns after his Greatest Deed,*
> *Death shall claim him. Fame eternal shall be his,*
> *Not for his Life, but his Death.*

To her father — indeed, to the world — Cangrande was the Greyhound. He himself had believed it for years. Yet it seemed it was not the Scaliger but his heir who was destined to slay the she-wolf and be remembered for his own death.

Waiting, Antonia saw her younger brother in the crowd. Leaving his studies in Florence, Jacopo had returned to Verona for this day's events. Always ready with a laugh, he had sobered some in recent years, though he was still without occupation. The only member of their family to go home to Florence, he was on his way to becoming a prominent man of no substance, famous only for his father. As opposed to Pietro, who was unable to choke down his pride, and yet was destined to become a man of real import.

Antonia caught a glimpse of a living *memento mori* in the crowd. Among the many faces near the cathedral door was Tharwat al-Dhaamin. The threats of violence that had driven him from Verona two years ago were nowhere in evidence now. *But then, he's not as fearsome as once he was,* thought Antonia, looking at the patch that covered the Moor's left eye. It might have made him more sinister, had not his shoulders become slumped and his frame less robust. He looked suddenly old, as if the years had finally caught up to him. Instead of fearing the dusky-skinned astrologer, the people of Verona could now pity him.

Arriving, the knights dismounted and their horses were led away. There was young Detto, looking as crushed as a hound that's lost its master. Not far behind him, Antonia saw her older brother step out of his stirrup and onto the cobbled stones. Pietro met her eye, but there was nothing for it but to plunge ahead with this travesty of matrimony.

Next to dismount were Cangrande and Carrara. The first time she had seen Marsilio da Carrara, thirteen years before, he'd been engaged in a duel with her brother, so she had little liking for him. But it was the smiling and waving Cangrande who received the bulk of her ire. It was *his* fault, of course, that Cesco had been brought to Verona too early. *His* fault that Cesco had been tasked past enduring. *His* fault that Cesco's heart was now a wreckage, perhaps beyond mending.

If his heart was in tatters, Cesco certainly did not show it. Halting just behind the Capitano, the young bridegroom waved and grinned as if he were the victor of some great battle.

By his side was the day's other groom. Antonia had to tamp down her revulsion at the sight of Mastino. She was certain he had known of Fuchs' crimes, condoned them, perhaps even ordered them. Bile rose in her throat as she imagined him laughing as Fuchs shared how she had fought, cried, tried to strike back. She knew it was an un-Christian thought, but if it were ever in Antonia's power to do Mastino ill, she would welcome the chance.

Stepping down from their snowy mounts, Cesco and Mastino climbed the three short stairs to the church doors. Antonia could almost have touched Cesco as he passed. He smiled at her, but the smile passed on to the other sisters. Nothing personal, no meaning.

The main duty of the clergy was to witness the oaths exchanged and verify that neither couple had an unacceptable degree of consanguinity. This last task had Antonia feeling quite ill, but Cesco showed only humble delight as he received his blessing from the Bishop.

At a signal, the doors of the Duomo opened. From within the great cathedral emerged the bridal party, with the families of both girls dressed in lavish splendour. Cesco's future father-in-law appeared to have already been drinking, for there was a sloppy smile plastered across his face.

Children emerged, bearing the precious Venetian bridal chalices. Antonia half-willed one of them to trip, break the glass vessel, and so curse the marriage. But both children were lamentably sure-footed.

The music reached a fevered pitch, heralding the arrival of the brides. Heavily veiled, like the grooms the ladies were dressed in matching cloth of silver and black, save for the single ribbon of blue to indicate their purity. Antonia saw the one adorning Cesco's bride-to-be and wanted to scream.

Mastino was the first to greet his intended. On the arm of her cousin, Taddea da Carrara allowed her hand to pass to her new master, who kissed the proffered wrist and stepped close to lift the veil, displaying his bride to the people of Verona.

It would have been perfect had she been beautiful. But she had the too-tight face of her famous father, the late *Il Grande* da Carrara. Her whole head was longer front to back than it was tall, making her short-chinned and hawkishly-nosed. In her father, the features had made him stern and serious. In the daughter, the effect was just the same. The smile on her face seemed strained and out of place. But she had been expertly painted, and she had one attribute eternal to beauty – youth.

All eyes turned to Cesco as he stepped forward to greet his own bride. She was holding shyly back just inside the cathedral doors, balking at this, the ultimate moment. But Cesco knelt before her and said something Antonia could not hear. In spite of herself, his bride laughed. Standing, Cesco held out his hand. She slipped her fingers into his and together they stepped forward for the crowd's approval. Cesco reached across and lifted her veil. The masses cheered, and many were the sighs of *aww* and *how precious* from the combined citizens of Padua and Verona.

If youth was any measure to gauge a bride's beauty by, Cesco's betrothed was the fairest in the land.

She was all of five years old.

TWO

Padua
Two Months Earlier

D ETTO RACED AHEAD of Cangrande and Ser Alaghieri
to the room where he'd left Cesco and his love Lia just hours
before, embracing like the lovers they were. Wrenching open the
door, he now saw only Lia, dressing herself in men's garb. She was
quite alone.

"Where's Cesco?" Even those words caught in Detto's throat.
He had trouble looking at her.

"Gone." Lacing up the masculine doublet, Lia's fingers shook.
Her breathing was ragged. For a moment Detto thought there had
been some row, some lucky, wonderful break between the lovers. Then
he saw his own horror reflected in her face. *She knows. Somehow, she
knows.*

They'd met only a handful of times, Detto and Rosalia Rienzi.
For most of those meetings, she'd been disguised as a boy. That had
held true last night, as they'd traveled from Verona to Padua, two lads
on a midnight ride.

Detto had just recently been entrusted with this, Cesco's closest secret. As the true architect of the peace between Verona and
Padua, Cesco had claimed the right to marry where he liked. He had
chosen a girl who had threatened to kill him on several occasions,
once holding a knife to his throat. Typical Cesco.

Detto was still young enough to be resentful of his friend's
fascination with the opposite sex. But, seeing them together, Detto
witnessed the change in his friend. Less acid, more humour. More

bark, less bite. That edgy wit was tempered, still sharp, but no longer careless. It had all seemed so right. Just hours ago, Detto had left Lia and Cesco looking as joyful as any couple on the eve of their wedding.

But then Detto had told Cangrande the girl's name, and it had all gone wrong. Dragged into a side chamber of the great palace of Padua's bishop, set aside for the Scaliger's use, Cangrande had pressed him again for the girl's name.

"R–Rienzi," Detto had stuttered. "Rosalia Rienzi."

The Scaliger spoke as if in a war. "Where is he, Detto?"

"What's the matter?" demanded Detto in return, unwilling to betray his friend, even to his famous and fearsome uncle.

"Where is he?!"

"You're scaring the boy," said Ser Alaghieri, having followed in concern. "And me, for that matter. What's wrong?"

Cangrande was brusquely commanding. "Cesco cannot marry the Rienzi girl."

Stunned, it was on the tip of Detto's tongue to shout, *You promised!* But the look of anguish on Cangrande's face checked him. This was not cruelty. This was something else.

Ser Alaghieri was also studying the Scaliger's face. "Why not? You promised him his choice."

"He cannot marry *this* girl." Cangrande's emphasis was full of unspoken import.

Ser Alaghieri frowned, then his eyes widened. "You bastard."

Cangrande's gaze would have made paper curl. "Bastard is indeed the word of the hour."

Detto looked back and forth between them. "What? What?"

Without taking his eyes from Cangrande, Ser Alaghieri spoke. "He's saying, Detto, that the Church will forbid this marriage. That God has forbidden it. That even the idea is sinful."

Enraged on Cesco's behalf, Detto could not understand. "Why sinful?"

"Because," said Ser Alaghieri through gritted teeth, "this Rienzi girl isn't a Rienzi at all. She's a bastard."

"But how would Uncle Francesco know that...?" Detto's eyes glazed over as the floor fell away from his feet. He felt sick. "Oh."

"Thank you, Pietro," remarked Cangrande. "I was attempting to shield him. Not that it will be secret long. But I was hoping to spare Detto here the shame of this. If I can, I'll spare Cesco and the girl as well. Let them think I've gone back on my word. Let them blame me."

Not even when Cesco had lain at death's door, poison running through his veins, had Ser Alaghieri seemed so sick at heart. "You *are* to blame."

"Then let them blame me in a way that absolves them of this sin. Can we agree on that? Detto, say nothing of this to anyone. Let it be me. I'll be the unpredictable, unreliable Scaliger once more. Tell everyone I've forbidden the marriage because of Rienzi's loathing for me. I'll say I need the boy to make a political match to some Paduan girl. Pietro, we *must* keep this quiet, if we can. Hopefully no one will remember that I once had a dalliance with Rienzi's wife."

Pietro nodded his head in mute assent, but Detto was still struggling with the thought. "So that's why she wanted to kill you. Because her father hated you. But she didn't know why."

"Tried to kill who, me?"

"Yes," said Detto. "It was Lia who attacked you in the snow after you went to the forge two years ago, and she tried again in Trent – that was why the bridge fell, we were chasing her and stirred up trouble. She was trying to murder you, to please her father."

"Not realizing she was angling to become a female Oedipus. But naturally Cesco chooses a girl who wants me dead. A fine choice of brides." Cangrande looked too sick to be amused. He leaned his face close to Detto's. "Now – where is he?"

And Detto had lied. The moment his uncle and Ser Alaghieri set off to one of the Carrarese palaces, Detto had raced back to a casa owned by Baptista Minola, only to find Lia shaking and Cesco vanished.

If she knows, Cesco knows, too. Unwilling, his eyes moved to the bed, still rumpled and disordered. Gorge rising, Detto quickly turned his gaze to the window. The day had started so clear, but storm clouds were threatening. Apt.

Finished lacing her boots, Lia stood. "I need a horse." Her voice was remarkably steady. But then, she was a remarkable woman. From a remarkable family.

Detto's own treble wasn't as strong as hers, but he managed to say, "I'll take you."

"I'd rather be alone." It came out harsh.

Detto looked right at her. "He'd want me to."

Lia bit her lower lip, then nodded. "Now, please."

Detto swiftly led her to the nearest stable. They had to get out of Padua before she was confronted by the Scaliger. Detto could not imagine a worse scene. She had tried to kill Cangrande several times before, but never had she had such cause.

Being the nephew of the great Cangrande was enough to procure them horses on a promise. Mounted, they trotted in silence out the gate and across the ancient bridge spanning the Bacchiglione river. When the rain began, it was a mercy, filling their terrible silence with the sounds of a weeping heaven.

♦ ◊ ♦

For the whole of that day and most of the next, as the rains came and went, there was no sign of either Cesco or Detto. The latter, it was quickly discovered, had taken two horses and ridden off with another boy, one that did not quite match Cesco's description. Cangrande grunted when he realized who the mystery rider had to be. "One problem solved, at least. Though doubtless I will have to deal with Rienzi sometime soon."

Loath to fan the rampant flame of rumour, it was given out that the cousins were off enjoying themselves, as teens were wont to do. To a worried Pietro, Cangrande said, "Credit the boy with his due share of ingenuity. We'll not find him until he wants to be found. He'll reappear when he chooses. Search, by all means. He won't thank you for it. You'll merely draw more attention to his absence."

Pietro grudgingly acknowledged the truth of this. He wished for the old days, when Cesco never moved without his shadow, the Moor. But Tharwat was no longer spry enough to spy, and Cesco knew all the Moor's vanishing tricks.

Pietro filled the time by seeking out the famous Paduan doctor of law Bellario, and having a spirited debate on all manner of legal concepts. Bellario was less interested in justice than in wringing all semantic meaning from a law, whereas Pietro was more interested in the spirit of the law itself. It led to a discussion of the laws upon which all laws were based, the Ten Commandments, and the difference between the Greek, Hebrew, and Latin translations, as well as the importance of the ordering. The excellence of the conversation was almost enough to distract Pietro from worrying over Cesco's continued absence for almost five minutes at a time.

Bellario enjoyed the discourse as well, and said so. "Rarely have I had such spirited debate outside my own family. And of them, it is only the females who show any real instinct for the Law. I have a cousin in Bellamonte who, were she a man, would make me look to my laurels. Her father, a very legal man, had ridiculous notions of marriage contracts. But he was more of my thinking – literal interpretations. Which I would think you would agree with, being the son of a poet! We will never know the author's intent beyond the written word. So it is the written word in which we must place our trust."

"That assumes the author is infallible in his wording. Some, like my father, were. Others are not."

"Yet if they took the trouble to write the law out, surely they put thought into the wording. Words matter, Ser Pietro."

"On that we agree," Pietro said.

On the morning of the Thirteenth of September, just three days after his triumphal entrance into the city, Cangrande was on the balcony of a palace owned by an obscenely wealthy old Paduan called Gremio, socializing with a handful of august locals. They'd begun by discussing his plan to build a magnificent palace on land owned by the exiled Scrovegni family, but had moved on to disputing the value of different regional vineyards.

"I was recently given a lesson in the history of Italian wines," remarked Cangrande. "By a local friar, no less. Never met a man so learned in plants. He is an herbalist, but has French blood in his veins, and so owns a natural attraction to wine. Quite the philosopher, too. Told me that Italian wine-making was modest until the defeat of Carthage. It was the Carthaginian slaves who taught the Romans how to mass-produce wine. It became such a successful industry that the Romans outlawed it anywhere outside Italy."

"They understood trade, the Romans did," observed Gremio, eagerly inserting himself into the discussion. "Supply and demand! Cut off the supply and wait for the demand."

"Indeed," remarked Cangrande with an arched eyebrow. "They applied that to many industries – wine, grain, even armaments."

Gremio blenched. The hunched old man (who'd ludicrously embraced the new style of hose that included extra fabric at the groin) had conspired during wartime to secretly buy arms from Antonio Capulletto. That under-the-table dealing had nearly cost Capulletto everything, but he'd redeemed himself in the eleventh hour to retain the Scaliger's trust.

Now the covetous, niggardly, wizened old Gremio wished to impress Cangrande, assure him that he would be as good a friend in peace as he was an enemy in war. For his part, Cangrande was content to let Gremio sweat.

"What is your favourite wine, my lord?" asked Filippo da Peraga. This young noble had been one of Carrara's companions for the secret peace-making in Venice, and was eager to use the peace to climb the social ladder of the Scaliger's favour.

"Wine is like sex," said Cangrande. "The worst I ever had was wonderful. There's nothing like a good Carinena from Aragon. I developed a taste for Spanish wine some years ago, while traveling." He smiled in private amusement. "I've sent away for wines from as far afield as Trebizond. But lately I've become partial to the local vintage made in the Greek style. *Acinatico*, they call it. It's made in Valpolicella - the Valley of the Cellars - and created from three different kinds of grape grown along the Adige."

Gremio clapped his hands. "I have some! Shall I—?" Cangrande waved his assent.

"Greek style?" Already Peraga had seen that Cangrande loved explaining things.

"They employ partially dried grapes. I've often said vintners should make wine from raisins, so it will be aged automatically." Everyone laughed dutifully, Gremio hardest and longest. "Perhaps I grow nostalgic, but I think there is no finer wine than a good Veronese —" Cangrande's eyes flicked to the doorway. "Ah! You must excuse me, gentlemen. If Ser Alaghieri is here, it must be business. He has little interest in wine. Which is a shame, as such a methodical fellow would prove a capital wine-maker."

Bowing to Gremio, Pietro apologized. "I'm afraid I must borrow the Capitano for a moment."

Retiring down the stairs into Gremio's garden, Cangrande threw back the contents of his goblet and began to refill it from the carafe he'd brought with him. "Has he been found?"

"Detto has. Turned up this morning, saddle-sore and exhausted. He got the girl back to my sister's convent in Verona. Bailardino's shouting at him right now."

"Nothing quite as raw as the relief of a frightened father. All that frantic energy bursting forth in such an inverse manner."

"You don't seem particularly frantic," observed Pietro, who was. He hadn't slept but three hours these two nights.

"Because there is nothing to be done. What, shall I wear concern like a doublet, for all to see? Should I earn sympathy by displaying anxiety? No, I choose to reserve my energy until it's needed." Cangrande sighed. "Pietro, I am truly sorry for him. For them both. Believe me, you have no idea how sorry I am that Cesco won't be marrying for love."

Pietro's tone was flat. "Yes, I do. I've seen the charts."

Cangrande's face hardened. "I forget. You know all my secrets."

That forced a laugh devoid of amusement. "If that were true, I'd be dead. But on top of astrology, there's the prophecy. The oracle predicted three great loves will bring Verona down."

The Scaliger pulled a face. "If she hadn't been murdered already,

I'd be tempted just for that. Everyone assumes the Capulletto-Montecchio mess to be the first love. The whole of Verona is pregnant with fear of some second great, disastrous love."

"You don't think this is it?"

"How on earth should I know? But if it is, you'll be doing no favours bruiting it about. Not only will it shame the lad and lass — not to mention me — it will also have everyone thinking Doomsday is around the corner." He drank. "Curious, isn't it? Loves, like deaths, do seem to come in threes. Well, for whatever reason, I am sorry for them. I wish…" Cangrande's voice trailed off, eyes upon a sky rubbed raw after two days of rain. Then he shook himself like a startled hound. "It leaves us with another problem. The double-wedding has been announced. Mastino to Taddea and Cesco to some mystery girl. If we cancel one, it would be a stain to the gloss of our new peace."

"What are you going to do?" asked Pietro.

"The only thing I can," shrugged Cangrande. "Find another bride for him."

"No need for that!"

They both turned to behold Cesco entering the garden, a saunter in his step, a carefree smiled plastered across his face. "Morning, my lord. Morning, Nuncle. Never you fear, I've taken care of matters, and smartly too. I'm sure you'll approve." Taking up a goblet and filling it to the brim, Cesco echoed the Scaliger by quaffing it off at once.

Pietro stared past the bravado, trying to see into the boy's mind. His face was mild, but there was a curious slackness to his frame. His ever-abundant energy was absent, replaced by something more languid. He looked as though he hadn't a care in the world.

Cangrande showed no sign of concern whatsoever. "The prodigious prodigal. It is good to see you whole."

"What, should I have torn out my eyes and thrown myself from the city gates to wander the barren wastes of the Feltro for three year? I have better things to do."

"Indeed. Greek style suits grapes better than you. When you say you've taken care of it..?"

Cesco wiped the wine from his lips with two fingers, pinching and flicking the drops away. "Well, as you said just now, the weddings have been announced. It would damage my new peace to call one off."

Pietro noted '*my* new peace,' but he was more concerned for what Cesco had in mind. "You're not marrying—"

Cesco cut sharply across his foster-father. "I'm delighted to announce my betrothal to Maddelena, youngest daughter of Pietro de Rossi. Not only a pillar of the Paduan community and close ally of the Carrarese, but my lord Pietro's brother Rolando is the current ruler of Parma. In many ways, he will remind you of yourself in your youth. Just twenty-five, and already a Podestà. And as I am quite used to calling a man named Pietro 'father,' it all fits swimmingly. I've just returned from his casa here in the city. He came to witness your happy advent, with no inkling he'd be so blessed as to join the Scaligeri clan. Needless to say, he is overcome with joy at the match. He even overlooked my birth, since Ser Alaghieri so successfully lobbied to have me legitimized." Bowing ironically to Pietro, Cesco smacked his lips. "Thirsty working, this matrimony." He held out his goblet.

Cangrande hesitated before refilling the proffered vessel. "A trifle young, isn't she?"

"A shade, perhaps." Cesco's eyes were a cloudy green, the pale ring around them dull. Pietro wondered if the boy had been indulging in something stronger than wine. *Damn you, Tharwat.* Aloud, Pietro asked, "How young?"

"Not yet a woman," said Cangrande.

Cesco clucked his tongue. "Tch. She has not seen the change of six summers, true. But her lineage is impeccable. The spitting image of her father."

The target was unmistakable, but Cangrande showed no sign of being hit. "A commendably clear-eyed solution. All three Rossi brothers are young, ambitious, and capable. And they are, by tradition, Guelph."

"A foot in the enemy camp. It was a choice between them and the Lupi clan. I liked the symmetry of that – the Greyhound's heir married to the daughter of a wolf. But they had no eligible maidens at hand. Alas."

And Rossi sounds like Rienzi, thought Pietro with depressed admiration. *If there's any hint of the story going around, everyone will think the name was garbled along the way. How can he think so clear, when his heart is broken?*

Cangrande was looking more and more pleased. "The Rossi will certainly do. With one wed to my heir, they'll dedicate themselves to building Verona for your children. Not that I expect any children for years. You'll treat her well?"

"But of course! This is like adopting a child instead of making one. With your help, I'll set up a suitable household for her. I, however, hope to fill the intervening time perfecting the sweet arts of war. We'll begin with Treviso. I was reading Josephus' account of the siege of Jerusalem, and I was thinking we might learn something from the way Titus placed his legions—"

"Wait a moment. There is something I must say." Cangrande placed a hand on his heir's shoulder. "Cesco, you have no idea how truly sorry I am."

Cesco slipped out from beneath that weighty hand. "The Scaliger, sorry? Whatever for? I hope I get around half as well at your age. But I can hardly blame you for adultery. Without it, I should not exist myself. I too was conceived on the wrong side of the sheets. If anything, she has the better claim, being my elder." Cangrande opened his mouth, but Cesco waved him off. "No no, I beg you, let us employ the proverb of gilt, glimmering silence. There is nothing more to say, is there?" In spite of the crooked smile and jaunty tone, Cesco's gaze was blistering. "Besides, there's a great deal to be done. Wars and weddings to wage, wagers to win, wenches to woo, leaving woes to wither in the womb. So let's be about it, hop hop. *'Be ye doers of the word, and not hearers only.'* First, if you are free this hour, sans any random Paduan wives to seduce, Maddelena's father wishes to fix the contract. Try not to sleep with the mother until after the ceremony."

Cangrande barked out a laugh. "Serves me right for feeling sorry for you! Do you care about anything at all?"

Smiling still, Cesco answered with a single, deliberate, "No."

Slowly, Cangrande nodded. "Good for you. It makes everything easier. Lead me on."

The matched duo departed side-by-side, leaving Pietro feeling cold in the bright autumn sun.

Later that night, Pietro had sought out the two men he trusted most. Upon a time, he would have imagined those roles to be claimed by the pair he'd been knighted with, ridden into battle beside, shared wounds with – Capulletto and Montecchio. But their mutual estrangement had estranged him as well, and while his eight year exile to Ravenna had not cooled their individual friendships, it was two other men with whom Pietro had shared a much more difficult battle – the raising of Cesco.

One was a grizzled, bald, fork-bearded Italian shaped like a barrel. The *jourdan* hanging on a cord about his neck marked him as a physician. Ser Dottore Giuseppe Morsicato, knight, surgeon, and private physician to the Nogarola family. His gruff practicality and open querulousness made him a poor dissembler. Being too honest himself, Pietro appreciated someone he knew wouldn't lie to him. They had shared much.

But not as much as Pietro had shared with the Moor. Tall and dark-skinned, the old man had ancient scars about his throat, and more recent ones about his hands and ankles. It was these that prevented him from following the boy as he had in years gone by. These, and his missing eye, the sewn gap covered with a patch. He was also missing several teeth on one side. These newer insults to his flesh had been inflicted just last year, while he and Pietro were in France, facing not just peril of the body, but of the soul. Tharwat al-Dhaamin was the one man Pietro was certain would always be there to help in a crisis. Which was strange, as the Moor was the last living member of the order of Hashashins – Assassins.

It was odd for Pietro to look at the pair and realize the blunt doctor and the crippled assassin were his closest intimates. Almost as odd to be an honoured guest in a palace belonging to a man he'd once fought a duel with, faced three times in battle, the man who'd given Pietro a deep, puckered scar on his thigh that still ached when he ran. But Cesco had arranged this peace so completely that Marsilio da Carrara was now forced to honour Pietro Alaghieri, much as it might stick in the Paduan's gullet.

Dismissing the servants, the trio sat in Carrara's guest suite, pouring their own wine and snacking on cheese and Golden Morsels. Pietro had already informed them of Cesco's ill-fated romance, and now he related the news of the day – Cesco's betrothal to the Rossi girl.

"Good God!" sputtered Morsicato. "Five years old?"

"Keep your voice down, for God's sake." Pietro cast a glance at the door.

"Five?" repeated Morsicato, his hush not hiding his outrage. "That's worse than Capulletto!"

Antony Capulletto had married an eleven year-old. Only Pietro and Cangrande knew that Antony had been blackmailed into it by the girl's relations, who had learned of his arms deal with Padua. Secrets upon secrets. *How many can I carry?*

"It is closest to the chart we feared," rumbled the Moor in his broken voice. "The darkest fate." Though known around the world by many names, in almost every guise Tharwat was a respected astrologer. He had made charts for many people – and for Cesco, many charts.

Stubbornly, Pietro shook his head. "It could still be the middle path. The twin stars, crossing in the sky." At the hour of Cesco's birth, there had been reports of stars falling in the sky. Several reports described one star, and a single report described the opposite. Each affected Cesco's fate, one for the better, one for the worse. It had been Pietro who had suggested there might have been two stars, both good and ill.

The best chart, the one they had hoped for, granted Cesco happiness at the cost of his brilliance. If he married for love, he would live long and do great things, but not rise as high as some of the darker charts. Now, with that promising fate denied, Pietro clung to the idea of a hard but not awful middle path.

"Fate has a way of thwarting the plans of men," said Tharwat. "The stars have led him here. He will not love another."

The doctor had no use for stars. "This isn't birth, this is blood! A brilliant boy, born of a brilliant father, looking for a love as brilliant as himself. How natural that he thought he'd found it in his sister?"

"It's not natural at all," protested Pietro. "This isn't Egypt, they're not Ptolomies! Christ Jesus, it worse than sin, it's…"

"I'm not saying it's *good*. I'm saying we can't think that the boy is condemned to a life of misery because of an unlucky choice in loves. Not for his first choice, at any rate," he added sourly, stroking his beard.

"Nor should we condemn him for this new marriage," replied Tharwat softly. "No, listen, doctor. This may be the best thing for him. He is hurt. He will not, now, marry for love. So he is taking a wife that frees him from playing the part of a husband."

"What about the little girl?" demanded Morsicato. "What is Cesco thinking, dragging a child into the viper-pit of Verona?"

"She will be treated as a princess. They will certainly not share a room until she is of age. Ten years. What changes will be wrought in them both in that time?"

"Ask the stars," grunted Morsicato.

"I have, and shall continue to."

Pietro said, "He means to throw himself into the war with Treviso."

"The Capitano will let him. To a point," added Tharwat.

"Yes," agreed Morsicato at once. "To a point. When the great hound feels himself being eclipsed, he'll send the pup back with his tail between his legs."

Pietro held his goblet tight, his wine undrunk. "I'm not sure.

Cangrande seems genuinely grieved. I know he was hoping that Cesco would marry for love, and so prove once and for all that he is not the Greyhound. But there was something else. He looked – uncertain."

"Unusual, for the Capitano." Though firmly tied to Verona's ruling family, the doctor had long since stopped being an admirer of Cangrande della Scala. Or for that matter, of his patron's wife, the Scaliger's sister. Both of them had conspired to ruin lives and wreck dreams. All for the sake of a prophecy.

Remarkably, it was Tharwat who had the most sympathy for Cangrande. "The Scaliger has finally come to care for the boy. Having opened himself, he feels the boy's plight. He received a blight at the same age. From me."

Pietro knew what this meant. Tharwat had shown the fifteen year-old Cangrande his true star chart, revealing to the gifted boy that he was not, in fact, the fabled Greyhound, as he'd been led to believe. "You told him the truth."

"The truth often wounds more than a lie. Look to what the truth has cost Cesco."

"It can't have been delivered kindly, coming from that bastard Mastino," observed Morsicato.

"No," said Pietro, who hated to imagine that scene, and couldn't stop. "But Cesco won't talk of it. At least, not to me."

"I doubt he'll mention it to anyone," said Tharwat heavily. "Ever private, this will make him moreso."

"How did he seem today?" asked Morsicato.

"Almost like himself," answered Pietro. "Quick. Sarcastic. Amused. But – careless. As if nothing had weight. I've never seen him drink wine before."

"Better wine than that awful hashish." Morsicato cast an accusing look at the Moor. But Tharwat did not choose to again debate his practice of giving the boy a careful mixture of hashish, poppy-seeds, and various other herbs.

His bait not taken, the doctor asked, "How many people know?"

"Only a few. Most think there was a mix-up in the names. For those who know everything, it's us three, the Scaliger, Bailardino and Detto – which means Katerina will know. Rienzi, of course. And Mastino."

"Bastard," grunted Morsicato. "Do we know how Mastino discovered the truth?"

"Fuchs. He'd been following Cesco for months. And, as we now know, he was also behind the disappearance of Cesco's mother."

Cesco's mother, the mysterious foreigner called Maria, she of the green eyes and lilting accent, had been in Pietro's presence only twice. Once, when she handed her infant over to Cangrande's care, and again three years ago, when she had been introduced to Cesco in the guise of a handmaiden. Then she had disappeared. Tharwat had tried to trace her, only to find blood stains and a mysterious jumble of letters carved into the wood where she'd been bound. Pietro and Tharwat had struggled for years to decypher the code, and failed. Whatever secrets she had tried to convey, they were beyond Cesco's protectors.

But not now beyond his enemies. "If Mastino knows whatever secrets she was hiding, why not use them?"

"He's done enough already," said Tharwat. "No, he'll hold them close to hurt Cesco at some later date."

"I wish we knew how to defend him."

Morsicato pulled a wry face. "We could always ask Cangrande, or Katerina."

Tharwat was unamused. "It is up to us. Protect him, and smoke out the secrets, once and for ever."

There was little more to say. Feeling the weight of both the years and their hearts, they'd all retired for the night.

In his darkened room, Pietro had moved from bed to table to window to chair, cursing Cangrande, cursing Fortune, cursing the stars in Heaven. Even, unthinkably, cursing God. Filled with impotent anger, Pietro was reminded of Cianfa Donati, laying on the floor of his father's Hell, giving God the fig. Amusingly, Cesco had tweaked that man's namesake, preventing the living Cianfa Donati from absconding with Dante's bones.

But it was the vivid image of the poetic Donati that lived in Pietro's mind. He'd never before been angry enough to lay the blame for earthly woes at the Lord's feet. Yet this was such a perverse circumstance, so utterly random. Of all the girls in the world, that Cesco should fall in love with Cangrande's secret daughter? The blame could go only to God, or to Satan.

Yet Satan had no power in the world, save that allowed to him by God to test Mankind. God had allowed this. For the first time since his miraculous readmittance to the faith, Pietro felt alienated from the Lord, something he had never experienced, not even when excommunicated by the Pope himself. Denied the Church, denied the society of priests and friars and nuns, Pietro had still felt God's presence in his life.

That presence was darker now, and Pietro was angry. *This is my son. He has already been tested more than any boy should. Brilliant, clever, he can light up the world. Why, O Lord, do you task him so?*

As if in answer, Pietro remembered another son, tested by his father, tested beyond endurance. A son deserving of love and honour, but given ridicule and death.

Cesco is hardly Christ-like, mused Pietro. *Nor am I Abraham, willing to sacrifice my son for the Lord. Cesco may not be the son of my flesh, but he is the son of my heart. No, God — I will not give up my son. That's asking too much. I am not you, and Cesco is not the Savior.*

But Cesco did have a destiny. If he was indeed the Greyhound, he was to bring about *'a power unknown since before the Fall of Man.'* These events were merely shaping him for it, just as a sword is hammered into shape and bathed in fire. What does it matter to the knight what the sword feels, so long as it cuts? The tool is required. It must be strong.

Pietro had gone to bed that night impotently raging at the injustice of it all.

◆　　◇　　◆

Standing now in the brisk November air, Pietro watched the two couples wave to the assembled masses. They were unconsciously arranged in order of age. Standing on the left was Taddea, twenty-four years old, then Mastino, twenty, followed by Cesco, fourteen, and Maddelena, five. It was absurd. Worse, it made Cesco seem small, Mastino grand.

This was not the first time Pietro had seen the grooms with their brides. The formal betrothal of Mastino and Taddea on the steps of Padua's own Duomo had been followed by the blessing of Cesco and Maddelena, with the Paduan cleric pronouncing, *"Benedictio annuli ante hostium templi."* Even then Pietro had found himself comparing the grown Mastino to the growing Cesco. Would Verona prefer a handsome young man to a wild youth barely starting to shave?

Lost in his mind, Pietro nearly missed the signal to enter the great cathedral. The interior was brighter than most, thanks to the polished coloured marble, rose and white. Past the nave, the apse was enclosed by a semi-circular white marble arcade in the crossing between the transepts.

To the right was the tomb of Pope Lucio III, who had died in Verona while ordering preparations for the Third Crusade. Over his elaborate sarcophagus hung a twin to the object hanging in the archway between the Piazza della Erbe and the Piazza dei Signori

– a long curved bone taken from an ancient monster that the city had risen up to vanquish. Pietro wondered whose bone it really was. Some giant creature, obviously. But there was no such thing as monsters. At least, not that kind. *The true monsters are men, doing monstrous deeds.*

Everyone was taking their assigned places. Pietro's seat was beside a thin-faced soldier with just one eye, sewn shut. Across him was an equally Germanic looking fellow – Prince Rupert, the Emperor's nephew. Pietro had met the young man in Rome, but not this fearsome companion. About to introduce himself, Pietro was forestalled by a flourish of trumpets.

With an eye towards theatricality, the wedding was not taking place within the curved arcade of the apse, but at the altar fifteen feet in front of it. The families sat on a raised platform inside the apse, neatly framed by the arch overlooked by two saints. It was like Greek theatre, performed in the round, which meant the families had their backs turned to the interior altar. But it was hardly the first time Cangrande had turned his back on God.

That was unfair, of course. Choirs often performed facing outwards, towards the congregation. But the raised platform within the apse was specially made for this day to allow every member of the Scaligeri, Carrara, and Rossi to see, and be seen in return.

The women had already been here, awaiting the arrival of their triumphal men. On the left-hand side sat Carrara's sister Cunizza, his wife Bartolomea of the exiled Scrovegni clan, and his aunt Elisabetta, mother of Mastino's bride.

Here too sat the mother of Cesco's bride. Madonna Rossi sat wedged between her two elder daughters Luisa and Sibilia. Both were already betrothed and therefore unavailable, though either would have been far more age appropriate.

The right-hand side held the whole Carrara clan, save those still in exile. Marsilio's wife, Bartolomea Manfredo Scrovegni, wore a look of apprehensive contentment. Some of her family had recently been exiled, which doubtless explained the apprehension. That, and the fact that she had yet to bear her husband a child. She might count herself fortunate that he had not chosen to tie this knot with one of his natural daughters. He had chosen his cousin Taddea instead.

The other cousins were present, daughters of the late Giacomo *Il Grande* da Carrara. Likewise Marsilio's sisters Cunizza and Rigoberna were here, with their husbands Tiso Camposapiero and Antonio da Lozzo – another of Nico's cousins who had refused to join him in changing colours.

With them sat Montecchio and his wife and son. Gianozza della Bella was cousin to the Carrara clan. Once it had been thought that her marriage would help seal a peace, but it had hardly lasted two years, and had launched a new if bloodless war within Verona's walls between her intended and her usurping groom. Pietro knew that Capulletto would spend the whole service looking at her, and that Mari would spend it scowling back.

With Rossi on the left and Carrara on the right, the Scaligeri were left to fill the center, perfectly framed by the arch. Waiting beside her husband's seat, Giovanna da Svevia was looking grave. Doubtless Cangrande's wife wished it was her great-nephew now walking up the aisle. She had long lobbied for Paride to supplant Cesco as her husband's heir. The blood of Emperor Frederick II ran in her veins. Fortunately, Paride had inherited none of her vaulting ambition. There he was, smiling and bright, seated between his aunt and Mastino's elder brother, the affable Alberto.

Behind, in a rare circumstance, all three of Mastino's sisters were present: Verde, Caterina, and Albuina. Caterina was seventeen years old, Albuina sixteen, both ripe for political matches, no longer resigned to the convent they had been raised in. They gazed at the crowd of knights, lords, and dignitaries, wondering which among them would win their uncle's favour and so their hands.

Both hoped they would not end up like their sister Verde, whose political match to a handsome man had gone sour. Rizardo da Camino was somewhere among the great nobility in the crowd, not given a place in the front. The Camino family were nobles of Treviso, and Cangrande had traded his niece for a foothold in that resistant city. But within months of the wedding the city had thrown out Rizardo's father, thus ending the hopes of a bloodless transfer of power.

That reversal hadn't been enough to end Cangrande's liking of Rizardo, of course. No, that had come four years ago when Rizardo had considered changing sides and fighting against Cangrande. After having his castle and lands seized, Rizardo sheepishly returned to the fold. Since then, Verde's husband had not been allowed a place of prominence in Veronese society.

Detto and his brother Valentino were both upon the dais, along with their father, the genial and warlike Bailardino Nogarola. Cangrande's brother-in-law, foster-father, and best friend, Bail was remarkably energetic for a man now somewhere past fifty. His hair was still thick, if whitened. Catching Pietro's eye, Bail winked and threw a gesture of a cup to his lips. *When does the drinking start?*

Pietro smothered a laugh.

Striding up the aisle, Cangrande took his place at the center of the dais. On his right hand was his wife. On his sinister side, his sister.

Katerina della Scala *in* Nogarola, mistress of Vicenza, Bailardino's wife, Detto's mother, and once Cesco's foster-mother. Long ago, Pietro had fallen in a kind of longing for this beautiful, older, married woman. Not that he'd ever acted upon his feelings. Bailardino was a friend, and Pietro's respect for everyone involved kept his emotions well within the prison of his ribs. His was the perfect Courtly Love, the love from afar, performing great deeds in her name without any hope of recompense.

For fourteen years Pietro had engaged in no romance, no dalliance, no love-affair – not even when one was offered in the most explicit terms. He told himself he was honourable. But he feared his reluctance to engage in carnality was because he had so terribly misjudged this first love of his.

He now knew this lady for what she was – a murderess, a plotter, a schemer, a woman who cared no more for the people she manipulated than a chess player did for the pawns on the board. She'd employed Tharwat to make Cesco's star-charts. She'd raised her own brother to believe he was *Il Veltro* in a cruel test of her methods. She'd even once sent murderers to kill baby Cesco in the crib. This was a fact known only to Pietro and Cangrande. Her reasoning was cold-heartedly sound – if Cesco was indeed the Greyhound of prophecy, he would survive, and the fearful mother would entrust the child to Katerina's care. If he were not, then best discover it soon by letting the child die.

It had worked. The child had come into her hands. Cesco still bore the invisible scars of her mothering.

Astonishingly, knowledge of all this had done nothing to alter Pietro's feelings for her, only made those feelings easier to resist. Often he wondered what was wrong within him, what part of him was broken, that he would place his romantic feelings into such an unworthy vessel.

Even now, with the marks of a stroke still evident in the corner of her mouth and the gloved hands hiding the terrible burns on her left arm, Katerina della Scala's face was where Pietro's eyes went.

But she was not looking back at him. Her eyes were fixed upon the altar between them where Mastino and Taddea knelt for the first blessing. Taddea's face was heavy with make-up, and her hairline had been plucked to make her brow high and proud. She positively glowed, as well she might – she was marrying a handsome member of the most powerful family in Lombardy, perhaps all Italy.

To their left, Cesco patted Maddelena's small hand as he turned her to face the Bishop. Where Mastino and Taddea exchanged elaborate oaths, Cesco and Maddelena's exchange was pure simplicity:

"I give my self to you, in loyal matrimony," said Cesco.

"And I receive it," Maddelena replied, frowning in concentration to get it out right. There were tears of fright on her lashes, and her gaze kept straying to the many people watching her. She almost forgot to add, "I give my self to you."

Cesco smiled at her reassuringly. "And I receive it." She gave a quavering smile back, and he whispered something private in her ear, forcing her to smother a giggle.

They exchanged rings, and with more prayers and thanksgivings for peace and harmony, union and order, the trumpets outside blared to life once more, signaling the start of the revels.

As the cheers broke out, drowning even the music, Pietro looked from face to face. Cesco's masque showed nothing but amused mirth. Cangrande displayed much the same, but there was a trace of resignation as well. Detto looked stricken. Pietro knew that somewhere behind him Morsicato and Antonia were gritting their teeth and restraining tears. Outside, Tharwat's ravaged face would be stone.

Among all who knew of Cesco's ill-fated romance, Katerina alone showed no regret. Her face carried something far more radiant, far more suffusing. Her face bore triumph.

Pietro recalled a moment, years ago, when he'd seen the same look on Cangrande's face. They had thought Cesco dead, and therefore the prophecy undone.

Now it was the sister's turn to revel, not in the breaking of the prophecy, but in the assurance of it.

Cesco had married. But not for love.

He was the Greyhound.

THREE

AS THE CEREMONY ENDED, the elder nobility breathed a unanimous sigh of relief. For them, the important part of the day was complete. The seal was set on peace.

But for the young men dressed in purple and gold, the day had hardly begun. They surged towards the exits, eager to transfer themselves to where their main event would occur – the Arena. Now that matrimony was achieved, it was time for the knighting.

Rising from his place of honour, Pietro watched the exodus of prospective knights with a crooked smile. He'd worn similar colours once – doublet, hose, cape, and hat, all tailored just to him. For years it had been his best attire, worn for the most elegant and momentous occasions. Though garish and showy, those garments had marked one of the proudest days in Pietro's life.

It was therefore a bittersweet sensation to see so many young men garbed in clothes just as rich, right down to the small tassels on the cape that ended in balls of real gold. Preferring the purple and silver he had worn to the ostentatious gold bedecking these lads, Pietro couldn't resist a chuckle. Gone were his days of fancy hats and expensive hose. His one sartorial quirk was his continued use of trousers, a habit he'd picked up after the wound to his thigh. He'd grown used to them, and now they were as much a part of his persona as the slight limp the wound had given him.

A voice in his ear said, "Are you thinking what I'm thinking?"

"That they aren't half the men we were?" Turning, Pietro

embraced Mariotto Montecchio.

"Exactly!" Thumping Pietro's back, Mari turned to the young-ster at his elbow. "Ser Alaghieri and I *earned* our knighthood. We had already fought in a great battle and taken wounds!"

"Yes, father." Mari's auditor was his seven year-old son, Romeo. The boy had a guileless, open face, with his father's smile and colour-ing, but his mother's long lashes and limpid blue eyes. He was a figure stepped from some Giotto fresco, too comely to be real. But he laughed readily enough, and away from his mother he seemed like an able, quick-witted boy.

"The best day of my life," reflected Mari. "Knighthood, I came in second in the Horse Palio, won the Foot Palio, and met your mother. Honours and love – what more could a man wish?"

Of course Montecchio would be happy today. Not only in prominence for his marriage ties to Carrara, but he had just amassed a new fortune. The Capitano had bought every knight a new *destrier*, the necessary warhorse, and a new palfrey, to carry the knight's gear. Pietro wondered if Mari had any beasts left in his stables.

In addition to the horses, the Scaliger had bestowed each new knight with a suit of armour, a full case of weapons, two fur-lined cloaks, two suits of purple and gold, and a trunk full of daily necessi-ties from socks to wax candles. All the new cavalieres were lodged at Cangrande's expense, each looked after by a page and two stewards. Unheard of largesse, but for Cangrande it was a standard bequest – a young Pietro Alaghieri had received just such gifts fourteen years earlier.

Politeness demanded that Pietro ask after Gianozza, presently chatting with her Carrara cousins, but there was too much bitterness on his tongue to form the words. Mari counted that as the best day of his life? How could he ignore the fact that he'd soiled his honour by betraying his best friend? *But then, honour doesn't mean as much to some men as others.*

That's not fair, said a chiding voice in Pietro's head. *Some men just have different definitions of it.* For Mari, love mattered more than friendship.

As if in answer, a rough, deep voice said, "I imagine Pietro counts the day after among his best. After all, that was the day he enshrined himself forever in Verona's lore by fighting a duel. For love and honour both." Antonio Capulletto had been standing with his back to them in the crush of bodies, waiting for Mari to depart before talking to Pietro. Stung by Mari's words, he now turned to face them.

"Pietro's sense of loyalty does him credit," said Mari acidly. "Even when he wishes to sever a tie, he will not."

"Just what I was thinking," countered Antony.

These were the moments Pietro hated most. Both men still counted him as their brother-in-arms, always vying for his loyalty.

Fortunately there was an avenue of reminiscence that might preserve at least a veneer of harmony. "I must admit, I feel odd seeing Carrara in Verona again. I'm tempted to finish what we started that day."

Antony said, "I'm not sure he'd take you up on it, hero that you are."

"We'd have to challenge him to a horse race first," said Mari to Antony, who actually grinned in spite of himself. Pietro felt a moment of lightness – a shared memory, one that wasn't instantly tarnished by their lost friendship.

"You'd have to find a way to keep your saddle this time."

Mari looked Antony up and down. "Well, I couldn't join you in yours anymore." Antony had bulked up greatly since their teenage years.

"There's to be a *mêlée* this afternoon," said Antony. "Afterwards we could invite Carrara to take a little ride, for old time's sake..."

"But if he didn't come back, it *might* soil the gloss of this day," said Mari with wistful sadness. "And Pietro worked so hard for this peace."

Though the idea had originated with Antonia and been implemented by Cesco, Pietro was the one credited for the so-called *Pax Verona*. It had the added benefit of eliminating one of the many death-sentences that lay over him. The lifting of his excommunication had removed another, leaving only Florence hungering for Pietro's head.

The possibility of another peace made Pietro long to lunge forward, grab them both and cry out, *This! This is what you were meant to be!* Comrades, fellows, companions, friends, brothers! For a scant six months, these two had been inseparable, almost as close as Cesco and Detto. Then Mari had been stupid, Antony unforgiving, and the result was thirteen years of wasted time.

Uncomfortable with this amity, Antony was the first to give in to his baser self. "Don't worry, peacock. *I* would never act to ruin a friend's great day. Besides, you could hardly challenge a close kinsman."

Mari's face hardened. Choosing to ignore Antony, he addressed Pietro. "It must have been difficult for your boy, taking a child to wife. But at least it was a political match, forced on him. I can't imagine he'd take a bride so young by choice." Antony's bride had been eleven at the time of their marriage. Mariotto didn't know that that marriage, too, had been made under duress.

Pietro closed his eyes. He should have known. These wounds were too well-tended. Even were they not, trust once lost is almost impossible to regain.

Antony opened his mouth to retort when a small voice said, "Lord Capulletto? I beg your pardon, my lord, but it is an honour to meet you at last." The speaker was young Romeo, who was making a perfect leg. "I hear reports of you from my father's friends, and he's often told me of your exploits together. I'm sorry I have not had the chance to meet you before now."

It was quite a speech for a seven year-old, and said with such an open face and genuine warmth that the bemused Antony paused, caught short by this unfeigned politeness. Or perhaps it was that the boy gazed at him with Gianozza's eyes.

Sensing he was doing well, Romeo pressed on. "I should also say, my mother speaks quite highly of you. She often laments that you do not call upon us."

Just like that, the moment was broken. Antony's face contorted and he brushed past the boy, plunging himself into the crowd.

Young Romeo's face crumpled, his lip beginning to quaver. "I only told the truth."

"I'm sure you did," answered Pietro kindly.

"Then why did he—?"

"Because he's an ass," said Mariotto, adding in a mutter, "Rude to my son…"

Pietro rested a hand on Romeo's shoulder. "You did nothing wrong. Some hurts just go too deep."

Romeo continued to look weepy. Blaming himself for something he had no control over, he was taking Capulletto's pain as his own. Pietro reminded himself of something his sister had once told him – that Gianozza was determined to raise her son to truly *feel*. Whatever that meant.

Mari took a dimmer view of his son's high emotions. "Romeo! Stop it. Now. What do we ask ourselves?"

"'Is this worth crying over?'" parroted Romeo, trying hard to steel himself.

"Quite right. Are you hurt? Are you dying? Is someone you love dying? No. Then cure yourself of this."

"Mother says—"

Mariotto knelt. "I know what your mother says. Listen to what *I'm* saying. Is this the person you want to be? Your feelings do you credit, but does crying solve anything?"

"No."

"Does it help anything?"

"No."

"Then it's an indulgence, isn't it?"

Romeo ducked his head. "Yes."

Mari pressed his son close, ruffling the boy's fine dark hair. "I applaud your attempt to make peace. But Lord Capulletto is trapped in the amber of his feelings. He lets his emotions rule him. Do you want to be like him?"

"No," said Romeo, squirming uncomfortably.

"Good." Mariotto rose. "Go play with Benvolio. I'll see you at the knighting ceremony."

Relieved, Romeo disappeared into the crowd to look for his cousin. Mariotto turned a rueful gaze to Pietro, who smiled in return. "You were very patient. More than my father would have been."

"If I thought I could beat it out of him, I would." From his face, Mari was only half-joking. "I've never met a child as self-judging. I hope he toughens up. He's got a brain, and a good arm. And on a horse... well, he's a natural Montecchio. But all the same I worry about him."

Tempting as it was to point out that the boy would not exist had not Mariotto let *his* emotions rule him, Pietro refrained. Instead he looked for an egress that would not have him waiting with the huge crowd, jostling to get out the main doors. Everyone was talking, in no rush at all. Sick at heart, Pietro had no interest in small talk.

There was a door to the north that no one was using. It was a longer exit, traveling as it did through the ancient church that had stood here before the rise of the Duomo. Pietro passed through it. At once the noise lessened. He walked over a floor mosaiced with flowery geometric shapes. There was comfort in such images. So often art depicted a story fraught with meaning – Biblical, classical, local. It was pleasant to look down and see the careful repetition of patterns, of shapes that held no message, nothing to interpret or digest. It simply was what it appeared to be.

Genuflecting to the saints resting here under their rose-marbled tombs, he came to an open-air courtyard, the space between old and new buildings. On an impulse he strolled into the original church. Somehow it felt more real than the grand edifice at his back. Simpler. Christ had been a simple man, and while it was fitting for his followers to raise great buildings in his name, Pietro could not help but think that the son of God would have appreciated the humble austerity of this building. Brick and layered stone, with plain white-washing to lighten them. There were frescoes here and there, but they did not detract from the plain wooden benches. The light was wonderful, coming from high windows rather than tapers.

And there, in the center, was the great octagonal baptismal font. Made from a single piece of marble, the craftsmanship was incredible, with the carved panels telling the story of Christ's early life across its eight sides. Pietro had always admired this piece. So often Christ was depicted on the cross, or dead. But though miraculous, it was not the manner of Christ's death that mattered, but rather his life.

A voice behind him said, "Shall we baptize you? Make you a true son of Verona?"

Pietro did not need to turn. "No, Madonna. I have been baptized already."

"But not for years." Katerina came close to stand beside him, looking down. "It isn't tempting to start again? Take a new name? What would you choose?"

"I am content with my own name, thank you."

"Of course you are. Pietro, *petrus*, the rock. You alone remain firm in a changing world. So what brings you here? A little early to be thinking of christening any children from today's union. Or do you, against all rumour, have one of your own on the way? Shall I congratulate you?"

Colouring, Pietro said, "I was waiting for the crowd to thin."

"And contemplating the parallels, no doubt, between the younger groom and Our Savior. Let's see — here is the Annunciation. I was not present for that, of course, but I imagine angels descended to proclaim the coming of *Il Veltro*. The visit to Mary — or Maria, as it happens. Apt. His birth, the shepherds. Briolotto's work is rude, but evocative. Ah, but here are the Magi — do you not think Tharwat would make an excellent Magi? And the good doctor Morsicato looks quite Oriental, with his forked beard. And you for a third. Did you bring the myrrh?"

Pietro pointed to the next panel. "Herod, ordering the massacre of the innocents."

"How dreadful, to order a child's death. O," cried Katerina in feigned shock. "You mean to make a comparison. Well, my brother is always saying I long to be a man. Were I a man, I think I'd quite like to be king. And here is the event we both were present for — the baptism of our little savior."

Pietro had indeed been there when Cesco was given a new name, one different from the one bestowed by his mother. That name was lost with her, a secret taken to her grave.

Turning, Pietro bowed. Talking to Katerina always tired him. He was not Cangrande, he was uninterested in scoring points, to be tallied after death. "Clearly, I am intruding. I shall leave you in peace, lady."

Katerina looked disappointed as he stepped out into the brisk air. The lady was obviously looking for someone with whom she could share her victory. Pietro was the wrong man. He cared more for the living boy than any fantastical prophecy.

His groom was waiting in the wide yard outside, still crushingly occupied. Mounting, Pietro's horse sidled into another man's steed. "I crave your pardon."

It was the grizzled foreigner who had held a place of honour equal to Pietro's own. "But of course," replied the thickly accented voice. Like the Moor, he had a sewn eye. But he disdained the patch, letting all the world see the puckered scar that sagged inwards to empty socket.

Pietro introduced himself, and the man did likewise. "Berthold von Neifen, Count of Marstetten, Imperial Vicar of Italy. And Ser Pietro Alaghieri needs no pardon from me. How did you like the wedding?"

"I appreciated its speed," said Pietro.

Berthold grunted. "I imagine Prince Franz feels the same." Franz was the emperor's name for Cesco. "For a young man, there is more excitement to be had in the coming hours." This was very true. The real draw of the afternoon was the great *mêlée*, a contest between two fully armed and armoured forces, each trying to capture the other's colours.

"Prince Rupert is there already, eager to ride into the fray. Ah, to be young and invincible," sighed Berthold, who was nearer forty than thirty. "I understand young Franz was injured in the last great tourney here, before he began his sojourn with his majesty the emperor."

Pietro opened his gloved palms. "I wouldn't know. I was in France at the time."

"Of course," said Berthold, politely acknowledging Pietro's trials before the pope. "Fra Bonagratia is a great admirer of yours. As is his grace the emperor, who honours you not only for bringing such worthy men as Bonagratia and the English Occam into his sphere, but also for your influence on young Franz, who is as beloved at court as his father is mistrusted."

"Still?" asked Pietro before he could catch himself. Cesco had betrayed the emperor's trust by trying to prevent Ludwig from burning Cangrande's forge, a petty blow from a petty man.

"His grace understands the pull of a powerful father." Berthold blinked his single eye. Or was it a wink? "He looks forward to Franz attaining his majority and, in due time, his full rights in Verona."

The message was unmistakable. Ludwig was waiting for the day when Cesco was made Capitano before elevating the city to its rightful place in the empire.

Berthold returned to his former theme. "But I am surprised you are not participating! What are you, thirty, thirty-one? In your prime!"

Pietro bowed his head. "You are kind. But so many souls are desperate to enter, and the new knights are to be given places of prominence. It seems churlish to take away a younger man's chance at glory."

"Especially since your own glory has been earned by necessity, in the trials of true combat. Like any man's should be," added Berthold approvingly. "Come, shall we go?"

They rode along, Berthold recounting tourneys he had seen and contested. Pietro listened with only half an ear. His mind was on the *mêlée*, praying it would shake Cesco out of his doldrums. In the wake of that horrible morning in Padua, Pietro had been fearful of some desperate, self-imposed trial, a wild act of daring like those Cesco had performed in the past. But for two whole months Cangrande's heir had been tame, quiet, docile. Diligent in study, determined in knightly drills, obedient in company, languid in private. Rather than spar verbally or physically with his elders as was his wont, he'd spent his free hours reading in the nearby monastery. After fourteen years of constant surprise, Pietro felt more frightened by Cesco's placid normalcy than he'd ever been by any madcap flight of daring, and felt a perverse desire for Cesco to do something scold-worthy.

But first they would have to reach the site. "Follow me, my lord." Abandoning the main street, Pietro led the way down a route known to locals, the *via Pigna* – 'pinecone street', so named for the Roman statue of a pinecone adorning the entrance. Mariotto lived on this street, and now so did Cesco, with a house purchased for him and his little bride. Which was too absurd to think about, so Pietro pressed on, wending his way like a native through the seeming cul-de-sacs and shadowed tunnels until he arrived at the great Arena of Verona.

Sight of it brought back so many memories – races, duels, prophecies, plays. But with this morning's nightmare still fresh in his brain, Pietro was reminded of his father's poetic dream in *Purgatorio*. Clutched by a giant eagle, Dante had been carried into the air:

Poi mi parea che, poi rotata un poco, *Then it seemed to me that after wheeling awhile*
 terribil come folgor discendesse,   *it plunged down terrible as lightning,*
 e me rapisse suso infino al foco.   *and carried me straight to the sphere of fire.*

 Ivi parea che ella e io ardesse;   *There it seemed that it and I were both aflame,*
e si lo 'ncendio imaginato cosse,   *and the imagined burning was so hot*
che convenne che 'l sonno si rompesse. *my sleep was broken and gave way.*

Some took the eagle literally, but Pietro knew it was a metaphor for Divine Grace. The fires of the sun were purgative – hence *Purgatorio*, a place where the soul was purged of sin. The penitent was meant to come out stronger on the other side. Pietro could only hope this would be true for Cesco. So far, he had not yet emerged from the fire.

◆ ◇ ◆

"Move aside, you lot!" A guard in Scaligeri livery used the shaft of his halberd to push back his section of the crowd. Gapers of every nationality pushed back, not to mention beggars looking for a shower of gold from the famously open-handed Capitano. But this path was reserved for the great nobles of Verona, who didn't need to be bothered by such as these. "Back. Back!"

Among those pressed backwards was a hooded figure with crooked shoulders and a fierce limp. Everyone who caught his sunken eye flinched and many made a sign to ward off evil.

As the first family of Verona finally came this way, the guard grew more energetic in his shoving. The Capitano rode beside the lady Giovanna, while the heir held the reins for his little bride's mount. Mastino was coupled with his Carrarese bride, while Alberto rode with his two unmarried sisters. Paride was next, with his cousin Verde and her disgraced husband Rizardo.

Next came the Nogarola clan, bound to the Scaligeri by politics, affection, and blood. A man, his Scaligeri wife, and their two sons. The lads were dressed in their knightly gear, their father proud as a lion, the lady sitting serenely sideways in her saddle as propriety dictated.

Fortune placed the twisted man on the right hand side of the procession. Had he been on the left, his eyes might not have narrowed in recognition. Resisting the liveried guard's jostling, he pointed his calloused forefinger towards the woman. "Who is that?"

"Show respect!" The guard slapped the pointing hand down. The man's Bergamo accent was almost impenetrable. Had he understood the question, he might not have answered it. As it was he snapped, "That is Donna Katerina da Nogarola, the Greyhound's sister, lady of Vicenza and mother to two of the new knights today. Now get back!"

As if under a spell, the cripple endured the shoving senselessly. After so long, all unlooked for, it had come. He had a name. He knew where to find her.

He stared until she was out of sight, wondering that she could not feel the intensity of his gaze. When at last she vanished from sight around the corner, Girolamo the Diviner turned and hobbled away through the crowd. He had some thinking to do.

♦   ◊   ♦

Having survived the latest earthquake without damage, the Arena was as impressive as ever. Second in size only to the Colosseum in Rome, this marvel of Roman engineering was superior in one vital respect – it was still functional. That was something that continued to amaze Pietro. In Rome, ruins were ruins, treated with reverence and open for pilgrims and gawkers with a sense of history. In Verona, the ruins weren't allowed to be ruins. Ancient arches were incorporated into new buildings, and if possible every structure was still in use. It was the difference between a necropolis and a metropolis. One was for the past, set aside for the dead. The other was for the living to carve out a future from the bones of history.

The Arena was the perfect example of this. Over a thousand years old, the inspiration for Dante's Hell could still hold thirty thousand people in its concentric rings of seats.

Today it was filled to overflowing. As the seats stretched all the way down to the Arena floor, low walls had been erected to protect the baser spectators from the deeds of the combatants. Though these protective walls had slats to allow viewing, they remained the least desirable seats. The best were in the fourth row on the center of each side – or else in the balconies above the two tunnel entrances on opposite ends of the Arena.

Berthold's appointed place was on the far balcony, so Pietro parted politely with the German. Elbow to elbow with the masses, Pietro climbed to the nearer balcony, the Scaliger's own.

Reaching it, he looked down and tried not to imagine a river of blood and a sea of centaurs. Instead he focused on his neighbours. Marsilio da Carrara was not far away, seated at the very front. The Paduan shot Pietro an amused smile and Pietro returned an ironic nod. This was their first time together in this structure since their duel. Perhaps time did indeed heal all wounds. Then he noticed Antony take up a seat far to the right, so he might not sit too close to Mari. *Not all wounds.*

Pietro's reserved place was just behind the front row. There were so many friendly faces here: Petruchio, Castelbarco, Nico da Lozzo. The first two were proud as peacocks, their sons being among those knighted this day, while Nico seemed to have grown a full foot in stature, so high did he hold his head. He had the right, vindicated in his decision to join Cangrande's faction at the start of this long war.

Petruchio was pointing to where his wife and daughters were seated, further up along the Arena's cascade of seats. "Poor sinless creatures. They don't get to be planted as deeply in Hell."

"Sinners always get the best seats," remarked Nico.

Petruchio grinned through his beard. "Well, we paid for them."

"Or we will," said Pietro, and everyone laughed.

Pleased with his small witticism, Pietro felt someone take a seat beside him and shifted automatically to make room along the stone bench. Turning, he came face to face with a much more recent nemesis than Carrara.

"Such pleasant weather for a November wedding," said Ambassador Dandolo of Venice. "But then, the Veronese always have the luck, do they not?"

The Ambassador spoke pleasantly, as if he had not once thrown Pietro into a lightless cell at the base of the Doge's palace, where rats had swarmed up through the grate of the foul Venetian waters to nip at Pietro's toes and fingers.

"If Verona has luck, it's because we make it." Pietro immediately regretted his sharp tone. He didn't want to give the Venetian the satisfaction.

"I must remember that in the future. Destroy the luckmakers, destroy the luck."

"Do you mean you wish to destroy your hosts?"

"On the contrary," replied Dandolo, eyes twinkling over his patrician nose, "I wish to learn from them."

This was not their first meeting since Pietro's escape from the Doge's palace. They had seen each other two months past, when Cangrande and Carrara had traveled to Venice to formalize this peace. Then, Pietro had been braced for Dandolo's cutting kindness and solicitude. Today, prepared for a different kind of trial, he found this unwelcome neighbour unnerving. Though he did experience a moment of gladness that his sister would not be attending. She hated Dandolo, less for what he had done to her brother than for the part he'd played in their father's untimely demise.

Pretending to look back to the Arena floor, Pietro's eyes paused at the Scaliger, who was now ascending to the balcony. Was Dandolo's presence some kind of taunt? A means of putting Pietro down yet again? But why? What was the message?

An internal voice very like his father's said, *It needn't always be about you.* Perhaps Pietro was not the victim here, but the weapon. Placing Dandolo beside a man he had wronged was hardly polite.

Well, if Pietro was here to discomfit the Venetian ambassador, he was more than happy to oblige. "I'm sad to say our mutual friends Dottore Morsicato and Tharwat al-Dhaamin will not be joining us for the ceremony," said Pietro lightly. "If you are in a learning mood, you could hardly have better teachers."

"Tharwat? Is that the man I knew as Theodoro of Cadiz? I thought I saw the renowned astrologer outside the church. I am delighted to hear he did not drown. Though, if what I saw was any indication, he has seen hard times of late. If I am to learn luck-making, I do not think I should apply to him. His luck seems to be of a most disastrous nature. Though perhaps it is a part of his profession. I was entertaining a diviner just last evening. He had a true gift, but was most disfigured — not by birth, but by mistreatment. Fortune must not look kindly at those who divulge her secrets."

"It might not be Fortune," offered Pietro. "Truth-tellers are often plagued by lesser men. Those who do not like the truth when they hear it."

"Does anyone want the unvarnished truth? I think the truth about any man would scald his soul and make his children disown him. Not you, of course, Ser Alaghieri. Everyone knows you to be honest to a fault."

"Whose fault?" demanded Nico across Pietro.

"Sorry," said Petruchio, pretending to break wind. "My groom gave me some beef and mustard this morning."

Cangrande arrived, clasping hands and slapping shoulders. Hearing Petruchio's comment, he pointed to Dandolo. "Perhaps Venice should make Lord Bonaventura a citizen as well, my Lord Dandolo. He could double the speed of your sails with a single expulsion."

Petruchio shook his hands in mock triumph. "The fart that

launched a thousand ships!"

Ignoring the continued brand of raillery that often occurred in the company of men, Dandolo retuned to his conversation with Pietro. "Our friend the Moor, I should like to speak to him. Where is he now?"

Tharwat and Morsicato had chosen to remain in the tunnels below, watching for danger. The last time Cesco had participated in Arena games, treachery had nearly claimed his young life. But that was not for Dandolo's ears. "They have better seats, closer to the action."

"Further down in Hell," said Nico across him.

Dandolo pressed on. "Indeed, I recall that Theodoro — forgive me, Tharwat — was always at the heart of any conflict. It must be difficult. Since the rise of this Orhan in Anatolia, Muslims have been more and more persecuted in Italy. I recall he was once attacked in Venice just for being a Moor. The Doge saved his life," added Dandolo pointedly.

"Yes, the Doge is certainly known for his hospitality," said Pietro. "And I will say, it is hard being a stranger in a strange place, full of plots and dishonest men. Fortunately, Tharwat knows a good doctor."

Being the second time Morsicato had been mentioned, Dandolo picked up the hint. "This doctor, you say he is our mutual friend. Yet I do not recall him."

"You met him once, for an afternoon. Though you might not recognize him, now his beard has returned."

Understanding dawned. "Ah yes, of course. Please tell them both I would be delighted to enjoy their company again."

"I am sure they will take that invitation in the spirit it was tendered."

"Excellent. Oh look. They are taking their places."

Pleased that Dandolo had been the first to change topics, Pietro followed the outstretched finger towards the purple-and-gold-clad men gathering at the center of the Arena. Amazed at how many there were, he did a quick count. "Thirty-nine! That must be the most knights created at a single time in Italian history."

"I believe the record is fifty-two. Azzo and Francesco d'Este created that many in Ferrara. 1294, I think. But this is certainly the most in modern times," added Dandolo, deigning to soften the correction with a patronizing smile.

Quelling the urge to hit the old man with his elbow, Pietro watched as the mitered Bishop Francis came forward to face the knights-to-be. He had been young and newly arrived in Verona at Pietro's knighting, and there was still a good spring in his step. Now, as then, he began the ceremony by reciting the Commandments of Chivalry:

Thou shalt believe all that the Church teaches,
and shalt observe all its directions.
Thou shalt defend the Church.
Thou shalt respect all weaknesses,
and shalt constitute thyself the defender of them.
Thou shalt love the country in the which thou wast born.
Thou shalt not recoil before thine enemy.
Thou shalt make war against the Infidel
without cessation, and without mercy.
Thou shalt perform scrupulously thy feudal duties,
if they be not contrary to the laws of God.
Thou shalt never lie,
and shall remain faithful to thy pledged word.
Thou shalt be generous, and give largess to everyone.
Thou shalt be everywhere and always the champion of
the Right and the Good against Injustice and Evil.

Next came the Chivalric Code. When Pietro had been created a knight, he'd been charged to proclaim two tenets of the Code. He'd chosen *'Live a life that is worthy of respect and honour'* and *'Protect the innocent'*. Having been extemporaneous choices, it was strange to think how prescient those words had been.

With so many new knights today, each had to name only one. An unworthy splinter of Pietro's heart hoped Cesco might pick one of his foster-father's choices. But Cesco had ever been his own man.

Among the prospective knights, the Paduans were given primacy of place for the ceremony, and so had their choice of tenets. Cangrande's close kin would go last.

"My eyes are not what they were," confessed Dandolo in Pietro's ear. "Who is first to speak?"

Pietro did not believe the Venetian for a moment – Dandolo, admit a weakness? "Ubertino da Carrara."

"Ah, Marsilio's less-troublesome cousin, new-reconciled. It will be interesting to hear his choice of tenets."

From the Arena floor, Ubertino's voice rang out. "Show respect to authority." A publicly contrite message that Marsilio applauded.

Next came Pietro Rossi, Cesco's father-in-law, who chose *Exhibit Courage in word and deed*, followed by his brother Marsilietto, who settled on *Live for freedom, justice and all that is good*. The youngest Rossi brother, Rolando, said, "Never abandon a friend, ally, or noble cause."

Dandolo squinted. "And who is next?"

Now Pietro was certain Dandolo was play-acting. "Obizzo d'Este and his brother Rainaldo."

"Ah! Quite the political coup, to have them present after your master's mistreatment of their brother-in-law." The Estensi had tied themselves to the star of the late Passerino Bonaccolsi through his marriage to their sister Alisia. It was widely considered that the Scaliger had performed an unusually craven and despicable deed in cutting off his former friend Passerino, going so far as to supply troops to help unseat him. But Pietro knew that, this one time at least, Cangrande was blameless. Bonaccolsi had tried to murder both Cesco and Cangrande. He deserved his fate.

Alisia was now a widow, Mantua belonged to Cangrande, and the Scaliger was courting the Estensi to shore up his support.

As Bonaccolsi's murderous plots had been made with the aid of the Venetian beside him, Pietro decided to twist Dandolo's tail. "Perhaps they don't wish to be blamed for his compact with Venice."

"Compact? What compact is that, Ser Alaghieri? You have some proof, I trust, to arraign me in your master's court?"

"If I had proof, I would have produced it before now. No, you are quite safe, my lord. But please do not insult me by feigning innocence. I recall hearing the plot from your own lips."

"You were more reluctant then to allow me to refer to the Scaliger as your master. Have we re-affixed our star?"

"No, just less interested in quibbling. We're missing the ceremony."

Several more knights had gone, uttering innocuous oaths – *Avoid Lying, Avoid Cheating, Avoid Torture, Exhibit Self-Control, Die with Valour, Respect Women*. A man called Jacobo dal Verme took one of Pietro's own, *Protect the Innocent*. Whereas his brother, Pietro dal Verme, declared, "Exhibit courage in word and deed!"

Dandolo pointed. "There's one of ours." And indeed, a Venetian called Nicolo Foscari was at that moment proclaiming, "Administer Justice!"

At last they reached the Veronese faction, the crowd cheering loudly for each one. Hortensio Bonaventura stepped forward and declaimed in a trumpeting voice, "Exhibit manners!" At which his father hooted.

Hortensio grinned as his brother, young Petruchio, took his place. His oath, "Despise pecuniary reward," had everyone howling with laughter. His namesake had famously gone to Padua to take a wealthy wife, and had returned with not only his gold, but his soulmate.

Other famous men had sons in this crowd. That redoubtable Veronese statesman, Guglielmo da Castelbarco, beamed like the summer sun as his own son proclaimed, "Be respectful of host, women, and honour!" It could have been their family motto.

Surprisingly, Valentino Nogarola chose, "Always maintain one's principles," whereas his brother's oath was warmly predictable. "Never betray a confidence or comrade!" Detto uttered it with great feeling, and Pietro appreciated the young man's continued loyalty. Cesco seemed to take no notice.

Last came the four Scaligeri heirs. The youngest was first. Paride della Scala was turning into a handsome fellow, if a little lacking in colour. His oath was straightforward, like the uncomplicated lad who said it: "Die with honour!"

Next came Alberto della Scala. Though he was Mastino's elder brother, Alberto was not insulted to be given a less prominent place. It was his brother's wedding day, after all. His frown was due to the paucity of choices left. It was considered poor form to repeat one already spoken. Finally he smiled. "Crush the monsters that steal our land and rob our people. *La Costa!*"

"*La Costa!!!*" roared the crowd, reveling in this local lore. *La Costa* was the name of an arched tunnel where hung the monstrous bone whose twin Pietro had seen just an hour ago.

Finally came the two bridegrooms. Mastino's choice was a cumbersome one, but Pietro was among those few who knew how well it fit. He spoke deliberately, enunciating each word. "Never use a weapon or stratagem on an opponent not equal to the attack."

At last came Cesco's turn. Pietro had lost track of which oaths had been spoken. What was left?

The fourteen year-old shook his longish mane of curling chestnut hair, smiled at the crowd, and spoke in a voice that carried from end to end. "If you cannot bend Heaven, raise Hell."

Startled looks, confused murmurs. A low hum rumbled all around as people questioned, repeated, and parsed what Cangrande's heir had said. This was not a proper oath, not one of the tenets of Chivalry! Few in the huge crowd would recognize it as a line paraphrased from Virgil. But the original context meant little. This oath, uttered in this place, on this day, was contrary to every aspect of Chivalry.

Dandolo was sitting upright. Bailardino shot a look at Pietro, who felt his heart beating faster. Was this it? Was this the moment when Cesco broke free of his indolent malaise?

At the front of the balcony, Cangrande rose. "We admire your creativity, Francesco della Scala. And also your love for the classics. But for the sake of form, choose a more traditional oath."

Cesco gave an elaborate shrug. "Avenge the wronged." With that, he returned to his place in the line as the clapping crowd discussed the portents of what Cesco had done.

It quite took the gloss from the final knighting as Cangrande turned and, drawing his father's famous sword, placed the blade on the shoulder of Marsilio da Carrara. Marsilio's choice of oath rang out through the packed stadium. "Live to serve God, Capitano, and country and all they hold dear!"

Satisfied, the Arena crowd applauded for what felt like ages. Eventually Cangrande gestured for silence, then turned to address the new knights below, reciting the same words his father had once spoken to him. "There is more to being a knight than skill at arms. To become a knight is to take upon you the responsibility of being God's sword of justice here on earth. A knight does not enrich himself. He does not, as many today do, seek fame or dress in the finest apparel." Here he paused, bowing his head in acknowledgement of his own sartorial habits, and how he had dressed these new knights. But when he held up his hand for silence, he continued in a serious vein. "A knight rights wrongs. A knight protects the innocent. A knight listens to the words of the Lord. Do you understand this?"

"We do," proclaimed the assembled youths.

"Then take the communion offered you and be one with the Lord." All the new knights ate the bread and drank the wine offered by the priests, and Cangrande proclaimed, "I bestow on each and every one of you the highest honour Verona can bestow. I name you Cavalieri del Mastino!"

Excitement began to build. The moment these knights finished basking in the crowd's adulation, they would go off to arm themselves for the *mêlée*.

On the edge of his stone seat, Pietro girded himself for the coming battle. He did not know what he wished for most – his ward's safety, or a return of the daring Cesco of old.

He noticed Dandolo rising to depart, and suddenly recalled his earlier comments about a diviner. A chill crept along Pietro's spine. What had he been divining?

◆   ◇   ◆

Now he had a name, Girolamo could do so much more. He'd searched for almost a decade, ever since the gift first revealed itself. But all he had was the vaguest memory of her face, hidden in shadow, her voice, muffled, and the scent of lavender. He'd tried both the church where she'd summoned them and the house they'd been dispatched to, without success. But armed with a name, the little stone at the end of the chain was swinging true.

It hung over a rough map of Verona. He asked, and it swung to where she was now. But everyone knew where she would be. There were times, even now, when he mistrusted. It had been wrong before. So he asked it where she was lodged. It showed him that, hovering over a different part of the map.

A roar from the Arena shook Girolamo's concentration. Knowing from experience how hard that concentration was to restore once lost, he stood up in the alleyway where he was hunched and tucked his pendulum away. Then he set out in the direction of that it had pointed him.

FOUR

IT WAS OVER almost before it had begun. Armour shining under the November sun, the two armies lined up. Not wishing to pit Paduan against Veronese on such a day, leadership was bestowed upon the new bridegrooms, the Scaliger's heir in charge of one army, his nephew commanding the other. Each had loyal Paduan knights to protect them, and the flags they carried were not of cities or families, but of solid hues – purple and gold.

Pietro expected Cesco to take this opportunity to revenge himself upon Mastino – an expectation clearly shared by Mastino himself, who kept shooting mistrusting glances at Cesco as the armies lined up. But though his army did well, Cesco himself refused to draw his sword, instead playing a very skillful game of cat-and-mouse with Mastino's army. Riding hither and yon, he let himself be chased around the Arena in a dazzling display of horsemanship. The crowd laughed at his antics, everyone remarking that it was an amusing strategy, if hardly a daring one. His foolishness demoralized his army, which quickly fell to Mastino's swords. Once his defenders were dispatched, disarmed and dismounted, Mastino's forces quickly cornered Cesco, who cheerfully yielded his banner to his cousin's waiting hand. "How you must love me, cousin!"

"Love you?" asked Mastino, pulling off his helmet to frown.

"*Amor vincit omnia*. You have conquered, and therefore you love. I feel bathed in my family's love today, don't you? Hoist, hoist, the masses are waiting."

Mastino obediently hoisted the banner of the vanquished side, and the masses bellowed their approval. Reaping the victor's accolades, Mastino found he could not smile. He had waited so long to be knighted, to be finally given his due. Yet both knighthood and victory seemed tarnished. Cesco had not truly tried, and there was no sweetness in beating an apathetic foe.

He had a weapon yet, should he choose to employ it. A weapon that would stir up Cesco against the world. The trouble was the double-bladed nature of that weapon, which could as easily cut his own heartstrings as the bastard's. Best to wait, and devise other traps to prod the bastard into.

One person who did not wait to prod Cesco was Cangrande. Almost the moment the *mêlée* was ended, the Capitano di Verona exited his balcony to greet his heir in the tunnels below. Neither demurred when Pietro joined them.

Dismounting and tugging off his helmet, Cesco gave them a lopsided smile, reminiscent of Pietro's own. "Alas, though I was defeated, it's no dishonour to the Scaligeri. I was beaten by one of our own."

Cangrande gazed down at his heir. Despite the young man's recent growth, it was doubtful he would ever reach the Capitano's magnificent height. One eyebrow arched. *"Fléctere si néqueo súperos Acheronta movebo."*

Cesco slapped his forehead dramatically. "Thank you! I couldn't remember the exact quote. Hence the mistranslation."

"If I cannot bend Heaven, I will raise Hell. Do you wish to explain it?"

Pulling off his mailed gauntlets, Cesco blinked. "Why, don't you understand it?"

"You hardly raised Hell in the *mêlée. Audentes fortuna iuvat.*"

Pulling his tabard over his head, Cesco shrugged. "Fortune may favour the bold, my lord, but she's already made clear her feelings about me. I don't see any point in wasting time wooing a bitch like her."

"That will be good to remember, as I make dispositions for the war with Treviso."

Cesco shrugged again as a servant unbuckled his *petta,* the breastplate with family seal etched in acid upon it. "I'll find something useful to do, wherever you set me."

"I daresay you will." Pietro understood why Cangrande's brow was furrowed. The Scaliger usually had more power to exert in these clashes. But Cesco seemed not to care how the conversation went.

"What a great success today has been," observed Cesco lightly. *"Sit Verona potens Itala virtute propago."* Let Verona's offspring be powerful, by Italian valour.

Cangrande placed a hand on Cesco's shoulder. "Cesco — it grows easier. *Experto crédite.*" Trust one who has gone through it.

Cesco patted the hand. "My, we are in a Virgilian vein! Grandfather Dante would be proud. Let me conclude, then, with an observation as true thirteen hundred years ago as it is today. *Quisque suos patimur Manes.*"

Pietro winced. He knew the quote well, had himself taught it to the boy years ago. *Each of us bears our own Hell.*

Cangrande sucked in a long breath. "It's you against the world, eh?"

"I hope I'm not against anyone! Except hunger. Isn't it time to feast? My bride should be done with her nap by now. Capitano. Nuncle." With a bow and a salute, Cesco departed, immediately joined by Detto, Paride, and the rest of the pack of Verona's new knights.

Pietro watched Cesco vanish around the curved walls of the catacombed tunnels, then experienced something unprecedented. The Scaliger placed a friendly arm about his shoulders. "He'll come out of it. *Ómnia fert aetas.*"

It was kindly said. *Time bears away all things.* But Pietro could not help noting that the Scaliger did not add the other half of Virgil's phrase: *'Animum quoque.' Even our minds.*

Pietro's response was as churlish as the Scaliger's had been kind. "I thought you wanted him broken."

Cangrande allowed his hand to slip. "So I did. I must be more careful what I wish for. Never fear, there will be some great trial soon. If not, I will invent one. The boy is too much himself to remain in this sullen vein for long."

Pietro hoped that was true. He dreaded what would happen when the pent up anger and frustration burst its dam. Like flood water, it would not care where it directed itself. Nor upon whom.

◆   ◊   ◆

The evening feast was magnificent. The food was delectable, the wine superb, and the entertainment the finest in the land. If this was to be Manuel's final bow, he had gone beyond the dreams of entertainers crafting an ongoing spectacle that would pay the performers for a year and be talked of forever.

The dwarfish Jew himself led the first round of revels, singing:

Wedding is great Juno's crown
O blessed bond of board and bed
'Tis Hymen peoples every town,
High wedlock then be honoured:
Honour, high honour and renown
To Hymen, God of every town!

"To Hymen!" cried the male revelers (and a few of the bolder feminine ones as well).

With so many people to host, the planners had eschewed any of the palaces. Cramped within doors, some great person would of necessity be snubbed. Instead, the tables were set up in the open air of the Piazza dei Signori, with braziers full of spiced wood warming the air.

"Ah! Now comes the true event!" Ever the lover of good food, Morsicato tucked in with delight at each new confection and dish presented, the creation of which was a task that had taxed the creativity of the Scaligeri cooks for a full month. As was the custom, each course was brought in on horseback, making an *entrée*, as the French called it, to great applause.

Cangrande's personal chef, the soft-spoken genius of the saucepan Giorgio Gioco, had crafted the banquet's menu and overseen the preparation. For this, the most significant meal in Verona's history, he had firmly embraced the theory of Four Humours cuisine. The enormous feast offered a variety of dishes to balance Melancholy, Choler, Phlegm, and Blood. Melancholic foods were cold and dry, while choleric foods were hot and dry. Phlegmatic meals were cold and moist, whereas bloody foods were hot and moist.

Most often a cook would pair fish, a phlegmatic food, with a hot and piquant sauce, balancing the cool moistness with choler. Today each course balanced the next, with wave after wave of culinary delight: dried venison, roast turtle dove, eel, oysters steamed in milk, cold quail and fatty pork, sautéed radicchio with mushrooms, duck breast with oranges, plums, and apples, filleted horseflesh and cheese soup, iced wild hare and boiled duck stuffed with lamb and glazed in butter and beer.

Once discussion of the *mêlée* was exhausted, conversation turned to the wedding ceremony. Lord Bonaventura seemed especially taken with the vows. Turning to Cesco, seated with his new Rossi relations, Petruchio called, "Twenty-three words! I commend you, my young lord! The best vows ever!"

"He's just glad we got to the feast faster," confided his wife Kate.

"Actually, I'm just interested in getting back to my mistress." This was Petruchio's favourite joke of late. An avid falconer, he had fallen in love with a beautiful long-winged lanner, which he had named Comare – a common word for 'mistress'.

"Air her all you like, she won't rake you the way I will." The buxom red-head covertly stabbed her husband with a knife in the thigh, making him jump.

"The ceremony had to be short," replied Cesco over his shoulder. "That's a lot to memorize. Isn't it, Maddelena?"

His little bride was beside him, flanked on her other side by her nurse. A cute child, she was slightly chubby, with dark brown hair neither straight nor curly. Cesco winked as she hid her face behind her hands. "Alas, I am too old for her. Imagine, being forced to marry someone three times your age! I am positively ancient!" He slipped an orange wedge between her fingers and she began eating it.

"Say thank you to your husband, Maddelena," said Madonna Rossi, seated close by.

Dutifully Maddelena said, "Thank you, husband." Her sisters tittered at her and she flushed, not knowing why it had been funny.

But her husband wasn't laughing as he leaned close. "Call me Cesco. Or, even better, Francesco. No one calls me Francesco. It'll be a secret between us."

Maddelena nodded. Her eyes were watery. She had finally been made to understand that she wouldn't be going home again. Her nurse would come with her, and a maid, but she was going to live in a strange house with this strange boy she'd met once at a church in Padua.

Cesco began cutting her meat for her. "It'll be like having a brother, only you get to order me around. You can have your mother and sisters to visit whenever you like. Do you like dogs?" She nodded. "We've got a lot of dogs. We can get you one of your own. A puppy. Would you like that?"

"I'd like a cat better," she said with a half-timid glance.

Cesco winced, but said, "A cat it shall be. Christ Jesus, a cat among all the hounds."

Nico da Lozzo grinned good-naturedly at the young couple. "What a sweet child. I hope she grows into a beauty, like her mother." He nodded to the lady, who smiled politely back.

"Cesco can always find one if she doesn't," observed Petruchio, earning him a wifely slap on the back of his head.

Ruffling Maddelena's hair playfully, Cesco twisted around to address Petruchio. "I've taken you as my example. I'm out to make a friend of my bride."

"You'll have an easier time taming her than I did," said Petruchio. "Maybe that's the secret. Get them while they're young!"

"Old, am I?" huffed Kate.

Petruchio chucked her under the chin. "Never. That would mean I'm getting older, which is patently absurd."

"Yet you are withered," observed Kate, a tight grin spreading.

"Tis with cares," replied Petruchio, his smile matching hers.

"I care not." They said it together and howled, to the bewildered eye-rolling of those around them. The strangest couple, those two.

♦   ◊   ♦

Pietro was seated with his brother Jacopo and the lords Castelbarco and Capulletto – Montecchio was seated with the Carrara clan, his relatives by law. The conversation was carried mostly by Poco and the uncommonly ebullient Castelbarco. For Pietro, the day was full of despair, while for Antony it was too much a reminder of losses past. Tessa, Capulletto's lady wife, was being deliberately engaged by Castelbarco's own considerate spouse while Antony stared at the Carrara table with a sullen expression.

"How are you finding life in Florence, Master Jacopo?" asked Castelbarco. "Is the city much changed under your new charter?"

"Much, and very little. The city grows, the people remain the same. I do hope the new system succeeds, but I don't see how it can. Drawing lots for public office? What will that do, but create one happy man and a thousand jealous ones? Government by chance."

"Which is why they limited the terms of office, no? Two months only?"

"Yes, and no officer can be succeeded by a member of his own family. It's all meant to stop the factions. But the Signoria is still in control of the drawing of lots. Already there are cries of rigging. It's an ingenious system, certainly – for those at the top of the ladder to keep those below squabbling over the rungs. But it has halted the violence, for now. I think all the fighting was interfering too much with trade. That couldn't be allowed."

"A cynic," remarked Castelbarco.

Jacopo shrugged. "A realist. We Florentines may be a stiff-necked bunch, but we are clear-eyed in matters of business. Which is why I think my brother is more at home in Verona. He is a Romantic at heart."

"Romantic?" Pietro frowned, puzzled. He considered himself a lawyer.

Poco showed his teeth. "Secret missions, martyrdom, adventure, peril! Above all, honour. You are made for the court of King Arthur. I don't doubt that in a few hundred years your deeds will be sung in legend."

"Hear hear," said Antony, grinning. "I had a song written for him once. I should have it appended to continue his tale."

"You're all mad," said Pietro, flushing.

His brother clicked his tongue. "Tch. A pity that stiff neck can't bend enough to make nice with the Signoria da Firenze. Think of the riches that would be heaped upon him."

"I don't need riches," said Pietro.

Poco turned in mock appeal to Castelbarco and Capulletto. "See? Not a true son of Florence. He doesn't care for money."

Antony clapped a hand to Pietro's shoulder. "Fortunately, he is already rich."

"He could be richer still, if he could just choke down that pride of his."

"I humbled myself in Avignon to escape the condemnation of God," said Pietro abstractedly. "I can live with the ire of my birthplace."

"The German theologian Eckhart was not so fortunate, I hear," said Castelbarco.

"Yes," said Pietro. The news had come over the summer. Not officially executed, but dead in custody.

"I've heard the name," said Poco. "Was he accused of heresy as well? Did you meet him?"

"Yes, and no," admitted Pietro. "There were orders for his trial while I was in Avignon, but our paths did not cross."

"Do you know much about his heresy?" asked Castelbarco.

"Supposed heresy," corrected Pietro with lawyerly precision. "No, I've not read his works. Did it have to do with Christ's poverty?" It was the *bête-noir* of the Avignon church under John XXII, which had amassed astonishing wealth selling indulgences.

"A little. He wrote that to be full of things is to be empty of God."

"That would do it," said Pietro, sipping lightly at his wine.

"Ah," said Castelbarco with relish, "but he followed the thought to its natural conclusion. That we are all beings of nothingness. God is the font of all life, our lives are merely borrowed. Being borrowed, we are mere reflections, poor images of God Himself. Not that, to Eckhart, God resembles man. God exists as God only when we pray, when action is required. The rest of the time God is a force of life, greater than human conception."

"I have always thought it was the folly of Man to try to understand the nature of God," said Pietro.

Castelbarco wagged a bony finger at Pietro. "Which was Meister Eckhart's point exactly. He said Man must live without asking why. That only in abandoning the pursuit of God can one discover the true *Gottheit*, which is beyond God Himself. The fecund source of all life."

"No wonder he was condemned," murmured Poco. "Abandon God to find God? Bad for papal business."

"I'm certain I'm butchering his meaning. I am no theologian," added Castelbarco defensively.

Pietro restrained a grin. *God Logic* was often sneered at, even by those who practiced it most. "Which, according to Eckhart, means you are enlightened."

"I will confess, his view of an over-abundant God is appealing. But we see too much in life that is cruel to believe that God is overflowing with love."

"It seems cruel to us," said Pietro, again forced to remember this day. "But what if the cruelty has purpose?"

"Cruelty comes from ignorance, or indifference. I choose to believe the Lord our God is neither."

"Cruelty can come from selfishness as well," said Antony, whom Pietro had not thought to be listening. "Most often it does."

"Truth is truth," said Poco, raising his cup.

As they all drank, Pietro reflected that Antony was correct. Castelbarco as well. Ignorance, selfishness, indifference – all kinds of cruelty stemmed from those roots.

But there were times that cruelty was simple caprice. A dark laugh by evil stars. Without cause, just the malice of Fortune. There was no use in raging against that kind of injustice. For how could one take revenge on the stars?

♦　◊　♦

The revels stretched on into the evening. More and more torches were lighted. The piazza outside the Scaligeri palaces, filled with the new knights and their families, was the stage for singing, dancing, laughter, contests, wagers, and the occasional brawl. Fire-eaters and sword-swallowers performed along the steps. The crowd exulted in the acrobatic feats of the tumblers. Fortune-tellers set up at the edges, predicting glory equal to the size of the coin pressed in their palms.

One of them was within a stone's throw of Donna Katerina, watching as his little teardrop of stone made its circles and told its stories. Twice he was removed by the guards, told that his visage was upsetting some of the women. But he simply took up some new station near the lady. He made certain he was between her and the house where the pendulum said she was lodged. She could not go home without passing him.

♦   ◊   ♦

While Cesco's table kept quiet, so as not to frighten little Maddelena, Mastino and Taddea were performing the proper duties of their station, circulating among the hundreds of guests and greeting famous faces.

Carrara was pleased to see them behave so smoothly, and said as much to Cangrande. "It bodes well for their public life."

"And their private?" asked the Scaliger.

Carrara pursed his lips. "What does it matter, so long as they behave properly in company?"

"There is no one less proper in company than Kate and her Petruchio. Yet I deem them the perfect marriage of Padua and Verona."

Glancing at his own wife, childless these several years, Carrara pulled a face. "Not all of us are lucky enough to be matched in spirit as Dante and Beatrice. We must settle for show."

Cangrande curled his eyes towards his own wife. "True enough. Please excuse me – mention of Dante puts me in mind of something." Catching the eye of his Master of Revels, Cangrande gave a signal. Laying a sly finger alongside his nose, Manuel disappeared.

A few minutes later Pietro was holding forth on a recent legal opinion issued by the famous Bellario of Padua when he saw Manuel approaching, lute in hand. With him came a small young woman, barely taller than the Master of Revels himself. Commanding silence with a hand, Manuel began to pluck the instrument's strings in a mournful tune, but with threads of hope woven through it.

Upon her cue, the female singer opened her mouth and the most incredible voice sprang forth: rich and full, earthy and entirely unexpected from such a shy waif. She sang words Pietro had never heard before – a new composition:

O anima cortese Mantoana
Di cui la fama ancor nel mondo dura
E durerà quanto 'l mondo lontana
L'amico mio, e non de la ventura
Ne la diserta piaggia è impedito
Sì nel cammin, che volt' è per paura
E temo che non sia già sì smarrito
Ch'io mi sia tardi al soccorso levata
Per quello ch'i' ho di lui nel cielo udito
Or movi, e con la tua parola ornata
E con ciò c'ha mestieri al suo campare
L'aiuta si ch'i' ne sia consolata
I'son Beatrice che ti faccio andare
Vegno del loco ove tornar disio
Amor mi mosse, che mi fa parlare.

O courteous Mantuan soul
Whose fame still lasts in the world
And will last as far as the world will go;
My friend, not the friend of fortune,
On the deserted shore is so blocked
In his journey that he has turned back for fear,
And I am afraid that he may be already so lost
That I have risen too late to help him
According to what I have heard of him in Heaven.
Now go and with your ornamented speech
And whatever else is needed for his escape
Help him, so that I may be consoled.
I am Beatrice who causes you to go;
I come from the place where I long to return,
Love has moved me and makes me speak.

It took Pietro no time at all to recognize the story, one told from a new perspective. He found his eyes welling, moved by this beautiful tribute to his father and the great *Commedia*. Before he knew it, both his brother and sister were by his side, and Cesco too, as they all listened to the Ballad of Beatrice, Dante's great love, the lady whose very name Antonia had taken for her holy vows. In it, the heavenly bearer of light and hope told of Dante's journey from *her* point of view, starting with her plea to Virgil to rescue Dante from the she-wolf, and ending with her final words of parting in Paradise.

It was a gift beyond price. And though Pietro knew the tune was Manuel's, a glance told him the words had been fashioned by Cangrande himself. A reward for years of service, a public acknowledgement of this peace, a private apology for all the betrayals, all the pain and anguish. In his inimitable way, Cangrande was making amends.

That planted an unwelcome doubt in Pietro's mind. Remorse was so uncharacteristic in the Scaliger, so utterly foreign to his nature, that something quite terrible must have happened. Did he feel Cesco's pain so deeply? Or was there something more?

Forcing those troubled thoughts aside for the time being, Pietro allowed himself to enjoy these poetic lyrics set to a haunting tune. Beatrice sang of dressing to meet with Dante on his journey, donning a white veil, a green cape, all over her flame-red dress — white for faith, green for hope, and red for charity. Then she placed upon her head a crown of olive leaves, the traditional crown of Pallas Athena, goddess of wisdom.

Unable to resist, Cesco plucked a rebec and bow from one of the idle musicians and began lightly sawing away in counterpoint to

Manuel's tune. They did not often have the chance to play together, these two. When they did, they were like two hands on the same sword, working in unison to cut the heartstrings and pluck the soul straight from out the body.

Flooded with emotion, Pietro watched this boy — *his* boy! — show another of his countless careless skills. His sister's hand crept into his. This was their child. His pain was their sorrow, his victories their pride. They had raised him, and now they wept as much for him as for the song. Pietro listened and watched, savouring, wishing this moment would last forever.

Beatrice brought Dante as far as she could go, ushering him into the Sun, the Heaven of pure light, intellect and joy married in perfect love and harmony. In the song she handed him off, not to San Bernardo as in the poem, but to God Himself, who welcomed the great poet home.

Part homage, part eulogy, the song ended on a long drawn-out note from Cesco's rebec, a note that had even Manuel's eyes clouding with tears. When it was finished there lingered only a hush, a raw shared breath as hundreds upon hundreds of souls clung to what they had just heard. Pietro's eyes were closed, his sister's hand clasped tightly in his own, wishing for so many things, grateful for so many more.

The applause started, and Pietro erupted to his feet with the rest. The girl singer blushed and smiled shyly, and Pietro knew that he would spend a large part of his now-considerable wealth to keep her in health so that she might sing this song her whole life long. He met eyes with Manuel. "Thank you."

"Say nothing. There is no greater joy than a gift properly appreciated."

Pietro turned to Cangrande. The Scaliger's famous *allegria* was strangely absent. Though the corners of his mouth were curled up and not down, he looked — sad, almost mournful. He, too, had been moved. Meeting Pietro's eyes, he did not hesitate, but walked up and over the table between them to embrace his favourite knight.

Pietro hugged him fiercely back, awash in conflict, grateful and resentful, happy and relieved, angry and wistful all at once. It was catharsis, an ending to so many hurts and hopes.

But when Cangrande turned to embrace Cesco, the boy was already shaking hands with other revelers, accepting their congratulations, as if the whole thing had been his idea. Cangrande barked out a short laugh. "Now I know how Zeus felt when his thunder was stolen."

Pietro wiped his eye. "It was marvelous."

Cangrande waved this aside with the back of his hand. "It occurs to me, Pietro, that this is what Verona lacks."

"What?"

"A poet. Your father is the closest we have come to literate fame, and that is reflected light – a Florentine falcon nesting in our towers. Mantua has Virgil. Why is there no great Veronese poet? What are we failing to do?"

"Perhaps it is Verona's destiny to inspire great art, not create it," suggested Pietro.

Cangrande mused at that before shaking his head. "Nevertheless, I must do something. I will add a professorship of Rhetoric to our six chairs. Perhaps that will elevate the discourse and lead to more scholarship." He snapped his fingers. "And you! Pietro, you know every winter month one of the six chairs must hold a public disputation on some matter under their banner. This past month it was arithmetic. Will you do me the great honour of leading a public debate of poetry next month? Use your father's text by all means. I need your help to make Verona not simply a military power but an artistic one."

Pietro balked. "I'm no poet. You should ask Cesco."

Cangrande cast a glance in his heir's direction. "I don't want to ask too much of him at present."

"I think it would be better to keep him busy than to let him wallow."

"You may be right. But I have kept him busy for as long as he's been in my power. I thought a lack of orders might show understanding."

"It also might show him you think he needs coddling. How would you have taken it, at his age?"

In spite of himself, Cangrande grinned. "I would have bitten off the nose of any man who tried to coddle me. Point well taken."

As the sea of praise ebbed, Cesco was returning to the Rossi table, where he excused himself. "My lords, forgive me if I depart for a time. My bride is understandably tired. It's time to tuck her in and tell her a story." There were good-natured barbs as men offered to accompany him to their home in a mock version of the traditional bridal procession. Taking Maddelena by the hand, Cesco added, "Don't fret, fellows. My wife won't lose her head like any common maid." That ribald comment was quite lost on the little bride, as it was meant to be.

"When you return," called Cangrande, "we'll find someone

here who'll help you celebrate your wedding night. We have willing dames enough!"

"Which no one knows better than you." There was no bite to Cesco's reply, only cheerful banter. But his words had several effects. Some men laughed outright, while others hid their faces behind their hands as they glanced at the Scaliger's imperious wife, blithely ignoring the implication. Well, she'd had enough practice at that! Cangrande's own laughter seemed just a little forced, while his sister's smile was completely genuine. Pietro saw Detto wince.

The young bridegroom escorted Maddelena out of the piazza towards their new home, hardly a stone's throw away. The little girl was attended by her sisters, her nurse, and several other servants. Madonna Rossi wept silently while the bride's father made determined conversation with his brothers, trying not to watch his littlest girl leave. It was a great match for them, but now the moment had come, he could not help feeling the tug of loss.

Between the song and the parting, things had become more maudlin than festive. "Come Manuel!" cried Nico. "Give us something lively, that we might caper!" The aged jester obliged, and soon the square was singing a spritely *ballata*.

Against his will, Pietro was forced to dance. Women flocked to him, married and unmarried both. Fathers introduced their daughters, brothers their sisters. It was a heady sensation, as he did not think of himself as either handsome or charming. But while Cangrande was the victor and Carrara the honoured guest, Pietro Alaghieri was the brilliant architect of this peace. Exiled Florentine, poet's son, knight, duelist, soldier, banneret, lawyer, judge, scholar, rich beyond most men's dreams. What did it matter if he was a clumsy dancer, or easily embarrassed? Of all the bachelors in Verona, he was the most sought after.

Spinning from partner to partner, he touched hands, stepping close then away. Sometimes a forward partner would brush her body nearer than was necessary, or drop a hand to rest on his arm, his shoulder, his chest. One even stroked his thigh. Pietro had to laugh at himself for being scandalized.

He eventually pleaded his bad leg and staggered off through the drinking contests and clusters of revelers. Dice had appeared on almost every table. It was like the best Christmas, a joyous Easter. And tonight was not the culmination, but merely the start of two more months of promised festivities that would last past the New Year. Some visitors would doubtless depart tomorrow, but the vast majority would stay on to partake in the hunts, sports, salons, and feasts that would go on until Twelfth Night.

He spied Donna Katerina, sitting alone. She caught his eye, and he could not resist her wave of summons. Sitting beside her on the bench, he took his ease.

"It is wonderful to see you dance," said the lady.

"I doubt I cut a very impressive figure," he replied, removing his hat to mop his brow.

"On the contrary, you are quite heroic. I am almost tempted to thwart all these feminine hopes and drag you away for joyous congress." He blinked, and she laughed at him. "O Pietro! For someone who has engaged in the sordid business of spying, your face is as a book to be read by all! A lover would do you such good."

"If you say so, lady."

Katerina studied him, amused. "Why did we never have an affair, you and I?"

An invisible fist clenched his throat. "Because I admire your husband."

"That cannot be the sole reason. Is it my many crimes?"

Pietro decided to answer truthfully. "Partly. But also that affairs, by their nature, must end."

"And you would not want it to," she said with a glow of delight. "That may be the most flattering praise I have ever received."

Flushing, Pietro shook his head sharply. "This is a poor topic on such a joyful day."

"Perhaps it is that, having achieved all my hopes, I seek a little piece of personal joy myself."

All her hopes. Cesco, locked in a sham of a marriage, bound to a fate he did not even know awaited him. Rising, Pietro bowed to her. He could not even think of an excuse as he stalked away, hearing her rippling laughter behind him.

He pushed through the people, his mood sour. *I should have taken Cesco abroad, to France or Spain, or sent him to the Imperial court. Anywhere but here, where he is the pawn of his family and the thrice-damned stars.*

The aged astrologer kept to the edge of the festivities, like a gargoyle in an old French town, watchful and immobile. Too often in the past a revel had turned to danger. Once, in this very square, Tharwat had faced down an angry leopard, though it was Ser Alaghieri who bore the beast's scars. The eight month-old Cesco had been pitched to its mercies by Cangrande's bastard brother, Gregorio

Pathino. Pathino was dead, but there were many other foes out there, beyond Verona's walls.

And even more within them. Tharwat's eyes returned often to Ambassador Dandolo, deep in conversation with the one-eyed Berthold. Venice and the Emperor had an uneasy relationship, but could possibly be united in their fear of Verona's rise. Out of such mutual interests were born strange bedfellows.

From the foreigners, the Moor looked closer to home. Mastino, now shaking hands and smiling, had proved himself more dangerous than Tharwat had expected. He had imagined the young man to be able only to inflict obvious and petty harms. Mastino feared killing his kin, and so the Moor had written off any real potential harm from that quarter. Clearly a mistake.

Someone who had not stinted at attempted murder was the Scaliger's wife, Giovanna. Finding her in the crowd, he was surprised when she met his gaze and, navigating the twirling dancers, approached him. Tharwat bowed. "Madonna. My congratulations on a most joyous day."

"Is it joyous?" asked Giovanna da Svevia. "Certainly it's frantic. But is seeing my husband's bastard married and made a knight a cause for joy?"

"For many, yes."

"For you, certainly. The culmination of years of scheming."

"The schemes are not mine, lady," said Tharwat stoically. "They belong to the stars."

"A convenient answer." The years had not been kind to Giovanna. Much older than her husband, her face had creased and withered. With her hair hidden under her flowing caul of gauze and silk, she looked severe even in repose. When, as now, she scowled, the lines bunched and multiplied.

Her eyes traveled to her good-sister, the lady Katerina, now talking with some hunchbacked mountebank. "I know whose schemes they are. The bitch-mother."

"Cesco is not her son, lady," rasped the Moor from his scarred throat.

"Which makes it all the more inexplicable. Her son, I could understand. But her brother's by-blow? Why trouble herself over him at all? There have been plenty others, and she's never cared a fig. Nor has he. Now all that has changed. You know that he's brought out two more bastards for the revels. It's as though he's determined to humiliate me."

"I am certain that is not his intent. He means to show the

whole strength of Verona's first family. I note that Paride has a place of honour."

"Yes." Giovanna's gaze fell upon her great-nephew, who danced with skill for one so young. "And he is knighted, which is as it should be." Returning her formidable gaze to Tharwat, she said, "It is of Paride I wished to speak. We made a bargain once. That when Cesco was elevated, he would take pains to raise Paride with him."

"You believe that time has come."

"I do. I wish Paride to become one of the Heir's intimates. If I could have my way, he would displace Katerina's son as the Heir's bosom friend. But I know she wove those threads early on. It would take a sword to cleave them."

"I pray that is not a threat."

Giovanna studied him, her eye lingering upon his eyepatch and slightly hunched shoulders. "If it were, would I be so foolish as to mention it? You are not so fearful as once you were, but I know enough of your history to respect even a shadow of your self." She smiled. "But it is heartening to hear that you pray. I did not know that a heathen astrologer ever bent knee to the Lord."

Tharwat said nothing, gazing out his remaining eye with stolid placidity.

Giovanna's lips curled. "So much for goading. My demand stands. Paride must be included in whatever Cesco plans next."

Now it was the Moor's turn to twitch a smile. "I do not believe he makes plans, Madonna. He is a creature of spontaneity. But I shall pass along your request. Though, knowing the two boys, I doubt any closeness will occur. They are as unlike as men may be."

"I do not care for genuine closeness. I care for raising Paride's station. Do that, and I care nothing if they try to murder each other in private."

"You should," said the Moor. "Because we both know which would win."

✦　◊　✦

Flushed and sweating from exertion, Cangrande dropped into a seat beside his sister. He waved off the hunchbacked diviner with a pair of coins. "Go to, man, and avoid her. She has too much truck with your kind as it stands."

The cripple backed away, but held the lady's gaze until he was swallowed by the crowd. Busy waving for more wine, Cangrande missed the look.

"You should be dancing with delight, my dear. Does your stroke prevent you? Surely Bail will carry you. Your own Bailata. Ha!"

"I don't doubt it." Unlike Katerina's limp, the slur from her stroke had long vanished. "But if you keep drinking the way you are, Francesco, he'll need his strength to carry you into the palace."

"They usually employ a cart. Lord, my head is swimming. If the Trevisians fell upon us tonight, they could win the war before it started."

"Another man might find that a sobering thought."

"Another man might not fight as well drunk as sober. You seem agitated. I thought today was your coronation. You should be well-pleased."

Her features realigned. "Am I not? Both my sons are knighted today. Though some might say they're too young for the honour you've done them. I'm not complaining, brother dear, but little Valentino has done nothing to deserve knighting."

"Few ever do," replied Cangrande as he waved to the crowded tables and dancing guests. "I was younger than either of them when our father knighted me. Besides, when are we going to have another such chance to trot out the whole family? See those two over there," he pointed. "My sons."

"Their names?"

"Bartolomeo and Ziliberto."

"Not Alboino?"

"No." Cangrande's grin became a touch more feral. "I can only imagine Mastino's reaction were I to name one of my offspring after his father."

"Yet he will appreciate you naming one after his uncle? I think the omission will be a point of contention."

"Very well. I shall go out tonight and father a new one to call Alboino. Does that please you?"

Katerina studied the two young men. "They are very alike. Do they have the same mother?"

Cangrande looked abashed. "Their mothers are sisters."

"Making them both brothers and cousins. Technical incest. That is repulsive." Katerina's nose wrinkled, yet she did not pursue this with the vigour he expected. "How old?"

"Barto is sixteen, Berto is just shy of Cesco — fourteen next month."

"What are they like?"

"They are like themselves. Which is to say, nothing like me. Barto is a follower, and Berto is the follower of a follower."

"Cesco has met them?"

"In passing. He didn't seem very interested. But I thought it was time to bring all my natural children into the fold."

"Including your daughters? How many are there?"

Theatrically, Cangrande counted on his fingers. "Margherita, Francheschina, Lucia, and —" he paused, then snapped his fingers together. "Giustina! Not to mention the infamous Rosalia, of course."

"No Katerina, I notice."

"Hurt?"

"Honoured, I think. Did you invite any of them?"

"And tempt the wrath of Fate? No, that was a narrow escape as it was. Why taunt him more? Poor boy."

Katerina stared unseeing into the crowd. "It would be worse if he ever knew the whole story."

Cangrande's head snapped away from the revels, the full weight of his attention landing on her. "Which is why we must make certain that our little Greyhound never hears it, no?"

"I quite agree," said Katerina, still not looking at him.

Cangrande studied her distraction. Then, hailed, he produced a flash of teeth and flung himself back into the dance while she remained behind.

Her distraction had not made her oblivious to his use of the title. Unprompted, her brother had applied the name Greyhound to Cesco. That was a victory in itself.

♦   ◊   ♦

Through a gap in the revelers, Pietro spied his sister sitting on the stairs by the old well at the far end of the square, deep discussion with a Franciscan friar. Looking at him now, it was difficult for Pietro to see the gangly, frightened young man who'd come to Verona fourteen years ago. But Fra Lorenzo was still handsome, even if he'd added pounds and lost hair — his tonsure was more expansive than strictly necessary.

Lorenzo spied Pietro threading through the milling throng and his smile faded. It was understandable. Pietro had once resorted to blackmailing the friar with a piece of his sordid French past. A deed that caused Pietro deep shame.

Rising, Fra Lorenzo forced himself to be complimentary. "Ser Alaghieri, you've worked a miracle. Blessed be the peace-makers."

"Thank you. I had little to do with it. It was Suor Beatrice's notion, funneled through Cesco. I'm just here to reap the praise."

"Your sister is a remarkable woman. The Dominicans are fortunate to have her." Fra Lorenzo's face darkened. "I half expected her to have company at the convent."

Pietro frowned for a moment before enlightenment struck. He looked accusingly at Antonia, who raised a defensive hand. "He knew already! Arranged for them to meet, even."

"Oh," said Pietro, forcing himself to be calm. "Forgive me, Father. You understand, I'm sure, the desire to keep that story to as few hearers as possible."

"Better than most," said Fra Lorenzo. "And if there is blame, I accept my share. I have a soft spot for young lovers – as you are well aware."

Knowing the friar's past, Pietro *did* understand. "I don't think there can be blame. This was set in their stars."

His sister gave him a piercing look. But there was no denying the power of those charts. Not anymore.

He glanced back to where Katerina sat. Standing beside this disused well in the *volto dei Centurioni*, next to Pietro's first home here in Verona, they were elevated by a step and so could look down on the bobbing and weaving heads to see her issuing orders to a servant. As if she had no more concerns in the world. She had believed in those charts all along – and helped them come true.

"The question of the girl troubles me," said Lorenzo, picking up his earlier thought. "I hoped she would seek the cloister. But since she went back to her father, I've heard nothing from her. God knows I've written. Has he gone to check on her? Has anyone?"

Shamefully, Pietro hadn't even considered it. But then he did not know her, had only a vague recollection of meeting her after the burning of the forge. "It's understandable that Cesco hasn't contacted her."

"It is," agreed Lorenzo. "And I'd like you both to see it stays that way. He's not entirely to be trusted. Not in his current state."

Pietro's brows came together. "What state is that?"

"Surely you know."

Pietro realized he did. "The hashish." Just how many of their secrets did the Friar know?

"I work with herbs, I recognize the signs. It might have been moderate, even healthy, before the peace. But now?" Fra Lorenzo looked momentarily furtive. "Actually, I think it is partly my fault. I convinced him to swear an oath. If God granted him his heart's desire, he was to abandon the filthy habit forever."

"And his heart's desire was this girl," groaned Pietro.

"She has a name," said Antonia. "Lia."

Pietro ignored this. "So, having kept his side of the bargain, he's decided that God has broken His, and is embracing the substance to punish God. Never mind that he's punishing himself more. Dammit!"

"No need to blaspheme," said Lorenzo sharply.

"The Devil there isn't! Is there any other meddling you'd like to share?"

Antonia laid a hand on her brother's arm. "Pietro. It is not his fault. You said it yourself. It was in their stars."

Pietro opened his mouth to find only ashes. He glanced again at Katerina, a great wad of emotion lodged in his throat.

He was rescued from this awkward pause by the arrival of Detto. The Friar congratulated young Nogarola on his knighthood. "Thank you," answered Detto perfunctorily. "Has anyone seen Cesco?"

Frowning, Pietro scanned the crowd. "He didn't come back?"

"No." That one word was fraught with meaning.

"He might not be in the mood for company," said Fra Lorenzo.

"He might also be feeling the strain of the day," said Antonia.

But Pietro was recalling another day in Cesco's life when he'd been thwarted, hurt. A child in arms, barely walking, he'd been ignored by Donna Katerina and had retaliated by threatening to fall out a window. During the years in Ravenna, such blatant self-destruction had moderated itself into mere recklessness. But now? "Find him. Quietly. Don't raise a fuss."

Their first stop was Cesco's lavish new mansion along the *via Pigna*. The girl and her servants were all there, but of Cesco there was no sign. He'd left her at the door with a brotherly kiss on the forehead, then headed back in the direction of the revelry. He'd never arrived.

"Hiding, or abducted?" asked Antonia, striding back towards the noise.

"I don't know which is worse," said Pietro. "Yes, I do. Come on."

They searched the palaces, the nearby taverns, the stables, all his known bolt-holes, without success. It was his wedding night, and while the whole city celebrated the peace he'd brought about, Cesco had vanished.

FIVE

Rising from her seat in the open square, Katerina da Nogarola begged to be excused from the festivities. "I grow exhausted with joy. No, Bail, you stay, enjoy the night. It's barely a dozen steps to our house."

This was perfectly true. The Casa da Nogarola was at the end of the alley that contained her family's private church, Santa Maria Antica. With two servants to light her way, she traversed the alley slowly, leaning upon her cane – her clumsiness was more evident when she was tired. Earlier tonight she had thought of her feathered mattress with a worrying anticipation. *Time enough to sleep when we are dead.*

She missed her former grace and majesty. More than anything, her stroke five years earlier had made her feel ugly, more disfigured than diseased. Hence tonight's flirtations with Pietro. Unkind? Perhaps. But while her infirmities were a price she accepted, Katerina missed feeling attractive, and Ser Alaghieri had always been an excellent bolster for her sagging feminine pride.

Neither fatigue nor pride mattered now. That damned diviner. After all these years, to appear tonight, of all nights! Fortune had a dark sense of the absurd.

Anxiousness churned her blood and she paused to steel herself beside the white and cream layered marble of Santa Maria Antica. Her eyes fell upon the freestanding marble sarcophagi of her uncle, father, and eldest brother. *Apt,* she thought. *Too bloody apt.*

Fashioned from expensive rose marble, the monuments were unadorned save for the family crest and their names – Mastino, Alberto, and Bartolomeo. Her middle brother Alboino was not entombed here. There wasn't much cause to remember him, save for fathering the namesakes of Alberto and Mastino. And for dying young, thereby forcing her littlest brother to take over the city before his time. Cangrande had been just twenty when he was made the leader of Verona. The burden would have broken any other man. But on this day, with the cheers and singing and joy echoing throughout the streets, it was hard not to see the hand of Fate, of Fortune, or even God.

My hand, she thought. *I have been the instrument of Fortune. Is she now finished with me? Is she truly that fickle?*

Her thoughts roiled in anticipation of the meeting to come. It would be dangerous. She could be exposed. But exposure would not be too high a price for the glory of this day. She had succeeded.

Impulsively, Katerina ran her gloved left hand over the stone of her father's tomb. She had some sensation in two of her fingers, but the rest were numbed by the terrible burns of long ago. Like her other infirmities, she resented the scars, but accepted them as the fee for her part in the great wheel. She had a goal, a duty, a purpose. She was meant to guide the Greyhound to his great destiny. It had been foretold, the greatest gift ever. The greatest privilege.

There is always a price. My scars, my stroke, they were mine. Cesco is paying his tonight. He will never thank Fortune, or me. But one day he may understand.

Though the cripple awaited her, Katerina lingered a moment more beside the marble casket of her father. A hard man, and a devout one – despite the fact that he had littered the Feltro with his bastards.

Bastard. Bastardy was such an interesting concept. Base born. But if they were truly base, why were bastards so often formed better than the legitimate heirs?

Legitimate. A word ripe for mockery. The product of legal mating – as if a ring and a vow made the coupling of man and woman legitimate. In having Cesco declared legitimate, her brother had set a dangerous precedent. If bastards could inherit, the wheel could turn and crush the nobility. Yet what choice had they had, really? Better a bastard than ruin. Her family had always been pragmatic.

Katerina's two feeling fingers traced the shape of her father's name. He was not a man to talk of Fortune. For him, it had all been God's will. Alberto della Scala had been far more religious than any of his children. His legitimate children, at any rate. Oh, her brother liked his shows of piety for the Virgin, but he was as often out of church on a Sunday as in it. The Pope's fault, for being too free with his excommunications. Barred from services, a man might realize that with the Church or without it, the world rolled on just the same. The dwarfish pope was undermining his own institution, eroding his own power by wielding it too carelessly. *There's a lesson in that.*

Turning from her father's resting place, Katerina gazed upon her eldest brother's marble tomb. Bartolomeo had been her favourite. All of Francesco's mirth, none of his rage. Francesco awed his people, but Bartolomeo had loved them, genuinely loved them all. It appeared in his every smile, a smile not half so bewitching as Francesco's, but far more genuine. He had wanted nothing from Katerina. At her request, he had placed Francesco in her care. She'd been so young, then. Just married, still in her teens. *Nearly thirty years ago.*

Katerina shivered. Without the warmth of bodies and braziers, the cold pressed in. But having paid homage to the two men resting here, she felt obliged to face the third. Mastino. The Mastiff. The first Scaligeri to rule Verona, having taken it by force from the malevolent Ezzelino da Romano. Mastino, the first Scaligeri master of Verona.

She had never met her uncle. His was the legacy they were all indebted to, and eager to run from. Wild, free, and fierce, he had died untimely, like most men in her family. Murdered in the *volto dei Centurioni* alongside Bail's father. Two families knit together by blood shared and blood spilled.

There was the year of his death, engraved upon the marble. 1277. He'd held Verona together for eighteen years, a record beaten only by her father, the devout Alberto.

Eighteen years. That's how long Francesco will have ruled when he takes Treviso next summer.

Enough. She had an appointment, one that could not wait. Leaving the dead behind, she carried on towards the Casa Nogarola, already within sight. Inside, a servant took her shawl. "You have a visitor, Madonna. He offered the correct password—"

"I am expecting him," said Katerina. "I shall meet him alone."

"He is in the waiting room upstairs, Madonna."

Her escort doused their lamps and departed as the servant lit a candle for her. The rest of the servants were out, attending her husband and sons, or else partaking of the revels themselves. This resulted in a pleasant silence, marred only by the thump of her cane and the awkward fall of her step. It also meant they would not be overheard.

Reaching the top step she saw a lamp was lit in the waiting room. Further down the hall a second light emanated from beneath her study door. There were standing orders that no one was to enter Katerina's study without her express permission. Bailardino, of course, went where he pleased, but when in Verona he preferred to spend his hours in one of her brother's palaces, not here in this cramped casa. No one else had the right to enter her domain uninvited.

A rush of fear filled her, propelling her to the door, her good hand fumbling at the latch and throwing the portal open. "Get out of here at once—!" she began, then stopped short.

Her study was a shambles – documents everywhere, cushions askew, the detritus of the bookshelves across the floor. A fire was blazing in the hearth, and another in a brazier upon the other side of the room, creating a positive wall of heat.

In the middle of the room, Cesco was seated in her favourite chair, feet propped upon a stool, several heavy parchments in his lap. "I let myself in. I didn't think you'd refuse. But I'll go in a moment."

"I was expecting someone else. Stay, by all means." Katerina took a moment to conceal her surprise. And her delight. She surveyed the shambles. "Was there another earthquake?"

Cesco didn't look up. "Yes. God appeared long enough to sneeze, and the foundations of the world were rocked."

"You'll clean all this, of course."

"In another life, perhaps." Cesco held up a parchment, the least faded. "This one seems to keep me busy." He gestured at another. "This one, too."

Katerina closed the door behind her, the cripple forgotten. Now the moment was upon them, she refused to be interrupted. "Where is your bride?"

"Tucked in bed with her rattle and blanket. I was heading for a whorehouse but ended up here instead."

Katerina examined the room. "And you needed to destroy the room because it lacked willing feminine pulchritude?"

"I was hoping to find Lord Nogarola's trove of erotic drawings. My education is lacking."

"We keep them in my bedroom."

"To arouse him, when you fail to. Sensible."

She was too pleased to be insulted. "I did not know you could read star-charts."

Cesco raised his eyes just long enough to deliver a look of withering scorn, then returned to tracing a finger along a coloured line upon one chart.

Katerina took a step closer, but did not sit. This was a conversation best had on her feet. "I simply meant I wouldn't have thought Tharwat would teach you. He didn't want this information in your hands, you see."

He did not rise to that bait. "You were expecting someone else, I take it. Feel free to find them. I'm fine on my own."

"You need not be on your own, ever. You have me."

"I have never been more lonely than in your company." He said it absently, but the malice was palpable.

"Shall I send for Tharwat to help you decipher?"

Cesco clicked his tongue. "Go, by all means. But you'll be wasting his time, and mine. He and Nuncle Pietro use astrology for all of their codes. I broke those years ago. It was safer to simply keep my birthday from me. I see it's June Thirteenth. Gemini Ascendant, the Moon squared with Mercury and Jupiter both, while trining with Mars and sextilling with Venus, which itself is opposed to Mars. I have very little relationship with Saturn I see. Mercury again, trined with Pluto, making me a master of cause and effect, which I should call the obvious. Venus opposed to Saturn. Does that make me unstable, or just filthy-minded? Ah! Mercury is conjunct with Jupiter."

"Hence your love of knowledge. And words," added Katerina.

"Tasty, tasty words." His eyes continued across the parchment. She waited until his eyes stopped moving. "So – what do you think?"

Setting the three charts neatly aside, Cesco straightened in the chair, crossed his legs, and rested his folded hands upon his knee. "I think it will be a short winter, but hard."

Katerina frowned. "What?"

"Just making polite conversation."

"Politeness doesn't suit you," said Katerina.

"Fine, you crippled mewling cunt."

Katerina's hand tightened on her cane. *"What?"*

"Just making impolite conversation. It's that, or no conversation at all. And I have the feeling, Donna Katerina, that you'd disapprove of silence above all else. You've waited far too long for me to see these." Glancing around, he cocked his head. "I know this room so well. I almost died here, you know. My very first night in Verona I was in a truckle bed by that wall, gasping and dying of poison. Nasty poison, too. Scorpion venom, mashed mouse, hellebore, and so much more. You weren't present, of course, as you were feigning your illness, waging whatever private war you deem more important than actually solving the problems at hand. But this was my sickroom, dear Auntie. For two whole weeks your sons watched as I was bled and fed and washed and nursed back to life. I always think of this as the Poison Room. A room full of venom and death."

"Poetic," observed Katerina. "But then, look who raised you."

"A pity no one shared these with me back then. It might have helped to know I needn't fear death — at least, not for a few more years." He lifted the nearest chart and pointed. "Death, without death. What on earth is that? No, don't speak. I prefer to work it out on my own. That way I know I can trust the source."

A lifetime of clashing with her brother had taught her how to engage such a speech. "Self-pity doesn't suit you."

"But I wear it so well! Self-pity is the only kind I'll allow. Certainly not the pity of others."

"Good, as I won't offer you any."

"I wasn't asking, you droop-faced bitch."

Katerina's jaw hardened. "Cesco—"

"I'm merely being accurate. You've had a stroke, and you are the mother-figure to Cangrande, the Greyhound. In terms of pure logic, that makes you a droop-faced bitch, does it not? Here we are, the bastard and the bitch. The confrontation so longed for by the bitch, and not at all by the bastard."

"Then why come?" When Cesco made a face as if the question were too foolish to answer, Katerina corrected herself. "Why today? Why not any time in the last two months?"

"I was arming myself."

"What with?"

"Knowledge. The only weapon worth having."

"Is that why you've deigned to see them? When last we spoke, you were determined not to know your future."

Languid in his seat, Cesco's smile did not reach his eyes. "Ah, but that was before the blessed goddess Fortuna made her declaration of war against me. If I am to don my invisible armour and march into the field, I need to understand the terrain." He gestured at the heavy rolls of parchment. "I know now what these are. Not star-charts. They're maps. Maps of how the battle will be fought. I was foolish to ignore them. Wars are won, not in numbers, but by strategy and intelligence. Had I taken up your kind offer, I might not have lost the first engagement. So I am here, setting aside pride to glean what my foe has in store for me."

"The stars are not your enemy, Cesco."

"Pity, as I'm determined to be theirs."

"They only mean to guide you to greatness. To your destiny."

Cesco looked upon her for a long time, considering, as if only now seeing her clearly. Then he shrugged.

"What?" asked Katerina.

"I never took you for a foole." He rose as if about to depart, then seemed to reconsider. "I am curious about one thing. When you were tempting me to bite the apple, Eve, lo these many years, you laid out the reason for the multiple charts – the night I was born, there were conflicting aerial omens. These charts are the varied results. Good, bad, muddied. I understand all that. What interests me is why you had these made in the first place. Why such a focus upon me, one of the Greyhound's many bastards littered all over the Feltro? How did you even know my chart would matter?" She opened her mouth, but he held up his hand. "No no, please. I might have mentioned that I prefer to work it out on my own. If I ask you no questions, you'll tell me no lies."

"I have never lied to you," said Katerina.

"Of course you have. Everyone lies. About everything. It helps to know that. Gives me a sense of the rules."

"Information was withheld until you were old enough to accept it."

"What, that I have a variable nature? I could have told you that at five. I probably did."

"You had to be old enough to accept the price."

"Price?"

"The fee of greatness. It is a terrible privilege – to be given a life with true purpose. There is always a price. For you, the cost was your happiness. In return, you will shape the world in ways I cannot imagine."

Cesco looked constricted within his skin. "And your price? Was that the hatred of all those you've mothered?"

That cut close to bone, but she remained relentless. "I have sacrificed much to bring you to your destiny."

He was as tall as she, thin and spry and hard. "Yes, but who were you willing to sacrifice? Not yourself."

"I have burned for you. Quite literally."

"Ah, you've heard I like older women, and of my own family."

"Cesco!"

His voice had dropped this summer, making his laugh richly deep. "Shock? From you? Astonishing. If you have burned, it was on a pyre of your own making."

"No. The pyre made by the stars, to forge your destiny."

"This destiny you keep mentioning – apart from a questionable death, there's no sign of it here."

Katerina arched a brow. "Here was I, thinking you were clever. Or does your love of insult so clutter your brain that you cannot see the obvious?"

This time her goading was successful. Cesco spoke slowly. "You said once that these charts were a weapon. A weapon I could use against Cangrande. They hurt him – how? He does not care if misfortune is heaped upon my head, so he cannot be lamenting the hardships these predict. I cannot say I envy my future self. Or rather, any of my possible future selves. Except this one." He held up a parchment, the honeyed wax of the broken seal making it bob awkwardly at one end. "But I think it's time to be done with fantasy," he added, and tossed that star-chart into the fire.

Katerina lunged forward before catching herself. He was right. The chart that predicted happiness, peace, marriage for love, was no longer possible. Yet she watched it burn with strange reluctance. She had guarded these charts for fourteen years, cherished them, pored over them. To see one burn was frightening. Never again would she behold those intersecting multi-coloured lines, so harmonious and beautiful. And false.

"The fee you mentioned." As the parchment crackled, Cesco started to pace, continuing his deductive monologue. "So Cangrande is wounded by these charts, not for my sake, but for his."

"Or Verona's," she observed.

"In his mind they're one and the same. Thus my brief life and brush with greatness somehow diminishes him. How? Everything I achieve reflects well on him. Yet he was pushing me towards that fate," he said, pointing at the blackened and curling parchment, "even seemed pleased if I could be happy. He was sad, today. Whereas you, Madonna, you found it possible to smile. I beheld the radiance of your joy quite clearly over my darling bride's head."

"I was happy for the day," replied Katerina. "A victory for Verona."

"You were happy in Fortuna's victory over me. As happy as the Capitano was sad. Because if I do not marry for love, I will achieve a greatness, one that might even eclipse him. Because if I have this greatness thrust upon me, then somehow he is less than…" He paused on a half-drawn breath. With a startled laugh, he smiled to himself. "Son of a bitch. I'm the Greyhound."

"Yes." Katerina swelled with triumph. "After today, that is certain."

Hearing her pride, his smile faded. "And what does it matter to you who the Greyhound is?"

Katerina della Scala raised her chin. "It was foretold that I would be mother to the Greyhound, guide him and shape him. Shape you."

"With your brother as your *quintana*, honing your lance. No wonder he hates you so." Shaking himself, Cesco became brisk. "Well, thank you, droopy bitch, for safeguarding my future. So many questions answered. *Felix qui potuit rerum cognóscere causas.* It's a Virgilian kind of day." With a theatrical shrug, he glanced at the remaining parchments. "Myself, I'm more interested in palmistry. At least those lines stay where I can see them."

Katerina crossed closer. "You cannot deny your destiny."

"That would make me like himself, wouldn't it? I understand him so much better now. You are quite the conniving cunt, aren't you?"

"When I need to be."

"And when you don't, as well."

"Now that it is certain, now that we are sure – it is time for you to come to me. Pietro and Francesco have had their time. It is *my* destiny to shape you, to mold you, to prepare you. Come and live in Vicenza – or wherever you like. Rome. Florence. Even Padua! Come to me, and let us be what we are meant to be."

He frowned at her. "What about your actual sons, children of your flesh. Why not extend this offer to them?"

"Bring Detto, of course. He has no place in the prophecy outside his friendship with you. But he can be at your side as you and I explore all the possibilities Fortune has in store for you!"

The moment held, suspended like a snowflake on a still night. Then Cesco laughed full in her face. "Do not wish to be my mother, Katerina della Scala. It's dangerous employment. We still haven't found my real lady mother's body. Somewhere meaningful, Fuchs hinted. *Horresco réferens.* Truth be told, I rather wish it had been you in her place. I liked her, that one time you allowed us to meet." He crossed to a sideboard and poured himself a drink. "Ah well! *Varium et mutabile semper femina.*"

Owning an excellent education, Katerina scoffed. "I am hardly fickle."

"I wasn't referring to you. But it's past midnight, Virgil's day is over. I think Horace had it right. *If a man's fortune does not fit him, it is like a bad shoe. If too large it trips him, if too small it pinches him.* I find mine pinches."

"Too small?"

"Much. I have no interest in the leopard, the lion, or the she-

wolf. What have they ever done to me? The she-hound, however..."
He suddenly hurled the goblet to clatter against the far wall in a flash
of crimson and silver. Against her will, Katerina shouted. She could
not see what happened next — he was a blur of motion. But she felt
the shock and staggered, her right cheek throbbing.

Cesco rubbed the back of his hand with detached interest.
"Never struck a woman before. Strange. Doesn't feel any different
than striking a man." He brought his eyes up to meet hers. "*Párcere
subiectis et debellare superbos.* Spare the meek, but subdue the arrogant. I didn't know till now it was a genderless distinction."

Touching her throbbing cheek, Katerina was horrified to find
tears in her eyes. "Cesco — you must let me guide you..."

"I must, must I?" His hands were shaking. "*Infandum, regina,
iubes renovare dolorem.* I think what I must do is die, and before that,
suffer. I need no guidance for either, thank you."

Something was burning in the room — was it the parchment?
"Why fight Fate? What good does that do?"

Cesco wore the hint of a smile upon his upper lip. "Who says
I have to do good?"

Ignoring the growing smell, Katerina began to recite: "*'He will
unite the land with Wit, Wisdom, and Courage, and bring to Italy, the
home of men, a Power unknown since before the Fall of Man.'*"

Braced for another blow, she was utterly unprepared for laughter. Cruel, mocking laughter. "That's your reply? Truly? Oh my poor,
poor, foolish Auntie. I suckled at the poetic teats of Dante Alaghieri.
I knew the double-edged swords of words before I ever lifted a blade
of steel! 'Look to your walls of wood.' 'Who will win the battle?
A great king.' 'Beware the earthborn serpent coming behind thee.'
Prophecies are never clear. They can't be! Otherwise men would
know what they mean."

The smell was growing worse. "What are you saying?"

"Wit, Wisdom, Courage — you can have all of those things and
yet not be Good, or Just, or Kind. A witty man distracts his foes. A
wise man eliminates them altogether. And a couragous man dares do
anything for his own good. Words have meaning beyond those we
want them to have. Did you never stop to consider what power there
was before the Fall of Man?"

Katerina felt a flush of numbness. Absurdly, she started to
hiccough. Fighting to breathe, she answered, "There was Paradise."

"True. But, my dear, sweet, charmingly naïve Auntie, there was
also Lucifer." Then he was gone, brushing past her and through the
door.

Katerina stood entirely still, breathing in and out of her throbbing jaw. The smell was worse than before. One of her eyes went out of focus. The hiccoughs grew more fierce. Suddenly overcome, Katerina sank to her knees, dazed and lightheaded. Her eyes latched upon the bent goblet on the floor. Above it, the tapestry was stained with crimson.

Too late, she understood. He would not come to her. Her part in his life was over. She was an empty vessel now. It was horrible, at this late date, to be utterly unsure of what she had wrought.

There was the latch of a door from the next room, and slow footsteps. Out of her one focused eye, she beheld the sunken face of the diviner gazing down at her.

"Well. If this is not Fortune's whip, I'm damned."

Through his thick Bergamo accent, it was near impossible to understand him. But his malice was unmistakable, and she was quite unable to call out.

With pain, he knelt his deformed body close and whispered, "Tell me that is not the boy you hired me to kill."

SIX

A RED–HEADED PADUAN sat in a taverna around the corner from the *via Stella*, on the east side of Verona. A flagon of wine stood before him, untouched. As it represented the last of his coin, he wanted to savour it.

All around him were other visiting Paduans. Lacking the social status to stay in the nicer parts of the city, they were here in a converted farmhouse to celebrate the double wedding that was their seal of perpetual security.

The war had been far harder on Padua than on Verona. Foreign overlords, constantly changing factions, murder in the streets, abductions for ransom, and taxes, taxes, taxes, all flowing into foreign coffers. With the promise of all that ending, of being united for the first time with the great tyrant of Verona, these men looked forward to victory in war, glory in peace, and prosperity in their daily lives.

Tonight their delight overflowed, and many Paduans had gathered here to sing songs and raise cups to the Scaliger, to Carrara, and to the *Pax Verona*.

Watching these joyful knock-heads from his perch on the former hayloft that now served as a balcony, the red-headed Paduan scanned their faces, their clothes, their carriage. He was looking for a friend. Not a friend he knew. A new friend, a young fellow with wide eyes and an open purse. Because the red-headed Paduan was out of funds. Again.

There was only one fellow in the place who appeared at all

promising. But he looked familiar, too, with his mane of curling chestnut hair, big green eyes and wiry frame. *Did I already touch him for money? Or his father, or uncles?* The fellow was young, more than a boy but less than a man. He sat alone on a barrel in the far corner of the hayloft, a small meal set on another barrel before him, singing softly to himself as he drank. He seemed an inexpert drinker, stopping often to allow his head to catch up to his tongue.

He does look familiar. Damn. The Paduan had to be careful. He owed so much to so many…

But there was nothing for it. Better to walk over now with a full flagon than an empty one. Standing, he left his bench and ducked under the beams to cross to the young man's side. The teenager looked up, and the Paduan raised his cup. "To the *Pax Verona*, young master."

The teen pulled a face. "Figs."

"Not a fan of peace?"

"Peace is boring. Just the hush between wars."

Veronese, from his accent. Little chance, then, of an old debt. Good. Dragging another barrel close, the Paduan sat himself upon it. "You've been to war, then?" he asked in an encouraging voice. Always good to get them talking.

"I'm always at war." The teen's blurred eyes narrowed at his new companion. The Paduan knew the figure he cut. Handsome enough, with thick locks of wavy red hair and a beard in need of trimming. He wasn't rich, which would be clear from his clothes. If he were noble he would be closer to the center of the city. But his sword was polished and his boots well-soled. Well-born, but of no consequence.

"I know what you mean. I saw my first war eleven years ago. Been fighting ever since. On the losing side." Oblique flattery.

The teen showed his teeth. "At war with your purse, from the looks of you. Is it alms you seek? Or do you think I'm one of your *bardassi*? Sorry, I'm a married man."

The Paduan flushed. This insult had grown up around Padua these last thirty years, that each young Paduan male had to spend time being buggered by a student at the University. *Damn students, tarring us all with their filth.* Yet he found a smile. "Married? My condolences."

"Not a proponent of matrimony?"

"I deplore it! Better a death sentence, and that's the truth."

"One and the same. Either way, you don't get out of it alive."

The Paduan's laugh was not at all forced. "I knew I liked you!

Though I'd have said you were too young for vows."

"Not as young as some brides."

"Indeed," said the Paduan, seizing the topic. "Have you heard about the Greyhound's heir and his bride? Of course you have, you live here. Poor lad. Must be hard, these political matches."

Drinking deeply, the young fellow looked up from his cup. "They say he chose her."

"Truly? Why would he want a wife too young to use for his pleasure?"

"Maybe he's a *bardasso*," offered the fellow lightly. "Buggered by everyone, he's looking for a girl with a boy's backside. Or maybe he's chosen perfectly. He's now free to take his pleasures from the world, without reproach."

"I didn't think of it that way," answered the Paduan amiably. "Viewed in that light, it's genius. All the benefits of marriage with the liberty of bachelorhood. But what happens when she grows older? They all do, you know."

The teenager shrugged. "I expect he'll be dead by then, so it doesn't fret him."

"That's rather grim."

"I'm in a grim mood." The teen set his cup down and held out a hand. "Franz."

The red-headed Paduan grasped the arm. "I'm—"

"Ahenobarbus, of course. He of the red hair and red mood. So you fought in the wars, Ahenobarbus?"

Quaffing the rest of his drink, the Paduan nodded. "I did. Joined when I was about your age, and ran with my tail between my legs at the second battle of Vicenza." He laughed at the memory. "I saw your Capitano then, in a floppy hat disguised as a Spaniard. Even saw the Count of San Bonifacio cut down by his own men."

"That must have been frightening."

"O, it was, it was! But I got myself a fine horse out of it, so I won't complain. Had that beast for seven years. Bastard," he added with feeling.

"The horse?" asked Franz, amused.

"Lord Carrara. I lost the horse defending him during the Denti uprising. He never replaced it. I daresay your capitano would have been more generous."

"I daresay you're right. He's generous to a fault. Everyone else's fault. Here," said Franz, flipping a gold florin into the air. "Buy us a pitcher and some meat."

The impoverished Paduan considered putting on a show of

protest, but it didn't feel needed. Snatching the coin from the air, he navigated the ladder from the loft and then threaded the crowd to the innkeeper's side. He ordered wine, meat, and mustard – typical tavern fare.

Not wanting to return empty-handed, the Paduan waited for the food. If the teenager was trying to be rid of him, now was his chance to slip away. The Paduan would not resent it, not with a pitcher and a plate of meat.

The innkeeper himself was a German with an Alpine accent, so his mustard was thicker than the kind Italians favoured, doubtless filled with honey and pepper. But the meat was blackened on the outside and raw within, and looked delicious. Because he didn't have the proper silver to change a gold coin (or so he said), the innkeeper added a bowl of nuts to the tray.

The Paduan took the platter to a pulley, which others hoisted while he climbed the ladder, pitcher in hand. Franz was not only still there, but had been joined by a second teen, larger but with a younger-looking face. The newcomer stopped talking as the red-headed stranger arrived with the flagon of wine.

"Ahenobarbus," said Franz, "this is Tänzer."

"Tänzer?" asked the second teen.

"There's no easy translation for Detto. Must be such a burden, having 'Nickname' for a nickname. Or perhaps it's freeing! You can choose any name you like. You can be Leonhard, Lion Brave! Or would you prefer a Roman name like Ahenobarbus here? We can call you Secundus. Secundus Manlius Cunctator. Cunc-tay-tor. How that word excels. *'The One Who Holds Back'*. Apt. Or, better, Nasica. Signor Nosy. Are you sharing that wine?"

The Paduan was still standing, the jug held stupidly in his hand. He passed it over and resumed his seat on the barrel. To the newcomer he said, "Well met, whatever he names you."

Under the cloak, the second teen wore the purple and gold of a new knight. Franz clearly swam with important fish.

The newcomer was studying the Paduan with a jaundiced eye. Again he was being sized up as a possible pederast. Best to take care of that at once. "After we sup, shall we find some feminine company? Oh wait, Franz said he was married."

"Not as married as that," replied Franz with a grin. "And it seems we need look no further."

Below, there was a sudden invasion of feminine flesh passing through the taverna door. These were salad days for the whores of Verona, now as bold as the sororities of Florence, bells jangling on their wrists and ankles.

Grinning, the red-headed Paduan recited the old chestnut about church bells and brothel bells. "The bells call a man to repent what the bells call him to do."

Franz laughed loudly, but his friend winced. The Paduan hoped distaste would drive this fellow off, so that he might worm his way into Franz's good graces. He was already liking the teen enormously. He spoke with an edge, and was free with his purse.

"You'll have to forgive Signor Nosy's prudery," said Franz. "He was knighted today, and he's feeling the weight of his oath. Does being ennobled make you feel any different?"

"No," said Signor Nosy.

"Me either." Franz raised his cup. "Truth is truth."

The Paduan bit into his meat to cover his surprise. So Franz had also been one of the many new knights created today. Why had he shed his knightly raiments? With them on, he wouldn't pay for a single drink tonight.

Franz continued to needle his friend. "You'll have to watch out for Tänzer around those women. They come from a cat-house, and he's Vicentine — he eats cats."

Signor Nosy rolled his eyes as the red-head frowned. "Eats cats?"

"You don't know the old saying? *Venessiani gran signori, Padovani gran dottori, Visentini magna gatti...*"

"That's stupid," interjected Signor Nosy.

"I don't know," said the Paduan, chuckling. "I don't mind being called a great doctor."

"You're not a doctor, are you?" asked Franz at once.

"No, but I can cure a toothache."

"Good." Franz jerked a thumb at his friend. "He gives me one. Tell me, Signor Nosy, how did you find me?"

Signor Nosy shrugged. "I looked for someplace loud, crowded, and anonymous. Alone, but not alone. Anywhere closer to the palaces and you'd be recognized."

"Whereas here anonymity is almost guaranteed. Innkeeper, another cup for my friend! In fact, more wine for all my elevated friends!" Franz waved at everyone on the hayloft and was answered by cheers from the reveling Paduans.

Below, one set of eyes was fixed on them. The red-headed Paduan thought it might be someone to whom he owed money. But no, he'd remember those eyes. They were grey as slate, odd in such a cheerful face, like two dollops of ice on a lazy summer's day. The red-head nodded, and the fellow saluted with his cup.

Signor Nosy said, "Everyone's looking for you."

Franz snorted. "Doubtless imagining me sulking on some roof-top, howling at the moon, when I should be at home curled up with my wife. But I'm no Capulletto. I like my women older." As he spoke, Franz's gaze drifted to the hilarity surrounding one woman's ascent up the ladder to the loft, with drunken Paduans angling to see if she wore small clothes under her skirts. Her arrival coincided with the wine Franz had ordered, so the noise on the hayloft only grew.

Suddenly Franz yelled, "Vopiscus!"

"What?" asked the Paduan, trying to catch the woman's eye.

"Secundus Manlius Vopiscus! That's your name, Detto. Second born, manly, and the survivor of twins."

Signor Nosy, whose real name seemed to be Detto, frowned. "I'm not a twin."

"Egg friend, then," said Franz, eyes rolling back in his head as he drank deeply. "Castor and Pollux, the heavenly twins. Gemini. I was born under their sign — our sign. But Castor died." Franz reached out to affectionately scruff at Detto's hair. "Poor Pollux, what will you do with no Jupiter to appeal to? He shan't make us stars, I fear. Of if he does, I'll revolt. I'm too revolting to be a star."

"You're talking nonsense," said Detto.

"I don't talk nonsense. I talk French, and Latin, and German, and Heathen, and Babble, and Dirty, but never nonsense. I see no sense in it." Franz giggled at himself.

"We should depart," said Detto.

"I'm not sure he can stand," observed the Paduan.

"I cannot," said Franz. "I cannot stand it."

"You can," said Detto. "Just give me your arm."

" *'Sing, O clear-voiced Muse,'*" declaimed Franz loudly, " *'of Castor and Polydeuces, the Tyndaridae, who sprang from Olympian Zeus. Beneath the heights of Taygetus stately Leda bare them'* — well, she bared all for the touch of feathers, didn't she? Come, let's crush another cup."

The red-headed Paduan reached for the pitcher, but Detto intercepted him. "I think you've had enough."

Franz snarled, then grinned at the woman softly jingling at the next table, sitting in a lap and stroking the ego of an inebriated Paduan. Reaching out, Franz pulled her over. She toppled into him, managing to place her bosoms full in his face. He laughed. "Hello, Leda. Shall we make a feather bed?"

As she tittered, probably at the size of Franz's purse, her former paramour began to protest, but the red-head distracted him the half-full pitcher and the bowl of nuts the innkeeper had given him. The drunkard subsided, but Franz was oblivious, his gaze lingering on the woman's cleavage, ample and perfectly rounded, pressed together and threatening to overflow the strictures of her garments.

The wench had already sized up the teenager, noting the expensive white clothes beneath the cloak, the quality of his haircut and his healthy skin. Smiling, she cooed in his ear. "Want me to make you a man, little boy?"

"I was made one by a maid sweeter than you," said Franz. "But I lack instruction. She taught me very little. Indeed, she was like a sister to me. What's your name, my sweet?"

Almost by rote she responded, "What do you want it to be?"

"Dear dear," said Franz, "a weighty choice. Not Leda, for then both Vopiscus and I would want you to hatch us. No – don't look at him, he might eat you! He's from a race of notorious pussy-eaters. A flower, I think. A lily? But no, forgive me! You smell so sweet, you must be a Rose. What do you say, Tänzer? Is her name Rose?" Detto turned away, and Franz laughed. "He's probably right. Better no names at all. Anonymous. Alone, but not alone. Don't you agree, sweetheart?" His hand moved inside her packed bodice.

"Whatever you say, love," she murmured, nuzzling his neck.

"Then I say let's revel it as bravely as the best. Ahenobarbus, find a wench and prove yourself worthy of your name. Pollux Vopiscus can sing and dance the while. *Balla balla.*"

However engrossed he pretended to be in the woman's flesh, Franz was deliberately goading his friend – the word meant both *dance* and *lie*. Tänzer's jaw was clenched so tight his teeth might crack. "I thought she meant something to you."

Franz shrugged. "I am disappointment personified."

"I hope not," murmured the wench. In answer, Franz shifted her weight in his lap. She looked surprised, then pleased. Franz nuzzled her breasts, one of which was now bare. "*Qui finem quaeris amoris cedit amor rebus; res age, tutus eris.*"

Hearing the word *amor*, the girl giggled, thinking herself complimented. Behind them, at the near table, there was a cracking sound as the drunk Paduan split a nut with the flat of his blade.

Over the girl's shoulder Franz said, "By the way, Detto, I struck your mother."

Detto blinked. "What?"

Crack went another nut. Franz pulled some of the wench's hair from between his lips. "*'Beneath the heights of Taygetus stately Leda bare them, when the dark-clouded Son of Kronos had privily bent her to his will.'* You heard me. If you want to fight for her honour, do it quick. I won't be able to stand much longer."

"Seems you're standing just fine, love," said the wench in a husky voice.

Cesco's tone was a little husky too. "Truth is truth."

Detto's brow was taut. "Cesco, what are you saying?"

The Paduan noted the name. *Cesco? Why does that name sound familiar?* Amid the laughter and shouts, another nut cracked open.

Through her hair and behind his groping hands, Franz was talking again. "I'm saying, and rather clearly, in the face of all this, that I struck your mother. Your dignity and status as a knight demands that you challenge me and earn your name, Vopiscus. But if you're going to do it, please do it now. I'm about to be very occupied."

Cesco. Short for Francesco.

The blood drained from Detto's face. "Is she dead?"

"Not unless she died of shock. I'm sure I wounded her vast and bottomless pride. Nonetheless, she was struck a blow by my hand. You should try at least to take the hand."

Detto gritted his teeth. "I know what you're doing. The answer is no."

Franz's hands were cupping the wench's buttocks, and her fingers were between them. "That's not her answer. What about you, Ahenobarbus? Is your temper as fiery as your hair?"

Francesco. A new knight named Francesco, whose friend was called Detto. Tänzer — that was German for dancer. In Italian, 'ballare' was to dance. Ballare Detto... Lost in these thoughts, the Paduan was brought up short. "What?"

Another nut cracked as Franz disengaged his face from the wench's bosom to glance his way. "Are you only here to fleece a golden lamb of his unwon coin, or do you have designs on the poor lamb's flesh as well? Is that the kind of man you are? A despoiler of boys, a denuder of purses, and a denier of all that's true and good?"

"What?" Halfway through connecting the tiles of a mental mosaic, the Paduan was staggered by this flurry of insults.

Disappointed the red-head wasn't reaching for his sword, Franz sighed. "Fine. Someone else, then."

Another nut cracked. Roughly dumping the half-dressed wench from his lap, Franz stood on his barrel, his points in great disorder. Wheeling about, his forefinger extended accusingly. "You!"

Masticating the opened nuts, the nearest drunk was working to crack another against the tabletop. His difficulty came from the stupidity of his fingers – the nuts kept slipping away.

"Oi!" cried the wench, rising without bothering to cover herself.

Franz continued to point at the drunk with the nuts and knife. "You! Yes, you! You sodding, sopping lackwit! I'm talking to you!"

Realizing he was the object of the teen's ire, the drunk reddened. "What?"

"I want you to answer a question. Be warned, though! This is a question that would puzzle a giant of intellect, a genius of Abelardian wit, the divinely-inspired Odysseus himself, and may well be past a drooling deviant drudge like you. So think careful, if think you can, and answer me one thing."

The drunk wasn't sure if he should strangle the teen or laugh. "Yes?"

Franz pointed to the bowl. "Are those hazel-nuts?"

Utterly befuddled, the man looked stupidly down at the scattered husks littering the table. "What?"

"A brilliant reply. It purchases time without the golden sin of silence. Nothing is more sinful than silence, save stupidity. Are. Those. Hazel. Nuts?"

"Aye," answered the drunk. His companions laughed, but the drunk was growing wrathful.

Warningly, Detto said, "Cesco…"

The young knight paid him no heed. Squatting, he put his face close to the drunk's. "What do you think you are doing?"

Now the drunk was truculent in his defensiveness. "What?"

"What! Again, what! Why not 'how', or better, 'why'! Why is the key! Why is always the answer. Every question worth asking starts with a why, and a wherefore – for a wherefore must ever follow a why. For example, why do you break those nuts? Wherefore do you think you have the right?"

With a wary smile the drunk looked around, wondering if this was some sort of joke.

"I have given you the why and the wherefore. Now here is the 'how'. How dare you?" said Franz loudly. Under the eye of every patron both above and below, he pointed at his friend. "You see him?"

"Yeah, I sees 'im."

"Do you sees what colour his eyes are?"

The drunk blinked. *"What?"*

"His eyes. What colour are they?"

The inebriated fellow squinted at Detto in the dim light. "Brown?"

"Wrong." Franz's fist snapped forward with all the strength of his shoulder and hip behind it. The drunk's nose burst in a shower of blood.

Franz rubbed his knuckles. "They're hazel."

The shock was palpable, and short. As one the assembled Paduans lurched forward to avenge their comrade. Stools and benches flew, tables were overturned, and the innkeeper dove through a short door behind the bar to run for help, leaving his wife swatting at the brawlers with a stout stave.

"Verona!" cried Franz in wild joy as the bleeding drunk threw himself forward and tackled the teen to the floor.

Something in Franz's face completed the red-head's mental picture. He'd seen almost the same expression eleven years earlier, under a floppy hat, rallying Vicenza's troops. Whatever he called himself − Franz, Castor, Cesco − this was the Greyhound's heir.

Oh fut.

The few Veronese in the taverna leapt up to fight without knowing why. But they were closer to the door, far from the hayloft where the red-head was now trapped with this young lunatic.

Detto was already on his feet, protecting his friend's right side, fending off blows and delivering his own. The red-head had seen Bailardino Nogarola in battle over the years, and this boy had inherited his father's basic frame, if not yet all the muscle. Moreover, he wasn't drunk, which couldn't be said of their opponents.

Franz freed himself from the drunk's tackle and leapt over the table to heel someone clambering up the ladder. "Paduans are nut-suckers!"

Signor Nosy slammed someone head-first into the brick wall at his back, then toppled him over the rail on the crowd below.

As they surged to join in, the outraged Paduans obeyed the unspoken rule of tavern brawls − trays and stools and flagons and even food were acceptable for combat, but a naked blade was dishonourable. Everyone scrambled to ascend to the hayloft, needing to get in a blow for Padua, for honour, for fun. The two wenches on the upper level were swearing and laughing, throwing blows with the rest of them.

A fist came winging at the young Scaliger's head. Without thinking, Ahenobarbus caught it, then grasped the assailant by the ear and bashed his head into the man next to him. Bludgeoning two more of his countrymen, the red-head twisted to fall in beside Cesco at the top of the ladder, warding off blows with the aid of a platter. Suddenly he was fighting alongside the newly-knighted, newly-wed, clearly mad prince of Verona.

Who was singing:

> *You graves of grisly ghosts*
> *your charge from coffins send*
> *From roaring rout in Pluto's costs*
> *you Furies up ascend.*
>
> *You trampling steeds of Hell*
> *come tear a woeful wight,*
> *Whose hapless hap no tongue can tell*
> *nor pen can well indict.*
>
> *I hate this loathsome life*
> *O Atropos draw nigh,*
> *Untwist the thread of mortal strife*
> *send death and let me die.*

As he sang, he leapt high, grasping a wooden strut and swinging into a kick that scissored the air, pushing one foe forward and another back. Releasing a hand, he swung around to drive his heel into a third man's ear before dropping back onto a barrel, facing away from the fight. He grinned at Signor Nosy. "Tell me this isn't better."

Incredibly, the younger knight laughed. Elbowing a drunk in the face, he called out, "Pick a better song!"

The young prince obeyed, taking up a martial air now famous across the Feltro:

> *Indeed a crown*
> *Verona wears,*
> *This trumpet blown*
> *This deed declares!*

Signor Nosy joined in:

> *Warhorse and charger,*
> *Fighting man, banner,*
> *Cuirass and sword,*
> *All a-charging!*

Betraying his homeland, the red-head burst into song as well:

> *Hear the tramp, tramp,*
> *Foot soldiers stamp.*
> *Tramp tramp tramp tramp tramp!*
> *Hear how they go!*

The hayloft was an excellent defensible position, with only the ladder to barrier with their bodies. They ducked as hard hunks of bread came flying at them, slapping and tweaking those who attempted to climb while struggling against the dozen or so at their backs. Some industrious Paduan below thought to use the pulley, but Cesco added his weight to the rope and the man hit his head on the beam before plummeting back into the crowd.

Ahenobarbus was about to punch the man clambering up onto the loft from someone's shoulders when that man immediately turned and kicked his human-ladder in the face. It was the fellow with the slate eyes from below. He joined in, taking up position on the red-head's left.

"You're mad to join us!"

"I like long odds!" called slate-eyes, catching a blow on his forearm and butting his attacker with his forehead. His accent was Paduan — another turncoat, but without the shabbiness of appearance that Ahenobarbus owned. Perhaps he was seeking another kind of favour. *Bardasso*, thought Ahenobarbus uncharitably. But slate-eyes quickly proved himself capable, knowing not to hit with his fist but with elbows and knees. He was swift, and devious, fighting left-handed. Even in extremis his face was mild and cheerful. With his help, they were able to dispatch the last of those above while fending off the assault from below.

Franz appeared at the red-head's side. "Well done, *maestro!* Give these scholars a lesson in brawling!"

Ahenobarbus called out, "What are Veronese?"

"What?" demanded Franz, ducking.

"*Venessiani gran signori, Padovani gran dottori, Visentini magna gatti...* what about the Veronese?"

Franz burst with mirth. "*Veronesi tutti matti!*"

Venetians are great lords, Paduans great scholars, Vicentines eat cats, and Veronese are all crazy! "Truth is truth!"

The taverna door burst open to allow a flood of gold-and-azure-clad soldiers. Cangrande had ordered his militia to keep these kinds of brawls to a minimum. Had these militiamen been solely Veronese, they might have fallen in on the side of the outnumbered locals. But the foresighted Scaliger had brought in Mantuans, Paduans, and Vicentines to help guard his city. Hence as they pummeled their way into the old barn, they struck everyone indiscriminately.

Ahenobarbus saw them coming. "We should scarper."

In obvious agreement, Detto turned to the high window over his shoulder. Leaping into the wooden beams, he threw it wide.

"Come on!"

Slate-eyes started to retreat from the balcony's edge. Ignoring them all, Franz continued to slam the bloodied nutcracker's head against a barrel, only to be knocked down by a blow to his own head. He shook himself, lashed out with a foot, and said, "Not leaving!!" He whisked off his cloak and used it to wrap up an incoming blow, then kicked his assailant through its muffling folds.

One leg into the open air, Detto wavered, then climbed down from the window and leapt back into the fray. The red-headed Paduan shared a look with his slate-eyed countryman, and they returned to protecting the young maniac's backs.

By the time the militiamen had the main floor quelled, the quartet on the hayloft were battered and bloodied, but grinning. Staves forced them back from the edge as the guards clambered up the ladder. Ahenobarbus and slate-eyes stepped back, hands in the air, but Franz and Signor Nosy fought them as well, only subsiding after receiving several blows more damaging than all the punches they had endured.

The room was a shambles. Men with broken heads or limbs were being carried and chivvied out of doors. The victorious quartet sank to the planks side-by-side, Franz's arm wrapped around his cousin's shoulder as they all coughed and clutched their ribs, giggling when they found the air.

"O, good idea," gasped Ahenobarbus.

"Idea," repeated Franz, then retched.

"Don't puke on me, you bastard!" groaned Signor Nosy, kicking him away.

For some reason the young prince found this hysterically funny. In the middle of vomiting up copious amounts of wine, he managed to spew more liquid from his nose. He aimed over the edge, and those below howled as the regurgitated nastiness pelted their heads and shoulders.

The red-head felt around his mouth with his tongue. His teeth were all accounted for, so he felt free to grin. "You are, both of you, mad."

Franz cuffed his face with his forearm. "I told you — *Veronesi tutti matti!*"

The militiamen were questioning the innkeeper, who had returned to survey the wreckage of his establishment. He pointed a furious finger at the young man whose feet were kicking idly over the edge of the hayloft. "Them! They started this!"

Signor Nosy threw up his hands. "Me? What did I do?"

"They were your eyes," observed Franz. Both he and Ahenobarbus burst into laughter.

A militiaman on the hayloft hauled Franz up by the scruff of his neck. Without moving to intervene, slate-eyes said, "Best handle him with care."

"Who the devil are you?" demanded the head militiaman from below.

"It's not who I am that matters. That's the Scaliger's heir you've got there."

"By the hair," said Franz, which started both teens on a new laughing spurt.

Over the murmurs of the vanquished, the lead militiaman crossed closer. "What did you say?"

Ahenobarbus took over answering. "That's Francesco della Scala, married this morning to Lord Carrara's cousin, and bannerman in the mêlée today. That's his friend, Bailardetto Nogarola, also knighted today."

Clutching his broken nose, the nutcracker appeared from behind a barrel. "You're lying."

"Yes, lying," chuckled Franz. "Throw me in the gaol." He then doubled over to spew the final contents of his stomach forth, forcing the militiaman below to jump backwards as the liquid splashed his boots.

Some were eyeing Signor Nosy's knightly attire and Franz's fine clothes. His cloak removed, the Scaligeri ladder was plainly embroidered on the back of the instigator's doublet.

"*Merda,*" said the militia leader, a Mantuan.

"He starteb ib," said the Paduan nutcracker in a nasally whine. "We didn'b dnow — how coulb we dnow?"

"By using your eyes," said the red-head. *I should have known the moment I saw him.*

"What the hell is he doing out here?" asked one militiaman of another.

"And on his wedding night!" added one of the brawlers.

Sensing it might be politic to come to the prince's defence, the lead militiaman snapped, "Remember who his bride is?"

Things quickly became more formal. The lead guard ascended to examine the two teens closely, taking in Ahenobarbus as well. "You're with them?"

A moment of hesitation was relieved when Franz — or rather, Cesco — said, "No one is with me. They're all against me."

"He's with us," said Signor Nosy, nee Detto.

The guard nodded once. *Sotto voce*, he said, "Get him home."

"Home is where the heart is," said Cesco, enunciating carefully over his split lip.

"And where is that?" asked Ahenobarbus.

"If you find out, please let me know. I've lost my hart."

Detto winced, but Ahenobarbus heard the strain of a familiar tune. "Oh-ho! Soured for love?"

"Figs," said Cesco. "Just a poor hunter."

"Here was I, thinking I was saving the Greyhound's heir. Some dog you turned out to be. No teeth, but lots of wag."

Cesco glanced up. "A witty Paduan! A rare breed indeed!"

"I have wit enough not to pick fights for no reason."

"But not enough to stay away when they start," observed slate-eyes.

"A hit!" cried Cesco. "And from the quiet corner to boot!"

Having invested his evening, Ahenobarbus was not well pleased to have to share with this last-minute joiner. "I have a soft spot for soft heads." He helped Detto to his feet. "Here, let me take them. Innkeep, I'm sure if you present the matter at the palace, you'll be well compensated."

Slate-eyes cast his cool gaze over the brawlers below. "The rest of you – I'd keep my mouths shut."

The leader of the militia gave this Paduan a hard glare. "And what's your name?"

"I'm Salvatore da Battaglia."

"Battaglia?" said the heir, amused. "No wonder you're quick to join a fight."

Salvatore offered a humble bow, his cheerful face expanding with his smile. "Quick to end one, my lord."

"Ha! Welcome, Ser Salvatore, knight of the battle. And you, Ahenobarbus? What name did your mother give you?"

"She never called me anything, my lord. She had little time for me. My father, either. But my uncle was a good Christian soul, and had me baptized."

"And what name did your noble uncle bestow upon you?"

The red-head made a mocking half-bow. "Benedick, my lord. I am Signor Benedick, of Padua."

♦   ◊   ♦

Under an escort of city guards, they headed towards Cesco's new house on the *via Pigna*. The mirthful quartet were reliving the fight when a figure stepped from the shadows into their path. A massive Moor, dressed all in blacks and greys, with a sword upon his back and a patch on his eye.

Benedick and Salvatore's feet jumped back even as their hands jumped to their swords. "Jesuchristo!"

The two young princes were unmoved. Cesco pursed his lips in a sour expression. "Ah, as foretold, Death has come to claim me. Where is your pale horse?"

Seeing them in the light of a nearby hanging brazier, the Moor's brow furrowed. His voice grated like a metal spoon against a bowl. "Were you attacked?"

Cesco shrugged. "More attacking than attacked."

"*Tutti matti*," murmured Benedick.

The Moor was grave. "We were looking for you…"

"Men's eyes were made to look," answered Cesco lightly. "Yours especially were shaped, it seems, to look only for me."

The one eye fixed on the other prince. "Not you. Bailardetto, you should go home at once. I'm so very sorry."

Arrested, Detto blinked. Cesco raised his eyebrows. "For what crime?"

"Donna Katerina," answered the Moor. "She's had another stroke."

SEVEN

Sunday, 27 November 1328

IT WAS LATE MORNING when Pietro arose, head aching fit to burst from an excess of wine. His house was quiet, but the street outside was bustling with life, music, and more. Recalling that the revels would continue on into the New Year, he groaned, pouring himself a cup of water and draining it. *I don't know if I'll survive it.*

This house was still vaguely unfamiliar to Pietro. Bought months earlier, he had not furnished it himself, leaving the choice of tapestries, chairs, desks, and even his bed to the ever-willing Tullio d'Isola, so practiced in serving the Scaligeri that furnishing a house was the work of an afternoon. The unfortunate result was that, though he had paid for everything, nothing felt like it belonged to him – essentially making him a guest in his own home.

But his clothes were certainly his, well-tailored farsettos, fine tunics, and his habitual trousers rather than the conventional hose. Of late he had invested in excellent boots, and had made the mistake of wearing a new pair for the wedding. Today the balls of his feet roared in anger, and his heels felt as sore as his stomach. Dressing for Sunday services, he pulled on an older pair of boots and ventured down the stairs, feeling wobbly. *Food. I need food.*

In the kitchens he was surprised to find his brother already up and about. "Morning!" chirped Poco.

"Morning," groaned Pietro dully. "You're more alive than I am."

Poco grinned. "I have more experience, and more determined

entrails. Any sign of Cesco?"

Pietro grunted. "Tharwat sent a note just before dawn to say he'd finally gone home."

"And Donna Katerina?"

Pietro felt a tightness in his chest that had nothing to do with drink. But after last night, he had given himself permission not to rush to her side. "Morsicato will let us know when he has a prognosis."

"Any notion who did it?" The state of the room and the bruise on the lady's cheek had caused Bail to roar about intruders, thieves using the revels as opportunity to ransack noble homes. Surprised, they had struck the lady of the house as they fled, causing her current pitiable condition.

Pietro did not want to give voice to his suspicions. "She was discovered by a cripple she had invited to the house — a diviner. He says he heard voices, then found her on the floor and raised the alarum."

"Is he a suspect?"

"Not so far. He was definitely there by her wish. The room was ransacked. But she hasn't awakened to tell us what happened."

"Christ. Heaven help the bastard when they find him. Bailardino will tear him limb from limb."

"Mm." Pietro's mind was on his conversation with the lady at the feast. *If I had gone home with her...*

"You need to hire a staff," said Poco grumpily as he fought the fireplace to remove a deformed lump that smelled like burnt bread. "A cook will do you wonders."

"You can stay on, if you like," offered Pietro, using his hands to balance himself against the tabletop. His head beat like a drum. The light from the open windows was dazzling.

Poco studied his handiwork. "I don't think you'd want me."

"Look at it this way," offered Pietro, smelling the burnt bread in the air. "There's certainly room for improvement."

Joke as he liked, Pietro knew his brother was correct. During the decade he'd lived in Ravenna, he'd had a household staff. But those had been mainly hired to cater to his father, and then to look after Cesco. Growing up poor, having spent most of his life in one exile or another, traveling from place to place, Pietro was used to fending for himself. Habit saw him eating meals at inns and taverns, or at the houses of friends, or else contenting himself with meat and cheese. Once he'd had a very competent steward to look after his personal needs, but his life had been so nomadic these last few years that he had released the fellow, along with the cook and groom. Whenever he arrived in some city, be it Avignon or Rome, he hired a local lad to act as his manservant during the day, and fended for himself after dark. When in Verona, he housed his horses in Scaligeri stables, kept his arms and books in Scaligeri abodes, and allowed himself to be looked after by Scaligeri servants. *That must change.*

Pietro knew full well why he was so resistant. His mistrust of servants grew from his former page, Fazio, who had been revealed as a spy for Cangrande's wife. Ever since, he'd been reluctant to put too much trust in anyone under his roof. If someone could be bought by him to do a job, they could also be bought by someone else for a different job.

Yet look at the Scaliger's servants. Tullio, Ziliberto, Aventino, Manuel. Loyal to the last inch. That's what I need. Someone I can depend on. Someone devoted and trustworthy. But where will I find—

"What you really need is a wife," said Poco.

Startled, Pietro laughed. "A what?"

"A wife," repeated Poco, sliding onto the bench nestled between the table and the wall. "You know – spouse, bride, consort, helpmeet, mate, nag, scold. A Kate to your Petruchio. Someone to play the *chatelaine* and run the house while you're off doing knightly deeds."

Hearing mockery, Pietro was quick to defend himself. "I'm not interested in marrying anyone just now, thank you."

"Pity." Busy cutting the blackened bread in hope of something edible inside, Poco glanced his brother's way. "If for no other reason than it would relieve a little of your pent-up tension."

Pietro flushed. Katerina had offered that very thing. "Just because I'm not out tom-catting after every available hemline—"

"I'd be surprised if you've ever seen what's under a hemline, much less enjoyed it."

That hit remarkably close to home. But Pietro was not about to admit his utter lack of experience in this one field wherein his brother had long-since surpassed him. Mulishly, he exploited an old rumour. "What, didn't you hear about me and Petrarch's sister Lucia?"

Pausing his excavation of the bread, Jacopo's expression was part amused, part offended. "Brother, have we met? Do we know each other at all? Even if I believed for one second that you would ever lay a finger on Lucia, the sister of your friend, your host, in whose house you were living as a guest – if I believed it for even the briefest fluttering of my heart, I would know by your actions that it was a tissue of lies. If there were any truth to it, you would have married the girl instantly. You could teach morality to Aesop, honour to Charlemagne. The very idea," added Poco with a wry chuckle as he searched for some olive oil to soak his burnt bread in.

Pietro slid along the bench to sit beside his brother. "Jacopo, I – thank you. But I'm not as moral as you make me sound."

"Mayhaps not, but you work at it every hour of every day. You'd never allow such an accusation to stain your honour, not while you had the power to fix it." Poco paused, then pointed a finger. "Ah. Father's trick. Sending me off on a side-road to avoid the real topic."

Pietro hadn't intended any such trick. "The real topic being?"

"Marriage." Setting his bread aside, Poco folded his arms and leaned back against the wall. "I was watching the wedding and knighting yesterday, feeling very happy. I know, I know, it's hardly a perfect match! But in the grand scheme of things it's good, both for him and for the city. But especially for you. Because you're free."

"Free?" asked Pietro.

"You were, what, twenty when Cangrande gave you Cesco to raise? Well, you did it! He's raised! He'll be fifteen next summer, a grown man. He's Cangrande's heir – legitimate, thanks to you – a knight and a married man. His whole future is laid out for him. Which means it's time for you to start thinking about your own."

Pietro took a hunk of blackened bread and tried sopping it in oil to make it less rock-like. "What about *your* future?"

Poco shrugged. "When I want a wife I'll find one. I'm not like you. I don't know what I want to be. I'm not a poet, I'm no knight, certainly not a famous banneret. I'm not a lawyer, my mind doesn't work that way. You now have an international reputation at law. You argued before the Pope and won! I'm going to end up what I was probably always going to be, a low-level member of the laity with a modest income of my own. I'll always have father's name to trade on, so I'll never be poor. But Pietro, you're the heir. The family depends on you. You're the one who has to carry on. You've had fifteen years of Cangrande's gold filling your coffers, and you inherited the lion's share of father's wealth."

"He didn't have much," objected Pietro.

"Fine, but you also got mother's land and the house in Florence." It was where Poco was currently living. "You're rich and famous – not just for whose son you are, but also for yourself."

Pietro was suddenly feeling acutely self-conscious. "This can't be my little brother talking! This sounds more like Antonia."

Poco nodded. "We've discussed it. Imperia agrees with me." *Imperia* had always been his nickname for his little sister, forever bossing him around.

Pietro groaned. "A two-pronged attack! Well, if you're worried about heirs, you've left enough of them about…"

Poco startled his brother by slapping his hands together. "Dammit, Pietro, listen! I'm serious! You're thirty-two years old, the same age father was when you were born. And by that time he'd already had Giovanni." This was their late elder brother whose death had elevated Pietro to the role of Dante's heir. "You know cousin Durante already has a son about ten years old, and another just a few years behind?"

"No," said Pietro, frowning. Durante Alighieri was Pietro's first cousin, the son of Dante's half-brother Franco. It had been Franco who had paid the fee in Jacopo's name to lift the order of exile and allow Dante's youngest son to return to Florence.

"Little Franco and Gabriello," confirmed Poco. "Do you want them to be the ones to carry the Alighieri name into the future?"

"Alaghieri," corrected Pietro.

Poco made an exasperated sound. "Sweet Jesus, Pietro, stop! I know father used the old pronunciation. But he did it out of pride, of pique. Do you think that, if Florence had allowed him to return, he wouldn't have changed his name back to Alighieri?"

"They didn't allow him to return, though," countered Pietro. "What they did do was send some grave-robbers to try and steal his body."

Poco's face screwed up. *"What?"*

"Didn't you hear that one? Cianfa Donati tried to steal father's bones."

"Cianfa?" echoed Poco, aghast. "He's been so friendly to me…"

"I'm not surprised. He's afraid you can expose him. He brought grave-robbers all the way from Florence to Ravenna, and they were breaking into the chapel when Cesco scared them off."

"That bastard!" Poco frowned some more, then shook his head. "Distractions! Save it for later, hear what I'm saying now. Whatever you call yourself, you will always be known as an Alighieri from Florence. And Cesco is not your son, and definitely not your heir. He's a della Scala. You need to settle down and carry on the family name."

Sitting side by side with his little brother, his back against the wall, Pietro stared. "You've been thinking."

"I have," agreed Poco. "I get a lot of attention in Florence for being Dante's son. I'm invited everywhere, for his sake. And it's made me think a lot about the family." He pulled a face, and the expression that emerged was bleak. "While you've been doing great and important things, I've been wasting my time."

"You've been enjoying yourself," said Pietro uncertainly.

"Yes," agreed Poco with a sad laugh. "Yet no one composed a song for *my* sake. No one cares what my opinion may be. I'm not important. You are."

Leaning in, Pietro wrapped his arm about his brother's shoulders. "You're important to me," he said, and surprised himself by meaning it. They had always been at odds, quarreling as brothers will. But it seemed that Pietro's little brother was finally – *finally* – growing up.

Poco beat his head gently against Pietro's shoulder. "I mean it, brother. You've done all you can for him. Time to take care of yourself for once. Find happiness. Build a life. Make father proud."

A heartfelt plea. Had it come from nearly anyone else – Antonia, Morsicato, even Cesco himself – Pietro could have dismissed it. Somehow, coming from Poco, it had weight.

Yet Poco did not know about Cesco's broken heart. Pietro wanted to see the boy to the other side of this. And then there was the question of Cesco's mother. She was dead, they now knew. But they did not know who she was, or the nature of the arrangement between herself and the Scaliger that demanded such secrecy.

When we have those answers, thought Pietro. *When all the questions are behind us, and he is happy, healthy, and whole. Then I can look after myself.*

Aloud, Pietro gave a soft chuckle. "You like the new crest, though?"

Poco grinned and patted his brother on the shoulder. "I *love* the new crest. An excellent start." He looked down at the bread they had failed to make a meal of. "Shall we step across to the Four Swords and buy a decent breakfast?"

Pietro had planned to visit the Nogarola house before church. But he decided he owed his brother a decent meal and some overdue friendship. "Let's. But take the bread. There are still some buildings that must be rebuilt, and that would make a fine keystone."

Poco lifted the half-loaf and struck Pietro with it.

◆   ◇   ◆

"Explain yourself."

"What part?" asked Cesco with smiling politeness. He'd been summoned to the Domus Nova in the early morning, but arrived in his own time.

Cangrande was upon the dais, sitting in his chair of office, reading over papers as though Cesco were a petitioner the Scaliger did not have time for. "Tell me about the brawl. You look as though you've been dragged through a knothole."

"I was defending a fellow knight's honour," answered Cesco through his puffed lip. "As any good knight should."

"Mm." Cangrande signed the document and picked up another. "And what was the mortal insult that caused such a rumpus?"

"The dastardly villain impugned Ser Bailardetto's heritage, his nationality, even his race."

"And how did he manage all that?"

"By cracking hazel-nuts at the next table over."

Cangrande's eyes came up from the page before him. "Say that again."

Cesco did, relating the whole exchange.

Cangrande pursed his lips. "Interesting. By your standard, if someone beats his dog, I must challenge him for whipping my sister."

"Only if she were a real bitch," said Cesco.

Cangrande picked up another paper to peruse. "It is in poor taste to mock the infirm."

"I learned my taste from you."

"Then moderate your tastes to match mine."

Standing at a little remove, Benedick listened, slack-jawed. Detto was off waiting for some news of his mother — the same woman that Cesco had just referred to as a bitch. But to Benedick's extreme discomfort, Cesco had invited him and Salvatore for the interview with Verona's Capitano. "As my witnesses," he'd said.

Dressed in borrowed clothes finer than any he'd owned in his life, Benedick hoped he displayed the proper amount of deference. He had to resist brushing his unruly red hair out of his eyes. Salvatore seemed equally uneasy. But the Scaliger had given the two Paduans only a cursory glance before ignoring them thoroughly.

And why shouldn't he? Born to a relative nobody, a distant relation of a former Paduan Anziani, *Signore* Benedetto da Padova owned little more than his sword and the clothes he'd been drinking in. The clothes were shabby but the sword was good. Worn but well cared-for, passed on when his wise and amusing uncle had died. Father and mother unremembered, though his mother was still alive, somewhere. She'd broken his father's heart, running away with a traveling merchant when Benedick was just a baby. His father had become ghostified, a mere shell, and it had fallen to Benedick's uncle, a confirmed bachelor, to raise a young man nobody else wanted.

They had become as much friends as relations, and the old man had mentored Benedick in the arts of war, drinking, and wagering. Benedick's only natural talent lay in talking, but without the money for an education or a law degree, there was nothing for it but to join the military.

Sadly, his nationality meant he'd joined the Paduan army. Being on the losing side of a fifteen-year war meant little glory and less wealth. Peace having come at last, he'd journeyed to Verona knowing there was another war in the offing. What he truly wanted was a contract with a fine *condottiero*. But instead of training in some enterprising mercenary leader's band, he stood now watching a family duel, desperately hoping he had affixed his future to an ascending star and not a shooting one.

Signing another document and passing it off, the Scaliger leaned forward. "You've caused me a problem."

Cesco offered a crooked half-smile. "Not a serious one."

"True, the Paduans aren't howling for your blood. But they are upset. Carrara came to see me about it, as did your father-in-law. Both are concerned about fights breaking out between our citizens. I reminded them that dueling is outlawed in Verona."

"That doesn't hold for Padua," observed Cesco.

"True," admitted Cangrande. "And since I said I'd let them be governed by their own laws, I can't change that fact, though I have gently suggested they amend their laws on this matter to match our own. Which still leaves me with a problem."

"Would that be me?"

"It would." Rising, Cangrande began to pace. "You may be the architect of this peace — no protestations, please. We both know the truth." Cangrande glanced at Benedick and Salvatore. "Gentlemen, if you breathe a word of this to your fellow citizens I'll hunt you down and peel the skin off your noses."

Incongruously, Benedick bowed. "Yes, lord." Salvatore did the same.

Looking momentarily amused, Cangrande returned to his pacing. "As I say, Ser Francesco, you may have brought all this about, but no one knows it, nor can anyone be told. If you're picking fights with Paduans, people will think we are not united in peace, that the next generation will manhandle the city of Padua in a way distasteful to its citizens."

"All that is perfectly true, O Capitano. But if you consider a little longer, you'll realize I did you a service."

"A service? Stop that!"

Cesco had been blowing his nose into his hat. He replaced it, looking unabashed. "You needed something like this. You have ordained this blessed peace, and have doubtless assured your place in Heaven with the other lambs and doves. Angels are this moment weeping tears of joy for your very being." Bouncing on the balls of his feet, hands clasped tightly behind his back, Cesco looked as if he wanted to fall in step with the Scaliger. "But on Earth, not everyone is as rapturous. There are Veronese unthrilled with the *Pax Verona*. Our soldiers, for example. No booty, no women, no reward for all their years of labour. They long to see some Paduan blood spilled, even if only in a bar-brawl. You can't do it. But your heir splitting his knuckles on a few Paduan chins will boost their morale. Thus when you give the order to besiege Treviso, they'll march with contented hearts."

Cangrande had ceased pacing. "Clever. *If* that's why you did it."

Cesco was all smiles and blinking eyes. "Whyever else?"

Cangrande answered question with question. "What happened between you and the lady Katerina?"

"Who is to say anything happened?"

"The room was dismantled in a way that tells me you were there. What did you and my dear sibling discuss?"

Cesco shrugged. "She showed me my stars, and I thanked her."

"With the back of your hand?"

"Yes. My poor hand nearly broke on the granite of her chin. But she was perfectly well when I departed."

They gazed at each other for a long moment. Finally Cangrande seemed to accept his heir's word. Yet when he spoke, there was a dire metal in the Scaliger's tone that made both Benedick and Salvatore step involuntarily backwards. "Did you learn anything of interest?"

Cesco ceased fidgeting to stare directly at the Scaliger. "Some doggerel about evanescence. Nothing very important. Nothing that *matters*."

Benedick had no notion what they were talking about, but the way they were gazing at each other belied Cesco's words. It clearly mattered very much.

Slowly Cangrande began to smile — not his famous *allegria*, something more canine. "You're quite right. It matters not a whit. It changes nothing."

"Nothing," agreed Cesco.

Resuming his seat, Cangrande became brisk. "Glossing over your striking my lady sister, what you say about morale makes a fair amount of sense. But it's an excuse invented after the fact. We both know why you picked a fight. I advise you to choose worthier targets in the future. Never strike downwards. Don't waste time on pointless battles. Fight ones that are important."

"And if none of them are?"

"Then find one that is." The Scaliger picked up another document. "That will be all, Ser Francesco."

Dismissed, Cesco turned on his heel and strolled out, the two Paduans in his wake.

It was outside the Domus Nova that Benedick realized that, whatever else, Cesco had been right about the soldiers' mood. The instant the young prince appeared in the Piazza dei Signori, he was cheered. Not loudly, but with wry appreciative laughter. Several men shook the heir's hand or clapped his shoulder.

Cesco clasped his hands above his head as if he'd won some great victory. "Thank you! Thank you!"

Trailing just behind the young lord, Benedick nodded at the soldiers and citizens as if they should recognize him. These were men he had to get to know, tie himself to, share humourous stories with. That was Benedick's greatest skill – the witty story. He'd charmed more than one commander over campfires and long marches. Now he had to work on these Veronese, earn their trust and approval.

There was no time like the present. "You should have heard it! Ser Francesco walks in as if he owns the place – which he might, I suppose…"

Cesco and Salvatore both listened as Benedick related the events of the previous night, embellishing the loutishness of his fellow Paduans and adding several feats of daring and phrases of insult that young Cesco had neither performed nor uttered, but sounded exceedingly well. He also made several mentions of his own participation in the brawl, and referred to Salvatore's late conversion to the cause – a slight wrapped in a compliment.

Dragging Salvatore over, Cesco clapped Benedick on the shoulder. "That's right. I have discovered two honest Paduans – three, if you count my wife. But then the young are always honest. Mendacity comes with age, like vinegar in wine. These two are the rare vintage of truth and valour. Though with one being red-headed and the other being left-handed, combined they would rival Odysseus! So what say you, friends? Shall we make these two honorary Veronese? April is a long way off, but we can visit San Zeno. You know how to swim? For Zeno, baptism required full immersion. And then fishing. Always, fishing."

"He was another Peter?" asked Salvatore. "A fisher of men?"

"I think he just liked fish. As a holy man, we should not impute he was a lover of the Devil's furrow, which often smells of fish. Though it begs the question, are women of the sea? Are we, lovers of women, sailors?"

"Seaman?" asked Benedick lightly. He was answered with groans.

"See, men?" replied Cesco, addressing the crowd. "Though born in Padua, they are Veronese in their hearts, if not their minds. For while no Veronese mind would resort to such poor wordplay as a pun when a *double-entendre* was at hand, yet his heart is given only to fish, like the blessed San Zeno who fished in the Adige for followers and for meals alike. O, he liked his fish, did Zeno, and who can blame him? Fish is fair, not foul, while fowl is foul, not fair. So if Signor Benedick praises the fish, not the fowl, there is nothing foul about him, and he is fishified as the most true Veronese, baptized by the patron saint of fishers. Which, in turn, means that Verona is a city of whoremongers. For though Vicentines eat all the pussies, it's the Veronese angle to hook the fish on their long and sturdy rods!"

Like the rest, Benedick was breathless with laughter. "Peace, peace! Your word play hurts my head!"

Cesco raised his eyebrows. "I took you for a lover of words."

"He's a lover of talk," opined Salvatore. "Very different."

"Whereas you are an opportunist of cant, Salvatore! You bide your time and pounce when the target is ripe."

Salvatore's cheerful face was mild. "What better way to hit the target?"

"I lack your patience. I make my targets before I hit them. Sadly for poor Benedetto here, he makes such a rich target!"

Benedick rubbed his neck. "Only because I'm not rich in other ways. I can't afford five-florin-phrases."

"That was almost flowery! But you are right, my prosaic Paduan, you are a man built for prose. Plain-talking and plain-dealing. Come, shall we dine, masters? The Paduans are buying."

Benedick gulped. "We are?"

Cesco put an arm about his shoulders. "Of course! They've rebuilt the brothel beside the cheesemaker's, and both have dishes I've been dying to sample. I have three years of eating to catch up on, and fourteen years worth of sinning to commit. I'll give you some five-florin-phrases to redeem along the way. *Allons-y!*"

♦   ◊   ♦

A street over, in the Casa Nogarola, Detto stared at a fresco of geometric shapes, waiting for news of his mother. His brother Valentino had fallen asleep, head nestled into the crook of a corner seat. Detto wished he could do the same, but he was wrestling with a thing that threatened to pull him in a hundred different directions at once.

Cesco said he hit her.

For all his devotion to his cousin, Detto's love was not entirely blind. He wasn't jealous of Cesco's wit, nor of his superior horsemanship, nor his burgeoning attractiveness. A year Cesco's junior, Detto himself was handsomely dark, while Cesco was just emerging from a most awkward period where his whole face seemed to be made up of eyes, nose, and lips. Even with the extra six inches Cesco had grown this year, Detto still owned more strength and size than his cousin. Cesco might be a more clever fighter, but Detto was fairly certain he was the better warrior. Cesco was selfish in battle, did not think of those around him, whereas Detto had a sense of himself in the whole, and far more discipline.

A goldfinch appeared at the window, a late flier heading south for the winter. Automatically Detto lifted a finger. The bird cocked its head, then lifted off to flutter down onto his second knuckle. Detto trilled at it, and it chirruped back. This was the special thing about Detto. His rapport with animals. Dogs followed him wherever he went, abandoning their masters to trot in Detto's wake. He had become an excellent falconer, and that was only partly due to his time squiring Lord Petruchio. He could woo a hare from its hole, calm a bolted horse, and, as now, charm a bird to his hand. Cesco openly envied Detto's 'animal magic'. That envy made it easy for Detto to quell any momentary burst of awe or resentment for his friend's many gifts.

Last night was different. That had not been Cesco excelling. That had been Cesco lashing out. Raw and naked, the rage that had occasionally showed itself over the years was close to the surface now. That brawl last night had been senseless, pointless. Something Cesco had never been. Even in the maddest escapade, there had been some reason, some cause.

He has cause to lash out at the whole world now. Was that the reason he struck my mother? Or was that pointless as well?

The truth was that Detto feared his mother. He loved his father, with whom he had an excellent rapport. But his mother was an awful figure, much more like the Scaliger. For two years he had barely seen her at all as she recovered from her stroke, and Detto was ashamed to admit he remembered those years fondly. He knew his rosy view of that time was partly due to spending it in Ravenna with Cesco. But he also wondered if those years had been a relief because he had not needed to fear his mother.

Somewhere deep within himself, Detto knew he could not trust his mother. A terrible thing, to know you cannot rely upon a parent. But she had always showed more interest in Cesco than in either of the sons of her body.

Why was I never jealous of that? he wondered now. *I should have been, shouldn't I? But no, I was—*

Relieved, thought Detto. *I was relieved that it wasn't me she was focused on. Because I never wanted her to look at me the way she looks at him. The way a hawk eyes a hare.*

Footsteps above made Detto cast the goldfinch off his finger through the window. The two doctors Fracastoro and Morsicato descended, followed by Detto's father. Their voices were low, but Detto heard Morsicato saying, "She needs rest, is all. We've been here before. And once someone has a stroke, they're prone to more. Whatever is broken in the brain often leads to repetition."

Broken in the brain. Is that the cause? Is mama mad?

Bailardino approached his sons. Detto nudged Val, who woke with a snort, looking around. "Boys, your mother will recover. Whatever bastard hit her last night, they brought on another stroke. It doesn't seem as bad as last time. She can speak, a little."

"I'd wait to talk to her, though," advised Morsicato quickly. "As I was telling your father, she requires rest."

"But she'll live?" asked Val plaintively.

"She should," said doctor Fracastoro, patting the eleven year-old on the shoulder. "She knows the road ahead. So do you."

"Doctor," said Detto carefully, addressing Morsicato, "did – did she say who struck her? Was anyone with her?"

"She had a visitor, they tell me," answered Morsicato. "A cripple, a diviner she'd requested to call after the revels."

"A diviner now," grunted Bailardino. "As if astrology weren't bad enough."

"Could he have done it?" pressed Detto.

"He's the one who called for help," said Fracastoro, taking up the tale. "He said he heard arguing in the next room, and only went to help when he heard the blow. He did not know with whom she'd argued."

Bail frowned at his son. "Do you know who it was?"

Detto shook his head. "I'm just asking…"

Bailardino's face grew red. "Fut! That little bastard! He hit your mother, didn't he? *Didn't he?*"

Morsicato laid a calming hand on his lord's arm. "Bail, keep your voice low…"

But Bailardino was incapable of hearing anything at that moment. "Your cousin came here last night and struck her, didn't he? That's why she says she doesn't know who hit her. Of course she'd lie to protect him. Did he strike her, then ransack the place to make it look like a robbery? Answer me, boy!"

Detto ducked his head. "He said something, just before the brawl—"

"Christ! You knew! You knew, and didn't avenge her honour? What kind of knight are you? What kind of son?"

Confused, Valentino said, "Cesco hit mama?"

"I didn't say that," answered Detto quickly. But he'd let it out.

"That bastard!" roared Bailardino "Hitting a woman! An ill woman, a woman who has been like a mother to him! Not even Cangrande in all his anger… *Fut!*" He pointed a shaking finger at Detto. "I'm telling you, stay away from him from now on!"

Detto's own sense of grievance swelled within him. "You can't tell me what to do!"

"Oh yes I can! I'm your father!"

"I'm a knight!"

"Knight or not, you're not so big that I can't wallop you!"

Detto squared himself. "I'd like to see you try it!"

Bail in a rage was a frightening sight. For all his geniality, he was a terror on the battlefield. Valentino backed up a pace while the two doctors looked on helplessly. "You let that bastard strike your mother!"

"I wasn't there! But I'm sure he had good cause," added Detto desperately.

Bailardino purpled. "*Cause!* What cause is there to strike a woman? What cause is there to hit your mother that you could ever approve? Tell me! Tell me what excuses this! Tell me what could make you take his side, after this!" Detto said nothing. "I'm waiting! Answer me! That incestual little toad strikes your mother and you don't even..!"

Confusion gave way to indignant fury. "Don't you call him that!"

"Shut your insolent mouth, boy! I'm the master of this house, not you! As long as you bear my name you'll defend this family's honour! God, I have to say this? What kind of son are you?"

"One who's sick of the games this family plays! Of course Cesco's angry! I'm angry! You hate it too, I know you do – the secrets, the lies, the games! It's all the Scaligeri do! I'm terrified because I'm half Scaliger myself!"

"What," sneered Bailardino, "do you want to marry a sister, too? Pity I wasn't out siring bastards! Then you and your friend could both have a lust for incest!"

Detto punched his father in the face.

Too astonished to move, Morsicato, Fracastoro, and Valentino stared. Bailardino himself seemed more shocked by the deed than the pain.

"There!" shouted Detto. "You and mama are a matched set!"

Bailardino pinched his nose. His fingers came away bloody. "Get out," he said softly. "Get out, now."

"Gladly!" cried Detto, wishing he wasn't saying it even as the word passed the hedge of his teeth. He turned to go, but Morsicato restrained him. "Detto, calm down!"

"Lord Nogarola," said Fracastoro in his best doctor calm.

"Detto, Papa..." pleaded Valentino.

Detto pushed Morsicato off him and started for the door. "I'm going to Cesco's!"

That stirred Bailardino to a rage, and the blood smearing the lower half of his face made him all the more frightening. "I'll disown you! I mean it! You stay away from him!"

Detto turned in defiance. "Do it. I dare you. Disown me." With that Detto stalked from his family's house, half-afraid his father would take him at his word.

Upstairs, Donna Katerina lay in her sickbed and listened. Another woman might have wept. But Detto's mother was still, unable to move her left side, her bruised jaw not aching because she couldn't feel it. In her mind she was turning matters over and over. For her mind felt no different. She tried to think, abjuring both her physical and emotional pain.

The fault was hers. Hers, and the diviner's. She had received worse blows in her life. It was the fear of exposure – that, and the fear of what might happen should Cesco ever learn the truth. Now that it was done, now that he could not go back – no. He could not learn of it now. She would not permit it.

The diviner could ruin everything. She had to see him.

When her husband cautiously cracked the door to check on her, she tried to produce a smile. Ugly and lopsided, to be sure, but she had to soothe Bail as best she could. He could not go to war against the boy. The boy would surely win. He couldn't not. He was the Greyhound.

"It was*sh* not Ce*sh*co," slurred the lady out of the right side of her mouth.

Bail remained mulishly in the doorway, a cloth at his bleeding nose. "You wouldn't tell me if it was."

"It was*sh* not him." She could see that Bail did not believe her. "Come here."

Reluctantly he obeyed, dropping into a seat. "You heard?"

"Who didn't?" she answered. "Detto i*sh* young, and confu*sh*ed."

"It's Cesco I want to throttle. Oh, deny it all you like. He confessed it to Detto. Cangrande was never like this." Katerina snorted at that, and Bail relented a little. "Wild to be sure, and insolent. But never – never vicious."

"Thi*sh ish* my brother you're talking about?"

It did not elicit the laugh she had hoped for. "I know you two sparred – but he never hit you! He wouldn't have dared! How can Cesco be so much worse than he was?"

"My brother was*sh* never in love," said Donna Katerina. "Now lis*sh*ten, there is s*sh*omething I want you to do for me."

EIGHT

THE TROUBLE WITH THE PADUANS seemed likely
to die out of its own accord until a second brawl broke out the
following day, this time in the open street.

Sitting on an outdoor balcony with Detto, Benedick and
Salvatore, Cesco scruffed the neck of one of his pack, a fine old greyhound called Icarus that had been part of Ser Alaghieri's household
in Ravenna. The dog had insisted on coming out today and was now
sprawled, eyes closed, basking in the rays of his master's attention.

Banners lined the streets, cracking in the wind funneling
between the buildings. Each long cloth was alternately emblazoned
with the crests of Verona, Padua, Vicenza, and Mantua, but they all
bore the Scaligeri ladder and hound.

Beneath the banners the city remained crowded — the lowest
estimate of foreigners was at well over five thousand. The mobs were
so massive that rich and poor visitors had to encamp themselves in
arcades, or put up tents in city squares. The Arena's arched tunnels
were a fashionable place to sleep, something that hadn't been done
in over a hundred years.

All around them the ongoing revels were in full force. Laughter
and singing came from all corners. But the party on the balcony
was subdued, drinking watered wine and passing irrelevant talk.
Cesco drew out Benedick and Salvatore for personal information,
but there was no urgency to it. Benedick had a lost mother, which
Cesco admitted to mirroring, and Salvatore a sister, which Cesco also

obliquely admitted. "Would I had married to gain me more a sister than a wife."

Frowning at that, Detto nursed the knuckles he'd split on his father's teeth. Everyone had heard about the falling out between Lord Nogarola and his eldest son, but his arrival had gone unremarked by Cesco, an unusual show of tact. Arriving home stinking of sex and wine, he had merely accepted his cousin's presence as if there was naught amiss with the world.

Cesco's little wife had dutifully attended church this morning with her family, as if her circumstances were unchanged. Cesco felt no pressing need to join her, so the quartet lounged on the balcony of his new abode, a fine mansion along the *via Pigna*, just a few blocks north of the Piazza dei Signori and within a stone's throw of the Duomo. He had been offered the mansion that had once belonged to Federigo della Scala, but Cesco had declined – he had no desire to inhabit the home of a man he'd help kill.

"It's not superstition," he told Detto. "Just poor taste."

Instead, his new abode was a three-story casa that was easily fortified, with a massive arch to a courtyard and a private stable. The large white stones clashed with the faux crenellations so popular these days. "Like a crown on an albino pig," Cesco had observed. The interior twisted and turned, having been converted from older buildings into a single residence.

The middle floor was reserved for his wife and her nurse, leaving the highest level for Cesco to haunt. Among the amenities were rose marble floors bearing the Scaligeri crest in white, frescoed images of the deaths of Iphigenia and Hector, and a long balcony that ran the length of the building, overlooking the street below.

One quirk of geography was that he shared a roof with his neighbor, Lord Montecchio. Cesco had once snuck into the Casa Montecchio through an unconventional portal – the death door, a sealed exit used only for the departure of those without mortal cares. He had knocked at death's door, and little Romeo had admitted him and helped him steal a horse.

The event had clearly made quite an impression on little Romeo, who was ever pestering Cesco for another adventure. It had been a promise lightly made, and not yet fulfilled to the lad's satisfaction.

The boy was waving shyly from the window of his father's house, and Cesco raised two fingers in salute. The seven year-old's face broke into an unrestrained grin. "Have you come to steal another horse?"

"Borrow," corrected Cesco, clucking his tongue. "I only borrow horses. Everyone knows the Montecchi are the real horse thieves."

Unoffended, Romeo's eyes flashed in delight. "Voiceless, you mean? We only went hoarse a-shouting when you came a-stealing."

"I only came a-stealing to make you start a-shouting."

"Watch out, or you'll get steel for stealing."

"Who will give it me? You?"

"Aye," said little Romeo, "I."

Cesco threw up his hands in mock dismay. "Ai ai ai! Thy steel doth steal my steel!"

"Better than your steel stealing our steeds! When can we ride?"

"Whenever you like," said Cesco. "I have no demands on my time at present."

"Tomorrow!"

Cesco tilted his head sideways. "Alas, I fear I may be lashed by a legal leviathan on the morrow. But soon, Signor Romeo, we shall ride as though Verona's gates as though the Devil were breathing down our necks!"

At that moment Gianozza appeared at Romeo's window. Casting a disapproving look at Cesco, she chivvied her young son back inside.

"You're kind to humour him," said Benedick.

Cesco shrugged. "There is enough unkindness for children in the world."

Detto had picked up on something else. "Lashed for what?"

Cesco lifted his full cup to his puffy lip without a word. Then he frowned as someone coughed. Icarus leapt up at once and began barking, causing Cesco to wince and clutch his head. Detto reached out a hand and started stroking Icarus' sleek neck. Glancing at his friend, Detto saw something smouldering.

A group of Paduans were sauntering along the street below, their nationality obvious from their accents and the feathers in their caps, worn over the right ear – the Guelph ear. Despite their submission to Verona, they were adamant in their support of the Pope over the Emperor.

Laughing and cavorting in high spirits, one of them had swallowed a gulp of wine badly, the liquid clogging his throat, and was now coughing loudly to the amusement of his fellows.

Cesco leaned over the stone rail and pointed an accusing finger. "You!"

Bleary eyes came up. "Yes?"

"You woke my hound! Apologize!"

Two Paduans laughed, and one gave Cesco the fig. The rest ignored him.

A mistake. Quicker than anyone could credit, Cesco was over the rail and sliding down a banner to drop into their midst. "You will cough your way into a coffin, *signore*! *Za!*" He kicked the cougher in the back of the knee, sending him earthwards, then ducked as the first blow came at his head.

After a stunned pause, Benedick, Salvatore, and Detto raced to his aid, though only Salvatore did the trick with the banner — the other two took the stairs three at a time and burst out of doors, fists flying. In moments they were joined by several more Veronese, eager to help the Greyhound's heir dispense rough justice. Dicing at a nearby tavern, Petruchio's twin sons were quick to fall in. Cangrande's two bastards, Barto and Berto, heard the uproar from where they were watching a mime and came to aid their father's heir.

More Paduans and Veronese streamed into the wide street, and soon the city guards arrived to put a stop to the violence, quelling many combatants with staves and clubs. When it was over, Cesco invited all involved, Paduan and Veronese alike, to drink at his expense. But only the Veronese were invited to join him in his home, where no one's cup was disgraced with water.

Returning from church, the party containing his little wife was waylaid by the steward and wisely decided to retire to the guest lodgings where her father was staying instead. The revels went on late into the night, and Icarus was encouraged to bark as often as he pleased.

◆   ◊   ◆

"You cannot find him?" asked the lady in her sickbed.

"Not for lack of trying," answered Bailardino soothingly. "He's probably frightened that he will be blamed, and so has fled the city."

"No," said Katerina urgently. "No, he took s*sh*omething he will want to profit from."

Bail's nose was still red, and one eye was blackened. It made his grimace more fearsome. "He stole?"

"He did," said Katerina, closing her eyes. "Paper. Paper that i*sh* of no import. Not now. But find him. Find him for me."

Bail had tried, but the crippled diviner was nowhere to be found.

◆   ◊   ◆

That Bail could not discover so memorable a person was surprising. More surprising still was his present location – at the door of the fine casa that housed the Venetian Embassy. Purchased three years ago, when Ambassador Dandolo became wary of entrusting his person to the Scaligeri guest palace, it was both exceedingly elegant and convenient, owning a very Venetian exit – a door leading to a covered porch with moorings for a boat along the edge of the Adige. A prudent precaution.

Ambassador Francesco Dandolo half-listened to his wife's description of a tapestry she had bought that morning while he considered what he had set in motion three days earlier, on the eve of the wedding. He was not used to doubting his choices. But this one was fraught. Could it be a trick? Could it *not* be a trick?

It was a risk he would not have taken, were it not for Cangrande. A man whose ambition stretched the sides of the world. Under Dandolo's advice, Venice had offered him the citizenship so that any deed he performed could be said to be an honour to Venice.

So long as those deeds are not against Venice. The coming war with Treviso, which Cangrande would doubtless win, would remove the last check on Verona's power. With all of Northern Italy united under him, there was no telling what this upstart dog could achieve, or where his sword might next point. South, to Florence, Pisa, and Rome? North, to the Empire? West, towards Torino? Or east, towards Venice? The man was unpredictable, and disruptive. He was like a king of old, an Alexander, who wished to conquer for conquering's sake. He was not a man of business, of sense. Such men could be predicted. Upon such men the world depended. Men like Dandolo.

Venice could not allow Verona to dominate the Feltro. Past plots had failed. Worse, they had been detected.

That was our mistake, thought Dandolo with clear-eyed criticism. *By making moves against him, we elevated him. Venice is best when she does not acknowledge her foes. The wolf is never troubled by the sheep. But when a giant tries to swat a fly, the fly feels important.*

The irony was that, had Venice done nothing, the Scaliger might well have fallen. These Scaligeri had no worse foes than their own kin. The war between Cangrande, Katerina, Giovanna, Mastino, and little Cesco might well have ruined them all without outside machinations. It was an interesting notion, and one that pleased the classicist within him. As Homer had put it: 'Men are so quick to blame the gods, for they say that we devise their misery. But they themselves – in their depravity – design grief greater than the griefs that fate assigns.'

Then had come this offer from within the Scaliger's own ranks. It had been tried before. But Bonaccolsi had failed, and been punished for it. He was dead, his family crushed, his name extinguished from the rolls of history. All because he had dared to oppose Cangrande. As ruthless in private as he was publically genial. A worthy foe.

If a man is measured by the quality of his enemies, I am a great man indeed. But then, so is he.

Dandolo did not fear for his own person. But he did fear what the Scaliger could do to his reputation. Which is why he had waited months to decide the question that irritated his intestines the way a grain of sand rubbed at an oyster. He could only pray for a pearl.

To act, or do nothing. That was the crux of it. Cangrande was a threat to Venice. With the Doge ailing and Dandolo all but assured elevation to that noble office, his reputation would be set by the next few years of his life. His decisions now mattered.

Odd that, of all things, a diviner should have made up his mind. But then, his mind had been made up already. He needed no plumb on a string to decide him, only to spur him on. After all, if he failed in this, it was only money. As Virgil said, Fate always found a way.

Both the ambassador's musings and his wife's recitation were interrupted by a knocking below. When he heard his steward say, "Take alms and be gone," Dandolo doubted it was anything to interest him. So he was mildly surprised when, a minute on, his steward tapped on the door. "Yes?"

"There is a man to see you. The diviner of the other night. He asks for another audience."

As his wife clapped in delight, Dandolo arched a patrician eyebrow. "Has he a new bauble to try? Or is it a premonition? By all means, show him in. No, my dear, you stay here and wait for your delivery – I'll see him downstairs."

Dandolo was not one to enjoy coincidence. He had just been thinking of the man, and he appears? Was that, too, part of the diviner's art? Was all of this an attempt by the Scaliger to entrap him into some mischief? He certainly employed such creatures – the Moor, for example.

Or was this simply another huckster interested in the patronage of a future doge? Very likely. Certainly, if he were here for any sordid purpose, he wouldn't have come in daylight to the front door. The embassy was doubtless under observation, as Cangrande was whenever he came to Venice. *We'd be imbeciles not to spy on each other.*

He met the man in the spacious room on the ground floor

used for such audiences. No one could see in these windows from the street, and the walls and doors were thick. He had forgotten how awful the man's face was to behold, and sight of it made Dandolo want to look elsewhere. He did not, fixing the uninjured eye with his gaze.

The diviner made as good a bow as he was able. Whatever else, the man was not faking his disability. Powerful in his upper body, he was twisted in his hips, with one leg withered and turned inwards.

Dandolo clasped his hands behind his back, looking majestic in his heavy fur-lined robe. "Girolamo, is it not?"

"It is, my lord. You are kind to remember it."

"You made an impression."

"I hope it was my art, not my face, that did so."

Wit, or resentment? "It was both."

The man's lip curled downwards as he plucked his cowl forward. Resentment, then.

"Have you come to ply your trade again? My wife is upstairs."

"No, my lord. I have come—" The man broke off, glancing at the steward who showed no sign of leaving. Nor did Dandolo dismiss him. Understanding he was not to have a private audience with the Venetian ambassador, Girolamo's face contorted to match his body as he framed his remarks. "The other night you asked if I had always been a diviner. I told you I was not."

"You said the gift came after your injuries, I recall."

"Yes. But I did not say what my employment had been prior to my taking up the pendulum." His thick Bergamo accent did not aid his discourse. Fortunately, he was taking his time, choosing every word carefully. "Before I discovered my gift, I did such work as a man might not wish to admit. I have lived with thieves and scoundrels. I was one myself. As you see, I paid the price."

"A fearful one. A mark of Cain, is it?"

"Yes," admitted Girolamo. "I was a criminal. I engaged in crimes. I was on my way to such a crime when I was felled. Pure happenstance. Or divine justice. I have never known. But as I lay recovering, the power of the diviner awakened within me. Before that, I was one such a highborn lord as yourself should never have admitted into your presence."

"I assume there is a reason you are telling me this now. I'm sure you do not wish to confess to your past crimes at this late date."

"But I do," said Girolamo. "To one, at least. But I am afraid that I will be silenced before I can speak of it."

"Does this crime have to do with Venice?"

"No, my lord. It involves Verona, and Padua. A great lady, and a noble child. Fourteen years ago."

It was not difficult to guess the identity of the child. "Does this tale revolve around Verona's heir?"

"It does."

"I see. And the lady?"

"Donna Katerina della Scala."

"Who was burgled, and struck," supplied the steward.

The eye in the sunken socket was fixed on Dandolo. "I was the one who called for help. I did not strike her."

"But you know who did."

"It is not for that reason I am here."

Dandolo studied the man. "You are seeking protection."

"And justice."

Dandolo considered, then made up his mind at least to hear the man. "Pray, sit down."

The story was plain enough, and the better for being so. Yet it was incredible. Part of it was surely true. Another part could be confirmed easily enough. It was less damaging than it might have been. And it was a very long time ago, now. Still, the lady had wanted it concealed. What did she fear, if his story came to light?

To act, or do nothing. Here was another opportunity to act, gifted as upon a platter. Dandolo could not see the outcome, and mistrusted overturning rocks when they might conceal adders.

And yet, the chance to bring down the heir... For in the desperation of his confinement, Pietro Alaghieri had revealed one very interesting fact. Cangrande was *not* the Greyhound of prophecy. It was the boy, now a married man and a knight. If Cangrande had risen thus high without the backing of Fate, how much higher would this boy rise? Would it not be better to crush him now, like an unhatched serpent in the shell? Or was there a middle path? A way to let these Scaligeri destroy themselves? Yes. Better, by far, to let them wrangle than to soil his own hands on this business.

"Do you trust me?" asked the ambassador. "Does your divination extend that far?"

The man hesitated, then said, "Of course, my lord. I place myself at your mercy."

"Then I will ask you to tell your story to one other, and we shall let him decide how best to deal with it. He is a man intimately interested in justice, and knows all the parties involved. I shall send for him. In the meantime, if you are willing, you might even while away an hour amusing my wife with more displays of your art. I am engaged for supper, but I will ask this man to step around late tonight. Tomorrow, before dawn, we will send you to Venice."

As Girolamo murmured his thanks, Dandolo turned to his steward, issuing orders. Perhaps Fate had indeed found a way.

◆　◊　◆

Cangrande chose to deal with Cesco's latest misbehavior publicly, in the judicial square beside the Giurisconsulti. Rousing them from their cups, he so chastised the young knights that rumours began to fly of Paduan favouritism. Cesco took an especially hard tongue-lashing, to which he made no reply, standing with his chin held high, staring stoically forward.

Immediately following, Pietro made a private appeal. Dressed in his lawyer's robes, he tried to be as understanding as possible, begging Cesco not to let recent events blight his ascending star. Pietro made the case that pointless violence would not aid Cesco's cause. Nor would it salve his pain.

Cesco listened politely, smiled sweetly, and agreed with everything his foster-father said, then sauntered off whistling to join Detto, the Bonaventura twins, Cangrande's two unlegitimized sons, and those two Paduans who had inexplicably attached themselves to Cesco's train. Watching him go, Pietro knew he had achieved nothing. *Well, I wanted him to stir from his torpor. Be careful what you pray for. The answer may be yes.*

Sure enough, the next day Cesco was at it again, stirring up trouble over imagined slights and preposterous causes. Cangrande threw his hands into the air and raged about the palace, quite aware of his impotence. Short of throwing the boy in prison, and half the young men of the city with him, there was nothing to be done.

◆　◊　◆

Mastino was late rising that day, having again explored his wedded bed after a rather arduous amorous session the night before. More than pleasure – and thankfully, despite her looks, it *was* a pleasure – he had a duty to perform. His aim was to get Taddea pregnant as soon as humanly possible. Cesco was Cangrande's heir, but would have no heir of his own for several years to come. If anything should happen to the little shit, or should he throw only girls, Mastino would be next in line, and any child of his after him. Oh, there was Alberto, of course. But no one could think of elevating Mastino's brother to Capitano, at least not alone. It was good to know that his elder brother was no obstacle to Mastino's own advancement.

No, it was vital that Taddea have a child, and soon. If Mastino's only advantage was age, he meant to use it. It did not hurt that Cesco was making such an ass of himself. But after his performance during the summer's earthquake, the city was willing to overlook much. And as his idiocy was rooted in Veronese patriotism, the people were choosing to be charmed. He had that Scaligeri magic Cangrande had made famous – the cheerful willfulness that excused even the poorest behavior. If he defecated in the street, the stupid plebs would put the result on a pedestal and praise its shape and colour.

If it continued, though, the effect would pall. Mastino had to be sure that, when the time came, he was seen as a sober alternative to the wild and unreliable bastard. To that end, he had to be out of the house each day, doing knightly deeds, looking every inch the prince.

Today he donned a thick suede farsetto, dyed an expensive black. The doublet's sleeves were slashed, displaying the ruffles of his burgundy tunic beneath. His hose were charcoal grey, and his boots so black they shone. His belt was jeweled, matching the ruby in his hat, both gifts from far off admirers. He enjoyed looking fine, and now in his twenties he was man enough to carry off the best clothes.

Yet another wedding gift awaited him in his study. They were still arriving, and from the most surprising places. Philip VI, the new King of France, had sent a remarkable scabbard, lined with fox-fur and studded with emeralds. The ruler of the Byzantine Empire, Andronicus II Palaeologus, had sent a flight of hawks. John III, Duke of Brabant, had sent a full suit of jousting armour in the latest style. King Magnus II of Sweden had sent a jeweled bow strung with a golden cord – utterly impractical, but charming nonetheless.

Today's gift came from Poland. As his servants unpacked it, Mastino gasped. It was a magnificent saddle lined in bear-hide, with *arciones* of solid silver. Admiring it, he hated himself for wondering what the Polish king had sent to Cesco. Surely it could be nothing so fine.

There was a knock below, and moments later Mastino's steward arrived to announce his sister Verde. *Fut.* He had put her off twice already, contriving to be out. Unable to duck this interview any longer, he assented to seeing her.

Verde swept into the room in her headlong manner, eyes hungry. With her curling dark hair beneath the gauzy sheath covering her head, with her bright and flawless smile, with her hazel eyes twinkling mirth and malice, she was a beautiful woman in repose. The trouble was that, like so many members of their family, she was seldom still.

As now, when she paced the room, looking at the saddle from all angles. "I had no idea you were so well regarded."

Having studied stillness, Mastino now modeled it for his sibling. "And a good morning to you."

"Is it still morning? I wonder that you are still indoors, the hour is so late. Your crest should be a dormouse." Verde ran a finger along one of the silver *arciones*. "Who is it from?"

"The King of Poland."

Unimpressed, she crossed to the window and stared out, her breath fogging the glass. "He has a funny name, doesn't he? What is he called?"

Mastino chuckled. "Władysław the Elbow-high."

Tracing a two-headed eagle on the steamed glass, Verde's scornful laughter came from the back of her throat. "Why, in heaven's name? Is he that short?"

"I have no notion," answered Mastino tersely. He did not enjoy visits from his sister, was much happier when she was exiled to her husband's lands. Sadly, her husband was incapable of holding his lands without Scaligeri aid. Which meant they had come to Verona for the whole winter.

Verde threw herself into the seat he had not offered. "I hear our cousin is practicing swords today. You do not mean to join him?"

"Your power to grasp the obvious remains undimmed."

"Mm. I thought you made a point of competing in all contests."

"Not ones held by the Heir."

"Not ones you can't win, you mean."

Mastino stiffened. "I don't mind losing. I mind looking small."

"He does make you look that, doesn't he?"

"Not at the wedding."

"No, though age will rectify that. But he made a mockery of you at the knighting, and he's all anyone can talk about since. He has a talent for fame that eludes you."

"Fame is a double-edged sword."

"At least it's a sword, not a club, blunt and useless."

Mastino grinned without feeling. "Depends upon the club. What do you want?"

"I? Nothing much. Fame, a little power. Most of all I want respect. I am tired of these jabs at my husband. As if I had a choice in marrying him. But as I am shackled, I mean to see him prosper."

"Or, failing that, at least see him not the butt of a dozen jokes."

"Yes," she said, wiggling her toes in her shoes. "That would be a decent start. I had rather hoped you would have eclipsed our uncle's bastard by now."

"So that I could honour your husband by bringing him into my company?" Mastino's smile held more feeling now. "It may happen. Fortune is a fickle bitch."

Verde pulled a face. "Vulgar as ever. Are you really content to put your future into the hands of fate?"

"Why not? Fate has been kinder to me than you. I, at least, have a satisfactory marriage."

Verde rose, and for a moment Mastino hoped she would depart. Instead she crossed to study a silver globe that had been a gift from the Venetian Dandolo years before. "I think it's preferable to craft one's own fate. Perhaps I should woo your rival. Take him to my bed, bind him to me."

Mastino grunted. "He does have a taste for family."

Still looking down, Verde stopped the spinning globe with a single finger. "Why haven't you spread *that* story?"

"I have my reasons."

"It appears to be weakness."

"That's the difference between us. You care about appearances."

Her eyes sweeping his fine attire from heel to head, Verde offered an ironic smile. "And you don't?"

"Not in things that matter. I care about results. I know when to use a weapon, and when to keep it sheathed." His voice dropped so that none but she could hear. "I promise you – the bastard will never rule Verona. I have the means. But until the time comes, I would be a foole to use it."

Verde studied him, his firm gaze, his stillness, and his coiled energy beneath, waiting for the right moment to burst forth. "Perhaps I have misjudged," she allowed.

"No 'perhaps' about it."

They heard a step and a voice in the hall without. Taddea was dressed and descending to begin her day. Verde took a slow breath. "Then you'd best create the time. I will not wait forever." At the inquiring knock, Verde called out to her sister-in-law, her smile free and uncalculating. They embraced and, with Mastino's permission, began making plans for the day. They left him standing alone beside the silver saddle that lacked only a mount to carry Mastino into glory.

But he knew where glory was to be found this day. Cursing, he went off to find some companions before braving the tiltyards.

♦   ◊   ♦

The swords were bated, the pourpoints were well padded. The tabards were ornate and garish, with devices of humour – a hare, a sheep, a duck, animals not noted for valour but for cowardice. It fit the mood of the event, full of boasts and hilarity. In the coming days would be more serious clashes of arms – jousts and duels of honour. Today was proposed as a practice bout, to recall for those out of martial habit the skills required. And to gain a few new ones.

The company cheered as each pair of duelists came together to clash. No shields, no bucklers, just flashing steel aiming for a touch, a disarm, a flourish. Barrels of stout German ale stood open to all, for that was the stipulation: each contestant must hold their goblet in their off hand, and the winner was judged by how little he had let spill at the end of three passes. He then had to drink off the remains and return to the queue to fight again. Thus the victors would each grow more drunk, evening the odds as the day wore on.

The tiltyards were packed, with three bouts happening at any given moment. Boys and idle men perched along the fence, gnawing food and taking wagers and hoping for some new madness to occur under their eyes.

Benedick wore a goose. Presented by Cesco with a mocking bow, the amused Paduan had donned it with pride. Cesco himself wore a curious device, newly stitched – a pair of falling stars and a winged puppy chasing them through the sky.

"I like mine better," said Benedick, cinching his belt over the long cloth that reached past his knees.

"I like his better too," said Salvatore, who was wearing a cluster of swarming bees.

"Shall we institute a rule?" asked young Petruchio. "The victor may strip the vanquished of his colours?" He was picking disdainfully at the golden threaded flea on his chest.

"Typical Bonaventura, changing rules halfway through the day!" taunted Cesco, who had already quaffed two cups. "Who are you betting on for the next bout?"

The latest contestants in the center section were Cesco's half-brother Barto and a massive mercenary called Yuri Castorani. He was a member of a *compagnia di ventura* under the command of the famous Otto the Burgundian. Come May, Otto's would be among the lead companies deployed by Cangrande against Treviso, with Yuri on his right hand.

But without a war to fight, the mercenaries that made up over half of Verona's forces were reveling it as bravely as the best, and had eagerly come out to join this display of prowess that was open to all comers.

"I shall never bet against a Scaligero," said Petruchio loyally, then cast his eyes over Yuri's massive frame. "So I'm not betting at all."

"Wisely, wisely," nodded Cesco. Indeed, Barto did not win the bout, and watched as Yuri cheerfully downed the contents of his cup, which had hardly spilled a drop.

Barto came over, panting. Like his near-brother Berto, and like Cesco, he was lean with strong nose, large eyes, and thick lips. But he had a pair of dimples in his cheeks that could only have come from his mother, and hair that bordered on black.

Berto had the hair, but not the dimples. He also owned a tremendous singing voice, when cajoled into using it. He slapped his winded brother on the arm. "That was terrible."

"He's got an arm like a battering ram," said Barto in awe. "Did you see? When I parried his first blow, I hit myself in the head."

"Trust me, we saw," said Salvatore, master of the sly hit — at least verbally. No one had yet seen his swordsmanship.

Next was Petruchio's twin, facing another mercenary from Otto's company, Fabio Scolari. Lighter and faster than Yuri, with a long tail of black hair knotted at the nape of his neck, Fabio quickly scored a victory in a flurry of moves too fast for the eye. The contents of Hortensio's cup ended up all over his pourpoint. Fabio downed his own drink, then rapped a wooden post with his knuckles as Yuri had done.

Yuri tugged Fabio's knotted hair as he passed. "You shouldn't show them all your tricks at once. Save some for later."

"I did," said Fabio, smoothing his sleek ebon hair back into place. "I'm going to steal a bolt from your quiver and fart at them. They'll spill their cups as they gag."

Yuri groaned. "Once! I did it once!"

"Five times, by my count. I know your farts too well," added Fabio. "You're more dangerous to the men behind you than in front of you. Tell me that's not how he won, my lord?" he said to Barto.

Barto was no one's lord, but forms of address were hard to navigate when dealing with the Scaliger's natural offspring. "I could only smell my own urine as I pissed myself," answered Barto, dimples flaring.

"Because he's big like a wall, and just as useful in the field," agreed Fabio. "It's how I stay alive, I dodge behind him for cover."

"Is that how, Fart-Catcher?" snorted Yuri. "I thought you used your bird bones to fly away while the rest of us earthbound idiots stay and fight like men."

"Like bears, farting and snuffling after fermented apples."

Everyone was beside themselves with laughter, and soon the pair agreed to a bout against each other. Cups in hand, it was a wild fight, alternately hilarious and awe-inspiring. Both were skilled, but in utterly different ways. Fabio danced and soared like an eagle, his shock of black hair trailing him like pinfeathers. Yuri hardly moved, allowing the blows to come to him and beating them back with the contemptuous ease of an annoyed bear, waiting for the moment to use his own speed.

Without taking his eyes from the contest, Cesco sidled over to Detto. "The eagle and the bear. Remind you of anyone?"

Despite his sullen mood, Detto's mouth twitched. He and Cesco were like this, Cesco moving light and free like the eagle, Detto grounded and strong like the bear. Different styles, very well matched. "The bear will win."

The bear did win, but only when the level in the cups were measured after the passes proved inconclusive. Fabio had spilled more than Yuri, and the victor downed his cup and knocked twice on the wooden post once again.

"Why do you do that?" asked Benedick.

"What?" replied Yuri.

"Knock after you drink."

Yuri let out a gust of raw mirth. "It's the rule in Otto's camp. *Ci non bussa, non gussa!*"

Uttered in the coarse Veronese dialect, it took Benedick a second longer than the natives to start laughing. Then his mind caught up and he had to clutch his sides as he joined everyone within earshot in draining their cups and knocking. A tradition was born — or rather a superstition. *If you don't knock, you don't fuck.*

Under their guffawing they missed the entrance of several men in fine clothes, armed and handsome for the day. Cesco heard the murmur from the fence and turned to behold his cousin Mastino approaching, accompanied by a company of knights and jousters including his brother Alberto and Castelbarco's son.

"Cousins! Ser Castelbarco! What a lovely surprise! Have you heard our knocking and come running?"

Not privy to the joke but understanding he was already being made the butt, Mastino said, "We've come to knock heads and send you running. We mean to show you how to handle a sword."

"If you mean to knock us with your heads, you have mistaken us for quintains. They are for your lances, not us. Unsheathe your lances at us, as we will indeed run."

"As all puppies do before mastiffs," said Mastino, examining Cesco's curious tabard.

"Naturally! Because puppies are hardly grown. But if they survive to enter their adult years, they have the advantage of youth over age – though not beauty! I am sure I own nothing so fine as that doublet. Or that belt! Jesu, what they must have cost. We must protect them from soiling, or else Barto might piss on them. Come, tabards for my beloved cousins!"

Fresh tabards were brought. Mastino first thought to be insulted by the image of a camel stitched across his until he heard his brother Alberto laughing at the one he'd drawn – an upside-down duck, tail in the air, head under water. Alberto donned his with pleasure, and Mastino saw that theirs were no more insulting than any worn today. In fact, he had done rather well. Young Castelbarco had been given a frolicking kitten playing with string.

The judges of the bouts were impartial, and sober, and the day progressed without any menace or more-than-normal raillery. Mastino took his bouts seriously, and not even downing three victorious cups could loosen his determination to keeping winning. Cesco was more light-hearted, playing the foole and losing as often as he won. But they never faced each other, and never attempted to.

There was one fellow who consistently angled to spar with Cesco, an angular teen of about his own height. Atop his tabard of a rat without a tail he wore a cowl and a high collar that muffled his mouth. As it was a chill day, it would not have been conspicuously suspicious, had he not been so determined to face Verona's heir. When Cesco recognized him, he started to laugh. "The cat! The cat! The cat has come calling! Oh, please, for the love of all that's good in this bad, bad world, Ser Castelbarco, give him your tabard! He mustn't wear the rat, but the pussy!"

Flushing, Thibault Capulletto threw back his cowl. His ice-blond hair caught the sun, causing several people to exclaim in delight. He was not often seen in public, and never in the lists, being steered towards a cloistered life by his uncle, Lord Capulletto. Which made no sense, as Capulletto's own children kept dying, save that pretty and hilarious wee girl, Giulietta. But without a male to carry on his name, no one understood what Antony Capulletto was thinking, sending this fearsome blond nephew to study at books when he clearly longed to study at swords. Had Capulletto hated his brother that much?

Thibault strode into the empty right-hand square, just vacated by Salvatore and an older Florentine here for the entertainment (Salvatore had won, being as adroit and patient in swords as he was in words). "Fight me, if you dare!"

Cesco laughed. "What would you want with me, pussy-cat? You don't want to face me, fresh from a fight and arm-weary. If you won, you'd never be able to boast about it."

It was true, and Thibault knew it. "Fine. Him, then." He was pointing at Detto, who shrugged and stepped into the list. His tabard bore a beetle.

Hands on hips, Cesco threw back his head. "O, you know not what you do, Master Thibault! Vicentines eat cats!"

Detto tossed a wry scowl Cesco's way and very nearly missed the sound of Thibault's sword hissing the air towards him. Detto stepped back, protesting. "I haven't even got my cup yet!"

"Eagerness is admirable in mouse-hunting. But I don't think you've ever been on that kind of hunt. You probably haven't learned to knock."

Thibault's cheeks flushed again. He and Detto were of an age, and though Detto was taller and thicker, Thibault did not lack for strength. The first blow was deceptively light, as it was only a feint for a second that caused liquid to slop over the edge of Detto's cup from the shock of the parry.

To everyone's surprise but his, Thibault was an excellent swordsman. His form was perfection, as if he had practiced all his life, because he had. Cesco himself declared, "This cat has a claw! Who knew?"

Thibault won the first touch, and lost the second only because Detto had more experience of the actual mechanics of sword-fighting against a real living body, rather than a shadow or a little girl. The third touch was inconclusive, as both he and Detto managed points after some very tricky engagements. Thibault had made an underhanded move straight from the Holkam Bible that, had the blades been sharp, would have pierced Detto's hip clear through. As it was there would be a nasty bruise. Men applauded, Cesco among them – there had long been debate over what the drawing had meant, and Thibault had clearly figured it out. Alas for him, Detto had at the same moment brought his sword down in a clout that again, had the swords not been bated, would have cleaved his skull. Instead it rocked Thibault, but he managed to keep his cup level, as Detto had not. With more liquid in his vessel, he was adjudged the winner. He drank and knocked and came strolling over, deliberately not rubbing his sore head under his helm. "What was that about eating cats?"

"Clearly you're a Veronese cat. No one would eat a cat that was insane." Cesco elbowed him in the shoulder. "Well done."

"I know it was well done," said Thibault at once, his colour rising. "I don't need your patronizing airs."

Cesco's brows rose even as his tone cooled. "Who was praising you? I was telling you how I like my meat. Well done. Go fetch me some."

"Fetch it yourself. I'm going to wait until your arm is rested, then I'll best you too."

"So it *is* my praise and admiration you're after," mused Cesco. "You just want me on my back when I do it. But I'm not your mouse, kitty kitty, and I can't stand to hear you mewling."

"Fight me," insisted Thibault.

"Make it worth my while," said Cesco, smiling sweetly, "and I might. Ah! Ruperto!"

Prince Rupert, nephew of the Holy Roman Emperor, strode aggressively into the yard, a glint in his eye, feigning fury. "You bastard of a bastard! How dare you withhold an invitation!"

Cesco bowed low. "Because I could not imagine luring you to such an event without a flourish of trumpets and a thousand trained elephants, cavorting for your amusement, your grace."

"Bugger that," said Rupert. "And it's you who likes absurdities, not me."

"Naturally, being absurd myself. But you're quite mistaken, I'm not a bastard anymore. I've been made legitimate. Which means I am more legitimate than you, who was born so. I earned my legitimacy. I have it in writing from the pope!"

Rupert had something of his uncle in him, at least in complexion, with his ruddy cheeks and reddish-blond hair. But his lips were less lugubrious, and he owned a jaw like a lantern, protruding wonderfully. He also had none of his uncle's insecurities, but rather the easy air of natural nobility. Studying Cesco, he laughed. "Well, clearly I've some catching up to do. Somebody give me a damn tabard, and fill my cup!"

"Fill it to overflowing!" called Cesco. "He's German, and would demand it anyway!"

"Give him drink!" cried someone. "Make him catch up!"

"Put it in my face!" shouted Rupert, pointing.

"In the face!" cheered everyone. "In the face!"

Benedick drew near to Detto, who was not too proud to rub

now at his hip, which would be stiff tomorrow. "That's the emperor's nephew? I thought Cangrande didn't get on with Ludwig."

Detto grunted. "He doesn't, at all. But Cesco lived for almost two years at the imperial court."

Benedick nodded. "And, being Cesco, he made lots of friends."

"No, he didn't. He made a lot of enemies. But because the Emperor was amused by him, everyone had to pretend to love him."

Benedick noted the sourness in Detto's voice, and wondered at the source. There were so many options. "And is this Rupert one of the pretenders?"

Detto pursed his lips, then relented. "I don't think so. Cesco likes him well enough, and he wrote a few times about the insane schemes they hatched in Trent." His lips twitched, and Benedick could be forgiven for thinking that Detto was jealous. He didn't know anything about bridges and oxen and cliff-climbing. He was new to Cesco. Detto did not fear being supplanted in his egg-friend's love. His concern was just as personal, but much deeper.

Detto's eye was caught by someone staring at him from within the masses of men queuing up to fight. As soon as Detto met his eye, the fellow looked away. It was hard to say under his helmet, but there was something familiar about him. Broad-shouldered and with a decent beard coming in, he had to be seventeen or eighteen years of age. The noseguard broke up the features, but there was something about the chin and the shape of the mouth that made Detto uneasy. He decided to keep an eye on that man, and noted that his tabard was adorned with a thistle.

The day lurched on, with all the fighters getting progressively more drunk. Targets became less precise, and so too were the parries. Several fingers were blackened with bruises, and one fellow lost a fingernail when he blocked too high and the force of the bated blade smashed his forefinger even through the gauntlet. A more serious injury happened when Salvatore nearly broke young Petruchio's jaw, and succeeded in knocking out one of his teeth. Another man had his nose flattened, and might well have lost it — he was carried off to the nearest doctor wheezing and weeping. Cesco applauded and urged the shaken nose-splitter to drink deeper.

The bouts became less frequent, and yet lasted longer, with much more panting and the occasional rush off to spew before continuing to fight, all the while holding the cup level so as not to spill. Though some men spilled deliberately, unable to countenance the thought of more ale.

Detto noted that the thistle-wearer was attempting to do what

Thibault had wanted — face Cesco in the list. He was more subtle about it, and it was impossible to tell if anyone else had noticed. He fought now and again, and won, but always presented himself quietly when Cesco was up for a turn. It looked like he was about to succeed when Cesco suddenly changed his mind and consented to face Thibault instead. Cesco seemed intent on winning, right up until the moment when he threw the contents of his cup in young Capulletto's face. "Whoops. Looks like I lost." And he sauntered away, whistling.

That deliberate loss knocked Cesco out of the final eight. Four pairs in the three lists, all laughing and swinging and walking carefully with their cups. Mastino was one, Castelbarco another, with the mercenaries Yuri and Fabio on the other side. A Spaniard lined up against the thistle-wearer, who was less drunk than most. The last pair were Prince Rupert and none other than Theobaldo Capulletto, the fearsome Thibault. If anyone was worried about protocol, it didn't show. Thibault lost to Rupert, who had the advantage of a few years of experience and a few inches of reach.

It might have become politically dangerous had Rupert faced Mastino, but Rupert was against Yuri, while Mastino faced the victorious thistle-wearer. Yuri won, earning him the right to face the victorious Mastino, but not before they both quaffed their full cups. Yuri swayed, lurched, and fell over, a huge smile on his face. Mastino was declared the victor, but all the slaps on his back were too much and he ended up heaving the contents of his stomach all over his retreating admirers.

Cesco knelt beside Yuri. "You did that deliberately."

Yuri popped open an eye. "Only so I didn't do it during the fight. Christ, stop the ground from spinning, I want to get off."

"Off the ground? Shall I carry you?"

"You couldn't manage me."

"Truth is truth. You'll have to stand."

"No," said Yuri happily, "I think I'll stay right here, if it's all the same to you, my lord."

"It's all the same to me," said Cesco. "But we're heading out to reap the benefits of all our knocking. If you can't knock..."

Yuri was on his feet in a trice. "I'm up, I'm up!"

Cesco grinned. "If you're standing, you can knock first." Putting his shoulder under Yuri's arm, he helped the mercenary up and led him away, the eyes of the thistle-wearer upon his back.

NINE

The invitation was surprising. Written in a fair hand, it was embossed with the seal of Venice, and signed by Dandolo himself.

Pietro had been staring at an open book he'd been excited to own — a legal treatise by the Paduan Bellario, whom Pietro had met in September. But he had not been reading, instead musing on Cesco's behavior, half wishing he were young enough to partake in things like mock duels, half wishing he had enough influence to quell the more lascivious sports Cesco was engaging in.

A knock had heralded this letter. Breaking the seal, Pietro felt his flesh crawl as he read the friendly greeting:

My dearest Ser Pietro,

Would you do me the kindness of calling at the Venetian Embassy this evening? I am certain you are busy for supper. Myself, I am committed to yet another magnificent feast, this time at the expense of Lord Carrara. But if you could find your way to call after you've supped, I would be glad to impart some trifling details of mutual interest. Please feel free to bring anyone of your choosing. So long as they are in your trust, they have my highest regard. Consider this my way of making amends for any misunderstanding between us.

Yours,
F. Dandolo

Though brief, there was so very much to chew upon. Dandolo was dining with Carrara? He wanted to relay something of 'mutual interest'? Pietro was to bring witnesses he could trust?

That last was a sign of good will. It was unlikely Dandolo would do anything to damage Pietro's person if there were others present. At once Pietro thought to invite Tharwat and Morsicato, but hesitated. They had once broken Pietro out of the Venetian prison. Taking them would expose them to arrest. But who else could he trust? Antonia, certainly. Poco, perhaps. His family. No one else. Certainly not Cangrande.

Pietro decided on a split company. One friend, one relation. For the friend, he chose Tharwat, who knew Dandolo and could better judge his intentions. The Venetian might be less apt to lie in the presence of an astrologer. For the relation he surprised himself by choosing his brother. Antonia's hatred of Dandolo was vitriolic. Besides, Poco was close to hand, staying in Pietro's home.

He sent a note around to Tharwat, then called up the stairs to his brother. "Poco! We're going out! Dress, and wear a sword."

The grandest bordello in Verona, *La Rosa Colta* – literally 'The Plucked Rose' – had collapsed in the late summer earthquake. From that moment, it was a race to see which was rebuilt first, the roof of the city's Duomo or the entire whorehouse. The Duomo won, but only because its foundations had been sounder.

But then, there was a healthy relationship between the Church and whores. Mother Church had ever turned a blind eye to brothels, considering them a necessary evil, a way for men to pay the Devil his due without turning to rape or sodomy. Often the Bishop of Verona would hold a special service for the town's whores, absolving them of their sins in return for their 'civic contributions'. In this, he quoted the recently-sainted Thomas Aquinas: *'If prostitution were to be suppressed, careless lusts would overthrow society.'*

This did not prevent them from being targets of scorn and the occasional campaign of outrage. But as the Scaliger himself was known to frequent *La Rosa Colta*, no one dared inveigh too heavily against the women within.

With so many foreigners coming to town, it was a matter of good monetary sense that The Plucked Rose should be finished before the wedding celebrations got underway. The best artisans and craftsmen had been rushed in to complete the work before the start of November. The end result was an architectural marvel. Windows of thick glass that allowed light but not sight, set in Arabian arches. Cheery cherrywood doors at street-level and similar grilles in the windows above. Multiple exits, should an irate wife come calling. The entirety was set behind a masterful fresco of flowers fresh with morning dew that looked for all the world like the parts of women that were usually covered.

With the rebuilt and expanded whorehouse came the need for expanding the clientele. Which meant finding new attractions. Willing dames were never a problem — there were always fallen young women who balked at a cloistered life. Some girls were sold by their families in their youth and raised to be whores, receiving training as an apprentice might in a guild. Some were widows of all ages in need of money, food, and shelter. Some were stolen from their beds in far off lands and sold into this life.

Such a one was Buthayna Warda. In her tender years, she had been the fairest dame in her village of Dahab, a seaside stop for the camel-riders and traders who made the trek from deeper Egypt. One of the traders noted her beauty and tried to purchase her to be his wife. Refused, he took her anyway. After enjoying her body, he had sold her to a Genoan slaver who specialized in whores. She had been fourteen years old.

That was two years past, and in those twenty-four months she had learned much of the world, and lost much of herself. She no longer even had her own name. Warda meant *'guardian'* in German, so it was discarded at once. She might have thought Buthayna a fit name for her enforced profession, but as it was not a fit name for an Italian tongue, she was christened Arabia.

The name, she realized too late, was a curse. Prized for her exotic beauty — dark skin, dark hair, dark eyes — she was reviled for what she represented. While there were some who admired the East, there were many more who feared and abhorred it. Some men would sink to their knees to profess her their muse, their goddess, their wonder. Others would take delight in degrading her, in literally fucking "all of Arabia".

That she was valuable she knew. Sold from Genoa to Pisa to Verona, each house grander than the last, her duties less onerous, her rewards more rich. Knowing that her life and comfort depended upon being a successful bedmate, she focused on that task and tried to think not at all of the life she might have lived but for the lust of one evil man. Thought was not her friend. Nor was memory. There was only the present.

Buthayna was newly arrived at *La Rosa Colta*, only here these last three weeks. The novelty for her was that this house was over-seen, not by men, but by two women, Madonna Rapida and Madonna Troppo. Of the two, Buthayna liked Rapida best, a short woman with stringy waves of black hair liberally mixed with grey. Her wide eyes crinkled with humour and her mouth had a full set of teeth. She often complained of shortness of breath, and if she lifted her arms too high, her hands would begin to shake.

Madonna Troppo was younger and brasher, with a false head of red hair that did not match her colouring. But her chest was so utterly impressive it seemed to arrive in a room minutes before the woman herself. Atop a still-slender waist and rounded hips, she was a disproportionate fever-dream of the feminine form.

Under the ministrations of these two women, business obvi-ously thrived. But they were not indiscriminate takers of coin, only admitting men of substance and discernment. A relief. Buthayna's first day of work had only involved two men, neither of whom smelled bad and who had left gifts of coin for her when they departed. Since then, it had been much the same. In her unoccupied time, she kept to a corner of the great chamber on the ground floor, watching and learning.

This chamber was wide, with carved pillars supporting the frescoed ceiling. This was not a place for dalliance, but for social camaraderie. Not every man wished to be abed the moment he entered. There was gambling, there were drinks and meats and sweets. There were even books, though most contained graphic drawings to accompany their most graphic descriptions.

Buthayna was pretending to read one such book when trouble entered, bruised and singing at the crest of a great tide of men. How she knew he was trouble, she could not say. He was young and thin – almost unhealthily thin – with a crop of curling brown hair and the first hatching of stubble upon his cheek and chin. Strong nose, strong lips, strong brows, each apart were good, but had not yet grown together into a whole.

The eyes dominated the face. Green as an unhappy sea, or a sickly-calm sky before a disastrous storm, they stood out wide and large, devouring the whole world and returning nothing but wry disdain. Buthayna felt a sudden frisson, a premonition of danger.

"Don't forget to knock," called green-eyed danger to the throng behind him, who all laughed.

"O ho," cried Madonna Rapida upon spying the mob of bruised and drunken men all reeking of sweat and ale. "Who is this that comes swaggering in like a lion before his pride?"

"Hush you, and check your eyes," cried Madonna Troppo. "That's no lion, but a great hound that comes to view a field of hares and hinds."

The young man – clearly someone of great importance – said, "As long as the hinds are not hairy, I will chase them to the bosom of the earth."

"O Jesu, my lord the prince!" cried Rapida in mock dismay. She curtsied deeply. "You are most welcome, my lord."

"I hope I shall be. My head is swimming, and I can hardly stand."

Troppo clucked her tongue. "Then turn yourself right around, for standing is required in this house."

"I am pleased to be thrown out, for I'd never stand to be a guest in a place that desires me."

"But this is a domicile of desire, my lord," said Rapida. "All men have tastes, and dogs too. And you'll be pleased, lord prince. There's not a hair on the hares here that doesn't belong there. And apart from us, there's not a bit of hare that's hoar."

Cesco burst into laughter. "A witty whore is nothing hoar! But peace, before I spend all my stamina in tilting against your titillating wits. I've been battered in the lists already. I came for a different sport."

"Tilt all you like," said Madonna Troppo. "We have bucklers to deflect your lance."

While Buthayna's knowledge of Italian had of necessity grown these last two years, she was finding it difficult to pierce the local accent and locate the words underneath, let alone the meaning. She saw rather than understood the introductions that were made, and that there was badinage and cleverness. She might get the cane across her shins for not rising demurely and greeting the two dozen men entering. But she held her book and remained where she was.

It was no use. Danger approached her, smiling. "What do you read, lady?"

Buthayna flushed. "I do not know, my lord. I read for the pictures."

"May I?" He twitched it from her fingers. "Ah! Catullus. Marvelous." Turning, he sang out, calling the others to reluctantly wrench their eyes from the half-covered women. "An ode to – what is your name?"

Buthayna flushed. "Arabia, my lord."

"Ha! Unlikely. What was thy name before?"

It took her a moment to realize he was not speaking Italian, but a form of Arabic. "Buthayna, my lord," she answered in the same tongue.

Winking, he turned to address the room. "An ode to Buthayna." And he read the poem, swapping out the name *Ipsithilla* for her own:

Amabo mea dulcis Buthayna	*Please, my sweet Buthayna*
meae deliciae, mei lepores,	*my delight, my charmer: I ask you*
iube ad te veniam meridiatum.	*to ask me to join your nap o' noon.*
et si iusseris, illud adiuvato,	*If you do so, grant me a favour,*
ne quis liminis obseret tabellam,	*let no-one bolt your door,*
neu tibi lubeat foras abire.	*and don't go to town on a whim,*
sed domi maneas paresque nobis	*but stay at home, and get ready*
novem continuas fututiones.	*for nine non-stop fuckifuckations.*
verum si quid ages, statim iubeto;	*Truly, if you should want it, say so right away:*
nam pransus iaceo et satur supinus	*because I've dined and am lying here, loaded,*
pertundo tunicamque palliumque	*about to make a hole in my tunic and cloak.*

"As am I!" called Barto, dimples like chasms in his cheeks, his arms around a woman from Ghent. Amid the laughter, she drew him by the hand up the stairs towards the private chambers.

Danger returned the book to Buthayna, eyeing her appreciatively. "Buthayna. *'Of beautiful and tender body'*. As you are. Are your other names as accurate?"

Again he was speaking Arabic, the kind the scholars used. She had not heard it often. It was beautiful. "Buthayna Warda."

"*Warda*. The Rose. A fit name for this place. *'Each Morn a thousand Roses brings, you say; Yes, but where leaves the Rose of Yesterday?'*" The testy eyes turned inwards for a moment, his mouth lingering on the word *rose*. He leaned forward and kissed her hand. "Well, my rose, tonight you will go unplucked by me." He passed on, choosing instead a woman in her late twenties, a veteran of the *bordello*.

Flushed in a way she had not been in ages, Buthayna marveled at the miracle of hearing her own tongue spoken to her. It was most unwelcome, dredging up thoughts and feelings best left buried.

Trouble swaggered up the stairs to the cheers of his fellows, some of whom were stretching, some calling for wine, some settling in to dice, but most eager to follow his lead. Yes, trouble was the very word for him. And while Buthayna felt grateful trouble had not chosen her this day, she also felt a nagging sense that Fate was playing with her.

Passed over by this young lord, she would have to work mightily to convince her employers she had not offended him, whoever he was. Not wishing to sully her reputation, she rose and set about attracting a suitor. She took the book with her, and asked a young man with dark hair to read it to her. He flushed and made an excuse, moving aside. Worse and worse. If she failed to win a client in this environment, she would be sold down, not up, hindering her goal of reaching Venice, which held the best brothels in Italy.

For Venice also had ships. Ships that could take her away to anywhere. With a smile on her face, she began seducing a cheerful-faced fellow with slate eyes. She was relieved when he allowed her to draw him upstairs, to the private rooms. She closed the door on the part of her mind that understood how perverse it was to be relieved.

◆　◊　◆

In addition to having the finest whorehouses, Venice also owned elegant abodes in other cities used for a different sort of prostitution – diplomacy.

After a light supper, Pietro, his brother Jacopo, and Tharwat al-Dhaamin walked through Verona's crowded streets and knocked on the door of the nearest of these. At once they were ushered up the stairs, into Dandolo's ornate office. Beneath the rich tapestries the walls were paneled in dark wood, a Venetian affectation that made sound less apt to carry.

Just arrived himself, Dandolo was standing on the carpet and donning a dressing gown of ermine and fox fur. With him was a woman in her middle years, fussing over the hem of her astonishing gown, which had picked up a trace of mud.

Dandolo opened his hands expansively as the trio entered his office. "Ah! My dear, may I introduce Ser Pietro Alaghieri, knight, lawyer, and the son of the great Dante. His brother, Signor Jacopo Alaghieri, of Florence. And this man is the famous astrologer Theodoro of Cadiz. Gentlemen, my wife Elisabetta, of the Cortarini family."

The lady curtsied, greeting each warmly in turn, until she came to Tharwat. "An astrologer!" exclaimed Elisabetta with delight. "Are you here to compare notes with the other?"

"The other," repeated Tharwat.

"The diviner. Oh dear, I see from Francesco's face that I have said something I should not. Pay me no mind, I'm sure. Old women are apt to prattle."

Some old women were, but surely not this one. Dandolo had clearly wished the subject introduced early. Nor was the lady's presence lacking in meaning. Dandolo would not do anything untoward with his wife in the house. The friendly greeting, the invitation of witnesses, the presence of his wife – the pains to which the Venetian was going to reassure only served to make Pietro warier still.

"My dear, we have some business to discuss. Perhaps you could send up some *vin brulé*?"

She had served her purpose. With kind words for them all, Elisabetta glided from the room. Pietro found himself impressed, thinking of his own mother, who had been just as homely but not nearly so elegant in manner. Perhaps years of training could mend the faults of birth. Or at least ameliorate them.

When the door was shut, Dandolo crossed to Tharwat. "May I say, while I deplore your injuries, I am glad to see you coping with them. Your light is too bright to be dimmed, even by the Church. I, too, have felt the displeasure of a pope. Though it was only my pride that was wounded, not my flesh."

Tharwat answered stoically. "I would have preferred an insult to my pride."

"Perhaps not. Injuries to the pride can often fester, and prove fatal." Dandolo seated himself, not behind his desk, but closer to hand. "Come, sit, please. I have a delicate matter to discuss. Ah, the wine."

A servant entered with a tray bearing four steaming goblets. Dandolo allowed them to choose their own, taking the last. He sipped it at once, then dismissed the servant. "I find nothing warms the way hot wine can. This particular mixture is one of my favourites. A full-bodied red wine infused with cinnamon and sugar, along with a good many cloves. Grated orange and lemon peels, along with a generous portion of Dutch *brandewijn*. Heat the whole mixture over a blazing fire and served scalding hot. Is something amusing, Signor Alaghieri?"

Poco was grinning to himself. "*Brandewijn* translates to 'burnt wine'. So you've heated burnt wine."

Surprised, Dandolo chuckled. "Making this twice burnt."

"You should call this *'Twice Shy'* then," said Pietro, sipping his own. It was delicious.

Dandolo leaned back and crossed one leg over the other. "I understand any reticence you may have. But as I said in my note, think of this as making amends. Tell me, who arranged the music for the wedding?"

The conversation meandered through mild topics, edging towards politics but never reaching unsafe ground. They talked of food and fashion, poetry and prose. Pietro and Dandolo had a brief and interesting debate over the odd Venetian law that excused a man for a crime if he committed it for love, rendering him out of his right mind. Through it all, Pietro noted that the Venetian was drinking very little. He might call this his favourite beverage, but he wanted to remain sober. Pietro did the same.

When polite conversation finally lagged, Tharwat reintroduced the topic they were clearly here to discuss. "My lord, your lady wife mentioned another of my profession. A diviner."

Dandolo continued to nurse his drink. "Ah yes. Perhaps you've seen him? The hulking cripple with the — forgive me, Maestro al-Dhaamin, I do not mean to be callous — with the sunken eye. The eve of the wedding he was admitted to amuse Elisabetta. I was struck by the truth of his answers, and discovered that his pendulum had a true gift. As true as such gifts can be. Again, forgive me. Unlike our renowned Doge Soranzo, I am not an adherent." Tharwat inclined his head to show his understanding. "This same man happened to be at the Casa Nogarola when Donna Katerina was felled by her unfortunate affliction. He called for help, and spoke of raised voices as he waited in the next room."

Pietro felt the blood drain from his face. Was this a witness against Cesco? Were they about to extorted?

Dandolo seemed to read his thoughts. "No, he claims not to know whose voice he heard. It is likely a lie, but that is of no matter. It is his presence in the Casa Nogarola that matters. Or rather, the reason for his presence."

Pietro was all attention. So, too, was Tharwat. Poco looked less intense, but certainly interested. "Do you intend to tell us that reason? Or shall we divine it?"

"Perhaps Maestro al-Dhaamin here could do. But I promise you that I could not. He was there at the request of Donna Katerina. He had approached her during the wedding revels, and she asked him to meet. I believe it was to pay him to vanish, but that is mere conjecture on my part. Certainly he took the precaution of leaving word where he was going with the traveling guild to which he belongs, so that they might know if he vanished. He did not say it, but I believe he feared for his life."

"If so, why approach her?" asked Tharwat.

"Justice, he claims. And certainly money, though if in the form of a bribe or patronage, I do not know. Alas, their talk never happened, for obvious reasons. Had she died, he might not have come to me. But because he has revealed his intent to the lady, he now fears for his life. Rightly, it seems, as I understand Lord Nogarola is hunting the whole city for this man. Having been here on Friday, he felt enough connection existed to come and beg for my protection."

Dandolo saw the skeptical arch of Pietro's brow. "My wariness then matches your own now. Was this a trap? A ruse? But I swear to you, it is Fate making fooles of us. I had nothing to do with any of this. And, I hope you'll note, the moment I heard his story, I wrote to you."

Pietro cursed, wishing he could be as impassive as Tharwat, and leave the cries and wide-eyes to Poco. He chose to pursue the most important point. "You said justice. For what crime?"

"I think you had best hear it from his own lips." Setting aside his half-drunk cup, Dandolo lifted a small bell from the table at his arm and rang it. To his steward he said, "Ask Signor Girolamo to join us."

When the steward had gone, Tharwat cleared his throat. "You said his was a true gift. Was his cause to speak to Donna Katerina connected to his divining?"

"No," answered Dandolo. "He said it was from events in the years before the gift arrived. I may mention that the question that led me to suspect the talent was genuine pertained to *Il Veltro*." He glanced at Poco. "May I speak freely?"

Pietro considered. Poco already knew most of their secrets. "Yes."

The Venetian inclined his head. "I had dined with Cangrande that evening, but not his heir. When I tested him by asking if I had dined with the Greyhound, his pendulum answered no. He seemed bemused, unaware that his bob had spoken the truth."

Pietro felt Tharwat's gaze travel to him, and realized he'd never told the Moor that Dandolo knew Cesco's destiny. In a moment of desperation three years earlier, begging to spare Cesco's life, Pietro had blurted it out.

"But it didn't," said Poco. "You were—"

"I'll explain later, Jacopo." The full name was used to convey seriousness. To his credit, Poco closed his mouth, though given enough time he should be able to work it out. "Signor Girolamo, you said. No family name? No city of origin?"

"He did not provide the former. The latter is all too clear. He is from Bergamo. Only a native to that horrible city is so grotesque to our language."

Pietro exchanged blank looks with Tharwat and Poco. Girolamo of Bergamo? The name meant nothing to them. "And he is here asking Venice's protection."

"Not Venice's. Mine. At first I suspected him of desiring only money. But there was a look in his eye that — well, I should not like to see such a look in the eye of anyone I had wronged."

It was tempting to say, *Look into my eye.* But the door was opening and the man himself was shuffling in. He looked like a child's toy that had been twisted. There was something amiss with his left leg and hip. It bent him, like a tree on a windblown mountain.

But it was his face that both drew and repelled the eye. The sunken area of his face was not exactly circular, but shaped, Pietro thought, like a horseshoe. In fact, put together, all the damage the man suffered could have been caused by being trampled. If that was the case, the poor bastard was lucky to be alive.

Girolamo did not remove his cowl, preferring to keep his battered visage in shadow. He was introduced, and invited to sit, which he did uncomfortably. He gazed at the patch over Tharwat's eye, and the scars on his throat, but said nothing.

"Signor Girolamo. Pray tell these gentlemen the tale you told me earlier today."

Frowning, the crippled diviner took a few moments to frame his tale. He seemed uncomfortable. "First, understand that I was not always – I seldom traveled in respectable circles. I mean, divining is not considered altogether good by the Church, but it's not illegal. But before, when I was younger..." He appealed to Dandolo.

The ambassador said curtly, "He was often engaged outside the law."

Pietro nodded, showing no judgment. He was too intrigued by the man's reluctance, which added to his credibility.

"Fourteen years ago, I was hired by a lady to commit a crime. A truly— you have to understand, I had no money—"

"We understand," said Pietro testily. "Consider us priests, and this is confession. Name the crime, and you will not be punished."

"Murder," said Girolamo at once. "I was hired to commit murder. The murder of a child."

Pietro stiffened, and Girolamo saw it. "I think I know the story you're going to tell. You were hired to go to a house in Padua and murder a newborn boy."

Girolamo's good eye widened. "How did you know that?"

"It was September, yes?" pressed Pietro. "1314? Just before the first Battle of Vicenza?"

"The night before it," said Girolamo, staring. "It was because of Vicenza that I am as you see now. How do you know?"

"I've heard part of this story from the other end. And since I know for a fact that you failed, I promise no harm will come to you. Please, tell us everything."

After all that, it wasn't much. Girolamo and his boon companion Ciolo, who was an old hand at this kind of thing, had been hired by a fine lady to kill a child. She told them the brat was her husband's bastard, born of a mistress who meant to usurp her place in Padua. She had promised them a whole chest of gold florins, enough riches that they would never have to work again. They had set out from Mantua, where the lady had found them, and ridden to Padua.

"I remember that night better than I do my own father's face," said Girolamo. "On the way into the city, it was eerie, quiet. No one in sight. We were just crossing the Ponte Molino when it happened. A whole army came riding out of the gates right at us. Ciolo jumped from his horse and dove into the river. I tried to turn around but didn't manage it. The horse was scared by all the noise and it reared, throwing me under the hooves. I don't remember much after that except pain. I was told later that people thought I was dead. It was only when they tried moving me that I cried out. They took me inside the city, to a doctor. It was weeks before I could walk again. I went to the house, but of course the job was long since finished. It was closed. Not a soul in it."

"And after the injury," said Tharwat, "you found you had the gift."

Girolamo stared at him. "Yes. If I'd had it before, I would have known to take another bridge. Maybe I did know. My hackles were up that night, and that's for sure. I thought it was nerves. I'd never killed anyone before."

"And you didn't that night," said Pietro.

Girolamo turned that sunken eye upon him. "You say the boy didn't die. I'm glad. I've always assumed Ciolo finished the job, and took the money. I thought I'd find him, somewhere. But he must have been smart and skipped off to Madeira or Crete or someplace well out of the way, where he could live in luxury."

Tharwat said, "You didn't try divining him?"

"I did. Nothing. Nor the lady. I never touched her. It helps if I know the person, or touch them. But I knew Ciolo, and I've never found him."

"Because he is dead," said Tharwat. "Killed that night."

Girolamo looked to Pietro, who nodded confirmation. It took him some time to accept that news, release a long-held rage. "Could have been worse, then."

Pietro took this as a signal that they might continue. "So you've lived from then to now without knowing anything about the child, or the woman who hired you. What changed?"

"I saw her, didn't I? On the street, after the wedding. And I shouldn't have, I know, but I went up to her during the revels, and told her who I was, and said she owed me. And if she didn't pay, I'd blab all I knew. She told me to wait at her house. I did, but she never came in. I heard her shouting down the hall, and when it got quiet I went to check on her, and she was on the ground drooling, with a huge welt blossoming on her cheek. I called for help, and it came. I was afraid they would think I'd done it. But they didn't."

Because it was Cesco. He'd ripped up the room. He'd argued with Donna Katerina. He'd struck her. On his wedding night. The night that sealed his fate.

"I heard today that the lady's husband was looking for me, and I came to Lord Dandolo here, hoping for protection. If she's awake, she'll want to make me quiet. She might even say it was me what struck her."

"Ser Alaghieri won't allow that to happen," said Dandolo. "He has a peculiarly strong sense of right and wrong. Admirable, especially in one so experienced of the world's multiplicitous injustices."

It could have been an insult. It could have been a compliment. Knowing Dandolo, it was both. It was also true. Pietro knew that Girolamo was not guilty of the attack on Donna Katerina. At the same time, he knew that the diviner was lying. He had heard more than he was admitting to. But that was for another time.

"No," said Pietro. "We won't allow that to happen. But I think it best if you leave Verona. Under Ambassador Dandolo's protection, of course. I will see what can be done to —" To what? Recompense the man for failing to commit a murder? For attempting to extort money from Donna Katerina? The stress of that might well have been what brought on the stroke. That, and Cesco... "— to make your life a little easier."

"Thank you, my lord," said Girolamo, bowing his head.

"There is a price. You must not speak of this to anyone outside this room. At least not until we have spoken to the lady." Girolamo grunted his assent. "And you must take us to that house. The house in Padua, where you were meant to go."

That caused the cripple to frown and Dandolo to arch an eyebrow. But Girolamo nodded his assent.

"One more thing," said Tharwat al-Dhaamin. "I must go with you."

Now it was Pietro's turn to frown. But he accepted Tharwat's statement, and would save questions for a more private occasion.

Retrieving his steaming drink, Dandolo sipped. "The lady is capable of answering questions?"

Pietro said, "Her ailment has not deprived her of speech, or thought."

"So it is genuine. Forgive my suspicious mind. I understand she has played the invalid before."

Pietro glowered as Tharwat replied, "When it was to her advantage. I see no advantage here."

"With these Scaligeri, it is hard to know." Dandolo raised the goblet in his hand. "Twice shy, you see."

They discussed arrangements for Girolamo's exit from the city, and Tharwat's part in it. At the last moment, Poco offered to join the party leaving the next morning. Pietro was pleased, if a little concerned. Poco had trouble concealing anything important, like his feelings, or a secret.

Rising, Dandolo escorted them to the door, saying privately to Pietro, "I prefer to not appear in this."

"Yes, I did hear poor Soranzo is ailing. We must not risk the reputation of one who means to be the next Doge." Dandolo smiled at Pietro's perspicacity. Hand upon the door's handle, Pietro paused. "I have to compliment you on this, at least. As friend and foe, you are unfailingly polite."

Dandolo remained entirely unruffled. "All of my actions are political, not personal. Here, it is in my political interests to help you, which pleases me. Personally I abhor bringing unhappiness to men I admire. But for the good of Venice, I cannot allow myself to feel anything. Reason must dictate my actions."

Pietro opened the door. "Whereas the Scaligeri feel everything."

◆   ◊   ◆

Slipping out of one of the private exits of *La Rosa Colta*, Cesco emerged into the chilly night quite alone. It had begun to snow, light flakes drifting down to melt as they touched his exposed flesh. He was acutely aware of the unexposed parts, and of the flush on his cheek. *Damn.* He hadn't yet achieved his goal. He longed to feel a postcoital nothing, a complete indifference to the act. If familiarity breeds contempt, he was not yet familiar enough.

Drink, he reminded himself. *Until then, drink, the Leathe of Life.* He lifted the skin of wine to his lips and slurped it down, splashing his fine doublet with crimson.

His step faltering, he tried to turn it into a little jig, giggling at himself. Realizing what an unmanly sound it was, he tried out different laughs until he found one that suited him. His first thought was Cangrande's laugh, deep and resonant. Then he found himself wondering if that was artifice, too. *When does artifice become reality? If you pretend a thing long enough, do you become it? What am I pretending to be now?*

It was a quiet night. For the first time in what seemed ages, Cesco was all alone. *Tutto solo.* He rested his spinning head by leaning it against the bricks of a house, watching the breath puff from between his lips. He tried to shape it, but it wasn't quite cold enough to be anything but a cloud. *I cannot even control the air in my lungs.*

Feeling steadier, he walked carefully along the street, his shoulder close to the wall lest his feet choose to lose their grip. Idly, he reflected on having brothers. Cesco had known of them, of course, had met Barto a few times in passing over the last three years. Barto was like a loyal hound, only with dimples, and Berto was like the little puppy chasing after the hound. They reminded him more of Detto's brother Val, or perhaps of cousin Alberto. Good-natured, warm, cheerful. Nothing particularly special. They lacked what he'd come to see as a quality unique to the Scaligeri, an indefinable something that was more curse than blessing. Cangrande and Katerina had it. Mastino had it. The late Federigo had had a sliver of it. Detto had it, but in more beneficent shades. Cesco himself had it.

Lia has it.

"Fut!" Shaking his head violently from side to side, he slammed his closed fist against the nearest wall. That damned awful, unrepentant corner of his brain had done it again, made him think of her! And once he was thinking of her, the sequence progressed as it always did. First he thought of their initial meeting, on a snowy night like this one. Then of their last, with such horror in her eyes that Cesco was surprised he had not dropped dead from her gaze. He wished he had, because now he was thinking of her body, the thin, lithe form that he had known so well. Too well...

He listened, hoping to hear the step he expected, a new fight to throw himself into. But there was nothing, no chance to blot out these images, purge these feelings that clawed at his brain whenever he was still. A fight, a drink, a race, a jest, a gamble, a paid lover — *any* sensation to drown his overactive imagination. The whores were especially important. Never the same one twice in a row, never one who talked too much or wanted to linger after. He needed to drown his memory of Lia's body in a sea of flesh, where limbs and breasts and that soft little nexus of birth and death all ran together into a nameless, faceless woman.

It seemed to be having the opposite effect. Instead of forgetting Lia in the arms of other women, he was remembering her more each time.

If there's no fight... He slipped a wafer from his belt and pushed it between his lips, tasting the bitter sweet as he chewed it. This was useful, too. Anything to erase thoughts of Lia. For Lia was always in his mind, always talking to him, always eating at him, always searing his thoughts with guilt and longing. *If I could take a knife and prise out the hunks of my brain on which she is written, all my pain would end—*

For an instant the world went bright, and he wondered if he had actually stabbed himself in the brain. Sliding down the wall into the snow, the pain focused on the front of his head. Groaning, he cursed.

He was answered with more pain, this time in his stomach as a boot-heel descended again and again. Cesco curled and covered up instinctively, and already his training was in action. He tried to catch the boot, missed, and so surged into a roll that tangled him up in his attacker's legs. The figure came tumbling to the ground, and Cesco pounded at him with elbows and knees, his jaw jutting out as he pulled air in his nose and mouth together.

His assailant broke free, and Cesco came wincing to his feet, focused and happy. The heat of action had burned away the wine fogging his brain. He dabbed at the growing lump on his forehead. "O, thank you, a thousand times, stranger. You have no idea how much I needed that. "

"Bastard." The other man was taller than Cesco, clearly older. He swung, and Cesco blocked and shoved the man back. "Bastard."

"Whom have I offended today?" asked Cesco lightly, even as he bent his knees and readied himself for the next blow. "Be ye Paduan? Veronese? Florentine? Venetian? English? French? Spanish? German? Oh, please be German. It's been nearly three months since I fought a German. Would you be the relative of the importunate Fuchs, who died bleeding like an animal at slaughter? Or are you someone looking to make a name for yourself? Whatever," said Cesco, rising to his full height, which was fuller than it used to be, "you are most welcome."

The man stepped back. "You don't even recognize me."

He had, of course. "Why should I? Did I usurp your bedmate in there? She's still there, although perhaps not able to walk for the next few hours. Though I be little, yet I am fierce."

"You bloody whoremonger. You didn't fight me today."

"Ah, is that you, thistle-down? I'm so sorry, I only fight those I know I can beat. It's the way to win. But perhaps that is not why you wanted to fight me? Is it to be close? Do you want to steal a kiss?"

The thistle-wearer from this afternoon looked first shocked, then disgusted. "You pervert. I'm here to win back my family's honour!"

"A blood feud! O excellent! Are we to be the new Montecchi and Capulletti? Alas, honour, thy name is as dust in my mouth. Dueling is verboten, my friend."

"When did you ever shy away from the forbidden?"

"You're so very right. I love eating the forbidden apple, filching the unbought sweetmeat in the market, plucking another man's rose—"

That brought out a cry of fury, accompanied by a knife, offering Cesco several moments' distraction and a wonderful clarity of focus. This would be a stupid death, and most deserved. But she wouldn't like it, and so Cesco didn't die. After ducking and evading and knocking the arm away, he stopped one blow at the elbow, twisted the wrist, and stripped the dagger away. He let it go skipping across the cobblestones. He didn't want to be armed. He didn't want this fight to be over. Not yet. However terrible, it was a connection.

The man was breathing hard. Too hard. Emotion had clenched his throat. Backing away, he spat, never taking his eyes from Cesco. Since he seemed unlikely to speak for the nonce, Cesco filled the space. "You seem to wish me to fly this life. But I am too, too wise. Have you never heard the tale of the girl who wanted to fly? A student at University offers to build her a tail, but it takes much repeated force, with the girl on all fours and the student hammering away. She tells him never to stop, day after day, until he gives her that tail." And he quoted the close of the dirty French poem:

Il remest o la damoisele	*Since what she told him gave him joy,*
Car la parole li fu bele,	*he stayed on in the girl's employ*
& de la queue s'entremist,	*and diligently worked her tail*
chascun jor .i. petit en fist;	*continuing to bang and flail*
tant l'empaint & tant I hurta	*away a little bit each day*
que la damoisele engrossa,	*till she was in a family way.*
& dit: «Clers, vos m'avez gabee!	*"Student," she says, "I've been deceived!*
La queue m'est el cors germeee:	*Thanks to you, I think I've conceived:*
je quit que je soie engroissiee.	*That tail of yours has germinated!*
Melement m'avez engignee!	*I've been cruelly manipulated!*
Je ne puis seulement aler —	*When I can scarcely walk upright,*
comment porroie je voler?	*what chance have I of taking flight?*
Empiriee sui durement.	*I've seen my lot steadily worsen.*
Bien savez engignier la gentl»	*You certainly can fool a person!"*

Li clers li dist: «Par saint Amant,　　　The student said, "By Saint Amant,
　Vos m'alez a grant tort blasment,　　Why turn on me? What do you want?
　Que, par la foi que je vos doi,　　You're not diminished in your stature
　　N'iestes pas descreüe en moi　　when big with child – that's only nature.
　se grosse iestes – ce est nature,　　You take my word for this, however,
　mes ce estoit grant demesure　　that it was prideful beyond measure
　que par l'air volïez voler;　　to think you could flight through the air,
　par trop en faites a blasmer.　　more shame to you! How did you dare?
　De poi estes apesantie.»　　Now you will be a bit less flighty."

"There's a tale of tails, and the hubris of wanting to soar, when it only makes you sore—"

He got no further. With an inchoate bellow of rage, the other man lunged. Cesco realized he might have miscalculated, and then he had no time to realize anything at all as he grappled and rolled and struggled with the thistle-knight, whose name Cesco knew all too well but was unwilling to utter. He hadn't known, hadn't been certain, that the family had known. Until today, when he saw this man in the lists, staring and attempting to fight him. He would have tried to kill, though it would have meant death for him too. Much better this way. If Cesco died, his killer would escape free. And he deserved this beating. This, and a thousand more.

She wouldn't want me to die. Or him.

The other man was beginning to suspect. Through the haze of rage and goading, he saw that Cesco was not taking the opportunities, not hitting the openings, fighting far less cleverly than he had in the lists today. "Fight me, you bastard! Fight me!"

"What do you think I'm doing?" demanded Cesco, half-choking, half-laughing. It felt so good, this release, this blessed pain and exertion. But it couldn't go on much longer. Someone would come, and the fellow was attacking Verona's princeling. He'd be hanged. She wouldn't like that.

Even now there were footsteps. Cesco was just about to fend the fellow off when his head exploded into a second sea of light. The thistle-knight was slamming his head against the cobblestones. Cesco plucked once at the man's sleeve, thinking to warn him. Then the man was dragged off and pummeled. *Please, don't let it be the guards…*

It wasn't. It was Prince Rupert, in the company of two of his Germanic fellows. And with them, Benedick and Detto. Always, Detto.

The thistle-knight was being roughly handled, and Cesco had to find the breath to halt them before they went too far. "Stop – let him go..." It was feeble, and no one seemed to hear. Cesco repeated it to the men kneeling at his arm. Holding a torch that stole the colour from his red hair, Benedick looked confused, but beside him Detto heard. He repeated the words, or at least one of them. "Stop! Stop! Cesco says to stop!"

"Of course," answered Rupert, politely grim. "I imagine he would like the pleasure himself."

There would be no pleasure in it now. The thistle-knight's face was already swelling, and the lower lip was cracked, and the left eye was shut and enormous. Cesco had done none of that. Part of him wished he had. With a Herculean effort, he rose to his feet. "Let him go."

"He was going to beat you to death!" protested Rupert.

"Are you blind? He was showing me a trick, and I slipped. He was helping me up, and he slipped." He hoped he wouldn't have to talk much longer. He was going to be sick.

"Slipped," repeated Rupert, uncertain of the Italian word.

Cesco repeated his statement in Bavarian German. It was utterly absurd, and yet absolutely clear that Cesco would not countenance this man being called to account. Shrugging, Rupert nodded to his men to let their prisoner go.

Loosed, the man staggered, stepping into the light from Benedick's brand. Detto let out a little gasp of understanding. But then, he'd met the fellow before. And the rest of his family.

"Should we not at least ask his name?" said Rupert.

"I know his name." Cesco's voice was severe, yet contrite. "The first among men. But I think my thanks for saving me from falling will have to wait until I am sober. Let him depart."

The thistle-knight looked first surprised, then disgusted. Cesco had known his name all along, and not fought back. Pulling his shoulders straight, Adamo Rienzi leveled an accusing finger at Cesco. "You're a coward."

It was on the tip of Cesco's tongue to make a coy remark, test the waters, find out how much Adamo knew. But to open those doors was to invite the storm. "I suppose I am."

Torchlit-face contorted in rage, the thistle-knight fell silent. Cesco could almost hear the fists clench and unclench. The five others waited. When the battered attacker made no move to continue, Cesco turned. "Detto, help me into some house. Any will do."

That stirred a comment. "You really don't care, do you? You used her and threw her away, and never cared for her at all."

I care enough for her not to kill her brother. Her other brother. But this answered one question. Adamo knew nothing of the incest. His father would, though. *Down and down.*

Rupert's face was suddenly amused. "Is that all? Some tryst gone awry?"

"Naturally," replied Cesco with exasperation. "He's a shepherd, and I despoiled his prize sheep. In the face. It was while *La Rosa Colta* was closed for repairs. Any port in a storm."

The Germans chuckled, but Adamo was shaking. "Stay away from her, you hear me? Stay away from all of us!"

"I have taken the golden fleece, Jason," said Cesco. "I need not sail again." *Stop talking, you idiot!*

"I mean it. Stay away from her husband's lands and ours, or you're a dead man, prince or no!"

Shock rippled through Cesco's body. He quickened his pace, hoping to turn the corner before his mouth betrayed him with a question or a cry. *Husband?*

"You threaten a prince?" asked Rupert darkly. A prince himself, he was clearly on the verge of continuing the beating.

"It's not a threat," said Cesco. "He knows I am allergic to sheep. I break out in a rash. I will not act rashly, I promise." *Husband?*

Of course. They would have married her off as quickly as they could, before the scandal got out. He recalled her saying her father planned for her to marry their neighbour. What was his name? Abramo Tiberio. "Old Bramo the wild-man," she had laughed. "He once tore a wolf's leg off with his bare hands, they say."

Husband. Lia, married. Rosalia Tiberio.

All's well then, thought Cesco savagely. *She's married, and so am I. Everything's worked out so well!*

As he staggered off between Benedick and Detto, he heard the bells from the nearby Duomo calling the monks to prayer. He was reminded of wedding bells, and could not help himself crying out into the night, "Congratulations to all newly-weds! Long may they suffer!"

◆   ◊   ◆

Not far away, in the home Cesco shared with his little bride, bells were also ringing, and feminine laughter fluted the air, but of a different sort than Cesco had heard at *La Rosa Colta.*

Little Maddelena was blindfolded, as were the household servants. Only the nurse Dahna's eyes were free. In exchange for her sight, the nurse was forced to wear small bells on her ankles and wrists, causing her to sound like a sleigh horse each time she moved.

The game was called *Tintinnio*, and the goal was for the blind-folded players to capture the jingling target as she hopped and jumped about, dodging as best she could. The best strategy was for the belled woman to find a place in the room to be absolutely still. But with a five year-old playing, winning was not the goal. Especially not if the five year-old in question was in dire need of distraction.

This was the most joy Maddelena had experienced since the wedding. Married nearly a week, she'd barely laid eyes on her husband since he'd walked her home. Occasionally she'd hear him on the other side of the house, or on some other floor. Once, coming back from church, she had witnessed a fight in the street that had frightened her so much that she'd hidden in her room all the next day, refusing to come down even for meals. Visiting, her mother and sisters were unable to shift her without using force. Not even her new kitten could make her smile, though she clutched it close when it let her.

It had been Dahna who had devised an answer. In her mid-twenties, she had lost her own child at birth and her husband the following year in a battle with Paduan exiles. She'd nursed this child from infancy, and knew her well. So Dahna set about luring Maddelena with games. She'd begun with the board game Fox and Geese, then moved into more physical play. As Cesco had left the staffing of his new home entirely to Cangrande's Grand Butler, the servants were all young and energetic, eager to please the future first lady of Verona.

For the last three days there had been games, crafts, and sweets, each as varied as the household could make them. Time enough for weaving and numbers when she grew older. It was vital to make the girl comfortable in this, her new home. With or without her husband's help.

In truth, the nurse was pleased that the master of the house showed no interest in his bride. Nor could he be expected to. A young man, knighted, just in his middle teens – what could he possibly care for the child-bride he'd been saddled with? Best to let him live his life on the upper floor and keep the young mistress out of sight.

This game, however, required room to play. The furniture in the main hall had been cleared so the staff of six and the little girl could stagger about with blindfolds. The old hound Icarus bolted this way and that, barking and snuffling at them as they bumped into him, hands outstretched. As Dahna jumped and ducked every which way, there much was laughter, and the nurse was considering if she should allow herself to be caught by her charge or the handsome cook called Vito when the front door opened.

Braced between the red-headed Paduan and the young Vicentine, the master of the house looked terrible. There was a pregnant moment as he stared at the gaggle of blindfolded servants racing about. Holding a handful of new snow to his head, he looked murderous, and Dahna braced herself for a savage tongue-lashing — or worse. Then she noticed that the snow was red with his blood.

Maddelena must have felt the chill air, or else had been peeking. Ceasing her quest for the bell-clad Dahna, she pulled the muffling folds from her eyes and cried out, "You're hurt!"

"I fell," said Cesco shortly.

Whipping their own blindfolds off, the servants abashedly fetched water and bandages for their master's wound. The amusingly-named steward Fidelio was all solicitousness. "Should we send for Doctor Morsicato?"

"No." Cesco took a seat upon the steps as they daubed the swelling lump on his brow. "He'd take an hour reforking his beard. And what would he do? Bleed me, scold me, and ask too many questions." Thus he forestalled any questions from his staff, clearly wondering if he'd started yet another fight.

Icarus appeared, nuzzling his master's hand. Cesco scruffed the dog's neck while his servants finished binding the wound. After a moment he glanced at his wife. "Up late, aren't you?"

Maddelena ducked her head shyly. It was Dahna who answered. "She's been having trouble sleeping. I decided to try exhausting her before bedtime."

"Trouble sleeping?" asked Cesco, wincing slightly as the hound pressed itself against him. Moving aside, he put an arm around Icarus and continued to pet it. "Is it falling asleep that's the problem, or staying asleep?"

"Falling asleep," replied Dahna.

Cesco sent her a look that clearly said, *Let the girl answer*, then repeated the question.

"Falling asleep," answered Maddelena.

"Lucky you," said Cesco. "My dreams wake me up. Of the two, I'd rather do without dreams." He glanced at the bells still dangling from Dahna's wrists and ankles. "Bells. You know what they say about bells?"

"No, what?" asked Maddelena.

Cesco winced and shook his head once. "I forget."

Fidelio, Vito, and the other servants were busily restoring the furniture while two girls rushed off to heat water in case the master would like to soak his injuries, as he often did. The red-headed Benedick looked perplexed, while the master's cousin was ashen-faced and sad.

Maddelena looked at the bustle and felt obliged to explain. "We were playing."

"*Tintinnio*? I used to play that at home in Ravenna, before we moved here. Drove you mad, didn't it, boy?" he added, leaning his face against the dog's head.

Maddelena's eyes went wide. He hadn't always lived here? He came from somewhere else, like her? And he used to play games?

Reading the question in her eyes, Cesco laughed. "I was a champion – I had a trick when I wore the bells that no one could ever match."

"What trick?" the little girl asked with real urgency.

"It's a secret."

Maddelena placed her hands on her hips and stomped her foot. "I'm your wife!"

Cesco burst out laughing, laughing so hard he couldn't stop, even as he clutched his ribs in pain. "Yes! Yes, you are," he answered at last, tears streaming down his face. Softly he repeated, "Yes you are. Fut!" Cesco leapt up as a small orange kitten rubbed against his legs. His foot twitched, but he refrained from kicking it. Instead he glared at Icarus. "Fat lot of good you are. You're supposed to protect me from it, not make friends."

Maddelena picked up her kitten and held it close. "Icarus likes him."

"A rank traitor. He was always a poor judge of character. Have you named it yet?"

"Could I call him Felix?" asked Maddelena softly.

"Why not? The house can use a little luck."

Maddelena reached out to take Cesco's hand. "Come and play! Show me your trick!"

Dahna was quick to intervene. "Maddelena, he's hurt. Leave him be."

Maddelena whipped her hand away from Cesco's. Told how to behave, she was afraid of being chastised for forgetting. "Forgive me, husband."

She was answered with a wan smile. "Francesco, remember? My friends call me Cesco. The Emperor calls me Franz. The citizens of Verona call me Prince. But at home, my wife may call me whatever she pleases."

Sensing she was not to be scolded, Maddelena returned to her plea. "Will you show me your trick?"

Leaning on his cousin, Cesco started up the stairs. "You don't want to learn any of my tricks."

Dahna saw her charge's face become watery, the bottom lip beginning to tremble. She knew too well that the girl could work herself up into some fierce tantrums. They had to be prevented before they began, or else would last an hour.

But just as Dahna was stepping forward to offer a distraction, she saw a hard determination pass over little Maddelena's face. As she was walked up to the sleeping chamber she shared with Dahna, the little girl muttered, "I will *make* him want to play with me."

II

AN INFINITE DEAL OF NOTHING

TEN

DAY BY DAY, Cesco's parade of public misbehavior escalated. On Wednesday he fell out with a Paduan for tying up his new shoes with old ribbons – "You ridicule Veronese cobblers, befouling their fine work with strings plucked from the river!" On Thursday he took violent umbrage over another's fine beard – "You mock my poor chin, that can barely sustain the fuzz of a peach!" On Friday he struck a Mantuan for sucking the meat from an egg – "Your slurping offends my ear as your face does mine eyes!" It was petulant, childish, and often hilarious. It was also driving the lord of Verona mad.

Fortunately, this was only an undercurrent in the flow of festivities. The marriage had launched a month-long celebration that would last past Christmas. Jousts, banquets, tourneys and tilts, plays and pageants followed one upon the next in rapid succession.

The *giostre* were spectacular, day after day of tilts and jousts, with men desperate to display their martial skill to the lord of Verona. Already a famous jouster, Mastino so excelled that he won the praise of both foreigners and locals. Cesco ran, but rarely seriously – he'd twist in the saddle at the last minute to duck an oncoming blow, or use his lance to vault himself over a barrier. He was amusing, but hardly the stuff of valour. He seemed to be auditioning for Manuel's job, not that of a warlord.

In other games, Cesco was much the same. In hunts, he lingered at the back, mocking the events, or else ran ahead in an animal skin to pretend to be the prey. In public contests with staves, knives, or swords, he was languid and careless. Not that he lost – more often than not, he emerged victorious. Yet the manner of victory seemed cheap, tawdry. He didn't cheat, exactly. But neither did he show his opponents respect. His insults were already passing into legend, and to receive one was fast becoming a badge of honour:

"He called me a fawning, mumming, demi-rogue!"

"Well, I'm a blot of unvirtuous bean-fed horse!"

Despite his antics, or perhaps because of them, Cesco began to amass quite a following. Nearly every youth of any standing vied for his attention and favour. Cesco seemed to be collecting pairs, two by two, like Noah. Two Paduans, in the persons of Benedick and Salvatore. Two Bonaventura, as young Petruchio and Hortensio were now part of his daily entourage. Two Scaligeri as, to the Scaliger's chagrin, Barto and Berto were now among his heir's retinue (no jealousy there, which was something). Two skilled mercenaries, as both Castorani and Scolari were now among Cesco's boon companions.

The exception to the rule of two was an occasional member of the band of troublemakers, Thibault Capulletto. Whenever Thibault was able to slip away from his tedious studies, he attached himself to whatever game or challenge was decreed for that day.

He was hardly alone. Other young men, aged thirteen to thirty, flocked to spend the treasure of their time with the foolish prince who would, one day, be master of Verona. Most of them would turn up in the pre-dawn light at the house on the *via Pigna* and wait for Cesco to emerge with their trial of the day. Then, when they were all exhausted and flushed with drink and exertion, those not in need of a doctor's care would return to carouse until the small hours, when they were turned out and forced to seek the confines of a tavern or a brothel.

There were exceptions to this growing cluster of young hotheads. Though he competed in the official public events, Mastino took no part in the revels that followed, feeling no desire to be eclipsed. Alberto refrained because his brother told him to, and Castelbarco the younger also abstained, spending more of his time with Mastino, whom he had known all his life and whom he admired for his sobriety. He was not alone.

Valentino da Nogarola was torn, but fear of his father's disapproval kept him from joining his brother in familial exile. Though furious, Detto's father had stopped short of disowning his eldest son. Bail had always been soft-hearted.

Cangrande was not, and yet he did not check his heir as he

might have done. Instead he tried to engage the young knight in matters of state, calling him to be present during councils or audiences. Cesco would lounge near the back making vulgar remarks of incredible invention, or singing bawdy songs to himself.

It was leaving one of these that he was plucked by the sleeve by Tullio d'Isola, Cangrande's long-suffering Grand Butler. Expecting to be called back for a rebuke, he was surprised when the aged fellow smiled politely and said, "I wish to be sure your household staff is meeting your needs, my lord."

Relaxing, Cesco nodded. "Indeed, try as I might, I can find no faults at all. They are expertly chosen. Though perhaps the cook is a shade too handsome. My wife's nurse can hardly keep her eyes off him."

Tullio nodded gravely. "Indeed, my lord, it was a strike against him. But Vito is a wizard among the pots. He was being courted by Donna Giovanna herself, but I managed to acquire him for you. I think he hopes one day to take Giorgio's place in the palace."

"Only if he ages poorly," said Cesco. "Otherwise he'll be spending too much time fending off females to preside over the palace pots. But just this week he introduced me to pine nut brittle. Why have I never eaten this before?"

"Too sweet for the Scaliger's taste," answered Tullio.

"Indeed? Perhaps he has too much sweet already. I shall try to offer him some sour."

Tullio's expression did not alter in the slightest, but his very blankness was a sign. The Grand Butler was quite devoted to his master.

Cesco laughed. "Fear not! Now, I haven't seen the Arūs of late. Has he called?"

"I have not seen him, my lord," said the Grand Butler. "Shall I send someone to seek him?"

"No. They are all busy looking for this famous crippled diviner. I wish I had seen him. He sounds monstrous. A matched pair, he and Tharwat. East and West, night and day, the stars and the pendulum. Oh hum. I suppose I shall have to chivvy myself."

"My lord?" asked Tullio politely.

"I was expecting to be reminded of an oath. But the Moor has let me down, as he was destined to do. So I must force myself to ask you this: where I might find master Paride? I must keep a promise I never made to let him suckle at my teat."

"I believe he is in palace, taking lessons."

Leaving the Domus Nova, Cesco crossed the Piazza dei Signoria and entered the palace. Three tall steps, a turn, and up the long stair-case with the frescoed deeds of valour of his family, from first to last. It was amazing to see how much art had changed in just thirty years. Giotto's influence. People looked less like ideals, more like people. Flaws were evident, and skin-colour was more natural. But it was the matter of perspective that seemed to have gained the most ground. Bodies today had the right proportions, and things vanished over the horizon just as they did in life. He knew that it was a matter of style, not talent. But he missed the grotesque shapes of men and horses in the old paintings.

He strolled down the long arcade on the second level, mullioned windows on each side. The servants and councilors bowed to him, and he took churlish satisfaction in not acknowledging them. He had more important things to do. More important, because they had no importance.

He opened the heavy wooden door to the chamber where, two years earlier, he had been given lessons at letters. Sure enough, there was his little cousin, bent dutifully over his book and copying out phrases from Latin into courtly French.

They did not know each other well, Paride and Cesco. It was not a result of coldness or any hostility. For the first year, Cesco had been kept busy by his hawking. The second year he'd spent at the imperial court. And since his return, he had been – distracted.

And Paride, nearly two years Cesco's junior, was just a little too *nice*. Painfully, perfectly polite. He was also the great-nephew of Cangrande's wife, Cesco's avowed enemy. Years earlier, that lady had colluded to exterminate her husband's heir. Threatened with exposure, she had extracted a vow from Tharwat on Cesco's behalf. On the night of the wedding, as Detto had raced off to his moth-er's bedside, the Moor had related his conversation with the lady, reminding Cesco of his obligation to admit Paride to his inner circle.

Though he was not one to be told what to do, this was an obligation that amused him. *Come, cos. Let's see how nice you really are.* Besides, according to the stars, Paride's life was linked to his. *Poor Paride.*

Walking up, Cesco rapped his little cousin on the pate. "Oi. What do you have planned today?"

Rubbing his scalp, Paride looked cautious. "Tutors all the morning, a ride this afternoon to look over my mother's holdings in the south."

"Skive off."

"I can't."

"You can. You just won't."

"To do what?"

"Play," said Cesco innocently.

Paride realized the date. "It's race day!"

Since his return from the imperial court earlier that year, Cesco had been holding races on alternate Fridays of each month in preparation for the Palio, the traditional dual contest peculiar to Verona, held the first weekend of Lent. March would be Cesco's first time riding in the Palio, and he meant to emerge victorious.

In answer to Paride's excited statement, Cesco grinned. "Indeed it is. Being the first Friday of the month, it's a horse race. But this time we're not racing through the city. We're going up."

"Up? Where?"

"*Re Theodorico.*" This was the local name for the Hill of San Pietro. Nine hundred years earlier, the Visigoth ruler Theodoric held northern Italy, and while his capital had been in Ravenna, his favourite city had been Verona. It was said you could see his sleeping form in the shape of the hill that rose above the city, across the Adige. "I'm feeling classical. Besides, the city is too jammed with people to race through. So we're heading to the Hill of San Pietro and holding a chariot-race."

Paride's eyes were wide. "A chariot race! And you want me?"

"Who do you think is going to pull the chariots? Come along, you booby! No one likes someone who always does as they're told!"

"If I go with you, I'm doing what you tell me."

"Fine. Don't come with me. I'll pull my own chariot."

Grinning, Paride left his books and inks behind and ventured out into the brisk air by his cousin's side.

The ride into the hills took two hours, so that it was noon before the racing began in earnest. It was a thrilling day, with the horses pelting between the trees on the hillside and the newly-made chariots slewing dangerously from side to side. They were one-person affairs, on two wheels, modeled after classical art. As no one had any experience riding them, there were no advantages. Several people were thrown clear, and there were many sprains and bruises, even a few broken bones. They were lucky to have avoided broken necks — Barto was gravely injured when a wheel hit a jutting rock and he was tossed into the air to land hard on that very same rock. Cesco himself was nearly killed as the traces snapped, sending the chariot skewing off sideways into a tree.

They took a break, and no one was anxious to remount those

deathtraps. "No wonder Colosseum races were exciting," opined Hortensio. "Death could snatch anyone."

"Can you imagine being at the siege of Troy and fighting on the back of one of those?" demanded Rupert, who had nearly slipped from the back of his chariot and been dragged, something his uncle the Holy Roman Emperor would not have enjoyed.

"In battle they had two," said Yuri, massaging a strain in his arm. "One to steer and one to fight."

"No, there was just one," said Salvatore.

"Were you there?" demanded Yuri.

"Yes," replied Salvatore in his flat affect. "I'm twelve hundred years old, under a witch's curse, doomed to talk to fooles."

"Ignobly doomed," said Fabio.

"Truth is truth," chimed Paride.

"In the face," added Cesco.

Berto glanced at him. "What's that you're chewing, brother?"

"Poison. Sweet, sweet poison." Cesco rose. "Shall we try it?"

"What?"

"A chariot battle."

"The horses are tired," said Detto, who had raced hard, but said little. He had seen the wafer Cesco had popped into his mouth and was glaring.

The Devil was looking out of Cesco's eyes again. "I wasn't thinking of using horses."

Within minutes they were up and drawing lots for teams of three — one to ride the chariot, and two to pull it. They use staves in place of spears, and re-enacted the Battle of Glisas, to much hilarity. They whacked at each other, sticking staves into the spokes of the chariots and striking the 'horses' on the shins and heads. The chariot guided by Detto ended up winning, with Paride and Yuri both panting and rubbing their sore bits, having been chosen as Detto's steeds.

His victory had been nearly usurped by Thibault Capulletto, driving his chariot with unaccustomed skill and endless vigour. Afterwards, Cesco had teased him. "You court disaster, Master Thibault, lining up against Ser Detto yet again. Do you so long to be masticated?"

Thibault scowled, Detto snorted, and Benedick demanded, "Where does that come from? Do they truly eat cats in Vicenza?"

"Hardly," replied Detto. "We once had a rat problem, and the city borrowed a hundred cats from Venice. When the rats returned to Venice—"

"Where they feel so at home," interjected Cesco.

"—the Venetians requested the cats be returned, in the same number. But the cats had all gone." Everyone started laughing, and even Detto looked abashed. "They asked where the cats had vanished to, and my father told the Venetians that once the rats had gone, we'd eaten them. It isn't true!" he cried over the jibes that followed. "They had just run off. But ever since…"

"Ever since, Vicenza has been known to have cat on the menu," laughed Benedick. "Your own fault!"

"His father's fault," corrected Cesco. "But Lord Nogarola never thought he'd be believed. He is a merry man, and never takes anything seriously. At least, not for long."

Detto looked downcast and angry, and the matter was let drop. Instead, inspired by some new madcap notion, on the way back from the heights, Cesco led his merry band to a small village to the north-east of the city. "I have never been," he remarked, "but it's my understanding this is where to make Veronese out of Paduans."

"I have no interest in having my penis shortened," said Benedick, who was beaten for that remark.

"Why here?" asked Salvatore, invoking circumspection rather than circumcision.

"This is where the blessed San Zeno first reached out to a flock, transforming pagans of the old gods into devoted children of the one and only. They say his baptismal font still runs. Are you ready for your bath?"

The church itself was rather ordinary. But they were not there for the church. Before the church there was a hole covered with a paving stone. Under the eyes of the local priest, who hoped for largesse from this young prince, the party shifted the stone to reveal a ladder leading down into darkness. Though there was still light in the sky, they lit lanterns and descended.

The walls were close, and the light from their lanterns flickered off damp build-ups of white calcium, left by the flowing water at their feet. It was surprisingly warm down here – the heat of the earth kept out the chill air from above.

"What was this place?" asked Benedick. "Did Zeno build it?"

Cesco shrugged, but it was Paride who answered. "No, he hid here. This was originally a Roman *hypogeum*."

"It means 'underground'," whispered Salvatore.

"I know what it means," answered Benedick tartly. "So, was this a tomb?"

"Part of the aqueduct," said Paride. "The locals think it was also a shrine to water nymphs."

"Here's hoping the nymphs are still here," said Petruchio with a lascivious chuckle.

"Why was he hiding?" asked Rupert.

Surprisingly, this time it was Thibault who answered. "While the people in the cities accepted the new religion from Rome, the people in the countryside were less willing to see God's true light. He hid here, holding services, until the faith spread."

"Like an inferno," said Cesco absently. He ducked through a broken bit of tunnel and out into a larger chamber that branched in three directions. He chose to go left, through an arch that opened into a room twice his height and large enough to stable four horses with ease.

Cesco's foot scuffed dirt from the floor, revealing small coloured tiles – the entire room was mosaiced in swirling crescent patterns of blue, red, yellow, green, brown, and white, all faded and dull now but still enough to marvel at. In some places the tiles had gone, revealing outlines carved into the concrete floor for the artisans to follow. Men had laboured down here, creating a place first to worship nature, and then God.

As the others joined him, their lanterns lit the perfectly curved walls enough to behold the faces that stared back at them, unseeing. Painted on the walls were curious scenes – curious because of their raw and unusual nature. These were not the staid church frescoes of today. Somehow by being less polished, less perfect, they were more honest.

Not that the faces showed emotion. Even in the most violent images, the faces were serene. And violent they were. The young men spent twenty minutes in this room, deciphering the stories the round walls depicted.

There seemed to be no order to their telling, yet there was a purpose, for a painted child lit the order of the stories from left to right around the room. In the first image, Christ invited six young men for Palm Sunday, where the young men lay out their coats for Christ to walk upon.

Next was King Nebuchadnezzar trying to force some Jews to adore an idol, which they shunned. Their punishment was to burn, depicted in the next framed scene, with the three young men bound and in the flames. But they did not burn – an angel appeared behind them, protecting them from the flames.

In the next frame King Herod ordered the slaughter of the innocents, and soldiers with jewels on their wrists smashed babies on stones.

The frame that followed caused a debate among the viewers. Some said it depicted the Nativity, with animals in a manger. Salvatore maintained that that biggest animal was not an ass but a large dog, while Paride and Thibault said that it wasn't the Nativity at all, but a depiction of Isaiah 1:3 *'The ox knows its owner, and a donkey recognizes its master's care. But Israel doesn't know its Master.'*

"How do you carry so much Biblical knowledge?" demanded Berto of Thibault. The younger man shrugged. He didn't like to say that his uncle meant him for a cloistered life, and was appalled to discover that some of the stories had sunk in.

Over the portal through which they had entered stood Christ and his Twelve Apostles. All the apostles held papers – the Word of God. That image that funneled up into the curved ceiling, with paintings of massive scrolls that hung like pipes overhead, the largest in red, then rising higher in blue, the final layers in yellow. Scrolls bearing the laws of Israel, the Word of God.

"You say this San Zeno was a teacher," asked Rupert. "I wonder if this was not his school."

Petruchio was more practical. "Why do these older frescoes look so much more real?"

"Perspective," said Cesco, craning his head up. "Something we lacked until very recently. See how things grow smaller in the distance? A visual trick. What's that hole?" Directly in the center of the ceiling was a funnel that provided a bare modicum of light to the chamber.

"We must be under the church," observed Berto.

"Let's keep exploring," said Detto.

They did, Cesco leading to the room across the main chamber, which held an altar of sorts. There were broken statues here, and the paintings had not survived as well. As in the previous room, there were marks on the walls of how high the water had risen in times of flood. They were almost at chin-level.

Back in the central area, Cesco ducked his head and started to travel along a narrow passage, opposite the way they had entered. Quickly both his shoulders were brushing the walls. His feet were wet. This was where the water originated, coming from the old Roman aqueduct and running through a carved channel to carry water through the shrine.

"It's almost a thousand years since Zeno was here," Cesco marveled, his voice echoing around him. "Yet the water still runs. Imagine that. Building something that stands for a thousand years."

"The Arena," said Detto at once.

"The Colosseum in Rome," offered Thibault.

"There are Roman ruins all over the world," said Petruchio.

"The Parthenon is still there," came Hortensio's voice from the shadows. "That's older than anything the Romans left."

"They say the pyramids in Egypt are older still," observed Paride.

"Which all begs the question — what have we built that will stand a thousand years from now? How will they remember us?" Cesco halted at a shape in the floor — the curved channel for the water ended in a small basin, barely two handspans wide. A hidden pipe fed the water at eighty litres a minute, according to the priest above. Though the tunnel continued into blackness, the water did not. "Benedick, Salvatore — time to make you proper Veronese."

It was a more solemn moment than he had intended — he'd hoped for a pool to throw them into. Instead they each knelt while he splashed cold water on their heads. There were a few weak jests but no laughter as they all turned about and retreated the way they had come. Then someone suggested they brace themselves for the cold above with wine. It was a welcome suggestion, and soon the chambers were ringing with songs whose lyrics were most unreligious.

Exiting at last, Cesco answered the priest's prayers with a small bag of gold, and they all remounted. Benedick looked up at the building that stood over the ancient site. "What is the name of this church?"

"The same as the village," replied Cesco, using his reins to turn his mount's head. "Santa Maria in Stelle."

Saint Mary in the Stars.

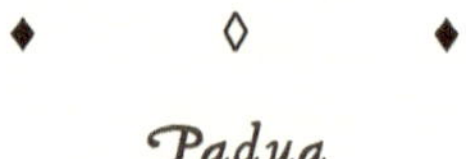

Padua

The cheer in Padua was greater than it had been in ages. Taxes were low, foreign soldiers were absent, there was construction on houses and churches instead of walls and fortifications. Best of all, the terror that had stalked the streets these last few years had vanished. No longer did one need weigh the risk of stepping outside their door, lest they have a hood thrown over their head and be beaten or kidnapped or murdered outright. The local convents no longer barred their doors against theft or violation.

All around the town the sentiment was the same — *We fought against the Scaliger for so long, when we could have had this?*

Thus the people of Padua had decided to decorate their city lavishly for the coming holy days. The bridges over the Bacchiglione were covered in lamps by night, and fresh greenery during the day. Mirrors were set up to reflect light in wild directions, and the red apples hanging from trees complimented the rose-marble in the city's major buildings.

Not only were the buildings made ornate, but the people as well. Masques (an unwelcome reminder of recent horrors) were forbidden, but colourful clothes, scarves, hats, and fripperies were in evidence everywhere. Long feathers sprouted from men's hats, and while they did not go so far in honouring their new overlord by switching the feather from the Guelph to the Ghibelline ear, several caps bore a ladder on the crown, a sign of just how much Padua now loved Cangrande. A love he continued to earn. While the celebrations in Verona would be unparalleled, the Paduans appreciated that their new lord had not forgotten them. Ornaments and sweets and toys were given away daily to any Paduan child who cared for one, and there were several public feasts hosted by the Carrara family, paid for by the Scaliger.

One such feast was in the air as the crippled Girolamo entered this city that he had loathed for nearly fifteen years. He twitched and fidgeted in the carriage. The jerks and bumps of the wheels on the bricks caused his twisted spine to ache, and every cheer from the crowds made him start. But he bit his lip and suffered in silence.

Not that the journey had been silent. The Florentine, Jacopo, had talked incessantly, and about nothing. He'd asked the questions they all asked – about the pendulum, about the future, about predictions. He'd talked of events in far-off places, about poems he had read or written, about women – dear lord, the talk of women! Girolamo hadn't had a woman in years. The few times he had paid for sex, the women had asked for darkness, or to be taken from behind, so that they might not look on his features. But with his hip he could not balance on his knees. His only pleasure came from being on his back, but that forced the women to look down upon him. Mostly they looked at the sky while feigning their pleasure. He'd stopped seeking that kind of comfort, but he missed women. There were some things for which the pendulum was no substitute.

The only respite came when Signor Alighieri fell asleep. That had been interesting. The Moor had sat, his one eye closed. But from his breathing Girolamo suspected he was awake. At last the diviner had spoken. "Do you divine?"

"I have," the Moor had answered, his eye still shut. "The results were mixed. The pendulum does not sing to me."

"But I heard you dabble in such things."

"I do," came the rasping voice, as painful to the ear as Girolamo's face was to the eye. "Dabble."

"In what way?"

"I chart the stars. They sing, and at times I hear their music."

"Isn't that just Greek math?"

Girolamo thought he had offended the Moor, the pause was so long. But the man was just framing his answer. "There are those who can play an instrument. And there are those to whom the instrument is a part of their being."

Girolamo had never heard it put so succinctly, and he knew at once that this was not a charlatan, a mountebank, but a fellow traveler, one to whom the mysteries of the world were always calling and only revealing themselves a wink at a time, like a painting seen through a tattered gauze at a distance. "People are always asking me for predictions. But that's not what the pendulum is best at. It likes facts, and the present — where is this person now, is this food poisoned, like that. Are the stars better?"

The eye opened. "At the future? Yes. But they are rarely certain, and often misleading. Ser Alaghieri says the stars are a book, but the reader can interpret them according to his own lights and prejudices. Only the author knows the truth, and He is silent."

"You believe in God?" asked Girolamo.

"Do you not?" asked the Moor.

"Is that an evasion or an answer?"

"I believe there is more to life than flesh. I choose to call that belief divine, though whether it is Allah or Yahweh or Jehovah or Jupiter, that is beyond me. I do not try to find the answer. I merely ask questions and receive the reply. Is that not what you find?"

Girolamo was silent for a while. "Yes. But if there is a God, then He is punishing me. What else is this face, this body, if not punishment? Which means the evil I've done will be put against the good, and I'll be damned."

"Only if you continue to do evil. Despite our companion's father, whom I knew well, I am uncertain of the afterlife, if there is such a thing."

"Mohammedans don't believe in Heaven?"

"I am speaking for myself," said the Moor. "And I have not said I am one of the Prophet's followers. Nor did I say I was an unbeliever. I merely said I was uncertain. Certainty is often a sign more of fear than of conviction. It is something the poet himself would say after he had taken his wine and stopped writing for the day. We would talk, he and I, late into the night. Ser Alaghieri as well, and his sister. We would debate, we would challenge, we would discuss. We came to few conclusions. I know Ser Alaghieri and Suor Beatrice felt strengthened in their faiths."

"And you?"

"I felt then as I do now, uncertain. I choose to believe in forces I cannot understand, any more than I understand what brings a gust of wind, or a drop of rain. Or a shooting star," he added, his rough voice trailing away.

He didn't know what had made him say it, but Girolamo confessed, "I saw them. The boy's charts. The ones he didn't burn. I took them."

The gaze came back into focus. "Did you understand them?"

"Not entirely. But I saw the differences. Something — something did not feel right."

"They are dark portents," said the Moor.

"No, I mean — when my pendulum wants to swing, but I'm asking the wrong question, my fingers itch. It was like that, holding the charts."

The Moor was silent for a long while. "I was right to come. We shall speak of this further. When our journey is finished."

That had certainly given Girolamo enough to think over for the remaining hours of bouncing carriage wheels and infrequent stops. They entered the city without trouble, crossing the dreaded Ponte Molino of terrible memory. From there, Girolamo instructed the driver how to reach their destination, carefully repeating words branded in his brain so long ago. He'd been to the house several times through the years, trying to prise free the reason he had been sent here. But he could not fathom what it was these men were seeking. They knew where the boy was, and who had ordered his murder. What did they want with an old house, long since abandoned?

Apparently the younger Alaghieri felt the same. Girolamo overheard him asking the Moor why the house mattered.

"It matters to your brother because it might reveal the identity of Cesco's mother, and why Cangrande has worked so hard to keep it secret. It matters to me because I may find someone who was present at his birth — a nurse, a servant. They may be able to give me better details. The hour, the colour of the sky, anything."

When the carriage came to a halt, Girolamo tried his best not to sigh in relief. Jacopo leapt from the carriage with the alacrity of the whole. Slower in exiting, Girolamo scuttled to the carriage door in his crabbed gait and clambered awkwardly to the ground. The Moor followed suit, looking less pained, but with the same careful movements of one who has been injured and now was cautious of his body.

Looking about, Girolamo pointed. "That's it."

"You're certain?" asked Jacopo.

"I'll remember the description until the day I die." Girolamo shifted. "In many ways, I died that day."

"Mmm." Jacopo plucked an apple from a tree and bit into it. The Florentine was uninterested in Girolamo's self-pity. Girolamo did not like being judged by men who had grown up in privilege and ease. Exile? What hardship was in that, against food and clothing and fame and a remarkable lack of want. Besides, he had already been judged by higher powers.

Chewing, Jacopo pointed to a symbol elegantly carved into the wall surrounding the house. "What's that?"

"A caduceus," answered the Moor in his low rumble. "Carried by the god Mercury, it granted him passage everywhere. It is a symbol of messengers. But since he could also descend to the underworld with it, some view it as a symbol of death."

Girolamo squinted at the carving with new interest. He had always taken it for a family crest, not some ancient symbol.

Jacopo remained puzzled. "I thought it was a symbol of medicine."

"One snake is healing. The sign of Asclepius. Two is Mercury."

"That's funny, considering the coin." Jacopo turned to the diviner. "What was the name of the family that lived here?"

Girolamo shook his head. "I could never learn. City lawyers aren't impressed by a cripple. And the caretaker was never willing to unbar the gates."

They banged on the wooden gate to the yard, but without answer. The Moor looked grim, and Girolamo felt his frustration. Once, they both could have swarmed over the wall with ease. But no longer.

"I can go to the city offices," suggested the Florentine. "As the brother of the crafter of the *Pax Verona*, I imagine they'll be most helpful."

The Moor nodded. "Do not use the Scaliger's name. It would be best if he remained unaware that we have discovered this place."

A statement that set Girolamo thinking.

♦   ◊   ♦

They arrived at the city long after nightfall, frozen, sore, and delighted. Several bottles of warming liquid were shared around, and they scuffled and brawled, cheerfully injuring each other with coarse jibes and heavy blows. Detto amused them all by relating the tale of the attempted theft of Dante's bones, and how Cesco had arranged to have the man behind the deed beaten until he cried, "I am a sore and sorry ass". The phrase tickled them all, and it became a goal to make other men say it.

Long after dark, Cesco returned Paride to the palace with a promise of more foolery on the morrow. He gave the frowning Giovanna a happy wave, then staggered back out of doors where Detto was waiting. "Well? Is he doomed?"

"Judging by his aunt's basilisk stare, he may be," admitted Cesco, chagrinned. "Damn. I like him! He *is* that nice. And perfectly innocent. Damn!"

"You were hoping he was another Mastino."

"Yes. But he's as genial as Alberto without the saving grace of sinfulness. Paride is practically perfect."

"So you'll corrupt him."

"I have to! Otherwise he'll never survive in this grinding mill of existence."

"You might have given him one of the Moor's little chews, then."

Cesco checked, then blew out his lips. "I thought we just agreed that he doesn't need poisoning. But they do ease the pain, if briefly. Would you like one?"

"No," said Detto sourly. "I thought you'd sworn them off."

"Why, Signor Nosy, when there are so many other things to swear by." Seeing Detto's expression, Cesco clucked his tongue. "Christ, if this is your victory face, I'd hate to see you if you'd lost. For mercy's sake, go to him."

"Who?"

"The Great Cham. Who do you imagine I mean? Your noble father, of course! As chariot champion you should be a preening peacock, not a sulking slug. You clearly are not made to have a filial rift. Go mend it."

"Mind your own affairs."

"I am," said Cesco tartly. "I have to look at your unhappy visage every hour of the day. It's putting me off my food."

"I should have known your concern was for your own appetites!" snapped Detto. "Would you like to throw me out, too? You'd eat better. Unless it's those damn wafers that turn your stomach."

"They ease the pain of your silent bellyaching."

"Then I'll leave!"

"Did I say that? No, cos, I'm simply saying that you won't be content until you have your father's approval again. So go get it. And visit your mother."

In a wrathful whisper Detto said, "Don't mention her."

"Very well."

Detto balled up a fist below Cesco's nose. "I mean it!"

"And I agreed."

Detto looked ready to throw a blow. But for once Cesco showed no sign of encouraging a brawl.

Waiting not far off, Benedick decided to interpose himself. "Where shall we dine? *La Rosa Colta?*"

"Why not?" asked Cesco, his eyes still on his cousin. "I like bathing in rosewater."

Turning sharply, Detto stalked away. Softly, Benedick asked, "What was that?"

"The reaping of my own harvest. The paying of my own coin. The rendering unto Caesar what was Caesar's."

Benedick took a breath. "I don't pretend to know his mind, my lord. But clearly he's hurting, so he wants to hurt everything, and everyone. He wants revenge, but can't say against what."

Cesco's brow furrowed. "How well you know us, Ahenobarbus, after so short an acquaintance. Do your insights apply to someone other than Detto?"

"Of course not," said Benedick at once.

They walked on in silence for a few moments. Then Cesco said, "Detto doesn't know what to be angry at. I do."

"What, then? Your noble father? Padua? Life? God?"

Cesco spread his hands in an encompassing gesture. "Them all together."

♦   ◊   ♦

"And what shall I tell your uncle, the emperor?" demanded Berthold von Neifen.

"Tell him that I am perfectly well, despite several knocks to my head."

"Is it rough sport? Or an attack?"

Rupert pulled a face of annoyance only used by the young. "If it's an attack, it is not on me. Ser Franz almost died today. He pushes himself to the utter limits of endurance, and we go with him. I don't think he cares if he lives or dies. It's inspiring."

"It's madness."

Rupert sighed as the servant tugged his boots free. "A glorious madness. Who wants to live past twenty-seven? Watch it, lout! My ankle is sore."

"Forgive me, my lord prince," said the servant.

Like the accomplished jouster he was, Berthold remained on target. "Is there any point to this constant exercise of imbecility? Sports and trials of manhood are one thing, but I do not recall him creating such brawls and scenes in the imperial court."

"Then you're not recalling correctly. He damages the most serene calms, crafts the most delicious diversions. True, he is escalating. But that comes with age. He is a man now, or almost, and wishes to prove himself one." Rupert waited for the door to close on the servant before removing something from his belt. "He eats these. I stole one when I was able. He says he has a taste for sweets, but it seems medicinal."

Grunting, Berthold took the wafer up. It was sticky to the touch. He took the smallest bite. "Sweet."

"It could be nothing," conceded Rupert.

"I'll send it to an alchemist. Meanwhile, are you any closer to your goal?"

"I am part of his retinue. He is distressingly egalitarian in his choice of company – men of no name held in equal esteem as a prince of the blood. He claims he prizes excellence above all else. As if excellence were not inherited. But I have reconciled myself, and am part of his fellowship. His cousin remains his closest adherent, yet there seems to be some sort of rift. I am attempting to exploit it, but there are many with the same goal. That red-headed Paduan for one. His natural brothers for others. He is the coming power, and everyone wants his ear and his favour."

"They must be yours."

"I'll get them," said Rupert confidently, laying back on his bed. He groaned. "If I don't die trying."

"Better he should die than you, my prince," said Berthold, moving towards the door.

"I was thinking much the same. Oh, Count? There is one thought I had. He is most eager for the war with Treviso."

"Such a war would only increase Verona's power."

"I know. So what if we were able to delay it?" His eyes closing, Rupert sighed. "Right in the face."

◆　◇　◆

Thibault Capulletto snuck into his house, his face raw from the wind and sore from unaccustomed smiling. To his amazement he had been welcomed into the heir's company, and joyfully taken part in the chariot races. He'd not won, which was troubling. But he'd certainly acquitted himself well, and had enjoyed the company of men doing deeds worthy of men. He was not the youngest – that honour went to Paride. But Thibault felt pride in holding his own against men twice his age, both in the field and afterwards, when they had called at a fancy cat-house (an education for Thibault, whose nurse had explained everything, and yet nothing).

"You should be at home here, O King of Cats," mocked Cesco, playing on Thibault's name, shared with the cat from the fabled tales of Renard the Fox.

But Thibault had not partaken in the alluring feminine flesh offered, preferring to play at dice with some of the others. His was not a reluctance to soil himself in vice. It was rather that he was in love, and in every youthful half-clad girl, Thibault saw only his uncle's wife, his own former betrothed, his dear and lovely Tessa.

Thibault had been engaged to Tessa since birth, but his uncle had broken the agreement to marry the girl himself. One of many usurping blows to the youthful blond hot-head, who should have inherited all his grandfather's estates and wealth. But his fat gouty grandfather had passed over his firstborn's heir, leaving all to Antony instead.

Thibault could have endured the loss of the money. But coupled with the loss of Tessa, it made him hate his beefy, ruddy uncle with the passion of a burning star. In the whorehouse, seeing women fondled and fondling, he burned all the hotter as he imagined his uncle doing those things to sweet Tessa's body. As he imagined doing those things himself, and having them done to him in return...

Whatever festering wound was salted in *La Rosa Colta*, the rest of the day had been a joy. At dawn the next day Thibault again made to slip out from the house – they had spoken of a wolf-baiting, followed by a race along the old Roman walls. He still balked at join-ing any group led by Cesco, a fellow he disliked almost as much as he admired. For Verona's heir was able to do everything Thibault longed to do – rebel, flout authority, and become a famous blade.

But for the first time in his life, Thibault felt included. Part of something larger than himself. And he meant to prove his worth. In six months, there would be no contest he would not win.

As he was setting out through the tunnel leading to the street, his uncle emerged from his office. "How now! Where are you off to?"

"Nowhere," was Thibault's mulish reply.

"Damn right, nowhere," answered Antony, flushing to the roots of his sandy-blond hair. "Get back inside. You should be studying your Latin."

Thibault despised Latin. Stories of Caesar and Aeneas were fine, but most of his reading was biblical. The moment Antony had a male heir, Thibault would be sent to some monastery high in the German hills, far from home, with little hope of escape. The bastard knew him well enough to know he'd try to run the moment he was gone.

But Thibault longed for war, for fame in battle, for honour and dignity and the way of the sword. There were some books he did not despise – his hidden stash of *fechtbuchs* from which he trained himself nightly. When he was meant to be scribbling his Latin, he was instead doing exercises to increase his strength. At thirteen, he was not yet strong enough to fight his uncle. But the day would come when he could make his own way in the world, and when it arrived, it would find him ready.

"Well?" demanded Thibault's uncle. "Get back to your books, boy."

"No," said Thibault. "I'm off to meet the heir."

His uncle's jaw clenched. "The Devil you say!"

"The Devil I don't," retorted Thibault, enjoying the outrage he was eliciting. "Yesterday I nearly won the chariot races!"

"What are you, a gladiator?" Antony swelled. "Do you have any idea how upset the Scaliger is by his son's antics? He's furious! That boy has injured the peace with the Paduans a dozen times in as many days! He's a prince, he can get up to what he likes. But no member of my household is going to be caught stirring up trouble. Get back inside!"

"I won't!" said Thibault defiantly.

He did not even see the blow that cuffed him to the ground. As he shook his head to clear it, his uncle gestured to a pair of men. "Take this idiot away and lock him in the tower. Bar the outer windows. Build him a fire, and give him his books. And if he burns them, burn him upon his own pyre."

As the men approached, hot tears coursed down Thibault's face. "Don't touch me. Don't touch me!"

"If he makes any noise, gag him." With that, Antony Capulletto stalked back into his office.

Frog-marched into the main building, Thibault saw his little cousin Giulietta come running out the door, looking at the light snow that had just begun to fall. Laughing until she saw him, her face became pitying.

It was shaming to him, being pitied by a three year-old. "Get out of it!" he shouted at her as he was marched past, back within the doors, up to his dreaded books.

Startled, Giulietta went running to her father to tell him what those men were doing to her cousin. "I know, dear," said Antony, patting her on the head with a tender smile. "Your cousin is too headstrong for his own good. You know what he wanted to do? Go out and start fights. He's not thinking clearly, is all. He thinks that fights and duels and swords are all there is to life."

"He does like swords," confided Giulietta. "He teaches me sometimes."

"Does he?" asked Antony, bemused. "Does he indeed? Well, I'm sure you're a better swordsman than he'll ever be. Now run along, poppet. Don't let him spoil your day."

Giulietta liked compliments, and as she toddled off to the main house, she decided that she would cheer her cousin up by asking him to play with her dolls. But when she approached, he was in serious conversation with her mother. Knowing better than to interrupt her mother at anything, Giulietta turned around to seek out her nurse instead. She did not see her mother countermand her husband's orders, nor did she witness Thibault slipping over the wall of the yard a few minutes later, where once he had struggled with a masqued lad who was now the heir to mischief and glory.

♦　◊　♦

The wolf-baiting started without the presence of young Capulletto, but he was not missed amid the great danger of the taunting of the beast. He arrived just in time to see the beast get loose, badly mauling Fabio's arm before Yuri stepped in to haul it back while Cesco stabbed it in the neck.

"And thus to Hell," he muttered.

When asked why he had ended their sport, he replied, "I needed the practice. Ah, here is the crafty kitten, come to collect the kill. He can bind Fabio's arm instead. Come, the rest of you, let us filch sweetmeats from the market before sweetening our own meats with piscine perfume! Wait — is that Paduan over there urinating? How dare he! Pissing on the very foundations of this great city! Shall we show him what we think of that? *Allez!*"

Detto, Rupert, Benedick, Salvatore, Petruchio, Hortensio, Paride, Yuri, Fabio, Berto, Barto, and Thibault. Thus formed Cesco's army of ne'er-do-wells, the next generation of Veronese knighthood. Flowers of courtesy, souls of chivalry, and vessels of chastity, they threatened the peace, filled the air with their blasphemies, and ended each day in a brothel, a brawl, or a bottle.

Even those who shook their heads in disgust had to admire the sheer energy, the boldness, the daring of the Heir. Though they scurried out of sight at Cesco's approach and shook their fists if his shenanigans invaded their daily lives, a strange sort of pride kindled in the hearts of the Veronese. He might be a Hellion, but he was *their* Hellion.

ELEVEN

The seventh day of December found the public once again feasting at the Scaliger's expense. Beneath a gently falling snow, six hundred Veronese peasants were given a banquet of culinary delights they had never dreamed existed.

Just arrived back in Verona, Bailardino stood looking down at the jubilant crowd from the palace balcony. "Good god, Francesco. How much is this costing you?"

Cangrande waved, causing the chilly revelers to cheer. "Castelbarco is beginning to squeal. When he bleats, I'll know I'm in trouble. Or rather, Treviso is."

Bail grunted. "Can't wait. My last war."

"You're not serious."

"I certainly am!" declared the barrel-chested soldier. "I'm nearer sixty than fifty, Pup."

"Pup!" laughed Cangrande. "I haven't heard that in eleven years. San Bonifacio used to call me that. The usurping puppy."

"Well, you're hardly a puppy anymore. You'll be forty in a few years. Grizzled."

Cangrande wrinkled his nose. "I'm in my prime. The Romans of Caesar's day thought that a man's life peaked at forty-one."

"War is a young man's sport. And our young men need it," added Bail darkly.

"Things no better with Detto?"

"We're not speaking. First time ever."

"He's at the right age to rebel. As I recall, I was particularly troublesome at thirteen."

"You've never not been troublesome. I remember saying you'd be better off with a jackass on your helm. But I thought – I don't know, I thought Detto and I would weather it better. I wonder, am I too old to be a father? I had more energy when we fostered you. Serves me right for—"

"Being a randy old goat?" Cangrande grinned.

Bail slapped at his friend's head. "That's your sister you're talking about."

"I think that's supposed to be *my* protest. Speaking of Katerina, how is she?"

"Settled at home in Vicenza, as comfortable as she can be. Face almost healed. For the rest, as you'd expect. Angry, frustrated, weak."

"The latter causes the former."

"I know. Sometimes I wonder if God is punishing her."

"For?"

"Poking about in the supernatural. That damned astrologer."

"The fault is not in the astrologer, but in the stars themselves," said Cangrande.

Ignoring philosophy, Bail continued in a practical vein. "Kat's still worked up over this diviner. How can such a man disappear?"

"With help. He was seen entering the Venetian embassy. He was not seen to depart, which means Dandolo smuggled him out. After being called upon by Ser Alaghieri and that damned astrologer. Did that catch your attention?"

"It did. Though it might be innocent. Pietro has more honesty in him than a stack of bibles. He might be hunting to avenge Kat's honour. He's always been soft on her. By the bye, she's insisting you ride out and talk to her. Promised I'd mention it."

"What, and miss my own revels?"

"Do it, please. I know how things are between you two. But she's most alive when talking to you."

"Or to Cesco."

Bailardino scowled. "I don't want that little shit anywhere near her. He's poison. Infects everything and everyone he touches."

Cangrande shook his head. "Whatever happened between them, Cesco didn't cause Kat's stroke. As you say, it was God's Will. You shouldn't cast blame where it isn't earned."

Bail pursed his lips. "Do you think it might have been this diviner? She wants to see him, badly. That could mean he was the one. She keeps saying it wasn't Cesco. But I don't see how a cripple could have hit her with such force."

"Sometimes weakness in one limb can lead to strength in others."

"And sometimes it just leads to more weakness," countered Bail.

With a final wave, Cangrande turned away from the crowd. "Come! Our feast awaits."

"At least we're eating indoors," said Bail, blowing warmth into his knuckles. "This snow doesn't seem to be relenting." Verona never got much more than a few dustings of snow each winter. This year it was beginning to accumulate. If it continued, the city would grind to a halt under a blanket of ice.

"I'm tempted to make a jest about Verona becoming an ice lake. But people might misinterpret and think to find Lucifer buried ass-upwards in the snow. But it is Hellish cold."

Owning no interest in poetry, Bail blew on his hands again. For the first time since his wife's stroke he was about to face Cesco, and his son. He wanted his hands ready.

♦　◊　♦

The notables of Verona gathered for another *fête* in a season that promised many such. This banquet was held in the north end of the palace, on the second level. The need for space had finally won out, and a wall had been knocked down in the old civic building to allow the palace to expand. Of course, Cangrande had also built a new palace, known as the Palazzo Cangrande, but the one on the east side of the Piazza dei Signori remained the heart of Scaligeri life. Most of the bedrooms had been moved to the new palace, making space for offices and meeting chambers. Cangrande himself retained a bedroom in this palace, as did his Constable, the redoubtable Massimiliano da Villafranca. Notably, Giovanna had her own suite of rooms in the new building, leaving Cangrande's bed free for whatever pleasure he chose to take.

In the olden days, the feasting hall had been below. But it had been airless and stone. This new one, converted from a meeting chamber, had huge windows along the south wall facing the public square. Four massive oak doors studded with iron opened east and west, one in each corner. Above the exterior doorframes were frescoes of the Madonna and Child – Cangrande was particularly devoted to images of the Virgin, and had built a church in her honour.

Inside, the high ceiling was ornately designed in crimson and gold geometric squares, while the walls were frescoed in similar designs but with far more colour. Candelabra adorned each wall, along with banners bearing the Scaligeri ladder, eagle, and hound surrounded by a gilt laurel wreath. Even the stands holding the banners were carved, a clawed foot below the ubiquitous ladder.

The floor was perhaps the most impressive feat. Cangrande eschewed the straw rushes often used to carpet public chambers. His floors were bare, but rather than stone slabs or mosaic tiles, the floor of this chamber was laid in wood that shone with polish that reflected the light from the blazing candles overhead.

Pietro Alaghieri took in the chamber with appreciation. In the light and heat of this room, the faces were all familiar to him. Most were friendly – Petruchio and his Kate; Castelbarco and his wife and grown son; Nico da Lozzo. There, at one end of a table, were Mariotto and his wife Gianozza, seated opposite Abbot Giuseppe, another of the many Scaligeri bastards of the previous generation who had taken the cowl and prospered. At the other side of the hall were Antonio and his heavily pregnant wife Tessa, facing the Bishop of Verona, a genial man called Francis. Montecchio and Capulletto were seated as far from each other as decorum allowed, with holy men to muzzle them, removed from the center of power as punishment for their never-ending (though happily bloodless) feud.

Places at the High Table were reserved for family and close Scaligeri friends. Pietro was among these, seated just three spots away from Cangrande's throne. Morsicato was absent tonight, still tending to Donna Katerina in Vicenza. And Tharwat and Poco had yet to return from Padua, though they had sent a note assuring Pietro they had found the house and were making inquiries. He tried not to feel excitement over what they might find. His face was too expressive, gave away too much.

But his guilelessness was nothing compared to Alberto della Scala's genial obliviousness, which had earned him the nickname Alblivious. Seated on Pietro's right, he was the cheerful barrier between Pietro and Mastino, who was naming people for his new wife Taddea. Beyond them sat Cangrande's niece Verde and her semi-disgraced husband Rizardo. *I wonder what they think of being so far removed from the center of the table?* Pietro noted that even the chair given Rizardo was an insult. Men had high-backed chairs, but Rizardo's bore the lower back of a woman's seat.

Of course, the heart of the feast was reserved for Cangrande and Cesco, with their wives flanking them. Like Cangrande, Cesco and Maddelena had not yet arrived. Beside the Scaliger's empty throne sat Giovanna, looking grave – she did not appear pleased to hear the latest adventures Paride had partaken in that morning. Unaware of her disapproval, he chatted away about the contest that had left him with a bruised chin that must have made his wide smile painful.

Next to Paride were two empty seats. One was clearly for Bailardino. But Katerina wasn't coming — had they miscounted chairs? *No,* realized Pietro. *It's for Detto. Seating him beside his estranged father — that should make for an entertaining meal.*

Beyond Detto's place sat Valentino, looking miserable. Forever second lute to his brother and Cesco, chasing after them in the role of tagalong, he had turned inwards, to books and study. Fitting for a second son. His father notwithstanding, it was rare that anyone other than the firstborn should become a lord — Bailardino eclipsing his elder brother was entirely due to his marriage with Katerina della Scala. And his one-armed brother had hardly suffered — for twenty years he'd been married to the Countess da Fogliano, and when he was not tending Vicenza for his little brother he was holding his wife's lands for Cangrande.

Though knighted, Val did not seem destined for war the way his father, uncle, and brother were. A second son himself, Pietro felt for young Valentino, just twelve years old. He hoped the boy would find his level, not have one forced upon him. When his own elder brother had died, Pietro had been ill-prepared to become his father's heir.

And if something happened to me? Poco would inherit. Not as terrible today as once it was. *Poco's right, though. I should marry, have a son of my own. Because however much I wish it, Cesco is not my heir.*

Think of the Devil and he appears. Cesco entered, followed by Detto, Prince Rupert, young Petruchio and Hortensio, the two Paduans, the two bastards, and the rest of his cohort. On Cesco's back, riding him like a horse, was his little wife, her hair frosted with snow. Slinging her to the ground, Cesco took a moment to dust it off, a sight that touched Pietro's heart.

They wended their way through the tables, one long one and four short, like an E with an extra tine. Cesco paused beside Mariotto and Gianozza. Donna Montecchio leapt up to kiss the little princess while Cesco shook Mariotto's arm. Mariotto said, "How is the horse?"

"Truly magnificent!" said a beaming Cesco. Mariotto's wedding gift had been a hot-blooded courser. The term 'hot-blooded' came from the fact that its father was a rather fine Arabian stallion Mariotto had purchased to cover his mares. From their ignominious origins as horse-thieves, the Montecchi had proven time and again their instincts for horseflesh.

Mari was visibly pleased. "Romeo wanted me to tell you *he* picked it."

Cesco's smile grew. "I'll be sure to return the compliment as soon as he's old enough."

"Be careful! His mother won't want him cavorting with your band of merry rakehells."

"Rakehells!" cried Cesco. "Lord Montecchio, I believe you have just christened us! Do you hear that, Detto? Hortensio?" He picked up a bowl of water and splashed it at the brothers Bonaventura. "I baptize you in the name of God's favourite, Lucifer. Henceforth, we shall be called the Rakehells!"

"O Christ," groaned Mariotto. "Well, at least you have a horse coloured for the place. Have you named him?"

"I call him Abastor." Hearing the name, Pietro frowned but said nothing.

Young Petruchio and Hortensio fell in beside their parents and their siblings, two sisters called Evelina and Vittoria. Vittoria was misty-eyed as she gazed at Cesco, and almost burst into sobs as he sent her a wink. Had he not known better, Pietro might have suspected the young prince of bedding Petruchio's firstborn. But the romance was all in the girl's head, and had to run its course. He hoped the arrival of the two Paduans, Benedick and Salvatore, at their table would distract her. Though neither seemed to be promising in their purses, they were at least pleasant.

Cangrande arrived with Bailardino, and they too worked their way up the hall, greeting men and wives. Bail embraced Pietro with one of his fierce bear-hugs – the man had lost none of his strength. He watched as Bail moved down the table to his place, and noted that Detto had switched seats with Val, so he would not have to sit beside his father. So much for *rapprochement*.

The High Table was a literal as well as a figurative name. On the one side the seats were set higher, allowing Cangrande and those sitting with him to have a view of the whole room. Eyes traveling across the feasting hall, Pietro was startled to spy a pair he did not know. Clearly a father and son, though the son was not yet a man – a squire's age, perhaps.

Greeting the Scaliger, Pietro inclined his head. "Who is that?"

Cangrande followed his gaze. "Ah, our new friend from Naples! Don Antonio Laurito di Napoli. He has come north to root himself in our fair city, bringing a sizable fortune with him."

"Don?" said Pietro, puzzled.

"You've clearly never been to Napoli. There's a sizable collection of Spanish merchants there, and since the Sicilian Vespers, several have ennobled themselves."

The Sicilian Vespers were a series of assassinations fifty years before on the island of Sicily, when the people had murdered the French-bred nobles belonging to King Charles, throwing the island into war. The king of Aragon had stepped in, and his heirs had ruled Sicily ever since.

"Not desirous of having their throats slashed, they have eschewed the term Signor, and especially Monsieur, instead styling themselves as Dons. Hence Don Laurito."

"Will he still use it?" asked Pietro. "You say he means to plant himself here."

"It's my understanding. He's made a sizable investment in a home and land. And he's brought his son. That's him, sitting beside his father. Proteus is his name."

"Proteus?" said Cesco, arriving to seat his little wife and himself between Cangrande and Pietro. "I believe I'm jealous. He has a better name than all of us. Downright mythical." He snapped his fingers. "What was the name my mother gave me?"

Cangrande arched an eyebrow. "Why do you ask?"

"I don't mean to insult the noble name of Francis," Cesco assured him. "But during one meeting with my mother, she called me something. Ser Alaghieri, surely you recall."

Pietro did. Since the age of three, Cesco had sported a single piece of jewelry, a talisman of sorts, an old Roman coin Pietro had found bearing the word *PAX* on one side. On the reverse was an image of the god Mercury. When Cesco had met his mother three years previously, she had commented on it:

"Mercurio. He suits you, my boy."

"True, I am light on my feet, even without the wings. But sadly all accounts have him tall, and I fear I shall never grow to great heights."

"The little Mercury, then. Mercutio."

She had owned a peculiar lilt to her voice, one that Pietro had never heard before or since. In addition to Mercutio, she'd called him strange words – *uirisg* and *mo chridh.*

Struck by the memory of a woman they now knew was murdered, the woman whose house Poco and Tharwat were now investigating, it was several seconds before Pietro spoke the name aloud. "Mercutio."

"Mercutio?" said Maddelena. "That's a funny name."

"It is, isn't it?" Cesco threw a mocking glare at Cangrande.

"Why couldn't you have named me that?"

"Clearly I was remiss," replied Cangrande. "Certainly it suits your current moodiness. Intemperate as you are clever, your mood shifts as if carried by golden wings. But we never know, when naming a child, what he will become."

"Do you not think that the name shapes the man? Pietro here is as stolid as the saint whose name he bears, the rock of faith and duty. My little Maddelena here is named for one of Christ's followers, who was purged of evil spirits. You yourself shed Francesco to become *Cane Grande*, larger than life."

"And you? What does Cesco signify?"

"An attempt to create a diminished version of your forgotten self."

"No wonder you long for another name. But alas, so long as you are my heir, you must bear mine. Diminished or no."

"If I renounce your throne, oh mighty one, may I choose my own name?"

"Certainly. Though I fail to see the value in that exchange. What's in a name? Call a sword a spade and it will cleave as deep. Names do not change a thing's nature."

"My father wouldn't agree," said Pietro, hoping to shift the talk to less combative ground. "When Antony's family took up the mantle of Capulletto, he foresaw the renewal of the old feud. He talked of numerology. Names have as much power as the stars."

Cesco groaned. "O excellent. Another unseen element trying to control me."

"Nothing is controlling you, boy," said Cangrande.

"Not for lack of trying," retorted Cesco. "I wonder how much Tharwat knows of numerology."

Cangrande snapped his fingers. "Ah! Speaking of Tharwat and Spanish Dons, I have news for him. Pietro, where is he? I expected to see him here tonight."

Was there an edge in the question? "He was called from the city, by his art. Shall I convey a message?"

"It is hardly urgent. I learned in a letter today that Don Pedro of Aragon is to call this month in Verona."

Pietro brightened. "I know he visited Tharwat in August."

"On matters of astrology, or a social call?"

"I don't know," said Pietro. "Perhaps both."

Cesco's interest was piqued. "How does a Spanish prince know our beloved Moor? Did he predict doom for him as well?"

Gently, gently. "I think Tharwat once met his father, King

Frederick. But as I understand it, Don Pedro came to Italy in search of a wife."

Cesco clutched Maddelena's shoulders. "He can't have mine!" Everyone laughed except the girl, who was shifting uncomfortably in her seat. She tugged at Cesco's sleeve. Bending over so she could whisper in his ear, he nodded, then waved for her nurse, standing along the wall with other servants. Dahna scurried forward, took the little girl by the hand, and they disappeared through a door cleverly concealed in the wall behind them at the end of the table. Clearly nature called.

Pietro said softly, "You are very kind to your wife."

Cesco raised his brows in surprise. "Should I beat her? She's a little young. Though I hear Lord Bonaventura has novel ideas about training a wife…"

"I'm simply noting you can control yourself when you choose."

Cesco filched a Golden Morsel from a passing tray. "In all of Verona, she is the only innocent. I am sure one day she will scheme and plot like the rest of us. But at the moment she is exactly what she seems. I value that. And she deserves no ill will."

"Whereas I do?"

"We all do," said Cesco.

"Even you?"

"*Especially* me."

Little Maddelena returned, and the feast progressed. As ever, there was laughter and merry-making, with Manuel's musicians underscoring the arrival of each course. The Master of Revels was evidently training his replacement, a skinny jester called Noam, a Hebrew like himself. There were three other young musicians, French, whom Manuel had employed for the duration of the festival. Their names were Simon, Hugh, and Jacques, and they played remarkably well together, though they stopped often to eat the free food. Owning a remarkable voice, Cangrande's natural son Berto joined them for the singing, and the eating. Now they were performing an amusingly dark tune that professed, however bad life was, it always had something worse to offer. *"So you think you've hit bottom? So you think you've hit bottom? O no. There's a bottom below…"*

Everyone was grateful for the music. Quite often these public feasts had an awkwardness to them by the name of Antonio Capulletto. When the nobles gathered as themselves, he was genial and loud, often joining Petruchio and Nico da Lozzo as the life of the party. But when wives were present, his time was spent mooning at Montecchio's wife and trying too hard to be witty, cunning, honourable, clever, and everything a man should be for her benefit.

Of late, things were even more awkward, with his fifteen year-old wife heavily pregnant with their fourth child. Two boys had expired in their cribs, smiting Capulletto's spirit each time. Only his daughter had thrived. He spent a good deal of time telling stories of his three year-old girl, whom he had named Giulietta in homage to Caesar's daughter, Julia, the perfect woman. It had also been his name for Gianozza — and thus a constant insult to his wife.

Of course, the usual centers of attention were the Capitano and his heir, who bantered quite pointedly. But when they disengaged, people were free to enjoy themselves. The meal was sumptuous as ever, with the Scaligeri cook, Giorgio Gioco, proving as inventive as the musicians. Talk of war with Treviso was mixed with news from other lands and more banal conversation — the signs of a hard winter, concerns over the upkeep of roads, a proposal for a new granary on the west side of the city.

"You should give it to Signor Benedick," said Cesco. "He lacks employment."

"I do not," said Benedick at once.

"That's true," said Prince Rupert. "He's a professional imbiber. He's drunk nightly."

"In the face," murmured Salvatore.

"With drinking the health of the Capitano and his Heir!" cried Benedick.

The tables broke out in applause and all the goblets were raised. Maddelena lifted her cup to imitate the others, but Cesco put a hand over the top of it. "Not with water. It's bad luck to salute with water."

"Be careful of saluting even with wine," warned Petruchio from the next table.

"Oh?" asked Cesco.

The bearded lord waved a hand at his wife. "My Kate and I had a salutary warning once, from a constable-turned-innkeeper in Brindisi. What was his name, my love?"

"Maurizio," replied Kate, amused.

"Yes! Maurizio. We were up drinking a sweet lemony concoction of his in the wee hours, and were about to make a salute when he stopped us. 'You must make eye-contact with your beloved when you salute,' he told us. 'Otherwise it's seven years bad sex!'" The hall erupted in laughter.

"Father!" chided Hortensio, while his twin groaned.

"A most dreadful curse!" cried Nico da Lozzo.

"Far worse than breaking a mirror," agreed Castelbarco.

"At last, a curse I need not fear!" roared Cesco, wiping a tear from his eye.

Petruchio was red-faced and slapping his knee. Beside him, his red-headed Kate smiled thinly. "It is the one superstition my husband takes deathly seriously."

"Black cats be damned," agreed Petruchio loudly. "I never cover my mouth when I sneeze – let demons try to enter my body! I leave doors open all over the house. But if someone lifts a cup, Kate's eyes had best be on mine, or I'll refuse to drink."

"And he hates refusing to drink," said Kate, pouring him a new cup. He did the same for her, and together they lifted their goblets and tossed them back, their eyes locked just inches from each other's face. There was a surge of noise from the watchers, one that increased when Petruchio threw his cup aside and grabbed his wife to kiss her full on the mouth. She kissed him back, and soon men's eyes sought for other places on which to land. Petruchio's close friend Nico da Lozzo groaned. "If they end up in coitus, we'd best have water ready to douse them."

The couple broke apart, allowing the meal to continue. Seeking a more cerebral vein, Cangrande said, "Pietro, have you chosen what canto you mean to read from this month?"

Pietro started. He had almost forgotten his promise at the wedding to hold a public reading and debate over his father's work. "I hadn't thought of it, my lord. I shall do so. Perhaps Cesco can help me choose," he added, looking at the young knight.

Cesco surprised him by offering several good suggestions, and they debated the merits of this canto or that until their voices were drowned by laughter from the end of the table. Verde was barking at something her husband Rizardo had said. Annoyed, Cangrande called loudly across to her. "Verde, has Rizardo said something witty?"

"He did, uncle," answered Verde proudly. "He said that taking Treviso would not be so difficult, as any chess player may take a castle."

Cangrande laughed louder than the jest warranted. "Write it down! It's likely to be both the first and last time Rizardo will indulge in wit. Unless – yes! Manuel! Do you have the patience for a second apprentice? For I swear, I think Rizardo will make an excellent foole."

Both Rizardo and Verde coloured, focusing on their plates as the other guests laughed at the expense of Cangrande's kinsman.

The feast concluded, the parties breaking up to find other revels or to stagger home with bellies full of food and heads full of wine. Maddelena had been sent off to bed an hour gone, freeing Cesco to pluck up Hugh's rebec and join the musicians, stirring the affair into something more raucous by singing lyrics from *Le Fabliaux*. The room was alternately scandalized and uproarious as they listened to the story, in which God, making the Earth, creates three orders of men — knights, clergy, and peasantry. As He departs, He is waylaid by the entertainers and the whores, who beg Him to bestow some provision for them. God, in His infinite wisdom, commends the entertainers to the care of the knights, while He tells the clergy to take care of the whores.

Selonc cestui commandement
ne font il nul trepassement,
car il les tienent totes chieres,
si les tientent a beles chieres
del miaus qu'il ont & del plus bel.
Selonc lou sen de mon fable
se vos l'avez bien entendu,
sont tuit li chevalier perdu,
qui les lecheors tienent vis
& d'aus les font sovent eschis.
Aler les font sovent deschauz,
mes putains ont peliçons chauz,
dobles mantiaus, dobles sorcoz.
Petit truevent de tiels escoz
li lecheor as chevaliers,
& si sont il molt bons parliers;
ne lor donent for viez drapiaus
& petit de lor bons morsiaus,
en gitant com as chiens lor rüent,
mes putains sovent robes müent,
avec les clers cochent & lievent,
& sor lor despanses enbrievent.
Li clerc lo font por aus salver,
mes li chevalier sont aver
as lecheors, si se traissent
quant del commendement Dieu issent.

In keeping with the Lord's decree,
the clergy supports harlotry,
holding these women in esteem
and making sure they get the cream
of all of Mother Church's riches.
Contrariwise, my fable teaches,
if you have understood it well,
as for the knights, they'll go to Hell.
They look with scorn on the performers,
who must live poorer than a dormouse
and go about without a pair
of shoes, while whores get furs to wear
and well-lined cloaks and fine attire.
The entertainers for their hire
get little enough of their lords.
For all their fine and noble words,
they give them only worn-out garments
and toss them, as they would to varmints,
of their fine dinners, scraps and messes,
while harlots often change their dresses,
sleep with their priests, and what they're fed
is counted in the overhead.
The priests do this for their souls' sake,
whereas the stingy knights forsake
the entertainers, and are damned
for violating God's command.

The members of the clergy, insultingly complimented, steadfastly ignored the song, while the knights threw food and cajoled the grinning singers, who were delighted to have the chance, under the blanket of the prince's protection, to say what they truly thought of the nobility.

Under the cover of the dirty ditty, Bail's son Valentino had moved across the room talking with the Don's son, Proteus. This left nothing but air between Detto and his father. But when Bail made a passing comment to someone across Detto, the young knight stood and joined Cesco with the musicians.

Pietro slipped into Cesco's vacated seat. "You heard what he's named his horse?"

Cangrande inclined his head. "Abastor? I'm not familiar with that one. Does it mean 'sire-slayer' or some such?"

Pietro was grim. "Abastor was one of Pluto's four steeds, and was said to run faster than the stars. The very name in Greek means both 'deprived of the light of day' and 'away from the stars'."

Cangrande chuckled darkly. "A poetic act of defiance. Good."

"Good?"

"It means he's fighting back in a better way than brawling."

"They're not mutually exclusive," warned Pietro.

A touch of two fingers on the Scaliger's shoulder gained his attention. Tullio d'Isola was there, murmuring in the Capitano's ear. With a nod, he leaned towards Pietro. "Follow in a moment. Bring Bail. No fuss. It may be nothing."

Cangrande departed through the small door at his back, and Pietro moved down the table to where Bail sat, watching his eldest singing ribald tunes. "He won't even look at me."

"He's probably embarrassed. It's harder to be forgiven than forgiving."

"Humph. Well, I'll not forgive the singing. He has a decent voice, but no sense of rhythm. Where did the puppy disappear to?"

"I was to bring you after him. He says it may be nothing."

"It's clearly not nothing." Bail threw back the contents of his goblet and said loudly, "God's bread, but I'm going to spew. Ser Pietro, you'll have to carry me!"

"Cart you, perhaps! But I'll never shift your bulk." Bail threw a mock blow, then accepted Pietro's shoulder as he pretended to stagger from the hall.

The moment they were out of sight, they straightened and followed a waiting servant to a side chamber. The first thing Pietro saw was a dark-wood octagonal table, almost the exact size of the baptismal font in the Duomo he had examined after the wedding. Pietro wondered at it, then saw who was standing beside it, being embraced by Cangrande. "Otto, you old cad, you bounder, you rogue! How are you?"

"Well, my lord Capitano," said Otto the Burgundian, sweeping into a deep bow. The leader of Cangrande's largest mercenary *compagnia*, he had served in all of the Paduan campaigns of the last several years. He had also chosen Cesco over Mastino when Cangrande had been thought dead, a reminder of how personable the boy could be, when he cared to try.

Otto greeted Pietro and Bail warmly, then sat in the indicated chair, a steaming mug of mulled wine warming his hands and face.

Cangrande sprawled in the chair opposite, his arm leaning on the octagonal table. "You missed the wedding, but there are plenty of revels left."

The mercenary leader was impassive. "You don't pay me to revel, lord."

"Remind me, then, what do I pay you for?"

"Fighting. And keeping you apprised of news."

Cangrande leaned back, pretending to brace himself for a flock of arrows. "Let fly."

"Gueccello Tempesta is on his way here from Treviso, under a flag of truce."

Bail's mouth twisted. "War hasn't even started yet!"

"He's taking no chances."

Cangrande was amused. "I take it he comes with terms."

"Or else to defect?" asked Pietro hopefully.

"Not to defect," said Otto with assurance. "And I think his terms are for you to jump in the Adige. He's coming to hurl his defiance in your teeth, but with the smooth polish of a diplomat."

"Which is not his wont," observed Cangrande. "What's to prevent me throwing him in a cell beneath the Giurisconsulti and taking Treviso while he's absent?"

Pietro didn't mind showing his exasperation. "A flag of truce!"

"His companion," said Otto shortly.

Cangrande puzzled for a moment, as did Pietro and Bail. Who would stand with Treviso against Verona? "Dandolo?"

Otto shook his head. "Ludwig. Or, to be specific, his right hand."

"*Berthold?* Ludwig sends Berthold to protect the man who has sworn to keep his city out of the empire? He offers protection to Tempesta, his enemy, to treat with me, his ally. Is he mad?"

Otto was silent. He was an impassive man in life, only passionate in the field.

Suddenly Cangrande's brow uncreased. Squinting as if in pain, he began swearing. A servant arrived with more wine for Otto, which Cangrande intercepted and kept.

No one noted the second figure who had entered after the servant until he spoke. "Otto! I didn't know you were in these parts!"

"Good to see you, my lord," said Otto, rising to bow gravely.

"Good to be seen," answered Cesco brightly. "But you must call me Ser François now – it is François in Burgundy, yes? – and remove your hat."

Otto's mouth twitched. "If you want my hat, take it."

"Would that I could, but I'd be afraid of frosting your hair with snow when you departed. I cause too many grey hairs already." Cesco's eyes darted between Cangrande and the Burgundian. "Dare I ask the news?"

"What do you not dare?" growled Bailardino.

Otto answered in an even tone. "Nothing of war. I am only a messenger."

"Nothing of war? How are your men to keep their skills sharp? I shall have to visit the camp and put them through their paces."

"You would be most welcome, Ser François," said Otto. "If only to allow Yuri and Fabio time to recover from their respite in town. Fabio's arm cannot carry a shield for at least a month."

"Indeed, François," interjected Cangrande, "your sport seems more dangerous than my wars."

"Because my sport has higher stakes."

Otto was not unaware of the daggers in the counter-talk, but did not mind placing his body between the sharpened edges. "Speaking of sport, my young lord, our last hunt has become legendary. Morando Bevilaqua still talks of how your arrow jostled his on the way towards the hart. He says you owe him a chance to regain his honour at the hunt."

"He wants to take my honour? What am I, a maid?"

"A lord with the wiles of a virtuous maid in an armed camp."

"In your camp, that's a wily maid indeed. Well, tell Bevilaqua I shall come, and he can attempt to take my maiden head." Even the impassive Otto could not restrain himself from laughing aloud, while Cangrande drank deeply and Bail scowled.

"Pardon, Nuncle." Crossing past Pietro to the octagonal table, Cesco helped himself to a goblet of wine and poured himself languidly into another chair, exactly matching the Scaliger's pose. "I take it Otto's news is dire. Has he had a better offer? If not, can I make one?"

"You cannot afford me," said Otto.

Cangrande offered a grimacing smile. "Otto knows to whom his loyalty is owed. No, it's Tempesta. He's on his way here with a flag of truce, in the company of your cyclopean friend."

Cesco frowned. "Tharwat? Is that where he's gone?"

Pietro blanched, but Cangrande clarified at once. "Berthold.

Though you're right, we seem to be collecting one-eyed acquaintances. Is it a statement on the myopia of our enemies? Their lack of vision?"

"I thought Tharwat's latest affliction was more an ironic expression of Divine Will. He's been peering into the future so long, he was bound to lose an eye. Our own Tiresias, or at least half of one. *'Blind who now has eyes, beggar who now is rich, he will grope his way toward a foreign soil, a stick tapping before him step by step.'* But not even Sophocles tortured the ears of his hearers with such a voice!"

Cangrande laughed even as he shook his head. "I'm a terrible person. Or you are. You see what this means?"

"That Ludwig is trying to out-maneuver you?" said Cesco in a bored voice. "Yes, it's obvious. Tap tap tap. Tempesta comes here under safe-conduct with the Emperor, whom you cannot defy, and declares his independence. Berthold allows you two to wrangle with each other, then steps in with the stunning hammer. He forces Tempesta to submit, not to you but direct to Ludwig. You're granted Treviso not through feat of arms but by Ludwig's good will. You'll have your title, but in a manner that robs you of the victory. I had no idea the *Pax Verona* bothered him so much."

"That, at least, is gratifying," admitted Cangrande. "He sees me as important enough to keep down."

"He needs Verona," said Cesco. "But he does not trust you. I'd say not to take it personally, but it's personal. You're far too skilled at wielding power for him to feel easy giving you any more. Which, I imagine, is why Rupert ingratiates himself with me. I am wooed from all corners. Except this one."

"That's the trick of wooing," said Cangrande. "Make the wooed come to you, and then there is no question of consent."

"I know that trick. And Ludwig does as well, that much I know. He will make any power unpalatable to you, but leave it there for future generations that are more pliable."

"Shall I just step aside now?" asked Cangrande in grand fashion, rising and offering his seat. "Or do you want it all baked into a proper cake first?"

"You must be drunk," replied Cesco dismissively. "Why would I want your duties? Remember, I'm the irresponsible one. Let me enjoy the last of my minority. When I'm a man, I'll shoulder a man's burdens. Besides, when have I ever been called pliable?"

Cangrande studied his heir. "Six months of idleness, and then what?"

Cesco quaffed the last of his wine. "Then Treviso."

"And after that?"

"What, should I angle to lose an eye as well? Who knows what the future holds? There's been too much scrying and spying, crying and plying. Indulge your enemies. But if it makes you less uneasy, Pater, when Tempesta comes I will remove myself. Otto, I accept your invitation. My Rakehells — how I like that name! — will sojourn at your camp."

Cangrande frowned. "Taking Rupert with you? What if I desire you both to remain here and blunt Berthold?"

Slapping his hands on his thighs, Cesco leapt up. "Federigo! Padua! The very ground under our feet! Must I do everything?" With that he stalked from the office without a glance for either Pietro or Bailardino, both of whom were frowning, if for different reasons. Only Pietro followed him out.

Cangrande made to pour himself another drink. Before it reached his lips, a phrase the boy had uttered bubbled to the surface of his brain. He smiled. "Indulge your enemies. I'll think I shall do just that. When is Tempesta arriving?"

"A week, I think. San Pompeius' Day, or thereabouts."

"Pompeius. Fitting for a pompous puss like Tempesta. Tullio, tell those musicians to gather their fellow performers. They'll not lament their ill-usage by Verona's knights after this. How does Petruchio put it? I shall kill them with kindness."

◆ ◇ ◆

Pietro reached Cesco along the stairs, the sound of the revels at their backs. "Cesco. Please, talk to me."

Cesco spun, balancing on his heels. "Why? Are you starved for conversation?"

"I don't think you see where all this is leading."

"On the contrary, my eyes are unblinkered. It was earlier that I chose blindness. Unseeing, I fell into an obvious trap."

The meaning was plain. "Love is not a trap."

Cesco scoffed. "Says the man whose sole romantic love was a woman who lied, used, and manipulated him, all the while knowing that she would never let him taste of her lips. I've known more women in the last fortnight than you have in your whole life."

Pietro blushed. "That would not be difficult."

"We both know I was not meant to be pure. If I am damned, I mean to enjoy it. I will indulge in all the arts of love until I can claim a laurel wreath."

"I thought you said love was a trap."

"You mistake love for passion, Nuncle."

"You said love."

"I said arts of love. Art is short for artifice. Fake. Unreal. Deceptive."

"Don't let Manuel hear you say that. Is music so false? Or poetry?"

"As false as the emotions they inspire. But perhaps I misspoke, Nuncle. I am not done with love. I am done with dreams. Now, if you'll excuse me..." He sauntered away, his step faltering slightly.

In no mood to rejoin the revels, Pietro exited the palace, reliving the conversation, wondering if he could have done better. Probably not.

Returning home, he saw the lamps lit in several windows that had been dark for over a week. Racing within, he discovered his brother had returned. "What's happened?"

Poco looked fit to burst with pride. "Brother! I have news."

"Tharwat's not with you?" demanded Pietro.

Poco rolled his eyes. "What, don't you trust me with even a message?"

"No. I mean, yes, of course. I was just concerned—"

"Tharwat is traveling on to Venice with the cripple. I don't think he wanted Girolamo about when you were told what we discovered. Tharwat says we should meet in Vicenza in a few days, where we won't be under as many eyes. You can say you're visiting Detto's mother. That way Morsicato can attend."

Pietro waved his brother to a chair. "Very well. Tell me everything."

Poco remained standing. "No, we're waiting on someone else. I don't want to tell it twice. She'll be here in a minute."

It took Pietro only a moment to realize whom Poco meant. He protested, demanding the news now. But, reveling in his unaccustomed role of spy and informant, Poco was determined to milk it to the last drop.

A knock came, and Pietro admitted a muffled figure in grey robes. *"Suora."*

"Brother," said Antonia, eyes twinkling. "Brother."

"Sister," answered Poco. "Just don't ever become an abbess. I don't think we could tolerate calling you 'Mother'."

"If I keep sneaking out of the convent, there'll be no danger of that. What's so urgent?"

"News from Padua. We found the house Cesco was born in, and the name of the man who owns it."

Pietro gripped the back of the chair he was standing behind. "Well?"

"It was bought two years ago."

"That isn't important," said Pietro at once. "We need to know who owned it fifteen years ago, not who owns it now."

"I think the current owner will interest you very much," said Poco with maddening superiority. "It belongs to one Niccolo Fucarile."

Antonia gasped, her hands flying to her mouth. Pietro felt less awe, but certainly it was a shock. A coincidence? No – the name was far too similar to the late, unlamented Nikolas Fuchs to be chalked up to chance.

Antonia was as white as scraped parchment. "What on earth could Fuchs want with a house in Padua?"

Thinking about it the whole journey, Poco had an answer ready. "Buying it himself afforded him the opportunity to search it. And you can be certain that the money came from Mastino. They never did anything apart. Hip-joined, those two."

Antonia shuddered again, but Pietro was too busy grappling with the implications of the purchase to notice. "He couldn't have visited it – he was too well-known in Padua as a Veronese."

"Have it searched, then," said Poco, helping himself to some roasted chicken. "It doesn't look lived-in. Shuttered, but with lit torches to keep thieves at bay."

"So you didn't get in?"

"Oh, we got in," answered Poco with sly pride. "On our third night I leapt the wall and opened the gate for Tharwat and Lamo."

"Lamo?"

"Girolamo. Lamo. Lame-o. I could call him gimpy, but that's in poor taste."

Pietro shook with an involuntary laugh. "Go on. What was inside?"

"Nothing of note. A few pieces of furniture in some of the rooms, whatever was too large to move. They had all been searched. Ashes of some papers in the fireplaces. Someone had even tried stripping some of the frescoes from the walls to see if there were messages beneath."

"Why did you bring this Girolamo with you?" asked Antonia. "He already knows more than he should about Cesco's past."

"He was told where in the house the baby's room would be. Tharwat wanted him to lead us there."

"And did you find anything?" asked Pietro.

"A crib. A small stuffed hound. Someone had split it open to see if there was a message inside. It's poor cloth guts were all over the floor. Tharwat said it was like an augury."

Pietro felt a bitter disappointment. "So there was nothing."

"Nothing at all. Except what Fuchs couldn't destroy." Poco face burned. "The name of the previous owner. It was in the sale records."

Alight with frustration, Pietro was ready to punch his little brother full in the face. "Yes?"

"The house belonged to a Signor Leonardino d'Amabilio, bought through a factor of a bank in Venice in the winter of 1313. December 10th," he added in answer to Antonia's next question.

Antonia did some swift math. "Seven months before Cesco's birth."

Pietro held up his hands, staring into the space before him. "Hold. Amabilio, Amabilio... That name — it tickles something in my memory. Amabilio. Mab..." In a rush, Pietro realized where he knew the name. "That was it!"

"What?"

"For years I've tried to remember the name Katerina gave Cesco's mother. Amabilio. That's it! Mab. M-A-B..."

Now it was Poco's turn to be confused. "What are you talking about?"

"The Mab in the message Tharwat discovered. Amabilio!"

"What message?" asked Antonia, even as Poco said, "Tharwat found a message? He didn't say anything!"

Pietro's eyes were unfocused. "Amabilio. Leonardino d'Amabilio. Poco, you're certain?"

"That's the name on the deed," repeated Poco. "Saw it myself."

Pietro clapped his brother on the shoulder. "That's excellent, Jacopo! Truly well done! We have a name! And you said Tharwat is in Venice? He'll go to the Jew. If he doesn't, I'll go myself! This is too important to miss."

"What are you talking about?"

"When Fuchs kidnapped Cesco's mother, Tharwat traced her to a shack in the country. He found blood. That's probably where she was murdered. But before her death, the lady used the last of her strength to carve a message into the floor where she was bound. A coded message."

"You never said!" cried Poco in outraged excitement. "What was it?"

"A series of letters forming a large 'M'." Pietro withdrew a paper from his person, a piece of writing well-perused over the years, copied from the scene of the murder. He passed it across to his brother, and Antonia drew close to study it.

M	R	C		T	S	M
A		A		T		A
B		V	X	D		B

"MAB," said Poco. "It's there, twice. What about the rest of it?"

"CAV, we think, is a warning. *Cave* – beware. For the rest, we're just guessing. But – something Cesco said tonight. MRC – *Mercutio.* That was what she called him. The little Mercury."

"'Mercutio beware.'" Antonia took the paper from Poco and raked it with her eyes. "VXD. Is that a number?"

"It is!" cried Poco. "It's from father's final writings – DXV, the five hundred, ten, and five! Father knew? Is that what this means?"

"I don't think so," answered Pietro, who had wrestled with this code for two long years.

"It can't be a coincidence," said Antonia warily. Here was a secret she and Pietro shared, that Poco did not. One that might hurt him, were he to discover it.

Understanding the question in her eyes, Pietro tried to answer obliquely. "I told her. I thought she should know what her son had done."

"What?" demanded Poco. "What?"

Pietro was silent. When his father had died seven years earlier – *Lord, has it been seven years?* – Cesco had been inconsolable. Not just for the death of the man he believed to be his grandfather, the greatest mind he ever expected to meet. The seven year-old had wept bitter tears because the poet had died with his life's work unfinished. The great *Commedia* had had no ending.

That thought kept them all up nights, none moreso than Cesco. The idea of an incomplete life, especially a gifted one, troubled the lad beyond words. For weeks he'd been edgy and skittish, wary of his normal risks and larks, lest his life also be cut short before its zenith.

This had changed when Pietro finally dared to enter his father's study, two whole months after the funeral. There he found the notes. Asking Cesco and Antonia to help, they had turned up a wooden box containing scraps of paper, messages chalked on pieces of wood, and wax tablets with carved letters. Words, phrases, thoughts that had tickled the poet over the years, all jumbled together in a mish-mosh without rhyme or reason.

"I didn't know he kept these," Pietro had observed at the time, marveling. His father's mind had always seemed a metal trap, containing all the effluvium of his creativity.

"Nor I," Antonia had answered.

But Cesco had known. "He was afraid, he said, of losing his memory, as old men do," the seven year-old had explained with the disdainful pity of the young. Without more words, he began spreading the notes out across the tiled floor. When Antonia tried to raise one and read it, he'd waved her off. "It's a puzzle. A word puzzle."

Sharing a long glance with his sister, they had both retired from their father's study. For weeks after, Cesco had laboured, his little brow furrowed, his mind bent to untangling the jumbled genius of the great poet. When at last he emerged, he had managed the unthinkable – he had crafted the last cantos of *Il Paradiso*, the close to the epic that had seemed so horribly unfinished.

They were not perfect – there were references Cesco did not understand, as well a couple understood only by himself. But with Pietro and Antonia poring over the pages with him – the scholar-knight and the *de facto* publisher who knew her father's work better than anyone – they finally got it as close to perfect as they dared.

The question was what to do next. It was already known that the great epic was unfinished. To appear after months with a completed manuscript would be suspect.

It was Cesco who hit upon the answer. Recreating the text in something like the poet's hand, they hid the pages in the bottom of a trunk and waited for Poco's next visit.

When, after three frustrating days of Poco not finding the treasure, days that tried everyone's patience to the limit, he finally went rummaging through their father's things and came up with the 'lost' cantos. He was so joyous, so proud in his discovery, that no one would suspect him of artifice. Pietro was mercilessly ridiculed for not finding the pages sooner, and Antonia was set to hiring copyists to publish the final third of their father's great epic.

And Cesco? Cesco had positively glowed. Returned to his carefree excesses and clever word games, he was once more the maddeningly troublesome child they knew and loved.

Now Antonia said to Pietro, "We have to tell him. It's time."

"Tell who? Time for what? What's going on?"

Pietro nodded. "Poco – sit down. We have a confession to make."

When they were through, their brother was justifiably furious. "You used me!" It was half an hour before he had stopped raging at them for their deception and they could return to the matter of the message.

Pietro had told Donna Maria of the role her son had played in penning the final part of Dante's *Commedia*. With that in mind, the lady might have used that knowledge to fashion her message. The VXD could alternately be read as DXV, a prophecy made towards the end of the epic poem. It was an ambiguous line, one that even they had not understood. Some thought it alluded to a number – five hundred, ten, and five. But the letters could also be transposed to read *DUX* – the Duke. Another name for Prince.

Antonia pressed the paper down upon the table, uncreasing the folds to lay it flat. "Why are the letters backwards, though?"

"Tharwat once suggested they were mirrored. That the message actually read MAB MRC CAV DUX DTT MST MAB."

"DTT?" said Poco. "Did she mean Detto? Is she warning him against his best friend?"

Pietro voiced what he had long suspected. "I think we're all so used to his name, we forget what it actually means. Detto means 'also known as' – a nickname."

"I know what it means," snapped Poco, still mulish.

It was Antonia who read it out clear. " '*Mercutio, beware the Prince known as Mastino.*'" And bookending the message was his mother's true name – Amabilio. Mab.

It was a disappointment, to say the least. After so long, such a plain message. The lady was warning her son of the man who had ordered her kidnapped and murdered. A warning no longer of use. They all knew Mastino wanted to destroy Cesco. There was no help for Cesco in his mother's final message.

But at least they had a name. Another thread for them to tug upon to see what would unravel.

TWELVE

IN THE BUILD-UP to the arrival of the Trevisian embassy, Cangrande attempted to keep his heir busy with civic duties. But somehow, even in the most innocuous task, Cesco could find some mischief to be made. Handed the dies to deliver to the town moneyer, he switched them and had instead his own image coined on the front, while the reverse side bore the words *'Il Veltro – Figlio d'un Cane'*. *The Greyhound – Son of a Bitch*. On a second coin, he had an image of Padua and the words *'Miseri Mortacci'*, meaning *Miserably Feeble Ancestors*. A third held the image of the *La Rosa Colta* and the single, hideously offensive word *'Fottere'* – *Fuck*. Laughing, the city embraced the new coins, especially the Paduan ones, causing Cangrande more embarrassment with his new allies.

Ordered to decorate the public trees on Advent Sunday, Cesco found fault with the apples, tearing them from the branches to pelt the nearest Paduans, making them run. "Faster, faster, for it is a fasting day!"

On another occasion, Cesco secretly rewrote the script for the Christmas mummers, whose duty it was to act out religious tales. In his version, Joseph and Mary became a bickering couple who never ceased arguing, back-biting and carping even as the Virgin gave birth to the Savior. Everyone was reminded of Lord Bonaventura and his mad wife, and there were several references to reinforce this – most especially the fact that Kate was Paduan by birth. The city laughed itself sick as Joseph hinted at his wife's infidelity with God, saying

Paduan women had been known to open their legs to far lesser men than the Lord. "Yes," replied the labouring mother, "including you!" Petruchio laughed so hard he immediately hired the players to repeat their performance at his house on Christmas Eve.

Cesco could hardly step out of his house without drawing a crowd, as everyone wondered what devilry he'd think of next. But this particular morning his devilry was not particularly devilish, though it threatened a fate similar to that of Lucifer – buried in ice. The weather had continued to grow cold, colder than any living Veronese could remember. For the first time ever there was a thin layer of ice across the Adige. Too thin to walk across, the boats were all forced to use staves to break it apart before moving up and down the river. Everything slowed, and trade was stunted.

Which made the Adige the perfect place for a free-for-all quarterstaff *mêlée* fought across the boats stuck in the river.

Atop of a stack of timber being ferried south, Cesco fended off an attacker on either side, plus the occasional snowball from the cheering onlookers on the bridge above. Hortensio was perhaps his deftest opponent, sliding his staff from long-form to short and back with ease. Salvatore was another who showed skill, having knocked Barto into the water moments before pressing Cesco hard on his sinister flank. All around them were the clack and clicks of wood striking wood. Two Rakehells had already dropped into the icy water, to be fished out and hurried to a fire before they chilled too badly. One of them was Thibault, who was heard to complain loudly that the quarterstaff was not a proper weapon for a man.

Detto was on the next boat over, having a spirited timber debate with young Petruchio, while Benedick remained at the edges, waiting to see who lasted longest while keeping himself fresh. Cesco taunted him. "Get in, Ahenobarbus, or you forfeit and buy all the drinks tonight!" Benedick leapt into the fray, showering Yuri with a series of blows, some of which connected with flesh, not wood. Enraged, Yuri used his greater weight to slam into the red-headed Paduan and then sweep his feet from under him with a flick of his staff. He was busy laughing at the splash Benedick made in the choppy water when Rupert caught him a blow upon his shin and levered him over and down amid the floating wafers of ice.

Wafer. Cesco wanted one. He didn't like wanting anything, but he wanted one of these, badly. Leaping backwards, he kept his pole spinning in one hand while the other dropped to a pouch. Ducking, he brought the wafer to his lips and felt a blessed relief, a rush of energy and an easing of the hunger. He wondered if the sensation were real or imagined. Regardless, it felt delicious.

"Snacking during a fight?" demanded Salvatore.

"I can't help it. I eat when I'm bored." Cesco flung himself into a wild attack against them both, striking them each several times inside their desperate parries. When at last he backed off, they responded with equal fury, and Cesco had to keep his staff spinning hand over hand to beat away the strikes angling for his head and feet.

"Barbarous *bardasso*," taunted Cesco at Salvatore, "you wield a stick as if you've been stuck! Thrust thrust thrust, is that all you can do?"

"Coarse, of course," said Salvatore coolly, not at all baited. "Not every Paduan offers themselves as targets — unlike some!" He swung hard, then reversed his blow, coming in to sweep Cesco's legs while Hortensio jabbed for the ribs.

Making a show of leaping over Salvatore's stave, Cesco beat aside Hortensio's attack. But his landing foot caught a patch of ice on the timber and he skidded down to the boat's edge, barely catching himself before he toppled overboard. Hortensio raced forward to press the advantage, but Salvatore had his eye on the larger prize and chose to knock Hortensio off the boat from behind before himself taking up a stand against Cesco. The delay gave Cesco just enough time to find solid footing, so he was prepared when Salvatore's extended stave came in for another jab.

There was a shout off to the side, followed by a splash and several cheers. Detto had been knocked into the water, probably by Rupert, who was among the last to remain dry. There was a second's silence, then someone said, "He's not coming up!"

Parrying hard, Cesco darted a glance in that direction. People were looking down on the spot where Detto had fallen, which was thick with broken ice. But the area around it was not broken, merely a flat sheet. If the current under the ice had pulled him, Detto could be trapped.

Parrying Salvatore again, Cesco was about to shout an order when he saw Detto's hand emerge, grasp Rupert by the ankle, and topple the German prince into the icy water.

Cesco's laugh was cut short by a crack across his shoulder. He hunched, making him prey to the butt end of Salvatore's staff already hooking his ankle and upending him. There was a moment of suspended time, flailing and grasping for something to hold. Then the drenching shock of the ice water as Cesco plunged beneath the surface.

He might have expected the current under the ice to be sluggish. Quite the opposite. The water around the Ponte Pietra always roiled, and with the uppermost layer frozen, the flow was even more determined beneath. Cesco swam for the light of the gap where he had fallen, struggling against the tug of the undertow. He was just about to break the surface when something struck him in the temple. His mouth opened, expelling needed air. He closed it, but not before swallowing a little water into his mouth. Lungs aching already, he shook his head, which felt bizarrely slow. He had slipped down under the sheet of ice, drifting away from the hole. He saw several staves breaking the level of ice where he had fallen and understood – he had been struck by one of the shafts attempting to free him by shattering the ice.

I could stay here, he thought. *Open my mouth and let go.* Already he was numb, the icy daggers of the cold becoming less painful, almost warming. *I could let go and thwart a whole host of prophecies. What would they think of that?*

Instead of struggling back towards the now desperate men plunging into the water where he had fallen, Cesco let himself be carried off down the river. *Stars, if you want me, here I am. Prove I matter. Prove that I have a destiny. I won't help unless you show me.*

He felt a shadow pass overhead and realized he was now under the Ponte Pietra. He banged into something hard. Feeling around, he knew it for the pillar supporting the ancient Roman bridge. A single shaft of reaching down told him the ice above him was weaker here, imperfect. All he had to do was try.

Perversely, he didn't want to. Yet he had asked for a sign, and been given one. Not passive rescue, but a chance to survive. He didn't want to, yet found himself pushing up, hard. The weak ice spidered under his fingers, and with a second push he was through. His head followed and he gasped, dragging air into his fiery lungs.

Shouts from up the river. What had been a long way off underwater seemed a ridiculously short distance now. He had barely traveled more than the length of a boat. As he was hauled up he wanted to make some smart remark, but his teeth were so busy chattering they chopped off any attempt at words. Sopping, Detto embraced him, then turned with the others towards the shore.

Salvatore arrived, bristling with concern. "Are you hurt, lord?"

"Only my p-p-pride." Cesco touched the spot on his temple where he'd been struck. "An-d-d-d my head-d-d."

"That was me," said Salvatore, mortified. "I was trying to break the ice."

"Next t-t-time, no s-s-saving," said Cesco. "Who w-won?"

Salvatore looked abashed. "I, my lord."

"Then you can b-build the fire."

Soon Cesco was with the other losers around the fire blazing along the riverbank, huddled under blankets and not wanting to move more than their toes. Cesco's face felt so raw it might have been burned, but he was surprisingly cheerful, and when he spied a frightened face amid the crowd at the edges of the fire, he called out. "Well m-m-met, young R-r-r-romulus, founder of R-r-rome who r-r-r-roams away from his m-minders."

Romeo Montecchio darted close to join the shivering Cesco. "You're not hurt?"

"Hurt? N-never. I'm just l-l-lacking Heaven's heat at present. Who's your f-friend?"

"Benvolio," said Romeo simply. Two years Romeo's elder, Benvolio Lenoti smiled in a free and open way.

"Oh, r-r-right – your cousin. Benvenito's s-son?"

Benvolio nodded as Romeo said, "Yes." His tone was hurt.

Seeing the sullenness, Cesco wanted to laugh. "What's the matter?"

"You never invite me to play," said Romeo, half-accusing, half-pouting.

"You wanted a s-swim? We can oblige. Someone, toss him in. Where are your minders?"

"We got away," said Romeo proudly.

Cesco ruffled the seven year-old's hair. "After my own heart. But you're not yet old enough to hunt with these heartless hinds."

The rest of the Rakehells laughed. Thinking they were laughing at him, Romeo threw off his child's coat, declaring, "I can do anything they can do, and better!" His small hands wrested the staff from Salvatore's fingers but, as he tried to spin it, he dropped it. Flushed with embarrassment, Romeo retrieved the staff and, holding it firmly, swung it at anyone around the fire who dared chuckle.

Rising, Cesco intercepted him before he could strike anyone. "Alright, alright! You don't need to prove anything to these fishy fooles. Let me dry off, then I'm game for whatever you have in mind. What do you want to do?"

Romeo's eyes brightened. "Horse race?"

Pulling another sticky chew from his belt and eating it, Cesco made a show of thinking. "You have an unfair advantage, being part equine yourself."

Romeo considered. "A flight of birds?"

"You know how to fly birds?" asked Hortensio, son of a famous falconer.

"Of course we do," insisted Romeo, clearly lying. "And Cesco's father has the best birds!"

"He certainly does," agreed Benedick, who had seen the menagerie, but might have also been thinking of the women Cangrande often had visit his rooms in the palace. His tone was salacious enough.

Only Detto saw Cesco stiffen at the mention of birds, and the memory it provoked. "How about a different kind of hunt?"

The eldritch air Cesco generated, the one that excited everyone near him, caused Romeo's face to light up as if an inner fire had blazed to life. "What kind?"

Leaning close, Cesco whispered in the child's ear. Romeo's watery blue eyes grew wide as he listened. Though he'd inherited his father's good looks, his eyes were his mother's in shape and quality. The boy's teeth flashed – his smile was just as bewitching as Cesco's, but in a completely different way. "Can we bring Benvolio?"

"If you think he can keep up." While Romeo ran to his cousin to share this plan, Cesco explained the idea to his companions. "A hunt. Within the city walls. No bows or edged weapons. No birds, no horses, only hounds and staves. The one who catches his prey wins my respect –" he got boos from the other Rakehells "– and a fifty Veronese silver." Cheers.

"And the prey?" Benedick suspected the answer.

Romeo and Benvolio came bounding up. Cesco placed a hand on their shoulders. "Me and my two friends. And Detto," he added, sending a questioning glance at his cousin, who nodded. "Two brace of cousins."

"When do we go?" Benedick was not eager to move.

Cesco sneezed, then grinned. "We all need to warm up first. Go home, change clothes. We start at my house in thirty minutes."

While everyone else scattered, Benedick elected to stay by the fire. "If I'm twice your age, I'm four times those lads'. There is a limit to those I call peer."

"Ah, but they're wealthy," cooed Cesco. "And of a fine house. Perhaps you should tell them a few tales, win them over. They could take care of you into your dotage."

Giving Cesco the fig, Benedick huddled under his blanket while everyone else moved away. Cesco and Detto walked back to the house on the *via Pigna*, Romeo and Benvolio prancing about in excitement, pretending to be hunted animals. Cesco started laughing. "Remind you of anyone?"

◆   ◊   ◆

"Ser Pietro? Suor Beatrice is here to see you."

"Thank you, Delphinos." Pietro had taken his brother's advice and hired a steward, one with high commendation from Tullio d'Isola. High, but not the highest. Pietro had passed over the first two choices. He did not like being suspicious, but disliked being taken in by his naturally trusting nature even more. He had also chosen Delphinos because he was not Italian, but Greek.

Setting aside the legal papers he had been studying, Pietro stood to greet his sister. "Where are you coming from?"

"I went to see my confessor."

"Fra Lorenzo." Pietro tried not to show his feelings, and failed.

Antonia pulled a face. "He feels much the same towards you. He recognizes that you are a good man, but he doesn't trust you."

"He should by now," said Pietro. "I haven't betrayed his secret."

"He believes it's because he holds several of ours, and you're afraid that if you expose him, he'll expose you."

"Fra Lorenzo is not the most trusting soul," said Pietro. "Nor particularly forgiving, for a Christian brother."

"He fears exposure for his past. And your brush with Bernardo Gui only heightened his unease. He was certain you would offer up his name in order to save yourself."

"Then he doesn't know me at all." Pietro had honestly not even considered such a thing.

"Which is what I tell him. Give him time. He is — he means well, and has been a good friend to me." Pietro heard something in her voice, but before he could frame a question she said, "When are you going to meet Tharwat?"

"When the lord of Treviso arrives. I'd rather not see what Cangrande has in store for him. Why? Do you want to come?"

Antonia shook her head. "I don't think I could get permission for that. But there is something that needs to be said."

Seeing her expression, Pietro braced himself. "Say it."

"Lia. As Lorenzo asked on Cesco's wedding night, where is Lia in all this? Has anyone even attempted to discover what happened to her?"

Pietro's stomach dropped, then began to roil. "I imagine Cangrande…"

"She's married."

Pietro sagged with relief. He had been afraid Antonia would say the girl was dead, murdered by her irate father. He could only imagine Cesco's reaction to that.

Antonia said, "One of us should see her."

"Oh. Yes." There was an expectant pause. "*You* know her."

"As I just mentioned, I cannot ride out of the city on a given day, *Ser* Pietro."

"What happened to the terror of Florence, the woman who made booksellers tremble?"

Antonia was not amused. "I am a novice in the service of the Church."

"I only I met her the once," he protested. "And it's in the opposite direction of Vicenza."

"Should I ask Cangrande? Or Cesco?"

Pietro raised his hands in defeat. "Very well. Before I meet with Tharwat and Morsicato, I will ride out and call on her."

"Thank you. In the meantime, I've had an idea. We're all worried about Cesco, and I am also concerned for Detto and that little girl. Cesco's wife, I mean. I think someone should be in that house that isn't a servant. I have discussed it with Abbess Verdiana, and though she shares my qualms, she has agreed. So I'm going to offer myself as a companion to little Maddelena. I don't think Ser Cesco will be quite so rambunctious with his Auntie Imperia in the same house!"

"An excellent idea!" said Pietro warmly, before adding, "He'll resent it."

"I know. But these are the dangerous months. He's so angry — not without cause. I had thought his quiet between September and the wedding was a good thing, that he was seeking understanding or even growing up a little. Now I see he was just waiting to spring into action. Do you know what he's doing?"

"Rebelling," said Pietro simply.

"Against what?"

"Whatever's at hand. Which is why he won't appreciate a novice coming to live in his house."

"I don't care if he appreciates me. We have to find a way to divert his energy, not keep on with these brawls and pranks. He was so quiet before the wedding. What was he doing, do you know?"

"He was at the Duomo — or rather at the monastery attached to it. For a time I was afraid he was going to become a monk." Realizing to whom he was speaking, he gave a crooked smile. "Forgive me, *Suora.* There is no higher calling, I am sure."

Antonia waved this off. "What was he doing?"

"Reading. When he broke his leg a couple years ago, the

Scaliger sent him to the monks to catalogue their books. Evidently some of those old papers caught his eye. He was there nearly every day in October and November, reading. I asked the monks about it. They said he was looking at copies of Greek and Roman manuscripts they had not even been through yet."

"Could it be Virgil? Or a lost play?"

"The monks didn't know, and I haven't asked Cesco."

"Is he becoming a bibliomancer?"

"That wouldn't be the worst thing. Wander the world hunting rare books, building Verona up into a new Library of Alexandria — that would be a feat worthy the Greyhound."

"A new age of Man. Perhaps we can help him find that road."

"How?"

"By buying books. I still know some collectors."

"What about copyists?"

Antonia frowned. "You want to become a publisher?"

"It keeps with the family business. But I wasn't thinking of myself."

"I can't! It would be a conflict of interest, not to mention disloyal, undercutting the work the sisters are doing—"

"Believe it or not, I wasn't thinking of you, either. I was thinking of Poco. We owe him something."

"Still angry, is he?"

"Furious. This might be a balm, and secure him an income. I'll provide the capital, you can give him the connections."

"And Cesco can choose the works to be copied. I like it. We'll have to approach them both in just the right way."

"I'll handle Poco. As for Cesco, I was actually hoping he might start writing. He has the skill."

"That would be a blessing," said Antonia.

"I was also thinking of using this symposium Cangrande roped me into doing tomorrow to draw Cesco out. The *Commedia* worked a miracle after father's death."

"You think it can do so a second time?"

"We'll find something," said Pietro with determination. "If I have to lie, cajole, cheat, or trick him into his old self, I'll do it. One thing I've learned — when pushed, I can fight as dirty as the Scaligeri."

◆　◇　◆

"Maddelena!" snapped Dahna in that sharp tone adults have that chills children to the bone. "Come away from the window. You'll catch your death!"

Dutifully the child turned away from the thick, imperfect glass and returned to the balls of string she was untangling. But she kept listening. At the passing of every horse, every carriage, every group of men, Maddelena would run to the window and look. For all the frustrations of disappointments, once a day there was joy. Francesco would come home, poke his head in the nursery to say hello, speak funny words, swear at her cat, then kiss her once on the forehead before heading to off to his rooms. It was something her father had never done, nor her siblings, and she liked the attention.

Today she had heard him come back around mid-day, but he hadn't stopped in to visit, only change his clothes. She heard that he'd been swimming. She couldn't wait until she was old enough to go play in the streets with Francesco and his friends. She wanted to learn to swim. Francesco would teach her. Francesco was better than anybody at everything. There wasn't anything Maddelena's husband couldn't do, and she was proud when he picked her up and teased her, calling her wife.

Maddelena felt so foolish now when she thought about before the wedding. She'd cried and cried, protesting she didn't want to leave her toys, her house, her nurse. It was Francesco who had knelt down and stuck his head under the table and told her she could bring all her toys, and her nurse too. As for her house, it was really her father's house, whereas if she got married she'd have her own house and she'd only have to share it with Francesco and his friends. She could go visit her father in Parma whenever she liked, or her sisters in Padua, and she could have friends come and stay with her, and have a cook of her own to make whatever she wanted, whenever she wanted.

"Cake?" she'd asked.

"Breakfast, noon, and night," Francesco had told her. "Cake until you can't stand the taste of it."

"I'll never not like cake!" she'd told him forcefully.

"Then it's a good thing I like cake too." She'd giggled, and after that it was fun, putting on pretty dresses and having people make a fuss over her. She'd cried a couple of times during the wedding day, and she felt stupid about that, but since then life had been joyful. Of course, she didn't have cake every day – that would be silly. And her days were almost exactly the same: lessons and playtime with her nurse, weaving, naps, church, meals, prayers, and bed. But most days Francesco would appear from nowhere, bestowing Maddelena's world with a beam of sunshine that made everything else go away.

Yet when she heard him with other people, he sounded different. He wasn't happy. In fact, Maddelena thought he was sad. He pretended not to be, and he fooled everyone because he was so good at pretending — but he was sad.

So was Detto. Maddelena liked Detto, though he didn't spend much time with her. At first she'd thought he didn't like her, but then she saw that he was shy with everyone except animals. And when they were alone, Cesco didn't pretend as much.

Maddelena wondered why Cesco pretended to be happy when he was with her. She was his wife! He didn't have to pretend with her. Dahna told her again and again it was her duty to grow up to be a good wife and make her husband happy. But she knew she didn't have to wait to grow up, she could make him happy *now*. She could draw for him, or sew pictures like in the tapestries that hung from the walls. She could sing — he liked singing, she knew.

She worried that he didn't really like her. He could do anything — everything. All she could do was weave a little and sing and play with blocks and make messes and pray. Maybe he didn't really like her, but since he'd already married her there was nothing he could do so he just pretended to like her and all the time tried to think of ways to stay away from home.

I'm going to ask him, she decided. *I'll ask him why he's sad, and then I'll fix it, and he'll love me and not need to pretend anymore. I'll ask him.*

♦   ◊   ♦

Venice

Girolamo was eating better than he had ever eaten in his life. Mostly fish, of course, but fish in such quantities and with such marvelous sauces that he would never dream of complaining.

The Venetian had kept his promise, lodging the crippled diviner at a fine private establishment set aside for guests of the Serenissima. He had already had an interview with the ailing Doge, who had wisely refrained from asking personal questions — his end was near, he needed no oracle to tell him that. Instead they had discussed parts of the world where Venice had business interests. They had also discussed the lawsuit that had all Venetians buzzing, brought by a Hebrew money-lender against a prominent merchant. "I will have to hear it. My last act of justice will be most unjust, I fear. Unless you can divine an answer to my dilemma?"

Girolamo had shaken his head. "The pendulum does not deal

with such things as law, your grace. Perhaps the merchant should consult an astronomer. They are better at predictions."

"There was an astrologer once," Doge Soranzo had reminisced. "A Moor called Theodoro with such terrible scars on his neck. He made me the best chart I have ever seen. And it was so true – right up to now. I plan to be buried with it. My map to the heavens."

A warning look from Dandolo prevented Girolamo from mentioning that the Moor in question was at that moment within the city. Where Tharwat went each morning was a mystery even the pendulum could not answer with precision. Somewhere in the Jewish quarter, the area on the map called the Yellow Crescent. He thought that Dandolo too might have been trying to trace the Moor's movements, with even less success.

Whatever the reason for the Moor's continued presence in Venice, Girolamo was grateful. They had spent the last few evenings in deep discussion of their mutual arts, in a way different than Girolamo had ever experienced. Most often when trading talk with other diviners, it was tricks for finding clues for desired answers, or ways to manipulate the pendulum to make it swing in the correct direction. Deceits. Girolamo had used his fair share of them when pleasing some idiot with a fat purse. But his gift was real, and he did not appreciate methods of deception, however useful.

With the Moor, though, the talk had been of that invisible curtain, the veil between the world they could see and the world that existed just at the edges of their sight. They had different experiences, but of a similar nature, and both were fascinated to find someone with a real talent. The last one Tharwat had met had died over a decade before, he said. "In my arms."

Not that talent was particularly rare. Both of them had met men and even women who had a vague sense of that other world. But the ability to sense that world and translate that sense into language was so rare, Tharwat was able to name only a dozen men in his life who had owned such talent. For Girolamo, he had known only one before now, a member of a merchant family in Genoa called Mario Giustiniani. Disowned by his family, he had plied his trade around the south of Italy and discovered Girolamo's talent by what had seemed chance.

"In truth, his pendulum brought him to me, so that he might train me," Girolamo had explained. It was not something he would have said to another man, but the Moor had not looked skeptical or shocked. "He was aging, and wanted to pass along his knowledge to one who shared his gift. I had nothing else, obviously. I was a mere beggar with an itching finger. It was Mario who taught me what the itch meant, and how to obey it. He also warned me of its dangers."

"I had a similar experience," Tharwat had told him. "Pain and suffering, followed by the revelation of a gift and a wise teacher to guide me through it. What became of your mentor? Is he still living?"

"No," said Girolamo. "His cousin married into another banking family, and he was able to return to Genoa before his passing."

"What family?"

"Adorno." The Moor's eyes had shifted at that, and Girolamo had nodded. "You feel it too?"

"Yes. A powerful name."

It was moments such as that, moments of inexplicably shared understanding, which made Girolamo lament the coming departure of the Moor. Tomorrow, the day after, one day soon Tharwat al-Dhaamin would leave Venice to meet Ser Alaghieri, and Girolamo would remain here, safe. Even had he been invited, the diviner would not have dared venture into Vicenza. Donna Katerina was there, and her husband was searching for him. But he did not want the Moor to leave. Perhaps it was more than just the shared skill. For Tharwat was the only man he had met in fifteen years who did not shy away from looking into Girolamo's ruined face.

He heard a shuffled step and a knock on the door, and at once said, "Come." The Moor entered. "Any luck?"

"Yes," said Tharwat, unwrapping the muffling folds of his cloak and scarves. "But no help." And he did not say more on the subject. Instead he crossed to warm himself by the glowing brazier.

"There is fish," offered Girolamo.

"Thank you. My last meal in Venice, at least for some time. I leave tomorrow."

Disappointed, Girolamo ducked his head, muttering low wishes for a safe journey. He focused on his fish, but could no longer taste it.

"I understand why you would not wish to leave here," said Tharwat. "But if I can guarantee your safety, would you consider joining me?"

Girolamo was pleased, but wary. "Can you guarantee my safety?"

"I think so. Let me speak to the lady. If all is safe, I will send to you. You may, of course, choose not to come. But I have valued our time here. I think the stars brought us together for a reason. I would like to explore that."

Girolamo looked up from his fish. "I would like that as well."

◆   ◊   ◆

The hunt through the city was brilliant, with the quartet dodging their pursuers, throwing off the scent of dogs, clambering through windows and under buildings. They used tunnels no one knew about, remains left by the Romans a thousand years past. Cangrande had restored the ancient baths under his palace, but other than that had paid little attention to the old Roman streets beneath the current city. Some of those streets still existed, and Cesco led the way to exploring them. So it was a double adventure, and ended in a day all four would treasure.

At the appointed hour of capitulation, the failed hunters offered their praise to the successful quarry, then the knights brought the two boys home, right next door to Cesco's abode. As he passed it, Cesco knocked on the death door. No one answered.

Inside, Casa Montecchio was in a mild frenzy, with Gianozza ordering the servants to start hunting the streets for her wayward son. Arriving in the yard, the two young boys were clutched to her chest as if she had feared them lost at sea. Cesco stared up at the evening sky while Detto explained the innocent nature of the game and Romeo and Benvolio described the excitement, the thrill, the genius of it. Lady Montecchio wept her relief. Her husband, who appreciated boyish adventures, was delighted and praised the quartet for such an inventive (and harmless) sport. Cesco and Detto departed the Montecchio house with smiles and waves following them, Romeo and Benvolio clamouring to do it again tomorrow.

"I don't like him," said Gianozza stiffly, running her fingers through Romeo's hair as if he'd been gone a year.

"I do," said Romeo, a little breathless with his defiance.

◆　◇　◆

Next door, Cesco was greeted by little Maddelena, who was red-eyed. Dahna was attempting to restrain her, but she broke free and raced forward to halt just before her husband, hands upon her hips. "Francesco, you have to get rid of Vito!"

"Get rid of Vito?" echoed her husband. "Why, has he been distracting Dahna again?" At his shoulder, Detto grinned. Vito was exceedingly handsome.

"He slapped me!"

Cesco's frown held more than a hint of anger. "Why?"

Maddelena flushed and repeated, "He slapped me."

"On your face?"

Maddelena bit her lip. "On my wrist."

"Where was this?"

"In the kitchen. It's my kitchen, you said so!"

"Yes, but it's his domain. Were you touching something hot?"

"No." Then she confessed, "I wanted a sweet, that's all."

"A sweet?"

"Some of that pine nut brittle he makes for you."

"You were trying to steal a sweet?"

Maddelena sensed this was going badly. "I – I wasn't – he struck me! He said it was only for you, and that he'd make something else for me. But I wanted to taste it!"

"I thought you didn't like it," said Francesco.

She flushed again. "You like it."

"And you want to like what I like. That's very sweet. But unnecessary." He ruffled her hair. "You are yourself."

Feeling better, she dragged him into the sitting room and listened to him talk about the game of hide-and-seek he had just played, and his swim earlier in the day, and his new horse that he was enjoying so much. As he spoke he absently flipped an empty cup between his hands. When he noticed that her eyes never left the cup he snatched up three balls of yarn and began to juggle them in the air. Maddelena clapped her hands. "Higher! Higher!"

Enjoying Maddelena's delight, he said, "Want to see what they see? Detto, come here."

Before she knew what was happening she was flying in the air, tossed back and forth between her husband and his cousin. She squealed in gleeful terror, and when they put her down she grabbed Cesco's hands. "Again! Again!"

After the third time through this exercise, she grabbed him about the neck and swung around to his back, legs kicking for purchase. Half-choking, Cesco dashed about the room in a mock attempt to throw her off before collapsing onto the floor on his belly. "Peace, wife! I am not a pony!"

She hopped off to crouch and gaze into his face, her expression greedy. "Can I have a pony?"

"Only if he can juggle, too."

"Ponies can't juggle," she informed him. "They don't have hands."

"Really? It must be very sad not to be able to juggle. You should learn to juggle for them."

Maddelena nodded seriously. Kneeling beside him, she tucked her feet under her skirts and placed her hands properly in her lap. "Husband?"

Cocking an eye at Detto, Cesco sat up straight. "Yes, wife?"

"Do you like me?"

He ruffled her braided hair. "What a ridiculous question. Of course I do!"

Maddelena ducked from under his hand. "I wasn't sure. I'm so little."

"True. You should try to grow some more. Luckily, I like children. They never lie about anything important, and they don't pretend to be something they're not."

Maddelena's little brow furrowed. "What if I get older?"

"You will," said Francesco. "Even I cannot beat back time — though for you I'd try."

She liked that. "Will you still like me when I'm old like you?"

That sent him into peals of laughter and even Detto was smiling. "If you're still like you are now — sweet and honest, clever and blunt — I'm sure I will."

A wide smile crossed her face. Good. He liked her. Now she could ask him why he was sad. But first she leaned forward to kiss Francesco the way her nurse always kissed her, on the eyelid.

Suddenly she found herself hurled backwards against a chair. She slammed into it and slid to the floor, the breath knocked form her body. She opened her eyes to see Francesco staring down at her, aghast. Then he was gone. Detto called for her nurse before chasing after his friend.

It was only when she was alone that she began to cry, weeping full-bodied tears and wailing like the child she was. Nor would she tell Dahna what the problem was. She just bawled until she fell asleep. Her husband had left the house and did not return all night.

The next morning, Maddelena received presents: two new dresses, a lovely painted doll from France, a stuffed bunny with long floppy ears, and a real live pony named Boco. And Vito was preparing all her favourite dishes.

She was overjoyed by the gifts, of course. But she never saw Francesco all that day, and he sent no message. Maddelena understood the gifts were his way of saying he was sorry.

She was the one who was sorry. She'd done something wrong. She'd made him sadder. She tried to wait up that night to apologize, but fell asleep long before he got home.

In the morning she rode her pony. That afternoon, keeping it a secret from everyone but her pony, Maddelena began to teach herself to juggle.

THIRTEEN

The people of Verona were growing tired of revels. It seemed constant merrymaking could be as tedious as toil. But the promise of poetic hellfire lured even the most weary citizens into the public square to hear Dante's works read aloud by his heirs.

To make up for the secrets kept from Poco, the two Alaghieri siblings brought him in to discuss the publishing venture, and to help choose which part of *L'Inferno* was most likely to bring Cesco out of his torpor. They settled on the fourth canto, devoted to philosophers and poets, relegated to the least horrible place in Hell.

"The crowd will be disappointed," said Pietro. "No horrors, no grotesque tortures.

"Well, it does have something the unwashed will appreciate," observed Poco. "An earthquake."

Antonia pulled a face. "You shouldn't joke. It was horrible."

"But it was Cesco's finest hour," countered Pietro. "He rallied the city and helped stave off panic. Hopefully they'll remember it, and think of him fondly."

Apparently the Scaliger was placing equal faith in the healing power of a poetic Hell. "Both public and private chastisement have proved less than fruitful," he said, "so let us take advantage of the boy's flair for dramatics and hope something can stir him beyond a fight or a pair of breasts. Though we should refrain from inviting him. It's the best way to ensure he comes."

The setting for the reading was not the Piazza dei Signori, but rather the Piazza del Comune just to the south. Smaller, it was more enclosed, allowing voices to reverberate off the buildings. Massive braziers were set all around the square, and the snow had been swept away. Cheery spices were burnt to improve the biting air, and the square was dotted with trees ornamented with apples.

A stage was set on the square's western end, with a podium to rest the text upon and three chairs for the poet's family. Cangrande himself was stationed not upon the stage, but rather on a raised platform of his own, seated upon a backless chair in the pose of a Roman consul, signifying his role as audience, not performer.

The crowd's size was impressive, Pietro noted. Far better attended than the handful of public readings his father himself had given here in his life. There were nearly as many people as at a public execution. Men perched in windows, atop the crenellated roof-edges, upon every plinth and pedestal available. Women came with stools to rest upon, and children sat upon on their fathers' shoulders.

One such child was young Romeo. Montecchio had brought both his son and his nephew Benvolio, the two youths still glowing after their adventure the day before. Less happily, he had also brought Romeo's mother, though Pietro supposed it was to be expected. It had been *L'Inferno* that had brought Mari and Gianozza together in the middle of the night of that long-ago Palio. Lord, was that almost fifteen years past?

More surprising was the presence of Capulletto and his wife. Tessa Guarini *in* Capulletto was now at least close to a respectable age. Fifteen, she was again swollen with child. Perhaps this time Antony's son would survive past crib-age. Odd that their girl child, born when Tessa was just twelve, should have lived when the two boys had died within days of their birth. *Morsicato is always saying girl babies are hardier than boys. Which makes no sense, being the weaker sex.*

Biding his time with distractions to quell the stage-fright roiling his bowels, Pietro considered the women he knew. Katerina, Antonia, Giovanna, even Gianozza and Tessa there — all were formidable forces in their own ways, capable of surviving what would kill most men. Was it Original Sin that made them so hardy? Or had God granted them an extra strength to endure their inferior position in His great plan? *Perhaps we should revise our notion of weakness.*

Noon drew near without sign of Cesco or his Rakehells. But the people could not be kept waiting. Feeling the trepidation he always did when facing a crowd, and recalling the last two public readings he had done were before an Inquisitor and an Emperor,

Pietro rose from his seat and strode to the pedestal, where the heavy book was open to the appropriate page.

After the applause subsided, Pietro thanked the Scaliger and the other notables in the crowd – Castelbarco, Bonaventura and his wife Kate, Antonio and Mariotto (of the two, he made sure to thank Antony first, to avoid him storming off in a huff), and a half-dozen other important men.

He gave a brief introduction, summarizing the events of *L'Inferno* to this point – Dante waking in a dark forest and being greeted by the dead poet Virgil, who led the living poet away from the dangers of the Lion, the Leopard, and the She-Wolf by the only route available – down into Hell, promising to guide Dante to his ultimate destination, Heaven, and reunite him with his long lost love, the lady Beatrice.

After passing through the famous gate bearing the dark inscription *Lasciate ogne speranza, voi ch'intrate*, and seeing the ranks of the Uncommitted – those who did neither good nor evil in their lives (including those angels who took no sides in Lucifer's rebellion) – Dante and Virgil cross the river Acheron. "But the act of crossing sends Dante into unconsciousness – and thus we arrive at the Fourth Canto, wherein Dante awakes to find himself in Limbo." With that, Pietro cleared his throat and began to read:

Ruppemi l'alto sonno ne la testa
un greve truono, sì ch'io mi riscossi
come persona ch'è per forza desta;

A heavy thunderclap broke my deep sleep
so that I started up like one
shaken awake by force

e l'occhio riposato intorno mossi,
dritto levato, e fiso riguardai
per conoscer lo loco dov' io fossi.

With rested eyes, I stood
and looked about me, then fixed my gaze
to make out where I was.

Vero è che 'n su la proda mi trovai
de la valle d'abisso dolorosa
che 'ntrono accoglie d'infiniti guai.

I found myself upon the brink
of an abyss of suffering
filled with the roar of endless woe.

Oscura e profonda era e nebulosa
tanto che, per ficcar lo viso a fondo,
io non vi discernea alcuna cosa.

It was full of vapour, dark and deep.
Straining my eyes toward the bottom,
I could see nothing.

'Or discendiam qua giù nel cieco
mondo,' cominciò il poeta tutto smorto.
'Io sarò primo, e tu sarai secondo.'

'Now let us descend into the blind world
down there,' began the poet, gone pale.
'I will be first and you come after.'

Just as Pietro was finishing these lines, Cesco and his Rakehells entered the square. Ruddy-cheeked and tousle-haired as though they'd been riding – or romping – they were respectful if cocksure as they strode boldly towards the front benches and shouldered themselves into seats.

Pietro's relief that the bait had been swallowed was tempered by the boy's demeanor. His very stride had changed. Always Cesco had posessed a purposeful gait, light on his feet, always someone with a destination. Now his careless lope proclaimed a truculence that pained Pietro's heart.

Not faltering, Pietro carried on through the events of the Canto – Virgil explaining that those who dwelt herein were only guilty of not knowing Christ in their lives, either through dying before baptism or else having been born before the Savior came to provide Grace to the world; Dante asking if any had ever been saved from this place, and Virgil recounting the Harrowing of Hell, when Christ came down to bring the great Hebrews up into Heaven – Adam, Abel, Noah, Moses, Abraham, David and his children, along with others who knew the truth of God and deserved to be brought to join Him above.

Pietro carried on to read of the four spirits that approach Dante and Virgil:

Lo buon maestro cominciò a dire:　　　　The good master spoke: 'Take note
'Mira colui con quella spada in mano,　of him who holds that sword in hand
che vien dinanzi ai tre sì come sire:　and comes as lord before the three:

quelli è Omero poeta sovrano;　　'He is Homer, sovereign poet.
l'altro è Orazio satiro che vene;　Next comes Horace the satirist,
Ovidio è 'l terzo, e l'ultimo Lucano.'　Ovid is third, the last is Lucan.'

At this point the ancient poets did Dante honour, inducting the living man into their ranks and making him the sixth great poet of all eternity. Then, coming to the foot of a massive castle, the dead poets ushered Dante in and at once he found himself inside an Elysian meadow alongside other great historical figures – Electra, Hector, Aeneas, Caesar, Camilla, Penthesilea, Latinus and his daughter Lavinia, the first Brutus with Lucretia at his side, Julia, Marcia, Cornelia and, sitting alone, Saladin.

Pietro read of the approach of Aristotle, with Socrates and Plato, Democritus, and the other great philosophers, followed by the legendary mathematicians Euclid, Ptolemy, Galen, Hippocrates, Avicenna, and Averroes.

The Canto concluded with two stanzas, as Dante was forced to leave this exalted company:

Io non posso ritrar di tutti a pieno,　　I cannot give account of all of them,
però che sì mi caccia il lungo tema,　for the length of my theme so drives me on
che molte volte al fatto il dir vien meno.　that often the telling comes short of the fact.

La sesta compagnia in due si scema: *The company of six falls off to two*
per altra via mi mena il savio duca,   *and my wise leader brings me another way*
fuor de la queta, ne l'aura che trema.   *out of the still, into the trembling, air.*
'E vegno in parte ove non è che luca.   *And I come to a place where nothing shines.*

"From here, the poet descends into Hell itself." Closing the book, Pietro bowed to Cangrande, making a deep leg to his father's last and greatest patron, who put his hands together, a signal for the crowd. Under the applause, Pietro could not help recalling his first day in Verona, when they had all lounged upon Cangrande's loggia and debated this very text.

The Bishop of Verona began the discussion by posing a leading question about light. "Tell me, you Alaghieri who knew him so well, why does your father describe Hell as a *cieco mondo* — a 'blind world'. Are we meant to take this literally? Are the denizens of Hell blind?"

"I imagine," said Cangrande, "that he means they are blinded by the smoke of hellfire."

Pietro inclined his head. "I'm sure my lord Scaliger is correct. However I think my father meant something more metaphorical. He was likely referring to a poetic lack of Light. Outside of all the torments and suffering, it seems to me that this lack is the very definition of Hell."

"How so?" asked Cangrande.

"I often heard my father say that Hell is not truly defined by those who are condemned to be there," said Pietro, "but rather by He who is not. Hell is, quite simply, the absence of God."

"Ah!" cried Cangrande, leaning forward. "God is Light, and if all light comes from God above, then the only light in Hell is reflected, or produced by flame. Bishop, do you not approve?"

"Very well said, my lord," nodded Bishop Francis. "I imagine that this would be torture enough — to stand there and feel the lack of God's divine love would be an emptiness that would stifle the boldest soul."

"You speak to two former excommunicants," remarked Cangrande with a half-grin. "Both Pietro and I know the pain of which you speak most personally."

If it had been awkward for the Bishop to hold sway over a city whose lord had been excommunicated, he chose to laugh. "So you must feel the Light all the more full now that you are both back in His sight."

Cangrande's full *allegria* flashed, whiter than the snow clinging to the rooftops. "Yes! Like the poet himself, Pietro and I have braved Hell, and are returned to Heaven. By which I mean, Verona." The crowd laughed, and there were smiles all around. Pietro saw Cesco roll his eyes.

"But what about the *Limbicoli*?" This came from Lord Castelbarco. "Why does the noble poet place so many ancient figures among those in Limbo, rather than lower in Hell?"

Pietro waited, hoping Cesco would answer. But the prince of Verona was looking blankly expectant, listening without the remotest hint of participation. It fell to Antonia to respond. "The poet disagrees with the blessed San Tommasso, who says that Limbo is filled by only two classes of men – Hebrew saints and unbaptized infants. Instead we are given the great pagans, the learned men who were never afforded the comfort of knowing the light of Christ."

"I see that," nodded Castelbarco. "Yet there is one who troubles me. Why is the infidel general Saladin placed in Limbo, rather than lower with his master?"

Pietro knew why, though he could not speak it aloud. His father had abhorred Islam as much as any Christian – though that had tempered over the years he lived with Tharwat al-Dhaamin. But it had been Muslims who had preserved Aristotle and much of the great philosophy, science, and especially poetry lost to the West when Rome fell. Honouring Saladin, the greatest of the Muslims, was the poet's way of acknowledging a debt humanity owed to the Infidel. It was no accident that the very next person introduced after the Muslim was Aristotle himself.

There followed some spirited debate over the life of Saladin, with Cangrande and several others attempting to reconcile his dignity against his deeds in fighting against Christianity. They concluded that, though he was a Muslim, his acts had been so chivalrous and so enlightened that he deserved to be among the noblest of the damned. Because, as Cangrande noted, "Damned is still damned." Still Cesco said nothing.

A humble man in the crowd asked why Homer carried a sword. This question was answered by Mariotto's wife, the poetry-loving Gianozza. "The sword in Homer's hand indicates he is an epic poet," she explained, standing up. Now in her thirtieth year, she was as beautiful as ever, stopping the breath of men even with her raven hair covered and out of sight. "Also he is the greatest among them, and wrote of the greatest deeds in the history of men – the siege of Troy, from which all other history has sprung. It is only fitting he is honoured with a sword." Antony applauded her answer, much to his wife's dismay. Cesco applauded too, if wryly.

Giving up hope that Cesco would partake in this discussion,

Pietro let himself be drawn into a debate with Fra Lorenzo over *scïenzïa* versus *arte*, the first indicating knowledge, while the second and greater word alluded to the ability to express that knowledge – infinitely harder. "It is easier to know than to share that knowledge."

"Which is why the Lord has granted these great poets – as well as the philosophers and mathematicians – the lightest punishment in Hell," added Poco with surprising clarity. His time in Florence had done him well. "Their abilities mitigate their torment."

"Damned is still damned," repeated Cangrande. Men laughed, and it began to be the catchphrase for the afternoon, as time and again men brought the conversation back to the fact that, however great and able these men were, they were all still damned.

After an hour of vigourous talk and countertalk, and a few shouting matches that almost came to blows, the event showed signs of heading for a natural conclusion. Pietro saw Cesco whisper something to his band of Rakehells and they moved to depart ahead of the rest of the crowd.

Cangrande saw it, too. "Francesco della Scala! You are uncommonly silent – especially for someone raised at the poet's knee. You have as much right as any to comment on his epic work. Surely you have some thoughts to share with us."

All eyes turned to Cesco, whose face showed innocent surprise. "I doubt I have anything of value to offer this illustrious gathering. Certainly there are none better than Ser Alaghieri, Suor Beatrice, and Signor Jacopo to enlighten us all to the poet's meaning. And for good measure, we have heard from Donna Montecchio, as learned as anyone in the field of romantic poetry. I marvel at the education I've had here today."

"And I marvel at such unaccustomed modesty," answered Cangrande with an oblique smile. "You have nothing to add?"

Cesco considered for a moment, then gave a brief shrug. "Far be it from me to criticize the poem. It is a fantastic piece of craftsmanship, unparalleled in modern times. Yet it behooves us to remember it is, in fact, only a poem. One that takes as its premise a flawed notion."

"And what notion is that?"

Cesco's posture remained nonchalant, but there was a fierce flicker in the depths of his eyes. "The notion that there is any such thing as Heaven and Hell."

The crowd grew very still, and no wonder. Heaven and Hell were central to the Christian faith. Priests and monks and bishops spoke of them daily. Without the promise of Heaven and the threat of Hell, how were men supposed to know right from wrong?

Bishop Francis was on his feet, as was Fra Lorenzo. Men were muttering, the mutters rising to shouts of outrage. Eyes turned to Cangrande, who held out his hands, smiling reprovingly. "This is what happens when you raise a prince at the knee of a poet. Or perhaps minor heresies run in the family. But remember, all, this is a discussion of poetry, not God's law."

Cesco flashed a thin-lipped smile. "See? I told you I had nothing of value to add." With that he turned and exited the square, followed by his band of Rakehells – a name that suddenly had new meaning.

The crowd dispersed, everyone discussing in low voices what Cesco had posited. Bishop Francis crossed to have words with Cangrande, looking for a way to stem the tide of unrest. Mariotto was kneeling to have a stern conversation with little Romeo, who was frowning in puzzled thought.

On the stage, Pietro kept his face neutral. Antonia was less successful than her brother. Her wide eyes and clenched jaw bespoke her feelings. It was Poco who turned his back to the crowd so he might chuckle. "Twelve words. Just twelve words, and he's caused more of a stir than father did with the whole poem."

Pietro, too, appreciated the skill with which Cesco had thwarted their obvious attempt to draw him out. *Be careful what you wish for...*

Antonia managed to keep her voice low, though it did nothing to soften her sharp tone. "He'll be murdered! The Church will condemn him as a heretic!"

Poco was dismissive. "This was a discussion of poetry. He can simply say he was—"

"What, being poetic? Poco, part of the reason it was so easy for the Church to rule against Pietro was our father's work. Not that he wrote anything outside of Church doctrine," she added hastily. "But any poem is open to interpretation. And in Cesco—"

"In Cesco, they have both Cangrande's heir and my foster-son," finished Pietro. "Damned on both sides."

"This will make it harder for the Abbess to condone my staying there."

"Or easier," said Pietro. "You are trying to correct his wayward thoughts, and protect his little bride."

Antonia looked like a geyser, steaming before the eruption. "But for Heaven's sake, why would he say such a thing?"

Poco and Pietro both stared at her. Was she serious? Surely she recalled the many evenings in Ravenna where their father had posed just the same question. Was there a Heaven? Was there a God? The great mind had wrestled with the problem, and come down on the side of *Yes*. But it had not stopped him from trying to reconcile the natural world with the divine one. Pietro recalled his own struggle, practicing his legal skill as he argued for God while his genius father played the Devil's Advocate, trying to strike down the underpinnings of faith. In many ways, the *Commedia* itself was the poet's attempt to make sense of the relationship between God and Man.

If it was hard for me, what must have it been like for Cesco, all of six years old, to listen as we all discussed and debated? What did he absorb? A prodigy with a quick and nimble mind, the boy must have heard the arguments and set about deciding for himself. *And his recent bitter reversals have made up his mind.*

"He's not just challenging his father and the stars," said Pietro in wonder. "He's determined to take the battle right to Heaven's door."

"Aim high or go home." Cangrande stepped onto the low stage to join them. "I was just assuring the good Bishop there that my wayward heir will be in Church come Sunday, and again on Wednesday. Can you divine what the sermons will be?"

Antonia was not amused. "This was a mistake."

"Was it?" asked Cangrande grandly. "On the contrary, I found the whole thing scintillating. As your late father would have, had he been here. The reading was excellent – you mimic him well, Pietro, albeit unconsciously, I'm sure."

Antonia was insistent. "But Cesco—"

"—showed more life in that moment than we've seen in ages. For three weeks he has reserved his liveliness for back alley brawls and petty pranks. Better this forum for his outrages than public violence. If the price is unity with the Church, well," he glanced wryly towards Pietro, "we've slipped across that ice before. We should do this again after Twelfth Night."

"Perhaps not so public next time?" suggested Pietro.

Cangrande tapped a finger alongside his nose. "Wisely. Wisely."

"If it's not public, how do we get him to come?" asked Poco shrewdly.

"By inviting the Bishop, of course. Having thrown down his gauntlet, I imagine Cesco will want to engage in single combat."

"Against the Bishop?"

Pietro shook his head. "Against God."

FOURTEEN

HAVING BEEN EDIFIED by poetic mischief-making, the Rakehells went straight back to raising the Hell that Cesco denied existed. Lining up at the arches of the ancient Arena, they agreed on a track and mounted their steeds. Some horses, like Benedick's and Thibault's, were borrowed from Cesco's stables, but most were the property of their noble riders.

For Cesco this was an important race, for he was fully airing Abastor for the first time. Beside him was Detto atop a brown stallion he'd named for the steed of Roland, paladin to Charlemagne, made famous in *The Song of Roland*. In Italian Roland was *Orlando*, and his horse Veillantif became *Vegliantino*.

When Detto had named him on the day of the knighting, Cesco had been bemused by the choice. "Really? A man famous only for failing to protect the emperor's rear?"

"He allowed the emperor time to get to safety," Detto had answered.

Cesco had blown through his lips. "Then called him back as he died! Was there ever a less useful death than Roland's? He didn't even die fighting. He blew a horn so hard his head erupted. And he lost all his men."

"That was no fault of his horse," Detto had said, patting his steed's neck. Cesco had been forced to confess the truth of this.

The route today was through the Porta Lioni, up the *via Cappello*, then left through the Porta Borsari, around San Zeno, and back south to the Arena. Cesco offered a pair of golden spurs to the victor, but that was less important than winning the praise of their fellow Rakehells, especially their leader.

Positions were chosen by lot, six rows of four horsemen riding abreast. The flag dropped and everyone kicked, their breath misting the air. The race was made more treacherous by the new snow on the ground. The horses were shod with heavier shoes, the better to not slip on the cobblestone and marble route. One horse and rider did just that, ending both the horse's life and the rider's ability to walk for months to come. It was a knight from Brindisi come for the revels, and he was bitterly cursing the snow as he was taken to his inn in a cart.

"If you want to run the race, you run the risk," said Cesco with a shrug.

Still getting to know one another, Cesco and Abastor were not the victors. That prize went to Detto and his dun-coloured Vegliantino.

"That's twice in a week," groused Cesco. "I'm beginning to think about arranging an accident for you before the Palio."

"If you do, I'll make sure you get the same, and it won't be an accident."

Second place went to Salvatore. To him, Cesco was more magnanimous. "Well run! Had Detto not caught that last turn, you would have taken the spurs."

"Thank you, my lord," said the Paduan in his even tone as Cesco passed him a bag of silver.

Detto received the congratulations of his peers with a wan smile that disappeared when Cesco made a show of presenting him with the golden spurs. "This Orlando came in first, not last, and still has his wits about him! Congratulations!"

"Thanks," said Detto simply, face expressionless. It was up to Cesco to grab his wrist and hoist the trophy triumphantly into the air, allowing the others to cheer.

Young Petruchio was shaking his head. "The Veronese are not doing well. Twice, we lose to the cat-eater."

Hortensio agreed. "Perhaps we should devise a sport that a cat cannot win."

Grins, nodding heads. Cesco said, "Very well. What shall it be? Something that the horse cannot win for him. A wrestling match – no, he's enormous. A cat-batting? A goose pull?"

"Goose pull! Goose pull!" roared the Rakehells.

"Could it not be a battle of wits?" pleaded Benedick plaintively. "Something *I* have a chance of winning."

Cesco began to recite: "'*The voice of the wild goose, caught by the bait, cries out...*'" He stopped suddenly, his eyes glazing over. Then he shook himself. "But what can the Egyptians of old teach us that we do not already know? We shall order the good Ziliberto to find us a prime goose and we shall pull it, or the goose shall pull us, and in the end we shall end with our ends ended and our bottoms bottomed. Which is as much to say—"

"Goosed," groaned Benedick.

Cesco grinned. "Why do you honk so, gander?"

"He who would pun would pick a pocket."

The jests that followed had them all grinning, and the laughter lasted right up to the moment that Cesco and Detto returned to the house on the *via Pigna*. Doffing their outer wear, they were greeted by Cesco's new steward.

"Suor Beatrice called, my lord," said Fidelio, handing over a slip of paper. "She left this."

Cesco read it at a glance, then cursed, throwing his hands dramatically into the air. "Fine! So long as she doesn't bring her Abbess with her." With that curious declaration, he stormed off to change clothes.

Detto hurried after him. "What is it?"

"A holy houseguest," muttered Cesco, pulling off his hose so forcefully that it tore. There was a knock on the door. "What!" The door opened and a woman gasped. "I said 'what,' not 'come in'!"

The door closed again at once. Through it Dahna said, "You're not having another feast, are you, lord?"

"What do you care if I do?" demanded Cesco.

"It's my lady – your wife. She got into your pine nut brittle and is unwell now. Too much sweet."

"I thought I smelled vomit on the stairs," said Cesco unconcernedly.

"Yes," said Dahna through the door. "Well, she's napping, so any noise..."

"We're going out," said Detto before Cesco could erupt.

The chastened nurse disappeared, followed by Cesco's shout of, "And keep her away from my pine nut brittle!" He continued to mutter, throwing his damp clothes across the room. "There's nothing that's actually mine. Why should there be. I mean, it's my house, my name, my life. But no, people come and stay whenever they choose, eat my treats, steal my pleasures. *Fut!*"

"I can go," said Detto softly.

Cesco froze, then took a deep breath. "No. You're entitled. And you don't steal from me," he added, pulling on fresh hose.

"I don't like the taste of it, is all," said Detto. "I'm guessing your aunt Antonia has invited herself to stay?"

"To help look after my wife, she says. Really, to muzzle me. But how can I refuse?"

"You could make the little girl stay with her parents until she's of age."

"Can't," said Cesco, pulling on a new tunic. "She's got to live in my house until she bears a child. Then there's no chance it's not mine. The Capitano wants no doubt about the bloodline. They tell me seven or eight years and she'll be ready, but I think I'll wait a little longer." He shrugged as he pulled on tall boots over the fresh hose. "Whatever. I plan to be away as much as possible for the next ten years – we've got wars to wage, fiends to foil, and stars to startle. You won't credit it, but I'd much prefer to do battle with my sword, rather than my words. Hm – all you have to do is move the 's' and words become a sword. So the pen is the mate of the sword, not its master. Or perhaps it means that words said are equal to a sword – dead!" He chuckled and held up his hands apologetically. "Took it too far. But it was a good start to something...*God dammit!!!*" he added, leaping a foot into the air and clutching his chest as the fluffy cat Felix went streaking past his legs.

Detto couldn't restrain a laugh. Cesco gave him the fig.

♦   ◊   ♦

After delivering her message, Antonia returned to the convent of Santa Maria in Organo. Entering, she took a breath of homecoming. Of safety. For three years she had lived within these walls, and for two of those years she had served as personal aide to Abbess Verdiana. Her call here was twofold – first, to check upon the progress of the bibles being lovingly copied by her fellow sisters, a lucrative project that also brought great esteem to the holy house. Second, she had promised to report to her mistress before she departed.

Early in their acquaintance, Abbess Verdiana had treated Suor Beatrice coldly, keeping the headstrong novice at arm's length. But after learning of the rape, the wizened lady had taken the wounded sister into her care, given her renewed sense of purpose and duty, helping her find God's grace again.

There was only one condition. Antonia had made a vow there should be no secrets between them. At first it had felt like a betrayal. But she had come to see it as cleansing.

All was well in the copyists' room. Books were proceeding apace, the sisters were being as diligent and exact as the best lay scribes she had hired in Florence. After praising the finished pages and making sure they had an ample supply of chalk and ink, Antonia marched across the chilly yard to the Abbess' solar.

It did not surprise her that the door was shut, as the Abbess would often closet herself away. Antonia took herself to the small chapel just outside the solar and knelt. She first prayed God for forgiveness, then asked the Virgin for protection and guidance for Cesco and all those working to aid him in his quest to become whole.

After twenty minutes she heard a door open. Finishing her prayer, Antonia rose and found herself facing a woman dressed in exquisite fashion. Their eyes connected, and Antonia felt an unwelcome swell of shock and dislike. She curtsied. "Madonna."

Giovanna da Svevia barely inclined her head. "Suor Beatrice. An unexpected delight." Her smile was as frosty as the air outside. It had been this woman, Cangrande's powerful and aging wife, who had contrived with the Count of San Bonifacio to have Cesco murdered years before, hoping to clear a path for Paride to be the Scaliger's heir. Found out, she had shown no remorse. Nor had she made her dislike of young Cesco's role in Veronese life a secret. His recent behavior was clearly a source of satisfaction for her, as she said, "I understand you are attempting to tame the young knight. May God aid you in all your endeavours."

Abbess Verdiana appeared, tiny and hump-backed with age. Blinking once, she said, "Suora, you come in a happy time. Donna Giovanna called to offer us gifts in honour of Santa Lucia's day, and I am at a loss how to make best use of them. I am certain you will have several excellent ideas." Santa Lucia's day was very important in the lives of the Veronese, marking as it did the day of the year with the least light in the sky, and the longest night.

Antonia curtsied again, but made no reply.

Bidding farewell to the first lady of the city, the Abbess returned from seeing her to the convent gate and ushered Antonia into the solar. The door closed, she said, "I shall be sorry to lose you. But I hope your presence will quell the prince's exuberance. You joining his household will hopefully lessen today's perception that he does not believe in the Lord our God." Verdiana pursed her lips. "His words were most troubling. I don't know which would be worse – if he were to say such things to provoke, or if he believed them."

"If he believed them, surely."

"Such belief is misguided, not malicious," said the Abbess.

"Malice is harder to correct. Unless it is not malice at all, but madness."

"Madness? Cesco is not mad."

"What of his addiction to the drug. It has lessened?"

Antonia frowned. "I – cannot say. If he indulges, it is not in my presence. But I can see traces of it in his eyes. He hides it well, but it is there if you look for it."

"So he spends his time out of his senses, either in drink, in brawls, or in a *bordello*, if the reports are true."

Antonia bowed her head. "I am afraid they are."

The Abbess made a tutting sound. "In one way, I deplore it. But it may be for the best. He is a married man, and cannot yet partake of his wedded bed. One cannot entirely condemn him for sowing his youthful oats. It is natural. Does he take Bailardetto with him?"

"No," answered Antonia. "But I think that is Detto's choice."

"I am relieved to hear not all the young men of Verona are indulging in the fleshpots."

"Detto seems subdued, due to the rift with his father. And he is younger than Cesco."

"Yet perhaps wiser. What of the young prince's other companions?"

"They are young men. They are respectful in my presence, but take little note of my advice. Or my disapproval."

"Name them, please. These Rakehells."

Antonia ran through the list of them, starting with the noblest, Prince Rupert, and descending to the least noble, the two Paduans. "Signor Salvatore is quiet, but not dull. He often enjoys the last word in a debate. He reminds one of a cat, watching for the moment to pounce. But he has a very cheerful face, in spite of it."

"And what of the other Paduan, this Benedick? Has your dislike of him grown?"

Antonia's brow furrowed. "I think him a better man than I first judged him. He is a devoted friend to Cesco, though he does have a tendency towards flattery that I deplore. He jests too much, mostly at the expense of women. In public I have been twice forced to put him down. Oddly, he seems to enjoy the repartee."

"I'm sure," said Verdiana knowingly. "And you?"

Blushing, Antonia confessed she enjoyed the verbal sparring. It reminded her of exchanges with an old friend, Petruchio's cousin Ferdinando, who had died before they had been able to explore any other mutual likings.

"I see," said the Abbess gravely. "Are you in danger of falling into a relationship with this man?"

A sharp laugh bubbled out of Antonia. "Goodness, no! Mother Abbess, I know very well who I am, and I see him more clearly than he sees himself. I pray for him, but he is not the man for me, and I would never be the woman for him. I belong to the Lord."

"Truly? Did you not tell me that you helped the Heir and his lover over the summer because you yourself did not act swiftly enough in the matter of your own heart?"

Antonia bowed her head. "And I am punished for it daily, Mother Abbess." It was true.

The Abbess seemed satisfied. "Come, help me sort out these goods that Donna Giovanna brought to us, and determine where they are of best use."

Following her mistress, Suor Beatrice hid her unease. Servants could have easily delivered these goods. For what reason had the first lady of Verona come calling at this little convent? What had Giovanna been discussing with the Abbess?

For two years Antonia had poured all her secrets into this holy vessel, from Cesco's indulgence in hashish to the horror of the incest. It had been her oath, her sacred vow made before God, to keep no secrets.

It occurred to her for the first time that there had been no oath of reciprocity.

✦   ◊   ✦

Pisa

Another Beatrice heard a commotion outside her door and started down the stairs, wiping her hands quickly down her skirts. She'd heard the horses, but thought they were passing by. She had been busily mending the broken window, hammering wood over the shattered pane. The glass had been poorly blown, it seemed, and not equal to this unusual cold.

Riders? To see me? Beatrice de'Lionati had no notion who had come calling on her. She had seen almost no one since her mother's passing, months earlier, and as the money ran out had dispensed with most of the household staff. She'd kept her maid and the old grounds-keeper, but had taken up the cooking and cleaning herself. The time was fast approaching when she would have to sell this small house and find her way in the world. Which might have been daunting for an unwed orphan girl of twenty-three. But to Beatrice it was a cross between an adventure and an inconvenience.

Passing another window as she descended, Beatrice noted that her visitor's servants remained outside, seeing to the mounts. His retinue alone was impressive, and a little daunting. Was there a bill unpaid? Some debt owed that she had missed? Full of wary trepidation, she opened the door to the sitting room.

The visitor, dressed in fine clothes, had taken the time to brush the muck of travel from his boots and change his doublet and hose before calling. More than his excellent attire, he had a proud chin and a complexion bespoke a lack of lack. Yet there was something that wore on him, as if he had suffered a recent reversal.

When Beatrice opened the door, he was looking over the books on the shelf with evident interest. He turned at once and bowed. "Donna Beatrice. I am Don Pedro of Aragon. Forgive me for intruding. Your noble uncle, Leonato de'Leonati, asked me to call upon you and beg your company back to his estate in Messina. I expect he wrote to you?"

Trouble evaporating on the air, she had to laugh. "If he did, it never found me. You are most welcome, Don Pedro. And let me state that I will be ready to leave just as soon as your horses are rested."

♦ ◊ ♦

Outside Lyons, France

Across the Alps, hooves beat the road, echoing around the steeply ascending landscape.

Looking over his shoulder, the fugitive slipped in the mud of the road. Scrambling on all fours, he lunged for cover, chest bursting. Thank Heaven he was fit, without an ounce of fat on his light bones. But he'd been running for so long!

In fact, Benjamin had been on the run since taking ship twelve days earlier. Last night he'd spied the hunters loitering outside his inn. He'd hoped to fool them by leaving his horse stabled and slipping away in darkness. But no, they'd figured it out. *Damn damn damnady damn damn.*

The horses were racing nearer. The night was moonless, and the road was curved. They weren't yet in sight. Benjamin had seconds to decide. He couldn't hope to outrun pursuit on the open road. But horses couldn't climb – nor could they swim. That was the choice: turn right and scale the rise of the Alps, or throw himself into the Savoy River and swim.

It wasn't the damp that made him shy of the water. He was already soaked through, and the receding tide of his hair was plastered down with sweat. He might soon wet himself. But outside the drenching, the Savoy would take him back the way he had come, away from his destination. Nor was he a strong swimmer.

The climb was an equally dangerous choice. They might have bows. Even a well-placed rock could fell him.

Choose!

Veering right, Benjamin scrabbled at the steep incline, fingers digging for a hold. He grasped low scrub, looking up to where trees grew, wondering if he could reach them in time. Within moments his mud-spattered hose were torn to tatters by nettles and branches. Already he was regretting his choice, but it was too late to go back. The horses were just around the bend. A few more moments…

Wriggling fingers of fire lit the nearest rocks and shrubs. Like a deer sensing onrushing hunters, the fugitive froze face down along the hillside, prone between the low branches of bracken.

As the horses approached, the torches cast a nightmarish light over the ground. *Let them pass, let them pass, O God, I will never sing that song again, you know which song, the bad one, I swear, just please for the love of all that I hold dear, let them pass…*

But God must have approved the song, or disapproved of the singer, because the hunters reined just down the slope and slightly ahead of their prey.

Cursing mentally, Benjamin had another conversation with God about the nature of requests, and of how perhaps it was unfair to judge a man for a song, no matter how vulgar, or for what he'd done with that lady's maid in the castle at Devon, and yes he'd done it several times, but once you're damned, why stop…?

"Why stop?" The question made Benjamin jolt. But the speaker wasn't talking of the maid, he was asking why they had halted. As it was a question of some importance to the still figure on the slope, he listened.

The answer was unhelpful. "Quiet. The Italian's thinking."

The Italian? That's who they sent? Drat drat drat! Unwillingly, the fugitive turned his head. Yes, there he was. The Italian, who wasn't Italian. His father had been an Italian adventurer who'd taken a Scotswoman to wife. The result was this odd little man with the Italian name – Aiello, the Scot.

Aiello was frightening, despite the fact that he shouldn't be. He had a face more suited to a foole than a villain. One eye opened comically wider than the other, and the beard he wore was thin, not closing the distance between his chin and lips. He had a frantic, frenetic energy, like a bird in a rough wind.

The Scot's restlessness made his horse skittish under him as Aiello scanned the ground. Doing the same, Benjamin saw with horror the tiny trickles of earth he'd knocked loose as he'd climbed. But how had Aiello seen these traces in the dark? Was the hunter that skilled?

Slowly the Scot's head came up, tracing the path directly to Benjamin's hiding place. Their eyes met and Aiello smiled. It was a private moment, suspended in time. Benjamin could see Aiello take the time to frame the perfect words. The pause seemed to last an eternity. Then, finally, Aiello said, "Hello, pretty."

Benjamin bolted. Not uphill, but back down across the path. Diving between the legs of Aiello's horse, he sprinted to the road's edge and threw himself in a flailing dive into the water of the Savoy.

The enormous splash in the chilly water was punishing, but Benjamin scrambled like a dog upwards, trying to recall everything he'd ever known about swimming. When he broke the surface, he was already a quarter-mile downstream of his pursuers. Over the rush of the water, Benjamin heard shouts as they wheeled their horses about to follow him. He tried to swim with the current, traveling faster and faster away from the Alps and his chosen path. Behind him, the horses had to follow the winding road, while he just had to keep his head above the waters that were carrying him away from his destination. But if he was to deliver his message, he first had to remain alive.

He heard Aiello's voice far behind him, its odd lilt echoing around the silence of the hills. "Nobody rests until we have the bastard Montagu's head on a pike!"

♦   ◊   ♦

News came that the emissary from Treviso would be arriving within the next two days. "The goose will have to wait. We're off to Illasi." Cesco made preparations to depart, knowing full well that Suor Beatrice would use his absence as the perfect opportunity to move into his house.

Cesco was not alone in being plagued by the redoubtable Antonia. Word had come that Tharwat was returning to Vicenza, which had Pietro packing to join him. But before he could go west, he had a most uncomfortable promise to keep to his sister. He recalled something Cangrande often said. "Family is a wretched nuisance."

Then he realized that the phrase was far too apt for this particular situation.

FIFTEEN

ALL UNWILLING, Pietro Alaghieri set out in the pre-dawn darkness to call upon Cangrande's bastard daughter, Cesco's forbidden love, Rosalia Rienzi.

Tiberio, he corrected himself at once. *Donna Tiberio. Rosalia Rienzi in Tiberio.*

Pietro had met the girl exactly once, at her father's house, and taken no notice of her at all. Though he dreaded the coming meeting, he felt a natural curiosity as to what qualities this young woman held that had caused Cesco to craft the *Pax Verona* in order to marry her. Only to have that cup dashed from his lips.

Lucky, thought Pietro. *What if they had married in secret? How much worse would that have been? Not that we'd have had any trouble having the marriage annulled. The one ground that will always revoke a bond is consanguinity…*

Forcing those unhappy thoughts from his mind, Pietro focused on the immediate question plaguing him – what excuse to craft. He couldn't go to the girl outright. There was no possible claim of prior friendship. If he'd been going to her father's house, it would have been easy enough to ask after the rebuilding of the forge, burned down earlier in the year. Though Pietro was glad enough not to have to face that particular Geyron, whose triple-heads would all have spit fire at the mention of Cesco and Cangrande.

Still, the visit required some plausible reason for calling. Making some inquiries, Pietro learned that Abramo Tiberio owned a parcel of land north of the Lago di Garda that he was offering to sell. It would make perfect sense for Ser Pietro Alaghieri to be looking for a place to build the estate long due him. It did not guarantee an interview with Donna Tiberio, but it was all he could think of.

He needed to move swiftly. After this, he had to reverse course towards Vicenza for his interview with Tharwat and Morsicato. Trying not to curse his holy sister, he mostly succeeded. Because she was correct, this journey had to be made.

But it was a hard journey to make in December. He kept to the northbound road between Monte Baldo and Monti Lessini. This took him up past Mori as he turned east. Here he came across the Slavini di San Marco, adjoining the village of the same name. Huge blocks of stone lay heaped in a confused pile, as though left by some monstrous child who had not tidied his toys. Pietro's father had referenced this landslip in *L'Inferno*, when he and Virgil were about to descend to the level of wrath:

Qual è quella ruina che nel fianco As on the rockslide that still marks the flank
di qua da Trento l'Adice percosse,   of the Adige, this side of Trent,
o per tremoto o per sostegno manco, whether by earthquake or erosion at the base,

che da cima del monte, onde si mosse, from the mountain-top they slid away from
al piano è sì la roccia discoscesa, the shattered boulders strew the precipice
ch'alcuna via darebbe a chi sù fosse: and thus give footing to one coming down

 cotal di quel burrato era la scesa. just so was the descent down in that ravine.

This whole territory had made a huge impression on his father – perhaps because twenty-five years ago he had traveled this route as he left Italy for France. The poet had feared this was the last he would ever see of his beloved Italy, and it had stayed with him ever after. As he had fashioned Virgil to speak of it:

Suso in Italia bella giace un laco, 'High in fair Italy, at the foot of the alps
a piè de l'Alpe che serra Lamagna that form a border with Germany near Tyrol,
sovra Tiralli, c'ha nome Benaco. lies a lake they call Benàco.

Per mille fonti, credo, e più si bagna 'By a thousand springs and more, I think, the land
tra Garda e Val Camonica e Pennino between Garda, Val Camonica, and Pennino
de l'acqua che nel detto laco stagna. is bathed by waters settling in that lake.

Benàco was the old name for the *Lago di Garda*. The passage continued on for five more stanzas, a remarkable length for such a pastoral scene. It had clearly meant a great deal to the poet.

But Dante had passed this way in Spring, when the snow-melts had the lake overflowing and the land was a verdant green. Coming in winter, it was a chill and forbidding place. The wind funneled down from the Alps, howling in Pietro's ears like the cries of the wrathful at the bottom of an infernal ravine.

It was slow going, and he spent the night at a tavern, warming numbed fingers too stupid to undo the ties of his cloak. The food was plain and fairly awful, but welcome nonetheless. He might have pressed on to the house, but had no desire to arrive after nightfall where he was not expected and likely unwelcome.

He decided to make his story resonate by trying it out on the tavern's owner. In reply, the man said, "It's good land, but wild. Like old Bramo himself. Begging your pardon, Ser."

Pietro waved this off – he never felt comfortable receiving the deference due his station. "What can you tell me about him?"

"A hard man. Like he stepped from the old days, you know? Cares nothing for these modern times. The old ways – *'stone and steel, hearth and home, fox and hound may never roam.'* Makes him a bit raw, m'lord. But fair. He'll not cheat you."

Pietro was not fearful of that. He was afraid of being torn limb from limb.

◆   ◊   ◆

Before their planned departure the next day, Cesco arranged for a visit to the baths under the Scaligeri palace. "To loosen my frozen limbs. *Mens sana in corpore sano.*"

Detto couldn't help saying, "Perhaps the one will lead to the other."

"Ha! Doubtful. I'll meet you there. I have someplace to call first."

"Where?"

"A place I'd prefer you didn't go. You'll spoil my gardening."

Which Detto took to mean *La Rosa Colta.* He dressed and headed down the stairs, passing as he did the two small trunks that carried Suor Beatrice's worldly goods. She was being installed at the end of the hall on the same floor as Maddelena, her ostensible charge. The lady herself would arrive that night. Just in time for Cesco to vanish from her reach, if only for a week. They'd be back in time for Christmas.

There was singing in the streets, and mimes, and jugglers, all still plying their trades at the Scaliger's expense. It was known that Verona was rich, but even so, this constant flurry of entertainments must have been draining the vaults. Castelbarco, in charge of the city purse, must have been counting the days until Twelfth Night and the end of these extravagances. Fortunately, Verona had investments in arms, in spice, and in wine. Come summer, all of it would come in and refill the depleted coffers.

Below the palace, Cangrande's father had excavated the Roman ruins of a bath. Somehow the knowledge of how to run them had been lost, along with all the other knowledge that had been vanquished by the arrival of the barbarians nearly a thousand years ago. Upon becoming Capitano, one of Cangrande's first acts had been to send to the great ruins at Caldiero down the road, setting his best engineers to reconstructing the place in hopes of reviving at least a piece of Roman greatness.

There was no need at present for the frigidarium, but the calidarium was a popular destination for Verona's elite, where the steam made bodies almost invisible. But first one had to undress and dip into the tepidarium to acclimatize the body to the warmth.

Detto was shirtless and just removing his boots when he spied a figure coming through the steam. Though the face was obscured, he knew the outline. He stopped in mid-tug. "Fut."

Entering the low-ceilinged room filled with ancient pillars and tiles, Bailardino stared at his son. "I was told to meet Cangrande here."

"I was told to meet Cesco." Detto's jaw was clenched so tight, it was hard to speak.

There was a lingering silence as the sound of rushing water and heating pumps gurgled all around them.

"You have something to say to me?" asked Bail.

"No." Detto pulled his boot back into place and stalked from the baths, struggling back into his clothes as he pushed past his sire. Bailardino did nothing to stop his son from departing. When he had gone, Bail sat on a bench and sighed. "Fut."

"Ah, Arabia. I should like to visit there. I am not Christian enough, it seems. I must go Crusading."

Buthayna had known it the moment he had entered *La Rosa Colta*. The young prince had eyes only for her. Sad eyes, angry, full of storms. Full of trouble.

She did not know why she felt such hesitation when considering him in her bed, his skin on hers. Inured to the bad breath, poor hygiene, fat bellies, cruel tempers, and bestial desires of men three times her age, the idea of a handsome young lord should have been a relief. Yet she found herself trembling as she took his hand and led him up the stairs.

Each room in *La Rosa Colta* was done up in a different style.

There was an Egyptian room, and an African, as well as Greek, Roman, French, and Spanish. The girls changed rooms as often as they changed their outfits. But the room assigned to Buthayna was hers alone. The girl called Arabia had sole ownership of the Arabian room. It contained grilles in geometric patterns, gauzy curtains, and hanging chalices of incense, a vulgar parody of her culture.

As she lit the tapers and set the scent wafting, he poured himself some wine. "Do you mind if we speak in your tongue? I get very little practice."

"As my lord pleases."

He switched to Arabic. "Wilt thou enjoy the coming holy days?"

"Yes, my lord."

"Despite not being wholly holy to thee. But thou hast beheld Christ's Mass before?"

"I have."

"I imagine thou were a gift given many times."

Her practiced smile was knowing. "A pleasure for all, my lord."

"I'm sure. Shall we?" He set about disrobing in such a matter-of-fact way, she felt compelled to do the same.

Naked, men's bodies were traitors. His casual tone was belied by his obvious excitement. Yet beyond his erection, he was a series of hard planes and sinewy muscle, thin as a corded whip. She was surprised by the number of scars on his youthful body.

As she took in his appearance, so did he hers. "Very well formed, my Arabia. Shall I bring a Crusade to thy shores?" He came close and kissed her, softly at first, then more fiercely. She twined her arms about him and pressed herself close, as if she were as hungry for his touch as for air.

But in moments her mouth was alone and she was upon her back, gazing at the ceiling in the dim light from the brazier. She tried to slither further up the bed to give him a perch, but he pulled her back to the bed's edge. Kneeling, he pressed his face between her legs. "The Devil's furrow. I'm making a study. My poor attempt to become an expert. Thine is dark and fulsome, with a proud mane like a panther's. I could almost braid it." His voice became muffled as his mouth set to work, yet somehow he continued talking. It sounded like poetry.

Though accustomed to sex, Buthayna was not immune to sensation. She felt one physical reaction she wanted to resist. But she knew she had to perform, so she arched and moaned in pleasure.

Cesco sat up and slapped her thigh, hard. "Stop that. Thou dost behave like a whore."

Startled, she couldn't help an incredulous laugh. "My lord, I *am* a whore."

Fixing on something in his teeth, he worked it with his tongue. "Ah, I forget. Know, whore, I prefer honesty. If I do not please thee, do not act pleased. I will take no offence. Frankly, I'm here for mine own pleasure, not for thine. That's what the coin is for. As the great Abu Bakr says, *'Intentions count in thine actions.'*"

Buthayna's composure slipped a little at hearing the Prophet's companion quoted, in such a setting. But his bluntness was strangely refreshing. "And what are thy intentions, my lord?"

"To lose myself in thee. If thou dost care to join me, welcome. But if thou wouldst rather read, I can call for more light and some books. I know the best poems."

She stared at him in disbelief. Grinning, he started reciting a verse in French, a language she barely knew. She heard the names of God, woman, and the Devil, but very little else that made sense. As he spoke, he pressed himself inside her. Still standing, he held her legs and took himself to his climax, rocking in time with his spoken verse. Buthayna tried to take him at his word, but habit was too ingrained, and she found herself feigning delight as he reached his zenith. Looking down upon her, he laughed and Buthayna felt foolish. He knew she had been feigning.

Collapsing beside her, he sighed happily. "I thank thee, Arabia. A most successful Crusade. I have come to batter at Jerusalem, like the great Titus. Though I left no walls wailing, I hope."

Not understanding, she echoed him. "I thank thee, my lord."

"Does Arabia thank the Crusader? I think not. Except for leaving her alone. Shall I depart?"

"As my lord pleases."

"I shall be pleased to stay awhile, relishing my temporary conquest. After that, I'll return home to see what a shambles I've left behind me. It's what Crusaders do."

Such talk was dangerous for one of her skin. "What was the poem, my lord?"

"The creation of the cunt, dug with the Devil's spade. Everything sounds beautiful in French."

"It is most mellifluous, my lord."

"A mellifluous malevolence, is France." She could hear the sleep in his tone. "Perhaps I should go there. Or to Arabia – the true Arabia. Will she welcome me, do you think? Or must I pay? What coin will she ask?"

"No coin, my lord," she said, stroking his hair in the dim red glow. "All men are free there."

"As I am not. There is a weight that stakes me to this ground. I cannot move, cannot fly, cannot die." She felt him quiver, a stuttered breath. "We are much alike. Neither free, both at the beck and call of men not half our worth. And so very, very alone."

Feeling daring, Buthayna at last said something not scripted for a whore. Another saying of the great Abu Bakr. "*'Solitude is better than the society of evil persons.'*"

He stiffened, and for a moment she feared what would come next. But at last, in a voice thick with unshed tears, he asked, "And what if the evil person is the one in solitude? Is it because he did evil that he is alone?"

Before she could reply he had stood and quickly dressed. There were no jibes now, no cocksure smiles, no disarming quotes. In moments he was gone, leaving her to tidy up herself and the room for whoever next came calling.

Buthayna finally understood the danger he posed. It was not danger to her flesh. It was danger to her soul. For there was nothing more destructive to a professional whore than to fall in love.

♦   ◊   ♦

Detto was pacing Cesco's chamber when the master of the house returned. He heard his cousin's voice on the stairs and, when the door opened, Detto punched him full in the face. "You go too far!"

"*Che cazzo!*" Cesco launched himself at Detto, and the two pummeled at each other with such fury that Maddelena wept and Antonia ordered the servants to fetch buckets of water to douse the pair. Before cold water could be thrown over them, however, Detto had bolted himself in his room, leaving Cesco bleeding in two places and nursing a twisted wrist.

"Fut," said Cesco thickly. Opening the window, he broke off an icicle and pressed it to his swollen lip. "Welcome to the asylum."

"What was that about?" demanded Antonia.

"I thought it would help."

"What?" Antonia's tone was edged as she straightened up the wreckage of the room.

"Detto and Lord Nogarola. I tried to effect a little reconciliation. Obviously I failed."

From stern, Antonia's heart swelled. He was not lost — not yet.

Seeing her expression, Cesco snorted and turned away to stare out the window at the lowering sky. "I wonder if it wouldn't be better that the della Scala and Nogarola families had left their friendship down at the bottom of the well in the *volto dei Centurioni*. Friendship's Tomb, they could call it, and..."

Antonia set down the chair she was righting. "What is it?"

"I know where she is," he said simply.

"Who?"

Cesco shook his head and refused to say more.

♦   ◊   ♦

Pietro slept hard that night in the best bed the taverner owned, which was not particularly good. At dawn he set out gifted with sausage and a stone flask of hot wine. Clearly the man hoped to soon have this famous knight for a neighbour.

Approaching the rustic home nestled into a sloping hill that continued higher behind it, Pietro's feelings of otherworldliness only grew. The tavern-keeper hadn't exaggerated. Far from modern, this was something from a time past, a hard structure for a hard place. The wind whipped around stone walls that rose and rose into defensible positions. Not a castle, but neither was it a *casa*. This was a fortified position behind a long wall, a place where the local farmers and landholders could gather when threatened. The grounds even held a small church, complete with a bell and a graveyard.

Climbing the steep, exposed track up towards the Tiberio estate, Pietro was seen long before he arrived, and he was not surprised as he entered the gated yard to find himself greeted by the master of the house. What did surprise him was the size and shape of the man, whom he had met in passing but never truly noticed. Tiberio was a tall man in his middle fifties with a heavy paunch to his middle and a long bristling beard that jutted in all directions. His white hair was braided into a coil that almost reached his belt-line. Here, among the cold winds and snow-covered earth, he looked like Old Man Winter, wild, fierce, and awful.

Dismounting without invitation, Pietro offered his arm. Tiberio kept his thumbs hooked on his belt. Pietro dropped his arm with more gratitude than resentment — those hands looked fit to break bricks. "Lord Tiberio, the best of the day to you. My name is Pietro Alaghieri. I hear you've got some land for sale hereabouts. I'd like to look it over."

Tiberio stared at him, then jerked his head down the hill. "Down there. I'll have someone show it to you."

Pietro nodded absently, looking around and rubbing his gloved hands together. "Brisk. Could I trouble you for a warm drink before setting out?"

"You're here to talk to the girl," said Tiberio roughly.

Pietro blinked, taken aback by the blunt answer. "I assure you, I'm here to consider buying—"

Tiberio laughed. "I'll bet not. Buy it or don't, as you please. Hell, if that's truly why you're here, I'll give it to you and welcome. You can be on your way." Seeing Pietro's consternation, he bared his brown teeth. "No, that's not why you're here. You're here to bother my wife. Yes, I know all about it. I know she fell for the Greyhound's little son, who promptly threw her over. Little whoremonger. Like father, like son, I guess."

Pietro kept his mouth firmly shut. It made little difference to Tiberio. Words continued to pour forth from that wild beard. "I knew all about it when I married her, and I don't need you poking around in genteel ways and stirring the whole hornets' nest into the air. So piss off and tell the Greyhound and his pup to sniff other asses than ours."

Pietro considered doing just that. But he had promised to check on the girl – he had to at least see her. *Truth is better than lies.* "I'm not here for Cangrande or Francesco."

"The Devil you're not."

"The Devil has nothing to do with it. I'm here for my sister. She's a novice at the convent of Santa Maria in Organo, and she came to look fondly on Rosalia during the aftermath of the earthquake. She would be here herself, but a young nun can't travel alone on a whim. I promised her I would make certain Donna Tiberio was well. You can listen to the whole interview."

"Can I?" glowered Tiberio. "Big of you."

"I mean, there's nothing that is not for your ears. I merely promised my sister I would check on Rosalia's welfare."

Tiberio continued to stare in silence, under the heavy gaze of all his household men and several serving women. At last he said, "You can have five minutes. And for that, you'll buy the land at the price I name."

Unable to argue, Pietro followed Tiberio into the house.

The interior was less raw than the outside would indicate. Pietro noted that much of the furnishings – wall hangings, cushioned chairs, pillows – were new. So at least Tiberio had been kind enough to outfit his home for his bride.

"If she doesn't want to see you, you won't force her."

"Last thing I would want," answered Pietro.

Showing Pietro into his study, Tiberio left him – watched – while he went to fetch his wife. Pietro stood, back straight, hat in his hands, staring at the fire, feeling the warmth on his face. The stone fireplace was carved with five grotesque hooded heads, some with eyes closed, as if they were modeled after decapitated monks.

The door opened behind him. Turning, Pietro felt the bottom fall out of his stomach. Steeling himself, he forced a smile. "Donna Tiberio. A pleasure to meet you."

Rosalia Rienzi *in* Tiberio glided forward across the rushes. She was dressed in a russet panel gown that covered her from neck to toe, almost swallowing her hands. Her hair was hidden, as a married woman's should be. But now that he looked for it, Pietro saw what should have been obvious to the world. *Those eyes...*

Below her chin, on the exposed skin of her throat, hung a coin. The facing side held the image of the old Roman god Mercury. Pietro knew it well. He had found that coin buried in the wood of an ancient bench on the very night Cesco had come into his life. For a few years it had hung about the neck of Pietro's loyal hound, giving him the name Mercurio. When that hound had died saving Pietro and Cesco, the child had taken it as his own. For ten years it had been Cesco's only token, his sole superstition. And he'd given it to her. And she wore it still.

Rosalia extended her hand for him to bend over. "We have met, Ser Alaghieri. When the forge burned, you stayed at my father's estate." Was there a hitch when she said 'my father'?

"Of course. It is lovely to see you again."

"Is it?" She crossed to one of the cushioned stools and lowered herself gracefully. "I thought the silence from Verona was a kindness. But I see now that was merely neglect."

That cut like a knife. Taking a stool not too close to her, he said, "If my presence is unkind, it is my doing alone. No one knows I'm here, save my sister."

He thought he saw her rigid expression soften a little. "How is Suor Beatrice? Is she quite recovered?"

Pietro frowned. "Recovered? I don't know to what you're referring. Has she been ill?"

Lia looked away. "Ah. My mistake. Please thank her for her concern, and tell her I am as well as is possible on this earth."

This was not the first time that Pietro had sensed there was some secret his sister was hiding. But now was not the time to probe that question.

"Donna Tiberio, please forgive an impertinence. Is there any other message I should make? To Fra Lorenzo, perhaps? I understand you knew him while you were in Verona."

"No, I have no message for anyone in Verona. But I do have a question." Her eyes fixed upon him, and the intensity of her gaze made Pietro want to turn away. "Is he happy?"

How blunt. How brave. But what to answer? Should he lie? Would that please her? Or should he craft a non-committal reply, one that could mean anything or nothing?

The answer was already plain upon his face. "No. He is not."

Leaning against the wall, Tiberio grunted. But Rosalia said nothing. Her eyes were clear and bright. There was no look of satisfaction. There was no expression at all, as if she had traveled deep within herself.

Pietro sat, wanting to speak further, to justify Cesco's wild actions, which she'd surely heard about. Speak of his suffering, his rage, his need for revenge. Make him less odious, less wanton.

But in her lack of expression, Pietro saw complete understanding. More than that, he perceived a contained rage of her own. If this visit told Pietro anything, it was that her cause was even greater than Cesco's. She obviously understood every event in Verona these last months, and could even feel compassion for the one person whose pain matched her own.

I shouldn't have come. I've poured salt in an endless wound. There's nothing here that can be healed.

Pietro bowed his head. "I'd best go. Forgive me for disturbing your home. And congratulations on your marriage."

He had started for the door, which Tiberio opened, when Rosalia stood. "Ser Alaghieri. I ask one thing. That you tell no one – not even your sister – what you saw here."

It was as if a fist gripped his throat. "Donna Tiberio, I swear it."

The image that Pietro carried away with him as he rode down the steep track was of her standing there, side-lit by the fire, her hair hidden, her form unmistakable under the long gown.

Donna Tiberio was several months pregnant.

SIXTEEN

AS PLANNED, while the lord of Treviso and his imperial companion approached Verona, Cesco and his Rakehells decamped for the castle of Illasi, where Otto's men were wintering. Close enough to Vicenza to enjoy a city's pleasures but far enough to not engender unease, the two hundred of men in Otto's command were more then amenable to a few days of winter sports.

The mercenary army was a relatively new phenomenon in Italy. For the last two hundred years, men had returned from Crusading with no notion of a life outside warfare. Arriving at the ports in southern Italy, they had taken up residence in the land, despite mostly being German, Spanish, French, Flemish, Catalonian, or even English. At first they had formed *masnade*, bands of brigands, little better than highway robbers. As local cities had no standing armies, it seemed wiser to pay the local *masnada* off. First it was only payment for 'protection'. Then to attack a rival city. Through this had arisen the notion of a contract army, and *condottiero* had come to mean both 'contractor' and 'warlord-for-hire' in command of a *compagnia di ventura*.

Otto the Burgundian was a *condottiero*. Having left his native Bruges for a Crusade that had never taken place, he had spent three years waiting around Brindisi for ships to take him to the Holy Land. When at last he was certain no ships were coming, he took command of the soldiers of his company and decided to make up for those lost three years by extorting money from the local cities that had driven them to poverty during their stay.

That had been twelve years ago. His reputation had grown so swiftly that he had been invited to Lombardy to take part in the Paduan wars, first on the side of Padua. But when Padua could no longer pay, Cangrande had bought his services, and Otto had never had cause to regret the alteration of allegiance. He much preferred fighting on the winning side.

Local men like Yuri and Fabio had joined the *compagnia*, making up for the natural attrition in such a company. Men died, men were wounded, men retired, men ran off. Otto's company of Burgundians were now almost half Italian, many of whom were Veronese. But there were Paduans in his company, as well as Trevisians, Mantuans, Vicentines, Venetians, Pisans, Romans, Florentines — men disaffected with their lot who saw the chance for riches and fame in the military. Without a national army to join, the *condottieri* offered escape for men who longed to do more than push a plow or scribble notes for their masters.

Winter was always a dull time for the company. Though they were not paid as well during these months, as they were not fighting, Cangrande did allow them use of his land to remain and hone their skills. There were some who had wanted to travel south again, to warmer climes. But Otto had remained, sensing that loyalty to Verona would not go unrewarded.

Now, as he rode into the camp alongside the heir, Otto felt both amusement and unease. The unease stemmed from his fear that he would be dragged into the on-going battle between the boy and his sire. The amusement grew from what the boy was wearing.

Cesco arrived at the camp in a fancy gown, his long hair braided under a caul with fake braids sticking out beneath. He was also sporting a black eye and several bruises, which only added to the ridiculousness of his attire. All the other Rakehells were dressed in mock-armour, save Benedick, dressed as red-wigged Guenivere. Ludicrously, neither Cesco nor Benedick had shaved.

Detto was there, dressed as a wizard. Like Cesco, he bore marks of the scuffle. They had not passed a single word on the ride overland, Cesco spending his time baiting Otto, Detto riding silently in the back.

Dropping from his sidesaddle perch, Cesco curtsied to the parade of soldiers. "I am Ninianna, the Lady of the Lake, and I bear a magic sword. I know many of you are practiced in tugging your swords, but to tug this one free you'll have to win the joust we are to hold."

All eyes turned to Otto, who nodded. He had given his approval to this sport. "Yes yes," said Cesco, annoyed, "we have the imprimatur of Sir Owain. Now, Galahad, Lancelot, tell them the rules."

Yuri and Fabio started explaining the details of the joust. Hoisting his excessive fake bosoms into place, Cesco flounced across to Morando Bevilaqua, the best rider in the bunch. "I hear you're after my honour. But can you joust sidesaddle?" A grin cracking the paint on his face, Cesco waved a hand and another dress was produced. Yuri was howling with laughter as Morando embraced the spirit of the day and donned the offered gown.

Lists were constructed with practiced ease, and the day descended into dangerous hilarity. Jousting sidesaddle was insane, but soon all men wished to have a go, and there were many broken heads and arms by the end of the day.

Soon the winter camp of Cangrande's best mercenary army was entirely debauched, for Cesco had ordered a wagon of women to follow them, and for the whole next day they switched from re-enacting the French legends of Arthur to the mad revels of the Saturnalia in ancient Rome under Nero.

Already in a foul mood, Detto had little taste for such things. He was enough of a romantic to want to love a woman, like the poets said, and he was self-aware enough to know he would not respect himself if he succumbed to the fleshly pleasures just for the sake of pleasure itself. It seemed his time in Ser Alaghieri's household had placed more of a stamp on his soul than on Cesco's. Or perhaps he hadn't lost as much.

Striding through the camp filled with singing and shouts in both masculine and feminine registers, Detto waited for a moment when no one would notice he was gone. When at last he was certain his absence would not be remarked upon, he mounted his horse and rode out of the camp, alone. In spite of his anger, he had a task to perform.

✦   ◊   ✦

Still shaken from his visit to Tiberio's estate, Pietro arrived at Morsicato's house in Vicenza for a conference of what he considered Cesco's inner circle. Tharwat was present, and Pietro shook him by the hand as he stamped the snow off his feet. "Have you ever seen the like?"

"Not in the Feltro," replied Tharwat.

Their host ushered them into his study. "You'll have to forgive Esta for not tending to us. She's feeling poorly."

"Again?" asked Pietro. "I'm so sorry."

"Her stomach plagues her at times, but she's well enough." After returning from Ravenna, Morsicato's wife had suffered from some unknown but debilitating illness that kept her husband occupied most of the time, to the detriment of his profession. Suspiciously, the illness had vanished when Cesco had gone off to the Imperial Court. Pietro often wondered if the nurse or someone in the household – a cook perhaps – was on a second paylist belonging to Cangrande, or Mastino, or the like. He'd voiced his concerns, and Morsicato had investigated. But there was no sign that the staff was anything other than what they seemed.

"It looks to be chronic, not poison. At least, it's not in the food they prepare for her. I've been eating what she eats, and I'm fine." The doctor did not sound pleased – he'd have preferred poison to some mysterious disease he could not identify.

As the trio convened over wine, bread, and cheese, Pietro inquired after Donna Katerina's health.

"She's resting comfortably," said Morsicato, wrinkling his nose at the cheese he'd found hanging from a hook in his kitchen. "The lady knows what lies ahead, and she's frustrated not to be past this already."

Once they were settled, Pietro said, "We have several matters to discuss. Tharwat, you've told Morsicato what you discovered in Padua? Good, then maybe we should start by hearing what you learned in Venice."

"Very little," said Tharwat in his low rasp. "The Jew is not feeling helpful towards anyone since his daughter's flight."

The Jew in question was a relative of Manuel, a money-lender called Shalakh who had often done business with Cangrande. He had been mildly helpful in the past, disbursing the secret monies for Cesco's upkeep during their years in Ravenna. At the end of August he had given them the name of the bank in England where Cesco's mother had lodged her money. That same day his daughter had run off with a gentile. His loss had been Cesco's gain – in the search for the missing girl, Cesco had been rescued from the clutches of the villainous Fuchs. An accident of timing, but a happy one.

Now, it seemed, Shalakh's thirst for vengeance was preventing him from aiding them further. "He is obsessed with a lawsuit he is bringing against a merchant who was somehow involved. He would not see me for several days, and when he did he said he knew nothing of the purchase of the house in Padua. He is lying," said Tharwat baldly. "I said the name Amabilio and saw a flicker of recognition.

But he claimed not to remember it. He is hurt, angry, and taking his revenge against anyone who crosses his path."

"Like someone else we know," observed Pietro.

Morsicato was more attentive. "Wait – is this the merchant we saw that day? Antonio something."

"Ansaldo. Antonio Ansaldo, yes. He stood surety for a sizeable loan for his friend, under curious terms. If he did not repay the loan within three months, he would have to give Shalakh—"

"A pound of his flesh," said Morsicato, who had heard the terms of the bargain and had misgivings at the time. Now he felt sick.

Pietro was utterly horrified. "What kind of surety is that? No judge would allow that to stand!"

"Under the laws of Venice, it seems, it is perfectly legal," said Tharwat. "Ansaldo had no fear of failing the bond, and did not take the terms seriously. But it seems his ships failed to return within the allotted time, and he is now in the gaol, his life in the balance. The trial is set for the day after tomorrow. Perhaps when the Jew's vengeance is slaked, he will be more amenable."

"You mean," said Pietro, "after he has killed this man we might be able to get what we're after?"

"Yes," said Tharwat. "You might even go and offer Shalakh legal advice. It would gain his favour."

"Help him commit murder?" demanded Pietro, incredulous.

"Or talk him into accepting the money he is offered. There are many people willing to pay the sum owed."

"And you think Pietro can convince him, when he wouldn't even listen to you?" demanded Morsicato. "Pietro's a Christian. You, at least, are not."

"I serve Christians. He has no sympathy for me. But in truth, I doubt anyone could succeed. Shalakh is determined to extract the penalty of flesh. Only his daughter's return could soothe him, and she has vanished with her Christian husband."

"This is dreadful," said Pietro. "To get the information we need, I'd have to help that little bastard kill a fellow Christian, when what I'd like to do is go and represent this Antonio myself."

"That would ensure we never get the information we require."

"Hang the information," exclaimed Pietro. "This is a man's life!"

There was a moment's pause, then Tharwat said, "It has nothing to do with us. I advise we wait until the trial is decided. Afterwards, whatever the decision, the Jew may be more pliable."

It was an answer that Pietro disliked. "I'm going to Venice

tonight. I'll see what can be done."

Tharwat opened his hands, indicating the decision was not his to make. "Shall we return to the matter of Cesco?"

Pietro had to calm his unsettled head before nodding. "Yes. Cesco's mother. We have a name, at last."

"What does it matter?" asked Morsicato. "He's been legitimized. He's the heir. What does it matter now who his mother was?"

Pietro pressed his lips together. "I feel in my soul that something about her is vitally important. Otherwise why keep it such a mystery?"

"Then start at the beginning. Why did Cangrande take Cesco in?" asked Morsicato.

"Because he's the Greyhound," said Tharwat.

"We didn't have proof of that until recently. How did they know it was him? And why did his mother give him up?"

"That's one question we know the answer to," said Pietro. "She did it to protect him. There was an attempt on his life."

Morsicato grunted. "Made by Donna Katerina, through this cripple. Chess moves, to bring Cesco into her sphere."

"Yes, we are aware of Katerina's motivations," said Pietro, setting aside the moral implications — they had debated them many times over the years. "She wanted to fulfill her destiny to raise the Greyhound. But Cangrande had no such desire. For him, if Cesco lived in ignorance and ignominy, all the better. So why bring Cesco into his household and acknowledge him publicly?"

"You mean why Cesco and not one of his other bastards?" Chewing his beard, Morsicato pointed a thoughtful finger. "There's a question. Barto is older."

Pietro turned. "Tharwat?"

The Moor frowned. "I was asked to make charts for the boy two months after his birth. They were already fixed upon him. I was not consulted about the Scaliger's other natural children."

"So even before the charts were made, he was important," mused Pietro. "I remember three years ago hearing them discuss some arrangement between Cangrande and Donna d'Amabilio. Whatever it was, it had strength enough to bind him."

"Love?" suggested Morsicato.

Pietro pulled a wry face. "Does it seem likely? If the Scaliger fell in love, he'd keep his lover close. And he'd have been more upset when she disappeared. No, there's something about this woman that we aren't meant to know. We still don't know her true name. Amabilio was her husband, I presume. So who was she? Royalty?

Someone's sister or daughter?"

Tharwat cleared his throat. "I am willing to travel to England to look into this bank. But it will take time."

Pietro shook his head. "We need you here. Because there's something more pressing to attend to."

"Cesco's behavior," grunted Morsicato.

"Yes. He's lashing out. Amusing and clever, but destructive."

"Subversive," said Tharwat. "We must find a channel for his anger."

"How?" asked Morsicato. "He's a knight now, not a squire. Everybody knows he's the heir. Nobody but the Capitano can rein him in, and so far Cangrande hasn't done a damn thing."

"He's tried," said Pietro. "Cesco's got quite a following — not just Detto and the rest of the young men, but among the older soldiers. He's out at Otto's camp right now, wooing them. Cangrande can't quash Cesco without alienating his *condottieri*, and he needs them for Treviso in the spring."

"Besides," added Morsicato, "short of murdering the boy or locking him in a cell, what could stop him? He's got the rage up, and like you said, Tharwat, he's bent on taking his revenge against anyone who crosses his path. It's a miracle that no one has died yet."

"It is up to us," rasped the Moor. "We must try to mend him."

"Is he a tool that's broken?" asked Morsicato.

"Others see him as just that. Which is the problem."

Pietro waved this aside, trying not to remember the smiling, happy young man he'd brought to Verona three summers ago. "How do we reach him? I've tried the direct approach. Every time I make to talk to him, I'm met with a wave and smile and he's gone, surrounded by his Rakehells."

"Could be worse," said Morsicato, chuckling in spite of himself. "They could pelt you with urinated snowballs, the way they did that band of Paduan minstrels."

"If I call at his house," continued Pietro, "he's not home."

"Would you be," asked the doctor, "with a five year-old wife, her nurse, her maid, and a whole gaggle of women waiting for you?"

"You can't really be defending him?" demanded Pietro.

"No," said Morsicato evenly, "but I don't believe this is as dark as you seem to think. It might even be healthy. He's a young man — not even, he'll be a man next summer. If not for this knighthood and the marriage, he'd still be under Cangrande's roof and none of this happening. But he's got a taste of what he's always craved — freedom. Can you blame him for going a little wild?"

"You've changed," observed Pietro. "You used to be the one against letting his reins slip."

Morsicato shrugged. "Just observing a fact."

"That might have been true — this could be just adolescent rebellion writ large — but for his sudden taste for wine. And," Pietro shot a glance at the Moor, "for the hashish."

Pietro expected the doctor to begin raging. He had been furious when he'd discovered Tharwat was supplying the boy with small amounts of hashish to give him strength and clarity, a skill passed on from the Moor's own youth. For the last two years, much against his will, the doctor had been forced to make the little sticky brown wafers for their ward.

But the doctor looked strangely smug, even as the Moor defended his decision. "It is a discipline. I thought over-indulgence it was a lesson he had learned. If this was a mistake, it was mine."

Morsicato grinned. "The good news is that we don't need to fear that much. Ever since I took control of his doses, I've reduced the amount of the hashish a little each month. At the same time, I've continued with the other herbs — ginger root, anise, laurel, basil, tansy — as well as nightshade, hellebore, monkshood and even a small amount of hemlock."

"You're poisoning him?" demanded Pietro.

"Building his tolerance for poisons, actually. As long as he eats the wafers in moderation, he'll be resistant to ever being poisoned again."

Now it was Tharwat's turn to look angry. "You fool."

Morsicato's barrel chest swelled. "I'm the fool? I'm not the one who started him eating—"

"You reduced the hashish. But his eyes proclaim him a lotus-eater, or so swears Fra Lorenzo."

Morsicato made a rude noise. "What does a friar know about medicine?"

"A good deal, according to Antonia," said Pietro. "She's told me about a theory he has, that plants are like men, good and evil in one."

"Not very original."

Tharwat clapped his hands for attention, then spoke in a very low, measured tone. "Doctor — by reducing the hashish, you have thrown the mixture out of balance. He will not feel the relief the herb brings."

"And he will be weaned off of it!" stated Morsicato triumphantly.

"No," said the Moor. "He will just eat more of it, chasing the clarity and energy he had before. And poison himself in the bargain."

The doctor blanched. Pietro stared at them both. "So now he's being poisoned by us."

In his gravest tone, Tharwat said, "Doctor, I need you to show me your current mixture, and we must consult on how to revise it in the future."

"Why not just stop giving it to him?" asked Pietro.

It was Morsicato who answered. "If he *has* been over-indulging, it would do more harm than good. He cannot just stop. I was trying to wean him off the filthy stuff, which is the way to do it. I told him how often he should take it…"

"But being Cesco, he's hardly going to follow rules. Especially after Lia." Pietro closed his eyes. "Our meddling does more harm than good. It's a wonder he's still alive."

"So we ply him with better distractions than the ones he has chosen," said Tharwat.

"Pity the war won't start again for months," said Morsicato. "Nothing like a war for a young man. But races and contests seem to amuse him. Shall we invent more?"

"He can do that himself," said Pietro. "I want to engage his mind."

"It's not his mind that's broken," said Tharwat. "It's his heart."

They sat for a time, looking blankly at one another, bereft of ideas.

"Normally I'd say find him a wife," said Morsicato.

"He has one," said Pietro.

"A lover then. Someone to dedicate himself to. To do great deeds for. Turn chivalry into something useful."

Pietro shook his head. "Too soon."

"Well, at least we can address the medicine. I have an idea that will solve everything."

"Excellent." Pietro rose. "While you do that, I'll ride to Venice."

"And do what?" asked Tharwat.

"I'll know when I get there."

The Moor was grave, but understanding. "You are a good man, who cannot see an injustice without intervening." He paused. "You may see Girolamo. If he asks, will you deliver a message for me? Tell him I have not yet secured the lady's permission."

"Permission for what?" asked Morsicato gruffly.

"To join me here. To become my apprentice." Both Pietro and Morsicato exclaimed their surprise, and Tharwat explained, "The

Scaliger is not the only man who thinks of his legacy."

Morsicato was swearing, but Pietro put their mutual objection in plain terms. "Why would you take in a murderer?"

Tharwat shook his head. "He did not commit murder."

"He tried to kill Cesco!"

"Had he done that, doctor, I would not let him live. But he did not reach the point of attempting it. Intention is not action. Who knows what he would have done when he had arrived that house? All I know is that the stars have put him in our orbit, and he has much to offer. In exchange, I mean to teach him. If I read the stars right I have only a little longer on this earth. And Cesco will soon be leaving our orbits. I want someone to carry on when I am gone, someone to read the stars and help as best he can."

That dire statement elicited a fresh round of protests, though these were more muted. "You've seen your death?" asked Morsicato.

"What do you mean, leave our orbits?" demanded Pietro.

"Ser Alaghieri, you recall the night you rescued Cesco from Pathino from the cave?"

"Am I likely to forget it? I still have nightmares. More since Pathino's death. I think he wanted me to do the deed so he could haunt me."

"I told you then that I had seen the intersection of your life and the boy's. That you were meant to raise him, mold him, give him a foundation for his life."

"Yes." Pietro recalled the conversation all too clearly. It was just after his illusions about Cangrande and Katerina had been shattered, before he'd called upon the raving Count of San Bonifacio. "You also said you had seen your own death. On the chart with the twin stars."

"Yes. If that chart is correct, I do not have much longer here. No, doctor, it is not at hand. I may have a year or more. Before it comes, there is a divergence."

Pietro frowned, parsing that statement. "A divergence."

"Yes. Your influence over the boy is coming to an end. Your line and his part ways."

Chilled, Pietro puzzled over that statement and its possible meanings. "Do I die? Does he?"

Tharwat shook his head. "Not for many years. But recent events have shown which of his charts is more likely true. Both remaining charts indicate a break from you."

"And from you?"

"For a time. Ours realign more swiftly than yours."

"But they do realign?"

"On one chart, yes. Briefly."

"You're certain?" demanded Pietro.

Tharwat opened his hands. "This is Cesco. His stars are as tricky as he himself."

"So you don't really know anything."

Tharwat ran his hands over his head. "I may be mistaken, of course. But you should be prepared."

Pietro wanted to protest, debate, argue. But how did one argue with the heavens? *A man may control his actions, but not his stars.* Still he had to ask, "Why?"

Tharwat shook his head. "He is in rebellion. And what is more natural than to rebel against your father?"

Pietro took several slow, deep breaths. "Thank you for that. Is there nothing I can do?"

"Wait. Watch. Be yourself. All will unfold as the stars dictate."

Pietro did not like the sound of that. So far the stars had been remarkably unkind.

◆　◇　◆

Not far off, in the palace of Vicenza, Detto climbed the stairs to the room set aside for his mother's convalescence. He hesitated at the door, feeling conflicted. A dog wandered up and he knelt to pet it. Over the edge of the low balcony he looked down into the open central atrium with the fountain of the three muses. He remembered playing in that fountain with Cesco on their first arrival together, when all the secrets were revealed. He had been so happy, then. How had things gone so badly?

"Oh!" Emerging from the sickroom, the nurse was startled to see her mistress' son. "Ser Bailardetto! She'll be so pleased to see you."

"I'm sure." Rising from the happy dog rolling on the tiled floor, Detto entered.

As a boy, he had feared this room. Now he found himself resenting it. His mother's first stroke had occurred when he was little, nearly seven years earlier. Half his life, then, he had known her to have that twisted face, slack and expressionless on the left, fierce and beetling on the right.

Donna Katerina was propped up in bed, surrounded by distractions – a chess match half-completed, a book, papers, quill, and ink on a small tray. Being confined was a terrible thing for an active mind.

"A welcome early Chrish*t*mas gift. Come and tell me tale*sh* from the court."

Obediently Detto sat in the nurse's vacated chair and told her about the talk from Verona. When she inevitably asked of Cesco, Detto was brief, mentioning the contests without speaking of anything more personal.

After a time, Katerina lifted a hand. He took it. "Detto – my mortality i*sh* on my mind. My body i*sh* weak. If it fail*sh* me, if I am not here, there i*sh* shomething you mu*sh*t do for me."

"Anything, mother."

Minutes later Detto was outside, clambering back onto his horse. It was the middle of the day, and he pelted out of the gates of Vicenza with tears in his eyes. He did not turn back towards Illasi.

SEVENTEEN

From the moment they entered his city, Cangrande embraced Guecello Tempesta and Berthold von Neifen as long-lost brothers, throwing them into revel after revel. For the last two days they and their companions had been run through a gauntlet of hunts, jousts, dances, concerts, plays, acrobatics, and feasts, feasts, feasts. Whenever they tried to gain a private audience, they found the Capitano di Verona unavoidably detained elsewhere.

Utterly flummoxed, the two men began to appreciate Cangrande's strategy. As there were not yet any open hostilities between Verona and Treviso, there was no means to force the issue without Treviso itself declaring war. Tempesta was tempted, but he knew his own people would revolt if he were perceived to be dragging the Greyhound to their gates.

Berthold had thought to goad the Scaliger to take offence by bringing Riccardo Annibaldi, a Roman who had insulted Cangrande before the emperor. But the master of Verona was too wily to take that bait, and got in first by repeating the story before Riccardo could mention it, thus making himself the butt of the joke.

Another element added to the potion was Cangrande's invitation of his cousin-in-law Rizardo to join them. Rizardo da Camino was of the famous family Tempesta had helped overthrow to gain control of Treviso. His marriage to Cangrande's niece had promised a foothold in the city. A promise denied by Tempesta's coup.

The inclusion of Rizardo in their company could have easily

been an insult, a possible opportunity for Tempesta to pick a quarrel that would incite the argument he was here to have. But Cangrande had invited Rizardo so that he might belittle him, mock him, give him such a tongue-flaying that he could hardly stand for shame. "Thank the Virgin that it was you who took Treviso's reins, Gueccello! Can you imagine if Rizardo here had inherited? The city would be a crater, smited by God above for pure ineptitude. Though I cannot commend you for foisting him off on me. It was most unkind. Family! Such a wretched bother."

It was all so skillfully done, Berthold acknowledged the Scaliger's victory by announcing his intent to return to Rome. Losing his protection, Tempesta had no choice but to prepare his own departure as well, his hopes for independence utterly dashed. Killed through kindness.

◆　◇　◆

"Say, Otto," said Cesco, leaning against the tree. "Who's the best rider in the company?"

"Me," said Otto.

"Hmm. Who after you?"

"Morando Bevilaqua."

"Hm. And after him?"

"Yuri."

"I believe Morando is a sporting man."

Otto gave a sidelong glance. "If there's enough money in it. What do you propose?"

"A race, you against Yuri, Bevilaqua against me. The winning pair to race each other."

There was no hint of interest in Otto's expression. "The prize?"

"I don't know – enough to make it worth it, not enough to race dirty."

Otto thought for a moment. "Winner gets his pick of the loser's horses."

"Is that enough?" asked Cesco.

Otto shrugged. "Throw in gold if you want."

"Agreed. What do you say?"

Otto glanced at the sky. "Hard on the horses in this weather."

"Short course, then."

"Not much skill in a short course."

Cesco threw up his hands. "Then forget the whole thing! I just wanted a little diversion."

Otto made a snorting sound. "Short course, quick turns, no

saddle, hands tied."

"Bridle?"

"Yes."

"Spurs?"

"No."

"Done!"

Informed, the two other racers agreed at once. Both had eyes for Abastor, sleek and black and beautiful. As the track was laid out, word passed through the rest of the *compagnia* and all arrived in time to watch the first race between Otto and Yuri.

Both were excellent riders, not more than a hair's difference between them. Otto won, but only just. He accepted the cheers with his usual indifference, which made his men cheer all the more.

Next came Cesco and Morando Bevilaqua. They knew each other only a little from hunting and the previous day's mock joust. Bevilaqua was twice Cesco's age, and though there was no shame in losing to a prince, he was eager to win.

The flag fell and both men kicked. Bevilaqua rode with all the tricks of an experienced rider – not dangerous, not even mean-spirited, just the common bumping and jostles. Once he 'accidentally' kicked Abastor's mouth, forcing Cesco to miss a crucial turn.

Cesco had tricks of his own. He hadn't forgotten the months of secret practice learning the skills of the *jighitovka*, and he'd picked up more from the acrobats at the imperial court. Without a saddle to hold him, he clung on to Abastor's side as the horse bolted under a low branch and then leapt a stone fence to regain the lead to win.

Bevilaqua came over to congratulate him, grinning ruefully. "I don't know who's more envious, me or my horse. She wishes she had such a rider!"

The final race occurred under the eyes of Otto's whole army. Yuri dropped a flag and Cesco and Otto bolted forward, neck and neck. There were no tricks, no ploys, just hard riding. Otto took the same course Cesco had around the track, it being clearly the shortest, so there was no difference between them as they rounded the final turn and headed towards the finish line.

Suddenly Abastor seemed to lose wind, and Cesco sagged for a moment, allowing Otto to win by a head.

They were cheered and feted. But when it came time for him to take his prize, Otto refused. "Keep your horse."

"But you won!" protested Cesco.

"I don't like charity," groused Otto.

As they were out of general hearing, Cesco ducked his head. "I did it for me, not you. Treviso is coming, and I want the respect of the men. But not so much that they resent me. So help me by taking the damn horse."

Otto studied Cesco for a long moment, his face betraying nothing. "The men are impressed enough. Keep your horse. With it all tricked-out, I couldn't satisfy it. Like bedding Cleopatra — after Caesar, who can compare?"

Cesco grinned. "Why, Otto — that was positively loquacious!"

The Burgundian's expression did not change at all. "Not for you."

◆　◇　◆

It was nearly thirty miles from Vicenza to Venice by the main road. Pietro stopped in Padua for the night, something he could not have done just six months earlier. He dined with Petruchio's father-in-law, the cheerful Baptista Minola, who was concerned for his grandsons Petruchio and Hortensio. "These sports they indulge in with the young prince — they sound dangerous." Pietro did his level best to assuage the old man's fears, refraining from voicing his own.

Arriving in Venice at noon the next day, Pietro found himself at a loss. What was he doing here? Venice had judges and lawyers aplenty. And any meddling he did would hurt his chances of tracing Cesco's mother. But it was like a physical pull, the tug of action. He needed to come to the aid of this man, so unjustly imprisoned and likely to receive an even more unjust end. Pietro wondered if it made him a good man, as Tharwat said, or a foole? *A man can be more than one thing.*

He considered going first to the Yellow Crescent, but rejected the notion almost at once. He was not deluded enough to think he had the means to dissuade Shalakh from his grotesque revenge. Instead he turned towards the gaol, which stood beneath the Doge's palace. A place he knew intimately.

To his surprise, he was admitted. He tried to still his quaking knees as he descended into the basement where he had spent three months as a prisoner. He was astonished at how very afraid of the place he was, as if the stones, remembering the one who had escaped, would swallow him up and reclaim the man who had gotten away.

Antonio Ansaldo's cell was nicer than Pietro's had been. He was permitted light, heat, blankets, bed, even books. Pietro felt a stab of resentment that he schooled into gratitude — no one should have to endure what Pietro had. Certainly rats would not trouble this man.

Ansaldo was also allowed visitors. At the moment he was enjoying the company of a lean, provocative man with an odd style of hair, balding in the front and long in the back. Introductions were made. Pietro shook Ansaldo's hand, then the lean man's, who was called Salerio.

It was the latter who said, "Forgive me, Ser Alaghieri, if I seem ungracious, but why are you here?"

Pietro was bald in his answer. "I came to offer whatever assistance I can provide. If money will help, that I'll give and gladly. If you require legal advice, I have acted as a judge in Vicenza and argued cases successfully before the Papal Court."

Rather than answer, Salerio turned to Ansaldo, pointing at Pietro. "You see? Here's a man unknown to you, yet willing to plead your case. Word is that the Doge has sent to the famous Bellario in Padua to argue on your behalf! They're all willing to fight! Why aren't you?"

"I have offered Shalakh gold." Ansaldo's voice was calm, almost serene. "He wants my life. There is nothing at law to say he cannot have it."

"Bassanio arrives tonight!" exclaimed Salerio. "What kind of a welcome is this, to discover his closest friend willing to die for a debt incurred in his name!"

For the first time, Antonio looked alive. "Was he successful? Did he win the lady's hand?"

Salerio was astonished and frustrated at once. "Not only her hand but her love! He says they are married, and he could not be more joyful in her. And you mean to soil the gloss of their marriage by going willingly to this yellow devil's revenge?"

But Antonio merely smiled. "If Bassanio is happy, my life is a fair price. Ser Alaghieri, sit, please. Talk to me about your father. I've never read his *Commedia*, and it seems now I will never find the time."

It was a strange afternoon, with Salerio urging Ansaldo to fight, while the condemned man plied Pietro with questions of poetry, especially on the structure of the sonnet. For his part, Pietro tried several times to address the matter at hand, only to find himself skillfully forestalled. It was as if the merchant wanted to die.

It was late evening when more visitors arrived, stains of travel still on their persons. Antonio arose at once to throw his arms about a tall man with dark hair and a strong chin. "Bassanio! I wish you all joy of your marriage!"

"Joy?" cried Bassanio, clutching his friend's shoulders. "How can I feel joy seeing you in this place for a debt that is mine. I should be in here, not you!"

"Your wife would not approve of that, I think," said Antonio, though he was smiling.

Two other men were introduced, Gratiano and Solanio. They pleaded with Pietro to argue Ansaldo's case in spite of his wishes. "If Bellario does not come, I will," he promised them.

"I thought you said you had done business with the Jew," answered Antonio. "I do not want to put you in a position to hurt your interests."

"Justice is more important than personal interest." From another man it would have sounded pompous – Pietro felt like an idiot saying it. But the others seemed to accept his earnest intent.

Antonio was earnest only in his questioning of Bassanio, cajoling from him a detailed description of his wooing of the maid of Bellamonte. They heard of her beauty, of her biting wit, of her description of her previous suitors, mocking them all. "If I had not loved her image, I would have loved her for her mind – how she made me laugh! But after several days of talk, it was time to face the test, the trial set down by her father. If I had delayed any longer, I could not have bourne it, the uncertainty. She felt much the same, but was fearful, lest I should choose poorly and be banished forever from her sight."

"Little chance of that." Gratiano grinned. "The fix was in."

"Fix?" asked Antonio.

"She was determined he would be her husband," explained Gratiano, "so she helped him with the riddle of the caskets."

"I would have guessed correctly in any case!" protested Bassanio.

Gratiano shook his head. "What, and insult her?"

"What was the riddle?" asked Pietro.

"Three caskets, one of gold, one of silver, and one of lead. The task was to guess which one contained her image."

"I guessed correctly," mumbled Bassanio mulishly. "Without her help."

Gratiano barked out a laugh. "It surely didn't hurt that, while you were making up your mind, she sang a song in which every line ended in a rhyme for 'lead'!"

While the others joined him in laughter, Bassanio protested, "I wasn't even listening to the song!"

"So you find your maid leaden?" chided Salerio.

"A base metal for Base-anio," teased Gratiano.

"Women always enjoy being called base," agreed Solanio.

Antonio waved them off. "If Bassanio says he guessed on his own, he did. Do not question him."

It came to Pietro that he did not much like Bassanio, or indeed any of Antonio's friends. But they were devoted enough to him, and spent a good portion of the evening abusing the Jew in terms that had even Pietro frowning. As Verona had a thriving Hebrew population, he had too much experience of individual Jews, and never credited stories of well-poisoning or of the use of lepers to spread disease among Christian lands. Yes, Shalakh was behaving as a devil now, and had always been abrasive in all his dealings with Pietro. But a race should not be judged by a single representative. Nor was it fair to condemn them for excelling in the one occupation they were allowed under the law, that of usury.

Antonio himself was vitriolic in his hatred of Jews. Which made Pietro wonder how he had ever permitted himself to fall into the power of a man he clearly despised. As he watched, a suspicion began to form.

At last the gaoler came, politely requesting the visitors to depart. Bassanio protested, but Antonio told his friend to leave. "My fate awaits me."

"I'll be there tomorrow," said Bassanio at once. "I promise you, I won't let him harm you. If I have to kill the Jew myself, I'll do it and gladly."

"You won't," declared Antonio at once. "You will not die for me. I am not afraid of what tomorrow brings. But I will be happy to see you there. Come, and bear witness. I ask nothing more."

As the others took their leave, Pietro told the gaoler to give him five minutes more. "I have legal advice I must impart."

The gaoler remembered Ser Alaghieri well from his time here, he consented – he had treated the knight roughly in those long-past days, and was clearly uncomfortable facing someone he had kicked when down.

Alone, Pietro chose his words carefully. "Signor Antonio, I spy one hope. There is a defence no one mentioned. One that can exempt you from all penalty from this bond."

Antonio Ansaldo looked up in milder surprise than one would expect from a drowning man thrown a rope. "What is that?"

"There is a law unique to Venice. One that excuses a man from all deeds – not a blanket of immunity, but a mitigating factor. If proven, it renders a man legally out of his senses. If we could prove you were out of your senses when you signed that bond, the Doge would have reason enough to nullify it."

"Out of my senses," repeated Antonio softly. "I think I know the law you mean."

"Yes. In Venice, a man is less culpable for a crime if he commits the crime for love."

"For love," repeated Antonio. "How would that apply to me?"

Pietro said nothing, just waited for the merchant to meet his gaze. When at last Antonio did, his eyes were full of tears. "Is it so obvious?"

"I don't think any of your friends know, if that's what you mean," said Pietro. "It was obvious to me, but sometimes outside eyes are able to see what familiar ones are blind to."

The tears remained, unfalling. His lip trembled. "What good will it do, to speak? It would humiliate him, possibly even repulse him."

"You'd rather die than speak the truth?"

"I'd rather go to my death knowing I have his good will and friendship than live with his disgust and disdain." And from that position the merchant of Venice could not be budged.

As the gaoler returned, Pietro made one last attempt. "Will you at least let me represent you?"

"Only if you vow never to mention what we just discussed, now or after my death. Otherwise I will have you barred from the proceedings."

Pietro shook his head. But he understood, and before departing he gave his word. He left the cells feeling a deep despair. How terrible to love, and not be able to say so.

Is that not like Cesco and Lia? Like my own feelings for Donna Katerina? How could God allow such feelings to grow?

It struck Pietro that all the sorrows of the world came from men loving where they should not.

♦   ◊   ♦

"What shall we do tomorrow?" asked Salvatore at the camp in Illasi.

"Not drink," said Cesco, whose head was swimming. After the race he had tried to match Yuri cup for cup, but had not the head and had ended in spewing, much to the amusement of the mercenaries.

"Are there diversions to be had?" asked Rupert.

"Detto would know," said Berto. "He's from these parts. Where is he?"

"In Vicenza, I imagine," said Cesco dismissively. "Paying his filial respects."

"Detto?" demanded Barto, cuffing Berto on the ear. "Why ask him, when we have two Paduans sitting right here. What about it, Benedick? Salvatore? Where is the best sport hereabouts? What deviltry can we get into?"

Benedick and Salvatore exchanged glances. "The Euganei Hills offers good hunting," suggested Benedick.

"Been hunting," said Cesco. "Next!"

"There are also several ancient spas up there," offered Salvatore. "The *Terme Euganee*. We could try to get one working..."

Cesco was not interested in baths. "That's work, not play. Next!"

"We could sneak into the Citadella's walls," offered Benedick, referring to the walled city that had been a thorn in Verona's paw all through the war.

"And do what, raise the ladder and hound banner? It already flies. There is no joy conquering people who wish to be conquered. Next!"

"What about Correzzola?" asked Salvatore.

"Where?" asked Rupert.

"The Benedictine court at Correzzola," supplied Benedick, a little unwillingly.

"Sport? Benedictines?" Rupert was dubious.

"What they've built there is nothing short of miraculous. A whole community devoted to the poor. Farming, vintning, bread making, even horse breeding – all performed by the poor, for their own benefit. Some learn a trade to take into the world, some live there forever, working for their keep."

"In all the years of war, they've never been raided?" asked Rupert.

"Who would dare?" retorted Hortensio. "No one wants to incur the wrath of the Church."

"Uh-oh." His twin nudged him. "That's what you shouldn't have said. Our fearless prince has that gleam in his eye..."

Indeed he had. Everyone waited in gleeful expectation to see what mischief Cesco's fertile and agile brain invented.

♦   ◊   ♦

Exiting the Doge's palace, Pietro spied a familiar figure, one so incongruous that he was startled into exclaiming aloud. "Detto?"

In quiet conversation, Detto spun about, as astonished as Pietro. "Ser Alaghieri! What are you doing here?"

"I came to offer aid to a condemned man. What brings you

here? I thought you were with Cesco in Illasi."

As the other man bowed his departure, Detto's expression was so furtive, so guilty, that his answer was almost lost on Pietro's ears. "I had a message to deliver."

"To whom?"

Detto frowned, then shook his head. "I cannot say. I'm sorry."

Pietro's concern was doubling each second. He knew the face of the other man, had seen it before. "Does it have to do with Cesco? Is he here?"

"No," said Detto. "He's fine. I'm leaving to rejoin him in the morning."

"Well – come and dine with me, at least. I haven't eaten all day." Perhaps he could sound the young man out over food.

"Forgive me, no. I have to meet someone." Detto hurried off, leaving Pietro more disturbed in thought than he had ever been when a prisoner in this palace. For the man Detto had been talking to was Zanino. Dandolo's son and factor.

◆   ◇   ◆

As Berthold bade the Scaliger a final goodnight, he expressed his surprise at the absence of Verona's heir. "Ser Franz is so very skilled in such delights, so inventive, I fear these revels were incomplete without him. Rupert certainly thinks him a marvel. "

"I'm sorry to hear you were in any way dissatisfied," replied Cangrande with polite dismay. "Please stay, if you can! Cesco has taken himself off to entertain my army, though I imagine he's testing his mettle against theirs. You know young men, always eager for the next war, for advancement! But he'll be back soon enough, and I'm certain he would be delighted to see you eye to eye."

Berthold's polite smile became momentarily fixed. For forty-eight hours he had endured references to the mythical cyclops, to Odysseus, who blinded that same creature, to the Norse Odin, even been forced to watch a group of players perform *Oedipus Rex*. He had endured, knowing his taunting came from being outmaneuvered.

Cangrande turned to embrace Tempesta. "Guecello, my friend, I only wish you could remain longer. Verona's sole desire is to murder you – with joy! I swear, the next time we meet, I will besiege you with such sports that you'll find yourself begging for mercy."

Heading to their lavish rooms in the guest palace, Tempesta's gripes and pleas ringing in his ears, Berthold told himself that the Scaliger could have whatever victories he wanted now. His day was almost over. The boy Franz was the future. And one way or another, Franz would belong to the Emperor. Rupert would see to that.

♦　◊　♦

Rupert was at that moment engaged in an argument over a woman. Salvatore had brought a wench to camp, and Rupert was attempting to woo her away from the Paduan. When she refused, he was incensed — he was an imperial prince! How dare she choose a nobody Paduan over him?

The matter was settled when Salvatore volunteered to escort her from camp and expel her into the night. Rupert was gratified, and soon regretted his outburst. The two remained together, drinking and singing, through the night, while the rest of the Rakehells enjoyed themselves in their tents with less contentious companions.

♦　◊　♦

Back in the Scaligeri palace, Berthold would have been gratified to hear Cangrande's words to Castelbarco.

"Was it deliberate, do you think? Did he offer me the means to rid myself of this unwelcome embassage? Why not stay, then? He delights in thwarting me. Why not create the peace himself and take the credit this time? Instead he suggests a way to prevent peace from being achieved, allowing me to carry on as I planned. He even removes himself from the board so that I might carry out his design."

"The design was yours," said Castelbarco, who had been intimately involved in the forced entertainments of the last two days.

"He knew what he was doing, planting that seed. But then, I should have seen it for myself. Never give them a reason to protest, nor any opportunity to talk in private. Kill them with kindness. It's how I should have treated the Emperor when he came begging. Ah well. Live and learn. But Cesco! What is he up to?"

Castelbarco shrugged. "Perhaps he doesn't want peace."

Arrested, Cangrande's eyes widened at Castelbarco. Then he laughed. "I'm a fool! I thought it was about me. But no, you're correct, he's just looking for a fight. He has assured that Verona will go to war with Treviso. It's that simple."

But with Cesco, nothing was ever simple.

EIGHTEEN

The Road to Padua
Saturday, 17 December 1328

THEY LEFT LONG BEFORE DAWN, all ten of them abandoning their horses just a few miles south of Padua and transferring to a shoddy cart pulled by a pair of ancient horses that swayed when they stood still. Of the regular cast of Rakehells, only Paride, Thibault, and Detto were absent. Though Benedick was wishing he was elsewhere at present. "What's the sport in this?" he asked again as the cart rolled tremblingly for the southeast.

"Fooling them," said Cesco at once.

"Into giving alms to those in no need of them? That's un-Christian."

"*You* need them," said Rupert at once. Benedick's poverty was always a source of amusement to the German prince, who had never lacked funds in his life. "We could say we're collecting a fund for your future."

Benedick laughed with the rest, but it was hollow. The truth was that he had been to Correzzola before, with an empty belly and only lint in his purse. Without a horse, with only a sword, he had been forced to rely upon the generosity of the Benedictine monks at Correzzola for two whole months. They had been unfailingly kind, utterly without judgment, and it seemed poor sport to go and trick them out of aid that could be given to the deserving.

Shame kept Benedick from mentioning his time there, though there was every chance he would be recognized today. He would have to bluff then, or else confess. He didn't know which would hurt more.

Evidently Cesco saw something in his expression that bespoke the feeling, if not the cause. "There is no shame in not being rich. I haven't earned a groat in my life, and if Rupert has ever done an honest day's labour, I'll eat his hat."

Rupert took offence. "God gives to those He knows deserve. And those who take for themselves."

A chorus of voices cried out, "Take it in the face!"

Cesco wagged a finger. "Benedick here isn't cautious when it comes to the main chance. Tell them, *Signore*, of how you ended up with the horse of the Count of San Bonifacio."

Heads came up. Benedick recalled sharing that tale on the night he had met a young knight called Franz, and wished he hadn't — it was not the height of honour. But dutifully he told the tale of how Cangrande had tricked Marsilio da Carrara into thinking that Count Vinciguerra da San Bonifacio had betrayed the Paduan army in Vicenza. "He had dressed someone in the Count's armour to aid the Veronese hidden within the city. Carrara was convinced that the Count was a traitor, and when he came across the real Count during the retreat, Carrara cut him down. He fell from the saddle, bleeding badly. There was no help to be had, so I leapt into his saddle and saved his mount. An excellent steed." Benedick frowned. "Come to think of it, that mount died for Carrara as well. He took it from me during the Denti uprising, and it died under him — despite my best efforts. So in effect, he killed both the Count and his horse."

It was Salvatore that asked, "Who was it in the Count's armour? And where did they get his armour in the first place?"

"I suppose there's no harm in it now," said Cesco. "Carrara knows. No reason the world should not. It was Ser Pietro Alaghieri, who suffers a limp similar to the Count's and so could mimic his stance in the saddle."

"And his armour was captured a few years earlier, at the First Battle of Vicenza," said Petruchio. "Father told us the tale."

"Often," agreed Hortensio. "It appears the cowardly Count stripped it off and ran for his life, and Cangrande kept it safe until he needed it to amuse his enemies."

"I'm sure they were amused," said Salvatore softly.

Cesco elbowed the Paduan genially. "Now now! The war is over! Inferior as you Paduans proved, we are new allies, and can combine to defeat the true dolts of the world, the Germans!"

Both Paduans and Rupert all howled and the wrestling began, shaking the cart. Cesco ended pinned beneath Benedick and Rupert, one sitting on his head, the other punching him repeatedly in the ribs, just as they entered the unwalled confines of the monastery of Correzzola.

♦   ◊   ♦

Venice

After an unsettling night's sleep, full of that same dream again, Pietro woke early and dressed in his formal lawyer's robes of deep green, then set out for the Doge's palace. It was a chill morning, with mist rising from his mouth and his toes aching inside his boots.

There was already a crowd, one that filled all of the Piazza San Marco, and Pietro was barred from entering the palace by the sheer weight of the masses. The bells were ringing in the massive Basilica di San Marco, which abutted the Doge's palace. Pietro had heard those bells so often during his time in the cells, and taken comfort from them. He noted that the one still had that slight tremor to its cast that kept it ringing after its fellows, a lone vibration when the rest had stilled.

The arcade that fronted the palace was thronged, and looking up Pietro saw a huge number of the Venetian nobility in the loggia overlooking the piazza. Dandolo was there. *I wonder if he is glad he is not yet Doge — this would be a terrible decision to make. Save the man, or save the law.* Pietro knew that laws mattered more than men, because without law men were no more than beasts. But when the law was put to such perverse use, what good was it?

Sight of Dandolo brought to mind the conference between Detto and Zanino. Pietro tried to convince himself it was benign. He failed.

Pietro was edging around to try a different path when he felt a shift. All the heads on the loggia were turning towards the water. The crowd of Venetians grew still, and though there were no shouts now, the rumble of voices was far more menacing, almost like a growl.

Shalakh approached, ferried across the water from the Yellow Crescent. He stood in the center of the boat, flanked by guards sent to escort him to his appointment with Venetian justice. Pietro had expected Shalakh to seem smaller since the brutal betrayal of his daughter, but quite the reverse. The man was full of a fire that made him fearsome. Even his conveyance was foreboding. Gondolas were usually brightly coloured, reflecting hues of houses and classical tales. This gondola was black and sleek as an ebon night, as though

Death itself were carrying this man. Charon on the Ship of Shadows.

The boat arrived at the Piazzetta and the money-lender alighted onto the stone steps leading up to the Piazza San Marco. Though silent, the hostile gaze of the crowd abused the money-lender's clothes, his gait, his features. Shalakh paid them no mind, focused only on the doors to the Palazzo Ducale. He entered, and they were slammed shut behind him.

The crowd did not know what to do – wait or disperse? Surely it would not take much time. One way or another, it would be over quickly.

Pietro was making his way through the masses, though his lawyer's robes caused less deference than his knight's garb and sword would. He was close to the doors when he spied one of Antonio's friends, the one with the interchangeable name. "Solanio!" cried Pietro, hoping he got it right.

He had. Turning, the man angled to meet Pietro just in front of the doors. "Ser Alaghieri. Has it started?"

"Shalakh just arrived. Where are you coming from?"

"The road. A letter from Bellario arrived last night."

"Is he here?" asked Pietro with hope, looking over the heads of the crowd for the familiar Paduan face.

"Alas, no. He could not come. Sick, he writes. He has sent another doctor of law from Rome, with a letter of recommendation." Solanio did not sound particularly impressed, even as he waved his hand. There, just behind him, was a young fellow in green robes, accompanied by another youth in the red tunic and brown hood of a law clerk. They could have hardly had more than forty years between them. And that one was a doctor of law?

Pietro bowed and offered his name. The young fellow did the same. "Baldassare da Romano. This is my clerk, Nerio. It is an honour to meet you, Ser Pietro. I must congratulate you on crafting the recent peace. Blessed are the peacemakers, for they shall be called the children of God."

"You are very kind. I hope we shall see some peace made here today."

While they made introductions, Solanio explained who they were to the palace guards and the doors opened to admit them. Solanio raced ahead to announce their arrival. Pietro kept stride with the young lawyer. "You are from Rome?"

"I am," said Baldassare.

"I was in Rome during the Emperor's stay. Forgive me for saying so, you are very young."

"That is a fault that time will mend," said the youth without embarrassment.

"I meant no insult. Merely that I'm surprised no one introduced me to such a prodigy while I was there."

Baldassare made no answer to that, instead asking, "Do you plan to plead for the defence?"

"I have offered, if Bellario did not come." There was a moment of awkwardness.

"Well," said Baldassare at last, "he did not come. I will defer to you, if you wish, as my elder."

"Do you know any of the parties involved?" asked Pietro.

"I know neither the plaintiff nor the defendant. I have never laid eyes upon either."

"Whereas I have a prior relationship with one. It might be grounds for accusations of bias. I just want to be certain Signor Antonio receives the best defence possible."

"I'm sure you could be impartial," said Baldassare.

"It's the appearance of impropriety that concerns me. Also, I have spoken to Signor Antonio, and would be hamstrung by a conversation we had from presenting a defence that could remove the threat of death from his head." Baldassare cocked his head at that. "A quirk of Venetian law. I can say no more. If I step aside I don't want you to be hindered as I am. Did Bellario give you any instructions?"

"Do you know him?" asked Baldassare.

"I do, both in person and through his writings."

"Then you will likely know what his advice was," said Baldassare with a smile that dimpled like a boy's. It was not reassuring.

"Yes," said Pietro. "Literal interpretation. Find the hole in the wording."

"Precisely," said Baldassare. "Dottore Bellario is devoted to the language of contracts and law. He says that the answer is in the contract, and justice will only be perceived to occur if the contract is honoured."

"I haven't seen the contract," said Pietro.

"Nor have I. But I hope to."

Pietro pursed his lips. "Would you think me impertinent if I asked to see Bellario's letter of recommendation?"

"Not at all. Nerio?"

The dark-haired clerk produced the letter from a bundle in his arms. It bore Bellario's mark, but was not sealed. Pietro scanned it, and saw that Bellario did indeed recommend this youth in the most glowing terms. One line made Pietro smile: *'I beseech you, let his lack of years be no impediment to let him lack a reverend estimation; for I never knew so young a body with so old a head.'* Pietro could almost hear the Paduan saying it.

They heard running footsteps on the marble. Solanio came skidding to a halt before them. "The Doge is asking for Antonio's representatives." His eyes appealed to Pietro. Baldassare looked to him as well.

Pietro considered. Though a lawyer, he was not as devoted as some of his brethren to the practice of parsing each syllable of a contract, each line of a law. That was Bellario's field, and clearly this young fellow was cut from the same cloth. Perhaps that was the right approach for a situation like this. For if it was legal, the bond must be honoured. The law mattered more than the man.

Returning Bellario's letter, Pietro motioned to the clerk. "You should present that to the Doge at once, young Nerio. I shall speak to your master for a moment, then we shall be along." As Nerio went with Solanio in the direction of the main chamber, Pietro turned to Baldassare. "I will be there, should you need support. As a last resort, there is a clause we can invoke. But it would mean breaking my word to the accused. I would prefer not to do that. So this man's life is in your hands. You must see that his blood is not spilled."

Baldassare bowed. "I am honoured with your trust, Ser Alaghieri."

Together they walked towards the trial where the merchant's fate would be decided. The decision made, Pietro now fretted. Even if the young man failed, there was hope. Besides, Doge Soranzo would surely prevent an execution. Shalakh was not irrational, he would see sense before the ultimate moment. No amount of money was worth a man's life.

But this was not a matter of money. This was about revenge. And no man seeking revenge was rational.

♦   ◊   ♦

Correzola

The settlement was ancient, known in Roman times as *Civitas*, a term that meant many things. One definition was the union of the Roman and the Sabine people as members of a single society. But Cicero had defined it as a body of people, united by law.

After Roman law failed, the city was renamed and remained a sleepy hamlet until the founding of the Benedictine camp two hundred years earlier. Over the years it had grown, the brothers branching out into all fields of production – farming, milling, crafting, brewing, baking. When the first beggars had arrived, the spirit of Christ had not failed to welcome them, but at the price of labour.

The Rakehells arrived with no great Christian spirit, instead casting off the form God had given them in favour of playing at poverty. Some had created mock deformities, like a humped shoulder or an arm in a sling. Yuri was dragging his foot behind him at an awkward angle.

They were greeted with warmth and generosity, and soon any thought of mischief vanished. Here were no uptight monks in need of mockery, no declaiming abbots deserving a tweaked nose. It was a true commune, a community. The youths were soon fed and told to rest, and if they chose to work that afternoon, their help would be welcome.

Benedick was recognized, of course, and made all the more welcome by the monks, to the amusement of the other Rakehells. His embarrassment was intense enough to cause him to make himself scarce, joining in the loading of wagons full of livestock bound for Venice.

Salvatore approached Cesco, a loaf of bread under his arm and a stone bottle of ale in his hand. "Rupert was just talking to those men there," he said, pointing to a trio of wanderers preparing to depart. "They say there's a brothel up the road, but no willing dames within the compound."

Cesco shrugged as he accepted the bread and tore off a hunk. He wasn't feeling particularly lusty under such a grey sky. "I'm astonished this place survived the war."

"Who would raze it?" asked Salvatore, seating himself on a crate full of chickens. "Not your father."

"Certainly not," agreed Cesco. "I doubt he'd receive a reprieve from a second excommunication. But I meant that this place must have been over-run with the needy from Padua."

"They likely came, but didn't care to work for their bread."

Cesco arched one brow "Are you saying Paduans are shiftless, lazy, indolent buggerers?"

"No, that's what you're saying," answered Salvatore. Cesco always liked trying to get a rise from him, but his calm remained unperturbed. "It's funny that Benedick should have mentioned the Count of San Bonifacio."

"Why is that?"

"Because this place was started by one of his forebears," said Salvatore. "A couple centuries ago, a widow to one of the Counts bestowed this land on these monks."

"Really? But the Counts have traditionally been Veronese. Does this mean this is Verona's bread I'm eating, made from Veronese grain?"

Salvatore's cheerful face broke into a grin. "It used to be, and is again, thanks to the *Pax Verona*." He swallowed. "Does Detto know where we are? Will he be joining us?"

"I left word for him," said Cesco, in a tone that said he didn't much care. "Why?"

Salvatore shrugged. "I heard Rupert say something about him."

◆　◇　◆

Venice

Uninterested in the famous trial, Bailardetto da Nogarola departed Venice, huddling in a blanket as he was ferried across to the mainland where his horse was stabled. Running his hand over Vegliantino's neck, Detto asked the stable-boy, "Did he pass a good night?"

"All well, my lord."

"Good, good." Detto loved animals, and animals loved him. He could charm a fox from a hole, or a bird from a branch. It was just his nature, a strange but wonderful gift of Fortune, and one that he prized. Unlike some, he did not ever plan to let his gifts lay fallow.

Detto paid the stable-boy, not too much, but not too little. He did not wish to be remembered. He was here under a false name. A precaution that was rendered almost useless last night. What on earth was Ser Alaghieri doing in Venice? At the Doge's palace, even? He'd been a prisoner there, and therefore the last person Detto was afraid he'd run into.

It could have been a disaster, being stopped by Ser Alaghieri. But Detto had wormed away, though Nuncle Pietro (as Cesco called him) was nobody's foole.

When I get back, I'll have to say I met him. Then we can decide if we need to alter plans...

Fretting, Detto mounted Vegliantino and rode off in the direction of Vicenza.

◆   ◇   ◆

Vicenza

"I am afraid I have lo*sh*t the chart*sh*," said Donna Katerina to her guest.

"I have recovered them," said Tharwat, producing them. "All save one."

"It wa*ssh* burnt." Katerina's eyes were full of anger. "You found him? I*sh* he dead?"

"He is not, lady. He has told us all. He is no longer a threat to you. In fact, he may be a gift."

"How?" demanded the lady, hating her supine position, her utter helplessness.

"His is a true gift. Stronger than mine, for that art. He may be able, in the future, to take my role. When I have gone."

"Are you going?"

"Not yet. But one must plan."

"Indeed. What do you want?"

"Permission to let him travel freely with me, that I may instruct him."

"In exchange for what?"

"He will not reveal publicly that you tried to have the boy murdered. He will keep his silence."

"And the lady Maria? You will *ssh*top looking for her?"

Tharwat shook his head. "It is too late for that. Her name is known. It is only a matter of time."

"You mu*sh*t not look for her." She struggled to sit up, intent on relaying the importance of her words. "It will be ruin!"

"Whose ruin?"

But that she refused to answer. Just as she refused to allow the diviner freedom. "I will tell Bail he attacked me, that I wa*ssh* too afraid to *sh*peak. He will be hunted and killed!"

Shaking his head sadly, Tharwat rose to go. "He may be hunted. But he will live longer than either of us, lady."

◆   ◇   ◆

Venice

Inside the Doge's great chamber, Pietro moved along the wall of watchers. The Council of Ten was present as witnesses, as well as a dozen clerks and judges. Everyone was interested in seeing justice done.

A place was made for him. Almost against his will, he took it. The man to his left he only knew in passing, having met him at the peace talks in August. On his right was Francesco Dandolo.

"Ser Alaghieri," said Dandolo in low greeting. "How good of you to come. I was not aware you knew the principals in this case."

"I don't." Cangrande had always kept his use of Shalakh secret, and Pietro had done the same. As far as Ansaldo went, it was the truth. "But I heard of the case, and came to offer my aid."

"You are a good man. Did our most undivine friend reveal anything of use?"

"I understand he was perfectly truthful," said Pietro carefully. "Whether it was of any use, I cannot yet say." He did not like being indebted to someone who had once imprisoned him and tried to murder Cesco. But so far he had no reason to complain of Dandolo's behavior. He had to resist asking after Zanino. Direct questions would yield him nothing.

"I am glad to hear Girolamo was not dishonest in his confession," said Dandolo. "Though I worry about his accuracy. He predicted acquittal, but I don't see much hope for the merchant."

The Doge was shaking young Baldassare's hand and introducing him to both the plaintiff and the defendant. Pietro noted that the reports of the Doge's ailment were under-rated. He looked hollow, almost like a fruit that had been carved from within. He was rotting, and barely present. A healthy man might have had the strength to guide this trial to a happy conclusion. But it looked as if Soranzo was barely here in flesh, and not at all in spirit.

To the condemned man, Baldassare said, "Do you confess the bond?"

Antonio Ansaldo was dressed in simple hose, a loose shirt and vest, and boots, every inch the condemned man ready to meet his end. Chin high, he nodded. "I do."

Baldassare frowned. "Then the Jew must be merciful."

"On what compulsion must I?" demanded Shalakh angrily. "Tell me that."

Baldassare launched into a fine speech on the nature of mercy, of how it originated with God, and it was man's duty, if he sought mercy from above, to show it below. Pietro wished he had it written down, for it was excellent, all the moreso for being *extempore*. He felt the first stirrings of hope.

But the Hebrew remained unmoved. "The Christian Lord is a God of mercy. But great Jehovah, the Lord of my people, is a God of justice. Let my deeds fall upon my head. I crave the penalty and forfeit of my bond."

Baldassare gestured to Antonio. "Is he unable to discharge the money?"

Antonio's friend Bassanio bolted forward from the watchers. "Yes! I have twice the sum here. If that's not enough, I promise to pay ten times so much! Or my own flesh – take my hands, my head, my heart! If he refuses that, then he is not interested in justice, but revenge. I beg that you force this devil to accept payment. Bend the law, do a great right by doing a little wrong."

Baldassare shook his youthful head. "It cannot be. If the state breaks a law once, it is broken forever. The law is based on precedent, and from that little breaking many more will rush in and shatter the thing that keeps all men secure. It cannot be."

"A Daniel!" cried Shalakh, amazed and overjoyed. "A Daniel come to judgment! O wise young judge, how I honour you!"

Baldassare held out his hand. "Let me see this bond." Shalakh offered it willingly, and the young Roman studied it. "Master Shalakh, you will not accept ten times what is set down here as payment?"

"An oath, an oath," said Shalakh. "I have an oath in Heaven. I will not perjure my soul." Pietro wondered if he meant Antonio's oath to pay in flesh, or his own oath to exact revenge.

Baldassare looked up from the paper. "Then the bond is forfeit. Lawfully this Jew may claim a pound of flesh, to be cut by him near the merchant's heart. But Jew, be merciful. Take your money and let me tear up this bond."

"When it is paid in full, according to the law," said Shalakh smugly. His mouth was open and he was breathing hard, his gaze fixed on Antonio, who wanted this over. "I beg the court to offer judgment."

All eyes were upon the young Roman lawyer, who said simply, "Then prepare your bosom for his knife."

Again Shalakh cried his delight, drowning out the mutters of disbelief and horror from the watching court. "O noble judge! O excellent young man!"

Dandolo leaned close. "This is who Bellario sent?"

Pietro shook his head. "He's following the law."

"I was foolishly confident this would not happen," answered Dandolo. "Our friend Girolamo foretold an acquittal. Had he not gone, I would reprimand him."

"Gone?" Pietro felt a chill that had nothing to do with the proceedings.

"This morning, I'm told. I confess I was concerned I had been duped. He had been so fearful for his safety. But perhaps he did not trust my word. Did you speak to him?"

"No," said Pietro. When he'd arrived, he'd not felt compelled to seek out the crippled diviner. Now he wished he had.

♦　◊　♦

Girolamo was a slow traveler under the best conditions. He was no longer built for riding, and he was already aching from the contorted posture a saddle required of him.

But the pendulum had nearly flayed the skin from his fingers in the middle of the night as he tried to predict coming events, demanding he leave Venice at once. It frightened him, leaving the protective skirts of Francesco Dandolo. But what the pendulum was doing frightened him more. Ever since he'd met the Moor, his talent seemed to be more powerful, more demanding. He felt the swing of the small marble teardrop even when he was not holding the chain.

It was a grey day, heavy with the promise of yet more snow. He had tried to stay to the road, but the pendulum had pulled him off of it, southwards over land he had never seen before. Not Padua, then. Somewhere else.

He heard the hoofbeats before he saw them, and had enough time to take cover under a thick clump of evergreens, the kind known as Graveyard Cypresses. But it wasn't the name of the trees that had Girolamo clutching his reins. His pricking thumb told him this was danger. It was also why he was here. Under the cover of the trees, the diviner fingered the knife at his belt, waiting to strike.

♦　◊　♦

"If you have any words to offer, Ser Alaghieri," said Dandolo, "this is the moment."

It was indeed. Shalakh had produced a dagger, a strange blade, one that was forged not to be straight but rather to flow like waves. The Jew was now jiggling the weapon between a cutting grip and a stabbing one, trying to decide how best to rend Ansaldo's flesh.

Frowning, Pietro decided to act. He stepped away from the wall and tugged at the clerk Nerio's sleeve. When the young man turned, Pietro snatched the fellow's stylus and quickly carved a few words in the wax tablet. He then nodded urgently towards Baldassare, and Nerio quickly moved forward to show the message to his master.

Baldassare was telling Shalakh to order a doctor present to

stop the bleeding, but the Jew pointed out that the bond carried no such stipulation.

Nerio held the tablet out, and the Roman jurist read the words Pietro had written: *Venice is a city where crimes of love are forgiven.* It was as far as he could go without breaking his word.

Frowning, the young lawyer gazed at Pietro, then turned to Ansaldo. "Merchant, do you have any final words?"

"I am prepared." Antonio turned to his friend. "Bassanio, give me your hand. Don't look so sad! This is a happy fortune – I'm saved from growing old in poverty. Do me one favour – commend me to your wife. Tell her of me, speak me fair. Let her judge that her husband was not much loved in Venice. Don't grieve." He grinned with wry sadness. "I pay this debt with all my heart."

Tears of rage and despair stood shimmering in Bassanio's eyes. "Antonio, I love my wife with all my heart. But my wife, my life, all the world means nothing compared to my friendship with you. I would sacrifice them all willingly to this devil to save you."

Baldassare looked grave, almost angry. "Your wife would give you little thanks for that, if she were here."

Gratiano made a similar vow, and Nerio muttered something under his breath. Shalakh seemed to agree with the lawyer and his clerk. "Christians make terrible husbands. My daughter married one. Much joy may she have of him. Come, we trifle time! The sentence."

As Antonio was brought forward, his breast bared, Pietro tried to catch Baldassare's eye. Surely the youth understood the message. Ansaldo's declaration was as close to a statement of love as one man had ever made for another. Whatever shame would come, was it worth dying to avoid it? Perhaps the youth thought so. Certainly he was frowning, eyes downcast, unseeing, at the bond in his hand.

Shalakh had settled on a grip, and held the knife upwards, like a man about to carve a carcass. The steel rippled in the light from the high windows, reflecting upwards. In the shimmering glow it cast, the Jew looked quite demented in his delight.

Baldassare was still looking at the bond. "A pound of Signor Ansaldo's flesh is yours, Jew. The law demands it, and the court grants it."

"Most rightful judge," said Shalakh in a low tone, approaching Antonio.

"And you must cut this flesh from his breast, next to his heart. The law allows it, and the court grants it."

Pietro was horrified. The young lawyer suddenly seemed as eager as the Jew for Ansaldo to die.

"Most learned judge," hissed Shalakh. "You hear the sentence. Prepare."

The knife was raised. Pietro could bear it no longer. He opened his mouth...

"Tarry a little," said Baldassare, gazing down at the bond in his hands. There was a moment, a terrible moment, when he seemed to decide something. Then he raised his gaze to meet the Jew's. "This contract says nothing about blood. The words are expressly 'a pound of flesh'. So take it. But if you shed a drop of his blood, your life, lands, and goods will, by the law of Venice, be confiscate to the state."

Shouts from all around. At once the loud Gratiano began baiting Shalakh. "O upright judge! Mark, Jew. O learned judge!"

Shalakh looked ashen. "Is that the law?"

"We can show you the statute. You are so hungry for justice, we shall see you get more than you asked for."

Shalakh hesitated. The knife remained in his hand, trembling. He could strike, and have his revenge, at the cost of his life. Was the price too high?

At last he lowered the knife. "Fine. Pay the money and let the Christian go."

Bassanio started forward, but Baldassare waved him off. "You refused the money, several times. You demanded the forfeit named in the bond. So – take it. And see you take nothing more or less than one exact pound of his flesh. We'll have it weighed, and if it tips the scales by the estimation of a hair, your life, lands, and goods all belong to Venice."

"A Daniel! A second Daniel," cried Gratiano in jubilant mockery. Pietro wished he wouldn't, but understood the relief. He shared it.

Shalakh said, "Give me my principal, and let me go."

"I have it here," said Bassanio, offering his purse.

Baldassare intervened. "He has refused it in open court. He shall have justice, and his bond."

"Not even my principal?" asked Shalakh over Gratiano's crowing.

"Nothing," said Baldassare, "but what's in the bond. Take it at your peril."

Pietro had to stifle a laugh of amazement. The youth was not only brilliant, but brilliantly hard.

Shalakh threw his knife to the ground. "Keep it, and may it plague him. I'll stay no longer." He turned to leave, but Baldassare gestured to the guards to block his path.

"Tarry, Jew. The law has yet another hold on you. The laws of Venice decree that if any non-citizen attempts to take the life of a citizen, the injured party may seize one half his goods. The other half goes to the coffers of the Serenissima, and the offender's life depends on the mercy of the state. Down, therefore, and beg mercy of the Doge."

Gratiano was vicious in victory. "I'd say hang yourself, devil, but with what? You don't even have the price of a rope now!"

When Shalakh did not move, he was brought to his knees by the guards as Doge Soranzo stirred himself to speak. "So you might perceive the difference between yourself and a Christian, I pardon you your life. As for your goods, half belong to Signor Ansaldo. The other half due to the state we might reduce to a fine, depending on your behavior."

Shalakh shook his head. "You take my life if you take my livelihood."

Baldassare turned to the merchant whose life he had just preserved so magnificently. "What mercy does he deserve, Signor Antonio?"

Antonio stood, still bare-chested and drawn, looking down at the Jew. "If it pleases the noble Doge and the court, I am content with half his goods — providing that he renders the other half, upon his death, to his daughter's good Christian husband. And that he goes from this place directly into the Church of San Marco and is baptized a Christian."

"He shall do this," said the Doge, smiling, "or I'll recant my pardon of his life."

Baldassare handed the bond back to the kneeling man. "Are you content, Jew? Has justice been served?"

In a soft voice, Shalakh said, "I am content."

Pietro had never seen a man brought so low. The Shalakh Pietro knew would have been bristling, vowing to die rather than give up his faith. But the fight had gone from the old Jew. What his daughter's betrayal had begun, this day had ended. Pietro would have felt pity, had the man not just attempted to commit legal murder before their very eyes. Baldassare had offered the Jew every chance to avoid this humiliation. Surely this was justice. So why did it feel so wrong?

Baldassare turned to the many clerks along the wall. "Someone draw up a deed, giving all his goods at his death to his daughter's husband. He shall sign it now."

"Please," said Shalakh, "let me leave. I am not well. Send the deed after me, and I will sign it."

"Go," said Doge Soranzo, "but see you do. Guards, escort him to the Church."

Shalakh rose shakily to his feet and turned to go, only to find his path blocked by Gratiano. "Had I been your judge, you would be on your way to the gallows, not the baptismal font."

Shalakh said nothing in return. It was a sour note to end such a triumph. Ansaldo was embraced by his friends, and the Doge invited the young lawyer to dine with him, but the youth begged off. "I am expected in Padua this night, and must depart at once."

"A pity," said Soranzo, though from the look of him food had not passed his lips for some time. "Signor Ansaldo, gratify this gentlemen. You are deeply in his debt."

As Antonio, Bassanio, and the others crowded around the young lawyer, Pietro considered following Shalakh and asking again for information pertaining to the name Amabilio. But he could not bring himself to do it. The man had no reason to be forthcoming, not today. Perhaps not ever.

Dandolo pressed Pietro's arm. "I must attend the Doge. Should I send men to hunt our friend the cripple?"

Pietro shook his head. "I believe he has accepted an offer to study with Tharwat al-Dhaamin, to learn more of their mutual arts."

Dandolo sighed in measured relief. "That is good to know. Though what an unholy sight those two will be together. Forgive me for saying so, but I cannot imagine the court that would admit them for anything other than grotesque amusement."

"Until they have sampled their arts."

"True. But I tell you, soon Venice will have little time for the stars."

As Dandolo departed, Pietro found himself wishing the same were true of Verona.

From the clump of men surrounding the Roman lawyer, Pietro heard a stern tone originating from, of all men, Ansaldo, who should had cause to be joyful. "Bassanio, let him have the ring. He has earned it. Weigh my love against your promise to your wife, and value them by the scales."

"I'll buy the dearest ring in Venice and give it gladly," Bassanio was saying to Baldassare.

Baldassare seemed amused, not put out. "I see. Liberal in offers, conservative in practice. First you teach me to beg, then school me how to answer a beggar."

"Good signor, this ring was given to me by my wife, whose love I only just won. When she gave it to me she made me vow to neither sell, nor give, nor lose it."

Baldassare shrugged. "If she's not a mad-woman, she would understand. If she is, best you discover it now. But peace be with you." Baldassare motioned to his clerk and started for the door.

As Antonio continued to harangue his friend to give the ring in question to the lawyer who had saved his life, Pietro fell into step beside the young Roman. "Allow me to add my voice to the praise. I stand in awe of Bellario's method of reading the law. It is all in the language."

"Or in the omissions," agreed Baldassare as they traversed the hallway. "Sometimes they are not sins, but blessings."

"I confess, I was concerned," said Pietro. "You understood my message, I trust. I am glad now you did not follow my advice."

Baldassare said nothing for a moment, then took a breath. "I did not think it would benefit either the victim or his friends. And if it were known, it might provoke jealousy."

Pietro was surprised by that. "Jealousy? In whom?"

"In Bassanio's wife, for one. She would need a sign that her husband preferred her to his friend."

"Well, she has it," said Pietro. "Is that why you demanded the ring? To test his love?"

Baldassare was grinning again, complete with dimples. "It was a whim. But Antonio has offered to die for his love. I wanted to see if Bassanio was swayed by such devotion." He turned to Nerio, trailing along behind. "Go to the Jew's house and see the deed signed. I'll order the horses."

Nerio gave his master a baleful look, and Pietro wondered if the young clerk disliked horses. What, did he prefer to travel by carriage?

"You're heading back to give Bellario the news of your triumph? I'm off for Vicenza tonight, then on to Verona. I'd be happy to ride with you as far as Padua."

Baldassare looked startled, but recovered. "That is very kind, but we would only slow you down. We are not accustomed to the saddle."

"Not all knights are devils in the stirrups," laughed Pietro. "Come, I'd love to discuss the laws of Rome."

Baldassare pursed his lips. "Very well. Of course, we would be happy for the company. Nerio, go see that signed and—"

"Master Baldassare!" The urgent cry came from behind them.

The loud fellow Gratiano was racing across the marble floor to reach them. "I'm glad I caught you. Lord Bassanio has reconsidered, at Antonio's urging. Here is the ring you craved. And he invites you to stay to dinner."

Baldassare looked at the ring pressed into his small hand. The expression on his youthful face was wounded, not at all triumphant. "It cannot be." Then he started and said, more pleasantly, "I must leave at once. But I accept his gift with all my heart. Now, will you guide my clerk to Shalakh's house."

"Gladly," said Gratiano.

The lawyer and clerk stepped aside for a private conference, then Nerio left in the company of Gratiano while Baldassare fell into step again with Pietro.

"Did he pass your test, or fail it?" asked Pietro lightly.

Baldassare was gazing at the ring, a flush rising in his youthful cheek. "Who am I to judge?"

"You knew it was an impossible request," chided Pietro. "Either way he was bound to break faith."

"Yes," said the young lawyer, placing the ring on his finger. It fit perfectly. "But now I see whose love was stronger."

As they exited the palace into the open air of the Piazza San Marco, Pietro clapped the young fellow on the shoulder. "Just hope his wife never finds out!"

♦   ◊   ♦

It was growing late when the Rakehells departed the Benedictine commune, having performed labour in return for their genial entertainment. Cesco snuck into the abbot's cell, and there deposited a bag of gold.

Back in their borrowed cart, Benedick complimented Cesco's generosity. "They'll make good use of it."

"I'm sure," said Cesco. "Though I find myself utterly shattered in my delusions. I did not believe there were men alive who actually practiced what Christ taught. In a venal world, it is easier to believe all men are cads. Especially men of the cloth. Finding good ones do exist is quite disillusioning."

The sky had finally broken open, releasing the pent up snow that frosted their clothes, their beards, their eyelashes. They reached their horses and, paying the hire of the cart, remounted for their return to Illasi. Just as they did, they heard an inhuman cry carried on the wind of the evening air. It was joined by another, until it was a chorus of bloodcurdling song.

"Wolves," said Yuri.

Cesco clapped his gloved hands. "Sport! This day won't be a complete waste. Cangrande once slew several wolves as a lad, or so the bragging goes. I've a mind to return with pelts that will put his best furs to shame. Come, let's see what they're hunting, and turn the hunters into prey! Hya!" With a snap of the reins, he had Abastor racing at a gallop, the rest of the Rakehells in his wake.

◆　　◇　　◆

The two Romans did indeed ride slowly, as if they had no experience on horseback. Pietro had to keep his horse in check, and as the sun disappeared over the horizon he began thinking of houses in Padua where he could stay. "I might join you at Bellario's," he said. "You could avoid seeming immodest and allow me tell him the tale of your victory. If you don't mind my company."

Nerio shot Baldassare a glance, and the lawyer again looked uncomfortable. "It is not for me to invite you to another man's house."

Pietro sensed the Roman's reluctance. "He invited me to call whenever I was in Padua. But I don't mean to intrude on your friendship."

Baldassare took a breath. "More than friendship, actually. I did not want to say it before, Ser Alaghieri, but Bellario is my cousin."

"Truly? He didn't mention any relations in Rome. In fact, the only cousin he talked of was a female, a woman in Bellamonte who had as good a head for law as—"

It was like lightning. Bassanio had married a woman of Bellamonte. Bellario. The ring. The shape of this youth, outlined in shadow. Pietro breathed out a hiss, then started to laugh.

Discovered, the lady laughed as well. "Well, Nerissa, we're rumbled. I'm stunned we pulled it off for as long as we did."

"At least we can now stop pretending," said the clerk, pulling her cap from her head and releasing a tumble of hair. "O, how I wish we had side-saddles!"

Pietro was still laughing. "May I ask your name, Madonna?"

"I am called after Brutus' second wife, the lady who swallowed fire."

"Fitting." Pietro's grin broadened as he bowed his head to her. "A pleasure to meet you, Lady Portia."

The talk was much more relaxed after that. The women returned their voices to their usual trebles, and Pietro asked how they had invented their scheme. The only awkwardness was when

Pietro remembered the test of the ring. Or rings, as it seemed Nerissa, married to that lout Gratiano, had gotten her own ring back from him as well.

"I am sorry, lady, that I spoke at all," said Pietro honestly.

Portia waved it off. "It is a new marriage, against an old friendship. I see I have my work cut out for me. Trust me, it is not an error Bassanio will make a second time."

They were nearing a divide in the road when they saw torches and heard human cries and animal yelps. Pietro saw several men on horseback driving off a pack of wolves that had been feeding on a carcass in the snowy field beside the road.

There was a single cry that rose above the rest, a sound Pietro had heard only once before. "Stay here," he commanded, and set his horse into a gallop to the spot where the torches lit the landscape, reflecting off the silent falling snow. Spying a familiar red-head among the crowd, Pietro called out. Faces turned. Young Petruchio and Hortensio were there, looking angry and grave. Their hands dropped to their swords until he identified himself.

It was the red-headed Paduan who came up at a run. "He was attacked," said Benedick. "Caltrops in the road to lame his horse. It's dead, and he was stabbed and left to die in the snow. The wolves found him..."

"Who?" demanded Pietro, swinging from his saddle and racing towards the clump of men, surrounding the dead horse and the rider who had been cut from its saddle. "Who?"

Cesco was kneeling by the man's head. It had been his howl that had brought Pietro racing, a howl of despair and rage that Cesco had made on the night Pietro's father had died. Now it came again, and Pietro was terrified to see what had dragged it forth.

The figure on the ground belonged to Detto. The snow all around him was now longer white, but steeped in the crimson of his blood.

Beside him were the marks of footsteps. One of the footprints dragged a course through the snow, as if made by a cripple.

III

STRIVE WITH THINGS IMPOSSIBLE

NINETEEN

ANIMAL MAGIC had preserved Detto's body from the wolves. It was the only explanation. They had chosen to feed on the dead form of Vegliantino, the fine animal given by Cangrande to the young knight just three weeks earlier.

Pietro knelt close. Detto's face was pale and serene. There was no breath steaming from his lips, and his fingers were cold. But Pietro spied a small flutter under the skin of his neck. Life was still tethered to this body, if only by the slenderest thread. "He's alive!"

"Of course he's alive," said Cesco in a constricted tone. He was rubbing Detto's right hand to restore circulation. "He hasn't finished being my conscience. Have you, Detto?"

There was no answer. Pietro saw that someone had bound Detto's wound. The work was so rude, everyone else assumed Detto had done it himself. Pietro had a suspicion – a hope, really. He did not want to think that the cripple was behind this attack. It made no sense. None at all.

They quickly constructed a litter to drag Detto's unmoving form the rest of the way to Padua, where Salvatore had already been dispatched to wake all the doctors in the city.

"Here," said Yuri, reading the traces on the snowy ground. "Most of the attackers rode east, but one headed north."

"We'll follow the larger party," said Fabio, mounting swiftly. "We'll send word if we find the bastards."

"I'll join you," said Benedick.

"What about the lone man?" said Pietro, who had a feeling he knew who that was.

"We'll trace him," said Barto, signaling to his brother. Young Petruchio and his twin both joined the Scaligeri bastards as they tore off to the north.

The Paduans returned *en force*, Marsilio da Carrara in the lead, for this deed imperiled the new peace. Cangrande's nephew had been attacked within the Padovana. There would be no rest until the malefactors were hunted down.

Carrara greeted Pietro, who explained as much as he had been able to discern. "It was an ambush, set up in advance by several men. They wanted it to look like a robbery – Detto's sword, gold, and spurs are all gone."

"You don't believe it," said Carrara.

"No more than you. Robbers would not have murdered the horse. Someone has gone to a lot of trouble to attack Ser Nogarola."

"And yet they did not make sure of his death. Where do the tracks lead?"

"To Venice," said Pietro. "We've sent men."

"Did you trace their origin? We might learn something."

Pietro said they had not enough people for that, and Carrara sent off a pack of soldiers at once. Then he eyed Pietro's companions, women whose clothes looked peculiarly masculine under their cloaks. "And these are?"

"Two ladies I was escorting back to Padua. This lady here is the cousin of Dottore Bellario. Can I entrust them to your care? I'd prefer to stay here."

"I'll see them safely returned," said Carrara.

Pietro took his leave of Portia and Nerissa, then wondered what there was to do. He could think of so many things. But until they traced the malefactors, there was very little that was productive.

"What was Detto doing in Venice at all?" he asked Cesco, not for the first time.

But there were no answers to be had from that corner, or at least no real ones. "Buying passage out of this benighted land. But thankfully Charon asks too much coin."

"Cesco, if we knew why he was there—"

Though his eyes were red, the pupils for once looked almost clear. "How should I know? I am not his keeper."

Pietro tried another tack. "Cesco, if you know who did this—"

"I can think of two just offhand. No, three."

"Tell us, then, and we'll investigate."

"Let me know if you find anything. But you won't. I'll take care of it." And he had actually shoved Pietro out of his path.

Cesco was wrong – the knowledge that the cripple Girolamo was there was a good lead. One that Pietro had not yet shared with another soul.

Carrara's soldiers returned just as they were transporting Detto slowly towards the gates of Padua. "The tracks lead to Correzzola, my lord."

"Those are our tracks, idiot," snapped Rupert.

"No, prince," said the soldier. "Begging your pardon, but we saw your traces as well as theirs. They left earlier in the day, just as the snow started to fall."

"The party that left," said Cesco.

"What?"

"The party that left. That told Salvatore about the whorehouse. It was them."

"Did they think they were laying a trap for us?" asked Salvatore, confused.

"No," said Cesco. "They were hired to attack Detto when he came to join us. I mentioned I'd sent him word."

Sitting in his saddle before the walls of Padua, Pietro felt several unwelcome suspicions. "Hired by whom?"

"Salvatore," said Cesco, and all eyes turned towards the Paduan.

"Cesco – I mean, Ser Francesco," sputtered Salvatore with unaccustomed lack of calm, "you cannot think—"

"You said they had been speaking with Rupert."

All eyes turned to stare at the German prince. His mouth fell open for a moment, then he laughed. "I? Hire ruffians and vagabonds? To what end? What possible cause would I have to murder Ser Bailardetto?"

"To take his place," said Salvatore, breathing fast now. "To slip into the role of close companion to Verona's prince."

"And thus bring him closer to the emperor," said Pietro gravely.

Everyone was edging their horses away from the German now, and hands were freed, ready to drop to draw swords should the moment call for it. Rupert laughed again, but the bravado rang hollow – he sensed the change around him. "I didn't. Franz, I didn't do this. I couldn't – how would I have known to hire these men? How would I have known they were there?"

"We laid plans last night," said Salvatore. "You could have sent word in the middle of the night to meet you there."

"Going there was *your* suggestion," countered Rupert. "And

you talked to these men as well, it seems. I heard them talking of women and asked after local entertainments. Why did you speak to them, if not to give them orders? Why could it not have been you? Eh? Or Benedick, or any other Paduan! That makes far more sense, does it not? This was a Paduan attack, performed so near the city that was just conquered, with whose citizens Franz and his cousin have been brawling since the wedding. That is far more likely!"

It was a rare thing for a prince to have to recall who was his audience. But his speech was a mistake, uttered as it was before the Capitano da Padua. The last thing Marsilio da Carrara wanted was a rumour that this vile deed had been performed by Paduan hands. Far, far better to blame the Emperor, with whom Cangrande had a strained relationship already.

Without taking his gaze from Prince Rupert, Carrara half-turned his head towards Cesco. "Shall I arrest him?"

Through it all, Cesco had said nothing, his gaze level on Rupert. But his hands were shaking. "On what grounds? Suspicion? There is nothing like proof. Even if we catch the men who did it, there will be nothing, I'm sure."

"Franz," said Rupert in a half-laughing appeal. "We know each other. Would I do this?"

"Yes," said Cesco. "But I don't know if you did. Still, it might be best if you rejoined your uncle for a bit. Call your servants to Padua. Lord Carrara will offer you safe conduct to Rome. And Rupert?"

Turning his horse with a vengeful tug of his reins, the German prince had to look back over his shoulder. "Yes?"

"If Detto dies, I will burn down the world of whoever did it. I will flense the meat from their bones and wring every drop of blood before their eyes. I will hunt down their family, their friends, their cities, their God and destroy them all. Empires will fall, kingdoms will topple, and Heaven itself will weep, for all its citizens will be pushed down to Hell."

Rupert studied him, anger mingled with disappointment and humiliation. He chose to be clever, but there was no mirth in his tone. "I thought there was no Hell."

Cesco stared with eyes as wild as the open sea, as bright as the sun, as malevolent as an oncoming storm. "I'll make one. In the face."

"Come, Prince Rupert," said Carrara. "Let us see you safely out of our lands."

Rupert continued to look at Cesco, as if searching for something. Then he laughed and shrugged before allowing himself to be escorted away.

The rest of the party rode through the Porta Altinate, with its ornate recreation of a Roman Triumphal arch. Everyone was silent, focused on getting Detto to the doctors who would determine if Cesco would need to make good that terrible threat.

But as the party emerged from beneath the arch, their number had decreased by two. Cesco had paused in the shadows, and Pietro had noticed. The young man's hands were shaking, his breathing was fast. He looked like a man in the grip of a fever. Softly, Pietro said, "Are you well?"

Cesco clearly wished to be alone, but having failed that, he reached into the pouch on his belt and consumed one of those damned wafers. "I will be. All will be well. Well well well. Speaking of wells, there's something in Verona... But that can wait. Have you sent for fork-beard? He's presided over every disaster we've had, and no one's died yet. I think he's actually a witch – it can't be his medicine, he's not that clever. Can't even diagnose his own wife. But for stabbings he'll do."

"I sent for him, yes."

"Good. I'd rather not lose my only true friend in the entire world."

That was wounding. "I'm your friend."

Cesco looked Pietro dead in the eye. "I mean, the only person who has never lied to me."

♦   ◊   ♦

Having been called from Vicenza to tend the lad he'd known since birth, Morsicato shouldered past the Paduan doctors who had, in fact, done excellent work. He produced his signature cure for such injuries, the maggots that Pietro remembered all too well. But they had once preserved his leg from infection, and therefore amputation, so he welcomed the shuddering memory in the hope that Detto would live long enough to enjoy the fruits of their labours.

With the doctor came the astrologer. As soon as he could, Pietro took Tharwat aside and explained the traces he had seen.

The Moor was grave. "Do you suspect Girolamo of complicity in this?"

Pietro frowned. "The more I think of it, the more reasons I find not to suspect him. He was in Venice the night before, whereas these other men were in Correzzola. Someone bandaged Detto's wound after the attack. I think Girolamo found him, and tried to save him. But why leave Venice at all? Did you send for him?"

"No. I failed to procure the lady's guarantee of his safety. And if it is as you say, if he did preserve Detto's life, why run?"

"Girolamo was at the Nogarola house when Katerina had her stroke. He was once hired to murder Cesco. Seeing Detto in the snow, seeing the family crest on his person, he must have known how bad it would appear to us all. He would have considered himself ripe for hanging if he remained. Certainly Bailardino would not have waited for the law, but strung him up on the spot."

"So I think," said Tharwat.

Pietro started to speak, then stopped. The astrologer had been leading him on to the right conclusion — a maddening habit, especially in one who told fortunes. "Can you find him?"

The Moor shook his head. "My skill is not in the pendulum. I cannot find lost things, or it would not have taken me so long to find Pathino, or Donna d'Amabilio. But he will appear." He refrained from adding, *'When the stars decree.'* He knew Pietro's feelings about astrology at present.

Morsicato emerged from the sickroom after several hours to give them news. Detto was not dead — the wound had not been mortal — but had lost a great deal of blood. Had it not been for the rough bandage, he would have died in the snow. "Though I think the cold helped. Cold slows the flow of blood, so as bad as it was to be out there bleeding, had it been summer, he'd've been dead before we ever found him."

One positive outcome was that Bailardino now had a worthy excuse to forget his anger at his firstborn. He arrived in Padua at noon, the stains of travel marking him from heel to hip. Bursting into the sickroom, he knelt by the bed and gently brushed his son's hair. Cesco, who had barely left his cousin's side, moved now, letting the father in. In fact he left the room, forcing Bailardino to hunt him down in the palace for the inevitable confrontation.

Bail asked the same questions Pietro had posed, and though he asked in a louder voice and used more colourful terms, the answers were no more enlightening. Indeed, it took a great deal of convincing and talking to the other Rakehells before Bail was convinced it hadn't happened on some mad escapade. But then Rupert's name came up, and Bail set out to hunt down the German princeling, only to find that his target had already departed. He had known better than to linger.

"Well, that's the Emperor sorted," said Petruchio Bonaventura, who had ridden with Bailardino to see that his own sons were safe. "The Scaliger put on such a display of hospitality that one-eyed Berthold had to admit defeat. If this was Ludwig's other plan, it rebounded quite badly.

Cangrande had come as well, riding at a breakneck pace across the snowy ground to see his nephew. While Bail looked to his son, the Scaliger joined Carrara in organizing the hunt for the attackers. But they had vanished into the unwalled maze that was Venice, and the northbound lone rider had crossed a stream, and the tracks had vanished. Pietro did not mention the cripple, wanting to know the facts before he spoke.

Bail remained by his son's side, and Cesco quietly took up station across from him. After a time spent gazing at the young man they both loved, Bail said, "Thank you for trying. The baths, I mean. I assume that was you."

Unimpressed by the accusations hurled his way earlier, Cesco's voice was flat. "That must have hurt to say."

"More than you know," grunted Bail.

"It hurts him," said Cesco simply. "Whatever else you think of me, I don't want him hurt."

"You struck my wife." Bail waited, but when no answer came, he said, "You offer no excuse?"

Cesco shrugged. "Reasons. But no, no excuse."

Pulling a face, Bail seemed to seek out some excuse on his own. "She does like to meddle. Her and those damn charts. I'd be lying if I said I hadn't been tempted over the years." Fixing Cesco with a hard stare, Bail said, "Don't do it again."

"I can't imagine another reason so compelling."

Bailardino's brow remained furrowed in a manner foreign to his genial face. "You're harder than people think."

"Like the forged blade, I've been hammered into my present shape."

They were looking at each other, and so missed the first signs until they heard a voice, weak, from between them. "C—cia—"

Bail and Cesco both leaned close. "Yes, Detto? What is it?"

His eyes shut, his senses still absent, Detto mumbled, "*Cianfa dove fia rimaso?*"

Leaning back, Cesco began to laugh. In truth, he wanted to dance. Instead he went to find the doctors, who were never there when good things happened.

♦　◊　♦

When Detto woke clear-eyed for the first time on Tuesday morning, he accepted his father's presence without comment. Though knighted, he was still a boy, and needed his father in times of stress.

His father, and his best friend. He asked for Cesco, who was with the Scaliger but came at a run. Pausing at the door, he entered the room with a saunter and dropped onto a stool, shaking his head in disgust. "You didn't even capture a wolf."

"Capture one?" repeated Detto, a weak smile forming at the corners of his mouth. "I called them to keep me warm until my egg-friend arrived."

"That was your mistake, riding alone. Death came calling when I wasn't there. But it turns out we had it backwards. You're Castor, I'm Pollux."

"I don't feel immortal," said Detto, wincing.

"You should. You're the hero, and I'm destined to be the forgotten one."

"You did this to me on purpose," said Detto.

"I did," agreed Cesco. "Just to win the Palio."

"Next time, try a bribe."

Listening, Bail approved of this banter. But he could not long resist asking the important questions. "Who attacked you, lad? Tell me, so I can kill them."

Detto gave the best description he could. Three men, all hooded. Not soldiers, just men. "They killed Vegliantino, who couldn't run because he was lame."

"Caltrops," said Cesco, meaning the wicked spikes that had littered the road. "They lamed a couple of our horses as well."

Detto began to weep at the loss of his horse, and they spent time complimenting the animal, Bail promising to buy the finest steed Montecchio owned to replace it. The expending of emotion sent Detto back to unconsciousness, and he slept the rest of the day.

On Wednesday Morsicato said they could move him, if carefully. As they bundled Detto into a covered wagon, Cangrande ordered an escort of the best knights Padua had to offer for the short trip up the road to Vicenza. The Rakehells joined, and the enforced silence on the journey felt like a funeral procession. They all were hoping someone would attack, but no one did, though many peasants came out to line the road to doff their caps and pay their respects, which only added to the funereal air.

Rebelling, Cesco started to sing. The words were known to all the Rakehells by now, and they sang with gusto of the Devil crafting the privatest part of Eve.

"Damn," said Cangrande, laughing. "I'm going to have to hire a hundred more men to guard Verona's streets."

"To protect Cesco?" asked Pietro.

"To protect Verona *from* Cesco."

"He'll stay by Detto's bed, surely." Detto had remained at Cesco's side when Cesco was poisoned, and Pietro could not imagine Cesco doing anything else.

Cangrande disagreed. "He would, if Detto were in Verona. But think of with whom Detto will doubtless be sharing a room. I do not envision Cesco subjecting himself to that."

His words proved true. Cesco saw his best friend into the doors of the Nogarola palace, but did not cross the threshold into the chamber on the upper level where a second bed had been placed. Morsicato now had both his patients in one room, where Katerina could watch her son convalesce. "It might even motivate her recovery," the doctor had told the frantic father and husband.

Valentino came to stay, accompanied by his new friend Proteus. With the whole household buzzing, Cesco declared it no place for the Rakehells, and they decamped without paying their respects to their fallen comrade. The journey had been hard, and he was fast asleep, aided by the doctor's potions. So Cesco was not forced to face Detto's mother, a relief to all save perhaps the lady herself, who doubtless had something to say.

She did speak to her brother, if briefly. He emerged from the sickroom looking troubled.

Before the main party mounted for the ride to Verona, Morsicato offered Cesco a pouch. He made sure to scowl as he did, though the face he turned to Pietro was far lighter. "We've cracked it. A sure way to be certain he doesn't over-indulge."

"Yes?"

"I've laced each one with extract of poppy, much more than was in it before. If he takes more than two, he'll be asleep in no time." Morsicato walked off, chuckling to himself. But Pietro was not as certain of this plan. He imagined Cesco in some crisis, falling asleep when he most needed wakefulness. Still, slumber was preferable to constant brawls and madcap escapades. Pietro said nothing.

For the whole ride back to Verona, Cesco spent his time beside Salvatore, who spoke with uncommon feeling about Rupert's perfidy. Cesco himself was more phlegmatic. "It's Detto's own fault. He should not have been out alone. Ah well. The Rakehells have lost two members. That means I'm drinking for three. Come on, sluggards! Last one to *La Rosa Colta* buys the wine!" And he kicked Abastor into a gallop.

✦   ◊   ✦

The whole city had heard about Detto, of course. But the people of Verona seemed not to take it seriously. Those Rakehells were bound to get themselves injured, and he wasn't dead, was he? He was young and strong, he'd be up and around by Twelfth Night. No need to douse the candles and end the carols.

By now Antonia was ensconced in Cesco's house on the *via Pigna*, and had insinuated herself into the daily routines. Having used Maddelena as her excuse to move in, she hadn't expected to actually enjoy spending time with the girl. Not naturally maternal, she had always looked upon her role in raising Cesco as unique, because of his own uniqueness. She appreciated Detto for his good influence on Cesco, but never much cared for him until he became old enough to be a person in his own right.

To suddenly again be part of a five year-old's life was fascinating. Was it because Maddelena was a girl? Or was it age and experience that made Antonia appreciate the child's company? Was it simple nostalgia? Though clever, the girl was not at all like Cesco – not a prodigy, just a sweet girl thrust into unfamiliar circumstances.

The smart choice the household had made was to treat her as a child, and not lady of the house. Too much power invested early would skew the girl's personality. Instead the goal was to set her up more as a sister than a wife to Cesco. In that, Antonia found herself in whole-hearted agreement. He had always needed a sister.

The ill consequence, of course, was a lack of husbandly responsibility on Cesco's part. Had the girl been older, she could have insisted on formal dinners, on running the household, on managing the finances. All of those things might have curbed Cesco's more wild impulses. So instead of a wife, it was time for Auntie Imperia to step in and try to arrange these things.

For the last week she had worked with Dahna to create a new routine for Maddelena – Bible verses in the morning to learn to read and write, walks at mid-day, weaving after a nap, then supper and bed. These were interspersed with board games and some other physical activity, different each day. Maddelena was eager to ride her pony, so that was kept as a treat should all her other lessons be complete.

Maddelena was excited for Christmas, as her parents were coming back to visit her, and bringing her sisters and some more of her belongings that had been left behind. And she was to have a new dress, with panels, just like a real lady. Antonia had to smother a laugh at that, as well as at a dozen other things the child said.

Pietro arrived before Cesco, who had gone directly to the whorehouse. Glossing over that fact, Pietro quickly related everything, including the detail of the cripple that he had kept back from everyone except Morsicato and Tharwat. "I'll tell Poco tonight. Have you seen him?"

"Every day," answered Antonia. "He has a whole house full of copyists starting work. The Scaliger was only too happy to approve the project, and he smoothed things over with the guilds, who were unimpressed with so many of their best artisans being hired away to craft books. They don't see the profit in it."

"There may not be any," said Pietro. "There aren't that many actual libraries, and most of them are in monasteries. Though the Church can certainly afford books. What we've been talking about is copying obscure manuscripts, not popular ones. Things that were lost — poetry, letters, philosophical tracts, scientific treatises. The smattering of Virgil and Homer and more, the plays that were preserved in the corners of the Roman Empire when Rome fell — those things have changed our world. It's like we're all waking up from a bad dream. Imagine if we were at the heart of that reawakening."

"I don't know why you think I need convincing," said Antonia tartly. "It was my idea, if I recall."

Pietro ducked his head. "Sorry. I get defensive. What about you? How is your little charge?"

Antonia answered his smile with a sad one of her own. "Mostly, it's been charming. Though Maddelena thinks it's her fault Cesco left. She misses him dreadfully."

Pietro sighed. "Another poor soul caught in his wake."

"Yes," agreed Antonia.

"Still, it must be nice being in a house with a child again."

Antonia's smile widened. "It is. And she's quite bright — which is good, as I don't know how not to live with brilliance."

Pietro laughed at that. "Are you reconsidering the Order? Do you want a child of your own?"

Antonia's smile vanished. "No! No, no children for me." She visibly forced herself to relax. "What about you? It's past time you were married. I want some legitimate nieces and nephews."

Pietro groaned. "Well, if it helps, Antony says my namesake is doing well." Antony had accepted a bastard of Poco's into his country household as a servant. It sat ill with them both, that the first grandson of Dante should be raised to be a servant, and Pietro continued to toy with the notion of taking the boy into his own house. But unless he planned on naming the child his heir, it would be awkward. Perhaps in a few years.

Antonia returned to the important topic. "How is Cesco?"

Pietro's face hardened. "He remains – how to say it? Insolently carefree. He was delighted to hear that Ziliberto has found some geese. They're having a pull tomorrow."

Antonia's nose wrinkled in disgust. "A goose pull!"

Pietro opened his hands. "Better a goose than a man."

"But isn't it dangerous? They're vicious!"

"You would be too, in their place." Then Pietro relented. "Yes, it's dangerous. But no moreso than half the things he's done in his life. At least in this there are rules."

"It's a revolting practice."

"Again, better an animal than a man."

"Better an animal who has no choice, no voice, than a man who volunteers and could turn away if he chose?"

Pietro reddened. "I meant, better Cesco faces an animal than a man. Men are rarely what they seem. The goose will be true to its nature."

"And will Cesco be true to his? I remember him at eight weeping over a lame horse."

"Horses are different," said Pietro firmly. "You should have seen Detto weeping over Vegliantino."

"How is torturing a goose for sport better than beating a horse?"

"It just is," Pietro answered lamely. Her look could have frozen his bones and made them shatter. "It's a common sport. Better that than another brawl. Though even odds we'll have one of those before the day is out. Which is why I'm glad Poco's got the publishing venture churning. We need to draw out his better angels. Give him something to focus on rather than such sports as geese and brawls."

"And whores," said Antonia.

"And whores," agreed Pietro, blushing a little. Even after years in the convent, his sister retained her characteristic bluntness.

"Well, our last attempt was a disaster. Fra Lorenzo has been openly worrying for Cesco's soul."

"He's not alone," said Pietro, who misliked Fra Lorenzo's concern.

"What about Lia? You saw her?"

"I did." Pietro swallowed, and related as much of the interview as his promise allowed. As he spoke, he recalled Lia's concern for Antonia. *'How is Suor Beatrice? Is she quite recovered?'* Pietro mentioned the question, and saw Antonia whiten as she said, "I had a summer cold, is all. It was kind of her to ask." It was clearly a lie. But then, Pietro was lying, too. He did not mention Lia's pregnancy.

After an hour of talk, Pietro said farewell. His aching thighs and shoulders begged for his own bed. He was not as used to riding as once he had been. Antonia watched him leave, then walked up the stairs to read the next chapter of Luke to Maddelena before bed.

◆   ◊   ◆

Cesco was at that moment also heading for a bed, though not his own. Arriving at the whorehouse, he had first ordered food and spent a pleasant hour eating, drinking, and making merry. At last he beckoned to Madonna Troppo and said he should like to go crusading again. "I feel I did not do the West justice in battering down her gates. Besides, I get to practice my Arabic."

Buthayna was summoned, and she dutifully journeyed up the stairs to her private chamber with the prince of Verona on her arm. Alone, he was much more seductive this time, much more a common client. Only when it was over did he begin asking about her. Who was she? Where was she born? How had she left her home?

Buthayna attempted to avoid the questions, asking about his life instead. She made sure to ask after his cousin, but then proceeded to ply him with questions about his prowess in the saddle and with a sword. With most men, this succeeded. Men liked flattery. But Cesco simply stared at her. "It is impolite to answer questions with questions."

"Forgive me," said Buthayna. "But I am unimportant. My life is here now."

"And I am here now," he answered, stroking the line of her naked hip. "And thou art important to me."

Buthayna knew she should not believe him. He was young, and making lover's talk. But she experienced a quickening of her pulse all the same. In Italian she said, "That is so very sweet. But if you are here now, is there not something you would prefer my mouth be doing?"

He laughed and agreed. "But I warn you – I find puzzles most alluring."

He likes puzzles, she thought, pressing her lips against his flesh. *Then I must remain one.*

◆   ◊   ◆

"My lord Castelbarco, there is a fellow at the gate who says he needs to see the Scaliger."

"The Scaliger is indisposed." Upon arriving at his palace, Cangrande had sent for a woman he favoured and retired to his suite on the top-most floor with a barrel of wine. It was not an uncommon occurrence, and the meaning was understood without acknowledgement. "What kind of man is he?"

"He speaks fair French, and halting Italian," reported the guard. "Says he's from the English court."

England? That was odd. Then Castelbarco recalled a knight who had visited Verona a few years back, before the overthrow of the English king. Ser William Montagu, a relative of Montecchio's who had fought bravely in the tourney that year. Well, if he had come to be knighted, he was several weeks too late.

Still, the man came from the English court, with its boy king and his regents. Not insignificant. "Very well. Bring him to me."

The moment the man was ushered in, Castelbarco experienced a frisson of unease. This was not Montagu. The foreigner's left eye was slightly squinted, more an affectation than a defect. His thin beard was even across his jaw, but didn't quite bridge the gap twixt chin and mouth. But what made Castelbarco dislike the fellow was his energy, his bearing. He resembled nothing so much as a horse about to buck.

"Well?" demanded Castelbarco in French. "This had best not be yet another complaint about the levies on bolts of English cloth."

"No, my lord," said the man in smooth French. "Forgive me. I regret intruding upon your time, but I come with a message from His Majesty King Edward, third of his name, for Cangrande della Scala, Prince of Verona, Imperial Vicar of the Trevisian Mark. But for the urgent nature of the message, I should hardly be here. I'd much prefer to join the revels I saw on my way in," added the man with a chuckle.

This fellow liked talking almost as much as the Capitano. "And you are?"

"Ah! Forgive me. My name is Aiello of Edinburgh." With that title aired, he switched suddenly from courtly French to a ruder Italian dialect. One from the Feltro. "I must confess, I offered to come on this mission as I've never seen my father's country, and I was, how you say, curious."

"You said your mission was urgent?" asked Castelbarco leadingly, still in French.

"I did, because it is," answered Aiello gravely. "I come with news of a plot against the life of the Scaliger."

TWENTY

THE CITY LEARNED of the Rakehells' return at dawn the next morning, when the honking of geese awakened even the earliest risers. Some swore, some called down curses, and some threw on clothes and rushed into the street to see what devilment these young hellions had thought of now.

They began with the largest gander the Master of the Hunt had procured, well fed, long-necked, and powerful. Its grey feathers were greased in pig-fat, its wings pinioned with tight cords. Feet and beak bound, it was taken to the longest straight stretch of road in the city, the ancient Roman road that ran from Genoa to Trieste, the recently christened the *Corso Cangrande*.

Here a rope had been suspended between opposite windows on the second level, drawn taut. The struggling gander was hoisted feet first into the air and suspended by its legs so that it hung in the exact center of the street. At the last moment, the binding across its beak was whipped away and it immediately began to protest its treatment.

Already the contestants were arriving, their horses gathered on the eastern end of the wide canyon of buildings so the rising sun would not be in their eyes. The question of the morning was to glove or not to glove. Gloves would protect the fingers from the bite of the goose, but make gripping it all the more difficult.

"No metal gauntlets!" Cesco insisted, seeing two knights fitting them in place. "Unfair advantage. Leather, or skin. This is about skill."

"Skill," said Benedick dryly.

Cesco offered the Paduan a cutting glance before returning his attention to the mass of riders. He lifted an object into the air. "The victor takes the prize."

There were gasps and admiring coos. The reward was not only a bag of silver, but also a fine sword – not one from the Scaliger's ruined forge, but a Spanish-made longsword with an ornate hilt and guard. Men eyed it hungrily as he flashed it about in the air. "Very well. Shall I go first?"

Applauded, Cesco got Abastor into position. Ziliberto del Angelo, Cangrande's Master of the Hunt, dropped the flag, and Verona's heir started forward. He began in a slow trot, but after a few paces kicked the ebon steed under him into a run. He did not lean low, but kept himself straight-backed and slightly forward, his left hand mastering the reins as he flexed his right.

The goose struggled furiously, trying to free its wings. A clever bird, it nipped again and again at its bindings, succeeding only in injuring itself. If it heard the clatter of hoof-falls coming close, it did not yet know what the noise signified.

"I know how you feel, friend! Bound, cribbed, confined, contained, and angry! Let's see whose anger is bigger, yours or mine!" Hurtling closer, Cesco stood in his stirrups and reached up. His ungloved hand caught at the goose's curled neck. His fingers closed, trying to hang on as his horse carried him past. But the powerful neck of the greased goose pulled free and Cesco came away with only a slimy hand and an earful of jeers and jibes.

They drew lots for the honour of the next to ride. "Ser Hortensio," said Ziliberto, "your turn."

"You know," observed Cesco, returning to lounge in his saddle as Hortensio took his place behind the starting line, "in Roman times, the goose was revered."

Benedick was gazing at the struggling fowl down the road. "You don't say."

"I do say. When Gauls invaded the city, the dogs were all napping, and it was the geese that raised the alarum. Thus dogs were foul creatures and considered un-Roman, whereas geese were honoured."

"A shame for this goose, then," said Yuri, "that he was born so late."

Cesco grinned. "That is indeed a crime, to be born out of one's own time. I often wonder what age would suit me better."

"What's better than the present?" demanded Benedick.

Cesco shrugged. "I don't know. Sometimes I think on Roman

plumbing with longing."

Hortensio missed the bird entirely. The third contestant was Salvatore, whose fingers couldn't find purchase. Young Petruchio fared no better than his twin, losing his grip as soon as he touched the bird. Yuri got nipped by the angry gander who was beginning to understand the sport.

Cesco welcomed Yuri back by using the prize sword to mockingly knight him. "Were it in my power, I would make you a true Veronese knight."

"Because all of Verona's true knights have chafed palms," added Benedick.

Amid the blows aimed at Benedick's head, Cesco said, "I only meant you'd have to be crazy to pull the goose. And as they say of the Veronese..." He turned to Benedick, expectant.

"*Tutti matti,*" recited the Paduan dutifully.

More and more men were arriving, knights and soldiers eager for a chance to win the sword. Slightly thinner in width than was common, it had a deep fuller, making it lighter and faster than a common blade. Passed around from hand to waiting hand, it was both admired and derided.

"It's almost weightless!" marveled Cesco's half-brother Barto.

"It'll break on the first shield it meets," scowled Yuri, rubbing at his bleeding finger.

"A good edge," said Fabio, eyes narrowed in discernment.

The air was filled with ribald jests as more racers took turns at the goose. Some tried to grasp it with both hands, steering their mount with their knees. Some tried shortening their stirrups to gain height. Many came away with razored nips on their fingers and wrists, and the whole crowd erupted with laughter as Berto was lifted entirely out of his saddle by the powerful neck to which he desperately clung. He slipped to the earth and came limping away, too bruised to laugh.

"We should regrease the goose," remarked Hortensio.

"If we do, no one will win," answered Cesco. "Maestro del Angelo, you chose our foe well!" The Master of the Hunt inclined his head with a smile.

"It's lucky Detto isn't here," observed Benedick. "His soft heart for animals might have prevented the whole enterprise."

"Lucky, is it?" asked Cesco, his eyes narrowed.

Benedick flushed. "My mouth outpaced my brain. That was thoughtless."

"It was. Though you're right, Detto would not approve."

The Scaliger himself arrived, in the company of young Paride and several other knights, Alberto and Mastino among them. Begged to take a run at the goose, the Scaliger steadfastly declined. "I have an interview in a few minutes. Matters of state. Has my heir gone yet?"

"No," answered Cesco, "but it's receding a bit at the temples."

Cangrande smiled. "I've been plucking it out in case I'm to be greased and pulled as well."

"I'd like to see the man that would try to grease and pull you."

"No man, but women grease and pull me nightly."

Cesco groaned. "Damn! I set that up for you, and I was saving it for myself."

"That's the trick," replied Cangrande. "Never save any for yourself. Spend it all."

"May I try it, cos?" asked Paride politely, pointing to the sword in Cesco's hand.

"Do, cos," answered Cesco, passing it over. "So long as your aunt approves."

Flushing, Paride took up the sword with relish and sent it into a series of arcing *molinelli* that had even Cesco's eyebrows raised. "The mild Paride is unexpectedly deft with a sword. Interview with whom?"

Cangrande watched the windmilling sword in the youthful hands. "What, taking interest in matters of state? That's inconsistent."

"I am noted for my unreliability. With whom are you meeting?"

"An emissary from the English court. He's come to repossess the silver I pawned for your wedding clothes. I hope you weren't expecting a new suit for Christmas."

"Damn. I had them burned the next day. I'll just have to come to Christ's Mass in the nude."

"You'll frighten the few virgins Verona has left. Better to come as the ass."

"Better the ass than the goose. That's another man missed. Who's next? My lord Capitano?"

Cangrande shook his head. "I haven't the stomach. Besides, the goose is getting tired." It was true. The gander was now lolling limp between bouts, husbanding his resources.

Cesco twisted in his saddle to face Mastino. "It falls to you then, cousin. A tired opponent, trussed and eager to die – you must find it most appealing."

"Interesting," said Mastino. "I seem to recall that was actually your kind of prey."

Cesco's smile widened, but he said nothing at all to the reference to Federigo della Scala, whom Cesco had helped to murder. Mastino believed that act, the murder of a kinsman, had called down a curse upon Verona's heir. Cesco quite liked the security of Mastino's fear of earning a similar fate.

Something in his smile spurred Mastino. To the surprise of all, he kicked his horse into a gallop as he would have done on the tilt-yard. Standing his stirrups on his racing mount, he stretched out his right hand. For a moment he had a good grip on the gander's throat, but the bird twisted away at the last possible second, and Mastino halted a dozen yards on, empty-handed.

"Too bad, poor mastiff," called Cesco over the applause for a valiant attempt – he had certainly come closest. "The Romans had it right! Geese are cleverer than hounds!"

"Maybe we should change our crest," said Cangrande.

"What, like Alaghieri? Perhaps. Shall we ask him if that's a goose feather in his new crest?"

"A griffin's, I'm sure," said Cangrande. "Nothing but nobility for our Pietro. I must say, I approve of this far more than you goosing every foreigner in the city and gandering at all the ladies. Dare I hope Bailardetto's misfortune has sobered you?"

"Is that why my head aches so? Someone, pass me some wine!" Drinking, he offered the skin to Cangrande, who refused it. "Signor Benedick thinks it best that Detto is not here, as he would think we abuse the poor goose."

"Better the goose than the poor Paduans."

Mastino returned from the far end of the avenue, looking pleased with himself. "Whoever takes it, it will be thanks to me. I felt something snap as I held the neck."

"Shall you ride again?" asked Cesco brightly.

"No, cos. You take my leavings. Come, Alberto, Guglielmo." With his brother and young Castelbarco flanking him, Mastino departed.

"I'll be off as well. Thank you, Francesco, for inspiring me. I think I'll pass the word to Giorgio that I've a mind for a fine goose for supper."

"You'll eat what I kill?"

"So long as it isn't crow." Departing, Cangrande crossed paths with the Montecchi family, just leaving their home to venture out into the street a block over. Young Romeo rode beside his father, bright-eyed and eager. Unlike most lads his age, his mount was a full-sized animal. The Montecchi were descended from centaurs.

In answer to his son's pleading, Mariotto said, "No, Romeo. That goose will toss you into the air and swallow you whole."

"Will *you* ride, father?"

"Of course he won't," said a deep basso voice. Antony Capulletto checked his mount as he arrived. "Montecchio couldn't risk his pretty face being nipped off."

Montecchio bristled at being insulted in the presence of his son. "Romeo, hold on!" Lifting the lad from his own horse, Mariotto swung the boy around behind him in the saddle. Forcing his way to the front of the line, he kicked his heels hard.

His mount burst forward with a rush of speed typical of Montecchi stock. Cheering, Romeo grabbed his father's belt at the sides, not wanting to inhibit his father's hands. In one swift move, Mariotto reached up, grasped the gander's neck, and pulled, twisting as he did so. The honking ceased as the goose's head was pulled clean off the neck, misting the winter air behind the horse with a spray of blood.

Cheers arose, though there were also jibes from those who had been waiting in line. Antony scowled. "Typical Montecchio. Jumps in and shows off, taking what's other men's by right." With that, Capulletto cantered away, allowing Thibault to emerge from his hiding place in the crowd.

Returning with his triumphant father, Romeo said to Cesco, "Did you see?"

"I saw, little Romulus. It was you anchoring your father to the saddle that enabled the feat." Romeo smiled, enjoying the praise even if it wasn't true. "Lord Montecchio, the purse is yours. But I believe the sword should go to your saddle-mate."

Romeo looked to his father. "May I?"

Ruffling his son's hair, Mariotto's teeth flashed. "His mother won't like it. But it's about time he started practicing with steel."

Cesco made a show of presenting the Spanish sword to young Romeo, who drew it from its scabbard to the applause of those watching. "Wait until Benvolio sees this!"

Mariotto was looking about. "Where's the Capuan oaf? He needs to eat his words. I can offer him the goose, if he provides the gall to sauce it."

"He left," said Ziliberto shortly.

"Of course he did. For such a large man, he's awful small-spirited. Come, Romeo. Let's go tell your mother of our triumph."

As father and son cantered off, Benedick looked to Cesco. "What was Philemon's joke about geese?"

"*'What can a goose do that a duck cannot and a lawyer should?'* The answer is, stick its bill up its butt. Yes, Montecchio and Capulletto should try to remove their bills from their backsides before those bills come due. Come, a new goose, a new prize – a pair of hand axes. And it's your turn to ride, Ahenobarbus."

Benedick da Padua swallowed a gulp of air, shook his head to clear it of last night's wine, and trotted his horse into position. He took a long lead, easing his mount into a headlong run. His fingers were bare, his stirrups shortened, his head held high.

The goose was drawing closer, honking and writhing with frantic energy. Standing in the stirrups, Benedick reached out, willing his left hand to close at just the right moment—

He was momentarily distracted by a muffled figure above him, in the northern window. A flash of silver—

He closed his fist, and the instant he grasped the goose he felt his victory. His grip was firm, he had control of the animal and was pulling the goose along with him.

Too much goose! The head did not come off, but instead came crashing down on him whole. The long beak snapped at him as the struggling goose landed on his head. Then he was yanked hard backwards, the fowl pulled from Benedick's grip even as he himself was pulled from the saddle. He landed on his back in the center of the street, the wind battered from him. The trussed goose hit the ground at the same moment, frantically snapping at Benedick's extended fingers. Rolling away from the flopping bird, the Paduan scrambled to his feet and tried to understand what had gone wrong.

The rope on the northern building had come free just as he had gripped the bird. Benedick had held the living goose for the two yards it took for the left-hand end of the rope to go taut again. The rope had torn the goose from his grip, and the unexpected force of the tug had taken Benedick clear from his seat.

Seeing him on his feet, the assembled riders at both ends gave him the appropriate cheers and jeers. He waved and made a show of laughing. Waving made him notice how much his hands were bleeding.

While a new rope was found and the furious bird returned to its place, Cesco, Salvatore, and the others clustered around Benedick. "Could someone collect my horse?"

As several Rakehells rushed to obey, Cesco lifted the cord and examined the end. Coolly he said, "Someone cut this rope."

"Why do that?" asked Benedick.

"To cause an accident," said Cesco carelessly. "You didn't by chance see who it was in the window?"

"No," said Benedick.

"I guess Detto is not the only one with an objection to today's sport."

"Maybe they were objecting to something else," said young Petruchio. "Like Paduans. Or red-heads."

Benedick frowned. "Wait? You're saying someone wanted to hurt me?"

Cesco laughed darkly. "Signor Benedick, I thought the events of the last few days would have taught you. If someone isn't trying to commit murder, it wouldn't be Verona."

◆   ◊   ◆

In the great public chamber of the Domus Nova, Cangrande stood beside his throne of office. A servant brought him wine, which he did not offer to the man kneeling before him. "Who are you, and why should I listen to a word you say?"

"My name, lord, is Jon Aiello," said the man in halting but passable Italian. "And as for my credentials…" He produced a packet of sealed papers, which Castelbarco carried to the Scaliger.

Examining the seal, Cangrande's eyebrows lifted. "This is—"

"—the royal seal of the king of England, yes," said Aiello with a complacent smirk.

Unused to being interrupted by anyone outside his family, Cangrande's mouth turned down. As he broke the seal, he said, "Castelbarco says you are a countryman of ours?"

"Yes. My father, Giovanni, was part of the expedition your noble father sent to aid the Scottish warlord Uilliam Uallas – that is, William Wallace."

Castelbarco and Cangrande exchanged a glance. It was a piece of Veronese history that was not well known. A *compagnia di ventura* of Veronese soldiers had been hired to aid the Scottish rebellion. Thankful for the help, Wallace had sent Cangrande's father a token of his gratitude in the form of a golden medallion encrusted with pearls. That medallion had then been passed to one of Alberto's many mistresses, and thence on to her son Gregorio Pathino, who had tried several times to murder Cangrande's heir and stake his own claim to the leadership of Verona.

Few knew the details of that story, which had concluded the previous year, when Ser Alaghieri had executed Pathino at the Papal court in Avignon. Hearing this piece of Scottish-Veronese history, Cangrande was warily interested. "I see. Your father stayed, I take it?"

"As many did, my lord. He took a Scottish wife after the battle and spent the remainder of his life fighting for Wallace. He survived Falkirk, but caught the flux after the siege of Perth in 1303." Aiello seemed unmoved by his sire's demise.

"How old were you?"

"Four, my lord."

"So you followed in his footsteps, selling your sword?"

"Yes, my lord," said Aiello proudly.

"And how does a Scots-born mercenary come to me bearing the seal of the King of England?"

"It is a long story, my lord," said Aiello, for the first time showing unease.

"Summarize it, then. Briefly."

It was not brief. Three times Cangrande had to chivvy the man along in his tale, for, once started, it was impossible to hurry Aiello the Scot to the point. But the gist was that he had fought his first large battle when he was seventeen, which had been a crushing defeat of the English king Edward II at a place called Bannockburn. After that, he'd continued to fight for the Scots in both his native land and in Ireland.

There was a veiled admission of a falling out with the Scots king, Robert the Bruce, and a vainglorious account of his choice to join the rebellious forces of Roger Mortimer in France. Mortimer had once been Edward II's close friend (a phrase that had many meanings, though here it seemed to denote only companionship, not romance), but had then cuckolded his king, entering the bed of Queen Isabella. Isabella had traveled to her native France, taking the king's son with her as hostage. Mortimer, at Isabella's urging and with the French king's backing, had raised an army and invaded England.

Seeing a chance to regain favour with the Scottish court (or perhaps just to carve out a new place for himself), Aiello had joined the ranks of Mortimer's invading army and helped the traitorous knight depose his former friend and sovereign in favour of the young Edward III. In reality it was Mortimer, newly created Earl of March, and Isabella who today jointly ruled England in the name of Isabella's underage son. After a period of confinement, Edward II had been put to death in a manner most ignominious.

"Since then I have been in the employ of the king of England, doing special services. When it was time to send a warning to Verona, the Earl of March deemed me a natural choice."

"Yes. Your dire warning." At last they had reached the point of the conversation. "You say a fellow called Montagu is on his way here to murder me."

"Or procure your murder," added Aiello, a most unbecoming grin lingering in his eyes. He enjoyed holding the attention of great men.

"Very well, very well," said Cangrande testily. "Whatever the means, the aim is my death. Who is this Montagu? Is he —?"

"A relation to the knight who visited Verona three years past?" finished Aiello, interrupting again. "Yes. Benjamin Montagu is the half-brother of the man you met, but from the wrong side of the sheets. He was acknowledged as far as the old father could, and has even been seen at court."

"Heavens," said Cangrande, arching an eyebrow at Castelbarco. "A bastard at court. What has the world come to?"

"Exactly what I say, my lord," opined Aiello, oblivious to sarcasm. "I chased this bastard through France, but he's wily. I lost him near Lyons. I thought it would be best to come here and warn you."

"Why?" asked Cangrande.

Aiello pulled himself erect. "I may never have set foot in Italy before now, but I have not forgotten my heritage. I am proud to call myself a Veronese-Scots.

"No, I mean why is this Benjamin Montagu coming to kill me?"

Aiello shrugged. "I have no earthly notion."

Cangrande stared, momentarily speechless. Then he screwed his eyes up tight. "You come here telling me that the half-brother of my friend, Ser William Montagu, is on his way to Verona with the express desire to end my life, and you do not know why?"

Aiello bowed. "Yes."

Cangrande and Castelbarco shared another bemused glance. "Where is your proof?"

"If I had proof, my lord, I would have presented it." Aiello took on a confiding air. "Truth, my lord Scaliger — I was given these orders by the king himself. He seems to suspect Montagu's loyalty and thinks that, just as your father once sent aid to the Scottish rebels, Montagu might try to win troops for a similar rebellion in England."

"But that's absurd!" cried Cangrande, half-laughing. "Even if this is true — and I cannot imagine so noble a knight as William Montagu contriving to overthrow his king — again, even if this is true, how does my death get him troops?"

Aiello frowned for a moment, pursing his lips to one side of his face. "The king feels certain that, whatever friendship you have for him, you would not aid in the overthrow of an anointed monarch."

"Unlike your friend the Earl of March," observed Castelbarco, utterly unimpressed by this kind of betrayal.

That checked Aiello, but only for a moment. "It's known that Veronese bankers have invested a great deal in England, both before and after the recent unpleasantness. You would not risk their profits by supplying soldiers for more fighting."

Cangrande was nodding. Here, at least, was some sense.

"But Sir William Montagu has hinted that he made friends here in Verona, and with a change in regime, those friends might be able to sway a new capitano to do what your lordship would not – supply troops to overthrow the throne."

Cangrande sank back into his seat. "My head hurts. Thank you for this timely warning, Signor Aiello. Should he arrive, I shall interview the man closely, and then do what I must to ensure I get to the truth of this," – he almost said *nonsense* – "business. For the meantime, you are as welcome as the prodigal son. Feel free to join our Christmas revels."

"Please, my lord," said Aiello, bowing even as he spoke, "I would like to be present when you interrogate Montagu's bastard."

An unseemly request. "I'll consider it. You may go."

Bowing again, Aiello sauntered out the door. Castelbarco turned to Cangrande. "I cannot make heads or tails of the thing. Can you?"

Already stalking towards another exit, Cangrande threw up his hands. "Who can ever know with these Englishmen? They're mad! They make Italian politics look quaint. And s'truth, I can do without foreign intrigue. I have enough troubles on my hands here at home."

As he gathered up the English papers and followed in Cangrande's wake, Castelbarco wondered if his lord meant the trouble with the Paduans, Treviso, the Emperor, or with his heir.

◆   ◊   ◆

Little Maddelena was playing Fox and Geese with Suor Beatrice when she heard her husband and his friends enter below. "They're home!"

"Early," answered Antonia, frowning at the board. Maddelena was playing the red fox piece, while Antonia had thirteen white pegs representing geese. Four of them were already lost, having been 'eaten' by the fox jumping over them. The object was for the geese to capture the fox by surrounding it so it could neither move nor jump, while the fox tried to 'eat' all the geese until capture was impossible. She shifted a piece, trying to set up the fox to jump it, and waited for Maddelena to move.

But Maddelena was looking towards the door as they heard Cesco's voice on the stairs saying, "…must say, as plots go, this one was fairly lame. Meant more to humiliate than kill."

Antonia's head came up, and Maddelena's little brows knit. Passing the door, Cesco waved and continued to help his red-headed friend up the stairs.

Maddelena leapt up. "What happened to Signor Benedick?"

"Nipped by a goose. Like you're about to be. Look at the board – the good sister is trying to trap you."

Confused, Maddelena looked down and puzzled until she saw the trap. She pointed at Antonia. "Suora! You're trying to win!"

"Shouldn't she?" asked Cesco, lingering.

Maddelena looked at Suor Beatrice with appreciation. "I thought she was letting me win. Dahna always does."

"Where's the fun in that?" said Cesco as he continued past with Salvatore and Benedick.

Antonia stood. "I'll be right back, Maddelena. Don't move the pieces. I know where they all are." Maddelena pulled a face that made Antonia want to laugh. She passed up the stairs and saw the door to Cesco's chamber was open. "May I come in?"

"If you must," said Cesco, who was changing his shirt and doublet into something finer.

"I hope the goose won," she said briskly.

"Oh, it did," groaned Benedick.

Antonia still did not quite know what to make of Signor Benedick, who had so quickly joined the ranks of Cesco's intimate friends. He seemed a witty fellow, but also a man in perpetual need of coin. Salvatore was more understandable. He was calm, but of an age with the others. Whereas Benedick had ten years on them all.

Sitting at the edge of his bed, Cesco gazed at Antonia warily. "All moved in, then?"

"Yes. I don't own much."

"Of course not. Given all to the Lord. Well, welcome. May you have more success curbing my wife's baser instincts than you had with mine." He stood. "Speaking of base impulses, I think I'm in the mood to lay in a feathered bed. Salvatore? Care to accompany me? I don't think Benedick is interested. He's had enough goosing for one day. And Auntie Imperia is saving her appetite for the Christmas goose, which of course is more savoury as it belongs to God. Whereas the goose I mean to set honking is surely bound for Hell. Do I shock you?"

"Cesco," said Antonia, "you could only shock me if you took the cross."

He laughed brightly, his eyes shining. "It's tempting, just to say I've shocked you! But I think I have enough crosses to bear. Come Salvatore. Barto and the others are below."

"Wait for me, dammit." Benedick struggled to his feet and followed, leaving Antonia alone in Cesco's room. She noted Cesco had left behind the pouch in which he normally carried the little wafers Tharwat and Morsicato supplied him with, and she felt hope. He wasn't taking them. Perhaps the attack on Detto had shocked him to his senses. If so, was it wrong to thank God?

TWENTY-ONE

CHRISTMAS IN VERONA in the year 1328 was a time of extraordinary joy. Peace with Padua, the knighting and marriage of the Heir, money flowing freely from the palace coffers, the prospect of a quick and tidy war against Treviso and the fulfillment of the promise of Cangrande's early days — all of this combined to make the Veronese people feel brighter about the future than ever before.

If there was any unease, it didn't stem from the attack on the Nogarola lad, which was brushed aside as bandits. And how foolish, to be out alone. Really he'd brought it on himself. Prince Rupert's disappearance was linked to the disappointed Count Berthold's failure to sway Cangrande from waging war.

No, the unrest in Verona was caused by the clergy. Not the Bishop himself, but several of the lesser abbots and friars, all of whom had heard Verona's heir declare there was no such thing as Heaven, and no such thing as Hell. In the two weeks since the reading there had been many sermons and loud proclamations, some of them quite impassioned, complete with thumping fists and flying spittle. Hell was real, and it was vital that men understood what awaited them if they did not embrace the example set by their Savior.

"Did not God reach down and punish the young lord at once, by injuring his closest companion, his own flesh and blood, his cousin? Such is the punishment due blasphemers, whoremongers, and unchivalric knights!"

This came from the Abbot of San Zeno. Yet another Scaligeri

bastard, technically he was Cangrande's half-brother, though nearly twenty years the Scaliger's senior. Their mutual sire, Lord Alberto della Scala, had foisted this troublesome by-blow off on the monks of San Zeno at an early age. It seemed to be something of a habit with the Scaliger *paterfamilias* – he'd done the same with Gregorio Pathino, to terrible effect.

Unlike Pathino, Abbot Giuseppe was not mad, but he was cut from a similar cloth, being rabidly devout and painfully close-minded. Had the Abbot known Cesco was to be found nightly in the arms of a Muslim whore, his dark statements would have been even more direct. For after the attack on Detto, Cesco spent more and more time in the solace of a woman with whom he could speak in a tongue no one else shared.

To quell any doubts about Verona's prince, the Church was in great prominence that holiday season, with Cangrande attending Mass each day. Excuses were spoken everywhere – the prince was young, had been raised by a poet, and was resentful of the Church for excommunicating both his father and foster-father.

Certainly during the Christmas Eve and Day services at the Duomo Cesco showed no hint of heresy. Instead he was considerate of his little wife, bringing smiles to every face as he guided her up for communion. When he ostentatiously entered the confessional, there was even a smattering of applause. That he lingered within the wooden walls for nearly an hour was laughingly remarked upon, and many wished they had been a fly within those walls to hear the great number of sins he sought to expiate. At last he emerged, followed by the sweating and disconcerted Bishop.

The city was alternately concerned and charmed. On Christmas Day there was another petty fistfight in the road outside his house, which, far from becoming an avoided spot, drew onlookers hourly to see what mad quarrel he would invent next. At the same time, a story spread about the gift he had given his little wife – a pair of puppies named for her sisters, and a doll bearing her own name. "This way, you will always have sisters about you, and you can be sure Maddelena is well-cared for." The city's women wept just as much as she did.

There was an added benefit for Cesco, as the puppies chased the cat Felix all over the house, keeping the creature too occupied to cross Cesco's path.

Icarus was unimpressed with the puppies. "Your own fault! If you'd stop befriending cats, you'd not have been usurped."

◆   ◇   ◆

While the common people were discussing Hell and the heir, the court was more interested in the latest addition to its ranks. As an emissary of the English king, Aiello the Scot could hardly be hidden. He was astonishingly loquacious, and had just enough Italian to keep the conversation flowing during the Christmas feast, talking the ears off his unfortunate interlocutors.

As more and more men began listening to the Scotsman, Cangrande started to frown. When Castelbarco even waved the musicians off, that he could hear better, the Scaliger called out, "Guglielmo! What says our guest that you are so fascinated?"

Castelbarco stood. "My lord, he is telling us the tale of the Veronese soldiers who fought for Scotland against the English king Edward I."

"Indeed? It is a tale I know only the bones of. Perhaps we should all hear."

Visibly pleased, the Scotsman stood to face the main table. "I know only what I heard from my father, as I was then but a wayward gleam in his eye. In 1296, it was clear that a rebellion was brewing. Edward Longshanks of England had forced the Scots king to abdicate, and was claiming possession of Scotland as his right. He held many Scottish lords as prisoners and demanded the rest bend a knee to him. That's when a bowman called Wallace began agitating for open war with England."

As the man spoke, Pietro stiffened. He had not yet spoken to the man, and was suddenly eager to draw him aside. It was not the actual words that had him leaning forward. It was the formation of them. There was a lilt to his accent, one he had only heard once before. Pietro glanced at Cesco, who was likewise interested. A glance not lost on the Scaliger.

Aiello was still talking. "My father was among a band of mercenaries hired to join the Scottish forces for the coming war."

At the far end of the room, Antony Capulletto was incredulous. "How on earth did a Scotsman end up hiring a Veronese condottierro? And where did he get the money?"

"When you want to hire the best," replied Petruchio Bonaventura, to wry masculine cheers.

"*Tutti matti,*" murmured his wife, to appreciative feminine laughter.

Giovanna della Scala held up a hand. "I can illuminate this part of the tale. When the revolt began, Wallace sent a letter to Lübeck, asking for assistance from the Empire. My uncle was at the time in Lübeck—"

"My sweet, there are some here who may not know who your uncle was." Cangrande turned to address the crowd. "My wife's father was Conradin, grandson of Emperor Frederick II. Conradin's sister Margaret was married to Albert the Degenerate. Their son was also called Frederick – Frederick the Bitten. Why was that, dear?"

"Because, in a fit of anger over her husband's philanderings, she decided to jettison the cad by running off. But when taking leave of her little son, she was stricken by the pangs of parting. Determined that the boy should feel similar pain, she bit him on the cheek."

Cesco lifted a cup to her. "A dear happiness, then, that your own union has not been blessed."

Everyone who heard him looked away, save Paride, who gasped, and the fifty-nine year old Giovanna, who pretended she did not hear.

Scowling, Cangrande pressed on. "Upon Conradin's death, Frederick the Bitten took up his throne, and became protector of my spouse until God saw fit to deliver her to me. You will all recall that her sister was the grandmother of our beloved Paride here." Cangrande reached across to ruffle Paride's hair. "He died just five years past. Otherwise he would have been a great aid in my dealings with Ludwig. Anyway, this Frederick the Bitten, King of Sicily, Jerusalem, and Duke of Antioch is the man my wife calls uncle."

It wasn't often that Cangrande made such long-winded boasts of his ties to the Holy Roman Empire. He had conveniently glossed over the fact that Giovanna was herself illegitimate, and born after her father's death. Pietro suspected that such grandiosity would become more common in the days and weeks to come. Cangrande was laying the ground to step onto a wider stage. As soon as Treviso was his, there would be no stopping him.

Cangrande gestured for his wife to continue, and she smiled. "Thank you, husband. As I was saying, Uncle Frederick was in Lübeck, negotiating for the return of some land from King Adolf. He was unsuccessful, and angry. Under threat of being deposed, Adolf needed his alliance with England more than ever. To spite Adolf, Uncle Frederick funded a band of brave Italian and German soldiers to fight on the side of the Scots. He was already friendly with the Lord of Verona, and naturally asked for willing men."

Cangrande picked up the tale. "I take it, Signor Aiello, that your father was one of these hired swords."

Having waited with fidgety patience, Aiello was eager to again hold the reins of the tale. "He was, my lord. They arrived in the summer of 1297, and were present at the Battle of Stirling Bridge." He looked around, expecting the name to mean something. "Stirling Bridge? The huge rout of the English army? Despite being vastly outnumbered? A victory so complete that Wallace was able to have a baldric made from the English commander's skin?"

"Charming," drawled Nico da Lozzo.

"Like Hercules with the lion," said Petruchio.

"Only this lion belonged to England," joked his son.

Pietro did not join in the jesting. His mind felt like it was on fire. *All the talk of Scotland, and the medallion, the link to Pathino. We even knew she had been heading for England when she disappeared. Yet we never even considered Cesco's mother might be Scottish.* For this fact was suddenly clear to him.

Times like these made Pietro believe in the stars, in divine guidance from above. After years and years of waiting and wondering, of searching and simmering, all their questions were answered from several sources at once — the house, the name, and now the nationality. It had to be enough.

Arching an eyebrow at his favourite knight, Cangrande said, "Ser Alaghieri is entranced. Please, Signor Aiello, go on."

The dark-haired mercenary happily obeyed. "After that, Wallace led a raid into England itself. But he couldn't pay for the Italians to go with him, so they instead joined the guards on the Scottish border. Some liked Scotland so well that, when the campaigning season closed, they decided to remain. My father was one — he took a girl from Langholm to wife. Which meant, of course, he was present the next year for the Scots' defeat at Falkirk."

"What happened to this Wallace then?"

"He escaped the battle, and went to France, then to Rome."

"Passing through Verona on his way," added Cangrande laconically. "I remember meeting him. I was about eight. He seemed tall to me. Very broad-chested."

"He was a longbowman," agreed Aiello. "He'd have to be."

"Not that tall," said Castelbarco, squinting as though he could see back into time.

"What did he come here for?" asked Antony Capulletto.

"Money. Soldiers. Money and soldiers."

"Did he get them?"

"No," said Cangrande. "By then Adolf had been deposed. With no further need to stir up trouble against the king's English allies, Frederick the Bitten declined to send either gold or more men.

Though it seems Scotland gained several brave Veronese for all time," he added for Aiello's benefit. "We are grateful you've chosen to visit us, and I hope you will stay through the coming holy days."

Aiello preened. "My lord della Scala, it would be my deepest pleasure and honour."

Cangrande gave a wave to Manuel, who in turn signaled his apprentice Noam, who began to play. The other musicians followed suit. As the guests returned their attention to their plates and their neighbours, Cangrande faced Cesco and Pietro. "I assume by your expressions that you have made the logical deduction."

"Yes," said Cesco brightly. "I'm the son of William Wallace."

Cangrande barked out a laugh. "Only if he could impregnate from beyond the grave! He died nearly a decade before you were born."

"You're not Cangrande's son?" asked Maddelena, frowning.

Cesco turned towards his wife and rubbed a thumb across her crinkled brow. "It seems you've married a Scotsman," he said to her. "My mother was Scottish."

Maddelena looked around. "Oh. Where is she?"

"In Heaven," replied Cesco. "Somebody told me she died."

Maddelena grasped his hand. "I'm sorry. You must miss her so much."

Startled, Cesco patted her awkwardly. "It is difficult to miss someone you never knew." He gazed at Cangrande. "Still, it is a revelation."

"That you have Scots blood in your veins?" asked the Scaliger. "Why? Is it better than other blood? Wilder, perhaps. And more voluble," he added drily, glancing at Aiello.

"I must learn all I can about my new country."

"Perhaps you should visit."

"And leave my wedded wife at home to pine? Surely not."

Cangrande shrugged. "It was only an idea."

Cesco wagged a finger. "You'll not be rid of me so easily." He stood and slipped from the high table down to where Aiello the Scot was still hammering anyone who would listen with his combination of French and Italian. "Master Aiello, I wonder if you could help me."

Jumping to his feet, the Scotsman performed a flourishing bow. "My lord prince! If I can be of service, I will."

"Someone once threw words at me. I wonder if you know them. The first is – forgive me, I may mangle it – *siabrae*."

The Scotsman seemed taken aback. "*Siabrae!* Hunh. Yes, it's a Scots word. Rather like a mermaid, but a daemon."

"Indeed. Fascinating. And *uirisg?*"

Aiello's brows leapt skywards. "A rare word indeed. Sometimes it means a form of sprite, or water spirit. It's used in the Highlands, for creatures of the streams. But most often it means goblin. Wherever have you heard those words?"

"I forget," said Cesco, shaking the question off. "One final translation, if you please. *Mo chridh* – what does that mean?"

"*Mo chridh?* It means 'my heart'. A form of endearment."

Looking into the middle distance, Cesco said, "Thank you, Signor Aiello. From the bottom of my heart. Excuse me. Nature calls." With that, he left the bustling chamber.

Watching from the High Table, Cangrande slipped into the seat beside Pietro. "He has a new puzzle. Perhaps it will help to distract him."

Pietro stared for a long moment. "You could give him the rest of the pieces."

"And deprive him of his fun? You have the house now, and so you must have the name." Cangrande answered Pietro's look of surprise with an arched eyebrow. "My darling sister told me you possess the cripple. May you have joy of him. I've had enough prophecies for ten lifetimes. As for Cesco, he wouldn't believe the truth even if I told him. He is in a contradictory phase of the moon. May the Christmas star offer him a new light to follow."

"Like you, I think he's had enough of the stars."

Cangrande clucked his tongue. "As I learned long ago, it doesn't matter if we've had enough of them. It's when they've had enough of us that we should worry."

◆   ◊   ◆

Christmas Day was not the end of the holiday season, but the start. For twelve more days the joy would be spread in songs, in the ringing of the city's many bells, in drinks and warm sweets, in gifts and alms, in smiles and embraces.

"Saturnalia!" shouted Cesco. "Unbind Saturn's feet, let masters and servants change places, and set loose the Lord of Misrule. A most apt title, don't you think?"

Cangrande kept his own Lord of Misrule busy within the public view for every daylight hour of the next few days. Yet for each one, Cesco found a way to subvert the proceedings. At the feast of San Stephano, he read out the section of Acts recounting Stephano's testimony about Salvation, ending with the saint's own chastisement:

You stiffnecked and uncircumcised in heart and ears, you always resist the Holy Ghost: as your fathers did, so do you also. Which of the prophets have not your fathers persecuted? And they have slain them who foretold of the coming of the Just One; of whom you have been now the betrayers and murderers: Who have received the law by the disposition of angels, and have not kept it.

Pietro heard a heartfelt rebuke in that section, and had to smile when Cesco proclaimed, "Behold, I see the heavens opened, and the Son of man standing on the right hand of God." Cesco had ranged himself to stand upon Cangrande's right. Blasphemy in one sense, but one the assembled Veronese tolerated. Unlike Stephano, no one pelted him with stones.

At the feast of San Giovanni the Evangelist, Cesco had suborned Berto to join his voice to the choir, but in a key that undermined the musicality of the verses. Together with Cesco, they succeeded in turning the pious psalms into a drinking ditty. The trio of musicians Manuel was training joined in, to their master's dismay and the crowd's joy.

On the day of the Holy Innocents, the heir took his little wife to play with the children of city, devising a game of *Tintinnio* that ranged across the whole of the Piazza dei Signori and beyond. In that contest, he showed his wife the trick he'd employed as a boy, climbing high and leaping from plinth to plinth to frustrate the blindfolded seekers below. He ended with an admonishment. "Never willingly blind yourselves, children. For life is a game in which the rules are always broken."

On the day of San Tommaso, martyr of England, Cesco tried out a new tongue. Spending hours each day in talk with the visiting Scot, Cesco displayed his uncanny skill at languages by reading out a poem about the Englishman Becket. He read it again in French, that the message might not be lost. It was a warning of the power of tyrants — poignant, since Cangrande was seen as the perfect example of a good tyrant. He couched his words behind those of Aristotle: *'What it lies in our power to do, it lies in our power not to do.'*

"Exactly," said Cangrande in hearty agreement once the words were translated. "It has been my experience that the advice we give, we most often need to heed."

"Has it?" asked Cesco brightly as he settled into his place at table. "And what advice do you have for me, that you should heed? Is it 'Do not grow old?'"

"Actually, I find myself reminded of Epictetus. *'Make the best use of what is in your power, and take the rest that happens.'*"

At which Cesco laughed, and laughed. "Why so I do, *pater!* I take everything as it comes. Don't you?" The hashish was in strong evidence. His pupils were dark and wide, and he looked almost deranged.

Cesco did not participate vocally in the New Year's Eve revels, but he did dance, showing off his acrobatic prowess. He only subsided to listen intently to the songs of the Virgin – as her day, January 1st, fell on a Sunday this year, it was customary to move it up a day or two. Thus December 31st was both an honouring of the Madonna and an ushering out of a very fruitful year.

There was a play this night (using a script not tampered with by Cesco, penned by Cangrande himself) depicting the Virgin raising her troublesome child. It was an amusing pastiche of Cesco, and he himself laughed aloud several times. "If only I could turn the Rakehells into birds! Can you imagine the trouble we'd get up to?"

"Not a statue would be safe," agreed Cangrande.

Yet all the talk that evening was of the ailing health of the Venetian Doge, who had declined so dramatically these last weeks. The trial of the merchant Ansaldo had been his last public appearance, and he was not expected to live out the week.

The obvious successor was Francesco Dandolo, who seemed so friendly with the Scaliger in public, contrasting the rumours of assassination plots and imprisonment of Cangrande's trusted knights. Enough of the rumours were true that those in the know did not stem the tide. It was whispered in Verona that if Dandolo were to become Doge, it would mean war with Venice.

"Which the Scaliger will win," crowed young Petruchio.

His little sister Evelina was dubious. "No one has ever beaten Venice at war."

"She has no armies," said Hortensio.

"Nor walls," added his twin.

Evelina curled her lip downwards. "She's never needed them. As long as she has water and ships, the Serenissima will remain serenely unconcerned by war."

"You know these Scaligeri! Between the Capitano and the Hell-Hound—"

"Hell-Hound?" asked Vittoria, eldest of the four Bonaventura children.

"Cesco, obviously," retorted Evelina. "What a stupid name."

Hearing Cesco's name was enough to make Vittoria cloud up.

It still stung that she had never even been considered for his bride. In public feasts of this sort, where the men and women co-mingled, she often found herself looking at the central table and hoping the little bride would choke on her meal.

Looking up now, she noticed that the girl was falling asleep, and that her nurse was seated beside her in Cesco's place. "Where is the young prince?"

Petruchio and Hortensio glanced around. "Damn! He promised the next escapade would be ours!"

Turning from their adult conversation, their mother finally weighed in. "He is not your plaything, nor are you his keepers. Mind yourselves, and watch your blasphemies, or I'll have your father send you to the country house to muck out the stables. Again."

Vittoria looked smug, the twins crestfallen, and Evelina amused. Everyone thought their mother was mad, but to her children she seemed the sanest person in the world. In their youth, their playmates had often said that Kate was 'funny, but mean'. Most of the adults had stories to tell of her that made her sound utterly lunatic, which they claimed arose from her Paduan heritage.

In truth, her madness stemmed from a deep independence, a trait she tried to foster in her children, with varying degrees of success. So even when hushed, young Hortensio could not resist asking the question again. "But where is the Hell-Hound?"

♦   ◊   ♦

The same question (without the irreligious title) had been asked moments earlier at the High Table. Like the Bonaventura clan, Pietro had noticed the nurse Dahna in Cesco's seat. After unsuccessfully scanning the room for signs of unsuppressed revelry, he'd leaned over to Castelbarco. "Where's Cesco?"

Castelbarco shrugged. "No doubt we'll hear the shouting." With that, he returned to the conversation on his left.

Dissatisfied, Pietro was about to call for a servant when he sensed someone's presence at his shoulder. The man leaned forward, and Tharwat's broken voice rasped in his ear. "He has asked for us. Quietly."

Excusing himself, Pietro threw on his cloak and gloves and followed Tharwat out into the frigid air. The Piazza dei Signori was quiet. From the sound of it the Piazza delle Erbe still had some life in it, but this square faced by three Scaliger palaces, the city hall, and the house of justice was not a place frequented by the night owls of the city.

One figure, though, was present, if unexpected. Pietro started forward, but Morsicato waved his hand. "Detto's fine. Tender on his side, but fine. Wishing he was here, let me tell you. Christmas with his mother was more of an ordeal than the stabbing."

"I'm glad to hear he's well," said Pietro, blowing into his hands. "But then why—?"

"—am I here? Summoned. The note wasn't even coded. Just told me to be at the palace on New Year's Eve. Esta was unhappy, and unwell when I left. You don't know what he's up to?"

Pietro was about to reply when a voice greeted them from across the piazza. "Gentlemen! Over here!"

The odd party of three – the limping knight, the barrel-chested doctor with the forked beard, and the one-eyed Moor – kicked up small puffs of snow as they headed for the northwest corner to the ancient well where Cangrande's will had once been hidden.

"You came. I was worried you'd be too stupefied by the spirit of the season." Bundled up against the cold, Cesco was standing beside two iron crows, four buckets of boiling water, and a large sheet. He beckoned them onto the stone lip that ringed the ornately carved well. It was wide enough to fit all of them together, and Pietro had a fanciful moment wondering if they were going to descend. But the heavy stone lid covering it prevented them.

Morsicato stamped his feet, clapping his hands against the cold. "What are we doing here, boy?"

"Honouring the Virgin Mother, I think." Cesco handed Pietro one of the pry-bars. "Here. Help me with this."

With a confused look at the others, Morsicato bent to aid Cesco on his pry-bar while the Moor helped Pietro on his side. Together they laboured to raise the stone slab fitted into the octagonal mouth of the old well.

"Before I went to Otto's camp, I had a thought," said Cesco, "about one mystery."

"What is it?" asked Morsicato, straining.

"We'll know as soon as we get this open. Push!"

They obeyed, silent save for their groans and breathing. The singing from the next street felt oddly remote, other-worldly.

"Where's Signor Benedick?" gasped Pietro. "Your other Rakehells? They could be – *useful* – for once. "

Cesco wasn't yet breathing hard. "I may play the fool. Doesn't mean I am one. There's no need to share secrets with those who don't already know." With a last effort, he and the doctor heaved their end free. "Besides, this – is a family affair."

They shifted the rose-marble slab past the two pillars that held the winch and down onto cobblestones dusted with snow. Cesco next lifted one of the buckets and handed it to the Moor, who began pouring the steaming water down the well. They had to also knock ice off the chain before it would rise from its hook to be attached to the winch above.

"I hope your suppers are settled," said Cesco, gazing down mirthlessly. "This will be a dirty business."

Pietro realized that it wasn't just ice that was holding the chain down. Something heavy was attached to the other end.

"Is it the old metal box?" asked Morsicato, meaning the container for the will.

"Too heavy for that, surely," groaned Pietro as he got the winch working and hauled on it, dragging whatever was below up from the shadows to just below the level of their feet. Tharwat fetched a torch from a sconce around the corner. As they leaned in to see what it was, Pietro felt a ghoulish premonition.

A body. A body, wrapped in a leather hide, bound tight.

In a tone so hushed it sounded reverent, Pietro asked, "Who is it?"

Cesco leaned back, his eyes unfocused. "A lady of Scotland, I imagine."

"Christ Jesus," said Morsicato at the same moment Pietro murmured, "Oh Christ."

"I should have figured it out before," said Cesco woodenly. "Donna Maria's final resting place, courtesy of Signor Fuchs."

Shivering, Pietro gazed down at the bundle in the well. "Why here?"

"His way of giving me the fig. So much lovely symbolism – it's where the body of the first Mastino was unceremoniously dumped after his murder. And where Castelbarco hid Cangrande's will from Mastino. *Contrapasso.* Turnabout. Whatever you want to call it. My mother's body, hidden in plain sight. It's actually clever, in a blunt way."

After some debate they tied a rope around Cesco's waist. Pietro didn't want Cesco to be the one to go down, but being the smallest and the lightest, it made the most sense.

The body was badly decayed, and lay far below the water line. A seam of the leather wrapping had burst, leaking bits of the corpse into the water. Cesco had to dive again and again into icy liquid that contained floating pieces of his mother. Though he tried, the bones would not hold on to each other and in the end he had to bring her loose parts up piece by piece. He also retrieved as much of her clothing as he could identify. He vomited once, and his hands had surely lost their feeling, but he refused to come up until he was finished.

Wrapping the woman's body in the sheet Cesco had brought, the ghoulish quartet retired to Pietro's house. Cesco rightly did not want Maddelena to see the remains of her mother-in-law.

Evidently summoned as well, Antonia was waiting for them with food and drink. Cesco was told to go bathe while Pietro, Tharwat, and Morsicato took the corpse down to the cellar, where, like Cangrande's baths, the remnants of old Roman pillars rose from the floor. A table was brought, and the remains placed upon it.

"We should be doing this in a church," said Antonia.

"Time enough for churches," said Morsicato. "Give me more light, will you?"

They barely finished before Cesco entered the cellar. He found his mother's body lain out and wrapped in a clean sheet. "She looks small. Diminished in death. That's worth remembering."

"Cesco," said Pietro. "We are so sorry. We —"

"You didn't know. You only did what you thought was best. You were only thinking of me. Yes, I know it by heart." He turned to Tharwat, standing near the wall on the room's far side. "I need to think of a new quest for you. How about a piece of the true cross? Or maybe an impression of Prestor John's foot?"

"Cesco," said Pietro earnestly. "This might not be the moment, but we've learned something about her. Her name was Donna Maria d'Amabilio."

"M-A-B," said Cesco. He had been shown the coded message in August.

"It's time we told you about the cripple." And Pietro explained what Girolamo had told them, about the house they had found, and about his presence at the scene of Detto's assault.

"So you think he saved Detto's life? The first practical application of star-gazing I've heard of. I think I should trade you in," he added to Tharwat. "Like a tired horse. We can put you to stud, if you like."

"We have to find Girolamo first," said Tharwat, unoffended.

Pietro was less interested in the crippled diviner than in the question of Cesco's mother, now before them. "We know enough now to send to England and trace her movements."

"What does it matter?" Cesco took in their confused faces. "I'm honestly asking. What does it matter?"

Pietro's eyes narrowed. "We owe it to her."

"The dead have no debts."

"The living do," countered Pietro.

"Well, as her heir, I absolve you of this one. Because it doesn't matter. Fuchs is dead."

"What about her message to you? We think it's a warning against Mastino."

Cesco raised his brows dramatically. "I hardly need warning about him, do I?"

"What if Mastino was, in fact, behind it?"

"Then let God punish him," said Cesco mildly.

"You don't believe in God," said Antonia.

It was the first time those words had been spoken aloud, and they hovered for a long time in the cellar air.

"But you do," said Cesco at last. "You believe in Divine Retribution. Shouldn't we just leave Mastino to God?"

"The Lord works through Man," said Pietro.

"Then He's doing a pretty awful job. Besides, isn't the tale of your cripple proof enough of the power of Divine Retribution and Mercy? He planned to murder a child, he was punished, he has sought forgiveness, in a way, and he has been gifted with the Sight. Not that the Church approves of such things," he added.

Tharwat started to speak. "Girolamo—"

"—doesn't know anything about my mother. He knows about her house. He knows something damaging to Detto's mother. I'd like to see him shut up, for Detto's sake. But all of that has nothing to do with me. As far as my mother goes, he's told us all he knows." Looking at the corpse, Cesco swayed slightly. "Her story is ended. I'm leaving. There are too many ghosts here."

Pietro suspected the young knight was not talking about his mother's corpse. Cesco and Lia had used this house as a rendezvous. It could hold no good memories for him now.

"Cesco, wait." Antonia looked to her brother. "Tell him. He needs to know she's alright. Give him that balm."

Pietro did not want to, but she had forced his hand. "Cesco — before the attack on Detto, I went to see Rosalia."

In the door, Cesco gazed at him with no expression at all. "And?"

"She is well."

Wincing, Cesco pointed at the corpse. "She was, too. But we took her from the well, and must find her a grave. It shows the cost of meddling. Leave her be. One dead female relation is enough." He looked to the body on the table. *"Mo chridh."* With that, he exited.

Tharwat followed, leaving the others in the flickering light of the cellar. Antonia squeezed her folded arms. "We should have talked to him. About the hashish, if nothing else."

"He cannot be abusing it," said Morsicato with certainty. "The new wafers we've devised would put him to sleep before he could over-indulge."

"Did you see his eyes?" demanded Antonia.

"Drink," answered Morsicato with certainty. "It cannot be hashish."

Antonia was unswayed. "Then we should have confronted him about the drink. You don't live with him. He's like his father, there's always a goblet in his hand. But he's fourteen, not forty. He shouldn't be drunk at all!"

Pietro laid a hand on her arm. "He would not have heard us. Not tonight. Tonight was about his mother." When she opened her mouth to protest, he said, "Take comfort in this – when he needed help, he came to us."

Outside the bells were ringing. The new year had started.

◆　　◇　　◆

Falling in step beside Cesco on the street, Tharwat was silent.

"What?" demanded Cesco. "A new chart? A new drug? A new life?"

Tharwat kept his breath even. "If it becomes too much, there is an option."

"Death is always an option," retorted Cesco. But even that brought a frown to his lips. No one but Detto knew that he had once called Lia by the name of Death.

"Travel. Nothing frees the mind and the spirit like escaping the site of trouble. I have a letter from a friend. He is called Battuta. He has repeated his invitation to join him as he explores Arabia. It is an option."

"First Cangrande, now you. Everyone wants rid of me. But leaving is admitting defeat. How little you all know me." With that, Cesco increased his pace, and Tharwat let him go.

◆　　◇　　◆

In *La Rosa Colta*, Buthayna waited, and was not disappointed. But Cesco seemed uninterested in lovemaking. Instead they sat in darkness together, his back to her front, naked under a blanket, while he drank and recited lines from Dante, from Ovid, from other poets he did not trouble to name. Only one she knew, for it was in her own tongue:

> *Now the New Year reviving old Desires,*
> *The thoughtful Soul to Solitude retires,*
> *Where the White Hand of Moses on the Bough*
> *Puts out, and Jesus from the Ground suspires.*

And she held him as he wept. Only when the tears were done did he turn and enfold her into a more ardent embrace. Whatever it was that troubled him, it was her duty to give him solace. To her dismay, it was also her desire.

TWENTY-TWO

Sunday, 1 January 1329

To the people of Verona, the first day of January was something special. While the rest of the world carried on in the year 1328 until Easter, the Veronese calendar was yoked to the old Roman way. Hence the ushering in of 1329, a year everyone predicted would bring great things – victory over Treviso, newfound power and wealth for Verona, and all the blessings prosperity could bestow.

At noon Pietro called at Cesco's house, Poco in tow, nominally to escort their sister to the feast but really to draw Cesco into a discussion of publishing. They were somewhat successful, getting the names of a couple texts they might look into, until he realized what they were up to and told them they'd make more money just publishing translations of Catullus.

"Who?" asked Maddelena.

"He wrote about girls, but in Latin, so they can't read it."

"That's not fair," objected Maddelena.

"It isn't, is it?" agreed Cesco. "But Nuncle Poco can fix it. No one better."

A large group of servants bustled about them. Progress was slow – Maddelena had eschewed a carriage, determined to walk all six blocks. So Cesco had left Abastor behind, holding his wife's hand to keep her from slipping on the icy stones.

Some Rakehells arrived to act as an escort. Benedick walked on Maddelena's side, and Salvatore behind, ready to catch the little bride if she fell. Berto and Barto were discussing a hawk their father had just purchased.

At the center of the party was Detto. Arriving in Verona with his father for the celebrations, he'd come straight to Cesco's house on the *via Pigna*. He moved slowly, like someone five times his age. But he was upright, and his colour was excellent.

"Morsicato says the best antidote to illness is youth," repeated Detto.

"Thank heaven it isn't innocence," said Cesco, "or I'd be long dead. Hey ho, pincushion. It was very inconsiderate, not dying. Everyone was preparing to mourn you. I hear Valentino wrote a most eloquent eulogy. It was unkind of you to cause all that effort to be wasted."

"He'll have it when it's needed," answered Detto. "I was just tired of you getting all the attention."

"So you stabbed yourself?"

"Couldn't manage it. My skin is too thick. See, your words bounce right off."

"Are they so sharp?"

"Sharper than a real welcome."

Cesco grinned. "Wah wah. What do you expect? If I hug you, you'll pop like a bladder."

"Not from your hugs. They're soft and mild. Almost like your arms held no strength."

That brought Cesco into a mock scuffle, which ended in an embrace. After more welcomes and banter of sickbeds and stabbings, Benedick said, "While you were in Vicenza, Detto, what did you hear of the Doge?"

"That he is ailing," answered Detto, wincing a little from the rough play.

"I hear the world is ending," retorted Cesco.

"Is it?" asked Maddelena fearfully.

"No," replied her husband with a wink. "I mean to say, don't believe everything people say."

"Even what you say?" asked Maddelena.

"Especially what I say."

"Figs," said the little girl, repeating the mild oath he often employed. Cesco laughed, and she laughed with him. She was growing a little bolder in her husband's company.

"Still," continued Benedick, "isn't that bad? Dandolo as Doge? I thought you didn't like him."

"I don't, but for personal reasons. He was unkind to a friend of mine." Cesco's step faltered and his lips twitched in one of his lopsided smiles.

"What?" asked Benedick.

"Just thinking of the qualifications to be Doge. One must be a citizen. Nothing more."

"So?"

"Cangrande is a citizen. They made him one to honour the *Pax Verona*."

The Rakehells were all staring. Maddelena said, "Why did they do that?"

"It is the habit of men to give presents to people who scare them," explained Cesco. "Cangrande scares the Venetians, so they gave him the best present they could think of – they made him one of them."

"*You* gave him presents for Christmas," said Maddelena.

"I gave you presents, too," said Cesco. "Because you frighten me so."

"I do not, silly." Maddelena pressed her point. "Are *you* scared of him?"

"I used to be."

"Why aren't you now?"

"There is no longer anything he can take from me that I value."

If it was not lost on the adults, this flew directly over the little girl's head. "*I'm* not scared of him," she said firmly.

"You're braver than I was by far. After all, you married me!" In answer to which, Maddelena glowed.

Just behind them walked the three Alaghieri siblings. Antonia asked, "Tharwat is where?"

"On his way back to Padua, to make inquiries about Girolamo and Donna d'Amabilio. Someone may remember a Scotswoman."

"Cesco said the story was finished," said Antonia.

"As he just remarked," said Pietro softly, "don't believe everything you hear."

"Oh. Did Morsicato go with him? Or did he go to check on Donna Katerina?"

"Neither. He got a message this morning. Esta's unwell again."

Antonia shared a look with her brother. Hearing the mysterious illness had returned made both siblings wary. Pietro opened his hands. "He sends his regrets. He didn't want to leave." *Especially as he spent the whole night fruitlessly examining a corpse.*

"He'll be sad to miss this feast," said Poco. The doctor was known as a true appreciator of exquisite food.

Antonia said, "Perhaps we could ask for the recipes and send them to him to recreate."

"Recreate?" asked Cesco from before them. "I love to recreate. My favourite recreation is the creation of recreations for miscreants such as these Paduans here."

"Better a mis-creation than a re-creation," said Benedick.

"To be sure, it is always better to be original," agreed Cesco.

"Isn't that what Lucifer said?" asked Salvatore. The Rakehells all laughed, though Detto quickly stopped due to his side. Pietro and Antonia did not laugh at all.

They arrived at the palace in good order, and entered the feasting hall looking fine. Surprisingly, the first to greet them was Giovanna, Cangrande's wife. "Welcome, welcome. Hello, sweetheart," she said, kissing Maddelena on the cheek.

"Such uncharacteristic warmth, Madonna," said Cesco. "Are you quite well? Have you been possessed by the spirit of the season?"

"Another spirit entirely," she said with an unfaltering smile.

Cesco glanced behind him theatrically. "I sense a sword hovering over my neck."

Giovanna laughed. "What a wit you have, Ser Francesco. I have always admired that in you. It serves you well."

"As I don't have murder to fall back upon, I must rely on my wits."

Even at this her smile did not break. "As I say, very amusing. Ser Alaghieri, Suor Beatrice, Signor Alaghieri – welcome." She bussed them all on the cheek before moving along.

"That's worrying," said Pietro.

"It is," said Antonia, deeply suspicious.

"Be sure to have someone taste your food," replied Cesco.

Cangrande broke away from a cluster of lustrous lords to greet them. "Happy New Year!"

Straightening from his bow, Pietro said, "Lady Giovanna seems happy."

"As well she might! I have given permission for Ser Paride to journey abroad, in her company. They leave in late March, first for Germany to see her relations, then on to Paris. He has been accepted to study in the University there."

"Paris in Paris!" roared Poco.

Even Antonia smiled. "How apt."

"Let us hope he does not marry there," observed Cangrande. "For a fellow whose very name means 'married to death', it would be an unfortunate doubling of his destiny."

Cesco looked mildly amused. "I thought she had bargained to affix him on the tail of my comet."

"In light of your comet's current trajectory," said Cangrande, "she seems to have rethought that choice."

Cesco shrugged. "One less dour face. Nuncle, would you fancy a trip to Paris, too?" Without waiting for an answer, Cesco made to lead his bride to her seat at the High Table.

Cangrande forestalled him. "Dahna, will you see the lady seated? There is someone her husband must meet."

Curious, Cesco followed the Scaliger back to the knot of lords, who were surrounding a deeply tanned, nattily dressed man. "Ser Francesco, Ser Pietro, allow me to introduce Don Pedro of Aragon. Pedro, my heir, and Ser Pietro Alaghieri."

"A pleasure!" said Don Pedro, gripping their hands firmly in turn.

Cesco was tickled. "Pietro, Pedro. Pedro, Pietro."

"Settle down," said Cangrande.

But the Aragonese prince was unperturbed. His smile was not as glowing as Cangrande's, but quite sincere. "Congratulations on your recent wedding, young lord. I am sorry I missed it, believe you me. Ser Alaghieri, I hear of you from our mutual friend Theodoro of Cadiz."

This was an alias employed by Tharwat, one Pietro hadn't heard since Dandolo had mentioned it at the double wedding. "None of it is true."

"You are far too modest. You did not face down the Grand Inquisitor? You did not reveal a viper in the bosom of Avignon?"

"There are so many vipers there," said Pietro, "exposing one is no great chore."

"Ha! So there is *some* truth, at least. I hope you'll take revenge upon him by telling me tales of our quiet Moorish friend. He made a chart for me when I was only a lad."

Cesco's hand shot out to clasp Don Pedro by the wrist, folding his other hand over it as though consoling one deep in grief. "I am so very sorry."

"Settle down," repeated Cangrande.

"I'm wed," answered Cesco. "Isn't that settled enough?"

Not knowing what to say to that, Pedro continued to speak to Pietro. "We are to be neighbours this evening. A minor prince from Spain doesn't rate, I suppose!" His laugh was full-throated and infectious.

"Far more than a minor knight, I'm sure, no matter who

his father was," said Pietro with equal good humour. "I will be honoured. And who is this lady? Your wife?"

Beside the visiting prince stood a lovely woman in a rather ordinary green panel dress – though one that showed a great deal of décolletage. Her hair was free, marking her as unwed. She curtsied. "I could not wish to be so elevated. His grace is too fine for me."

Don Pedro made a contrite gesture. "I am remiss. My lords, allow me I introduce the lady Beatrice of Pisa."

Crowing, Cesco made a series of bows. "Donna Beatrice, Suor Beatrice. Beatrice, Beatrice. Pedro, Pietro. Beatrice, Pedro. Beatrice, Pietro."

Cangrande cuffed his heir lightly across the head. "Enough fooling."

"Is there ever enough fooling for a foole?" asked the Pisan Beatrice.

Rubbing his scalp, Cesco hooted. "A hit! Donna Beatrice, you'll fit in quite well. My bosomy lady, allow me to name my bosom friend Ser Bailardetto Nogarola."

"A pleasure," said Detto, bowing slightly over her hand.

"Salvatore da Battaglia."

"My lady."

"And this is Signor Benedick of Padua. Benedick, Beatrice. Possessor of blessing, here is the bringer of blessing herself."

Benedick's eyes had trouble settling on her face. "Charmed."

"I can tell," said Beatrice drily.

Disgusted, Antonia took Beatrice's arm. "What brings you to Verona?"

Don Pedro answered for them both. "The lady's uncle is a favourite of my father's, and she required an escort back home to Messina, in Sicily. I volunteered."

"I can see why," said Benedick with something like a leer.

Beatrice ignored him. "Like Aeneas, we arrive by a rather indirect route. In our case, we travel west to go east."

The literate in the crowd appreciated the comment. Benedick, however, was bright-eyed, a cocky half-grin on his lips. "Lady, if this is an indirect route home, is there a direct route to your favour?"

The lady measured and devoured him in a single glance. "I don't think I shall curtsey to you, *signore*, until you prove yourself a gentleman." With that, she turned her back on him.

Detto laughed in spite of himself. "Cut!"

"And bleeding," agreed Cesco.

Benedick rallied. "You must not know many gentlemen, else

you'd be better at conversation."

Don Pedro flushed a little, but the shaft was not aimed at him. Halting, Beatrice turned slowly. "No conversation is certainly preferable to this one." Again she turned away, to the admiring coos of the Rakehells.

Pietro's sister squeezed the arm of the newcomer. "Lady Beatrice, I think I like you."

"Suor Beatrice, I am honoured."

"How long are you staying?" asked Pietro.

Don Pedro gave a cheerful shrug. "As long as my presence is tolerated. How could I come to Italy and not visit the court of the famous Greyhound?"

"How indeed?" asked Cesco wryly.

Cangrande turned to speak to Castelbarco. Don Pedro pressed on. "I have heard so much of the glorious Palio, I feel I'd be a fool to miss it. I might even run."

Turning back, Cangrande pressed the Spaniard's shoulder. "You're most welcome. And you, Donna Beatrice."

"If only to see Signor Benedick laid so expertly low," added Cesco.

Soon they were all seated and, after prayers from the Bishop and Cangrande both, they set to. Cesco and Maddelena were once again near the throne of power. Detto was placed beside his father, his brother having elected to sit with his friend Proteus at a lower table. They said a brave greeting, and laughed together, the father solicitous of the son he had nearly lost. Cangrande teased them both. "If he starts cutting your meat for you, Detto, you know he's feeling maternal."

The table containing Pietro, Poco, the Prince of Aragon, and the two Beatrices was placed longways against the High Table, so what could have been exile actually meant those at the end were directly across from Cangrande. It meant Aiello the Scot was relegated to a far table. He looked put out, until he found his neighbor to be Antony Capulletto, with whom he had wanted to speak.

Asked his business in Italy, Don Pedro said, "I came to marry. But it did not come to pass."

"Whom were you to marry?"

Pedro frowned, as if considering his answer. At last he said, "The lady of Bellamonte."

Pietro cried out in surprise. "Bellamonte? You mean the lady Portia?"

The blood drained from Pedro's face. "You know of her?"

"We've met," said Pietro carefully. "On the road back from Venice, the night Detto was attacked," he added for the others.

Cesco recalled Pietro had been with two women, but his focus had been elsewhere. Still he said, "Didn't you say she was married?"

"To a Venetian called Bassanio." Pietro turned to the Spanish prince. "I am sorry if this injures you."

"Not at all." Don Pedro managed to produce a smile through his shock. "I am pleased the lady escaped her predicament."

"Now you *have* to tell us," said Petruchio Bonaventura, seated at the next table.

"If she is married, then I suppose the need for secrecy is over. The lady Portia is beautiful, witty and, if I speak truth, a trifle mean-spirited. But in fairness, her position was an impossible one. Before he died, her father created a test to choose a husband for her after he was gone. Three caskets, one of gold, one of silver, and one of lead. The man who chose the correct one could marry the woman."

Several men laughed heartily, while their wives looked on, aghast. "Good lord, that's arbitrary!" cried Petruchio. "Hm. I like it. Kate, shall we try it for Vittoria and Evelina?"

"Anything is better than the bartering you did with my father," said Kate. "I was a pig at market."

"A fat pig," said Petruchio.

"Fat!"

"I mean, rich! You judge a pig by its—" He put his head in his hands. "O God, I shall never have a moment's sleep again."

"On the contrary, husband," said Kate sweetly. "When you go to bed, sleep is all you will get."

Amid the laughter, Cangrande asked the obvious question. "Which did you choose?"

Don Pedro spoke with obvious reluctance. "I swore an oath not to reveal it. Even if she is married, I do not think I can say."

"I know which casket bore the prize," said Pietro. "I heard of it after, from Bassanio's friends, and I swore no oath. It was the lead."

"The lead?" said Don Pedro, puzzled. "A base metal? Truly?"

"It's unlike a Venetian to look at a woman and not think of gold," said Nico da Lozzo.

Debate started around the room, as to the merits of different metals. Under its cover Pietro confided, "If it helps balm the wound, lord prince, Bassanio had help discovering the correct one. The lady sang, and the rhymes were all for lead."

Don Pedro's mouth quirked. "I'm not certain it's a balm or an insult. She sang no song for me."

"You're well out of it, prince," said Benedick, usurping a seat designated for another. His intrusion was smoothly dealt with by the stewards, who created a new place setting where none was possible before. "Be it gold, silver, or lead, marriage is a yoke."

His words were for Don Pedro but his eyes were all for the lady Beatrice. Who ignored him entirely, enjoying a discussion of poetry with Dante's daughter.

To either his credit or his infamy, the red-headed Paduan did not give up the chase. All through the feast – a religious meal of fish and water with few real delights – he pressed Donna Beatrice for attention. He was each time shot down by a quick barb, but once or twice he gave as good as he got. Soon their raillery became a focus of amusement.

"It is a time of forbearance," said Beatrice after one particularly feeble assault. "Why don't you honour it by stilling your tongue?"

Wincing, Benedick turned to Antonia. "Tell me, Suora, what is it in the name Beatrice that makes women dislike me? For I swear I've never been this unpopular in my life."

"Perhaps because it is our duty to bring joy," answered Antonia, "and if we were to give you your head, your need for it would take up all our time."

"Well said!" laughed Donna Beatrice, lifting her glass of water in salute. Before she took a sip, however, Benedick placed his hand over the mouth of the cup and pushed it away. "I recently heard it was bad luck, saluting with water."

"Worse luck than your touch?"

"My touch? What's wrong with—"

"It must be the opposite of Midas' – from the state of you, any gold you have must turn to lead."

"Not to lead, if lead means marriage. For lead becomes iron, and I'll not be clapped in matrimonial chains."

"A dear happiness, then, that no woman is ever likely to imprison you within her walls."

That delicious double entendre was enjoyed by everyone present. Submitting to the ensuing guffaws with a good-nature, Benedick turned to the Spanish Prince. "My Lord, you likely think I'm a vagabond with a wagging tongue. But I can earn my keep."

"How?" asked Cesco lightly.

But Don Pedro was the soul of graciousness. "If you ever lack employment here, come to Aragon and show me. We can always use a good soldier – or a jester," he added.

"And the Prince scores a touch!" cried Poco.

"I would never spar with nobility," said Benedick with a small, seated bow. "Simply allow me to observe –"

"Observe the feast, please, and pass the fish," said Pietro. It was lame, but enough to garner a few chuckles.

"If he can bear to part with it," said the lady Beatrice. "Being so slippery, he must be a close relation."

Benedick blinked. "Am I fish?"

"No," said Beatrice, smiling lightly. "You're quite foul."

Cangrande barked once as Bailardino thumped the table. Cesco was hopping up and down in his seat as though he were the five year-old in the room. "Goosed, goosed, goosed!"

At the next table over, Petruchio turned. "Speaking of gooses, Kate," he said, and smacked his wife lightly on her cloth-covered buttocks.

"Geese," she said, her eyes swiveling after she'd settled back in her seat.

"Do they remind you of anyone?"

"Yes," said Kate. "Of characters from Aristophanes."

"Who?" asked Petruchio in mock dullness. "No, Kate, I mean us!"

"Perhaps. Only less boorish," said Kate, spilling his supper into his lap.

"More cerebral, I would have said," observed Nico da Lozzo.

"Give them time," replied Kate.

Standing to wipe the fish carcass from his hose, Petruchio addressed the young Prince of Aragon at his back. "Mark my words, lord, if they don't kill each other by sunrise, they're a good match."

"Only if I never wanted another moment's peace," retorted Benedick.

"Oh, is that the piece you coveted?" asked the lady. "That is not the impression you convey."

"I desire piece of mind only."

"It must be hard to find the peace, lacking the mind."

"Stop them, please!" cried Cangrande, wiping a tear from his eye. "Or I'll never keep the meal down."

"I'm in danger of the same thing," said Suor Beatrice, just realizing her namesake really did like the Paduan soldier. Her banter was a screen, and a good one.

Cangrande rose to make the rounds of the other tables, pausing to needle his niece's husband once more – he rarely missed an opportunity to make Rizardo the butt of some joke. Now it was for the beard Rizardo was attempting to grow. "Your chin looks unkempt, Rizardo! Next time you shave, try standing an inch or two closer to the blade."

As Rizardo attempted to laugh, Verde sent a glance in Mastino's direction. But her brother was deeply involved in discussion with Castelbarco's son about a new set of jousting lances he had received as a gift from Henry of Carinthia. So Verde stood, abandoning her seat to take a place next to Giovanna and launch a discussion of the new dresses she could purchase in Paris.

Prompted, Cesco used the Scaliger's absence to prod another target. "Ser Paride! I hear you are depriving us of your company."

Paride's joy was genuine. "I am quite excited. I've never been abroad."

"Nor I. But you must ask Ser Alaghieri to tell you all of the best attractions of Paris. Rest assured, cos, he would never venture into a place beneath his honour. Hm. Perhaps I should go with you – like a hound, I'd sniff out the best places to dine, and the best dishes."

"I did not know you were a gourmand, cousin," said Paride.

"Indeed I am!" said Cesco, winking at Giovanna. "I am learning all there is to know about stews, and flesh-pots."

Giovanna's expression was of resignation. "Can you help being coarse?"

"Of course not," said Cesco, tearing a piece of bread and helping his little wife mop up the oil on her plate.

"Ser Francesco," said Giovanna tartly. "At least in the presence of ladies, please end this nonsense."

"Nonsense?" asked Maddelena.

"Alas, she means I am insensible to sense. Sense-less." Not quite getting the joke, Maddelena smiled back anyway.

From the next table, Kate raised her voice. "Has anyone noticed that men retreat into wordplay when they have nothing to say."

"I certainly have," said Beatrice, looking at Benedick.

"Wordplay shows wit, an agile mind," he replied.

"Only if the words are well-played," observed Beatrice. "Any foole can try to be amusing, but few are."

"Dear lady, only a foole would argue with you."

"Dear me," said Beatrice, "and here was I, hoping you would."

Cesco snapped his fingers and pointed. "It's catching! Donna, if you wish to limit my wordplay, perhaps it would be best not to speak to me at all. That way, at least I cannot play off your words."

"Your silence would indeed be a blessing," said Giovanna.

Cesco opened his mouth to answer, but the blessing seemed ordained by the Lord. The large door in the corner of the room burst open and a messenger rushed in. "My lord!"

Cangrande said loudly, "What is it?"

"The Doge! The Doge is dead!"

This news set everyone to talking. It seemed that the night before, just hours ahead of the year 1329, Doge Soranzo had shuffled off the shackles of life and ascended to the canals of the sky.

Salvatore said, "What was your idea, Ser Francesco?"

Cesco looked blankly inquiring. "I forget."

"You suggested that, as the Scaliger is now a citizen of Venice, he should go stand for election as the next Doge."

Still across the room, Cangrande led the laughter at that. Feeling a stirring excitement, Pietro thought that this was just the kind of madcap adventure that might appeal to Cesco, an impossibly bold task that would be a slap in the face of the Venetians who had plotted so long against the people he held dear.

But Cesco just reclined in his chair. "Sounds exhausting."

"I quite agree," called Cangrande. "And I'm sure the vote is being held this very moment. Besides, what greater honour could there be than owning my current title? It is far greater to be Capitano di Verona than Venetian Doge. Or at least, it soon will be," he added with a wicked gleam.

"I'll drink to that!" said Petruchio. Finding his own cup empty, Petruchio stood and filched a goblet from the High Table where the Scaliger had left it. As was his practice, he did not lift the rim to his lips until he had locked eyes with his beloved wife, who smiled at him as she did the same. They drank as one, holding eyes that twinkled and sparked, containing a lifetime of love.

Setting the cup aside, Petruchio cuffed his bearded chin and started to laugh – or so it seemed. The laugh quickly became a cough. His face became a mottled red. Then he keeled over and dropped to the tiled floor, dead as a stone.

TWENTY-THREE

Tuesday, 3 January 1329

THE DEATH OF PETRUCHIO da Bonaventura and the attempted assassination of Cangrande cast a bleak pall over the remaining days of the Christmas season. The tension was palpable as everyone wondered who had tried to poison the Scaliger. Servants were questioned, of course, along with the cook Gioco, the stewards, the vintner – everyone who might have had the chance to drop something into the cup without drawing attention. But in a room full of witnesses, no one had seen anything.

For all the shock and sadness, there was another emotion in the air – anger. This had been no natural death, and certainly no accident. Every person in the hall knew that Petruchio had lifted a drink from the Scaliger's place, that the poison that had stripped their ranks of this beloved rogue had almost claimed a far greater victim.

Whoever had done the actual poisoning, the real question was who was behind it? Some men recalled Cesco being poisoned upon his entrance to Verona, and so leveled the accusation at Mastino. But what would it gain him to poison his uncle now? Why not months ago, when Cesco was neither a knight nor the anointed heir? The timing made no sense.

Some accused the Paduan exiles, angry over being barred a return to their homes. Others singled out Carrara, covetous of the top position. Still more accusing fingers pointed East, to where Francesco Dandolo had emerged victorious in the election for Venetian Doge, while others were pointed at the Visconti of Milan, suspected of attempting to poison the Emperor in just the same manner. Or was it Emperor Ludwig himself, angry at all the insults Cangrande had heaped upon him during the long stay in Italy? Hadn't his nephew already been accused of attacking a member of the Scaliger's family? And what about that Spanish prince, just arrived and seated only a few feet from the cup?

Most of these were external threats, political ones. Yet there were some who listened to the Abbot of San Zeno when he spoke of an evil spirit possessing someone near the Greyhound's throne. He was not so foolhardy to offer a name, but there was no doubt to whom he was referring. Who had been raised in the house of a man commonly believed to have walked through Hell? Who was every day attempting to undermine the recent peace by picking quarrels with Paduans? Who was seated beside the Scaliger through the meal? Most importantly, asked the Abbot, *cui bono?* Who stood to benefit?

Pietro asked the same question, though in a different way. Certain Cesco was innocent, Pietro wondered if the attempt had been aimed at removing both Cangrande and Cesco at once.

Was the attempt even real? Though his opinion of the Scaliger had softened of late, Pietro instinctively questioned the convenience of his being away from the table when the poison arrived. But Cangrande could hardly have known Petruchio would lift the cup, nor imagine anyone would drink his own wine – no one else would have had the audacity. It came as a painful relief to decide that Cangrande could not be blamed for this. *Probably.*

Another danger occurred to Pietro. What if it became known that Cesco had been dosed with poisons these last three years in order to build his immunity? Wouldn't that lead to more suspicion? Pietro had never imagined that a practice done to protect the boy could someday be used to attack the man.

Hurrying back to Verona to examine Petruchio's body, Morsicato concurred with Fracastoro as to the nature of the poison. "Hemlock. Simple and swift. Though it had to be a strong dose," the doctor added. "His breathing stopped almost at once."

Checking to be sure they were not overheard, Pietro asked, "Would Cesco's immunity have saved him?"

"I doubt it." Morsicato scrubbed his face with his hands. "Here's hoping we never find out." With that dark thought, he mounted to return home to his wife, still ailing. Which made Pietro wonder again about poison.

Suspicion grew not only in his mind, but in the minds of every man he met. It was as though the poison had seeped into everyone's brain, turning their thoughts against themselves. All of Verona was envenomed, and there would be no cure until the city had someone definitive to blame.

Inside the palace and the Domus Nova frank discussions of potential assassins were being held hourly. But there was a name no one had uttered, nor even thought of, a name not spoken until Cangrande called Pietro to his private suite on the top floor of the palace. Closing the door, Cangrande escorted Pietro to a closed window on the opposite side of the room and gave him mulled wine. He waited for Pietro to drink, and Pietro wondered if he was being tested somehow. Pietro sipped.

Cangrande nodded, then sat and took a long draught of his own. He then met Pietro's anxious eyes and said the name. "Rosalia Rienzi."

The breath escaped Pietro in a rush. *Rosalia!* Detto had mentioned her trying to murder the Scaliger on several occasions in the past. Surely she had an even stronger reason now. "You have proof?"

Cangrande shook his head. "Not even an ounce. I'm far from certain it is her. But you are the only man with whom I can discuss the possibility. I know you have seen her. Drink up, and tell me your thoughts."

The drink had not been a test. It had been meant kindly, fortifying Pietro for an unwelcome conversation. But wine did not steady Pietro's nerves, only dulled them. He set the drink aside. "If you know I saw her, you must know what I do."

A small furrow appeared between Cangrande's angelic blue eyes. "I know only that she married Old Bramo and disappeared behind his walls."

Pietro wrestled. He had sworn an oath, and he could only think that the last person she would want to know her secret was this man. Her father, who should be rejoicing at the coming birth of his own grandchild. Only that it was a double-grandchild, born of his two children, in incest. Pietro imagined it being born dead, or deformed, or monstrous. Or evil. He shook his head. "It is not my secret to tell. Only that I do not think she had anything to do with the poison."

"Is that wishful thinking, or reason?" Cangrande waited, but Pietro did not answer. "I could call her to court, under some pretext. Twelfth Night. The Palio."

Pietro blanched. "You don't want to do that."

Cangrande raised his brows. "So there is a secret, and the girl made the knight swear an oath to keep it. It is not petty, and will come out if she comes here... Tell me this – is she in contact with Cesco?"

"No," said Pietro with an absolute certainty.

Cangrande said nothing for a time, mulling it over. It did not take long for his active brain to reach the obvious conclusion. He winced, seeing unwilling confirmation in Pietro's too-expressive face. "Worse and worse. The poor child." The way it was said, Pietro had no notion which child he pitied.

Cangrande rose and refilled his goblet. "What you say – or rather, don't say – it doesn't help matters. If the girl is with child, then she has all the more reason to hate me."

"How would she even arrange it, from so far away?" Pietro was careful not to confirm the pregnancy, but he did not deny it either. The notion of Cangrande summoning Donna Tiberio was awful, and her answer would be worse. She might obey and so shame them all.

"It could be done. Remember, she is a Scaliger. Damn." Cangrande shook his head. "So small a thing..."

It took Pietro a moment to puzzle out Cangrande's meaning. Then, as if he were looking at a stone thrown into a still pond, Pietro saw the ripple of consequence, a chain of events that would drown all they had laboured to build. If Lia came, her pregnancy would be known. Were it known, either Lia or, more likely, Cesco would betray something to reveal the child as his. That might be amusing, proving no more than Tiberio to be a cuckold, unless someone were to remember that Cangrande had once slept with the girl's mother.

The pregnancy of Cangrande's daughter by Cesco was enough of a scandal that, even were he willing, the Bishop would not be able to cover it up. Instead the Abbot of San Zeno and the rest of the priests would seize upon this as proof that Cesco was damned – or perhaps claim it was the cause of his madness. In true Dominican fashion, they would attempt to remove the root of the evil. In this case, the girl. Cangrande's father had burned heretics in the Arena. It could easily happen again. And Cangrande would be helpless to prevent it, or risk losing the new protection of being back in God's sight. Were he to lose salvation a second time, there would be no reprieve. And therefore no larger ambitions. The Holy Roman Emperor might be able to appoint a new pope to crown him, but Cangrande could not. There was no ascent up the ladder of his ambition if this were known.

The rush of understanding was breathtaking – Pietro literally did not breathe for several moments as the whole series of events played out before his eyes. His heart was beating too fast. His head was pounding fit to burst. Was this what it was like, to be a Scaliger? To have a mind that played the game on such a grand scale, with consequences foreseen before the first piece moved? It was at once exhilarating and terrifying in equal parts.

Cangrande would not have the protection of the Emperor, who despised him, nor of his allies, whom he had conquered. In his mind's eye Pietro watched Venice join Padua and Treviso in confronting Verona, with Pisa, Mantua, and Lucca to the south taking up arms and Florence egging them on with funds and material. So swiftly the wheel could turn. Verona, ascending, would be ground into dust.

All because of an angry, pregnant girl.

"You cannot call her to Verona," said Pietro.

"And if it *is* her?"

"Send her a message, if you must. Or order Tiberio to take her away. To France, to Spain, somewhere. England! Send Tiberio to the English Court to find the truth of what Aiello says."

In spite of himself, Cangrande smiled. "Tiberio at a foreign court. I'd pay the price of admission. But it's winter. Do you propose to send a pregnant girl over the Alps at this time of year? Unless you mean that to solve the problem," added the Scaliger with an arched eyebrow.

Shocked, Pietro opened his mouth to say no, then realized how convenient a miscarriage would be. Surely God would prevent such a child from being born. Unless the priests were correct, and the Devil was at work here.

It was only a short leap from miscarriage to the potion women took to relieve themselves of unwanted pregnancies. "If you call her to Verona, she will think it is to murder her child."

"Only if she believes you have broken your vow – which you just have, by the way. But if I call everyone – her father, her brother, Tiberio, and all the other distant landholders in my domains – there will be no cause for outright suspicion. But that means Twelfth Night is too soon. The Palio, then."

"She'll be close to her time by March."

"Better the news of her pregnancy comes out now, I think. We will make a show of congratulating Tiberio on his coming heir, and gift him with a title or something. And it allows us to control the shock to Cesco's system. Not that he shows so much concern for us. But he is young, and angry. Almost as angry as I was at his age."

"The difference is that you had something to fight for. He has something to fight against."

"So clearly the poet's son, Ser Alaghieri. You are a master of the epigram. I should keep you on retainer for pithy sayings. 'A man may control his actions, if not his stars.' 'You had something to fight for, he against.' You sum up the world so well."

Pietro was not to be diverted. "Do not call her to Verona, my lord. She did not try to murder you."

"On the contrary, she tried to murder me several times already."

"But not with poison. Not now."

"We shall see. I like all the players on the board, you know that. I like to see their eyes."

A statement that reminded them both of Petruchio, who was to be buried the next day. He had died with his eyes locked on, not an enemy, but the love of his life.

Sensing the Scaliger's intent was to end the interview, Pietro held up a hand. "There is something else." There had been no time to speak of it, but it had to be addressed. "We found her. Donna Maria. She was in the well in the *volto dei Centurioni*."

He watched that information sink below Cangrande's surface. "Fuchs."

"We think so. She's been there some time, Morsicato says."

"Does he say how she died?"

"No way to know."

"And Cesco knows?"

"He's the one who figured it out."

Cangrande shook his head. "How much damage can he take? Even I was not so tasked."

"If you ask me, it's a wonder Mastino is still alive. Fuchs was his cats-paw."

"A point never far from my mind. Cesco is not normally known for his restraint. I worry what it portends." Cangrande shook his head as a wet dog might, and the light caught the first traces of silver at his temples. "But that's for the future. We must bury Petruchio, and it seems the lady as well."

"Her birth name would help," said Pietro, probing.

Cangrande smiled, if sadly. "Why, don't you have enough already? Bury her, by all means. But there will be no headstone."

"Why? What does it matter who she was?"

"Exactly. It doesn't." Cangrande looked gravely at Pietro. "It will not help him to know. Trust me."

Excusing himself, Pietro departed. Though he could not speak of the thing most forward in his mind, he did not want to be alone. But Antonia was living at Cesco's house. Morsicato was with Esta in Vicenza. Tharwat was still making his inquiries in Padua. This left only Poco, staying in Pietro's house. He could trust his brother, at least. Cold comfort on a cold night.

As Pietro trudged home, he resented the silence. It felt unnatural. The snowfall was again heavy, the night bitterly cold, colder than anyone could ever remember. It hurt to breathe.

He remembered Cesco's own laboured breathing three summers past. It had been the most horrible sound he'd ever heard. Which made Pietro think again of Petruchio's final moment. An airless death, with no chance to even utter last words. Horrific. A bad death.

But at least it hadn't lingered. Like the great Julius Caesar had once remarked, *'What matters the manner of death, so long as it's quick?'* In a world that esteemed a Good Death — in battle, in the saddle, sword in hand — it seemed to Pietro that how a man died mattered less than when. There was nothing more awful than a soul lost before his time.

♦   ◊   ♦

Wednesday, 4 January 1329

Petruchio's funeral was massively attended. The Lord of Bonaventura was one of the most beloved figures in Veronese life, always ready to offer a wager, a jest, or a roughly kind word. He was best known for the public spats with his wife, hilarious duels of wit from which he rarely emerged victorious, which seemed to make him ever-more joyful. The idea of one without the other was inconceivable. And yet it was now fact.

Known to be passionate and wild in nature, Katerina Minola *in* Bonaventura — whom her husband had teasingly called Kate — was surprisingly stoic through the service and burial. It was her daughter Vittoria who dissolved into absolute hysterics and had to be escorted from the Duomo. Her, and the late lord's groom, who blubbered as if he'd lost his own child. Petruchio's sons appeared stunned, ghosts in their skin. Only the youngest Bonaventura child modeled her behavior after their mother. Despite her red-hair, Evelina was cool and clear-eyed as they said prayers and carried her father to the family tomb just outside the city walls.

Bishop Francis was remarkably insightful as he intoned, "In a colourful city full of men of stature, Lord Bonaventura was perhaps the most robust-hearted man among us. He lived for each day, sucking the pleasure from it as one would the juice of a peach. His untidiness of manner was not slovenly. It was, instead, a statement of being. Loyal, fierce, mirthful, yet not vain or self-possessed. Never considered an intellectual — he would have scoffed at the idea — yet was there ever a man so blessed with confidence and self-knowledge? A man's man, who loved his hawks, his hounds, and his friends. He did not care what the world thought of him. He cared only for the good will of his God, his companions, his children, and most of all his wife. We must thank the Lord that He blessed us even for a time with such a presence, and that Petruchio's spirit will carry on in his four children, and in all our hearts. Verona will be less for the loss of his laughter."

The moment was punctuated by a long, unhappy cry. It was not a human sound, but the voice of Comare, Petruchio's favourite hunting hawk, shifting uneasily on her perch by the twins. It was this bird's sustained wail of sorrow, not her eldest child's tears, that broke Kate's composure. She lowered her head and wept in silence.

As they retired out of doors to escort the bier to the Bonaventura vault, Cangrande said to Pietro, "It seems to be a day for funerals."

For a moment Pietro thought he meant Donna Maria, who was still unburied in Pietro's basement. There had not been time to find a good place to inter her. Then he realized what the Scaliger meant. The late Doge Soranzo's state funeral was today. "Do you think this was Dandolo? An attempt to win before the battle was even begun?"

Cangrande shook his head, but not as a negative. "The trouble with owning so many enemies is never knowing which has distinguished themselves with a plot."

"You're employing tasters, I hope."

Cangrande pulled a face. "Much against my will. It means a little less spontaneity in life. And we've already lost enough of that," he added with a nod to the passing bier.

Pietro recalled the first time he had laid eyes on Bonaventura, surrounded by wedding revelers and lamenting his own lack of a wife. That day's bridegroom was also dead, having left only Paride behind him. *Sons without fathers.*

An uncommonly subdued Cesco rode alongside the bereaved twins through the snowy streets, across the Adige, and all the way to their family vault. The Paduan Salvatore rode beside the eldest Bonaventura child, the girl Vittoria. He held her hand, much to the consternation of her brothers. *When did that happen?* wondered Pietro.

From the time of the Romans, Veronese were not habitually buried within the city walls. One of the oldest Roman laws, never changed, read: *'hominem mortuum in urbe ne sepelito neve urito'* – *a dead man shall not be buried or cremated in the city.* Of course, as the city expanded, more and more ancient crypts were incorporated within its boundaries. And there were always exceptions – the Scaligeri had their sarcophagi in the city, and Castelbarco had already started construction of his eventual resting place just outside San Anastasia.

But for the rest, from knight to pauper, the body had to lie outside the city proper. Just as the living and the dead had to use different portals in a house, so the deceased could not set up camp near the dwellings of the quick. Which most took as fortunate, as there was no room within the city for elaborate crypts – the modern fashion was to mark a man's passing with a lavishly ornate monument to his life and memory.

The Bonaventura vault was barely a century old, making it relatively new by Veronese standards. Under the ornate stone cross that stood over the descending stairs, it bore a recently-engraved motto from a holy scholar destined for sainthood who shared Petruchio's family name: *'The voice of the heart must be heard more than the proceedings from the mouth.'* Petruchio had added that motto at the death of his father, and one could almost hear the wry voice booming the phrase now, with laughter.

As the ruling family, Cangrande, Cesco, Mastino, Alberto, and Paride joined the family and the Bishop within the tomb's walls. Dismounting, Pietro led his horse up the road a ways. Idly he looked up at the imposing metal doors of another family vault. The engraved name was hidden by snow. Depicted on the doors themselves were great deeds, done in the style of the famed doors of San Zeno. But instead of relating the acts of a saint, here were the acts of a family. The bronze was faded and worn on the oldest plates. But there were newer ones, two of which caught his eye. One was of a quartet of knights riding into battle. The other was of a knight in Verona's Arena, fighting valiantly. Both looked eerily familiar.

"How does it feel to be adopted?" Pietro turned to see Antony Capulletto gazing at the doors. "You'll forgive my father, I hope. He was so eager to add our deeds to that of the old family, he took some liberties. Since you were fighting on my behalf, technically your duel was a great Capulletto victory."

"Except that I lost," said Pietro.

Antony scoffed at that. "Carrara cheated. Fitting, as he was representing a cheater. To me, you'll always be the victor of that fight. And my friend." He walked over and stroked the clinging snow from the engraved letters over the doors. It was not *Capulletto*, but rather the older *Capelletto*.

"You didn't add any panels for your father or brother?"

"What did they do?" demanded Antony shortly. "Father made money. Luigi made that little sprog that drives me mad. Nothing worthy of being hammered into bronze. Though I will certainly be there – and for more than that ride with you and the Scaliger – and the bride-thief," he added grudgingly before carrying on. "Can you imagine your greatest deed being performed when you're under twenty? Spending the rest of your life living in the shadow of that? I can't. I need to do something grand. Look at the Scaliger. Look at your father! Great men, doing great things right up to the moment of death."

Pietro understood the bleak talk. "It's natural to be thinking of death today. I am. Legacy matters. But you've got a family. A daughter, and another child on the way. She must be close."

Antony grunted. "Days, they say. Let's hope this one lives."

"It will," said Pietro encouragingly.

"I've stopped getting my hopes up." Antony's brow darkened. "And I'm sending that little shit away to the country estate."

Confused for a moment, Pietro said, "Antony, you don't think that he——"

"I don't *know* it," said Antony gruffly. "But I can't help thinking it. Unworthy, I know. But as long as I lack a son, he's my heir. Just don't want to take any chances."

"But he dotes on Giulietta," protested Pietro.

"Giulietta isn't my male heir. Thibault is the only one who profits from the death of my sons. They're in here," he added, resting a hand on the right-hand door. "My sons, locked in the cold. In the dark. My poor boys."

Pietro reached out a reassuring hand. "They're not in the dark. They're with God."

"Not if your boy is right," said Antony, voice choked. "Not if it's all a lie."

The reading. The casual refutation of Heaven and Hell. It had even struck Antony, the least introspective or religious person hereabouts, making him doubt the existence of Heaven for his dead infant sons. *Cesco, do you even have a hint of the damage you're causing?*

Casting his eyes towards the tomb where Cesco had vanished, Pietro found himself watched. Mariotto Montecchio was gazing at his two old friends with obvious sadness. Was he feeling Antony's pain, even from afar? Could this be the link that repaired the chain between them?

But Mari's son was living, while Antony's were dead. Mariotto had everything — the wife Antony had coveted, the life that Antony wished to be living. Everything. And Pietro knew that so long as that was true, Mariotto could not be forgiven.

♦   ◊   ♦

The feast that night would go down in the history of Verona as one of the most magical moments in the city's history. Held at the Casa Bonaventura, it was not for the public, but for those friends and comrades of the bearded bellowing blowhard who had been so beloved. Kate had organized the evening, asking for help from Nico da Lozzo and Signor Hortensio of Padua, her husband's two greatest friends. They were each to speak, and she had told them in what vein they were to do it.

Long-faced with cheeks like a bellows, Hortensio began. "I don't know how to forgive Petruchio for this. I really don't. I wasn't even going to come today. I mean, why should I attend his funeral if the bastard's going to skip mine?"

Uneasy laughter, with shy looks to the widow. But Kate was grinning. Soon the laughter was less hesitant, more heartfelt as Hortensio heaped abuse on the dead man's head, all the while praising the things he had loved — his hawks, his hounds, his children, and his wife. There was a lot of focus on his wife — as much as they abused the dead man, there were an equal number of loving jibes at the madwoman from Padua.

When Hortensio finished, Manuel and Noam sang one of Petruchio's favourite drinking songs:

> *Be merry, be merry, my wife has all:*
> *For women are Shrews, both short and tall:*
> *'Tis merry in Hall, when Bears wag all;*
> *And welcome merry Shrovetide. Be merry, be merry.*
>
> *We shall do nothing but eat and make good cheer,*
> *And praise heaven for the merry year,*
> *When flesh is cheap and females dear,*
> *And lusty lads roam here and there so merr'ly.*

They ended in a C harmony, and the voices of the whole crowd sang the refrain with a heartiness that would have made the dead man proud.

Next it was Nico da Lozzo's turn. "There seems to have been some confusion this morning, as to whether Petruchio was supposed to be buried or cremated. I told Kate, take no chances. Do both. I mean, he'd be offended if he didn't find himself both below, and burning." It was unthinkable to mock Hellfire and damnation. And yet, for Petruchio, there was nothing more apt.

Nico continued, telling tales of his friend that were both scandalous and hilarious. He made much of the man's debts and his wagers before finally reaching the topic of Petruchio's marriage. "The real pity of Petruchio Bonaventura's life is that he wasn't born in Padua. Then he might have had some Veronese friends. As it is, he was too well known in Verona to make Veronese friends or take a Veronese wife. No one here would have him. No, while we all appreciate the *Pax Verona*, I think we can agree that the real conquest of Padua began when Petruchio went wife-hunting there. But, as we must also acknowledge, it was Verona that was conquered. Kate deflected Petruchio's lance with her ample bucklers, then did the unthinkable – out-talked him. Everyone here has heard them in their quarrels, talking over each other. Yet they maintained the impossible – they listened to each other even while they talked. Petruchio used to always tell me that Kate heard him. Not what he was saying, but what he meant. All of us long to be heard in that way. She brought out the best in him. He did the same for her. And while they are hardly the ideal couple – no great poems or lofty prose will ever be devoted to this pairing! – yet they have given us an example of unlikely people finding unlikely love. It was not chivalric – no one was less chivalrous than Petruchio! Yet in its best days it was even better. It was honest."

Another song, with everyone encouraged to sing along in their best impression of the deceased man. When Kate rose, there was an expectation. Hers was a reputation for wildness, humour, willfulness, selfishness, and audacity. Once she had stripped nude before a whole crowd of onlookers. While no one quite expected that of her this night, no one was quite prepared either for the performance she gave.

She began by abusing her husband's previous mourners, and the singers. Then she launched into a speech that had them all in tears – tears of joy, of sorrow, of shared pain and love and mirth. It was at its heart a speech of the agony of mortality, of love cut short, of the blazing unfairness of being cheated of a lifetime together.

"That he died drinking was a surprise to no one, really. But it was remarkably unkind. I've been drinking a lot these last three days, thinking I might join him. No, not because I cannot live without him, though I can't imagine how I will. Not because I must live on for my children, though I will, because I see so much of him in them. No, the reason I want to join him is because I have no one to lock eyes with now. Which means seven years bad sex." Kate's voice quavered even as she smiled, the tears staining her cheeks. "My children are looking at me in shock. Which, honestly, amazes me. You four know it was my sex with your father that brought you into this world, do you not? Yes, children, I regret to inform you that your father was nothing but a mother-fucker. But all the sex I have — and believe me," she added, in imitation of her husband's pelvic swagger, "I plan to have a lot of it — it will all be bad sex, because it won't be with him." And the tears came streaking down her face even as the howling mourners put their hands together in applause. Shocking, hilarious, and heartfelt — the perfect expression of the life of Petruchio.

It was a speech forever precious to those who were there, a gift given from the one who had suffered the greatest loss. Rather than be stoic, as she had been at church, she gave them catharsis, offering up just enough of her own pain to let the others feel it. Yet her pain was not so raw that it overwhelmed them, became a barrier to their own grief. If sacrifice meant to make something holy, she sacrificed her grief for them, to heal them, to comfort them. For those who perceived what she was doing, it was the most selfless act from a human being they had ever witnessed.

The drinks and food that followed were astonishingly cheerful. As the widow stood and allowed herself to be hugged, her hand to be clasped, doing more for those consoling than being consoled herself, the rest milled, hugging and raising their cups — though with an unwelcome measure of suspicion. Most men carried their own drinks, refilling them from their own bottles. Which meant everyone got drunk faster.

Kate's sister Bianca was present, come from Pisa with her husband Lucentio. She tried flirting with several men, then retired in a huff when she perceived that all the masculine attention was on her sister. Her father was red-faced with laughter at the jokes being told at his daughter's expense. He had never been more proud of her.

A feeling not shared by her eldest daughter, who slipped away to weep on the shoulder of another Paduan, Signor Salvatore. That the weeping ended in passionate kisses surprised her. But as Vittoria thought of the humiliations her mother had heaped upon her that night, she decided to rebel by letting the kisses grow into something more.

She was not alone in feeling scandalized. Several women, Madonna Montecchio and Madonna Castelbarco among them, were shocked. But then, Katerina Minola *in* Bonaventura had always been deemed mad. And certainly there seemed no shame in the proceedings, when even the Bishop of Verona had cried with laughter.

The night ended as it should have, with the city guards coming to disperse the loud and querulous crowd outside the Casa Bonaventura. For once it was not the Rakehells who were the cause of the trouble, but the elder generation – Nico, Hortensio, Pietro Alaghieri, and Castelbarco. The Scaliger himself was there when the guards came. He declared himself under arrest and then issued his own pardon in the same breath. And Mari and Antony showed that they were capable of setting their dislike aside for a night. As the drink flowed they even found themselves with their arms about each other, voices raised in harmony as the friends they should always have been. In the morning they would be sober, their amity forgotten. But for one night, they were again the comrades they had been when Petruchio had first met his mad wife.

It was a night that would have made the dead man proud to have lived.

TWENTY-FOUR

Friday, 6 January 1329

TWO DAYS AFTER the funeral, on Twelfth Night, the Feast of the Epiphany was a subdued affair. Planned as the pinnacle of the Christmas celebrations, the festivities were scrapped in favour of simplicity. No musicians, no jugglers, no actors. Instead they all retreated into the safe security of ritual, with the Bishop reading aloud: *Arise, be enlightened, O Jerusalem: for thy light is come, and the glory of the Lord is risen upon thee.*

In place of a lavish feast, Giorgio Gioco served a dish that every Veronese recognized as comfort food - boiled meats in *Pearà* sauce. A winter dish, it was made over a strong fire, allowing the heat to break up day-old bread mixed with butter, marrow from the *ossu buco* bone, and meat broth. After hours of slow boiling, cheese was added, along with nutmeg and a large amount of black pepper. The thicker the *Pearà*, the more it tasted like home, and childhood, and safety. Even if safety was only an illusion.

They buried Cesco's mother the following day. It was a small gathering – Cesco, Cangrande, Pietro, Antonia, Poco, and Detto. Cesco had decided on the place, one that only Cangrande and Detto had visited before. But the name was too apt to be ignored. *Santa Maria in Stelle.*

The priest of the old church was asked to say the prayers and bless the earth, but not told the surname of the woman he was laying to eternal rest. Her grave was not given a name either, but the marker was there. Someday perhaps her name might be added.

Cesco came dressed all in white, the garb of mourning. Cangrande chose to forego that colour, and declined the chance to speak for her, which Pietro found infuriating. On the ride back to the city he said so. "He's the only one who knew her at all!"

Cesco shrugged this off. "He doesn't want us to learn anything more. Do you think if we put him to the torture, he would relent? Because I have my doubts."

"Did he love her at all?" asked Detto.

"At least once," remarked Cesco. "Love is a motion of the loins, not the liver. Speaking of which, this is where I leave you." They had come to *La Rosa Colta*.

"Cesco," said Pietro sternly. "You should go home."

Cesco's jaw jutted, but he forced a smile. "I don't think my lady wife would approve of me bringing the whores back home with me." He glanced down the street, where he saw Benedick, Salvatore, Petruchio, Hortensio, Barto, and Berto. "Ah, the Rakehells have come to help me drown my filial sorrows. Perhaps I'll trade the rose for the sword. Come, lads! To the *Albergo delle Quattro Spade*! I must raise a cup to a lady and honour her name for me by being wavering in all my affections! To Donna Maria *in Stelle*! For my mother is now among the stars."

Seeing the revelry about to commence, Cangrande cantered close. "No trouble today."

Dismounting, Cesco handed his horse off. "Perhaps if you'd dressed the part, you could give instructions for how to mourn. As it is, I'll find my own way."

Cangrande stared after his heir for a long moment, then rode in the opposite direction.

The brawl that day was the worst yet. It took a host of city guards to separate the incensed Paduans from the hot-headed young nobles of Verona. The bereaved twins were especially vigourous in their fisticuffs, laying about them with verve. Four men had to be carried off in a cart, and Ziliberto della Scala had his arm set in a splint and a sling.

His white clothes both muddied and bloodied, Cesco was escorted to the main palace for a stinging rebuke, without any visible effect. The moment it was over, Pietro closeted himself with Cangrande. "It's getting worse."

"No," said Cangrande. "It is just that the tenor of the city's opinion has changed. Wild youth can be excused. But with the good Abbot of San Zeno talking of demonic possession, the people are less accepting." The Scaliger pulled a face. "Perhaps we should request an exorcism."

Pietro was not amused. "Can you gag the Abbot?"

"Not without igniting more rumours. I think we must hold that second salon soon."

"What, loose Cesco upon the Abbot full-force?"

"Fracastoro once told me it is sometimes better to make a disease worse, in order to cure it."

"And just hope it doesn't kill the patient."

"Truth is truth," said Cangrande. "Though at this moment I wonder who the patient is."

♦   ◊   ♦

Returning through the city center to change, Cesco and Detto were spied from a window. For weeks just the sight of Cesco had been enough to make Mastino scowl.

In all the heir's burgeoning notoriety, the people had utterly forgotten Mastino. Worse, he had begun to be openly mocked. His fine jousting armour, his gilt spurs, his fine clothes – gifts from far-off princes who understood his worth – were the butt of jokes around the city. He'd heard several men refer to him as a dandy, and to his face they over-praised his finery with barely-concealed sneers. The Scaliger's own heir owned nothing so fine – or if he did, he never showed it. Thinking he cut a fine figure, Mastino now understood he was seen as something of a buffoon. Which in turn made men question his ability. Was he truly as skilled at jousting and contests as he claimed? Hadn't the Heir *allowed* Mastino to win the *mêlée* on their joint wedding day?

Mastino had never spent much time thinking of his own father. Alboino had died sometime before Mastino's fourth birthday, and had never factored into the lives of the five children he'd left behind. Maybe Mastino's sisters thought of their parents. But the girls had been sent off to be raised by nuns, preparing them for a life as the political chattel they were. Mastino had never bothered to imagine what his father's life had been like – until Cesco had come to Verona.

As Mastino was to Cesco, so Alboino had been to Cangrande. The elder, rotting in the shadow of the brilliant younger. Mastino was determined not to end up like his father, dying untimely without a scrap of fame to his name. The parallel was exact, and damning.

Now Mastino sat impotently in the window seat and watched Cesco pass. It was all he did anymore – watch. And wait.

"My Lord?" asked his wife from their bed. "Are you well?"

"Fine. Tell them I'm ready for something to eat."

She dutifully rose from the bed and dressed. He didn't watch, and she left while Mastino seethed in quiet contemplation. He was perfectly aware that if any misfortune were to befall Cousin Cesco, he would be elevated to heir in an instant. Every day Mastino prayed that the next stupid, pointless prank would be Cesco's last. And each day saw Cesco survive, skin undamaged, fame growing. He rode bareback with his hands tied behind him, and yet didn't fall. He picked meaningless fights and came away no more than bruised. He played the foole with the Devil and came away unscathed. The boy was the personification of luck.

His best weapon was spent. Mastino had truly believed the revelation of Rosalia's parentage would have crushed the bastard. Instead the little prick was more cock-of-the-walk than ever. But then he'd always been lucky – look at the way he survived Fuchs' attempt to dispose of him.

Poor Fuchs – another reason to crush the bastard. Mastino sat back and imagined a day when he could call the little shit to account. But it would have to wait until the Scaliger was dead. Then, and only then, could Mastino act.

The one thing Cesco lacked, Mastino would cultivate.

Patience.

♦   ◊   ♦

"But why does Thibault have to go?" whined Giulietta.

Capulletto frowned, but took the time to squat down beside his daughter. "He has work to do, princess. He's getting older, and his studies aren't what they should be. Now now, my little Giulia," he said, tapping her nose as she began to protest, "I let him stay through Twelfth Night, just for you."

"But he won't see the baby!" the three year-old said.

That's the idea, Antony didn't say. Aloud, he was more circumspect. "Thibault is destined for a priesthood. Especially if this is a little brother to you. Then he'll stop being my heir and need some employment of his own. And if this is a sister, he still needs to work on his numbers and penmanship. Thibault hasn't learned his letters half as well as you have, and he's almost a man!"

Not being immune to flattery, Giulietta giggled and preened. Yet she remained doggedly fixed on her goal. "But can't he stay until the baby is born?"

"Since we don't know when that is, no," said Antony. "And he keeps getting into trouble – he was in another fight today, in the street. Better he should go and be taught manners than stay and be caught in the Devil's wake. No, Giulietta. Thibault must go." His tone had an air of finality, and by standing he showed her the topic was closed.

Which she accepted. Giulietta loved her cousin, but her father was as fair a man as existed upon the earth. With her nurse and the groom Andriolo – indeed, all the servants! – Giulietta's little world was filled with people who loved her.

The sole exception was her mother. Though she did not understand it, Giulietta felt her mother's coldness on a visceral level. Not that her mama was ever cruel – never mean, never shouting, never raising a hand. She was simply distant, uninterested. And nothing Giulietta could do would gain her mother's attention for more than a moment. Tears would earn her a call for the nurse. Laughter, a call for the nurse. Questions, a call for the nurse. There were times when Giulietta wished the nurse were her real mother.

But then she would not be the daughter of Lord Capulletto. Her darling papa was a bear of a man, a bull, a broad-shouldered but gentle beast who was only fierce in his loves. And he loved his daughter more than anything. It helped that he was as disdainful of Giulietta's mother as she was of her daughter. The little mind did not see a connection.

She noticed that her father was holding out his hand. She took it, feeling his large fingers wrapping protectively around her small ones. They started to walk together, and she gave a little skip. Laughing, he imitated her, and soon they were skipping side by side down the stairs and out into the enclosed yard.

There stood Thibault. He had neglected his hat despite the cold, and his ice-blond hair was bright in the slanting sunlight as he cinched the straps of his saddlebags. Beside him was Giulietta's mother, heavy with child. Her face looked warm and open – until she noticed her husband and daughter approaching. Then her face closed up tight and she stepped away to speak to one of the bustling servants.

Giulietta rushed up to give her cousin a hug about his thighs. "I wish you didn't have to go!"

He patted her head before disengaging her arms. "I'll miss you, snowflake. Stay away from the horses – you're so little, they might step on you. And look after your mother. She'll need you, since she won't have a man in the house."

Giulietta was about to ask, 'Where is father going to be?' when Thibault went flying backwards and struck the wall, sinking to the ground in a daze. Her father was shouting and rubbing his knuckles while her mother shouted back as she knelt beside Thibault, who was just beginning to stir.

Giulietta took a few fluttery steps, first to one side, then the other. She had never seen her father's face contorted in such fury. She knew he didn't like her cousin, but she wasn't sure what Thibault had done to deserve being yelled at. Then she saw the blood across Thibault's face and realized her father had struck him! With his hand! What had Thibault done?

Whatever it was, he now launched himself forward. Drawing a sword, Thibault thrust it at Giulietta's father. Giulietta screamed, as did her mother, though they were two quite different sounds, one fearful, the other excited.

Giulietta needn't have feared. Thirteen was no match for thirty-two. With two careless blows, Thibault was stunned, disarmed and turned, his right arm pinioned behind his back. Her father's arm curled about her cousin's throat. "You little shit!" he shouted in Thibault's ear. "You think because you race with princes that you are one? You're nothing. You'll never be master here, never a proper lord. I'll leave my estate to my girl sooner than you. Especially now you've raised a hand against me – thanks for that!" Her father's lips curled back into a smile. "I have cause, now. I could have you executed. Your life is in my hands. But I know you'll never be grateful. I've had little thanks for housing you, feeding you, sheltering you, raising you. Ten years, I've kept you alive. My brother would never have done as much for any son of mine. He tried to frame me for murder once, did you know that? Your perfect father, who hated me for being better than him."

Red-faced, Thibault sputtered, "Just like you hate me."

Giulietta's father hugged Thibault tighter, his big arms bulging. "Don't flatter yourself, whelp! What, you think I fear being eclipsed by a young hot-head like you?"

"Father!" gasped Giulietta. Thibault's face was purple now, his eyes bulging.

"Give you your head and you'd be dead in a month. But not before you wrecked this house and all I've built – *I* built, not your father! He never did anything but whine and watch from the shadows – just like you! Trying to stab an unarmed man – not too chivalrous!" The sound Thibault was making was barely voiced, just a gurgle. "A pity you couldn't have gone to live with your mother. But she didn't want you, boy! *She didn't want you.* No one wanted you. No one cares if you live or die!"

"Husband!" came an angry voice. "Let him go!"

Giulietta turned to see her mother holding a knife. It was at a strange angle, though. It wasn't threatening anything except her pretty gown. Pointed down, it looked like she was resting the tip on her own belly. Giulietta frowned. The baby was in there. Mother must have forgotten.

Her mother said, "Let him go."

Ashen faced, her father stared. "Is it even so?"

There was a terrible moment where it felt like Giulietta's stomach would stretch from end to end. Then there came a splash of water and her father gasped in surprise. Andriolo the groom had thrown a bucket of icy water over him. Sputtering, her father released Thibault, who sank to the ground. Giulietta's mother rushed to his side and helped him move away.

Seeing that her mother was holding Thibault, Giulietta went and wrapped her arms around her father. He was soaked, but she didn't care. If she could hold him back, he wouldn't hit Thibault anymore.

Amid more shouts and recriminations that followed, Thibault mounted. With blood flowing all across his face, he couldn't clamp his mouth shut the way he normally did. Instead he raised his chin and used the reins to start his horse moving. "Don't worry about me coming back!"

"You do and you're dead!" she heard her father say. Giulietta looked up at his flushed face. He glowered at Thibault's back as it disappeared through the tunnel and out to the street. Then with a final furious glare for his wife, he turned on his heel and stalked back into the house.

Without moving her head, Giulietta slid her eyes over towards her mother. Who was not crying, but standing with her eyes closed and taking long, deep breaths. Her hands were on her belly, but the knife was gone. Without a glance for her daughter, Tessa Capulletto trudged carefully through the snowy cobblestoned yard and into the house.

"How now, little one," said a soothing voice.

Giulietta jumped. Bigger and burlier even than her father, Andriolo swept her up and perched her upon his forearm, his other hand steadying her back. "Was that frightening? I suppose it was."

She could ask Andriolo, though it came out in a whisper. "What did Thibault do?"

"He was disrespectful. Deserved what he got," said Andriolo with assurance. "But you reap what you sow," he added with a covert glance at the house.

"What?"

Andriolo smiled into her face. "Nothing, pet. Just remember to mind your father. You'll never need fear, sweet thing like you. He dotes on you. Thibault's just jealous, and that makes him say stupid things."

She burst into tears, and he rocked her, cooing in her ear and petting her hair. She loosed all her fright into those tears until she was spent, shaking and hiccoughing. Finally she felt embarrassed. She didn't like to cry. Through her shuddering breath she said something.

Andriolo pressed his face closer. "What's that, poppet?"

"You g-gave father a b-b-bath," she repeated.

Andriolo laughed. "Well, we all need baths. Even great lords. All better now?" Receiving a nod, he put her down. "Sadly, I have to go get more water now. I was on my way to clean up the stables. Your father's off tonight with that Scotsman, and I still have yet to retrieve the new horses from –" He paused to glance up at something on the wall behind him, then put his nose close to her ear. "Don't tell anybody, but I'm buying some horses from the Montecchi stables."

Despite her stuttered breathing, Giulietta gasped. One thing she knew was to never speak to a Montecchio. They weren't to be trusted. Her father said so, and her father was always right. Hadn't Andriolo just said as much? "You can't!"

"They're very fine horses. The best. And shouldn't your father have the best horses? Just don't tell him they came from Montecchio's stables, jewel, and he'll never be the worse."

Giulietta nodded solemnly. She did not like secrets, but prided herself on her ability to keep them. It was right that her father had the best horses. And didn't this mean that Montecchio was losing them? Wasn't that a good thing?

"Now go inside and get warm. A nap will set you right." With a chuck under her chin, Andriolo walked away.

Standing alone in the yard, Giulietta looked up at the wall where the groom had glanced. It was a depiction of King David and Bathsheba. She was looking away, to where her husband Uriah was being killed in battle. Uriah looked just like her father. But David was dark and handsome, almost beautiful. Dressed in fine clothes, he was regal and noble and clearly loved Bathsheba. And he was very very sorry when, on the next wall of the mural cycle, he was punished by God for sending Uriah to his death just to marry Bathsheba.

Giulietta's father would sometimes stop to stare at the images of Bathsheba that ringed the yard. Her mother would, too, with a frown or a scowl. But her father would gaze on the image of the dark-haired woman with a sad smile, until he caught himself and shook it off.

Looking at the painted woman, Giulietta understood that this was the kind of woman men liked. Dark hair, dark eyes, pretty. Grabbing her own hair, she pulled strands of it before her eyes. Blonde. Not even an interesting blonde, like Thibault's. It was like straw. And none of it was the same! Some parts were lighter, some dark.

Grabbing a handful of snow, she started scrubbing at her hair, trying to make it less dirty. It glistened, and seemed to be a little darker now, not lighter. But darker was better, wasn't it?

Then she realized that the snow she had picked up had been stained with Thibault's blood. Blood that was now in her hair. She started screaming, and kept on until the nurse arrived to find out what all the fuss was about.

◆   ◊   ◆

In the Domus Nova, Cangrande was busy reading over state documents when Castelbarco entered. "You're late."

"My apologies, my lord Scaliger. I was detained."

"Business?"

Castelbarco shook his head. "The Scotsman. I've just escaped two hours of his self-important cant."

"The man does talk," agreed Cangrande, fully cognizant of the irony.

Castelbarco picked up papers, then sighed and lowered them. "Though I sometimes enjoy his company, I cannot bring myself to like the Scotsman."

"O, I like him well enough. It's just that I trust him not at all." Cangrande laughed. "These foreigners! Last year, Germans. Today, Spanish, English, and Scottish. All we need is for an embassy from the great Cham to arrive. Which reminds me – I'm due to sup with the Spanish Don this evening, at his request. I wonder what he wants."

"The price of being an ascending star," said Castelbarco. "Everyone wishes to tack themselves to your light."

Cangrande grinned. "So long as the star is not actually a comet, flaming across the sky only to vanish."

As it turned out, what the Spaniard wanted was so prosaic that

Cangrande found himself both moved and charmed.

The first part of the evening meal was spent in discussion of Spanish bladecraft. Pedro waxed eloquent on the history and virtues of Spanish forges. It was surprisingly pleasant talk. More than a decade younger, the Spanish Don had an easy haughtiness that might have been off-putting were he not so naturally assured. He wore authority almost as well as the Scaliger. Someday Don Pedro would be a most affable King of Aragon. Provided he lived so long.

"It's astonishing how easily I comprehend you," said Pedro at one point. "The open vowels of the Vicentines trip me up, and I've noted that Paduans don't roll their 'r's. I cannot comprehend anything said by a native of Bergamo."

"Nor can anyone," confided Cangrande.

"Yet I find the Veronese dialect mellifluous to my ear. Why is that?"

Cangrande flashed his famous smile. "I could say because it is a heavenly tongue. But the truth is, our local speech has a great deal in common with Spanish. It is why I once impersonated a Spanish notary – ah, you've heard the tale? I chose that role because it is easiest for me to mimic Spanish speech."

"But why is that? Was Verona founded by Spaniards?"

"Hardly!" laughed Cangrande. "I did ask one of the monks over at the Library. He directed me to a most learned amateur scholar, a layman not admitted to one of the guilds, called Rapelli. He showed me research that dates Verona back to pre-Roman times, when this land was populated with Etruscans. His theory is that the Veronese dialect remains true to its pre-Roman forebears."

"Fascinating. But what has that to do with Spain?"

"Now we're in the realm of pure conjecture, and entirely my own," admitted Cangrande. "Since the Etruscan tongue influenced the Roman language before being superseded, I think it clung to its roots here in Verona. And while Verona was not actually part of Rome until the fall of the Republic, troops from around Verona were certainly part of the legions who invaded Spain under Cato and the others. I just wonder whose duty it was to teach Latin to the conquered Spanish?" He shrugged. "I have asked the official scholars, but they know less than the amateur."

"As often happens," said Pedro wisely. "Because the amateur is self-taught, and is therefore untainted by the body of work that has shaped the thinking of the scholars. His view is unfettered, his thoughts from outside the confinement of accepted notions." Pedro laughed. "I imagine your friend Rapelli is not beloved by the scholars."

"They were unimpressed when I inducted him into their guild, it is true. But they seem more accepting now that they know I'm interested in his work. With my interest, gold follows. And being an outsider is not always a hindrance. I notice you are hardly a pariah here. And your lady friend is quite the favourite of the court. She's certainly enhancing Signor Benedick's reputation. He's never been so well-liked – though now I understand a little of why Cesco keeps him close."

Pedro pursed his lips. "He is amusing, to be sure. Quick-witted, and I hear valourous. But the lady is on her own for the first time in her life. Her mother is dead, you see, and with no living relative in Italy she passes into her uncle's care. I don't want her taken with someone unsuitable, not while she's my responsibility. It's up to her uncle to choose a husband for her." He saw Cangrande smile. "I've amused you."

"No no. You remind me of someone, is all. Another Pedro – Ser Alaghieri. He sees his duty in the world so much more clearly than the rest of us."

"I have been delighted to make his acquaintance. He is my father's most treasured correspondent. Though they've never met, the king is always entreating my brother and I to look to Ser Alaghieri as an example of decency and honour!"

"Your father does not exaggerate. Pietro is the best of us." The Scaliger's eyes took on a far-away look. "Hm. I should do something about that. Perhaps..." He chuckled in amusement. "Oh yes. So very perfect. But back to you, my young prince. You came to Italy for a wife. Having failed the lady of Bellamonte, do you mean to take the lady Beatrice for yourself?"

Pedro sipped his wine. "I daresay it's what old Leonato, her uncle, hoped for her – or rather, he hoped she'd marry my brother. His birth is nearer her state than mine. But as he's still serving as a squire, I offered to be her escort. Besides, it offered a chance to pay my respects to the Greyhound on the eve of his greatest victory."

Cangrande appreciated how delicately the Spanish prince had phrased the matter of Beatrice's birth. Pedro had not said 'my bastard brother' or even 'half-brother.' Yet Don Pedro's brother Juan had been born on the wrong side of the sheets, as the saying went. The brothers had been raised as equals, a tribute to the King of Aragon's fairness. But the fact remained that, legally, Don Juan stood to inherit nothing of his father's power or lands. Without ever impugn-ing Beatrice's honour, Pedro had conveyed the important information. The Prince of Aragon couldn't wed the illegitimate offspring of a minor Italian house, no matter how attractive and clever.

"Well," said Cangrande, "Benedick is a climber. His association with my heir seems to be one of self-interest. So perhaps once he finds out the lady is more of your brother's level, he might abandon the flirtation."

"An uncharitable suspicion, my lord. So thank you for saying it, because it was my thought as well." Laughing, Cangrande poured himself more wine. Don Pedro took a breath. "I have a problem—"

Cangrande quaffed his drink. "I know an excellent physician."

"Ha! No no, no. I am in a moral quandary, and find myself in need of advice."

"I'll be of any help I can."

Don Pedro clasped his hands before him. "I've taken an oath. A foolish oath, to be sure. But an oath nonetheless."

When Pedro paused, Cangrande urged him on. "What? What? I'm at the edge of my seat. Must you kill your father and marry your mother? What?"

"Ha. No. You mentioned the lady of Bellamonte. You've heard the whole matter by now – the caskets, the choice. But there is one part no one knows. There were conditions to those men wishing to undertake the trial."

"Never to reveal which casket you chose. I know."

"There's more. If I failed, I should leave her and never trouble her again."

"If she has wed, that dilemma is solved. Is there more?"

"Yes. I vowed never to woo a woman to be my wife."

The Scaliger whistled. "Quite an hazard of the die! All or nothing."

"Just so. Though I did not walk away with nothing." Reaching into the pouch at his belt, Pedro removed a small wooden ornament on a stick. It was the head of a jester, complete with coloured motley and little bells. The face itself was grotesque, at once mocking and mournful, pithy and pitying. "This was in the casket of silver, which bore the legend *'Who chooseth me shall get as much as he deserves.'* I thought myself deserving of all life has to offer. Including the woman. But when I opened the casket, this was what was inside." He rattled the foole's head. "And this."

Receiving a piece of paper, Cangrande opened it and read:

The fire seven times tried this:
Seven times tried that judgment is,

> *That did never choose amiss.*
> *Some there be that shadows kiss;*
> *Such have but a shadow's bliss:*
> *There be fooles alive, I wis,*
> *Silver'd o'er; and so was this.*
> *Take what wife you will to bed,*
> *I will ever be your head:*
> *So be gone: you are sped.*

Cangrande's eyes were alight. "Had I known about this, I would not have let Cesco wed in November, but sought this woman out and made him take his trials! O, to have met the father!"

Pedro's smile was thin. "Yes, a good jest. I simply wish it was not at my expense. But I got what I deserved." Again he shook the foole's head. "What I wish to know is if I am forever bound by my oath. Can I *never* marry? Or does the paper release me? It says take what wife I will to bed."

"Ah, but not whose wife you should take. No, forgive me. I'll attempt a serious answer. In truth, it lies with you to decide."

"Decide?"

"Decide if you wish to take the oath as literal, or as intended. This is the argument Pietro has been having with Bellario — the uncle of your failed bride. Do you adhere to the spirit of the oath, and never marry in your whole life? Or can you reconcile your nature to a more lawyerly reading of the text, where you cleave to the words, and yet undermine the meaning? It depends on the man you wish to be."

Pedro considered. "The man I wish to be would keep the oath in its entirety. But the man I am required to be by my rank and duties insists I find a chink in this armour. I must have heirs, to carry on after me. That is my duty. So I must keep my word, and yet still marry."

"I knew I liked you," said Cangrande approvingly. "And know that the lady's uncle would certainly agree. He is most literal-minded. Well then, allow an Italian to be your interpreter of this Italian oath. I think the number here is seven. Seven tries, seven judgments. I think seven years is your answer. That's without know-ing the mind of the author," he added.

"I cannot marry for seven years?" asked Pedro, aghast.

"No, you cannot woo a woman to be your wife for seven years. There's always an arranged marriage. I can attest to their effi-cacy — though perhaps you should try an age gap less chasmous than

Cesco's. Or mine! Also, it seems to me that if a woman wooed you, you could marry her. You cannot ask directly. But you may drop hints. Coy suggestions. Play the maid. Let yourself be pursued." Seeing the growing consternation on the Spaniard's face, Cangrande laughed to show he was jesting. "Well then, you've had my advice. Seven years. Now come! The wine stands beside you and the night is still young. Let us see if we can out-do my heir in mischief for once!"

♦   ◊   ♦

The revels were in full force when Cesco slipped out the rear door of the Four Swords. He'd spilled his purse on the table, so there was no more need for his presence. His bowels were in danger of loosening. Halfway home he threw up instead, the wine and fish disagreeing with other things in his system. The purge helped, but his thoughts remained fuzzy, his breathing labored. It was a common state for him these days. *Fourteen, and a drunkard. Perhaps that's my career. Always good to start training young.*

But it wasn't the wine. It was the wafers, those marvelous sticky chews Tharwat had given him to endure his hawking. The hawking was done, but the pain was worse. Pain not of the body, but of the soul.

Thinking of them, he reached into his pouch, only to realize he didn't need one. It seemed to be almost a constant now, the dizzying euphoria, the numbness to what others said or did. Numbness was welcome, as was euphoria. Whatever ill-effect it might bring, that was for tomorrow. Today was for today. What did it matter if he had momentary visions of infants with their throats cut, or Lia's face staring at him in horror? These were just waking nightmares, and nightmares were nothing new. He'd suffered terrible dreams all his life. Like all dreams, they began well. Then for no reason they twisted into something dark, ominous, and horrific. *Just like life,* he thought. *Just like love.*

The irony was that his hawking had been the only time in his life he hadn't dreamed. Too tired for his mind to be idle, too exhausted for the fantasies that came to plague him, he had slept deeply, bathing in Lethe's deep waters. Nuncle Pietro once remarked that parenting was the art of distraction. So was living. With enough distractions, one might forget one's self for a moment, a minute, even an hour.

Staggering alone into his home, he listened. No cries, no laughter, no wife, no nurse. He grunted as his servants pulled his boots from him and winced as one of them swung the lamp too close. He did not wait for slippers, but ascended to his chamber barefoot, his skin extra-sensitive to the chill tiles of the floor, the grainy stone of the steps.

Distracted as he was, he didn't realize until he was inside his chamber that it was occupied. Brother and sister. "*O cacat. In loco parentis.* What now?"

Antonia looked about. "Where are your companions?"

"Off warring and wooing," replied Cesco, crossing to pour himself some wine. "Detto is visiting his brother, and Petruchio and Hortensio are busy striving to replace their father in the gambler's books. Your namesake has entranced Signor Benedick, who flirts with her under the guise of visiting Don Pedro, but that's a stalking horse. Or a Judas goat. One of those animal metaphors."

"Is he a Judas for forsaking you?"

Cesco flashed a mirthless smile. "Casting me in the part of Christ seems unlikely."

"A Judas goat is a creature meant to tame wilder beings," said Pietro.

"Which makes you mine."

Nuncle Pietro crossed to place a hand on his shoulder. "Cesco. We buried your mother today."

"Did you? Was I there?"

Instead of saying anything, Pietro roughly grabbed the four-teen year-old's face. Cesco pulled away but the knight fought him until he could check the boy's pupils by the light of the lamp. Releasing Cesco as if burnt, he turned back to his sister. "He's in the thick of it. Lotus-eating. Look at his eyes. We won't get any sense out of him—"

Once he started laughing, Cesco found it impossible to stop. "Lotus-eating! Lotus-eating?!"

"It's not funny," said Antonia.

"Ah ha ha, if only I did eat the Lotus, Imperia! To sleep in apathy – it is a dream of mine. Hashish is a poor substitute."

Pietro was careful to keep his voice neutral. "Lorenzo said you had taken an oath to abjure it."

Amusement vanished. "Of course he did. You all gabble like geese over my secrets. I'm the only one secrets are kept from. Tell friar goose he should mind his own business, or he'll be pulled. I kept my side of the bargain. It was his God that broke faith."

"That's not how it works," said Antonia.

"Oh? Should we discuss what God has done to you?"

Antonia blanched. Nuncle Pietro didn't know what the threat was, but he clearly felt it, palpable in the room. Antonia didn't realize she was holding her breath until Cesco turned away to quaff his drink.

Pietro said, "You don't know what that terrible stuff is doing to you."

"I know what it's not doing," said Cesco, lifting the lid of a box and removing some pine-nut brittle to chew upon. "It's not lecturing me."

Pietro drew a deep breath, but Antonia laid a forestalling hand on her brother's arm. "Does it make it better?"

Biting into the sweet confection, Cesco shrugged. "For a moment. Then it's worse. Like drinking to alleviate a hangover. As long as the wine is flowing, all is well. The trick is to keep the river flowing."

Pietro crossed closer. "Cesco—"

Swallowing, Cesco closed his eyes. "Nuncle, you may relish being a rush-mat for men to trod upon. I am not you. Get out."

"Cesco!" said Antonia.

Throwing his half-empty goblet across the room, Cesco snarled. "God, how I hate that name!"

"It's the drug talking," said Pietro with scorn.

"No, dammit, it's me!" Cesco scrubbed his face with his hands. "Why should this worry you? The noble Moor gave it to me, the doctor continued in his absence. If you did not approve, you should not have been complicit. Why this sudden fear of what sustains me? A man cannot live off of prophecy alone. Nor can a Greyhound, it seems."

Pietro and Antonia shared a glance. "So you do know."

Filching a second sweet from the box, Cesco plopped down in a chair and gazed at the frosty window panes. "Yes. Despite the best efforts of my pack of keepers, I have learned the inevitable. What does it matter if I destroy myself? I have a *destiny*!" With his finger he traced looping figures on the glass. "Leopard. Lion. She-Wolf. Then death will claim me untimely. All I have to do is identify my three foes and I can be done with this farce called life." Wiping the figures away, he turned to face them. "Though now I wonder, could it be you? My keepers? Morsicato the Leopard, Pietro the Lion, and dear Sister Imperia the Wolf. If I murder you all right here and now, can I lie down and die in peace?"

There was such menace in his tone, such otherworldliness, such contempt, they were both taken aback. For the first time they actually felt fear. Not fear for him. Fear *of* him.

"Of course not," said Cesco, answering his own question. "You aren't important enough to be mythic beasts. You are just my deceivers, the ones who lie and lie in your throats for my own good. Is it any wonder that I do not have an impulse to candor?"

"You're being beastly," said Antonia.

"The beast in me is the best of me. Every cripple finds his own way of walking. This is mine. So leave me be. I mean it. *Get out!*" This last was shouted with such venom that the two adults took a united step back. "Fine. If you won't, I will." Cesco stalked to the door, exiting and slamming it after him.

"Well," said Pietro.

"Anything but well," answered Antonia. "If what the doctor says is true, shouldn't he be asleep by now?"

"Yes," answered Pietro. "Unless the doctor erred."

They looked at each other. There was nothing more to say tonight. Seeing her brother to the outer door, Antonia went upstairs to check on Maddelena.

Dahna was asleep on her side of the chamber. On the far end, the little girl was in bed, but something in how rigidly she held her white stuffed bunny proclaimed she was awake. "You should sleep, little one."

"And you should leave him alone," muttered Maddelena.

"What?"

The girl sat up sharply. "Why don't you leave him alone?"

Antonia leaned forward to stroke the five year-old's hair. "Because we love him. We don't want to see him get hurt. Or hurt himself."

"My husband is stronger than anyone," said Maddelena possessively, fiercely hugging her bunny.

"That's true," agreed Antonia. "Sometimes I wish he weren't so strong. Sometimes I wish he could let himself cry. Because someday all the pain he hides is going to overwhelm him and he'll feel all alone in the world."

"He won't be alone," said Maddelena. "He'll have me."

Antonia sighed. "That's sweet, little Maddelena. I hope you're right. I truly do."

A hammering on the door below caught them both short. In moments the steward arrived to announce young master Theobaldo Capulletto, commonly known as Thibault. He was bleeding, and seeking shelter for the night.

◆　◇　◆

There was no knock, no warning before Cesco came into Buthayna's room. She was with another man, who found himself hoisted mid-coitus by his hair and beaten across the threshold. The door slammed shut, but reopened so Cesco could toss the man's clothes out after.

It banged shut again, and he leaned against it, staring at her. "No one else. Whatever I must pay, you belong to me."

She gazed back at him, uncertain, restraining her heart from leaping with joy. As the frequency of his visits had increased, so too did her determination not to fall into the wanton's trap. Never love a client. Never.

He came to her and kissed her hard, with teeth and tongue and jaw. His hands moved with such force she would be bruised, and she responded in kind, biting his lips while her hands ripped at his shirt to rake him with her nails. It was angry lovemaking, loud and forceful. She thought her own hunger was artifice until she realized she was weeping with longing. Not for his body, but for his heart.

But she would not say it. She would not give up that last inch of her self, her dignity, her protection. Not unless he said it first.

Which he did. Curled behind her, spent and sleepy, his hands as soft as they had been rough, he traced the line of her arm with one finger. It was a moment she would remember forever – the sheets, the light of the taper, the scent of the incense, the feel of his body, the timbre of his voice. But most of all she remembered the words, spoken in her own tongue. *"Uḥibbuk."*

She suppressed the shuddering warmth that flowed through her. Reaching up, she trapped his hand against her arm, softly, tenderly. As was right, she responded in his own language. "I love you."

From that moment Buthayna knew she was lost.

She did not care.

TWENTY-FIVE

UNABLE TO FEEL his arms, Benjamin Montagu staggered down the road under a grey sky. He swayed, uncertain how he kept his feet beneath him, much less place one in front of the other. But he could see it now. His half-brother had spoken with reverence of Verona's fabled forty-eight towers. He was almost there.

Benjamin had been on foot ever since the cart driver had noticed an unwelcome rider and beaten him away with his crop. His own fault. The rocking of the wagon had lulled him to sleep, wonderful sleep. And even better, sleep while making progress! In the last three days of travel he had caught snippets of sleep in trees, once under that bridge when it had been too cold to brave the air. But sleeping in the back of a wagon, even a wagon of crated pigs, had been near heavenly. *How did he hear my snores over the grunting? Am I that loud?*

It had been a hard journey. Catching a chill from the river, he had been discovered and nursed to health by the farmer's wife – until her husband had taken umbrage at his wife's favourite method of warming Montagu. Escaping with his sword and shoes had been a miracle. He'd been on foot ever since.

Thinking of feet, his left foot was numb. He plopped himself down by the side of the road and massaged, not the foot, but the leg above it, welcoming the needles of pain as blood started flowing again. The temptation to stay seated was so great, but he dared not indulge it. He might fall into a never-ending sleep.

Struggling upright, he stalked back to the old Roman road. He had a vital message to deliver. He was only afraid the Scot had arrived before him. *It's been weeks. Maybe he turned about and went home—*

That sounds like horses. Benjamin longed for his own horse, safe in the stable in Lyons. He'd lost what little gold he'd had in the river, and it was a miracle he hadn't lost his sword.

Horses! screamed a voice in his head. He turned to spy six mounts galloping towards him.

Forgetting the cold, the pain, the exhaustion, Benjamin began to run.

♦   ◊   ♦

Beneath one of Verona's fabled towers, Benjamin's distant relative was skipping along, attempting to touch only non-snowy patches cleared on the ground. In his mind, if he landed in snow, he'd fall, not down, but upwards, into a cloud. *What if snow is actually fallen clouds? What if you could grab a handful of snow and be lifted into the sky?*

His thoughts in the air, Romeo Montecchio trailed along after his mother on the way to church. She made the trip daily, ostentatiously entering the confessional while her pretty seven year-old boy waited outside it. When he was smaller he'd just stood there, gazing at the walls, making up stories. He knew every fresco, every cross, every engraving, every fine fixture of this shrine. As he grew bolder, he started to explore.

The Basilica of San Zeno was a wonderful maze. The main chamber split at the boundary between the nave and the sanctuary, creating two tiers. The upper opened into the sanctuary proper. The lower, visible through the pillars that supported the sanctuary, led down into a cavernous enclosure where the holiest men and noblest Veronese lay at rest. The older sarcophagi were simple and plain, bearing rudely carved inscriptions. The newest bore ornate inlays of gold and silver, complete with elaborate crests.

Romeo had explored down there for weeks, always returning just as his mother emerged from unburdening her soul. By now he knew every stone, every inscription, and was ready for something new. Boldly leaving his mother behind, Romeo crossed to the descending stairs at the far left of the nave. Instead of following them down, he tugged on the door in the wall and exited the church, pulling his cloak tight.

The garden here was enclosed by the pillars of a walkway, with the monastery proper on the far side. A lone friar was toiling on hands and knees, re-wrapping some blighted shrubs. Romeo recognized him at once. Fra Lorenzo was a man whose frame was unsuited to his size, but that was due to the beer that Franciscans practically lived on. A favourite of Romeo's mother, Lorenzo had always been kind to Romeo, patting his head and sneaking him sweets.

The man's back was turned. It entered Romeo's head that it would be good sport to startle the holy man, and was about to call when someone beat him to it. "God give you good morning, brother!"

"*Benedicite,*" said Fra Lorenzo, automatically offering the greeting of the brothers of San Zeno, a Benedictine order. Then he saw who had hailed him. "My lord prince, an honour."

Romeo's face lit up. Leaving the cover of the walkway, he broke into a run. "Cesco!"

Himself startled, Cesco laughed and bowed. "Romulus! Did you leap the wall?"

"No, I just killed the brother that did." Skidding to a halt, Romeo bowed back, grinning, sure he'd found his adventure for the day.

"With so many brothers to choose from, how did you spy him out?"

"By finding the one without a hood."

"Because he was not a member of the brother hood. Ha! Well, whatever the cause, it is a holy delight to find you here."

"I've come to fill the unholy hole Adam left us with his bite of the apple."

"You'd best change your name then, to escape the apple."

Romeo frowned for a moment, thinking, then beamed. "Meaning I need a new appellation!"

"Right!"

"I shall apply myself to finding that new appellation, Cesco."

"Ser Francesco," corrected Fra Lorenzo, breaking into their badinage. "Even in wordplay, titles matter, my little lord."

"Quite right," agreed Cesco amiably, putting a hand around Romeo's shoulders. "Take our esteemed brother here. He could be called many things, but he prefers *Pater*, since he sees it as his duty to patronize the whole city. Take him just now – this is not even his garden, yet he feels compelled to meddle."

"I was asked," said the friar huffily.

"Which makes this a rare happenstance. Be warned, little Romeo, don't let the good friar into your life. He won't ever stop meddling."

Fra Lorenzo scowled. "Romeo has no need of my advice. He's a good boy – unlike some I could name."

"Could isn't would, and definitely not should. In the naming, wouldn't you shatter some oath or other?"

Finished wrapping the plant's base, Lorenzo lifted his shears to clip some stray leaves. "Ser della Scala, I hope you've come to pray. You aren't here nearly enough to atone for all your foolishness."

"I did my praying this morning, at an eastern altar."

"Humph. I suppose I must accept that oblique statement at face value. But if you have prayed, why are you here trampling these poor herbs?"

"I wanted you to explain something to me."

"And that is?"

"I was recently reminded of Omar Khayyám, and the dual nature of nature. I hoped you could enlighten me as to the theory of duality."

Lorenzo paused, frowning. "It is nothing new."

"Perhaps not. But Auntie Imperia – Suor Beatrice to you – says your view of it is unique."

"I am an herbalist. My observations come from working in my garden." Reaching out, he snapped a leaf from the white dog's blossom at his elbow. "Inside this plant there is both medicine and poison. If I crush it, mix a pinch of it with some other herbs it will cure several maladies. If I were to eat it whole, I would grow ill and possibly even die. Both these qualities live in my garden."

"Quite the Eden," said Cesco laconically.

Lorenzo was impervious to interjections as he warmed to his theme. "It strikes me that man has much in common with plants. The ability to do acts for good or ill – it is a question of use. If a gifted man used his gifts for selfish pursuits, no matter the reason, it would act like a slow poison on both the man and those close to him. If a man, for whatever reason, commits acts of charity and selflessness, it could cure a city, or even a whole land."

"Fascinating theory. And so similar to something... what was it? Ah well – it will come to me. Thank you, Friar, I feel enlightened."

"In lightened?" Romeo was still eager to play.

Cesco ruffled Romeo's hair. "Yes, a warm light fills me."

"All aglow."

"Better aglow than a-glowering," said Cesco with a sidelong glance at the friar.

"But you are lightened," pressed Romeo.

"Nearly weightless."

"Perhaps by wings on your heels."

Cesco winced. "Those were clipped long ago. I'm waiting for them to grow back. Until then, my lightening must come from a wick. Even a one as dry as this wholly holy man."

"My young lords," said Fra Lorenzo, "play with words as you please. I have work to do."

Cesco interposed himself between the holy man and the next plant. "One more thing. As you say, men, like plants, can have undesirable effects on their fellow man. That isn't limited to the young. The old and nominally wise can fall into the trap of doing evil, no matter their intent. Does the plant have intentions? Or is it just there, waiting to be used? Regardless, I wanted to warn you, some plants have thorns. Thorns that expose what lies beneath the surface."

Startled, Lorenzo's anger kindled beneath his tonsure. "Prince or no, take that tone with me again and you'll regret it."

"Regret will be catching, then. I'll pass it on to you. I know you Franciscans are all about good works. But take me off your list of charities. In this one instance, follow the guidance of my friend Benedick's namesake – separate yourself from worldly cares. Pray for me if you must, but leave it there."

Fra Lorenzo unconsciously cracked the knuckles of both fore-fingers under his thumbs. "I will do as my conscience dictates."

"That wasn't always the case, was it? I have heard whispers. Whispers of a city far, far away. A city in the hills of France, one with some very peculiar traditions – what, are you leaving?"

Fra Lorenzo had blanched, the shears trembling in his grip.

Romeo was confused. "What are you talking about?"

"Nothing!" said the Friar quickly, sweating despite the cold.

Cesco's tone remained jaunty. "O, our friar was once a sinner. Worse, really. We're all sinners, but Lorenzo was something more." He snapped his fingers. "*That's* why your plant-theology sounds so familiar! It's the doctrine of—"

"No!" gasped Lorenzo in a husky voice, looking over his shoulders.

Cesco grinned nastily. "Never let it be said, Romeo, that our dear Fra Lorenzo isn't perfect. Yes, always remember – he trained to be perfect, just like his father."

"I'll remember," said Romeo, not comprehending but eager to please.

Lorenzo stared at Cesco. "How – how did you—"

"I listen at keyholes."

"Please," said Lorenzo, wringing his hands.

"Don't beg, O holy perfection," mocked Cesco. "I'm no Inquisitor. Your little heresies are as safe from me as my secrets are from you. Put another way, I swear, *Pater Perfecte*, if my secrets are not mine alone, neither will yours be."

The Francisan swallowed. "God will not accept oaths to do sin."

"Sin?" Cesco feigned dismay. "You perplex me, you truly do. To do Evil is a sin. But according to San Giovanni, Evil's opposite isn't Good. It's Truth. All I threaten you with is Truth. How can that be a sin?" Cesco tapped Romeo's head with two fingers. "Remember, Romeo – perfect in every way." With that, Cesco departed the cloister.

Romeo was tempted to follow and ask what he meant, but he felt bad for the friar, who looked very upset. "Are you all right, father?"

Lorenzo mopped his brow, despite the cold. "Yes – yes, I'm fine. It's nothing."

"What's wrong with being perfect? I'd like to be perfect."

"Nobody's perfect, Romeo," said Lorenzo. "Certainly not me."

"Romeo!" Gianozza emerged from the church, her voice growing sharper as she spied her wayward son. "Romeo! For shame! Do you know how worried I was?"

Bending low, Lorenzo murmured swiftly in Romeo's ear. "Not a word, little Romeo. How would you like it if someone spread your secrets?"

"I don't know any secrets of yours," said Romeo.

"You know I *have* a secret," said Lorenzo. "That's enough of one, isn't it?"

Romeo's mother was making a bee-line through the gardens. "I won't tell," he murmured.

"Good boy." Patting Romeo's shoulder, Lorenzo intercepted the boy's mother. "I hope you'll forgive my presumption, Donna Montecchio. I asked Romeo to help me with my gardening."

Gianozza's annoyance melted. "Fra Lorenzo! I didn't know it was you. Of course you can take charge of him. I trust your judgment implicitly. In fact, if you like, I can send him to you each morning – he'll be here with me, and it will do him some good, I am sure, to spend time working among the brothers."

"I'd like that," said Lorenzo. "But I am only here once a week. My own garden keeps me occupied. I can tell him what to do when I'm absent. Is that agreeable to you, son?"

Eager to please, Romeo said it was and took his mother's hand to go. Over his shoulder he gave a broad wink to Lorenzo, who waved and smiled as if he was completely unconcerned.

It was a lie.

◆   ◊   ◆

Cesco arrived at his home to discover not only Detto and Antonia waiting for him, but a less-welcome houseguest. "When I promised my wife a cat," he observed, eyeing Thibault from heel to head, "I did not mean I'd take in any stray that came calling."

Detto said, "He and his uncle quarreled."

Cesco sighed. "And as I pioneered the sport, this is the natural nexus of young men with father issues."

"He is not my father," said Thibault with venom.

"Less shouting, please, or you'll wake the lady of the house from her nap," chided Cesco. For some reason this statement tickled him, and as he helped himself to some pine-nut brittle he giggled to himself. "O, how absurd! How wonderful! Of course, Thibault, you must stay. We'll fix you up with a bell, a saucer, and a ball of yarn…"

Thibault turned to leave, but Antonia forestalled him. "His tongue is wicked, but he means what he says. Stay."

"Yes, please! Or, better, we'll set you up with Benedick and Salvatore and the other provisional Veronese. Where are they, by the bye?"

◆   ◊   ◆

Benedick and Salvatore were at that moment in the company of Don Pedro of Aragon. Benedick was again relating his earliest venture into war, the sneak attack on Vicenza twelve years earlier. Pedro was listening to the great feats of Cangrande, but Benedick was trying to relate his own daring – though in fact he'd fought very little that day. Barely a man, he'd been a mere foot soldier, scaling the walls with the Count of San Bonifacio and helping open the gates for the invading forces of Marsilio da Carrara. "The Count died from wounds he received that day. In fact, he was stabbed by Carrara, who thought the Count had betrayed them."

"It was another part of the trick played by the Scaliger," said Salvatore. "Ser Alaghieri had dressed in the Count's armour and fought against the invading Paduans. Thus Carrara believed the Count was a traitor."

"Cunning," marveled Don Pedro. "And the Scaliger really did wear a disguise and wave the Paduans into the trap?"

Benedick grinned ruefully. "Completely true! I remember seeing him, though of course I didn't know it at the time."

"Amazing," said Don Pedro.

"Typical," said Salvatore with cool amusement.

From across the room the lady Beatrice stirred from her book. "I'm surprised the Paduans lost. With Signor Benedick on their side, how could they have failed?"

Benedick had deliberately sat with his back to her. Over his shoulder he said, "If only you had been there, lady, the enemy would have withered to dust before your basilisk stare."

Beatrice rolled her eyes but made no reply, so Benedick resumed his narrative. He had begun telling how he came to the rescue of Marsilio da Carrara during the Dente uprising when a noise in the street caught Salvatore's attention. "Did you hear that? It sounds like a brawl."

Benedick stood at once. "We'd best go see if Cesco needs help."

"Yes, do," said Beatrice. "So you can add saving Verona's heir to your litany of heroic deeds."

Caught wrong-footed, Benedick said, "A happy thing that you are not a man, lady. You would be hard-pressed to find a sword as sharp as your tongue." She opened her mouth and he held up a quick hand. "Save your rejoinders! I must go."

"I'll go with you," said Don Pedro, calling for his sword as he followed the two Rakehells out.

Beatrice remained behind, fuming. "Men! Always need the last word."

◆　◊　◆

In his house on the *via Pigna*, Cesco's head likewise came up at the sound of shouts and racing horses. "How now, what goes?"

"Whatever it is," said Detto, gazing down at the chessboard between them, "you'll be blamed for it."

Cesco reached for his boots. "Best earn the blame, then. Come on, kitty! Let's find you some yarn!"

Cesco, Detto, and Thibault barreled down the stairs, still struggling into their tall leather boots. Antonia appeared above them. "Cesco? You're not—"

"It's not me!" shouted Cesco over his shoulder.

Below, Maddelena was having her midday dinner when she saw her husband rush past the door. "Francesco? What's happening?"

Grabbing a sword from a rack beside the stair, Cesco threw its baldric over his shoulder. "I'll let you know, little princess, when I find out." With that he bolted forth without even a cloak.

In the street, city guardsmen were running after horsemen just turning a corner. Senseless of the cold, Cesco sprinted towards the sound with a whoop of pleasure. "A hunt! A hunt!"

Detto and Thibault were a step behind, having each grasped a cloak as well as a sword. Two blocks on they were joined by Benedick, Salvatore, and the Spanish prince and his men. The Paduans looked at Cesco in surprise. "What's going on?"

"No idea! Welcome to Verona, my lord! You wanted a Palio. *Ahí está!* On! On!" The chase turned down the *via Cappello*, a long straight stretch that allowed them to see the whole course.

"There's the hare!" Far ahead a thin figure on horseback was being pursued by five men with drawn swords, scattering merchants and buyers in all directions.

Unencumbered by armour, the sextet quickly outstripped the city guardsmen and Pedro's men, though they were unable to close the gap with the racing horses. Seeing the distant fugitive turn right, Cesco did the same, the others in his wake. Running parallel with the hunters and the hare, they scanned the gaps between the buildings to their left as they raced across slick marble paving stones.

Detto called out, "He'll have to turn at the Porta San Fermo!"

"Which way?" asked Benedick.

"This way, unless his horse can swim!" shouted Thibault, delighted.

"Save your breath," advised Salvatore.

The fugitive was trapped by the city's old Roman walls – the gates that allowed passage were barred by soldiers, who leveled their halberds. Twisting away at the last moment, the thin figure turned his horse's head northward to continue his flight, a path that had him galloping directly at the sextet.

With a chuckle, Cesco first began to slow, then twisted around to run away from the horsemen. Confused, the others stopped, leaping backwards to avoid being trampled as the first rider pelted past, followed by his five pursuers.

Running full tilt back the way he had come, Cesco kept looking over his shoulder. As the rider came level with him he lunged, grasping the saddle and jumping into the air. It was a trick the Rakehells had seen before, but Pedro's jaw dropped as he watched Cesco swing himself up and around the horse's rump to land straddling the beast, facing backwards. Cesco waved back at them as he was carried away.

The rider felt the bump at his back and turned to find a smiling young man perched behind him. "*Buongiorno, signore.* Wither are you bound?"

Not understanding Italian, the young man hesitated, then gasped in French, "Help me! I'm trying to reach the Greyhound!"

Twisting sideways, Cesco switched tongues. "You're luckier than you know. Turn right here. Whoops, nevermind!" The way back was blocked by yet more guardsmen. "Allow me, please." Reaching around the man, Cesco grasped the reins and turned the horse's head again southwards, back towards the Porta San Fermo, into the oncoming hunters with swords drawn.

"What are you doing?" demanded the man, but in English, a tongue Cesco was just learning.

"Trust, trust." Reaching up, Cesco pushed the man's head low. "Duck!" Angling the horse to the left side of the street, Cesco released the reins and drew his sword, an awkward gesture as it was trapped between their two bodies. But he whipped it free in time to block the blows of the two riders aiming for the fugitive's lowered head. He could not parry the stroke that slashed along the horse's right flank, instead lifting his legs. The fugitive's own leg was not so fortunate, though his wound was superficial.

The horse's was not. Staggering, the beast collapsed just at the mouth of the Porta San Fermo, where guards with halberds were poised to skewer anyone trying to get past. Cesco leapt clear, landing in a mound of frozen snow.

The horsemen at the far end of the street wheeled about. The guardsmen were coming near, too, points angled at the thin rider's chest. Cesco gave them a wry frown. "Leave him be!"

One Veronese soldier snarled, "Back away if you know what's good for you, boy! Our duty is to guard this gate!"

"Oh?" demanded Cesco, one eye on the approaching horsemen. "Who are you, to be so zealous over the this ancient stone portal, the builders? Forgive me Signor Valerius, Signor Caecilius, Signor Servilius, Signor Cornelius! I failed to recognize you! You've risen from your tombs to protect your creation against the intrusion of a dazed man?" Cesco placed his body in front of the fugitive, just staggering free from the saddle of the fallen horse, his leg covered in blood. Looking down the street at the hunters, Cesco grinned.

Intent on their prey, the riders took no note of the quintet running in the narrow street, and so were utterly surprised when Detto swung his sword out from under his cloak. Even at nearly fourteen he was strong, with thick arms like his father's. He used the flat of his blade to whack one rider in the chest, knocking him backwards in his saddle. Thibault's blade hissed the air and sliced the saddle's girth, sending the man flailing to the ground.

Pedro's target was not a man but the sword held in a stabbing position. It was a foolish man who stabbed on horseback – too easy for the blade to be ripped from your grip. Sliding his sword to the inside of the man's attack, Pedro let his blade ride up the length of the attacker's sword until it struck the crossguard, knocking the man's sword clean from his hand.

Benedick's method was simpler. Using the pommel of his sword, he punched a passing horse in the ear, sending that horse and rider careening into the man next to him, who was just then fending off a blow from Salvatore on his other side and did not veer in time. Salvatore leapt clear as the two horses crashed into the wall at his back.

That left Cesco facing just one oncoming assailant who held his sword high, ready for a crushing blow. As the horse thundered past, Cesco's sword hissed up in a defensive parry that met only air. Cesco was not the target.

The fugitive threw himself sideways behind a stone stairway leading upwards towards the top of the gate. The hunter reined in short of the threatening halberds and turned his mount about to try again. Cesco rushed forward, swinging his sword back and forth across the horse's line of sight. The hunter beat Cesco's blade aside and windmilled it around to come down on Cesco's bare head.

Catching it with a hanging parry, Cesco let the attack slide past him then jabbed his pommel. The man doubled over, winded, and Cesco reached out a hand to haul him from the saddle and onto the ground, where his pommel descended once more to render the man insensible.

Down the street the hunters had surrendered to the thicket of halberds that awaited them on both ends of the street. The four Rakehells and the Spanish Don were approaching, smiles all over their faces.

"Thank you. I cannot—" The cause of all the trouble tried to take a step, but collapsed in a heap, face skidding across the large marble paving stone.

The city guards swarmed, but Cesco waved them away from the limp fugitive. "Save your fetters of brass, brave souls, or you'll be in it when his hair returns." A reference to the Biblical Sampson – the fellow's hairline was in a losing war against his forehead.

"He'll be wanted for questioning," said the lead guardsman gruffly.

Cesco pulled a face. "For what, starving?"

"For racing through the streets and disobeying a lawful order to halt."

"I'll go with you, and gladly." Cesco strode up and tapped the device on the guard's tabard. "See this ladder? That's mine. Those colours? Mine too."

"Fut," said another guard. "It's the heir."

"Indeed," said Cesco. "And were I not, I'd still be a knight. And were I not, that fellow there is a knight, and the son of Lord Nogarola. And were he not, those two men over there are Paduans. Not much of a threat, I know, but still, he has red hair. That little one, he's not a man at all, he's a cat, with a nasty urge to scratch. And that man there? A prince of Aragon. And yet were we none of those things, were we the nameless, stationless plebs you took us for," said Cesco, building to a finish, "we would *still* be men enough to remove him from your hands as easily as we could remove the breath from your lungs and the blood from your livers!"

"Forgive us, Ser Francesco," said a third guard, stepping forward. "We were simply defending our gate."

With a dismissive grunt, Cesco turned to the captured men. "Who are you? Who is he? What had he done?"

None of them chose to answer. It was Benedick who pulled back the cowl from one head. "Cesco, am I right? Isn't this one of the Scot's men?"

Stepping close, Cesco squinted. "Indeed. And that answers the question of our fugitive's identity."

"It does?" asked Detto.

Cesco lifted the dazed man's chin. "What's your name?"

"*Quoi?*" replied the figure.

"*Comment appelez-vous?*"

"*Je m'appelle Ben.*"

"*Benjamin Montagu, non?*"

"*Oui.*"

"Montagu?" echoed Detto.

Continuing in French, Cesco asked, "Any relation to Ser William?"

The man nodded. "His brother. But..." The voice trailed off, not from fatigue but embarrassment.

"*Un bâtard,*" supplied Cesco. "Luckily for you, I have a soft spot for bastards. So does the Capitano, who is the biggest bastard of them all. Why were these men chasing you?"

Montagu pointed. "They tried to kill me! On the road. I

knocked one down and took his horse, then rode to beg protection."

"And you have it." Helping Montagu to rise, Cesco addressed the guards. "You're quite fortunate. Had you thrown this man in a cell, you would have been imprisoning a relation of Lord Montecchio. I suggest we take him to the Casa Montecchio instead. Mariotto can look after him, and take responsibility for his behavior. Besides," added Cesco, gesturing at Benjamin, "he is hardly a threat. Signor Salvatore, Signor Benedick, will you take him up?"

"My lord," said the most sensible guardsman, "please allow one of us to accompany you. What you say is likely true, but we would be in dereliction of our duty—"

Cesco cut across him. "By all means, come! As for the rest," he waved a hand at the Scot's men, "lock them up for attempted murder."

"His?" asked the first guard, pointing at Montagu.

"Mine! Now, shall we be gone? *Allons-y!*"

The doors to the Casa Montecchio were made of a light-coloured wood, studded with iron spikes and the Montecchi crest, an ornate horse's head that stared westwards. There was a commotion within as men armed themselves before pulling wide the gate. In answer to their demands, Cesco identified himself and called for the master of the house, who was just emerging, sword in hand. "Is the city under attack?"

"No, just the Montecchi," replied Cesco. "One, at least. Lord Mariotto Montecchio, allow me to introduce Benjamin Montagu, natural brother of your cousin Ser William Montagu."

"Third cousin, I think," said Mari, brows knitted as Benedick and Detto helped Montagu forward. Studying his face, Mari saw echoes of William's knightly features, right down to the small round ears. In flowing, courtly French he said, "Are you well, cousin? You look half done-in."

"I have walked from France, my lord," said Benjamin, his voice as thin as his frame.

"And he has been tasked this last hour in an attempt to deprive him of his life," added Cesco in Italian. "By the same people who claim he has come to murder the Capitano."

Hearing the word *capitano*, Benjamin said, "I have to see *le capitan*."

"Not today you don't," replied Mariotto with a frown. "Tonight you sleep, after you eat something. Then we'll see about arranging an audience." He nodded for his men to take Montagu into the house. Looking to Cesco, Mari said, "Thank you for bringing him to me. Does this make any sense to you?"

"Not yet," replied Cesco.

"Very exciting, this," mused Don Pedro. "Nothing so lively happens in Aragon."

"Verona has more than its share," said Cesco. "Mariotto, the fellow seems harmless enough. But if the Scot's story is true…"

"I could be welcoming in an assassin. I'll keep a guard on him until he has more strength and can tell us his side." Mari offered an ironic smile. "Now I regret not venturing forth at the hullabaloo. I thought it was just another of your madcap adventures."

"So it was," laughed Cesco. "Just not one of my making."

At the window above appeared an eager face under a crop of dark hair. "Father? What's wrong?"

Before Mariotto could answer, Cesco stepped back from the house and waved. "Hi ho, Romeo! Twice in a day. One might think it was destiny."

"Fateful," replied Romeo. "Full of fate."

"So full of fate is usually fatal," said Cesco.

Romeo shot back, "Fat with fatuous fatalities."

"Enough to make a man go fetal."

"Foetal, you mean, with tall foes all around."

"Thank heaven you don't have foes, they'd all be taller than you." Snapping his fingers, Cesco laughed. "But you do have a foe! I've brought the serpent into your orchard. Thibault the Cat, meet Romulus, who must be a wolf having been suckled by one. Wolf, cat, and dog — we are a menagerie!"

Mariotto was less amused. "Thibault Capulletto?"

Thibault bowed. "My lord."

"His uncle threw him out," confided Cesco in a mock whisper.

Mariotto visibly relaxed. "Typical of the man. Signor Theobaldo, you are welcome in this house."

"Damn," said Cesco. "I was hoping for something more exciting. But O, my Rakehells! We must feast the brave Spanish blade that has dared to join us in action! Come, Don Pedro - to the Four Swords!"

TWENTY-SIX

By Thursday the Englishman was well enough to present himself before Cangrande's inner circle. The essential Anziani of Verona were present – Castelbarco, Lozzo, Capulletto, and Alaghieri. So too was Mastino, taking a break from tiltyard practice to show an unaccustomed interest in foreign politics. Don Pedro was here as witness, as were Benedick, Salvatore, Thibault, and Detto.

Cangrande thanked Cesco for taking a break from his busy schedule of carousing and inciting violence to hear the case of the man whose liberty he had preserved. The heir's face showed mild curiosity, nothing more.

Aiello the Scot was present as well, in the role of accuser. All present knew the purported charges against the fugitive. Having learned of the enmity between Montecchio and Capulletto, Aiello had exploited it, spending the last weeks carousing with Lord Antony Capulletto. Finding the large, genial man so inclined, Aiello had hinted at possible lucrative contracts in Mortimer's England. Thus he had won Capulletto's devoted support. Not that Antony needed enticement. Opposing the Montecchi was his *raison d'etre*.

Mariotto escorted Benjamin forward. He had dressed his cousin's thin frame in the finest weeds, far better than anything Benjamin had ever owned. The Englishman had apparently grown up in a castle basement, strumming on a lute and teaching himself sword tricks late at night. It was only recently that he had been elevated to his brother's messenger. And that only out of necessity.

Having heard all the true details from the sick man's chapped lips, Mari knew what a farce this interview was sure to be. But for form's sake, the interview had to occur.

"State your name," said Cangrande in bored French.

"Benjamin Montagu, my lord."

"Brother of our friend William Montagu, chevalier of England."

"An acknowledged brother, yes. But without standing."

"What brings you to Verona?"

The pale blue eyes dropped a fraction, down and to the right, recalling the lie both his brother and Mariotto had coached him to say. "My health. Sir William told me of the restorative powers of the baths of Verona. I have been ailing, my lord, so my father sent me here to see if Italian waters could repair what English air has caused."

That produced a curled half-smile. "What is the nature of your ailment?"

Montagu flushed. "Premature aging." He removed his hat, displaying the hairline that was in full retreat from the advance of his forehead. That, combined with the many deep crinkles around his eyes did indeed make him look older than his years.

"How old are you?"

"Twenty-three, my lord." The effect of Benjamin's rueful smile was magical. It was formed as an artist might have painted it, big and youthful, filling the whole face with joy. Then it vanished as quickly as it had come. In repose, Benjamin was an oddity. In motion, and especially in happiness, he was undeniably attractive.

"I see," mused Cangrande. "When did your hair begin to thin?"

Again Montagu flushed. "At seventeen, my lord."

"We must have you talk to our physician. But that's for later. Your appearance may deceive. So may your words. We understand from this gentleman," he waved at the Scot, "that you are here, not to ensure your own health, but to deprive us of ours."

Even knowing it was coming, Benjamin coloured. "That is untrue, my lord!"

"Nothing you say is true, you pimply shit," said Aiello in English. If his words were not understood by the other men present, his tone certainly was.

"Ah yes," said Cangrande. "Our charming Scottish friend is your accuser, Monsieur Montagu. And he carries with him the seal of the king of England."

Benjamin looked angry at that, but said nothing.

Castelbarco stepped forward. "We are told you have come here to end the life of our illustrious Capitano."

Benjamin shook his head vigourously. "I swear by all that's holy that is not my purpose."

Capulletto grunted derisively. "We all know how valuable a Montecchio oath is. Why should this bastard be any different? Bad blood."

Mariotto purpled, but was restrained by Nico da Lozzo as Castelbarco continued the questioning. "Is it, then, to seek arms for an uprising against his majesty, your sovereign king?"

"Absolutely not," said Benjamin stoically.

"Then why are you here? Do you truly wish us to believe you traveled all this way just for your health?"

"I – I hoped to take service with the Scaliger." It was an acceptable lie, worked out beforehand. "There is no future for me in England."

"Nor here," murmured Aiello silkily, again in English.

"I cannot inherit, and my brother does not have the funds to aid me to some profession."

Cangrande chuckled. "Whereas I have both funds and a noted fondness for bastardy. What about the charges of horse-thieving and assault?"

"My lord, if there was an assault, I was the victim. I was walking up the road when six men on horseback waylaid me and drew their swords. I knocked one down and took his horse to throw myself at your mercy."

"You made quite a scene, entering the city."

"I regret it, lord. I truly do. But I was simply trying to preserve my life."

"It's true, lord Capitano," offered Don Pedro. "He never raised an arm against anyone. Whereas the Scot's men were quite zealous in attempting to remove his head from his shoulders."

"In an attempt to protect my host, the Capitano," insisted Aiello.

Cangrande waved the Scot to silence. "Well, Monsieur Montagu, here is what I shall do. I shall leave you at your liberty until I've written to your brother and to the king to ascertain where in all this the truth lies. But I have a warning for you." He pointed to Aiello. "And for you, Monsieur Aiello. Should any harm befall either of you, the other will be instantly put to death. I'll not have feuding in my city." There were coughs and everyone glanced away from Mari and Antony.

Benjamin appeared accepting of the edict, but Aiello bristled. "What if he dies by someone else's hand?"

Cangrande fixed Aiello with a hard gaze. "Best see he does not. For that hand ends two lives."

"And if he succeeds in his task, and murders you?"

Cangrande rose to his full height, a threatening act of dignity. "Monsieur Aiello, your bravery is manifest. For I must tell you, there are no men and only two women who dare to use such a tone with me."

Blanching, Aiello bowed. "Forgive me. I spoke in concern for your well-being."

"I see. Well, since you are so concerned, you'll be relieved to learn both your lives are tied to mine. Should I perish from this earth, I'll quickly have you both to attend me in Purgatory. Fortunately for us all, I employ food tasters these days. Now, is that all?"

The meeting dispersed with a grumbling Aiello following a subdued Montagu and Montecchio from the chamber. Capulletto lingered to glower at Thibault, who waved saucily to him, provoking a gale of laughter from Cesco.

Ten minutes later, Benjamin Montagu was closeted with Cangrande in a much less formal atmosphere. Leaving the Domus Nova and crossing the main public square, he and Mariotto had doubled back through the palace stables, around to a secret stairwell that had remained locked for thirteen years. Only Cangrande's steward had the key, and it was so long unused that it had hopefully been forgotten.

Still not recovered from his arduous journey, climbing the stairs exhausted Benjamin more than he'd expected. Emerging into Cangrande's loggia, Benjamin saw the Scaliger's heir seated beside Cangrande, along with Ser Alaghieri and Castelbarco. Benjamin bowed deeply. "Thank you for seeing me, my lord."

Cangrande noted his colour. "Are you still ill? Should this wait?"

"No, my lord. I'm fine."

"Then have a seat." Where before he had been frosty and disinterested, Cangrande was now solicitous. "I've had sunstroke and blistered feet both, so I know what you're feeling. Take your time. First, how is your brother?"

"Well in health, my lord."

"And in mind?"

"He is desperately concerned for the throne."

"So there is truth in what Aiello says? Your knightly brother seeks funds to raise a force to seize the English throne?"

"Not to seize it," said Benjamin doggedly. "To free it."

Cangrande exchanged looks with the others. "Free it? I do not understand."

When Benjamin failed to frame a suitable response, Mariotto spoke up. "What he means is that the English king, who is within a year or so of Prince Cesco here, does not rule. He is a puppet on the throne for his mother and her lover, Sir Roger Mortimer, the Earl of March. Is that not so?"

Benjamin nodded, pleased he had not had to speak so plainly. "Sir Montagu is loyal to the throne, but that loyalty does not extend to Sir Roger. It was not the king but Sir Roger who put the royal seal on that document the Scotsman gave you. Mortimer has claimed several estates for himself, and is on the way to becoming the richest man in England. He clearly wishes to build his power base before the king is old enough to demand his autonomy."

Castelbarco was bemused. "The queen allows this?"

"The queen is the one keeping her son in check. Or so it seems to my brother. They certainly have some power over him that keeps the king from moving against them. He is watched, his companions are limited, his freedom cribbed."

"I feel for him," said Cesco idly.

"So does this message come from your brother, or the king?" asked Castelbarco shrewdly.

"The king," replied Benjamin, himself a little awed.

"What does he want?"

"Money."

"Not soldiers?" asked Castelbarco.

"That would be counterproductive, my lord."

"Why?"

Cangrande supplied the answer himself. "Because the English king cannot bring Italian soldiers to fight his mother's French ones on English soil. But surely," he added, "an 'advisor' or two would be welcome?"

"Very much so," agreed Benjamin. "It would be more than kind."

"In addition to the money," said Cesco pointedly. "Not in lieu of it."

"He's the king of England!" protested Castelbarco. "He must have all the funds he needs."

"As Lord Protector of the realm, Mortimer controls the purse," Benjamin explained. "Mortimer's creatures manage the Treasury and make excuses any time the king tries to access his funds for anything other than his personal use. Even his bodyguards are Mortimer's men."

"I think I admire this Mortimer," said Cesco.

"You'd admire him less if he were Italian." Cangrande crossed to put a hand on Benjamin's shoulder. "Thank you for this message. I understand why this request cannot be made publicly. So we will continue this charade about your health — which is perfectly valid! Mariotto, take him to the baths today, and see that he goes every day until he is bursting with vitality. Meanwhile, I shall consider."

Mariotto led a grateful Benjamin out via the secret passage, and Cangrande saw it locked behind them. Then he turned to Castelbarco, Pietro, and Cesco. "Well?"

Pietro had remained silent through the interview. Now he said, "Whom do we believe?"

"I want to believe Montagu," said Cangrande. "But Aiello has documentation and authority on his side. And I find it hard to believe a king has so little power."

"A young king," observed Pietro. "Who has never experienced his power, and may not know how to wield it."

"And who is in awe of his mother," added Cangrande with a smile. "One sympathizes, if not respects."

Cesco cocked his head. "Truly? I thought you found mothers over-rated."

"How would I know, never having had one?" retorted Cangrande.

"Ah! That explains how I was denied a maternal figure. I was meant to follow your footsteps in all things."

"Right down to the suckling by a she-wolf."

Cesco grabbed his crotch. "She can suckle this."

It was a vulgar provocation, and both Castelbarco and Pietro blanched. But Cangrande remained calm. "I hear there's suddenly no shortage of suckling in your life, so perhaps we could return to the topic at hand. Do we send the money?"

"To whom?" retorted Cesco. "Ser Montagu? This circumscribed English king who lacks the will to break his bonds?"

"The funds," corrected Cangrande, "not the will."

Cesco pulled a face. "A strong will would find a way without funds."

"Then perhaps he needs someone to show him how to defy his circumstance."

"Someone skilled in such defiance?"

"Naturally."

"Naturally," echoed Cesco. "And a sea voyage might be good for one's health."

"Perfectly true."

"And calm the waters here at home at the same time."

"They do need calming."

"And perhaps return in a few years, time having healed all wounds."

"Old saws are not untrue for being old."

"Neither does age make them truer. The answer is no."

Slow to follow this exchange, both Pietro and Castelbarco realized that Cangrande was obliquely suggesting Cesco travel to England. He was more pointed now. "I do need to send someone to ascertain the truth in this."

"Then send someone who gives a damn." Rising, Cesco crossed to the door and exited. He had not asked leave to depart, but Cangrande was not about to start a battle over protocol. Especially one he would not win.

The Scaliger glanced at Pietro. "So much for that hope."

It pained Pietro to side with the Scaliger over Cesco, but he had to admit a voyage abroad was not the worst idea. It would allow the talk of demonic possession to fade, for the people to laugh at the memory of their young prince more than fear his approach. And it would remove him from the threats of poison or worse — the death of Petruchio, the near-fatal stabbing of Detto.

Perhaps it was just England that did not appeal to the young man. Could they entice him elsewhere? Send him away for as long as it took for his rage to cool, for his heart to heal. For Cesco to return to himself.

It did not occur to him — or perhaps he blocked the thought from his mind — that this might be the self Cesco was determined to become.

♦   ◊   ♦

"They want me to leave," said Cesco.

Buthayna pulled inwards a little. "Who wants that?"

He lay beside her, staring at the ceiling. "The Scaliger. Nuncle. The old folks."

"Where do they want you to go?"

Cesco's laugh was sour. "England."

"What's in England?"

"Nothing. There's nothing for me anywhere."

"Not even here?"

He rolled at once, placing his nose almost against hers so all she could see were his eyes. "Here there is everything." And he kissed her, and she kissed him back. But the fear did not leave her.

After a time he rolled onto his back. "Tell me about your home."

Buthayna had heard this request from many a man over the past two years. Always, she had spun a tale of a mystic and glorious land, full of exotic delights. These invariably pleased her clients. But this was different. Her beloved was asking. Instead of lying, she asked him, "Why?"

"Another friend suggested I travel East. I was trying to think of reasons to accept. I would need a guide…"

She brushed his hand aside. "You are not leaving."

"Am I not?"

"It would make life too easy for those who hate you."

"Perhaps I no longer care about making their lives difficult," he said. "So tell me."

Buthayna's brow furrowed. "There is not much to tell. It is a village, not a city. The market is miles away, shared with three other villages. The men fish and grow dates. The women weave. It is a simple place."

"Sounds heavenly."

She pinched him. "You would be bored the moment you arrived."

"Would I? Simplicity appeals to me. It's a dream I have – a simple life."

"But you could not live it."

"You're very cross today." Shrugging, Buthayna rose from the bed. He laughed at her. "You *are* cross."

"I do not like being tempted with empty promises."

"What empty promises?"

"Of being taken away. I am not so young that I have not heard such lies before."

Now he was angry. "Was I lying? I thought I was making a suggestion."

She had been dressing, her back to him. Now she turned. "Would you marry me? No, you cannot – you are wed."

"For now," said Cesco.

"For ever," she replied. "You are the heir to Verona. You will need the girl's father and her brothers. I have nothing to offer you—"

Cesco reached out a hand. "That's not true."

Buthayna pulled away. "You do not even pay for it. For you, there is no price."

"Clearly there is," growled Cesco, giving up and retrieving his own clothes. He dressed and departed in silence. The moment he was gone, Buthayna fell to her knees and wept. She had wanted reassurances. Instead she had pushed him away.

♦　　◊　　♦

Early the following week there was a knock at the door to Cesco's house on the *via Pigna*. It was still morning, and the master of the house was abed, as were Ser Detto and the other houseguest. Fidelio opened the door to find a huge man with arms like corded ropes and muck on his boots. With him was a bosomy woman in a nurse's wimple and a blonde child of about three. "Pardon us. We are looking for young Theobaldo Capulletto."

They were admitted and asked to wait, which they did. While someone was sent to wake Thibault, Antonia entered, drawn by the noise. Spying the little girl, she started. "Giulietta?"

"Suora?" said the little girl. "Why are you here?"

"I live here," said Antonia. "I'm looking after the prince's wife. What are you doing here?"

Giulietta looked down, and the nurse knelt to rub her back in a soothing manner. "Poor thing. She's afeard, Suora, that her brave cousin isn't well, and may not be coming back to her house. Her father says – well, you know him, he says a lot of things, some of which come true, some that don't, but he's said that he'll disown his nephew if he doesn't go off to his studies like a proper lad."

"He said more than that, Angelica," said her husband. "He means to stretch the boy's neck. That's what's got her fearful."

There was a foot on the stair, and Thibault entered warily.

"See, poppet?" said the nurse at once, pointing. "There he is, and just as strong and tall as ever you've seen him. He's got a bed here, I fathom, and they're feeding him regular-like..."

Giulietta rushed to throw her arms about her cousin's waist. "Thibault!" He patted her, both touched by the affection and embarrassed for it.

The conversation proceeded as most conversations with a three year-old will, with alternating understanding and stubbornness. Giulietta wanted her cousin home. They explained all the reasons it was better he be away just now, and she understood them, or said she did, then a minute later she was asking why.

"Is it nicer here?"

"It is for me," said Thibault.

"But aren't you lonely? I'm lonely."

"No. I have friends here, and there's even another little girl, so it feels like home. Only no one beats me here."

"Another little girl?"

Sensing a possible jealousy, the nurse Angelica said, "Would you like to meet her? Would that be possible?"

"Absolutely," said Antonia. "She's upstairs with her own nurse. Her name is Maddelena." Sending a servant upstairs, Antonia wondered why she had not thought of it before. Though destined to be the first lady of the city, Maddelena still needed friends. Who better than the daughter of one of Verona's great lords?

"Mama is going to have the baby soon," Giulietta told Thibault.

He looked to Angelica, who nodded. "A few days at most. Never fret, she's fine." Before becoming Giulietta's nurse, Angelica had raised both Thibault and Tessa, and knew the bond between them. Though Andriolo saw the trouble it caused, the nurse cherished it and thought it adorable, not dangerous.

Maddelena arrived, and everyone stood as she greeted them as the chatelaine should. Introduced to Giulietta, she smiled. "Hello. I have a cat, and some puppies. Would you like to see them?" Without waiting, Giulietta put her hand in Maddelena's and they went running off as fast as their layers of clothes allowed.

Antonia shook her head. "I'm an imbecile. They should have been together since the wedding."

"They're together now," said Angelica. "Dahna, was it? Would your little lady like to come visit our house next? Does she like sweets?"

Thibault slipped out of the room, away from this childish talk. In the hall he was stopped by Andriolo. "You alright, lad?"

Thibault nodded, his jaw clamped shut. He knew he should thank Andriolo for throwing the water on his uncle and thus breaking up the fight. It had probably saved Thibault's life. But that would mean admitting he'd needed help.

The older man did not seem to care if he was thanked. He ruffled Thibault's hair. "It's good for you, being among these Rakehells. If he could see past his mad, your uncle would approve. He was much the same in his youth."

"And look where that got everyone," retorted Thibault, ducking away.

"A fair point," agreed Andriolo. "So you make sure you don't follow in his footsteps."

Thibault scowled. "No danger in that."

TWENTY-SEVEN

CESCO AND HIS RAKEHELLS continued raising Cain throughout the city, and the denunciations from the pulpits became more pronounced. So Cangrande decided it was time to lance this particular boil, in the guise of another poetic salon.

This time the chosen site was within doors at the Scaligeri palace, and invitations went out to a select audience — men and women of intellect and poetic taste, not rabble who might misunderstand the stray malicious comment.

It was a debate to allow women at all. But Antonia was adamant she be present. "And after hearing of the last one, Abbess Verdiana plans to attend. Good luck barring the door to her."

"Mariotto's making noise about his wife," observed Pietro. "He'll never hear the end of it if she isn't there."

"Very well," growled Cangrande. "The nobility, the clergy, and wives."

"At least we'll be spared Donna Capulletto," said Castelbarco. Antony's wife had finally been brought to childbed, producing a healthy boy named Gianni. Never was a child so coddled, watched every second of the day lest he fall victim to the same crib death as his brothers.

Cangrande grunted. "I suppose that means we'll have to endure Antony's longing looks towards Gianozza. I wish she would run off with her groom or something equally foolish. Leave Verona — or just die! As time goes by, I can't help but think that we will only be freed from their nonsense by her death. Ah well. We cannot be fortunate in all things. Arrange for the salon, and let us hope for the best."

"Any other names?" asked Pietro, trying not to sound anxious.

Cangrande understood at once. "No. The general call will go out in March. Let's not add fuel to the fire before then."

So it was that towards the end of January the Scaliger's loggia was filled, as it had been so many times before, with the cream of Verona's crop. The only lack was the late Petruchio Bonaventura, whose boisterous laughter was missed by everyone present.

Just inside the door Cesco bumped shoulders with Mastino. Almost of a height now, Mastino gave Cesco the up-and-down. "You do not dress festively, cos."

Cesco indeed looked splendid in a black suede doublet with crimson piping, grey hose, fur-lined boots, and a hooded cape as black as night. "I dress to reflect my mood. Or my stomach," he added.

Mastino's brother Alberto clapped his hands. "I remember those days! One of the first tests of manhood is discovering your limits."

"Then here's hoping you will soon reach manhood, Cousin Alblivious." Everyone laughed, even Alberto, who loved wine, women, and song more than any man present.

Cesco threaded the press of people to where cushioned benches were set for the main players in today's little drama. The Scaliger was engaged in polite conversation with Capulletto and Castelbarco, but Antony paused long enough to frown at Thibault, entering in clothes borrowed from Cesco's own closet.

Cangrande patted Capulletto's shoulder. "It's a hard age, Antony. You remember, surely. One feels the need to rebel against everything. Isn't that so, boy?"

"It is," agreed Cesco. "Or should I defy you, just to prove your point?"

"Defiance is your natural state. It hardly needed puberty to set it in motion. Your dropping balls have only amplified your innermost self. I shudder to think what you'll be when you're full-grown."

"A pity you won't be here to see it." Heads turned at that remark, and even the Scaliger was momentarily at a loss for words.

Cesco looked around him in blank surprise. "The prophecy. The Greyhound is not meant to live but three days past his greatest deed. If the Capitano is indeed the Greyhound, then we must prepare ourselves to lose him. But not before he has won all that is due him."

Cangrande's face darkened. "We must all reconcile ourselves to our due. Shall we begin?"

Cesco deliberately seated himself opposite Bishop Francis, who sat beside Abbess Verdiana, Fra Lorenzo, and the aged Abbot Giuseppe. Pietro recalled his father engaging this man on their first day in Verona, belittling him for his lack of Aristotle and poor understanding of the art of theology — 'God logic'. The abbot's presence here boded nothing good.

Indeed, before Pietro could rise to read the chosen passage from *Purgatorio*, the aged abbot raised a hand. With a perfunctory request for audience, he said, "My lord Scaliger, pray forgive me. When this city last heard the words of the late poet, your son and heir made a statement that has caused consternation among the devout." He cast a glance at his superior, who was frowning. "Since no one has demanded an explanation of his words, I feel it is my duty before God to offer the lad a chance to renounce his heresy."

"While I confess to this uncommonly holy gathering that he can be troublesome, the lad is both a knight and a prince, *brother*," said Cangrande, giving weight to the word. "And will be referred to as such."

The abbot purpled, and Bishop Francis rose to aid his fellow ecclesiastic. "My lord, forgive the good abbot, do. Like the rest of your guests, I promise that I came to hear poetry, not hold an Inquisition." His mouth turned down. "Yet clearly some present have concerns. You and I understand the poetic nature of words, and how great literature often strives to seek drama in art, but means nothing for life. However, not every member of this august assembly has heard as much from your own lips. Perhaps you and Ser Alaghieri could spare a few words on the great questions of poetry."

Before either Cangrande or Pietro could speak, Cesco said, "Why address them, my lord bishop, when the demand was made of me? I am perfectly armed for an Inquisition."

The snake-pit already, thought Pietro.

The bishop had tried to deflect the moment, only to be thwarted by the very fellow he was trying to help. "Since you offer, Ser Francesco — you did surprise many of us with your most creative questioning of the existence of Heaven and Hell."

"Did I?" asked Cesco, blinking rapidly. "I thought it was fairly obvious. If not, allow me to elucidate. It is possible that I was simply responding to an omission in the roster of those languishing in Limbo. Or rather, a presence and an absence from the roster of noble *Limbicoli*."

"Whom do you mean?" asked Cangrande, waving the perplexed bishop to his seat.

Cesco rose, addressing the crowd. "The immortal poet mentions meeting the Laughing Philosopher, the great Mocker – Democritus, fellow of Aristotle, foe of Plato, father of Atoms. It was Democritus who first imagined that we are all made up of the same stuff as the stars, small bricks of matter molded into terrestrial forms. He noted that the basic elements of the universe – water, fire, earth, and air – have means to regenerate themselves. That inside a fallen oak are the elements to recreate the oak anew. That all things are made of these invisible yet solid atoms, and the rest is made of void. Atoms, and void." Cesco pointed. "I see from your face that you know."

Startled, Fra Lorenzo nodded warily. "Aye. Atoms and void – God's mortar and clay. That is the theory, though entirely unprovable."

"We shall never see an atom, that's true," agreed Cesco. "Yet in observing nature, we see that everything does indeed renew – trees from seeds, water from the sky, living creatures through sin." This elicited chuckles from his audience, but he did not pause long enough for the abbot to protest. "All this we glean from Democritus. Yet his natural successor is not in Limbo, but placed much further below. Nuncle, you know to whom I refer."

Sensing the road ahead, Pietro had to unclench his jaw to answer. "Epicurus."

"Epicurus! A name unfairly dragged in the mud of the ages. Thanks to high-living Romans, he is the father of a philosophy that has come to mean hedonism – wine, women, song, nothing more."

"Is there more?" asked Alberto della Scala, garnering a second ripple of laughter and easing some of the tension.

Cesco pointed two fingers at his cousin. "Exactly! His answer is that there is – and there isn't. He takes Democritus' thoughts on science and applies them to morality. If we are nothing but atoms, he argued, then when we die our atoms will disperse to be renewed again. If that is the case, then there can be neither Heaven nor Hell. When our selves cease to exist, the stuff that makes us is renewed. It was therefore the argument of Epicurus – who was no debauched soul, he actually lived rather modestly – it was his argument that we should live in the present time, appreciating the beauty of each day, because there is nothing after."

The abbot made to stand, but Bishop Francis placed a restraining hand on his knee. "He was a pagan who lived long before our Lord Jesus Christ and therefore never knew His truth."

"Yet the Epicurean philosophy was the basis for so many great men that followed, including many Christians. Atoms, not Adams, they said."

"For which crime he is placed in Hell," said Bishop Francis gravely.

"A place in which he did not believe," countered Cesco cheerfully. "Which begs a side question – if God depends upon faith, does a lack of faith weaken Him?"

The abbot broke his superior's restraint. "You speak heresy!"

"Fluently," replied Cesco. "But, my dear abbot, if you wish to condemn me, allow me to offer up more compelling causes for my coming crucifixion."

"Perhaps we should offer up some poetry, instead," suggested Pietro, half-rising with the large volume in his hands.

Cangrande waved him aside. "He'll say what he likes in any case. And, as he says, this is what the people came for."

"They should be serving boiling oil instead of wine," snarled Abbot Giuseppe as the crowd shifted in uneasy fascination.

Cangrande inclined his head to Cesco. "Please. Share your causes."

"That you might show me the error of my ways?"

"Always. As you show me the errors in mine."

Clasping his hands behind his back, Cesco spoke directly to the Scaliger, as if they were alone in the crowded loggia. "To my mind, lord, there are two pernicious notions that the Church has set down as the cornerstones of Christianity, foundations of our faith."

"Only two?" asked Cangrande lightly.

"Well, two to start. The first is the concept that knowledge is sinful. God cast Adam and Eve out of Paradise for eating fruit from the Tree of Knowledge. Therefore it is reasonable to conclude the act of learning is in itself evil, and must be avoided. Thus we are meant to be sheep, unable to read or write or think for ourselves. Education is dangerous. A useful stick with which to cudgel the unwashed masses. The educated thus keep the uneducated in check, forever living in ignorance."

Bishop Francis looked stricken. "My son, the Holy Mother Church extols intelligence as one of the highest virtues."

"Really? How often has Mother Church denounced works other than the Bible as being dangerous? Even Aristotle, whom we all agree is brilliance personified, was reviled for years."

"We don't all agree," growled the abbot.

Bishop Francis spoke over his neighbour. "Aristotle has been accepted as a great pagan thinker who simply did not know the light of Christ. Just as the poet portrays him."

"Yes," agreed Cesco, "when it became clear his works hold universal truths, Aristotle's thoughts were refashioned in a manner consistent with Church doctrine. His potential heresies are excused with the sop that he existed before Christ. Does that mean all thought since Christ is valueless? We twist ourselves to find means by which great works of the past can exist in harmony with the Church. Because anything that questions the modern interpretation of the Bible is dangerous to Church power."

"No," said the bishop gravely. "Because the Bible is the Word of God."

"And Aristotle is not? Intelligence, reason – these are God's greatest gifts. He gave them to us in order that we might use them. But the Church, in its cleverness, reverses that. We are told that reason is the enemy of faith. We are told that God gave us reason to test us. We are told we must reject reason in order to have faith." Cesco pointed to Pietro. "In Avignon, Ser Alaghieri befriended two holy men, Bonagratia of Bergamo and William of Occam. These men were held as papal prisoners and eventually drummed out of the Church itself for the crime of applying reason to the Bible. Who is more heretical, the man who rejects God's gifts, or the man who employs them to their fullest?"

Pietro shifted, uncomfortable because he did not disagree. Indeed, he had made a similar argument two years earlier before a papal Inquisitor. He felt he must speak. "It is true. They were reviled and accused of heresy despite their opinions having the weight of both reason and the Bible behind them."

"Describe them for us," invited Cangrande, thus silencing his heir for the moment.

Pietro did, with much focus on the question of the poverty of Christ, a heated debate at present. Antonia answered, followed by Castelbarco, which prompted more men to voice their opinions. Some sided with the Church. Startlingly, more took up the cause of reason. Cangrande himself posed several piercing questions, and the loggia became both more fraught and more relaxed. The topic was tense, but no longer did it feel as though a fourteen year-old was on trial.

Matters came to a head when the abbot said, "Returning to the root question of reason versus faith, it is no mistake that Eve and Adam were damned for eating the fruit of the Tree of Knowledge. Universal knowledge belongs to the Lord alone. He did not mean for us to share in it. It was our Original Sin, which has caused all the suffering since!"

Quiet until now, Cesco pointed. "Thank you for proving my point. You say that knowledge is sinful, the source of our woes. But was that the original sin? No, I don't think so. The original sin was God's, putting the tree there for them to be tempted in the first place."

Gasps. Even Cesco's Rakehells looked uncomfortable. Before more shouting and clerical denunciations could commence, Cangrande said, "If you were to reconcile them, Ser Francesco, how would you do it? Bend your reason to that. What lesson do you take?"

Cesco shrugged. "I have several thoughts. We refer to God as the Father. Our earthly fathers are responsible for teaching their children. I know of no good father who would place a poisoned apple in a child's room and say, 'Do not eat this.' It's nonsense. So perhaps God intended we should eat of the apple. Perhaps it was part of His plan that we should fall, that we might learn. Fathers are our teachers. Hard teachers, sometimes," he nodded to the Scaliger, whose mouth creased slightly. "But teachers. What father seeks his own son's destruction?"

"The father who fears being replaced by his offspring," answered Cangrande. "Kronos ate his children because he feared being usurped."

"Is that what we think of our God, whom we are told is a being of love? Is He so insecure on His heavenly throne that He planted the seed of Man's destruction in the Garden of Eden? Was it a trap? For if the Almighty is indeed all-knowing, He knew full well what would happen. The God we are told exists is not so cruel. So Adam and Eve were fulfilling their part in God's plan. What if He was attempting to teach them a lesson?"

Softly Antonia said, "What lesson?"

Cesco spread his hands theatrically. "How do I know? It is the folly of Man to say he knows the Will of God. I only posit that He gave us reason for a reason."

Fully engaged now in spite of himself, Pietro leaned forward in his cushioned seat. "What if it was not about the fruit at all? What if it was a lesson in free will? Because I disagree with you. His greatest gift is not reason. It is the opportunity to choose."

Cesco frowned, eyes turned inwards. "Well argued, Nuncle. What a mind the Church lost in you! Though it was your good fortune, as you would have doubtless suffered the same fate as Occam and Bonagratia. You are correct, free will is His greatest gift. But would He have offered us such a choice – eternal happiness or irreversible damnation – upon the bite of an apple? It seems too capricious, even for God."

Cangrande threw Cesco's own words back at him. "It is the folly of Man to say he knows the Will of God."

"And the damnation is far from irreversible," said Fra Lorenzo. "God offered us His only son, Jesus Christ, to provide a chance for redemption. Christ suffered, that we might be saved."

Cesco's answering smile was fierce. "Hah! I knew we'd reach it. The second pernicious notion."

Fra Lorenzo's powerful shoulders tensed. "Is it pernicious to say Christ died for our sins?"

"Not at all. Hm. Since this is meant to be a poetry reading, perhaps we should indulge. Nuncle, may I?" Foregoing the copy of *Purgatorio* in Pietro's hands, Cesco hefted the beautiful copy of *L'Inferno* and opened it to the back, turning pages rapidly. "Here we are! Canto Thirty-Four. The bottom-most pit of Hell, as far from Heaven as it is possible to go. Lucifer lies here, stuck in the ice where God cast him, his three mouths chewing the greatest of all villains – the betrayers. Virgil points to them each in turn:

'Quell' anima là sù c'ha maggior pena,' 'That soul up there who bears the greatest pain,'
 disse 'l maestro, 'è Giuda Scariotto,   said the master, 'is Judas Iscariot, who has
che 'l capo ha dentro e fuor le gambe mena. his head within and outside flails his legs.

De li altri due c'hanno il capo di sotto, 'As for the other two, whose heads are dangling
 quel che pende dal nero ceffo è Bruto: down, Brutus is hanging from the swarthy snout
vedi come si storce, e non fa motto!;   – see how he writhes and utters not a word! –

 e l'altro è Cassio, che par sì membruto. 'and from the other, Cassius, so large of limb.
 Ma la notte risurge, e oramai   But night is rising in the sky. It is time
è da partir, ché tutto avem veduto.'   for us to leave, for we have seen it all.'

Cesco closed the heavy volume. "The best thing about what the poet achieves here is the inherent implication of the nature of suffering. For suffering is the cornerstone of the Christian faith. The trials of Job. The sacrifice of Abraham. Moses and the Hebrews wandering in the desert for forty years. The Bible repeatedly makes the point that suffering leads to nobility, to greatness, to grace. There is no possibility of redemption without suffering. Whereas Dante shows clearly that suffering is just suffering. There is nothing noble to it."

Pietro's mouth was hanging agape. Nor was he alone. "There *is* nobility in suffering."

"No, Nuncle," said Cesco clearly, holding *L'Inferno* close to his chest. "There can be nobility in how a man handles adversity. Here we see Brutus suffering in silence. He is noble. But suffering did not make him so. Suffering *in itself* is not noble. How a man reacts to suffering shows his inborn nature. There is much suffering in the world, and the pain of life alone does not make one noble. Take me," he added, scanning particular faces in the assembly. "I have suffered. I think no one will argue that it has made me noble."

The vast majority of those in attendance believed he was referring to his 'hawking' at the hands of Cangrande. A handful knew better. For them, his admission of ignobility was less a confession than a statement of continued defiance. As was every word he had spoken this day.

Setting *L'Inferno* aside, Cesco drew himself up to summarize his heresy. "Education is damning, ignorance is blessed, and suffering ennobles. If I wanted to control a large group of people, I could ask for no better tools. In this way, I can maintain power, wealth, and authority. Ladies and gentlemen, I present to you the fearful power of religion."

The bishop could no longer restrain the abbot, and perhaps no longer wished to. Leaping up, Giuseppe leveled an accusing finger. "This is the Word of God you are condemning, young man!"

"Figs," said Cesco calmly. "It is the word of Man. The Bible was clearly written by men. God would not be so perverse. But Man can. God is not so fearful. But Man is. Especially men in power. An educated populace questions authority. That way danger lies — not for God, but for the tyrant. How better to keep a people docile than to keep them dull, stupid, and vapid? To tell them their poverty, their hunger, their pain will all be rewarded after they die. Whereas the much-maligned Epicurus eschews an after-life and urges us to find beauty and pleasure in the now."

We should never have done this, thought Pietro, barely breathing. *He will be racked and murdered, all to spite the stars.*

Yet is he wrong? This was the painful question rattling through Pietro's brain. All of Cesco's arguments had occurred to Pietro. Some had even passed his lips, in private. But he had never had the courage to voice them so forcefully, so fiercely.

"Questioning authority is not sinful," insisted Cesco. "It is the path to liberation. Christ himself questioned authority. Are we not supposed to emulate Christ? We focus so much upon how Christ died, when we should be heeding what He said and did."

Abbess Verdiana rose. "Ser Francesco, you have all the wit of your sire, and all the energy of youth. More, you have a questing mind that is wonderful to behold. I can only hope that in the days and years before you, you will set that mind to greater things than questioning the very fabric of our relationship with the Almighty. It is unworthy of one so deeply blessed with intellect and courage."

"I am perfectly comfortable with my hypocrisy, thank you." Turning to Cangrande, he raised his eyebrows. "Are we through?"

"Quite through." The way it was said, it meant many things. Then the Scaliger laughed. "I think if we listen any further, we'll have no convictions left. Come, everyone. A feast awaits. In the meantime, let us take my heir at his word, and pay renewed attention to the teachings of our Savior. Bishop Francis, would you like to lead us all in prayer?"

The Bishop took his cue from his patron. "Yes. For all the troubling arguments we have heard espoused by this brilliant if misguided young man, this is one I can heartily endorse. Let us pray to be more Christ-like in all our doings, to live the teachings of Christ as best we can, and do as He did — forgive and accept those who wrong Him, and pray for His guidance."

Cesco pulled a wry face as he realized he had given a sop that they could use to excuse much of what he had posited. He obediently knelt and listened as the Bishop recited the Latin prayer, though Pietro did not hear Cesco's voice as everyone else murmured Amen.

The crowd dispersed to discuss what they had heard. Would Verona under Cesco be wholly excommunicated, as Venice once had been? As, indeed, Verona had been in the days of Cangrande's father. It had taken the burning of hundreds of heretics in the Arena to expiate that sin. Would the Pope demand that Cesco recant his words, or else burn in like manner?

More, did he actually believe what he said? Wasn't there truth in it? Wasn't the Church in Avignon often more interested in wealth and power than in piety? Or was he doing what he always did these days, picking a fight to show his cleverness and daring?

We were fooles, thought Pietro. *We offered him a platform from which he could dare the world to condemn him.* Because Cesco knew what Dante had always maintained — the most dangerous thing in the world was a new idea. Ideas spread quicker than fires, quicker than disease, and could be far deadlier than either. And while questioning the Church and God was hardly new, it was not often done so publically, or with such vehemence, and such reasoned arguments. Perhaps it was the natural end to theology — apply enough logic to God, and there will be no God left.

Pietro was less concerned with theology at the moment. His sole focus was on protecting Cesco from himself. There was no question of sending him away — outside the protection of Verona, one speech such as that would have him dead.

Even inside Verona his safety was not assured. That Cesco was young was some protection. That he was a prince was far more. But the religious institution would only tolerate so much before it brought the sky crashing down.

Cangrande's wife ushered Paride away. "The sooner we are in France, the better," she was saying. Pietro saw Fra Lorenzo hurrying out, and understood why. If his secret were known, he would be in as much danger as Cesco.

Not everyone was anxious to leave. The abbot, abbess, and bishop all approached Cangrande for a private interview. There was no mistaking the gravity of their intent.

Across the loggia, Pietro met with Antonia and Poco. "He'll be hanged before Lent."

"Or *for* Lent." Grinning, Poco's eyes were wide as dinner trays. "That was the most exciting thing I've ever heard. Even father was never so daring."

Though shaking, Antonia was clear-eyed. "Father condemned bad priests and evil popes, never the whole Church."

There was awe in Poco's voice as he said, "All because of a thwarted love."

That sparked something in Pietro's memory. The oracle who had spoken at his knighting. *'Verona will be brought low by love.' Is this what she meant?*

♦   ◊   ♦

Word quickly spread of the gauntlet Cesco had thrown down to the Church. The Bishop did his level best to keep the sword of righteousness firmly it its sheath by grasping the least objectionable idea mentioned – following the teachings of Christ. The homily he delivered that Sunday was about the Sermon on the Mount. But at the same moment just to the west, the Abbot of San Zeno was loudly calling down hellfire on the Rakehells, a name no longer humourous.

Departing Verona in early February, Cangrande rode with a sizable guard to Vicenza. Arriving at his brother-in-law's palace, barely had he finished dragging his boots over the metal mud-scraper when his sister's steward invited him upstairs.

Katerina was upright, her hands folded, the gloved left over the naked right. Striding in, Cangrande hooked a stool with his foot and settled down. "You called. I came."

"Like a *sh*pirit invoked by conjuration," remarked Katerina. "*Sh*omeone trying to kill you again, I hear."

"Someone killed me once before?"

"Foole. Do you know who?"

"No idea. Though there's a story going around…"

"What shtory?"

"I'm just trying to get you to say the letter *'s'* as often as I can. No, the story is being spread by me. That it was Dandolo, in his first move as Doge. It is as much attacking as I can do, since he now has the means to compromise you."

Katerina's right brow furrowed, though the sinister side remained slack. "I did not expect them to live."

"He is crippled, if that is any consolation. But I forget, you've seen him. Very alive, and in an accusatory mood. Do you remember their names?"

"Ciolo Fi*sh*cella and Girolamo Pometti," she said at once.

"Nothing wrong with your memory, at least." He made to rise. "Well, I must—"

Katerina stiffened, lifting her good hand. "*Sh*omething more."

Settling back onto his stool, Cangrande smiled. "Say it."

The right corner of her mouth turned down. "The *Shcotsh*man."

"Ah, the Shcotshman. What about him?"

"A danger."

"One we did not anticipate, though I suppose we should have. He's a foole, and has told his story to the court. He knows nothing himself, but his very speech was a clue. Your fault again!" he added, pointing at her. "You're the one who summoned Maria to Verona four years ago. Had Pietro and Cesco not heard her speak, they would never have connected the stars into a constellation. Part of a constellation," he corrected.

"How much?"

"They know she was Scottish. They have the house and the name Amabilio. They even discovered her body. Fuchs hid it where Uncle Mastino and Bail's father were tossed after they were killed."

"Another clue."

"Yes, though they have not yet figured that out. Pietro is distracted by Cesco, who is in turn distracting himself with heresy."

"And Mas*sh*tino?"

"Ah, the Mastiff."

"He mus*sh*t know the truth about Maria."

"You mean that if Fuchs tortured Cesco's late mother, he likely passed the results on to his master. I have considered it, but not broached the topic. Knowing the lady, I do not think she would reveal any secret, no matter how tortured."

"Unless*h* it was a s*sh*ecret s*sh*e wanted revealed."

That caused Cangrande to frown. It was something he had not considered. But at last he shook his head. "Had he that bolt, I think he would have shot it in September. But even if he showed uncommon restraint, remember, it is hardly in Mastino's best interests to have those facts revealed. The secret does nothing to help him."

"Not while you are alive," said Katerina pointedly.

"After I die, the world of cares dies with me. I presume you have a contingency? You always do."

"I left order*sh* with Detto. A letter, hidden." Seeing her brother blench, she blew out her lips. "Have no fear. It will not be found until we are both gone."

"Some comfort at last. Though no comfort to my heir's present state."

"What can we do?"

Cangrande opened his hands. "Nothing but let the universe unfold. Never fear. The charts have declared themselves. The boy did not marry for love. Whatever happens next is what is meant to be."

Katerina's eyes glowed. "How i*sh* he?"

"Whole in body, brutalized in spirit. One sympathizes."

"It was*sh* never going to be painles*sh*."

Cangrande rose. "I suppose not. But it hurts to see."

"Are you wavering? You could *shave* him?"

"He barely needs to shave yet." Katerina made a snarling sound, and he laughed. "Oh, did you mean something else?"

There were tears of frustration in her eyes. "It i*sh* unchival-rou*sh* to mock the infirm."

"Nobody has ever accused me of chivalry. But to answer your question – no. Unwavering. Unmoving, and unmoved. As fixed as the North Star."

"Good. For if you wavered, you would be unmade."

Standing beside his sister's bed, Cangrande's face was lit by the low brazier beside her. It threw the sharp lines of his face into stark shadow, tinted with red. "I wonder. But we must see this through to the end."

"Yes," she said, struggling not to slur. "We have our destiny."

Cangrande leaned forward to kiss his sister on the forehead. "Everyone does. They just don't grip it so hard."

IV

Strange Capers

TWENTY-EIGHT

The weather at the end of February was as bitter as it had been in living memory. But a week later the cold broke, a huge relief to the men of Verona. The 8th of March was Ash Wednesday, which meant the following Sunday was the famous Palio, a pair of races through the streets of Verona, one on horseback, one on foot. As the second race was run in the nude, the warmer weather was appreciated. No one fancied getting frostbite on their privates.

For the last dozen years the majority of the betting had been on which would get in first, Capulletto and Montecchio. Having begun in the Palio, the twin races remained the only public outlet for their rivalry as each took his best horse and whipped it almost to death to beat the other, then stripped off his clothes and ran for his life in the footrace. Between them they had ten victories in fourteen years. Though the rest of Veronese nobility tried their best, few had their motivation.

This year promised something more. Marsilio da Carrara declared his intent to contest the Palio, prompting Ser Pietro Alaghieri to say he would join the horserace. The last time they had raced, he'd famously lost to the Paduan. The next day, they had dueled. The fact that Pietro could not run in the footrace was due to Carrara having shot him with a crossbow bolt just above the knee. Their enmity was supposedly a thing of the past, but in the Palio anything could happen.

Even more exciting, for the first time the Greyhound's Heir

was going to participate. Each past year he had applied to the Scaliger, and each year he'd been denied.

"*You* were allowed to race as a boy," Cesco had always protested.

"My father had three heirs," the Capitano always replied. "He could afford to lose one. I can't."

Knighted, married, living on his own and free to make his own way, there was now nothing to prevent Cesco from entering. For months he and the other Rakehells had been practicing, and the odds-makers were doing robust business. Yes, this year's Palio promised to be the best ever.

Ash Wednesday came, and the city spent the day in churches, praying. All eyes on him, Cesco knelt obediently by the Capitano's side, head bowed. All public displays of insolence had ended two weeks earlier, as had the whoring and brawling – a broad hint that he might miss the Palio due to being imprisoned had finally moderated the young prince's behavior.

Thus it was surprising, two days before the Palio, to hear shouts in the streets raised in alarum. Pietro heaved a sigh before exiting his front door and calling out, "What's happening? Is it the Rakehells?"

"If it is, they'll pay with blood this time!" called a lawyer who was shuffling down the street towards the Piazza dei Signori. "Lord Carrara has been attacked!"

Rushing to the palace, Pietro discovered that the Paduan Capitano was unhurt, but that his party had been set upon by a band of brigands wielding crossbows. "Dozens of bolts from under cover as we crossed the bridge by San Bonifacio," said Carrara, more angry than anxious. "Cowards killed two of my men! We chased them, but they had a boat and slipped down the river."

"Any notion who it was?"

"The exiles," said Carrara. "I'm sure of it. My men will hunt them down."

"You never know," observed Cangrande with a smile. "They might have been sent by Pietro here. A guarantee he won't have to face you in the Palio." A poor jest, but enough to lighten the mood. Soon they were sharing cups of wine and discussing Treviso, even as the countryside was scoured for the villainous ambushers, to no avail.

♦   ◊   ♦

The day of the Palio started out bright, but from an hour after dawn clouds were visible. They rolled in all through the morning's theatrical displays, and the first stray droplets slanted down just as the riders were mounting their horses on the floor of the Arena. With no new knights to create today, the speech the Scaliger gave was short. Telling them which coloured flags they were to follow, he gave the signal and they were off.

Pietro Alaghieri and Marsilio da Carrara both started strong. In anticipation of the day, Pietro had used his now-considerable funds to purchase a swift horse from Mariotto. But he was no longer seventeen. Past thirty now, the things that mattered so much in youth seemed less vital in age.

Carrara seemed to feel the same. No longer desperate to prove Paduan superiority, he rode with vigour but no heat. At several points he found himself smiling at Alaghieri, who unaccountably found himself smiling back. Partly due to the great peace they had wrought, and partly due to their added years, their rancor was gone. Neither man disgraced nor distinguished themselves, much to the disappointment of both the crowd and the bookmakers.

Their disappointment was enhanced by Capulletto's exuberant cheerfulness. Antony had paid no attention to the preparations for the race, talking his fool head off to every unwary ear about the brilliance of his little son, nearly two months old. According to him, Gianni was another Veronese prodigy. "He's trying to speak, I know it! And he can lift his head already. He'll be strong, my son. Certainly wore his mother out! She's barely out of bed. Ha! He'll be a force to reckon with, you wait and see!" Besotted, he gave no thought to the race until he was in the saddle, and hardly even then. He paid Montecchio no mind, and hardly frowned at all when he saw Thibault astride one of Cesco's horses.

Yet the race did not lack for excitement. From the start, a heated contest developed between Cesco's Rakehells and the companions of Mastino. Even without the late unlamented Fuchs, Mastino had a sizable following. In addition to some Veronese of his own years, he'd recruited foreign knights whom he had met upon the jousting circuit he so enjoyed. Inviting them for the Palio at his own expense, he had in effect hired his own small army of racers to rival that of Cesco.

Ever inventive, the Scaliger's track would give victory, not to the swiftest horse, but to the wiliest rider. There were few open stretches where a fast horse could gain ground. The course turned down narrow streets, under low tunnels, over obstacles. This race was all about angles, when to push and when to check, and the luck of being on the correct side for a turn.

At the halfway mark, six young men all vied for the lead. Of the Rakehells, Cesco and Detto were well away, with young Petruchio close on their heels, and Paride della Scala determined to make his name before he left for France. For Mastino's faction, there were only two – Mastino himself and Guglielmo del Castelbarco the younger, a quiet and stable fellow who seemed to be Mastino's genuine friend – something Castelbarco the elder could not fathom.

The rain made riding difficult. It came down in cold sheets, driving right into their faces. But none of the six gave up or checked. For Cesco, Detto, Petruchio, and Paride, this was their first Palio. For Mastino, who had won twice before, it was the upholding of that honour. For Castelbarco, who had ridden in the middle pack three years in a row, it was a chance to break free from his father's shadow and distinguish himself.

Cesco won, not for any trick or feat of daring, but for plain good horsemanship. Mastino entered the Arena two yards behind him, with Detto just overtaking him at the end. Paride and young Petruchio tied, while young Castelbarco's horse fell on the slick stones. Weeping, he was forced to order the beast killed.

The Rakehells all did well, coming in among the front ranks of the seventy-three horsemen who finished the race. They cheered their victory and their leader, whom they lifted on their shoulders for a parade around the Arena floor.

Set down at last in front of the Scaliger's balcony, Cesco found himself face-to-face with his cousin. "Congratulations," said Mastino gruffly.

"Thanks, cos! Cheer up. There's always the footrace to best me."

As Cesco marched off, Mastino murmured, "There's more than that."

Cesco received the victor's gilt crown and the red ribbon, called the Pride of Mercury. As the crown was placed on his head, he was singing to himself: "Indeed a crown Verona wears…" Ascending the Scaligeri balcony, he bestowed the crown upon his beaming little wife, seated under a canopy, at which point the crowd's hearts melted even as they themselves melted away to get out of the wet.

Cesco and the loser of the race, an old *cavaliere* named Adelmota, made the customary parade through the streets, the victor giving out alms while the loser rode a nag with the hock of cured meat for the superstitious in the throng to take shards from. The rest of the nobility returned to their homes to discard their soaked gowns, doublets, and hose, and dress for the feast that preceded the footrace.

On the way into palace, Suor Beatrice caught the eye of Fra Lorenzo. "You look sad, Brother. Are you well?"

Lorenzo started, but saw she was making polite, not intimate, conversation. "I miss horses. Watching the race, I mean. I've heard that some of my Benedictine brothers have participated, and I must confess a degree of jealousy. I don't mind going barefoot, and I've never had much use for money, but why on earth did the Holy Saint deny us the use of horses?"

"San Benedictus was much more practical," said Suor Beatrice of her Order's patron.

"Oh yes!" laughed Lorenzo from under his soaking cowl. "Seventy-three chapters of the Rule. Much more practical!"

"Our Blessed Saint was indeed very thorough," said Suor Beatrice tartly.

Lorenzo smiled. "I can see why you were drawn to that order."

"I take that as a compliment." She marched away, head held high in the rain. Which allowed him to return to fretting over the message he had just received.

The feast was as lavish as obedience to Lent could allow. There were a plethora of fishy-choices — Egerduse, salmon sautéed in red wine and vinegar with sugar, onions, and cloves; *bulbarelli*, a river fish from Mantua, in a galingale sauce; shrimp baked in a breaded confection; and Tart de Brymlet, a pie involving three types of boiled fish that were then minced and combined with figs and raisins washed in wine, as well as apples and pears, all placed under a sugared pastry shell. In addition to the ever-present Golden Morsels, there were all kinds of nuts — walnuts, pistachios, almonds — mixed with pears, peas, lentils, and fava beans. Pietro was amused to find the drink of choice was Dandolo's *Twice Burnt*, a drink Poco had made popular after sampling it in the Venetian embassy.

The only pall over the affair was the use of tasters, who had to sip or sample every dish before it could be brought to table. Pietro felt for the poor peasants. *They must be in Purgatory, tasting savoury dishes they've never imagined while wondering if each bite will be their last.*

But despite these living reminders of mortality, the mood was festive. The only person on edge was Pietro Alaghieri. Seated near the High Table, he swept the room with his eyes, taking in guests not seen at the court since the double wedding. There was Signor Martino, who lived to the south, nearer Mantua than Verona. He was the father of twin girls, and was currently deep in talks with Antony, glowing over his thriving son.

Across the room by a side table, Count Filipo Anselmo was harmonizing with his sisters, to the enjoyment of many. Old Lord Vitruvio had come down from his estate on the far side of the Lago di Garda, bringing his young French wife to display to all. Signor Placentio, the confirmed bachelor who was said to have an over-fondness for male company, had journeyed from his rich estates along with his sister.

Pietro was greeted warmly by Ser Serego, grown grizzled now, with more salt than pepper in his beard and hair. But he remained as genial as ever, recalling their first meeting during the Palio of 1315, where they had cursed and vied against each other so vehemently. Serego exhorted Pietro to come calling on his little estate at San Pietro in Cariano. "I have a daughter who longs to hear tales of your father."

Everyone, it seemed, had a daughter or a sister who was longing to hear of Pietro's father, his travels, his life's story. The noose of marriage was tightening. If he did not marry soon, he would be accused of living the same life as Signor Placentio.

Pietro found himself wondering when Verona had ever had so many eligible women? There was the lady Livia, who was said to have a great fortune, deep in conversation with the young Giulia – not Capulletto's daughter, but rather another of these young women who would soon be of age and seeking a spouse. She was making eyes at Valentino who was ensconced with his best friend Proteus, paying her no mind. Nor should he! Twelve was far too young for a man to even consider a spouse.

And thirty-one is too old. Not that there were any possible candidates tonight. However much their parents wanted to link their houses to his, these girls were all far too young for Pietro to even consider.

Blame Antony. Thanks to Capulletto's wedding an eleven year-old girl five years earlier, it was becoming fashionable for men to wed ever younger brides, barely in the flower of womanhood. Cesco's own wedding would do nothing to stem the tide.

Evidently still laid low from childbirth, Antony's wife was absent. But her brother was present. Signor Valentio Guarini, who like Antony had both a boy and a girl child, though a few years older than Antony's brood. He and Antony spent a long time laughing together.

Across the hall, it looked as if there might be a match in the offing. For weeks now Signor Lucio Villafranca, son of Cangrande's Constable, had been courting the vivacious Helena Lenoti, sister of Benvenito Lenoti, who was the husband of Aurelia Montecchio, who was sister to Mariotto. *These Veronese families,* thought Pietro, amused. *It's as bad as ancient Rome.*

Uncommonly, Benvenito was present tonight. Mariotto's brother-in-law usually spent his time at Mari's castle near Vicenza, breeding horseflesh. His visits to the city were rare, but every month or so he would make the ride to see his son Benvolio and sell a fine mare – the Montecchi rarely sold stallions. Naturally he'd come today to show off the finest of the family stock. Already he had a dozen offers on just one horse.

Turning his head once more, Pietro stiffened. *There they are.*

Not far away was the enormous round form of Gaspardo Rienzi, standing beside his son Adamo. Deep in discussion with them was a bearded mountain of a man Pietro recognized instantly. Abramo Tiberio.

The three men were here, but not the woman. Peering around, Pietro could see no sign of Rosalia. Which did not mean she was not here. It was hardly likely that she was standing. And she might be off in the company of the other wives.

Grasping a pair of goblets from a passing tray, Pietro walked boldly forward with a fixed smile. "Gentlemen. This is unexpected."

"I'm sure," growled Adamo.

Once, Gaspardo would have cuffed his boy for his rudeness. Instead he lifted his topmost chin. "The invitation was explicit."

"How goes the rebuilding?" The Rienzi family was in charge of Cangrande's forge, burned down last spring in a subtle imperial jab at Scaligeri power.

"Well enough," replied Gaspardo warily. "The foundation was solid. No expense is being spared. It should be back in operation by the fall."

"Indeed. And Signor Tiberio, you have received the price of your land? I hope to start building on it when the weather clears."

The huge man grunted. "It's yours now, do as you like."

Gritting his teeth, Pietro persevered. "I hope everyone is in health."

"My wife is fine, if that's what you mean," said Abramo coldly.

"She isn't here," said Pietro, daring to hope.

"She's in the city. Couldn't refuse a command from the great Greyhound. But she's resting." He looked accusingly at Pietro. "You promised her you wouldn't tell."

"A promise I kept, until the Scaliger planned to send for her. I tried to dissuade him. Cesco still doesn't know."

Unwilling to be mollified, Tiberio grunted. "Where is the little bastard?"

"You're not going to talk to him." There was a sudden hard

tone to Pietro's voice. He could imagine nothing worse than Cesco discovering Lia's pregnancy.

"I'm going to get stinking drunk. Now which one is he, so I can avoid him?"

Adamo pointed. "That's him there. With the little girl on his arm," he added in disgust.

"Don't point." Gaspardo knocked his son's hand down, covering the gesture by taking one of the goblets from Pietro's hand. "Let us survive the night, then get the hell away. Ser Alaghieri, no reflection on you. But you raised that – boy," – the fat man's mouth struggled to frame an inoffensive title – "and for obvious reasons we would prefer not to associate ourselves in any way with him, or you. Pardon us."

Pietro watch the trio move off with a slight relief. They meant no mischief. At least the older men did not. There was something in Adamo's eyes that said his restraint was imposed, not reasoned. Given a chance, he would likely slip his leash. Worse, Lia was in the city, a living sword of Damocles. Pietro hated to think what Cesco might do were he to learn of her presence.

Stopping by Morsicato, he found the doctor embroiled in a quiet debate with Fra Lorenzo over Cesco's use of hashish. The doctor spoke in an accusing tone. "I thought you were with us in insisting he must be weaned."

The friar looked like nothing so much as a rabbit caught in the open. "It is not for me to say. He is a man, or soon will be, and a knight. It is for him to make his own decisions."

Morsicato scowled. "Washing your hands of the matter, are you?"

"I suppose I am."

Pietro wanted to chastise the holy man, but there were too many open ears hereabouts. "Now is not the time for this discussion."

Swearing, the doctor stomped off. Turning away from the friar, Pietro spied another forlorn face. Normally at the heart of any revelry, Nico da Lozzo was leaning against the wall beside an ornate sconce done in the style of a snarling hound. *I wonder Cangrande doesn't get tired of the image.* "Ho, Nico. Not enjoying yourself?"

"It's not the same." Nico waffled a hand. "Everyone's acting as though it didn't happen. As though we didn't lose one of our own to some cowardly bastard. No one's even trying to find who did it!"

"That's not true," said Pietro reasonably. "Massimiliano has been scouring the city, the whole staff has been investigated, and there are tasters for everything. But with so many people there that night, it's almost impossible to know who had access to the cup." It had been the cup, not the flagon or the barrel. "The best hope, actually, is that he tries again."

Nico nodded. "I hope he does. I want to place my hands on him. Who do you think it was?"

"I suspect a different man every day. The trouble is that the Scaliger has no end of enemies. Was it the Doge? The Emperor? The Pope? The Trevisians? The Mantuans, in revenge for Bonaccolsi? There are too many choices, and who knows which one is nearest the mark."

Nico had grown disinterested. For him, the politics didn't matter. He had lost his best friend. He sighed. "Go join the festivities. I'm no good to anyone, the mood I'm—" Looking over Pietro's shoulder, Nico's face was startled. "She came."

Turning, Pietro saw Katerina Bonaventura, emerging from her mourning to re-enter Veronese life. Entering the hall with a son on either arm, Kate was greeted as though she were a returning monarch, back from some terrible war. Cangrande kissed her cheeks, followed immediately by her countryman Marsilio da Carrara.

Behind Kate came her daughters on the arms of their Paduan grandfather, Lord Baptista Minola, and the old family friend Hortensio, namesake of one of the twins. In fact, Katerina's whole family was present, including her beautiful but pinched-face sister Bianca. And if Bianca was here, then so too was — "Lucentio!"

Seeing the wave, Pietro's old schoolmate broke ranks, grinning. "Pietro! Or shall I say, Ser Alaghieri. I hoped I'd see you here. We didn't get to talk at the funeral. Congratulations on finishing the race today. I had intended to join in, but—" Glancing at his wife, he shook his head. She seemed to feel it, as she gave him a withering glare before smiling coyly at Pietro.

Pietro knew better than to smile back. Thanks to Petrarch, he'd already earned a reputation as despoiler of his friends' sisters. He wanted no rumours growing here at home. "It's not too late. You can run tonight. Tell her it's to honour Petruchio. She can hardly object."

"No, she'll just take her objections out in silences and..." Lucentio caught himself. "But look at this room! Paduans and Veronese, breaking bread. All thanks to you. It's hard to believe it was just six months ago that you appeared at my door with Carrara to negotiate the peace. Though someone is clearly trying to wreck it," he added darkly.

"Petruchio's loss was a blow to us all," said Pietro solemnly.

Lucentio nodded. "I owe him more than I can say. My purse may be richer without all his wagers, but my life will be poorer. Lord

Lozzo, it's good to see you again."

"And you," said Nico, clasping Lucentio's arm and exchanging the double kiss of friendship. "We've both lost a brother. You a brother-in-law, I a brother-in-arms."

"And a brother-in-love." Lucentio knew how close the severed bond had been.

Talk was hard at first, but Pietro and Lucentio filled the gap with reminiscences of their school days, half a lifetime earlier. From then the tables turned, with Nico and Lucentio talking of Petruchio's antics at Lucentio's wedding. "Though he was not the one who caused the biggest scene. Where is Antonio Capulletto?" Pietro pointed, and Lucentio chuckled. "That's him. Put on some pounds in the intervening years, but I'd know that frame anywhere."

Confused, Pietro looked to Nico for an explanation. "Capulletto and his uncle attended the wedding all uninvited. In masques," he added, smiling in spite of himself. "Overturned the entire desert table on Carrara. Don't tell Carrara, it might end the peace altogether. He was furious."

"I imagine!" laughed Pietro, wondering how this tale had escaped his ears. "How were you even there?"

Nico grinned. "Petruchio snuck me into the city. I bet him he couldn't, you see?"

Pietro demanded to hear the whole story. Anything that got Nico smiling again.

There were smiles near the center of the hall as well. Don Pedro of Aragon and Donna Beatrice had invited Signor Benedick to join them. Both the Pisan lady and the Paduan soldier understood they were being put on display.

"It seems we must sing for our supper," said Beatrice in an undertone.

Benedick grinned back at her. "We'd best, then — after that race, I'm famished."

"And drenched. In clichés, if not water."

They bantered for show, each scoring points and garnering applause. There was less bite tonight, perhaps because they were both aware of their status as entertainers. Or perhaps because of a mutual growing attraction? They did not admit it, but the pull was evident to all else present, making Don Pedro frown several times. During a lull in the bickering, he said, "Signor Benedick, tell me — have you ever considered becoming a lawyer, like Ser Alaghieri?"

Benedick blinked. "No, my lord, honestly it never occurred to me."

"You have a way with words, is my only reason."

"I am a soldier, lord. Nothing more."

"Nothing at all," agreed Beatrice. "Besides, there's more to lawyering than talking. One must be able to influence people towards one's cause. If Signor Benedick tried his hand at defending Saint Anselm on charges of theft, the jury would convict the saint of murder out of pure revulsion."

Seated nearby, Katerina Bonaventura laughed in approval, breaking the last seal of restraint. As in the ancient Olympics of Greece, a torch had been passed from bickering couple to bickering couple. Many expected a wedding within the hour. After all, the Palio had a reputation for secret assignations and stealthy marriages.

One wedding seemed promising – not Beatrice and Benedick, but rather the daughter of the late Petruchio and one of Cesco's Rakehells. Salvatore da Battaglia was seated beside the prim Vittoria, their heads close together. Pietro recalled them holding hands at her father's funeral. *Perhaps from tragedy, comedy will spring.*

The volume grew, threatening to drown the hammering of the chilly rain striking the palace roof. It was so hot in the smoky hall that layers of clothing were removed, some more risqué than others. Badinage, singing, and tales combined to make it a joyful gathering, despite the ominous presence of the tasters.

Pietro kept one eye on the Rienzi party, with occasional glances to where Cesco was laughing on the far side of the hall with his Rakehells. As long as those groups remained separate, all was well. Though Pietro wondered where Detto had gotten to – if anyone had the ability to check Cesco, it was his best friend and cousin.

Dinner was served, but people barely took time to chew as they argued, bantered, and wagered – it seemed that a dozen men were eager to fill the gap Petruchio had left in being Verona's bet-maker-in-chief. Even when Cangrande stood to make the prayer and salute, he was hardly noticed. It took the booming voice of Bailardino to swing everyone's attention around to the High Table. Cangrande made a prayer to the Virgin, his personal patron, and then allowed the Bishop to intone a longer prayer. Before raising his cup to propose a salute, he pressed the wine to his lips and drank. When he did not keel over, there was a slackening of tension. "Best get that out of the way. I would like to propose we drink to the man whose presence we are all missing. He was the perfect symbol of all we celebrate – a brave and cheerful Veronese married to a wild and willful Paduan, whose union was the envy of the world. Lord Carrara, may the marriage of our two cities be as fruitful and admirable as that of

Petruchio and his beloved Kate. To Petruchio Bonaventura!"

"Bonaventura!" roared a chorus of voices.

Lest anyone look around to see if someone was growing purple in the face, Cangrande pressed quickly on. "Before we finish our meals and the men get naked, I have another announcement. I had intended to wait, make this its own occasion. Because, as we all know, I am revered far and wide for my patience." Cangrande bowed his head under the ensuing jeers. "But with my friend Marsilio here, the moment seems far too apt. This is an occasion where we might right a very old wrong while at the same time rewarding one of our own. So please indulge me. This sort of thing is more commonly a matter of state, rarely done in spontaneous moments of exuberance." Cangrande looked about the expectant faces and found the one he sought. "Ser Pietro Alaghieri, step forward."

Startled, Pietro rose from his seat and came to face the High Table. He did not appreciate being the focus of so many eyes. *What fresh Hell is this?*

"Outside Verona, Pietro is known for his father. But we Veronese know him for himself. As brave a man as I've ever met. Unfailingly loyal. Unfortunately honest." Laughter. "Most of all, he is devoted to doing what he sees as right. His sense of duty binds him more than Aeneas' did, and the words of Virgil could easily apply to this knight before me:

<table>
<tr><td>Sum pius Aeneas,
raptos qui ex hoste
Penates classe veho mecum,
fama super aethera notus.
Italiam quaero patriam
et genus ab Iove summo.</td><td>I am Aeneas, duty-bound, and known
Above high air of heaven by my fame,
Carrying with me in my ships our gods
Of hearth and home, saved from the enemy.
I look for Italy to be my fatherland,
And my descent is from all-highest Jove.</td></tr>
</table>

"Pietro saved not the gods of Troy, but the future of Verona, taking my heir into hiding for eight long years. His descent is not from Jove, but from a man gifted by God with the power to create a word palace for Heaven to come to Man. Surely the duty-bound Pietro is as well known in that Heaven as ever Aeneas was. A pity that Verona already has a saint of his name, for surely Ser Alaghieri is worthy of canonization."

Pietro dropped his chin to hide his crimson cheeks. Heart racing, he waited for the hammer to fall. *Is he exiling me again?*

"Ha! See him now? That is another trait — no no, I do not refer to his modesty, which is all too genuine. I refer to his endurance. Uncomfortable as the good knight is to hear his praises sung, he will stand and take it as though it were a charge of cavalry. For Pietro knows how to endure. He has endured injury, exile, poverty, excommunication, unjust slurs, assaults on both his body and his character. More, he had to endure my heir's antics, and I must beg him to let me drink from the font that gave him his unmeasured patience! To mangle Virgil again, *Quidquid erit, superanda omnis fortuna ferendo est.*"

Here, at least, was a message Pietro understood. It was not for him, but for Cesco. *'Come what may, all bad fortune is to be conquered by endurance.'*

Across the table from where Pietro stood, Cangrande turned to his chief guest, Marsilio da Carrara. "My Lord, you had the misfortune to face this knight before he was a knight. You fought fairly on the field of battle, did you not?"

"We did," answered Carrara loudly. Clearly he had been informed of what was coming, and was playing his part. "He took me prisoner at the First Battle of Vicenza, fifteen years hence. It was I who wounded him, yet he treated me with honour, and released me at your request."

"Losing a fortune, in favour of honour," noted Cangrande. "Then you two dueled in the Arena, and Pietro was as gracious in defeat as he had been in victory."

I didn't lose, thought Pietro with a flash of annoyance. *You declared the duel inconclusive.* That was a technicality, though. Pietro had to admit that lying in the dirt with a dagger at your throat was a fairly clear sign of loss.

"And Lord Carrara, you must by now have heard the sequel to your first encounter. How, during the Second Battle of Vicenza, Ser Alaghieri wore the armour of the Count of San Bonifacio in an attempt to amuse you before the city's gates. It was Pietro who delayed you, and he who fought against you in the street alongside my forces."

Carrara's laughter was a little forced, but he managed it. Thankfully there was no mention of Pietro's hand in the Dente uprising, though Carrara knew full well that Pietro had tried to kill him in the street brawl four years ago. *What is happening?*

"The Count himself was wounded that day," continued Cangrande, omitting that it was Carrara who gave the aged Count his fatal wound. "Vinciguerra da San Bonifacio died a true son of Verona, brave and fierce in his patriotism, however misguided. He was an ally to Padua, and none fought harder than his father to overthrow the tyrant Ezzelino da Romano. With a temper as fiery as his head, his name meant 'In war, I win'. But we here today know that there are no winners in war. Peace is infinitely preferable. Yet in many ways, the Count's spirit embodies much of what we have achieved here – peace, prosperity, and a glowing future with Verona and Padua united to restore Italy to her rightful place as center of the world.

"Ser Pietro Alaghieri helped bring all this to pass. A lost son of Florence, a treasured son of Verona, a respected hero in Padua, Pietro set the seal on our newfound harmony with the *Pax Verona*. Now it is time for him to claim his reward."

Cangrande directed his gaze to the knight himself. "Ser Pietro Alaghieri, once you wore the armour belonging to the Count of San Bonifacio. Today I wish you to don that armour again. Not for anyone's amusement, nor in any act of deception, but in truth." Lifting his chin to bathe the assembly with his famous *allegria*, the Scaliger cried out, "Hear me now! I, Cangrande della Scala, Capitano di Verona and Vicar of the Trevisian Mark, hereby elevate Ser Pietro Alaghieri to the title of Count of San Bonifacio and lord of all the lands and deeds thereto. Praise be to God, and long live Count Alaghieri!"

It was impossible to know who cheered first as Pietro found himself swept into congratulatory embraces and kisses. The Bonaventura twins threw their caps into the air, Morsicato was slamming his hands together wildly, Bailardino leapt forward to crush Pietro in a bearish hug. Signor Benedick was on his feet, while his fellow Paduan Salvatore turned away from his courting to rise and applaud Pietro's elevation. He was weeping, odd in a man so phlegmatic.

There were tears in Pietro's own eyes as he accepted the sword Cangrande offered. He was then swept from hand to hand, thanking everyone for their praise, until he found himself embraced by Cesco. The pupils were distressingly large, but the rascal seemed quite himself as he kissed his foster-father on both cheeks. "I wish I had thought of it! Such poetic justice! But, as this seems to be another Virgilian evening – *Equo ne credite, Teucri! Quidquid id est, timeo Danaos et dona ferentes.*"

The quote was apt: '*Do not trust the horse, Trojans. Whatever it is, I fear the Grecians, even bearing gifts.*'

Pietro leaned close to whisper, "I was thinking the same thing."

◆   ◊   ◆

"You got my note." A statement of the obvious.

"You shouldn't be here," said Detto, dripping onto the rushes of the dimly lit room.

"No," agreed the room's sole inhabitant. "I was summoned. But I would have come in any case. I'm sure you understand why."

"It wasn't an attempt on Cesco," said Detto quickly. "And he's been poisoned before. He takes doses of something to prevent it happening again."

The figure rose from her chair, her back to the fire. Eyes adjusting to the darkness, Detto saw her profile against the flames. "O God."

Rosalia Rienzi rubbed a hand over her swollen belly. "Seven months gone."

Detto felt bloodless. "Cesco's."

"Yes."

There was such sadness in her tone that Detto had to hide behind his eyelids. "You can't see him."

"He can't see me, you mean."

"You *can't*," he said emphatically. Cesco couldn't be told. It would unhinge him even further.

"I must," said Lia.

"Do you still love him?" Detto didn't mean to ask, but the question forced itself upon him.

"Love?" echoed Lia. "I hate him. I detest him. I shake when I think of him. I want this last year back. But that's not possible."

"No," agreed Detto.

"I think – hate makes it easier. If I stopped hating, I'd only feel—"

"I know." His tone expressed his truth.

Sitting again, Lia folded her hands. "Poor Detto. Poor Cesco. Poor Rosalia. We're all too young to know such sorrow, aren't we? Because we all love. You and I, at least, don't live his life. He's a figure made for jealousy, envy, hatred, admiration."

"Pity."

That provoked a sad laugh. "How he would hate that! I cannot imagine a worse fate for him than to know he was pitied." Lia cocked her head slightly. "You are as loyal to him as you were when we met. Is he as loyal to you?"

"He's only disloyal to himself."

Lia sat for a long time, digesting that statement. "You should tell him so."

"He won't listen. And I can't make things better."

"No. No one can. We can only endure. Detto, I have to see him, but on my terms. I have made the arrangements. Do you trust me?"

"Secrets," said Detto. "I hate secrets."

Lia reached out a hand. "Detto – trust me. All will be well."

Even as he agreed, he knew she was wrong.

<h1 style="text-align:center">TWENTY-NINE</h1>

THE GENERAL HOPE was that the rain would end during the feast, or at least lessen. Instead it grew more torrential. Cangrande pulled his wizened steward d'Isola aside, whispering in his ear while scribbling notes onto a wax tablet, detailing last-minute alterations in the Foot Palio. When the Grand Butler returned some time later, the Capitano stood and announced it was time for the next race.

Busy being feted, Pietro did not see the start of the encounter he'd so dreaded. Marching up, Cesco was wringing Tiberio's hand before the big man knew it was taken. "I hear congratulations are in order! On behalf of my family, please allow me to offer my felicitations on your marriage."

While the shocked Tiberio struggled to find his breath, Adamo pulled back his arm to strike. His father closed a massive hand over his son's fist. "Not here!"

"No, he prefers back-streets and alleys, does our adamant Adamo," rejoined Cesco crisply. "He also likes taking men unawares. Signor Tiberio, shall I speak a word in your ear?" Shifting his body so the two Rienzi couldn't see him, Cesco stared up and up into the whiskered face. "Tell me she's well."

"As well as can be expected." Tiberio leaned forward to tower over Cesco. "I'm glad to have the chance of a word."

"You have something to say to me?"

"Just this. If you come near her, I'll murder you."

"You threaten well," said Cesco. "Not too much detail, just

plain words in a plain style, plainly delivered. Allow me to offer you a threat in return. If you do not treat her well, you're the one who'll be taking the measure of a grave. A big grave, to be sure. But a grave is a grave."

Tiberio's breath was slow as he controlled his aching fists. "On that we agree."

"Gravely." Cesco laughed. "Ah, I see the new Count counting the ways to part us. And he is correct, I must be going. The race, the race! Are you running tonight, Signor Tiberio? No? Perhaps your brother-in-love there can persuade you. For surely Adamo is racing! The first man thought nothing of his nudity until he ate of the Tree of Knowledge. A sin our Adamo has clearly never committed." Without even watching the barb go home, Cesco turned and slithered through the throng while the three northmen remained behind, seething.

Pietro passed them by with a wary look. Rienzi shook his head, but Tiberio chose to answer. "Keep him away from me. Next time, I'll kill him."

Saying nothing, Pietro continued to edge between bodies as he tried to catch up to Cesco, who was unlacing his doublet as he paused by Benedick's elbow. "Coming?"

Deep in banter, Benedick almost jumped off his bench. "Ah, no, lord." He loosed a fake-sounding sneeze. "I think I'm coming down with something. The race this afternoon."

Pulling a face, Cesco bowed sweetly to the lady and walked off, stripping as he went. Benedick raised his ruddy brows at Beatrice. "Lady, would you like to retire to the loggia and tell me more of what is wrong with me?"

"Are you truly not racing?"

Hearing a hint of disdain, he stood at once. "Of course I am."

Her smile was, if anything, even more disdainful. "What about your cold?"

"A passing chill. No doubt from your presence."

Beatrice pursed her lips. "No doubt. Very well. If you finish the race, I will tell you my life's story – provided you promise not to do the same. And not to interrupt."

"I promise the one, but not the other." Benedick grabbed her hand and impulsively kissed it, then turned and ran for the doors before she could speak.

The crowd outside was sparse, barely filling two-thirds of the Piazza dei Signori. Because the footrace didn't require ownership of a horse, it was usually the more contested event. This year, though, many men had decided to stay home. There was always next year. Of those determined souls remaining – nearly two hundred – most had already doffed their clothes, it being far more comfortable to stand shivering in the rain than to feel soaked clothing against their skin.

Reaching Cesco at last, Pietro found himself the recipient of the young man's clothes. "Take these for me, Nuncle. Though I must call you Count Nuncle now."

"That was stupid," said Pietro.

"Was it?" Cesco slapped his hands against his chest and hopped from foot to foot. "I thought it rather clever. Ah! The prodigal! Where have you been gadding?"

"Nowhere." Arriving, Detto pulled off his hose and tossed them to a servant. "What's happened?"

"He's been goading Rienzi and Tiberio," said Pietro quickly.

Detto winced. "Of course he has."

"Are you mad?" demanded Pietro of Cesco.

Before Cesco could frame a biting reply, Detto shook his head. "He did it to focus their hatred on him, not her."

Cesco made a gagging sound. "Is that the reason? I thought I was just an ass."

"Both things can be true," said Detto.

Handing Cesco's clothes off to the servant, Pietro was about to say something when there came a shout to follow the torches. Around the back of the palace, under the cover of a pillared walkway, Cangrande struggled to make himself heard. "Each year I am pressed to make innovations in the Palio. Last year the contestants had to climb through six windows across the city. The year before, you were chased by the city's children carrying sticks to beat you with, and not allowed to retaliate."

He inclined his head towards the naked Cesco, standing at the front of the crowd. "This being Ser Francesco's first year participating, I was determined to better myself. So this race contains not one new wrinkle, but three." Wry cheers, groans, mocks. "As I recall from our first meeting, Francesco has an affinity for rooftops. That being the case, I've designed a route that will please him immensely. Starting and ending on the palace roof, the contestants must reach eight different points around the city without ever once setting foot on the earth below."

Heads turned to look up at the wet clay tiles on the roofs above, and not a few racers wished they'd stayed home.

"Now, some roofs are too far away even for the nimblest of us to leap to. So wooden walkways have been put up, spanning the largest gaps. They're narrow, at most two feet wide. But don't follow them blindly – not all of them lead to the finish line!

"So much for the route. My second and third innovations were inspired by the weather. I cannot risk the lives of all my knights, soldiers, and bravest citizens. I have had the track reduced – you need to cover much less ground than I'd originally planned." He grinned. "To compensate for this, the track is not marked. I wouldn't want this to be too easy! Instead of markers or torches, I have ordered clues placed all around the city. It will require either brains enough to decypher them, or wit enough to follow someone who can. Of course, if you're following someone, you won't win, so use your heads! I can only plead with you all not to alter the clues when you find them, to give your fellow contestants a fair chance of winning." Already there were suspicious glances. "In this race, speed is second to wit. You must find the final clue, then return to me in the palace with the message it bears."

He waved to the servants setting out lengths of rope behind him. "The last innovation is a measure of both safety and challenge. Each man must take a partner. Using these coils behind me, every contestant must bind himself to his partner and remain bound for the entire course of the race. Anyone removing his tie or returning alone will be disqualified. This will let you help each other across the roofs, and also prevent anyone outstripping the slowest among you.

"I imagine this will take much longer than the usual Palio, so pace yourselves. Now, choose your partners and take up your cords!"

Like children picking team-mates for games of war, everyone leapt to take a partner. And, as with children, friendship mattered most. The brothers Bonaventura were a pair, of course. Nico da Lozzo bound himself to Petruchio's old friend Hortensio. Bailardino partnered his younger son, Valentino, too young by age but a knight and therefore qualified to run. Cangrande's bastards Barto and Berto were a pair. To the surprise of many, Mastino partnered Marsilio da Carrara. His brother Alberto chose Jacopo Alaghieri, of course. Since Poco's brother wouldn't be running, Don Pedro of Aragon accepted the partnership of Signor Benedick of Padua.

"Being Paduan, do you know the city at all?" inquired Don Pedro.

Benedick indicated Cesco. "After running around chasing himself, I know it better than I do my own."

Paride offered to partner Thibault, and Yuri naturally took

Fabio to run with. At the last moment, Abramo Tiberio appeared, more fearsome in his hairy nakedness. He tied himself to his wife's brother Adamo. Cesco's goads had worked, and the men meant to race and prove themselves his betters.

No one had asked to partner either Cesco or Detto, as their choices were a foregone conclusion. Without even a look they picked up a single rope. Unlike most of the others, Cesco didn't bind his end around his wrist, but rather his waist, cinching it tight. Detto did the same. Seeing the sense in this, several men unbound themselves to follow suit.

An amusing twist to the partnering – no one wanted to tie themselves to either Capulletto or Montecchio. Benvenito had already partnered young Castelbarco, and Antony's brother-in-law had partnered Signor Placentio. All else were unwilling to risk offending one over the other. So at the end of the dividing, they stood there, naked, each alone, each with a length of rope in his hand.

Seeing this, Cangrande said, "Antonio, Mariotto, I know that for years it has been your fondest wish to see each other at a rope's end – now is your chance!"

The roaring crowd waited, watching. Montecchio's jaw worked back and forth while Capulletto's fists clenched and unclenched. Finally Montecchio dropped his rope and held out his hand. Capulletto rolled his eyes and with an accusing look at many friends whipped the rope's end up towards Mari's face. Mariotto caught it and gave his former friend a chilly smile. They both went about binding themselves to each other, wrist connected to wrist. They were greeted with an ironic cheer.

Aiello the Scot was present, and was about to partner one of his mercenary fellows when Cangrande intervened. Bringing forward the reluctant Benjamin Montagu, he said, "Antony and Mari are a revelation. Our friend here planned not to participate, for fear of his life. As I'd like to be certain this young fellow returns unharmed, I will therefore place him in your care, Signor Aiello."

"Me?" demanded Aiello. "Why may I not partner Lord Capulletto, and let Lord Montecchio pair with his cousin?"

"Indeed," echoed Antony, "that would be more—"

"No," said Cangrande. "With each man responsible for his partner, I can imagine no better way to ensure all men return in safety. Now come, young Benjamin, strip! The race awaits!" Montagu obeyed, causing Cangrande to marvel. "Ah! We have discovered where all your hair has gone! It traveled from your head to your chest. And nethers. Good lord, it's almost cheating – you'll be dressed in a wool coat while everyone else races nude!" A huge round of laughter, while Montagu flushed in embarrassment.

Once all pairs were set, Cangrande clapped his hands. "You must begin by climbing the palace walls, for that roof is both start and finish. On your way up you can puzzle out the first clue. Again in honour of my Heir – and, by pure chance, my self – for your clues I have used the words of our mutual namesake, San Francesco. The first is this: *'Praise to thee, my Lord, for all thy creatures, Above all Brother Sun who brings us the day and lends us his light.'"*

"Say it again!" called someone near the back of the throng. Cangrande repeated it twice more, enjoying the nearly two hundred brows furrowed in concentration. Then he took a torch, stepped out into the rain, and threw it high into the air. "GO!"

Every naked man scrambled for the walls of the palace. Detto followed Cesco's lead around the side of the building where competition was less fierce. They were followed by a few others, including Benedick and Don Pedro, who had imitated Cesco's style of binding. Thus when they started their ascent, both arms were free to grasp the metal gate at the base of the wall. These gates had metal bands encircling the Scaligeri crest, the simple ladder. Cesco stuck his foot in the ladder's highest rung and heaved himself up. "A *scala* for a Scala."

As many contestants were discovering, it was much harder to climb quickly when bound to someone trying to climb in a different place at a different pace. For those tied arm to arm, it was especially dangerous. Some would be in the midst of ascending when their partner lunged for a window or cornice, jerking the rope and pulling them right off the wall. Often they would collide with another pair, and another, and all together they would topple back to the ground.

The rain was no help, either. In the rear of the Scaligeri palace, many were the falls and false starts among the hundred pairs. The side gate was far easier to grip, and less crowded. Achieving the top, Cesco and Detto were faced with a brick wall. Balancing their toes on the knobs of the gate's posts, their fingers sought handholds. But they weren't trying to climb upwards. They went hand over hand sideways, along the south wall of the palace, to a faux bridge between the first Scaligeri palace and the newer one built by Cangrande. A story lower than the roof, the fake bridge bore jutting crenellations. Perfect for looping a rope over.

Seeing what they were after, Benedick urged the Prince on. Already Cesco had wedged himself into the corner between the palace wall and the bridge and, using his free hand, was sending the slack of the rope arcing upwards. The rain-soaked rope missed once, but Cesco got it on the second try. "Go."

Detto immediately pushed off the wall and started climbing the rope. Cesco did the same, and Benedick held his breath, watching. A wrong tug from one would make the other lose his grip. But they timed their hands to grab at the same moment, left then right, and they reached the top as one.

A perilous three minutes later, Don Pedro and Benedick were at the top as well. It had taken Detto and Cesco half that long to reach the ledge eighteen feet overhead, and the roofline six feet above that. Red hair plastered to his skull, Benedick called up. "Hey! Give us poor foreigners a hint before you go!"

Cesco's head appeared, his longish hair falling across his eyes. "Brother Sun, he said. Have you seen the sun today?" Then he vanished.

Don Pedro looked blank. "Any idea?"

"Actually, yes," answered the Paduan. "Come on." They were about to try the ascent to the ledge when there was a panicked shout from the railing. Bailardino and Valentino had attempted the same ascent, but since their weights were so different, Val had been pulled high while Bail had plummeted down. The Lord of Vicenza now hung suspended five feet over the street. It might have been comical if his weight wasn't crushing Val against the crenellated rail. Val screamed as Bail yelled for help.

Pedro and Benedick dashed across the narrow bridge, feet padding on the wet concrete. Bending low, the Spaniard eased the pressure on the twelve year-old while the Paduan hauled on Bailardino's end of the rope. It was too slick, though, and kept slipping through his fingers.

A pair of thuds came from his left, and Cesco and Detto each grabbed at the rope in Benedick's fingers. Together they all heaved, and soon both father and son were on the narrow bridge, panting. Bail grasped Val close to him, stroking his soaked hair almost violently. Then he turned and crushed both Detto and Cesco with a bear-hug. "God bless you, boys! God bless!"

Cesco gasped something that sounded like, "So I'm forgiven?" but the last of his air failed him.

Bail turned to thank Pedro and Benedick. There were murmurs and congratulations, when a cool voice said, "Ah, not to damage the moment, but we're losing the race." Already on the ledge above, Cesco tugged Detto's end of the rope.

Indeed, voices could be heard from up on the roof. The first of those ascending the backside of the palace had achieved the top. Benedick thought he heard Capulletto's voice shouting in triumph.

"Go on ahead! We'll be along!" Turning to Val, Bail said, "Want to go on, son?"

"Yes!" Val ceased rubbing his ribs and ran for the wall. Pedro cupped his hands for him, but Val hesitated. "I don't need help," he said, adding, "my lord," in an attempt to remain polite.

"When you and your father get to the top, pull us up," said Don Pedro. "Then we'll be even."

Accepting the arrangement, Val called for his father to hurry up. Benedick watched them climb and sighed. Being a truly noble fellow, Don Pedro had decided to stay with the Nogarolese to look after father and son. That meant Benedick would, too. It wasn't a bad thing — it would gain him respect in many quarters — but it wasn't like winning the race.

But Cesco and Detto would do that, he was sure of it. So instead of forcing the climb, he made a joke, then another. The Prince grinned at him, and together they watched Bail push Val up to the ledge. By the time the quartet reached the roof, they were still ahead of two thirds of those climbing the backside of the palace.

But Cesco and Detto were long gone.

♦　　◊　　♦

Montecchio and Capulletto traversed one of the thin wooden walkways the Scaliger had mentioned. Less than two feet wide, it forced them to edge along sideways. Antony said, "Try not to fall."

"I'm not the one who weighs fifteen stone," retorted Mariotto, eyes on the drop below, nearly invisible in the rain.

"Twelve stone," grunted Antony. The rain made the temporary bridge quite slippery, so he slid his feet rather than stepped.

"I think the heirs are ahead of us."

"I told you that was a wrong turn!"

"We'd be in the lead if you moved faster!"

"We'd be pulped on the pavement if we moved as fast as you want!"

"I never knew you to lack courage. Well, once," Mari amended.

Without thinking Antony shoved Mariotto in the back. It was a little shove, so minor that it would have hardly offended the most sensitive honour. But it was enough. Losing his balance, Mariotto started to fall off the left side of the bridge. His flailing right arm went back and caught Antony in the chest, sending him over the bridge's right side just as Mari toppled over the left.

Falling, both had the foresight to grasp the rope with their free hands, so neither dislocated a shoulder. But it was still a wrenching stop, made worse by slamming into each other as they came down, bouncing off each other only to bang again, trying desperately to twist so their exposed genitals didn't meet. After a few moments they came to rest, each hanging by one arm, suspended two stories above the rain-soaked street.

"Great, Antony!" snarled Mariotto. "Goddamn great! O, well done!"

"Your fault!" retorted Antony.

"For telling the truth?"

"How now? You think I'm cowardly? I'll fight you here and now!" Releasing the rope with his free hand, Antony swung a wild punch at Mariotto's head. Ducking back, Mari swung a punch of his own, sending them both spinning and bumping as they shouted at each other.

Their shouts were answered. Hearing voices above them, both men instantly stopped their attacks. Mari grabbed Antony's shoulder at the same moment Antony grasped Mari's suspended arm. Clinging to each other, swaying in midair in the downpour, they listened.

"Watch your step," said Nico da Lozzo. "There's something across the bridge here."

"Thanks," replied Hortensio. "As if it isn't hard enough, someone laid a caltrop?"

Holding their breath, both Mari and Antony silently thanked God that the rain was hiding them from view. When the voices were gone, they looked at each other. "We've got to get out of here," said Mariotto in the same instant Antony said, "We've got to go." Mari resisted the grin bubbling beneath the surface of his lips, but when Antony loosed a half-stifled laugh it was over. Arms aching, they both started roaring, and were still howling in mid-air when the next group passed over the bridge.

"Who's down there!" called someone.

"Just us!" cried Mariotto.

"Nobody important!" called Antony.

"Do you need help?"

"No!" they both shouted, then fell about laughing again. The pair on the bridge shrugged and moved off.

Mari asked, "How do we do this?"

"Can you swing that way?" suggested Antony. "If we can reach that building over there…"

It took minutes to worm their rope sideways towards the nearer building. Finally it was done and they were perched on window-sills a story away from the rooftop.

"My arm is murder," groused Antony.

"Mine too," said Mari, massaging his wrist. "Want to stop?"

"Do you know what happens if we don't make it back?"

"We'll never live it down," agreed Mariotto. "Let's go then."

This time as they climbed they made jokes. Poor ones, as they were both treading lightly on this new peace. But it felt good. It felt right.

Each man had his best friend back.

◆　　◇　　◆

Having passed the first clue and already decyphered the second, Cesco and Detto were well in the lead. As hinted to Benedick, 'Brother Sun' referred to the monks at the Chapter Library of the Duomo. The Library itself was across the square from the Duomo, and thus reachable from the rooftops of the northeast part of the city. The 'sun' reference was double, since the fresco on the front of the building had both a sun high in the sky and the baby Christ in his mother's arms.

Inside the top floor windows, a single torch lit words scrawled in chalk:

> Love is he, radiant with great splendour,
> And speaks to us of thee, O Most High.

"It would be so easy," Cesco had mused softly.

"What, to erase the words? Leave that to Mastino," Detto had said.

Now they skirted buildings over-run with pushing and crawling men. In the rain they were invisible as Cesco led the way to the next location.

"Where are we headed?" asked Detto at last.

"Love, radiant with splendour. What rich building houses love?" They were already approaching their most familiar stopping point – *La Rosa Colta*. Cesco grinned. "Love he is, and speaks to us of thee, O Most High. Shall we?"

Acutely aware of his nakedness, Detto rolled with Cesco over the lip of the roof and onto a balcony that ran the whole length of the building. Every few feet there was another door. The noises from some rooms were quite distinct now, making Detto blush.

A door stood open at the end of the balcony, light streaming out. Above it was a painted Cupid, his bow drawn and ready.

Cesco made no gesture towards modesty as he passed through the open doors. "Good evening. I trust we're expected?"

The room was full of women in various states of undress. Some wore make-up, some wore wigs, some wore nothing at all. All were waiting for them, with Madonna Rapida and Madonna Troppo painted and primped for many promised guests.

"Poor babies," said Rapida, eyes crinkled. "They're all wet!"

"I can warm them up," offered Troppo.

"Greedy witch," answered Rapida. "We can do it together."

As Cesco walked deeper into the scented chamber, seeming to look for someone, Detto lingered as near the balcony door as the rope allowed.

"What's the matter, sweetie?" asked a young-looking girl with curled red hair. "Don't you like us?"

"No," said Detto, flushing. "I mean, of course, but..."

"But Bailardetto is a man of duty," said Cesco, "and we are on a mission. You have something for us?"

"It depends, dear Francesco," said Troppo in a husky voice. She walked to him and rubbed her hips against his pelvis. "Do you have something for us?"

Cesco looked down. "As you can see, Madonna, I do. I would make Priapus hide his head in shame. Isn't that right?" He wagged his hips to make his manhood nod. "He says that's right. But first, I hope you've got a message for us."

"We certainly do," said the young whore near Detto. She began whispering something in his ear that caused him to blush.

"I mean a message from the Capitano," Cesco clarified.

"The magic word." Rapida looked around at her companions to make certain they were ready, then led a joint recitation. *"You damned spirits! You can only do what the Hand of God allows!"*

Cesco grinned. "How appropriate. I hope you who are so skilled in *trucco* do not meant to trick us." In the Veronese tongue, the word for *make-up* was the same as for *trick*.

Rapida raised her palm. "Hand to God."

"Hand of God," said Detto from the doorway.

"Yes." Still Cesco seemed to be looking for someone. "Do you have it?"

"I think so. Let's go."

As Cesco continued to glance about, Madonna Troppo leaned and whispered in his ear. "She is not here, my lord. But she is not with another man, I promise you. Her chamber is empty."

Detto did not know to whom she referred, but Cesco was clearly put out. "Then we depart. Ladies, thank you for your hospitality. We'll be back – well, I will. My friend is virtuous to a fault. Keep the fires warm and yourselves warmer. I'll need to generate some heat."

The giggling women made kissing noises. As Detto withdrew, the red-headed girl attempted to pry his hands apart, hands that were having more and more trouble maintaining his modesty. On the balcony he accepted Cesco's boost to the roof, only to be humiliated as he turned to clamber up onto the tiles and got caught on the lower lip of the roof. Shifting his hips, he found his feet and used the rope to haul Cesco up.

They started west, towards the statue of a saint with obtrusively large hands. As they ran into a group of four, running together.

"Ho, Cesco!" cried Hortensio da Bonaventura.

"Ho!" called his brother, young Petruchio.

"Ho, Ser Pipsqueak!" called Nico da Lozzo.

"Ho, ho," said Hortensio da Padua.

"Ho. Ho. Ho. Ho!" called Cesco, greeting each in turn.

"Hello," said Detto dourly.

"Where are you fellows off to?" asked Cesco innocently.

"Don't give us that," said the elder Hortensio. "We're going where you've just been, and don't deny it!"

"Going to the whore-house," said young Petruchio happily.

"Ho ho," said Hortensio his brother.

"Nico, don't let them intimidate you," called Cesco.

"I'll try not to rise to their bait," retorted Nico da Lozzo.

"Just don't tell my wife, or she'll be a widow again," said Hortensio the elder with a note of real pleading. The four men laughed as they slipped over the edge and down to the balcony.

As Detto and Cesco traipsed across the rooftops, Cesco echoed the question the whore had posed. "What's the matter?"

Detto shook his head, his sodden hair whipping the rain away. "Just keep running."

♦　◊　♦

Amid the revels on the Scaligeri loggia, women were in great prominence. Most of the males were out there in the rain, leaving behind only men such as the senior Castelbarco, too aged to race, Cangrande della Scala, too important to race, or Salvatore, too enamoured to race. Even members of the clergy were participating in the Palio – forbidden to ride a horse, Fra Lorenzo was under no such restriction for his own feet, and was out there naked with the rest.

The feminine attention centered on Pietro. Gianozza Montecchio kissed him on both cheeks, and Antonia brought forward little Maddelena to curtsey to the new Count. Thanking the little girl, Pietro embraced his sister. "Now I have almost as many titles as you."

As she slapped him playfully on the shoulder, Castelbarco the elder appeared to punch him hard on the opposite arm. "What did you ever do to be made a Count?"

Pietro rubbed his bicep. "Does a title allow everyone to hit me?"

Gianozza Montecchio began rhapsodizing about the latest poet to catch her fancy — none other than Pietro's friend, Francesco Petrarca. He had started sending his shorter love rhymes to his friend Pietro, and Antonia had been foolish enough to share one with Gianozza. Now whenever they met she pestered her husband's friend to recite one of Petrarch's new lines, sighing deeply whenever the word 'love' passed his lips.

Other women were sighing too, but with more emphasis on the speaker than the words. Pietro looked to his sister for rescue, but she laughingly pled her duty to little Maddelena. "I'll have to take her home soon."

Escaping the poetic talk, Pietro sought a private word with the Scaliger. Crossing the loggia, he was suddenly waylaid by the Paduan Rakehell Salvatore, who rose from beside Vittoria to shake the new count's hand. "May I offer my congratulations?"

Pietro accepted the offered arm. "Thank you. You're not racing?"

The young man shook his head. *Sotto voce* he said, "I have another race to win. Vittoria is not much impressed with contests."

"With brothers and a father like hers, she must be tired of them. Well, best of luck. I hope her name brings you success."

"As much as your new name brings to you, Count."

Hmm. As he moved on, Pietro fretted. Was he truly ready to be a man of the land, to own and administer property, settle disputes, and lead men into war? His life to date had been one of itinerant travels. The longest he had ever spent in one place as an adult was his near-decade in Ravenna. Other than that, his life since exile had been spent in Paris, Pisa, Verona, Bologna, Avignon, and Verona again. *Now I am a man of substance. My heirs will be ennobled — if I ever have any.*

Reaching the Scaliger, he found the great man staring out a

window curtained with rain. "Count of San Bonifacio?"

Cangrande arched a mirth-filled eyebrow. "Does the title's previous owner bother you?"

Pietro recalled his one meeting with Vinciguerra da San Bonifacio. The corpulent older man had been raving nonsense: *"Come back and see me, boy, when I'm dead. I have stories to tell. I have a secret. It's one secret no one else knows. Not even your master! It's only mine. All mine. Two secrets, twins, entwined snakes! The caduceus! When I'm gone, someone has to know. I want to tell someone — someone who will suffer in the knowledge — someone who will, can, when the time is right, tell Cangrande the truth of it—"*

"Then tell me now," Pietro had said.

"No, no, no! You'll tell him too soon! Too soon! I have to have my secrets! Their lies killed me, so my lies have to live to kill their lies! And you, too, boy! You wore my armour! They told me! From beyond the grave I'll haunt you! Down, down down!"

Shivering now, Pietro did not share those recollections. Another prediction was itching at the base of his neck. "No. It's just — there's something Pathino said before he was executed. He said the Count of San Bonifacio was not finished with me. Was he prescient? Did he foresee this?"

"How could he? I just thought of it last month. It's past time someone took up the title. Twelve years is too long. The people of San Bonifacio will appreciate having a new lord. You don't have to live there, you know. Vinciguerra never did. I've held it for years. But now you have a castle, if you like of it. And you can buy yourself a fine villa somewhere and do whatever you like. Not that I imagine you'll ever settle into a life of ease. It's not in your nature."

"No more than in yours."

Cangrande's smile reached his eyes. "Some thanks this is! Here I bestow a heartfelt gift of my true affection, a statement of my valuance of your worth, and you squinny and wonder at my motives. In plain truth, I wanted to bind you to Verona. Whatever happens, the city will need you for all the days to come."

"Whatever happens?" echoed Pietro.

"Someone tried to poison me. As if I was not already approaching an age when one thinks about mortality. What was it your father said? 'Midway through the journey of our life, I came to myself in a dark wood, for the straight way was lost.' He was younger than I am now — and, alas, thirty-five did not prove the halfway point of his life." Cangrande shook his head. "You'll say the straight path was always lost to me."

"No," said Pietro with more compassion than he'd expected. "I'd say morbidity doesn't suit you. You've always been immortal, at least in your mind."

"You're wrong," said Cangrande, staring out at the rain. "I only wanted to be."

Interesting as the Scaliger's doubts were, Pietro had a more pressing mission. "Where is she?"

"At her husband's house in the city. Shall we?" Together they slipped out the side door of the hall and donned cloaks to take them to the interview neither was looking forward to.

♦　◊　♦

Giulietta did not like the rain. Her room was near the top of the tower, with a door to the hall and a small balcony looking down on the central courtyard. The rain lashed at her window, and though there was no thunder tonight, every few minutes the wind would pick up, howling around the corners of her tower, rattling the latches and brushing the covers on her bed.

A creak in the hall made Giulietta start. A footstep on the darkened wooden stair. Who could it be? Her father, home early from the feast? Or perhaps her nurse, come to cuddle her? Leaping up, Giulietta threw wide the door, face expectant, eyes ready to well with tears of relief. "Hello?"

It was not her father, nor her nurse Angelica, but her mother. At the look on her face, Giulietta wished she could close the door and disappear. "Mama? Where are you going?"

"Go back to sleep, Giulietta."

"Can't sleep," said the three year-old. "The wind," she added, ducking her head in shame. Tears gathered on her lashes, though they did not yet fall.

"Back to bed then."

"Mama," said Giulietta hesitantly. "Will you snuggle me?"

Giulietta did not expect the answer to be anything but no. Her mother had never snuggled her. But she was young enough to hope and scared enough to ask.

Surprisingly, her mother said, "Very well. This once." Entering Giulietta's room, she lay down beside her daughter on the large bed.

So happy she could hardly speak, Giulietta wriggled to press as close as she could. "Where were you going?"

"To check on your brother. But he's with Angelica, he can wait. Now hush, child. Go to sleep."

Giulietta closed her eyes. Her mother loved her! Not even the wind could steal her tonight, because her mother loved her! She kept sighing and cuddling closer, almost forcing her mother from the bed. But Tessa Guarini *in* Capulletto hung on to the last bastion at the edge of the mattress and stroked her daughter's hair. She was tempted to sing, but didn't know what the child liked. She settled on a song from her own childhood:

Ninna nanna, ninna oh	*Lullaby, lullaby, oo,*
Questo bimbo a chi lo dò?	*Who will I give this baby to?*
Se lo dò alla Befana,	*If I give him to the old hag,*
Se lo tiene una settimana.	*For a week she will keep him.*
Se lo do al lupo nero	*If I give him to the black wolf*
Se lo tiene un anno intero.	*For a whole year he'll keep him.*
Se lo do a lupo bianco	*If I give him to the white wolf*
Se lo tiene tanto tanto.	*For very long he'll keep him.*
Se lo dò all'uomo nero,	*If I give him to the bogeyman,*
Se lo tiene un anno intero.	*For a whole year he'll keep him.*
Ninna nanna, ninna oh...	*Lullaby, lullaby, ee...*

Giulietta felt a shiver run through her mother. Thinking she had forgotten the final lines, the little girl whispered:

Ninna nanna, ninna oh,	*Lullaby, lullaby, ee*
Questo bimbo me lo terrò!	*I will keep this baby for me!*

"Yes," said her mother, stroking Giulietta's hair. "Now go so sleep."

Giulietta nodded, feeling happier than she could remember.

♦   ◊   ♦

In the palace, Giovanna della Scala held a grand court, discussing her upcoming departure for Paris and all she meant to do there. At the other end of the loggia, two women found themselves together beside a tapestry depicting the siege of Troy. Donna Beatrice shifted uneasily. What to discuss with a widow? "My hair must be a fright. This kind of weather wreaks havoc upon it."

"You look fine," assured Kate Bonaventura. "Very natural."

"That's to say, unkempt. But thank you." They had not spoken since the night they had met, doubtless a most unwelcome memory for Kate. Unsure what else to say, Beatrice broached the nearest topic at hand. "Do you ever pity Helen?"

Kate laughed. "No! I know her all too well. A scheming, simpering little beauty who will as soon cut a man as kiss him. Selfish to the extreme." She pointed across the room. "Have you met my sister?"

Seeing the little beauty, Beatrice drew a breath of amused understanding. "Ah. I see. Well, I'll confess I've always pitied her just a little. 'The face that launched a thousand ships.' What a title to endure. How terrible, to have so many idiots dying for your sake."

"The chivalric ideal," agreed Kate. "What a pile of *controsenso*. A woman wants to be kissed. What good is adoration from afar?"

"Spoken like a woman who knows." It slipped past Beatrice's lips before she could recall it. "Oh! I'm sorry—"

Kate's expression was understanding, and though tears came, she was smiling. "No no, put your hands down. I'm not a fragile icicle to dissolve with a little heat. Not like herself over there," she added with a frown for Donna Montecchio. "I have loved and been loved. I refuse to mourn, but rather remember the love."

"That's – brave. Profound, in fact."

Wiping her eye, Kate fixed Beatrice with a basilisk gaze. "Do not mistake me. When it is known who did the deed, the Capitano had best keep him far away from these my hands."

Beatrice nodded. "I cannot help but wish sometimes that I was a man. I do not care for waiting. I'd rather be doing."

"A pity you've never met the Capitano's sister. In her youth she was as formidable as any man living. Wore armour into battle, and male attire on several occasions. She refused to be less than she could be, whatever her gender. A model for us all."

"Her husband didn't object?"

"Lord Nogarola said he enjoyed seeing her legs. My Petruchio often tried to entice me to dress as a man, for sport. He bet me that I couldn't pass for a man in a tavern for a whole evening."

Beatrice's eyes were as wide as her smile. "Did you do it?"

"Of course not." Kate gestured to her ample chest. "It would have been doomed to a ridiculous end. Not every bet must be won – something I never quite convinced him of." The smile was wistful, but not without joy.

"I am astonished, if I may say, at your equanimity."

"O, I wailed. I beat my chest and tore my hair for days. But he loved my hair. My chest as well. A poor way to honour him, doing harm to the things he loved. Which is why I so enjoyed your public displays of wit this evening. He would have appreciated it. Love should never be easy. Though," she added darkly, "some people make it too hard."

Beatrice's brow furrowed. "Was that aimed at me?"

"No," said Kate sadly. "For me. But what about you and Signor Benedick? He is a man of parts, yes?"

"Of parts, if you mean wit and looks and a nimble sword – or so I'm told, and not just by him. But if by parts you mean wealth, no."

"Does that trouble you?"

"Me?" repeated Beatrice in surprise. "Not at all! But it may vex him when he learns I have nothing to offer in way of land."

"You are unkind," chastised Kate. "Or else you do not think highly of him."

Beatrice looked away. "Too highly."

"Well then, if you will allow me to offer some advice? Focus on the aspects of your being that tempt him, and challenge him. Never be something you're not, because he won't like what he sees when the covers are lifted. Always remember – men are vain. They need to believe they are the best, the most valourous. 'This citadel must be taken, and I'm the only man alive who can!'"

"Is that what you did?"

"Hah! Yes, unknowingly. I was invested in my own independence, and the more I fought his wooing, the more he fought to win me. With jests, with mad deeds masked in kind words. It took me weeks to realize the game he was playing. The moment I recognized it, I set out to prove I was better at the game than he was. When I did, he accepted me as his partner. In a war of wills, we found a very happy peace."

"But not an easy one."

"Again, what in life that's worth doing is easy? But there are simple things to do that make a world of difference. The best thing I ever did was keep his reputation alive. We bantered and played in public, of course. But I never harmed his dignity. In fact, I upheld it. With mockery, yes. But with me fostering his reputation as a scoundrel, he did not have to remain one. Give the man the reputation he desires, and he is free to do as he likes. Reputation is far greater than wealth. And that is something you can give your Benedick. But first," added Kate, "let him prove himself worthy of you. Tell him the truth of your circumstances, and see if his affection cools. If it does, he is not the man for you."

Beatrice thanked Kate for her sage advice, then went off to fix her hair. Kate stood all alone, her eyes closed, shoulders bent. "Yes, I know. From me, of all people. But you don't get to criticize. You left without permission."

"Mama?" said Evelina, edging forward. "Are you talking to—?"

"Your father, yes." Kate drew herself upright. "It's not madness. But I'll never stop hearing his voice."

Evelina took her mother's hand. Kate squeezed it, then restored her brave face for the others.

♦ ◊ ♦

Across from the palace, Cesco and Detto reached the roof of the Domus Bladorum. Below was the well where Cesco's mother had been hidden. They said nothing of it as they made the short leap across to the next rooftop. Detto started to slip, but Cesco caught him by the wrist. "Careful."

Detto shook his hand free. "Do you doubt me so much? Can't I be trusted to do anything?"

"I have trouble sometimes," said Cesco slowly, "discerning how much of your anger with me is for show, and how much is real."

Detto pressed on. "Let's keep going."

They traversed the path above the Piazza delle Erbe. At the lip of the roof Cesco touched Detto's arm. "Wait a moment."

"What now?" said Detto harshly.

"This race. Think – we know the author..."

Detto understood. If they could guess the rest of the quotes, they might skip a step or two in the race. Detto tried to remember any pithy sayings attributed to San Francesco. "Wasn't there one about doing the impossible?"

"*'Start by doing what's necessary; then do what's possible, then suddenly you are doing the impossible.'* You see any help in that? No, nor I. What else?"

Detto frowned. "*'I have been everything unholy. If God can work through me –'*"

"*'– he can work through anyone,'*" Cesco finished. "That should be my motto. Does it bring any places to mind?"

"No," admitted Detto.

"I'm not doing any better," said Cesco. "There's the bit about injury and pardon, despair and hope, blah blah blah. Too vague..."

Detto stood upright. "The gloomy face."

Cesco slammed his wet palms together. "Perfect! *It is not fitting, when in God's service, to wear a gloomy face or chilling look.'* You know who that is, of course!"

Without another word, Detto led the way over the thin walkway of *La Costa,* from which hung the monstrous rib-bone, and towards the Torre dei Lamberti. In the square that joined it to the Palazzo Cangrande, there rested a fresco cycle of Pietro's father, the poet Dante, he of the most chilling look.

They were almost there when Cesco snapped his fingers. "Of course! *'I have sinned against my brother.'*" Detto stared at him. "A quote, not a confession." Cesco told him the context. "It makes the logical final stop, does it not?"

Together they reversed course and started running again, so focused at keeping their feet they failed to notice the knot of men following them below.

THIRTY

MONTAGU AND AIELLO ran along the rooftops in uncomfortable silence. Neither knew the city well enough to even hope for victory. Instead they followed the other runners and tried not to look each other in the eye. Or anywhere else.

"This way," said Aiello suddenly.

"Why that way?"

"Because, bastard, that's Mastino della Scala, with Lord Carrara beside him. They know where they're going. But if you have better ideas…"

Montagu responded by doubling his pace, leaving the older Aiello huffing to catch up. "Bastard."

"Yes, I am," agreed Montagu. "Your point?"

"My point is that you're a bastard, and are going to die a bastard's death."

It wasn't the slanting sheets of rain that made Montagu shiver. "Not in Verona."

"If you should disappear, it might go unnoticed. Poof. Vanished, like a shadow at nightfall."

"Like you did to Breon?"

Aiello managed to look both proud and wounded. "He stuck his finger in my meat pie. What did he expect? Stuck it right in there!"

"Stuck more than his finger in, I hear," answered Montagu.

Aiello swore, and Montagu feared he was about to be attacked.

Instead, the Scot began a diatribe on manners and fairness that lasted several city blocks. It was the strangest combination of outrage and indignation Montagu had ever heard, coming from the lips of a bounty hunter and murderer. Aiello concluded by remarking, "But that was personal, not business. I am paid to end your life. Scaliger or no, I am a man of my word."

I have to do something, thought Montagu.

♦   ◊   ♦

Mari and Antony had a salutary experience in the *La Rosa Colta*, laughing themselves sick, though not partaking of the offered enticements. Some of their fellow racers had abandoned the contest to remain there, and could be heard through the walls or glimpsed behind flimsy screens connected by lengths of rope.

Departing the whorehouse, the pair found themselves not too far behind the Bonaventura group, who had mistaken the whores' message and were only now heading towards the saint's statue.

"You know," said Mariotto, "we might just win this."

Antony rumbled with amusement. "We might at that! Wouldn't that shock the masses!"

They ran harder, and this time when one started to fall, the other helped him up.

♦   ◊   ♦

Back in the Scaligeri palace, Salvatore was talking in a low voice in Vittoria's ear when she let out a coo that had nothing to do with his words. "Oh, look at that. The little princess is falling asleep." Salvatore's attentions had miraculously cured her dislike of Maddelena.

Salvatore glanced over to where Maddelena was curled in her nurse's lap, trying valiantly to remain awake. Antonia and Dahna were making preparations to take the girl back to her home.

Salvatore rose. "Excuse me, Vittoria. As the sole friend of her husband present, I'd feel better if I escorted them." Vittoria pouted, and he flashed her a smile. "Cesco is Verona's heir, and my friend. I must look after his wife, as I'm sure he would do mine. When I have a wife."

From forsaken, Vittoria suddenly began to glow. Sitting close at hand, her sister Evelina made a vomiting noise, for which her mother scolded her.

♦   ◊   ♦

Cesco and Detto dropped together into the attic of a muleteer's shop three blocks from the river's edge. The way in was a sideways window in a cupola, and their eight-foot drop placed them center of an upper chamber.

Detto squinted along the walls, looking for some sign, some message. They were risking all on guessing the answer, and so far he saw nothing. "Are you sure about this?"

"No. But his dying words – 'I have sinned against my brother, the ass.' Wonderfully open to interpretation, don't you think?"

Detto had stopped listening. There was something warm near his ankle. Reaching carefully down, his fingers brushed the hot metal screen concealing a candle's light. "I think I found it." As Cesco approached, Detto removed the cover, and the flickering wick cast its light on the wall before them. Scrawled in dark paint was written:

The only ass here is you.

"Here's the problem," said Cesco. "I have no idea if that's the real message, or one meant just for me."

"No reason it can't be both."

"Hm. His messages are usually less subtle. And yours are growing ever more opaque." Detto turned away, and Cesco threw up his hands. "For Lucifer's sake! Do you want to strike me? Is that it?"

"You don't know anything," said Detto.

"Because you don't tell me anything! You moon and scowl and frown and play the perverse painted pillar of prevarication! Yes! I struck your mother! I refuse to apologize—"

"Who is asking you to?!" shouted Detto. "You think I'm so weak that I'd hold that grudge for months and months? If I wanted you to apologize, I'd beat you down until you begged to cry, 'I am a sore and sorry ass!'"

"You could try."

"Oh, you'd do it," said Detto loudly. "I know your tricks by now, God knows. But you don't know anything."

"What then? What the hell is your problem? Jesu, anyone would think you were the wronged party, *you* were the one the stars were conspiring against, *you* were the one with dashed dreams, *you* were the one who – who—"

The choked sob that escaped Cesco's lips might have checked anyone else. But Detto's own feelings were too pent up. The gates having fractionally opened, they now flooded forth. "It's all about you! Of course it is! You selfish git! You're the one wallowing in hurt feelings! You're the one wasting your everything! You think I don't see the wine, the women, the fighting, for what they are? You're diminishing everything you are because your feelings are hurt! Because Cesco is so deep! So important! He *feels* more than other people, his life matters more than anyone else's!"

"I don't think that—"

Detto squared his shoulders. "Well, you know what? It does! Your life *does* matter more than anyone else's. *That's* why I'm angry. I stand here, day after day, watching you soil yourself, spoil yourself, waste your gifts, squander the chance to become something great. The world has hurt you, so you hurt the world. But it wasn't the world, was it? There are maybe three or four people who invited your pain. Punish *them*! Not Fate, not the damned stars, not God. Fut! Other men moon or act morose, turn all their pain inside. But not Cesco! He has to hurt the people who care about him. Ser Alaghieri, Suor Beatrice, Ser Morsicato, Tharwat – do they deserve your wrath? What did they ever do but love you, rear you, raise you to be free enough to use your brain and see the world for what it is? You're so selfish that you'd turn the whip against your friends so they can share your pain!"

"My friends!" cried Cesco, stunned.

"Yes! People so eternally stupid that they stand by you even as you destroy yourself! What are you doing? Do you even know? What happened to your plans for Mastino and Venice? For your father? Are they still happening? Or are you just flailing like an infant with a toothache, wailing into the night?"

"Toothache! You don't know, you supercilious shit! You have no idea! You don't know what it is to love!"

"Of course I do, you stupid bastard! I love *you*! You're the only friend I have in the world, and my reward is the choice seat to watch you ruin your life! You want to know what's the matter with me? *I'm waiting for my friend to come back!*"

Cesco began tugging at the knot binding him to Detto. "The hell with this." But the wet knot was impossible to untie.

Detto grasped Cesco by the shoulders. "My mother gave me a message for you. It was her request, the night before I was attacked. *My* mother, who never gave a fig for me. If she died untimely, I was to tell you something. Her final words are for you. Not for Val. Not for me. Not for my father, even. We're the ones who... We're the ones... Why doesn't she have messages for us? I asked her that. You know what she answered? 'Because I have nothing to say to you.' So I went on to Venice and was attacked, on your business, knowing that even if I died, my mother had no message for anyone but you."

They stood naked before each other, with the cord binding them chest to chest across the divide.

"We're all waiting for you," said Detto. "I don't know for how much longer."

Still Cesco said nothing. Detto was wondering if he should say it, the thing he had promised to say. He licked his lips and drew a breath—

Cesco held up a hand. Detto heard it too. A scraping sound. He glanced up, wondering if some fellow racers had arrived. But no, the sound was definitely coming from below. There were footsteps on the stairs, and these feet were shod.

"In here," came a gruff whisper, barely audible over the patter of the rain above. "Spread out, and remember – no killing the prince."

Cesco flashed Detto a look. Anyone else might have showed fear. But Cesco's face bore relief, and pure joy.

♦   ◊   ♦

Hooded, Cangrande and Pietro were well concealed in the rain, and had no trouble avoiding notice as they approached the door of Lord Tiberio's house. Admitted before they finished knocking, they were shown up the stairs to a small chamber lit only by a fire. In its light, both men could see the figure seated in the chair. The figure, and the crossbow she held.

"Come in, father. Ser Alaghieri, step to the side. I'd hate for this to run through him and hit you."

"Hello, Rosalia. A pleasure to meet you at last." Unconcerned, Cangrande crossed to a side table and poured himself a generous helping of wine. "I presume I'm a fair target over here. The light's better." Lifting the cup, he paused. "Should I call a taster?"

"I'd drink some," answered Lia. "But it makes the baby kick."

"Then I shall have to risk it." Cangrande threw back the cup and waited, curious, before pouring himself another. "No. Poison did not seem your weapon. I recall a dagger."

"I did try poison once," she answered, her voice as level as his. "A blowgun. I tried it for weeks on the local animals, perfecting my aim. But my brother stopped me then as well."

Cangrande spoke sharply. "Don't call him that."

"Oh? Do you deny that is what he is?"

"I deny nothing. I just don't want Count Pietro here to vomit. His stomach isn't as strong as mine."

"Or mine," said Lia. "Count, is it? Congratulations. Is that the price you earned telling him I was carrying his first grandchild?"

Before Pietro could answer, Cangrande cut across him. "The good Count did not violate his oath. And he was only trying to prevent me from calling you here. He feared a scene such as this."

"I think it was a different scene he feared. Cesco burning the city to the ground."

"Which he would do for you, yes," agreed Cangrande. "I'm astonished, really, that it matters so much to him. He's fourteen. At his age I had slept with my sister half a hundred times."

♦   ◊   ♦

"Next time don't yell at me so loud," whispered Cesco. "Douse that light. Go left, stay low."

Detto had just closed the lamp's shutters when the door crashed open and four men burst into the room. Though it was dark, their posture said they were armed as they advanced into the room, searching.

Detto felt a jiggle on the rope. A signal. Detto crept left until the rope between him and Cesco was almost taught. Then, above the breathing of each unknown man, his ears caught a low whistle. Lurching forward, Detto pulled on the rope just as Cesco did the same.

Caught at their ankles, all four men flopped onto their stomachs. The leader took the brunt, a sharp crack declaring him out for the moment. His three compatriots clambered to their feet. One grasped the rope, dragging Detto towards him. There was nothing for it but to rush him head-on. Lowering his shoulder, he bolted forward.

As Detto made contact he heard a similar 'whoof' from close by – Cesco had come the some conclusion. Detto ducked what he hoped was a club and not a knife. In close, a club was all but useless. A knife was not.

A year wrestling with Cangrande had taught Cesco all manner of dirty tricks, which he had passed along to Detto. Making sure to keep a hand up to ward off blows, he swept a leg across one man's shin, drove his elbow into some soft flesh, and brought his knee up to follow a hard punch to the stomach.

Inches away, Detto heard Cesco's usual taunts while fighting. "You mewling pumpion! Craven scut-knocker!" It made Detto laugh.

Laughter proved dangerous, as a fist came at him, attracted by the sound. Head erupting with lights, Detto staggered back. The rope was both help and hindrance. Used correctly, it blocked attacks and could even be a weapon. But when one of his attackers grabbed and pulled, it was dangerous.

"Detto!" Suddenly there was light. Cesco was standing over the unshuttered candle, hands held low, shaped like a cup. "Up!"

Running forward at once, Detto stepped and Cesco heaved. Catching the edge of the high window, Detto wriggled through even as he felt the line at his waist shiver – Cesco was being attacked again.

Detto slid onto the tiles of the roof, scraping his whole body from shin to shoulder. He grasped the rope and began to pull. "Come on!"

Cesco must have jumped, because the line went slack before snapping taut. Suddenly the rope was digging into Detto's hands as he heaved. After several long seconds, Cesco emerged from the cupola, scrambling hand over hand. He slithered out onto the slick open roof and helped Detto pull the rope up between them. "Glad the rope is intact. No rope, no win."

Detto had to laugh. "I thought you wanted to quit."

Standing, Cesco touched his neck. "That was before someone tried to stop us winning. Who are they?"

"What, not friends of yours?" The way Cesco looked at his fingers, Detto knew his friend was bleeding. "How bad?"

Cesco used the falling rain to wash the blood away. "I'll live. Come on, they'll be –" He broke off to stomp on fingers gripping the windowsill. They heard a curse as the climber fell on the person below him.

"Fight, or win the race?" asked Detto.

Under the falling rain, Cesco cocked his head. "Is there any reason we can't do both?"

♦   ◊   ♦

Cangrande's words hung in the air, too horrible to contemplate. Pietro blanched, then gagged, clutching the table behind him.

The Scaliger shot him a pitying smile. "See? A weak stomach. Though I think I've finally cured the good Count of his unrequited smit."

Lia said, "You're not serious."

"Aren't I? Perhaps not. I thought it might goad you into pulling that trigger. Isn't that why you're holding it? To shoot me?"

"To protect myself," countered Lia. "And my child."

"At least you're breathing a little faster. Maybe if I upset you enough you'll miscarry. Wouldn't that be better for everyone? I can live a little longer without the title of *nonno*. Though it might make a good playmate for Cesco's wife. All in the family."

Pietro's head was reeling. "Stop it."

"Stop?" Cangrande's eyes never left his daughter. "I've never spoken to this girl before tonight. Yet she's tried to kill me on two separate occasions."

"Three," corrected Lia. She *was* breathing fast. "Once while you were hunting. I planned to shoot you dead, but you ran off to Mantua. Which left my brother instead."

"I told you, girl, don't call him that." Cangrande inclined his head. "But I remember that day well. Cesco was airing his little red hawk. And you were out to kill me, why?"

"My father – rather, my mother's husband – hates you, though I cannot imagine why. He sowed that hate into us, Adamo and me. I thought your death would cure him of his drinking and rage."

"Indeed? That would have been very Greek – to avenge your foster-father's honour, you murder your real father, all unknowing. The Furies would have come for you."

"Instead they gave me Cesco."

"Gave? I thought you took him. An older woman, dressed as a man. I've wondered if he does not incline that way. Did he have you dress in man's attire to make love?" Her silence made him laugh. "O, you did! How amusing. I had the feeling his whoring was a little too much protesting."

"Like yours? Is that why you bedded my mother, to prove you weren't attracted to her husband?"

Cangrande sputtered his wine. "I see why Cesco fell into your clutches! I suppose I should not cast the first stone. No, your mother was one of the loveliest women in the Feltro, with enormous breasts and the most marvelous dimples in her buttocks. Like a peach. Yum." Cangrande smacked his lips.

Lia took some time to answer. "Cesco said you were a brute."

"I hope you didn't talk about me during the act."

"Foreplay," retorted Lia. "He told what a drunken vainglorious ponce you were, and I got wet for him."

Cangrande's smile dimmed not at all, but Pietro knew from the wrinkle in his brow that the girl had scored. He wanted to cheer, but the talk was too awful to breathe, let alone utter a sound.

"Is that when you fell in love with him? As he abused me? Or was it was at first sight, when you held a dagger to his throat? Better your wrist had slipped then than to let him suffer as he suffers now."

Now the crossbow was quivering. "Whose fault is that?"

"Not mine," stated Cangrande confidently. "I wasn't the one

sneaking around and giving away my chaste treasure to a fickle prince. Your father knows whose child it is, and what such a union means. Does your husband? Will he accept a child born with three heads? You could name it Cerberus."

"He will accept it. He is a better man than you."

"Absolutely true," agreed Cangrande. "But if I am such a monster, and your mother was a slut, what kind of child could we have created but a monstrous whore?"

"Stop it." repeated Pietro. He'd finally realized what Cangrande was doing. "It wasn't her. You can see that. If she hasn't killed you by now, it wasn't her."

Back-lit by the fire, Lia looked between them, then sighed in anger. "You were goading me?"

Cangrande poured more wine. "I told you so."

"He's also trying to focus your hate on him," said Pietro. "Like father, like son."

"What?" It was said by both Cangrande and Lia. Even their inflection was the same.

"Earlier Cesco confronted your husband, and baited him. He wanted to focus all Tiberio's ire on him, lest any of it land on you. Cangrande is doing the same. If you hate him, you may forgive Cesco."

"So altruistic!" cried Cangrande. "Doesn't sound like me at all. Well daughter, the race will be over soon, and I must be there when it ends. People might talk. I don't expect to meet you again. Would you like a fatherly kiss before we part?"

"I want nothing from you," she told him.

"But I want something from you. Never contact him, never see him. He rages now, and that gives him strength. But he may weaken. Especially when he hears of the child. Be it a month from now, or a month of months, he'll hear, and he'll come for you. Do not see him. Let him be what he is destined to be. Let him alone." Lia was silent. "Promise me."

"I swear I will never let him see me," answered Lia stoically. "Or this child I carry. Is that all, father?"

"Almost. Just one thing more. I'd like to see your face."

Rosalia hesitated before rising. On her feet, Pietro could see how much the pregnancy had progressed since December. Her hair was coifed and covered, but her cheeks glowed with blossoming life.

Setting down his cup, Cangrande approached her and placed his hands on her shoulders. She did not back away, but the crossbow in her grip quivered a moment before lowering. Looking into her eyes, he allowed her to look into his. Then he kissed her under each eye. "It's not much. But every daughter should feel her father kiss her tears away at least once."

◆   ◊   ◆

Montagu slipped, and he caught himself at the expense of one of the clay roof tiles, which shattered under his knee.

Aiello hauled him to his feet. "Clumsy bastard, aren't you, bastard? Don't go dying on me now. Not when I plan to murder you in such a pretty, drawn-out way."

Montagu shoved him away with his shoulder and continued to follow Mastino and Carrara across the rooftop, hiding the thing in his hand.

◆   ◊   ◆

It was now just three short city blocks to the palace. Sliding down the angled rooftop, Detto and Cesco used their momentum to propel themselves across the gap to the next building. They landed just as the first head poked through the muleteer's cupola.

The two young knights would have been free and clear but for the rope. They passed a small chimney without noticing it, but seconds later the slack rope caught, yanking both hard. Their feet slid from under them and Detto's head struck the wet clay tiles, shattering a few.

"Jesus," said Detto dazedly.

"Hear him," said Cesco, echoing the prayer as he gasped for breath. The fall had dropped him on his back.

Hearing footfalls, they rolled just in time to dodge the kicks and blows from their pursuers.

◆   ◊   ◆

On the Scaliger's loggia, Gianozza Montecchio was sonorously reciting one of Petrarch's poems:

Son animali al mondo de sí altera	*There are creatures in the world with such other*
vista che 'ncontra 'l sol pur si difende;	*vision that it is protected from the full sun:*
altri, però che 'l gran lume gli offende,	*yet others, because the great light offends them*
non escon fuor se non verso la sera;	*cannot move around until the evening falls:*
et altri, col desio folle che spera	*and others with mad desire, that hope*
gioir forse nel foco, perché splende,	*perhaps to delight in fire, because it gleams,*
provan l'altra vertú, quella che 'encende:	*prove the other power, that which burns:*
lasso, e 'l mio loco è 'n questa ultima schera.	*alas, and my place is with these last.*

Ch'i' non son forte ad aspectar la luce
di questa donna, et non so fare schermi
di luoghi tenebrosi, o d' ore tarde:

però con gli occhi lagrimosi e 'nfermi
mio destino a vederla mi conduce;
et so ben ch'i' vo dietro a quel che m'arde.

I am not strong enough to gaze at the light
of that lady, and do not know how to make a screen
from shadowy places, or the late hour:

yet, with weeping and infirm eyes, my fate
leads me to look on her: and well I know
I wish to go beyond the fire that burns me.

◆　◊　◆

Their bodies slick from the still-falling rain, Cesco and Detto were able to slip from their opponents' grasping fingers. Cesco leapt this way and that, lifting tiles to use as shields and missiles.

The rope, which had been their foe, now turned ally, anchoring them and freeing them from fear of falling. Detto retreated a few steps, then launched himself feet first towards the nearest shape. Struck, the man hurtled backwards, his feet skimming the tiles until there were no more to skim and he plummeted three stories into the street, screaming all the way. A wet crunching thud and the screaming stopped.

The rope prevented Detto from following. But suddenly it jerked – another attacker had discovered it in the downpour and was now reeling Detto in. "Cesco!"

Cesco dropped his next missile to scuttle sideways across the roof, feeling his way almost blind in the falling rain. He crossed Detto's path and kept going, tugging on his end of the rope. The man pulling Detto flipped face-first onto the roof.

Released, Detto slipped backwards until the rope caught him. A body collided with his legs and fingers grasped at him, dragging him down to grapple. Cesco was close by, struggling with the other man who was trying to find a stranglehold about the prince's neck. "Where the hell are the others?"

◆　◊　◆

Back in the torrential downpour, Cangrande paused under a canopy. "Poor Pietro. The eternal witness. When I die, I'll have to wait for San Pietro to come and recount all my sins."

Pietro was glad his hood hid his face. "There are times I forget what a bastard you are."

"It's a good thing to remember. Especially for the Count of San Bonifacio."

"You were kind at the end."

"Which I'm sure I'll come to regret. I have always found that my regrets come from not being ruthless enough. But she is *sanguis meus* – blood of my blood. Quick, now. Back to the palace. We hardly want to be discovered here."

"I'll go my own way," said Pietro. "Antonia talked of taking Maddelena home. I want to be sure they arrived."

"Of course. There is a history of kidnapping on this night, and she's the perfect age for it."

Pietro had not considered that. He had only wanted to remove himself from the Scaliger's company. Now he hurried towards the *via Pigna*, a thunder in his ear that had nothing to do with rain.

♦   ◊   ♦

One of the clues Cesco and Detto had slipped led the other racers to the very edge of city walls, to the tower above the Ponte Pietra. Here, at the stone bridge dating back to the Roman Republic, was another clue – the one that would lead to the final message at the muleteer's shop.

Antony and Mari were already departing when Mastino and Carrara arrived, with Aiello and Montagu directly upon their heels. Montagu lagged behind.

"Come on, come on, you bastardly canker-blossom," urged Aiello, "sneck up!"

Ahead, Carrara said, "English is a musical language, is it not?" Mastino laughed, only to turn at the sound of a long wailing shout as someone toppled off the corner of the roof. Instantly both men lunged for the nearest figure, expecting him to be dragged off the edge as well.

But the nearer man didn't fall. Instead there was a splash as a body hit the icy waters four stories below.

"At least he missed the bridge," said Carrara.

"Won't make a difference," said Mastino. "Water's low this time of year. And there are rocks all around the bridge. How did it happen?"

"I don't know," said the survivor nervously. "He just – fell."

Mastino pulled up the slack rope. Had the knot slipped? He couldn't see it in the rain, but when his fingers reached the end of the braided cord he could feel frayed ends, unevenly severed. "This was cut."

"What?" demanded Aiello the Scot, pulling the rope from Mastino's fingers. "No. What? It can't be." His head came up. "You have to believe me. I didn't – I didn't!"

Carrara was grave. "We must give up the race and search for

the body. There's a chance he's still alive."

"And we have to bring this one to Cangrande," said Mastino darkly.

"No!" Shoving past them, Aiello leapt to the next building. They gave chase, but quickly lost him in the rain. Whatever else Aiello the Scot might be, he was an accomplished bounty hunter, and used to disappearing from sight.

◆　◊　◆

Pietro found all well at Cesco's house on the *via Pigna*. One look at his face had Antonia worrying, but he promised he would tell her everything on the morrow. "Tonight, I just couldn't." Antonia chose not to press. Tomorrow would do.

He had no desire to return to the palace, did not want to see Cangrande being jovial and bright. In one night the Scaliger had both made an enormously generous gift and planted a seed that would only fester over time. *He had not been serious, had he? He hadn't actually...*

But even if Cangrande were lying about that, the scene he had witnessed brought back all the worst moment of Pietro's life. Cangrande fighting Katerina on the rooftop in Vicenza, their words sharper than any blades.

The streets were not crowded, so Pietro was surprised when a cloaked figure jostled him, hitting him hard in the side and bowling him over. Instinctively Pietro reached for his sword, but the fellow staggered off, clearly the worse for wine. Clambering to his feet, Pietro winced – he might have cracked a rib. Another reason to go home.

But no. He had to see if Cesco made it back in one piece. And be certain Mari and Antony hadn't hanged each other with their rope. Feeling the weight of obligation, Pietro trudged back to the palace.

◆　◊　◆

Wresting furiously, Detto heard Cesco gasp and saw a hand around his cousin's throat. "No!" Heaving wildly, he kicked out. His heel caught the arm pressing Cesco down, but he also opened himself up to a violent blow that left him dazed.

Through the rain, came voices from across the roof.

"Do you hear something?" said Montecchio.

"Sounds like a fight," replied Capulletto. "Oi! What goes on there!"

It was all the distraction the two young knights required. Detto got underneath his foe's legs and, using the anchoring rope to pull himself upright, bodily lifted the man and tossed him over the roof's edge.

Throwing his elbow forward, Cesco clubbed his attacker in the throat, then used his knees to flip the man up and over the roof's edge. The scream was followed by a dull smacking sound from below.

"What's going on over there?" demanded Capulletto.

"Answer us, dammit!" echoed Montecchio.

"Help!" gasped Cesco, clearing his aching throat.

"Very funny, whoever you are!" called Montecchio. "But we're going to win! Come on, Antony – in here."

Panting, bruised and bleeding, Cesco grasped at Detto. "Hurt?"

"No!" He was, but not seriously.

"Then let's win!" Scrambling up, they unlooped the frayed rope from the chimney and started on their way again. But Detto grasped his cousin's shoulder. "Cesco – wait."

"Apologize later. We can win!"

"It isn't – I mean, there's something else." He paused. "Lia is in Verona."

It was his imagination. Through the rain, he certainly could not have heard his friend's heart stop. "Lia."

"She wants to see you. Tonight, after the race. She's arranged a place. San Zeno's."

The rain continued to fall, and Detto continued to shiver under it.

"Does she hate me so much?"

"She says hate makes it easier." There was so much more. But it was not his place to say it.

A whoop from the next building told them that Montecchio and Capulletto had emerged with the final message. Cesco shook himself like a dog, punching Detto lightly on the shoulder. "Thank you. I will see her after we win."

At the palace gate, Pietro was greeted by Signor Salvatore, the only Rakehell not racing tonight. Noting his still-soaking cloak, Pietro said, "I hear you walked my sister and the princess home. Thank you for your assistance."

Salvatore took the proffered arm and shook it heartily. "Not that it was needed. Still, now I can say I've been of service to the Count of San Bonifacio." His eyes narrowed as Pietro winced. "Are you unwell?"

"Some drunk knocked me over," said Pietro shortly, retrieving his hand. "I'll be fine. Come on, the race must be almost done."

♦   ◊   ♦

After finally falling asleep in her mother's arms, Giulietta was awakened by her nurse bursting into her room. The little girl's annoyance turned to panic when she perceived through the darkness that Angelica was weeping. "Madonna! Madonna!"

Tessa rose at once. "What's the matter?"

"He's gone! Alack the day, he's dead!"

Giulietta's eyes welled at once. "My father?"

"No, no no no! Worse. Far worse."

Giulietta was confounded. What could be worse than her father's death? But then she saw her mother's grim expression and gasped with horror.

♦   ◊   ♦

Cesco and Detto came hurtling through one palace window just as Mari and Antony swung in another, knocking over servants and onlookers alike. Capulletto started to fall backwards out of the window, but Montecchio caught him by the wrist and righted him on his feet. An ironic coda to a long-remembered wrong.

Having just himself returned, Cangrande approached, holding a pair of green ribbons. He looked from one pair to the other. "What is the final message?"

Shivering and bleeding, Cesco and Detto opened their mouths just as Mari and Antony chorused, "The only ass here is you!"

"And so it is!" cried Cangrande with good humour. "It is not every day that my people get to call me an ass with my full approval!" Cangrande eyed the shivering, panting figures of Antony and Mari. "But, ladies and gentlemen, I'm torn! Should I award the prize to two young men accustomed to working together? Or should it go to the pair that had more to overcome, including their pride? Who deserves it more?"

Standing in the door, holding his aching side as he shivered, Pietro felt a warm sunburst of hope. Could this be it? Was this the moment that all was mended? Opening his mouth, he shouted, "Capulletto and Montecchio!"

The cry was taken up by the whole loggia. "Capulletto and Montecchio! Capulletto and Montecchio!" The cheer went on and on, with laughter and cheers for the naked pair, huddled under blankets beside a brazier. They grinned like children, laughing as they had of old.

Cangrande waved for silence. "Ser Francesco, Ser Bailardetto, what do you say? Do you contest the will of the people?"

Detto shared a glance with Cesco. "Give it to them?"

"Yes, do," said Cesco. "All unknowing, they allowed us to finish. Let the victory fall on them!"

As the mostly feminine crowd applauded, Mariotto and Antony stood side-by-side to receive the ribbons of victory. "May this begin a new era," Cangrande said to them.

Pietro wasn't the first to reach them with his congratulations, but he made up for it in warmth, ignoring his pain as he hugged them both tightly. "About damned time."

Under three blankets, Cesco made his way through the congratulatory mob to stand beside Pietro. "I suppose it's because of the title that you had to voice your opposition to my victory."

Pietro noticed the ugly gash along Cesco's collarbone. "What happened?"

"We were assaulted." Cesco noted Pietro clutching his right side under the sopping cloak. "You?"

"Bowled over by a drunk. Who assaulted you? Were they arrested?"

"Probably angry Paduans trying to get their own back. I'll send some guards for them now. At least two aren't going anywhere. But I want to talk to them. And I have an appointment later. Where are my clothes?"

Cesco departed the loggia to dress, followed by Detto. A few minutes later Mastino and Carrara arrived with news of Montagu's murder and Aiello's flight. Cangrande ordered Aiello's men arrested until he could decide their fate. "And find that treacherous Scot," snarled the Capitano. "I should have known he'd be the flaw in our celebrations." He glanced over at the victorious duo and smiled thinly. "Though it seems as if nothing could spoil their night."

Wrapped in more warm blankets, Mariotto shook his sopping head, flinging water everywhere. "Watch that!" laughed Antony.

Throwing his hair back, Mariotto said disbelievingly, "We won."

"We did at that!" crowed Antony. "Just like old times. If we tried, we could—"

But what they might have done went unspoken. At that moment Gianozza pushed through the throng to throw her arms around Mariotto's neck, kissing him repeatedly. "Darling, I'm so proud of you!"

Pietro had never liked Mariotto's wife. Insipid, and self-centered. But he never actively hated her until now. Seeing what was happening, she could have stayed back. But no, she had to thrust herself into the moment like the lead in the theatre, demanding centerstage.

Flushed, Mari gently disengaged himself, settling his wife into the crook of his arm. He extended his other arm in a gesture of friendship.

Pietro watched Antony's eyes fix on the outstretched hand, then up to gaze at Gianozza. Capulletto's own hand came up, but to rip at the knot on his wrist with fingers and nails. The moment he was free, he rose and walked away.

The whole room watched him go, feeling only a sliver of Pietro's disappointment. Mariotto's son Romeo, who had a better sense of timing, now raced over to hug his father in congratulations. Mari tousled the boy's dark hair, but continued to gaze after his former friend.

Confounded, Cangrande was about to call after Antony when one of Capulletto's servants appeared at the door. Antony saw him and scowled. "What the devil do you — what's the matter?" The lad's eyes were red with weeping. Antony took a step backwards. "No. No. Please tell me, no—"

The lad shook his head. "He's gone, m'lord. Gone to Heaven."

Antony released a howl that was barely human. Suddenly no one felt like reveling. They all knew what it meant. Antony's young son, so strong and thriveful, had chosen this chilly, raining night to follow his brothers.

"Oh! Poor Antony!" Gianozza buried her face in Mariotto's shoulder. Antony turned to look at her. It was as though he were looking at the life that was denied him – the wife he loved, the son he could not seem to keep. His face a grotesque masque, he left the loggia with slumped shoulders, hardly able to breathe.

Pietro followed him out into the frescoed hall, unsure what to say. When he placed a foot upon the stair, he winced again. Taking his hand out from under his cloak, he marveled that the damp on his side should be so warm.

In the light of the braziers he saw the crimson on his fingers and palm. Twitching involuntarily, he looked around him in confusion before toppling down eight stairs to the tiled landing, blood slipping from the knife wound between his ribs.

THIRTY-ONE

The ensuing fight between Mariotto and his wife was destined to become a thing of legend. Challenging her decision to ruin such a moment, Mariotto berated her thoughtlessness. Gianozza countered by berating him for discounting her love, which superseded all boundaries. She accused him of no longer loving her, challenging him for their lack of lovemaking in recent days.

Young Romeo tried to come between his feuding parents, but was whisked aside by his aunt Aurelia, who sent him off in the company of his cousin Benvolio.

Mariotto decided that discretion was the better part of valour – his wife was enjoying the spectacle they were creating, and the best way to end her enjoyment was to end the encounter. Still naked under his blanket, he stormed from the loggia, the victor's ribbon hanging around his shoulder.

Thus it was Mariotto who found Pietro's unconscious form on the stairs. Hearing his shouts for aid, the whole palace was roused to an uproar. Had there been an attack within the palace walls?

"He was clutching his side since he came back," observed Salvatore, looking uncommonly frightened. "He said a drunkard knocked him down."

Morsicato appeared from below, where he and Fracastoro had a sickroom prepared – there were always broken bones and cuts to sort out after the Foot Palio. Ashen-faced, Morsicato said, "Quickly, bring him this way."

Among the men carrying Pietro, Cangrande remained when the doors were shut. Once the cloak had gone, the doctors saw Pietro's whole side was drenched in blood. As Morsicato began cutting Pietro's clothes away to find the wound, Cangrande said, "Someone will die for this."

♦ ◊ ♦

Upstairs, more racers appeared through the loggia's open windows, all repeating the phrase that would normally tickle the Scaliger's humour. Instead they spoke to his wife, presiding in Cangrande's absence.

Don Pedro and Benedick arrived just ahead of Bailardino and Val, but after the Bonaventura clan. Jubilant, they recited the phrase of victory. As they were pressed with covers and hot wine, young Petruchio demanded, "Why all the long faces?"

They heard of Capulletto's victory, and his loss. It was sobering. Then they were told of the near-mortal injury given to the new Count of San Bonifacio. Bail bolted from the chamber, while the Bonaventura twins leapt up. "This has to be connected to father's death!"

"Yes," agreed Verde della Scala, still waiting for her husband to return. "Round up all the drunks and torture them to reveal the names of their wine shops."

"Cesco was assaulted," added Salvatore from not far away. "He's gone to question the men. He'll get the truth." Young Hortensio's answering scowl was not for the words, but the sight of the Paduan holding his sister's hand.

Not far away, Signor Benedick was unlooping the rope at his waist. "An unfortunate end to an excellent race, my lord."

Huddled under a blanket, Don Pedro lifted his steaming goblet in sober salute. "There might have been another injury tonight – Lord Nogarola's son. Quick thinking."

"It was nothing – ah, the lady." Donna Beatrice was approaching through the jostling crowd.

Flushing at his nakedness, Don Pedro accepted her congratulations and excused himself to go dress. That left Benedick standing before her, shivering under his single blanket. "I didn't win."

"I disagree. You seem to have won the Prince's approval."

"Just his?"

"Indeed? Perhaps when you've dressed, we should see if you've won anyone else's."

Benedick grinned boldly. "Why wait?"

Who started the kiss was unknowable, but they maintained it for a long time. Then she slipped her hand into his and together they departed for a place more private to continue their wordless debate.

♦   ◊   ♦

One of the men had died, one had escaped, but two of the attackers were still near the muleskinner's, breathing but immobile. Cesco had them transported to the basement of the Giurisconsulti.

The Bonaventura twins were standing outside the building, faces fierce. "Cesco, your uncle Pietro has been stabbed."

There was no visible change in Cesco's features. So how did the temperature drop around them all? "Dead."

Young Petruchio shook his head. "Not when we left. The doctors were tending him. But he's lost a lot of blood."

"I talked to him," said Cesco blankly. "He was dying right in front of me, and I never knew."

"No one knew. Not even Ser Alaghieri."

"I see." With a disturbing suddenness, he was brisk. "Detto, do you mind forgoing the interrogation?"

"What do you need?"

"Armed guards at my door, and at Ser Alaghieri's — I should say, the Count's. Hortensio, Petruchio, I entrust that to you. Detto, Antonia must be told. And then a message sent to the Moor. Address it to Maestro Cadiz in Venice, it will find him, wherever he is."

"What about…?" Detto let his voice trail off.

Cesco drew a breath. "That can wait. Go now — and go together. There is an assassin out there, and this one is no friendly Moor."

They went. Turning, Cesco reopened the cellar door. To the guards he said, "Get out." Alone, Cesco advanced on the chained prisoner to his left. To the one on his right, he said, "Watch."

It did not take much. The battered men were Paduans, that much was clear by their accent. They pleaded no knowledge at all of the attack on Ser Alaghieri. They claimed to have been hired by a woman in her middle years, lean and hawkish, with brown hair streaked with iron.

It was not a description that resonated. "Who was she? Answer me."

"I don't know!" cried the tortured man as the broken bones in his fingers shifted.

"If you were not part of the attack on Ser Alaghieri, what about your actual commission. You were supposed to kidnap me."

"Yes!"

"Where were you to take me?"

"We don't know! We were to meet someone on the road north, by Quinto. They'll be gone by now. Someone was to pay us and take you."

"To where?"

"To where the girl is!"

"Tch," said Cesco reprovingly. "You said it was a woman."

"Not her," shouted the injured man. "We were supposed to tell you — if we were captured, tell you. Your great love. She is waiting with your mother, in the stars. Come alone."

Cesco had staggered back, ashen-faced. Lightning-quick he produced his dagger and stabbed the nearer man in the shoulder, twisting the blade. "Say that again! Say that again!"

Screams prevented words. It was the uninjured prisoner who said, "Your great love! That's what she said! She was taken tonight, same time as you were meant to be!"

"By whom!" Pushing the tortured man aside, Cesco withdrew the bloody dagger and advanced on the other. "Give me a name! A name!"

♦　◊　♦

A hammering on the door of Cesco's house roused the steward Fidelio. Unaware of any danger, he opened the portal, to be greeted by a huge figure holding a snuffling bundle in his arms. "Suor Beatrice. Get her, please."

Summoned, Antonia came quickly down the stairs, fearful of some mishap during the Palio. Instead she was greeted by Andriolo, the Capulletti groom. In his arms he held a weeping child. "Her brother died tonight. She can't be in that house. My wife is distraught. Can you and Dahna...?"

"Of course!" said Antonia at once, reaching out to accept the three year-old. "O, poor thing! Come along, Giulietta. We'll bring you to Maddelena. She'll be so happy to see you."

But she hadn't climbed five stairs before the door burst open to reveal Detto and the news he carried. "Ser Alaghieri — the Count, I mean — he's been stabbed. In the street. He's at the palace. Cesco wanted you to know."

Numbed, Antonia handed the little girl off to Vito the cook while she went to dress. By the time she returned, there were armed guards outside the door. The groom Andriolo offered to escort her to the palace, and she accepted. She passed quick words with Dahna, who promised to see both little girls settled safely in Maddelena's room, then joined Detto and Andriolo in the hammering rain as they raced back towards the palace, to where her brother lay bleeding his life away.

There, pleading another errand, Detto entrusted her to Andriolo's care. Antonia hardly noticed, so focused she was on reaching her brother's side and finding out who had done this thing.

♦　　◊　　♦

Returned from running, Fra Lorenzo donned his plain robes, feeling pleased with himself. He had not dared to hope he and Fra Giovanni would win, but they had finished in the middle of the pack, very respectable for two holy men who weren't getting younger.

Hearing the news, he sighed inwardly as he imagined Donna Gianozza's diatribe. At least he was not her confessor, a blessed relief.

Though it was un-Christian of him, he could not help feeling satisfied that Ser Alaghieri had received a measure of Divine Judgment. Everyone talked of the noble knight, not knowing he had once threatened Lorenzo with blackmail. But, Lorenzo reminded himself, since then Alaghieri had faced down Bernardo Gui. He could easily have traded Lorenzo's life for his own, but did not. No members of the Inquisition had arrived in Verona to root Lorenzo out. Alaghieri had kept his word. Besides, his sister had suffered enough already. So Lorenzo forced himself to set his grudge aside and offer up a prayer for the new Count.

His body decently covered, his kirtle cinched, Lorenzo procrastinated a moment, telling himself he was allowing his feet to warm. In truth he just did not want to go to his next appointment. So when he heard sniffling, he seized the chance to investigate.

Romeo Montecchio was huddled in a corner, arms wrapped about his knees. He was clearly in the aftermath of a great cry, his breath stuttered and hiccoughing.

Lorenzo knelt. "What ails you, lad?"

Romeo wiped his face with his sleeve, leaving trails behind on the fine suede. "Nothing!"

"Only imbeciles weep over nothing, and you're far from an imbecile. It's your father and mother, yes? They quarreled?" Romeo shrugged, a gesture that the good friar genuinely despised. "A shrug is not an answer. Even in trials, we must put words to our ailments, or we are no better than beasts."

"Yes," said Romeo. "They quarreled."

"As most couples do. You don't know how blessed you are, to have parents who have not quarreled before your eyes until now.

Seven years of harmony is a blessing of two thousand five hundred and some odd days. And do you weep, when you have lived such a blessing? I would call it rank ingratitude."

"I don't want to go home."

"Ever, or tonight?"

"Tonight."

Lorenzo nodded gruffly. "Understandable. Look, I have someplace to be. Why don't you come help me secure my plants, then you can curl up in the vestry and sleep. I'll tell your aunt."

What the impulse was to bring the boy to this meeting, Lorenzo could not afterwards say. As an ally? As a shield? As a witness? Whatever the reason, Verona would have cause to regret his decision to the end of time.

♦   ◊   ♦

Cangrande arrived at the Giurisconsulti to find both men dead. Drawing Cesco quickly outside, the Scaliger said, "You didn't have to—"

"I did," retorted Cesco. "Pietro?"

"Alive for the moment. He's having difficulty breathing. Had the wound been on his other side, he'd have died at once. These men, were they behind it?"

"They knew nothing about it. I was their quarry." Unconscious of the blood on his hands, Cesco began mounting the stairs two at a time. "A woman hired them. I have her description, and where she found them." Cesco relayed the information. "She was Paduan, by her accent."

"I can't think of anyone that fits."

"Nor I," admitted Cesco.

"Does this link to the poisoning?"

"They say no." Finding his cloak, Cesco pulled it on. "And truly, would they know? They're hired swords, not master spies. You know as well as I that Petruchio's death was done by someone inside that hall. Besides, if the woman who hired them was behind the poisoning, she'd be a fool to tell them so."

"But they were Paduans?"

"Yes. Nobodies. No name, nor standing. Scum."

Cangrande was grim. "I'll set Carrara onto their trail. He'll be desperate to help, and it might be linked to the attack on him."

"It might. Excuse me, I have to clean up."

The young knight was so anxious to leave that Cangrande was suspicious. "Did you learn anything useful?"

"They *were* holding back one detail," said Cesco, exiting into the rain. "The woman who hired them said they were working for the Count of San Bonifacio."

◆   ◊   ◆

"The Count remains in the sick-room, Suora," said Tullio d'Isola. "They deem it too dangerous to move him."

Antonia was admitted at once. There he was, his skin the colour of old parchment. Taking her brother's hand, she pressed her fingers against the wrist to feel the thready flutter of a man clinging to life. Lifting the blanket, she gazed at the bandages, freshly changed. There was no hint of blood. Was that because he had lost too much even to bleed? Or had they gotten to him in time?

"We burned the wound, then sewed it closed," explained Morsicato, lowering the blanket again.

"Will he live?"

Morsicato opened his mouth, then closed it, chewing on his beard. Fracastoro answered. "He has a chance. It was a little wound, made with a thin blade. His cloak and doublet blunted the blow. Had it been even half an inch deeper, he would not be with us now. So much damage from so little a thing," marveled the physician.

Collapsing onto a stool, Antonia took up a vigil on Pietro's left side, while Morsicato sat on the right. "I remember — when Cesco was poisoned, we kept rubbing his feet and hands to keep the blood flowing. Would that help?"

"It wouldn't hurt." She noted Fracastoro did not say it would help.

Jacopo entered, dripping and naked. She hugged him, then returned to rubbing Pietro's arm. As he dressed, Poco listened as the two doctors described the injury. "But the man problem is he lost so much blood. It all soaked into his clothes, and in the rain he never noticed."

"Can I give him my blood to replace his?" asked Antonia. "The Bible mentions it. And Ovid writes that Medea transferred blood to Jason's father to save his life."

"Do you have werewolf entrails?" asked Morsicato harshly.

"I'll find some," snapped Antonia.

The doctor ran his hands over his face, forking his beard again. "Sorry, sorry…"

Fracastoro filled the awkward gap. "Even if it could be done, blood transferred often does more harm than good. We don't know the properties of blood, or how to transfer it. They have tried making men drink blood to replace the quantities they've lost, but it has never helped."

"Perhaps it would make him a Greek *mormo*," said Poco with a grim attempt at levity. "If not living, then not dead."

"You're not amusing," snarled Morsicato.

"I'm not amused," replied Poco, pulling up a stool. "Can we not replace his blood somehow?"

Morsicato slapped his hand onto his knee. "Do you think we haven't discussed it? There's a Paduan — what was his name, Aventino? I can't think."

"Pietro d'Abano."

"Yes. Twenty years ago he did a study of blood transferral, and the use of cups and leeches."

"Well, where is he?" asked Poco urgently. "Have Carrara send for him!"

"He's dead," said Fracastoro. "Killed almost fifteen years ago by the Inquisition."

"For studying medicine?"

Morsicato's voice was hard. "For denying the existence of God."

♦　◊　♦

Cesco couldn't risk his own stable, his own house — too many eyes, too many questions. *Come alone.* That part resonated loudly. So he did not fetch Abastor for this ride. Fortunately after the morning's Palio there were stables full of swift mounts. He chose one, made sure of his arms, and went.

Leaving the city unseen was impossible. Men were hunting for Pietro's attacker, and more men were hunting the fugitive Aiello — Cesco guessed that from discussion of the 'missing Scot'. Something must have happened to Montagu.

It didn't matter. Only one thing mattered.

Lia is in Verona.

In the end he allowed himself to be seen. Identifying himself, he told the guards at the Ponte Pietra gate that he was on a mission for the Greyhound. Which was true. Turning his stolen horse towards Quinto, he raced north under the pelting rain, his mind blazing so hot it blistered.

Lia. Was this her doing? How would she have known about his mother? Had Detto told her that? What else had he told her? Who else had she been in contact with?

She wants to see you. Tonight, after the race. She's arranged a place. San Zeno's.

Lia had tried to murder his father — her father — had hated them all without knowing the truth. How much more must she hate them now? Had she been the drunkard who stabbed Nuncle Pietro in the street? She had played at being a man before.

But then who was the woman who hired the kidnappers? Killing them had been a risk. But had they lived, they would have told Cangrande and the others about the threat. His one true love.

Above it all, that one thought repeated over and over. *My one true love. How she must hate me, to do all this.*

The argumentative part of his mind reminded him that Lia might not be behind this. The obvious name was Mastino. He could have known where Fuchs hid the body, and been alerted when it was moved. He definitely knew about Lia. How he had relished telling them the truth of her birth, of their relationship. Did he have her now, as bait to lure Cesco to his death?

No. Lia was many things, but never helpless. She would not allow herself to be used in this way. Instead she had used Detto to send a message. San Zeno's. Not the church, but his original baptistery. With Donna Maria, in the stars.

She says hating makes it easier.

She was right. Cesco had just chosen other things to hate.

Detto arrived at just the wrong moment. Tiberio had returned home from the foot race to find his wife missing. Worse, the girl's father and brother were with him. In a rage, they accused Detto of helping the Scaliger spirit her away. Tiberio had his men clap Detto's arms and would not listen when Detto shouted his innocence. That was when Adamo started hitting him.

Manhandled, Detto said nothing about San Zeno. He could give Cesco and Lia that, at least.

Mariotto returned home, helpless and angry. Still covered in Pietro's blood, he didn't know where else to go. Yet he had no desire to face his wife. For the first time in fourteen years he was regretting his marriage. Always he had excused her excesses, made concession after concession to her whims and fears, her passions and her unhealthy need for attention. Tonight was like the breaking of a dam. Pent up resentments flooded through him. A thousand petty annoyances cascaded over his heart, hardening it towards the woman he had loved nearly half his life.

How could she have been so selfish? So stupid? *I could have had my friend back!*

And how selfish was he, thinking of his own loss when Pietro was lying close to death. When Antony had lost his son! *I should be there, comforting him...*

"Lord?"

Startled, Mari whirled about, hand dropping to his sword. "Who's there?"

A figure came forward. He was covered in a horse-blanket, but Mariotto knew that balding head with the small ears. "Benjamin! We thought you dead! Come, let's get you warm."

"You won't tell anyone I'm here? Not even the Capitano? If Aiello learns I'm alive—"

"I won't tell," promised Mariotto, glad to have someone he could actually help. Starting for his door, he halted suddenly. "Not here. My wife – is not discreet. We'll find you a place to recover, and then I'll send you home."

♦   ◊   ♦

In the palace, Pietro stirred, only to be dosed with the syrup of poppies and sent back into blissful oblivion.

If Antony Capulletto could have availed himself of the same, he would have welcomed it gladly. Hearing of Pietro's plight, he sent a lad with a note to ask after his friend. The lad was Pietro's own nephew, one of Poco's little bastards. Little Piero. A boy Antony had taken in, thinking to give his first son a playmate. But that son had died, and the next. And now Gianni. He could raise other men's sons. Just not his own.

He howled, then tried to sleep, then howled again. As glad as he was that his little Giulietta was not here to see him so unmanned, he missed her badly. It was like a physical need, to wrap her in his arms. In her place, he reached out to clutch his wife, red-eyed but stoic in her grief. The nurse Angelica was in utter hysterics, raising such a lamentation that Antony had her husband take her to the stables to mourn. He regretted it the moment she was gone, and called her back, and they wept together.

He'd sent for Fra Lorenzo, but was told the brother was out of the cloister at the moment, having disappeared after the footrace. Another brother came in his place to administer what succor he could.

When the comment was made that his wife was young and they might yet be blessed, Antony snapped. "What, and go through this again! Three times! Three times blessed, and three thousand times cursed! No – no more! I have my daughter. She is all the heir I require!"

Unable to remain in the house any longer, Antony crossed to the building he used as an office on the far side of the courtyard. Opening the door, he was startled by movement. He wasn't wearing a sword, but his hand dropped to his knife. "How now! Who's there?"

Aiello the Scot came forward, dressed in a blanket and a spare shirt Antony kept here. "Lord Capulletto, you must help me. I didn't – I didn't do it. I didn't touch him, I swear it!"

Stepping sideways, Antony put the table between them. "You hurt my son?"

"What? No – no, my lord, I mean Montagu!" Swiftly Aiello explained.

"If you did nothing, why did you run?"

"Because of how it looks! But I swear on my father's grave that I did nothing to harm a hair on his head. He must have cut the cord himself, then jumped so the blame would fall on me."

"Just like a Montecchio," said Antony reflexively. Then he shook his head. "I'll give you clothes and some silver, but then you must go. I am in no mood for intrigues."

Aiello wanted to argue, but the threat in Antony's eyes kept him silent. A few minutes later, dressed and armed with a small bag of silver, he hitched himself over the wall into the garden that backed up to the Capulletto house.

Leaving Antony alone with his grief.

♦ ◊ ♦

Quinto was a tiny hamlet, named for the simple fact that it was five Roman miles to the north of Verona. The kidnappers were supposed to bring him here, to the fork in the road a mile south of it. They had been told Quinto, but that was not the true destination. Cesco angled his horse instead to the right, towards Santa Maria in Stelle.

The village seemed deserted – it was night, and the rain was unrelenting. Up the steep incline, he arrived at the church, its back to the shadowy hills. There was no light within, nor without. If not for the rain, there would have been no sound.

Dismounting and throwing his saddlebag over his shoulder, Cesco tied his mount to a tree. Already his fingers in the gloves were numb. Kneeling low, he felt his way across the ground until he found the entrance to the hypogeum. It was sealed shut, the heavy stone slab bolted in place with new iron. Cesco had expected as much. There was another entrance he was meant to use.

Approaching the church, he suddenly wished he had a sticky-chew. He hadn't taken one before either race today, believing he did not need support. And he hadn't, for the races. But it had been a mistake not to carry them tonight. He needed clarity, and emotional distance. Especially now.

Word would have reached Cangrande, he would know Cesco had lied, that the prisoners had said more than he'd revealed. Hunting parties would be racing out. But in this weather there was no hope of them tracing his path. He was alone – which is how he was told to come.

Pushing the doors wide, Cesco entered the still church. There was a single candle lit just for him. It stood above a hole bored into the church floor. He recalled looking up from below, seeing that perfectly round gap reaching upwards in the room with all the frescoes. It had been surrounded by the painted scrolls. The Word of God.

A trail of dampness led into the church. Someone had been here recently, lighting the candle for him. Someone from out in the rain.

Following the path set for him, Cesco knelt beside the candle. He didn't bother looking into the shadows – if he was observed, there was nothing for it. Unlike the foot race, he had to run the whole course.

A sound caught his ear. Weeping. A woman. It came from somewhere far below. Could it be that Lia was a prisoner? Or was that what he was meant to think? He could shout. But that might alert someone below. Better to act in silence.

Two crossed metal strips barred passage into the hole. Cesco drew his sword and began levering them up. They were not strong, and once the bolts came loose he was able to bend them back, out of his way.

He was not a foole. Even with his mind whirling, he had paused in the stable long enough to grab what he would need. Producing a rope from the saddlebag, he looped it around the altar, then tied one end around his sword, which he then lowered into the darkness. He measured each length against his forearms, wrist to wrist. A man was about as tall as his armspan. The sword touched the tiles between the fourth and fifth length. Thus the drop was less than five times his own height. Twenty-five feet or so.

He lowered the saddlebags the same way, using the other end of the rope, which was now anchored below by two heavy objects. He noticed the saddlebags splashed as they touched down. The water was high in the ancient baptistery. So much for the torch he was going to drop down there. He would have to descend blind.

A larger man could not have done it. Detto could not have done it. But even though he had gained height this year, Cesco had grown no broader. Thin as a whip and just as lithe, he had only to bunch his shoulders as he slipped feet-first into the circular hole. He grabbed the two ropes, side by side, and lowered himself down. Before he vanished below, he reached out and snuffed the candle. No sense helping anyone watching.

It was tight, and for a moment he feared getting stuck – his cloak was clinging to the prickly bricks around him. But almost at once his feet felt open air and he let himself slip a little down the rope until his head was clear of the narrow tube. He breathed in the close air, and tasted the water before he felt it. Lowering himself, he found it was up to his knees.

It was pitch black, and he worried as he fumbled at the saddlebags that water had ruined his torch. But he'd packed it well against the rain, and unwrapping the outer cloth revealed the sticky pitch that would still burn well enough. He pressed it against the wall with his forearm while his fingers found the flints and sparked it to life.

The sobbing choked off at the first hint of light. "Who is there?" The wary voice was distant, echoey, hard to distinguish.

"Cesco," he said.

"Cesco? Cesco! I'm here! I'm here!"

There was no mistaking the fear. Just as there was no mistaking the voice. But Cesco had to see for himself. Flickering shadows danced as he splashed through the door, following the voice down the narrow tunnel to his left, the source of the water that was rising so high now. He had to bend double, the torch just above the water, its flames licking the curved rock that brushed his head.

She was chained on her knees, with a collar around her throat. The water was at her neck, and rising. Her face was terrified, bruised, and thin.

It was not Lia.

It was Buthayna.

THIRTY-TWO

There was no time to understand. She was clutching at him with her manacled hands, and he had to pull away lest she douse the torch. "Shh, shh," he repeated. "Listen – listen! Calm yourself. I'll get you out, but we need this light. Now let me think."

Buthayna quietened at once, and Cesco closed his eyes. Someone had stopped the flow out of the hypogeum, causing the water to rise. This was the work of not hours but days of preparation. It would be a long time to find the blockage – fool that he was, he hadn't looked for where the water went last time he was here. He'd only traced it to its source.

It was a place to start. "Listen, my Arabia, I need you to be calm. You must hold the light. I have to dive and slow the water from rising. I need you to keep the light from going out. Can you do that?" Shivering, she nodded.

How fast did this water run? Eighty litres a minute, the priest had said. Faster now, probably. The rain was making the water rise swiftly, something his enemy could not have counted on. Whoever his enemy was...

Later. Focus. Passing her the torch, he removed his cloak from his shoulders and, after filling his lungs with air, plunged into the water. At once his fingers found the stone channel and he traced it forward, past her. When he ran out of air, he put his foot in the trough and rose. "Almost," he said, hoping to reassure her, then submerged again.

This time he found it, the little gap in the floor where the ancient pipe provided the water nymphs with the source of their power. Taking his sodden cloak, he jammed it into the pipe's mouth, tucking the corners to wedge it deeply.

Rising, he returned to her. "That will stop the water." It was only half true — it would slow the rise. But there might be another pipe further along the tunnel, or his cloak might not be as waterproof as he hoped.

But the statement had the desired effect, the girl was calmer. He reached out to hold her for a moment, kissing her cheek. But when her mouth sought his, he pulled the torch from her grip and retreated. "I need my sword to get you free. I'll be back in no time at all. Be brave, Buthayna."

He left her there while he returned to the teaching chamber for his sword and bag.

Which were both gone.

♦   ◊   ♦

Adamo slapped Detto's face again. "Where is she?"

"I don't know!" repeated Detto through gritted teeth, straining against the ropes about his wrists. "If I knew, why did I come here to find her?"

That checked him, and Detto used the respite to roll his tongue around his mouth, exploring. A tooth was loose. "Bastard."

"We're not the bastards!" shouted Adamo, hitting Detto again.

One eye closing, Detto squinted up. "Do you really want to be caught beating the son of Bailardino Nogarola?"

"He's right," said old Bramo Tiberio. "About all of it. He wouldn't be here if he knew where she was." Pushing Adamo aside, the huge man knelt in front of his captive. "But he probably knows where his cousin is. Find the Greyhound's heir, find my wife." The man leaned close. His breath was atrocious. "Where is he, Ser Bailardetto? Where is the bastard?"

Detto's honest answer would not help him. "I left him at the Giurisconsulti. Ser Alaghieri was attacked tonight, and Cesco is interrogating two captured men."

"Then why were you here?"

"To tell Donna Tiberio—" Detto broke off.

"Tell her what?"

"Tell her that Cesco could not keep their appointment."

Adamo punched a wall in a fury, and old Rienzi swore repeatedly. Only Tiberio remained calm. "So she's gone to meet him, not knowing he's abandoned her again. How very like him. But let me tell you this, young man. If my wife comes to any mischief, I will kill him, and you, with my bare hands."

Seeing the power in those hands, Detto believed it. Still he said nothing of San Zeno.

♦   ◊   ♦

Benedick and Beatrice laughed with joy in a dark corner of the Scaliger's palace. The room was set aside for visiting dignitaries, but as it contained no luggage or waiting servants, they had invaded it, Beatrice leading Benedick by the hand. For once their tongues were not shaping insults, being otherwise occupied. Indeed, there was nothing between them now, not even the sheets of the bed as they slipped into it, joyful, scared, excited, and hopeful all at once. The candle remained lit, and she took the time to marvel at his hair. "I thought you wore a wig, or coloured it."

"Peace," said Benedick, pressing his mouth to hers once more.

♦   ◊   ♦

The newly-minted Count awoke terrified. He was back in the sweltering room full of sawed limbs and maggots. The sweet stink of herbs burning, the bitter taste in his mouth, the feel of sweat on his naked skin, it all conspired to transport him back fourteen years to his injury in the First Battle of Vicenza.

He sat up – or tried to. Barely had his stomach muscles clenched than he was gasping in pain. *O God! O God, what has happened?*

Hands were on him immediately, and voices he knew, but distant. Something sweet and sticky was poured into his mouth and he spat it out. *Poison! They're poisoning me!*

"Dammit! He's torn his stitches! Get his sister, someone!"

"Pietro? Pietro. It's Antonia. Shhh. Relax. Relax. You're going to get through this."

Pietro opened his eyes against the pain. It was like swimming up from the bottom of a river that was trying to sweep him away. "'Tonia?"

"Yes! Pietro, yes, it's me! Shhh. You're hurt, but they're helping you. You have to drink this. Please, drink this!"

He was impossibly thirsty, but could only take a shallow sip. "What—I—"

He drifted away again, only to find himself back on that balcony, with a hundred centaurs battling below. This time, Cesco didn't come. Pietro was alone, watching the struggle from on high, through a haze of smoke that slowly became wafting clouds. His head was impossibly light, and for the first time he could remember he was free of care…

♦   ◊   ♦

Cesco cursed. He'd left the sword and saddlebags tied to the two ends of the rope as an anchor. Had he been thinking at all, he'd have seen how easy it would be for the person above to haul them up. Not only was he without tools, he was trapped.

Though it wasted time, he stepped to just below the hole in the ceiling and raised his voice. "I don't suppose you want to give me a name! Or perhaps a cause?"

Not expecting an answer, he was not disappointed when none came. Instead he retraced his steps to the low tunnel and Buthayna. He still had the dagger at his waist. It would have to do.

"The water is rising," she said plaintively, keeping her chin above the waterline.

"You'll be free before it gets too high," he assured her, waggling the dagger. "I need you to hold the torch again." Seeing her frightened eyes, he switched to Arabic. "Smile, love. 'Dead yesterdays and unborn tomorrows, why fret about it if today be sweet?' Besides, you're certainly used to me going down."

She was too scared to laugh. He pressed her arm as he put the torch in her manacled hands, then dove. The first course was to trace the chain holding her neck in place. Though bound, her hands were not anchored. Once her neck was free, she could move.

The links ended in a metal plate, with massive bolts driven into the ancient stones. He tried to find purchase for his dagger, but there was no gap anywhere in which to start work. He tried digging at the stone itself, but the Romans had known better than to use a soft stone here, where it would erode.

He came up for air, shaking his head to clear it. The water droplets hissed as they struck the torch. Buthayna whimpered. "Sorry. Here, let me get behind you. You're used to that too." He grinned.

She did not. "You cannot save me. Say so."

"I just want to look at the collar. As someone was telling me earlier this evening, I make things too hard. It might be simpler this way."

It wasn't, but it was the best chance she had. He started prising the two metal halves apart with the tip of his dagger. It was steady work, but only engaged part of his mind. The other part was beginning to grapple with Lia's absence.

It could still be Lia. She could be mocking me, using the woman I now profess to love to show my hypocrisy, my faithlessness.

But other pieces were coming together. The attack on Detto – Lia could not have arranged that. She had been with Nuncle Pietro just before. *Unless she had the help of her husband, father, and brother...* Tracing that line of thinking to its end, he rejected it. If Adamo had a plan, he would not be so impulsive as to attack Cesco in the street. If Rienzi wanted to ruin Cangrande, why attack Detto? And if Tiberio had married the girl, he'd want her affair with Cesco to remain secret, or else be mocked for taking another man's leavings.

No, they had cause to hate, but no cause for this. Or to attack Detto. Or cut the goose free to injure Benedick. Or attack Carrara. Or disgrace Rupert...

Or stab Pietro.

Taken together for the first time, it was a breathtaking swath of destruction. Yet none of which had borne fruit. Not even the poisoning of Petruchio, which had missed its intended target. Which begged the question, was the person behind these deeds incompetent? Or were the failures by design?

Whoever it was, they had known about this place. About Cesco's mother. About Buthayna – but not Lia. That excused Mastino. *Of these crimes,* he reminded himself. The long game remained.

But Lia was not here. Even as his numbed hands worked the dagger into the metal collar, creating the first gap, Cesco felt a horrible relief to realize Lia was safe, free, not a part of whatever plots were swirling around him. He doubted he could be so calm were it her neck in this metal band, her chin just touching the still-rising water. He would be frantic, tearing at the metal with his nails and teeth. And Lia would have to calm him by mocking him, as she always did. *But Lia is not here. She is safe.*

His relief did nothing to dull the accusing ache growing within him. When the villain had said his true love, Cesco had never even thought of Buthayna.

◆ ◇ ◆

"You talked to her tonight," accused Tiberio. "The servants told me she had three visitors. You, and two cloaked men. Was one of them the heir?"

"No," said Detto. "I came before the race, and ever since we've been together. He did not even know she was in the city."

"Then how did they have an appointment?" demanded Adamo, certain he had caught Detto in a lie.

"I told him. During the race, I told him..." Again Detto trailed off.

Tiberio finished his sentence for him. "...told him she wanted to see him. So it was her notion, not his. Who were the other men?"

"I have no idea."

"And you don't know where they were to meet?"

"No," said Detto again, too forcefully.

Tiberio shook his head. "You're a poor liar, lad."

◆   ◊   ◆

In the Basilica San Zeno, lights burned. The lay brothers were all abed, but a few monks wandered the cloister, observing the hours and the rain. One was a visiting brother, come to tend the garden in the storm. He had brought Lord Montecchio's heir with him, and the lad worked hard, no doubt to distract himself from the events of the evening. That news had spread like a flood. Little wonder the boy was red-eyed and sullen.

No one objected when, after a half-hour's labour, Fra Lorenzo took the boy to shelter in the main body of the church. Though there were a few knowing looks. *Well,* they thought privately, *if the Pope himself had affixed a price to it...*

Inside, Lorenzo closed the door and, instructing Romeo to wait, made his way to the confessionals. "My dear? Has he come?"

There was a momentary pause. "No."

Lorenzo sighed. "As I told you when I arrived, Ser Alaghieri has been injured this night. Even a man so wild will feel the filial pull to his foster-father."

"Francesco will come," said Lia through the confessional door. "I know it."

"He cannot see you," warned Lorenzo.

"Fra Lorenzo," called Romeo from the far side of the great basilica. "To whom are you talking?"

"A penitent," answered Lorenzo, before confiding in the girl. "The son and heir of Lord Montecchio. He's here due to a family quarrel."

"Cesco's little *protégé*," said Lia.

"I'll fix him a bed in the vestry and return."

"Why not let him stay? We can console each other while we wait."

And, foole that he was, Lorenzo agreed.

◆   ◊   ◆

Cesco's hand slipped and the dagger skidded across Buthayna's shoulder, causing her to gasp and cry out. The torch rose, striking the ceiling, sending sparks everywhere, before it dipped. It hissed as it started to cross the waterline, and she quickly raised it again to preserve it. "I'm sorry, I'm sorry!"

"It's for me to be sorry," he answered in a flatter voice than he intended. "You've been dragged here to torture me. Seems we should have been more discreet. Tch. This poor dagger. I'm afraid it will never be useful again. But I've almost gotten these two pieces to separate." It wasn't true, he had only managed to create the tiniest of gaps.

"The water is still rising." It was lapping her chin now, and his hands were below the surface as he worked.

"I think our foe got more than he bargained for in this. He could not have anticipated the rain." She whimpered, and he clicked his tongue. "No, I mean that's good. He meant for me to get here and have enough time to save you. If the water's rising faster than he intended, he'll have to do something to help us both survive." Cesco did not mention the other possibility, that their intended slow death would merely be hastened. It was best to offer hope. "I don't suppose you know who abducted you?"

"Men. Two men. I didn't know them. They said they had a message from you."

"For me, morelike. I am sorry, Buthayna, that you are in this mess because there are people who bear me ill." He stopped talking for a time as he worked at the gap. "They didn't mention a woman, did they?"

"A woman?"

"I was attacked tonight as well. They were to bring me here and, I suppose, chain me up as well. They said they were hired by a Paduan woman in her middle years. Ah well. So many women despise me, it was only a matter of time…"

Still she said nothing. Lia would at least have laughed.

♦　◊　♦

"You know Cesco?" Romeo sounded dubious.

"I know how highly he speaks of you," answered Lia through the confessional wall. "Once he took me to see your house. He told me about the Death Door, and the brave young fellow who dared to open it and admit a daemon."

Romeo was surprised. "You *do* know him."

"Yes. He's coming here to meet me. How much happier will

he be to find you here as well."

Romeo looked to Fra Lorenzo for confirmation. "Cesco's coming here?"

The friar temporized. "He meant to, but it is a busy night." Spoken to Romeo, the words were meant for the woman within the wooden walls.

Romeo returned to Lia. "When did you last see him?"

"Several months now."

"So you haven't heard about the hunt we had?"

"Tell me," said Lia, trying to be bright in spite of her fear.

Romeo launched into a detailed description of the day, starting at the river and ending in their successful eluding of their hunters. He had to circle back several times as he recalled little bits of jest or poetry or song, all of which he shared. He only paused when he heard a snuffling sound. "Are you crying?"

"I don't mean to," came the answer through the door. "I just missed these stories. Exciting tales of adventure."

"Adventurous tales of excitement," answered Romeo. "Like a playful dog."

"Tails of excitement," laughed Lia through her tears. "He told me you were good with words."

"I am a weakish speller," admitted Romeo.

"Nobody's perfect."

"Fra Lorenzo is! Cesco said so."

"No—" said Lorenzo quickly.

"He did," insisted Romeo. "He said you trained to be perfect, just like your father. How can you train to be perfect? May I train, too?"

"You wouldn't want to. And besides, I failed. I am far from perfect."

"But your father was perfect. Cesco said it."

"Prince Francesco says lots of things. And none of them are to be heeded."

At once Lorenzo knew he had erred. Not only had the boy's face become mulish, but the silence from the confessional was deafening. If he had not protested so much, the import of his words might have gone unnoticed. As ever, his fear had trapped him.

"Romeo," said Lia, "I think I understand what the good brother means when he speaks of his father. He was not perfect, as you and I know the word. It was his title. Was it not, Fra Lorenzo?"

There it was. She knew. But, damned as she was by her own secret, she could not reveal his. And the boy was too young to understand.

"That's correct," said Lorenzo, before clarifying for the boy. "Cesco was making a joke, that's all. My father was a city prefect – it's a Latin word for officer or magistrate. That's all. He was making a joke. Like your wordplay."

Thinking he understood, Romeo subsided, returning his attentions to the lady inside the wooden box. "You didn't tell me your name."

"I'm Rosalia," came the answer, surprisingly truthful. "It's Latin. It means Rose."

"So you're Cesco's Rose." Romeo said it in all innocence. And yet it was enough to send the lady into a fresh bout of quiet tears.

Romeo had thought he was being kind. Self-judging as ever, he began welling up. He hated his own failings far more than those of others, and held himself accountable.

His father always told him, 'It's not the spill, it's the cleaning up after.' Romeo recalled the hugs he always got from his mother when he cried at home. Hugging made the sadness better, because it was shared. It had been awful to cry and not be hugged at the palace. A crying person needed a hug! And since both Rosalia and Romeo were crying—

Before anyone could stop him, Romeo had thrown open the confessional door and held out his arms. The friar's shout of "Romeo!" and the lady's gasp halted him. In the light from the candles nearby he could see her state, even through the muffling cloak. "You're pregnant!"

"Romeo, come away." Lorenzo closed the door quickly.

"Why?"

"Because it's a secret," sighed Lia. "My husband knows, but we don't want Cesco to find out."

"Is it a surprise?"

"More like unwelcome news," said Lorenzo. "Come now, Romeo. Why don't I set you up with a blanket in the vestry. I promise, if Cesco comes, I'll wake you."

It was a promise Lorenzo never meant to keep. Nor would he have to. Even Lia sensed it now. Cesco was not coming.

✦   ◊   ✦

The water was now at Buthayna's lips, and Cesco had only succeeded in creating a gap of perhaps half an inch in the two joins of the metal collar. The bolts were two inches long, so he was just a quarter of the way towards freeing her. "The rest will go faster," he assured her. "I can almost turn the blade sideways, and then I'll be able to lever it open."

Hands numb from the water, back aching from being hunched over, Cesco couldn't see. Smoke from the torch had nowhere to go but his eyes, which were watering. *Just what we need, more water.*

Another source of water was her tears. She was terrified, and rightly so. But she had suffered so horribly in the last years, she knew how to weep in silence. Cesco was grateful for that, at least. If she were rocking or shaking, his hand would slip again, and then…

There was a crack, and Cesco swore loudly. The blade of the dagger had snapped near the grip, rendering the implement all but useless. Buthayna turned and saw the broken weapon in his hand and closed her eyes. "Go, then. It is done. There is no way."

"Of course there's a way," snapped Cesco. "I can prise up a stone, or maybe…" He looked about them, his mind fogged and unbalanced. *I need a wafer.* That disturbed him, but he set it aside. What he truly needed was another tool. But there was none to be had. And the water continued to rise.

♦   ◊   ♦

"I hope you remembered to bolt the door."

"Whoops," said Benedick, and slipped at once out of the bed to do so. "Lucky."

"Twice lucky." There was a smile in her eyes, but an anxiousness as well as he slid into the bed beside her.

"I hope you are all right, Donna Beatrice."

"I most certainly am not," she answered, rolling onto her side to look at him. "Didn't you hear my muffled shouts for help?"

He laughed, then grew serious as his finger traced the line of her hip. "Lady — I cannot offer much…"

"A fair start."

"…and my name isn't much yet…"

"Lowering my expectations, good."

Benedick ran a distracted hand through his hair. "For God's sake, will you let me finish?"

"I thought you had finished. If you start this badly, you'll never make your purchase this way."

Benedick frowned. "Did I say…?"

"You didn't, and at the rate you're going you'll never get there. I'm helping."

Benedick's laughter was slightly tinged with scorn. "I'm sorry I don't live up to your expectations. I'm not as clever as these Scaligeri."

Beatrice snuggled close. "Comparisons are odious. Besides, I wouldn't like a man who is too clever. However could I maintain my dominance?"

"You'll run circles around any man," said Benedick.

"If he's lucky," said Beatrice.

"He'd be lucky to link your name to his."

"How so?"

Benedick frowned. "I just meant, you'll ennoble any husband you take."

"It will have to be by the nobility of my character," said Beatrice.

"But you have such a noble chest," he teased.

She laughed. "It's not much of a secret, I'm afraid. My mother was unwed. There was a man she loved, but something happened before they could marry – I think he died, but I never knew for certain. Anyway, I was born in secret and my grandfather sent us both away in shame."

"I see. And now?"

"My mother's brother inherited the estate in Sicily a few years ago. He's been trying to bring her home ever since. But mother refused. She had her pride, you see. It was only just now, when my mother finally succumbed to illness, that I agreed. There is nothing left for me in Italy."

"Who is this uncle, a famous lord?"

"Signor Leonato? No, he's a minor land-holder in Sicily – though I guess the king likes him. I've met him several times."

"The King of Aragon?"

She poked him with a finger. "My uncle! He came to visit us, begging mother to return home. But she always refused. Yet I should like to see Messina. It feels like home." She smiled at him. "That's my story."

"You're truly not noble?"

Beatrice's lips wound together in a tight smile. "In every way but birth, I assure you, I'm a proper young lady," laughed the naked woman.

"So I've noticed," said Benedick, smiling back. But his eyes were distant. "Well – it's getting late. You'll be missed."

Beatrice inched closer, angling for another kiss. "I won't tell if you won't."

"I'll never tell," said Benedick, leaning to kiss her on the cheek. "But I think I should get you back. We don't want to start any rumours."

Clear-eyed, she looked at him. "There won't be any rumours if you ask me the question you meant to."

Benedick blinked. "What question is that?"

Beatrice stared at him for a long moment. At last she said, "Nothing. Apparently you aren't as curious as I took you for."

"I'm as curious as the next man," said Benedick with a defensive laugh.

"Then perhaps I should wait for him," said Beatrice.

"Perhaps I should leave you to do it."

"Perhaps you should. Lord knows, I'd hate to stain your name. Mine, as you've heard, can bear it."

"Fine," said Benedick, playing the injured party. "But mark me, lady – you'll never find a husband with that temper of yours."

"Who said anything about a husband? Certainly not you!"

"Definitely not me," agreed Benedick, hauling on his clothes at speed. "Farewell, Donna Beatrice!"

"Go with God, Signor Benedick!"

He unbolted the door, poked his head out, then slammed it shut behind him, leaving Beatrice feeling naked indeed.

◆   ◊   ◆

Fra Lorenzo stayed with Romeo to be sure the boy went to sleep. He had not cried again – the distraction of Lia had worked, insofar as the lad was no longer fretting about his parents. That it had opened a new danger – well, it was too late to be helped now. Only contained. "Romeo, we must keep Rosalia's secret."

"I won't tattle," said Romeo, a little indignantly. "I'm not Benvolio."

"Of course you're not. But I wonder – do you understand the importance of secrets? Secrets are precious to the ones to whom they belong. They are shared out of love. Tonight you discovered a secret that was not meant for you. There's no danger, and you are not in any trouble. But Cesco will not be happy if he finds out Rosalia is with child."

"Because she's married to someone else, and the child will be his, not Cesco's." Romeo had the understanding of youth, helped by a lifetime of poetry at his mother's knee.

"Yes, the child will be her husband's," agreed Lorenzo, grateful he did not have to lie outright. "But if Prince Francesco learns of the child, he will be sad."

"So Cesco loves Rosalia."

"I'm afraid he does."

Another boy might have pointed out that Cesco was already married, and so was Rosalia. But in Romeo's world there was nothing odd about being in love with one person and then finding true love in another. That's where most real love happened, he knew. His mother's poems said so.

Content with such an orderly world, Romeo fell asleep. Lorenzo lingered, again procrastinating. But at last he mustered his courage and ventured back into the main basilica.

If he'd been hoping to find the girl deep in talk with the prince, he was disappointed. Nor had she fled into the night. She remained, quiet and patient, seated on a small pillow on the confessional bench, the door closed. "Hello daughter."

"I've enough fathers, thank you," said Lia. Then her voice became amused. "Prefect?"

"Yes," blustered Lorenzo at once. "Of a small town – near Genoa, actually. They love their Roman influences, the Genoese—"

"Fra Lorenzo, relax, I beg of you. I am in no state to spread anyone's secrets. That being the case, if you would care to unburden yourself of yours, I shall be happy to listen. I can do you no harm. The one person I might tell already knows, it seems. If it will ease your mind, I am here. I do not seem to be waiting for anything else."

It was not her sadness that moved him to do it. Rather, it was his own. He had never willingly revealed his past, not even in confession. But then, his father's last act before they parted had been to absolve Lorenzo. A final consolation.

To his surprise, he began to speak.

♦   ◊   ♦

Cesco left Buthayna with the torch. It was foolish, as it made his work harder, but it was the only comfort he could offer. He owed her that.

First he sought for a bit of metal around the portal he had come through on his sanctioned visit here. He wasted little time on that, though. Instead he tried to discover the blockage preventing the water from draining. If he could shift it, the water would pour out and save her. Standing utterly still, he felt for movement, any at all. But there was none. The blockage was truly complete. As it would have to be, for the level to be rising this way.

Growing frantic, Cesco returned to the Teaching Room and called upwards. "The rain is causing the water to rise too fast! Whatever your mistress had in mind, she did not intend us to die so swiftly! Throw down my sword, that I might free her from her bonds!

That way we'll drown together!"

Silence. He hoped he had at least offered his guardian amusement. Returning to Buthayna, he hunched down at her side, taking the torch as he uttered the hardest words he'd ever spoken. "I don't know what to do."

"It's alright." She was calm now, holding her head back. It was almost covered with water. "You tried."

"I wish it were me chained here."

"I don't. I'm glad you're here. It allows me to say I love you one last time."

His voice was constricted. "Don't."

"I love you, my dancer. *Hayet albi enta.* You are the life of my heart."

"Hush, Arabia. Save your breath."

"For what?" she asked as the water finally covered her face. It was the thinnest layer, but it sent water up her nose and she began to sputter.

Cesco quickly leaned down and pressed his mouth to hers, putting air into her lungs with a kiss.

♦   ◊   ♦

"It begins with a name. *Le Bon Guilhem.* That was what they called him. Handsome, bright, and good — at least that's what was said of him. He was the son of Pierre Authié, a man we now call heretic. Pierre was the head of a family which was a major force in the city of Ax in the Sebartès. It is odd, in fact, that the prince of Aragon should be here. The Authié family became famous in their defence of the Count of Foix, who was a vassal of both Aragon and France. While he was forced to submit to France in the end, the Authiés preserved his lands and title. Naturally their reputation flourished. But, like most who excel through innovation, they were unorthodox. The family had long been a member of the heretic sect called Albigensians, or Cathars.

"I imagine you've heard of the Cathars. Few, however, understand them. They believe Christ was not born of woman, but appeared like Diana, fully formed, the Word of God made flesh. They are very literal in their interpretation of texts, and so eschew transubstantiation, as that would mean the flesh and blood of Christ would be digested by men's bowels. They admit to only one sacrament, that of the *Consolamentum*, the final blessing before death that absolves all sin. If a man dies without the *Consolamentum*, his soul is reborn into a new body, and will continue this cycle until he receives this final blessing. It is for this reason that Cathars believe that the taking of any life, man or animal, is wrong. They may be cutting off a soul in search of grace.

"But then, the Cathars are against all violence, all shedding of blood. They seek to emulate Christ's meekness. They eat no meat, though they do eat fish, as fish do not copulate as beasts do, and so are not sinful. Their view of sin itself is different than ours. Copulation of any kind is sinful, and, forgive me, pregnant women are abhorred. But they view sex within marriage as just as sinful as that without it. Moreso, since those who engage in it are convinced they are not sinning. The Cathars would have excused your situation, my child, saying that there is nothing more sinful in a brother and a sister having sex than in any other couple."

For the first time, Lorenzo smiled, if wryly. "Pierre Authié was a man unafraid of sin. He had seven children by his wife, and two more by a mistress, the sister of a fellow notary in Ax. Her name was Monète Rouzy, and she was mother to le Bon Guilhem.

"Six years before the Papal Jubilee, Pierre voyaged with his youngest brother Guillaume to Cuneo here in Lombardy. There they were ordained Cathar priests, called Perfects. Le Bon Guilhem was with them, and three years later he returned, still a very young man, to Sebartès as their herald. They meant nothing less than to wage war against the Church. *Contemptus Mundi.*

"For ten years Pierre Authié, his brother, and his natural son lived as fugitives, though you would hardly have known it, so beloved they were by the locals. Those were heady years for le Bon Guilhem – both a celebrity and a criminal. Handsome and genial, he was much admired by the ladies of the Cathar faith. He sinned much, I'm afraid. He even loved, and was loved in return. But he could never remain long. The Church was aware of Authié's preaching, and determined to end it. The heretics had become so influential, you see, so very persuasive in their proclamations of their outlawed faith, that the Inquisitor Bernardo Gui proclaimed he had no higher goal than arresting Pierre Authié.

"With a price on his head, it was only a matter of time before Pierre was betrayed. It came at the hands of one he had trusted, known since he was a lad. Perhaps it was because he had known the fellow's mother carnally. But I think it was greed. The money was just too good. Besides, the fellow had been arrested, and was saving his own hide." Lorenzo paused for a time, clearly reliving ugly memories. "Pierre Authié was arrested in 1309, and burned at the stake the following year in Toulouse. It was a Thursday, the 9th of April.

Before they lit the pyre, he announced that, were he given the chance to preach, he would convert the entire mob come to see him burn. And, truth be told, he was not wrong. His tongue could woo fish from a river."

Another pause, during which Lia was silent while Lorenzo composed himself.

"On the very eve of his arrest, to save his son's life, Pierre told le Bon Guilhem to run. Guilhem's sister came to spirit him away, and he returned to Lombardy, which he remembered from when he was a boy. He took the cowl, and hid among those who had persecuted his family. He took a name for himself, one that seemed apropos. You know the story of San Lorenzo?"

Lia's voice was soft. "When asked to hand over the Church's treasure, he presented the sick and the poor."

"For which he was burned to death on a grid-iron," concluded Lorenzo, lest that fact escape her. "It seemed appropriate to le Bon Guilhem."

This whole time Lorenzo had spoken as if the story belonged to someone else. Lia honoured that choice as she framed a question. "Why did he choose Verona?"

"Lightning," answered Lorenzo. "They say if you stand in the place where lightning has struck, you will be unharmed. The Scaliger's father—" here he paused, almost saying 'your grandfather' "—Alberto della Scala, he burned two hundred Cathars in the Arena. The whole region was deemed cleansed. What better place to go to ground? Since then, he has strived to be a good son of the Church, while keeping faith with the commandment 'honour thy father'. He eats fish, but no meat. He tends to plants, as they are sinless, holding the potential for both good and evil in their roots. Just as man does."

Lorenzo was already regretting his volubility. After an awkward silence, Lia spoke. "Thank you, Fra Lorenzo. It is good to be reminded that all men have troubles. I hope le Bon Guilhem has found peace."

"If he has not," said Lorenzo, "it is through no one's fault but his own."

◆   ◇   ◆

In the guest palace, Don Pedro was aching all over from the race. In a robe, he summoned a servant and asked for water and bread. Then he noticed a light coming from beneath the door to Beatrice's sitting room. He knocked, and her maid answered. "Is she awake? I don't mean to disturb her."

Beatrice said something and the maid admitted him. The lady

was seated, still dressed in her finery from the evening, though a little bedraggled from the rain – it had certainly been at her hair, which was fallen from its caul. "I went to escort you home, lady, but could not find you."

"A pity, as I was all alone," said Beatrice tartly, wiping her eye. "My partner had gone to find a finer conversationalist. I'm afraid I didn't come up to his standards."

Frowning, Don Pedro sat beside her. "Lady – have you been crying?"

Beatrice removed her hands from her face as if scalded. "No, lord! Crying – me? The day I shed tears for any man is the day I shed my name! Especially a man such as Signor Benedick. He's as good as a trick horse that can canter sideways – there's no harness that can catch him but a golden one!" She brushed her skirts irritably. "A boor, one of these duelists without a kill to his name, all talk, no steel. Why, he talks as if he were the Scaliger's own right hand, rather than a limp hair cut from his head. Don't mention his name again!"

She had risen and exited to her bedchamber before Pedro could point out that he hadn't mentioned Benedick at all.

◆　◇　◆

Leaning close to Detto, Tiberio said, "It will be dawn soon. If my wife is absent at daybreak, it will be spoken of. Would that help your friend? If they planned to run off, they will have done so by now. If he did not go to her, then she is alone and frightened – of me, of her father, of discovery. I will not harm her. I knew we should not have come. The fault is mine. I will not blame her, Bailardetto. But I must see her safe. Please."

Reason worked where threats had not. "San Zeno's. She's at San Zeno's."

"Thank you," said Tiberio, reaching behind Detto to free his hands.

Adamo protested. "He could be lying!"

"He's not."

Standing, Detto rubbed life back into his wrists. There was an awkward moment where his captors considered begging or threatening him for silence. In the end, they hoped his own loyalty to Cesco would still his tongue.

He donned his cloak and, to their surprise, marched with them towards the Basilica di San Zeno. If Cesco was there, he would need a friend. If not, Detto had to be sure the girl was not harmed.

The rain had slackened at last, and the sky was lightening.

Steam rose from roofs as the hearthfires evaporated the water clinging to the tiles. Verona looked new, fresh, cleansed. The opposite of
how Detto felt.

They found Lia in the confessional, still talking with Fra
Lorenzo. Informed that her husband, father, and brother had come,
she emerged. Her face was neither fearful nor confident, but resigned.

Tiberio put a hand on her shoulder. "Good morrow, wife. Are
you well?"

"I am well, thank you, husband. Only tired. I have prayed all
night."

"A worthy thing," he said. "Come. Let me take you home."

Nodding, she made eye contact with Detto. "Ser Bailardetto,
thank you. And you, Fra Lorenzo. I have left a token of thanks behind.
I trust you will see it delivered."

"We will," said Lorenzo.

With a last look around, Lia allowed her family to remove her
from the basilica.

Detto stared after her. "He didn't come?" When Lorenzo shook
his head, Detto made to rush back to the palace to see what had
occurred during his captivity.

Lorenzo forestalled him. "Wait! Her token." From his robes he
withdrew a sealed letter. Taking it, Detto felt something heavy inside.
"Use your judgment, lad. It might do more harm than good."

◆   ◇   ◆

The sound came from far away. Voices raised, and the clash of
steel. Using what breath he had kept, Cesco called, "Help! Help! In
the cellar! For God's sake, help!!!" He paused to breathe into her
mouth again. She tried to pull away, ready to die, not wanting to
prolong her torment. Her head submerged, she could not hear rescue
coming.

Cesco dropped the torch hissing into the water as he used both
hands to hold her face and force her to take his breath. Fortunately,
her struggles were weak. The cold water had numbed them both,
though the chamber itself was warm. Had it been exposed to the air,
they might have already succumbed. But then they would not be so
trapped.

He wished that she could hear the noises from above. He called
again, gave her air, then called once more.

This time he was answered. "Cesco! Is that you?"

"Yes!!" Echoing around him, his very voice seemed trapped.
"Help! I need an iron crow, a sword, something – now!"

"We're coming!"

He couldn't tell whose voice it was, but was reassured by the use of the plural. Buthayna was now aware of his yelling. Her body tensed as he gave her breath again, with a comforting squeeze on her shoulder.

Splashes caught his attention, and he told them where to go. Flickering lights heralded their approach. Never before had Cesco been so glad to see his brothers Barto and Berto. With them was the Paduan Salvatore. He didn't bother to ask how they had found him, nor how they had squeezed through that narrow gap in the church floor. "Quick! Break her free of this collar!"

It took moments, and she struggled as air was forced from her in their attempts to free her. The water was close to the ceiling of the low tunnel now, forcing them to perform their work submerged.

With three sets of hands levering the pieces apart, the collar gave way at last. Buthayna came up gasping, shaking and weeping with relief. She clung to Cesco as he dragged her down to the large central chamber where they could stand upright.

Consoling her with one hand, Cesco looked to his fellow Rakehells. "Is there anyone up there?"

"One guard only. He's dead," added Barto.

"Damn." But he could not complain. He had killed those two men in the dungeon to keep them from telling anyone else the message that brought him here. Thinking of which, he frowned. "How did you find me?"

"We heard what gate you used and followed. There was an innkeeper who told Salvatore he saw a young man riding towards Quinto. We went there, but no one had seen you. Then we had the idea that you might have come here. We didn't know why."

"I couldn't say why myself." Their arrival seemed suspiciously miraculous. But now was not the moment to look a gift horse in the mouth. "If it's safe, let's get her out of here."

Above, he searched the dead man, but found nothing. They found the priest trussed in his solar and freed him before setting out for Verona. Buthayna rode in Cesco's lap, while the dead man was slung behind Salvatore's saddle. Cesco already knew that identification would be useless. The man was nothing.

During the whole ride back to Verona, his dizzied brain kept posing the same question: *What was the point?* He could find no answer, because another thought kept intruing to smote him to the heart.

I missed her.

❖   ◊   ❖

At the break of day, Giulietta was retrieved from the *via Pigna* and brought to her own home where she cried and cried. She hugged her father, doing her very best to help him through his grief. At one point she asked if they could send for Thibault. "He must be here. He's family."

For the first time, he felt a slight thawing for his nephew. His suspicions felt churlish now. "Yes, very well. Bring Thibault home."

As Giulietta rushed off to tell her mother the good news, Antony exited the house and dully crossed the yard to his office. The chill rain had finally ended, and the sky today was clear. The promise of Spring. But it was a promise already broken.

Among the papers his steward handed him was a note of condolence from Mariotto, kindly written, and full of offers of friendship and renewed camaraderie. Antony read it over, then threw it in the fire.

❖   ◊   ❖

Cesco's first stop in the city was San Zeno's. But the brothers were already at their labours, and no young married lady was waiting for him. Not anymore. He did find young Romeo, who seemed strangely quiet. Which suited Cesco, not in the mood to banter.

He had asked Barto and Berto to see Buthayna safely ensconced at *La Rosa Colta*. Himself, he felt the pull of the palace, and Ser Alaghieri. But his hands were shaking, his stomach in knots. He needed a wafer to calm him.

Need. It was a word that frightened him.

His home was full of frightened servants, all full of questions. He asked if there was news from the palace, or anywhere else. They said that Suor Beatrice had not yet returned, but that Ser Bailardetto was upstairs. Detto, who had seen Lia, whereas Cesco had bitten on the wrong lure.

With feet hardly heavier than his heart, Cesco ascended the stairs.

❖   ◊   ❖

The rising sun found the Piazza dei Signori thronged in silent vigil for Pietro Alaghieri, son of Dante, knight of the Mastiff, Count of San Bonifacio. The Veronese loved him for all the things he had done, and for himself. Was there any man more noble, more honourable, more devout – more Veronese! – than Pietro Alaghieri?

Somehow a rumour started that Ser Alaghieri had been attacked by Paduans, and lay now at death's door. Perhaps his foster-son had known all along that Paduans weren't to be trusted. Or perhaps the Scaliger's heir had brought this on with all his brawling. On one thing everyone agreed – if some treacherous Paduan backstabber had spilled the blood of the architect of the *Pax Verona*, the war would start anew.

♦   ◊   ♦

In the suite they shared, a roaring fire had been kept alive all night in case of the master's return. When Cesco entered, Detto sighed in relief. "You're alive."

"Am I? Someone erred, then."

"What happened?"

As he pulled off his ruined clothes, Cesco explained. It took remarkably little time to tell.

"And Salvatore, Barto, and Berto found you?"

"Just in time to drag us from a watery grave. Yet another near death. Though I think I was meant to save her. They didn't anticipate such heavy rain."

"Where is the – what is her name?"

Encased in a fresh tunic and hose, Cesco lingered at the box that contained the wafers. It stood beside the pine nut brittle he liked so well. "Buthayna."

"Where is she now?"

Opening the box, he took out a wafer. "*La Rosa Colta*. I placed some guards outside."

Detto ventured a smile. "That will spoil their business some-what."

"I'm glad you're amused. What about you? I half expected you to be leading the hunt for me."

"I would have, had I not been bound to a chair in Tiberio's house." That brought Cesco's head around sharply. Detto described the events since they had parted. "My own fault for calling there. I hoped to forestall her."

"And were forestalled yourself." Cesco paused, his face in shadow. He had not yet bitten. "And what of her?"

"Lia waited all night, until her husband came to collect her. They're heading back to the Tiberio estate at once."

"Did he hurt her?"

"He was gruff, but kind."

There was nothing to say to that. But there was something that needed saying. "You were correct tonight. Selfish. So very, very self-ish. The ideal word."

"I was wrong." Detto had spent hours wishing he hadn't said anything at all. Like all emotions, they were one thing when inside. Blood ran blue under the skin, but changed colour as soon as it touched the air. Things seemed so very different now. But how was Detto to have known all that would befall this terrible night?

"Figs. Everyone around me gets hurt. How many injuries must my friends endure because of me? Cangrande spoke sense. I should go. England, France, Spain – Arabia. Somewhere. I should just go." He sighed, closing his eyes. "But they'd find me. Wherever I went, the stars would find me. O, it would be so much better had I never been born!"

This was dangerous talk. In his current state Cesco might take it into his head to do something awful. "There is no one who wishes you had never lived."

"No one?" The retort came with bitter sharpness. "I can think of a dozen within a stone's throw. How many lives have I ruined just by living? How many are dead, or nearly died, because of me?" His eyes welled, and his voice became small. *"What's the matter with me?"*

There was only one thing to say. "Cesco – I have something for you. From Lia. She left it for you. I didn't know if I should deliver it. But she wanted you to have it."

Eyes opening slowly, Cesco saw the proffered paper, sealed with a crest he didn't know but that seared itself into his brain. The Tiberio device. Taking it, he broke the seal.

Something fell out. Detto recognized it. So did Cesco, who left it alone as he scanned the page in the firelight. Though he read it over twice, his expression remained fixed. "Most amusing. Wouldn't you say?" Without looking up, Cesco offered the paper across.

As Detto read, Cesco picked up the old Roman coin from the floor. Crossing to the window, he stared down into the street. In one hand was the little wafer. In the other, the coin. He flipped the metal disc into air, caught it, and looked at the upward face.

Mercurio.

Nodding to himself, Cesco walked to a trunk by his bed and removed a satchel. He stared at it for some time, then carried it to join the box full of wafers. "Burn these." Gripping the coin with white knuckles, he nodded at the letter. "That, too." Wrenching the door open, he vanished.

Detto advanced on the burning brazier. With a surge of vindi-cation, he tossed the package of sticky chews into the flames, then upended the contents of the box and watched as they sizzled, filling the air with a sickly scent.

But the letter remained in his hand, unburnt.

♦   ◊   ♦

In the makeshift hospital in the palace, the vigil was ongoing. They filled the empty space with stories of Pietro, gently mocking his earnest good nature, his devotion to fairness. Poco kept chastising the unconscious man. "Really, big brother? You won't even defend yourself? Come along, join the debate!"

They were relieved when Cesco arrived, looking wan. Detto arrived shortly thereafter. Both looked much the worse for wear, and the Scaliger demanded to know where they had been. Explaining his own dark adventure, Cesco concluded by saying, "Someone is toying with us."

"With you," said Cangrande. "With me and mine, it seems they are not toying at all. Carrara is on his way back to Padua to investigate those corpses. If he discovers who hired them, he will report at once."

"He won't," yawned Cesco. "Discover who it was, I mean. If we couldn't find a poisoner in a closed room, he certainly cannot find the correct woman in all of Padua. Is there anything more?"

"Nothing but to wait and see how Pietro fares."

"Nothing fair about it." Cesco crossed nearer the supine figure of Pietro. "As I learned earlier tonight, I find I much prefer being victim to being observer. Shouldn't he be awake by now?"

"We're keeping him asleep," said Morsicato. "If he wakes, he may tear his stitches again."

"What about maggots?" The doctor always prescribed maggots for deep wounds to keep the flesh from rotting.

"If he makes it through the next few days, we'll use them. No use until we know he'll live."

"He'll live," insisted Cesco. "If this were fore-ordained, the Moor would be here, hovering like Atropos with her shears."

Pietro shifted slightly, and everyone stilled, fearful of the ultimate moment. But then he sighed and relaxed back into sleep.

In several ways, Cesco looked more ill than Pietro. The blue of exhaustion hung about his eyes and lips. Knowing the signs, Morsicato quietly offered a little syrup of poppy to him, but the young knight steadfastly refused.

Cesco was not the only one showing the signs of fatigue. "Antonia, you should go get some sleep," advised the doctor.

"Not until Pietro decides whether to live or die."

"Alas, Ser Alaghieri is dead already," said Cesco bleakly. Everyone turned frantic eyes to him, and then to Pietro.

Cesco continued in a maudlin tone. "The great Scaligeri murdered him last night, put him in his grave. There is only the Count of San Bonifacio now."

Morsicato groaned, clutching his heart. "You little… don't do that!"

"I speak only the truth," said Cesco with a feeble smile.

"If only that were true," retorted Cangrande from near the door. "But you're right. He's the Count now."

Antonia shook her head. "That will take some getting used to."

"For all of us," said Pietro.

They turned to see him smiling weakly from behind closed eyes. Rushing forward, everyone began talking in low but chipper voices, welcoming him back to the land of the living.

Minutes later Cangrande made an announcement from the steps of the palace to those waiting without. Cheers went up, and bells began to ring.

Verona's greatest knight would live.

THIRTY-THREE

Legnano
Saturday, *19 March 1329*

PLYING HIS TRADE in the shelter of a tavern wall, Girolamo noticed the muffled figure watching him. No telling how long he had been there. After a half-hour under that stare, the stress started interfering with his pendulum. Lifting his stick, the crippled diviner limped across the street to confront those accusing eyes. "You found me. Divination?"

"I have not your skill," said Tharwat al-Dhaamin. "But I can read a map, and I know you by now."

In spite of himself, Girolamo laughed. "Comical. One cripple pursuing another."

"I am not here to chase you," said Tharwat in his broken voice. "Merely to ask what happened. And again offer to mentor you."

Girolamo's twisted face softened. Then he turned away, shrugging. "Come along. Slip me some coin and I'll buy us bread and wine. They won't serve you here."

They ate in the open air, under a sun that was warmer than any time in the last six months. A false spring, a lure to buds and shoots and those foolish animals young enough to mistake light for warmth.

"I thought the blame would land on me," confessed Girolamo gruffly. "I tried to save him."

"You did save him," said Tharwat. "He survived, thanks to you."

Girolamo nodded. "I know. The bob told me."

"Why were you there? Why did you leave Venice?"

"It was the pendulum." Girolamo held up his callused finger.

The scars were plain. "If I stayed in Venice, I was in mortal danger. Or so I thought. Instead it guided me to someone else in danger."

"Detto." Tharwat's brow creased. "But then, when he was safe, why not stay?"

"I told you…"

"I do not believe you. You had another reason for going to ground." Tharwat waited, his one eye level and hard.

At last, Girolamo wilted. "When I touched him, something happened. I'd never felt anything like it. A premonition. It wasn't until I was away that I asked the pendulum. Three people. Three people with a close blood tie to that boy — they're all going to die, and soon."

Tharwat did not argue. His own charts showed a great upheaval was at hand. "You did not care to warn them?"

Girolamo could not meet his eye. "Already I've been linked to two misfortunes to that family. You know the saying. Once is happenstance, twice is coincidence, three times is enemy action. How would anyone believe I was innocent, especially after I admitted to attempted murder! No, far better to remove myself until the damage was done."

"Except that, if you interposed yourself, you might have prevented the damage. Your pendulum can find poison, can it not? You could have saved Lord Bonaventura."

The cripple shook his head again, this time defensively. "Only if I was holding the cup. And the pendulum doesn't always answer the questions I ask! It tells me only what it wants me to know."

"You are mistaken. It tells you only what *you* want to know. It will not respond to questions when you are afraid of the answers." Tharwat drew a long breath. "You have a gift, Girolamo. One perhaps greater than mine. Certainly of more immediacy. But knowledge is only useful if acted upon. And that requires courage. If you find yours, come to me. I will be in Verona, attempting to stave off this future you saw."

"You can't," insisted Girolamo flatly. "Three deaths. The pendulum doesn't lie."

"Did it name those who will fall?"

"No," said Girolamo.

"Which means, deep down, you are afraid to know. But you see, there are many with a close blood tie to that young man. Some are worth saving. Others less so." Tharwat rose to his feet. "I would rather choose which of them will fall than let the stars decide. One thing I have learned in my life — the future is open, until it is past."

◆   ◇   ◆

For days after the close of the Palio, it was all anyone could speak of. A stabbing, an attempted kidnapping of the heir (again!), the near-reconciliation of Capulletto and Montecchio. The death of poor Capulletto's wee heir. It was enough to set tongues wagging.

After months of revels and foreigners, life at last returned to something resembling normalcy. Venders set up their stalls in the Piazza delle Erbe, and tradesmen went about the business of their guilds. There were cheerful greetings, but all in a Veronese tongue.

At the same time, nasty stories began to bubble up – Paduans being harassed, waylaid, knocked down. None of it so far amounted to much, but wearing a feather on the wrong side of one's cap or speaking without rolling one's 'r's became less and less advisable within Verona's walls.

Despite this, there was a sense of wellbeing in the air. The rains had banished the unnatural chill of that horrible winter. Spring came early, and labourers enjoyed working with their sleeves rolled to the elbow, their vests unlaced. Women went about without heavy mantles to cover their gowns. They had not realized how terrible the winter had been until it was behind them.

Cesco was occasionally seen in public, mostly trotting back and forth between his home and the palace. He was remarkably unquerulous. Some thought him frightened by the attack on his person. Others speculated that his spleen had all been building towards the Palio, and that having won both of the races (everyone knew he'd *allowed* the other pair to claim victory), he had no more need to ruckus. Not until Treviso.

Only one voice was unequivocal in condemnation. The Abbot of San Zeno maintained his stance that the heir was possessed by an evil spirit – just look at those suffering all around him!

This particular morning, Benedick went to the house on the *via Pigna*, only to discover the master absent. Thibault was there, packing up his few belongings for his return to his uncle's house. Hearing Benedick's intent, he volunteered to take Cesco's place. He was in no hurry to return to the *via Cappello*.

Along the way they collected Salvatore and the Bonaventura twins. At the river's edge they all donned leather armour and set to shows of swordsmanship.

"Christ," said Thibault after a couple of passes. "Here I thought my mood was foul. I've never seen your blade so quick."

"Eager for Treviso." Benedick was a head taller than the young man, who was about to turn fourteen.

"As am I, though I doubt I'll be allowed."

Still waking up, Salvatore splashed river water onto his face. "What happened to Donna Beatrice?"

Benedick lunged, forcing Thibault to leap aside, parrying. "Nothing happened to her."

Petruchio sat kicking his heels on the edge of the bridge. "I heard Don Pedro's party is departing today."

Twisting his blade to deceive, Benedick said nothing. Undeceived, Thibault caught the attack on his false edge and slid into a counter-thrust. "Wish I were going with them. Do you think the Spanish prince requires a squire?"

"You're too fair," said Hortensio, stretching his wrists and ankles for his turn. "You'd burn under a Spanish sun."

"I burn here," said Thibault.

"A day of departures," continued Salvatore. "Paride and the Scaliger's wife leave for France as well. We'll have to be finished and clean before they go. Unless you have somewhere else to be?" added Salvatore innocently.

"Nowhere," grunted Benedick. "That's a hit!"

"No!" cried Thibault.

"A hit," declared Salvatore.

"A hit," agreed Hortensio.

"I didn't see," admitted Petruchio.

Furious, Thibault touched blades, then brought a blow angling for Benedick's head. "Not going to say good-bye?"

Benedick beat this stroke away. "No."

"Good for you," called Hortensio. "Watching you these past weeks, I thought you were falling in love!"

"What? No!" said Benedick defensively as he tried to beat away a lunge.

Thibault recoiled from his deep stance. "*That* was a hit."

Benedick did not care, rounding on the others. "I'm a confirmed bachelor, as you all well know! I just — enjoy her mind."

Under the others' derisive hoots, Salvatore clucked his tongue. "Tch! That's when love's arrow pins you to the wall. Trust me, I know!" They spent some moments abusing his relationship with Vittoria. The twins had finally reconciled themselves to it, and rumour said the banns would be read sometime next week.

Points even, Thibault withdrew, giving his partner breathing space. Salvatore picked up a loose stone with his free hand and plopped it into the Adige. "So — why are we here?"

A little too innocently, Benedick said, "I need the practice."

"You certainly do," said Thibault.

Salvatore glossed over this. "Why so far from home?" They were by the Ponte Navi, close to the stews from which Benedick and Salvatore had first met Cesco.

"No reason." Hating being so transparent, Benedick raised his sword to Thibault. "Come on."

As Thibault engaged again, Hortensio grinned. "It's odd, isn't it, Ser Salvatore. If you're leaving the palaces, this is the easiest southbound bridge."

"Is it?" asked Salvatore in mock surprise. "By God, it is, and that's a fact!"

"Here's another fact for you," said Petruchio, still kicking his heels, "the other southern bridge is only accessible via this road."

"You're right, Ser Petruchio! If I were waiting for someone heading south, this is the place I'd choose to wait."

They were using single-handed swords. Benedick switched hands suddenly, making Thibault jump back.

Thibault seemed impressed. "Hm! Are you naturally ambidextrous?"

"Yes," said Benedick as he pressed Thibault back along the water's edge, up towards the bridge.

Thibault feinted right, then struck left with a much faster hand-switch than Benedick had achieved. It almost made the Paduan fall on his back avoiding it. "I taught myself." He waggled the blade in front of Benedick's nose. "Look upon it. Look upon it."

"Of course," continued Salvatore, "if one was going to, say, Spain, one might go north over the Alps, through France, and so down."

"That's true," said Hortensio. "But not if you were stopping in Sicily *en route*."

"No," said Petruchio, "in that case, one would take ship in Genoa or Ostia and relax the whole way."

Benedick's eyes flicked up to the road. A carriage was approaching.

"This isn't challenging enough," he said, flicking his point to make Thibault retreat. Turning, Benedick swung at Hortensio, who barely parried in time. Suddenly Benedick was facing two men at once, switching from one to the other with a furious series of blows.

Salvatore drew his blade and charged, while Petruchio jumped down from the bridge to join the fray. Benedick was driven back along the water's edge, face furrowed in concentration, holding his own against four enemies. He waded out to ankle depth to keep them from surrounding him and called a challenge. He blocked Thibault's stab, then swept the blade around to catch Petruchio's cut for his leg. Hortensio lunged, but fell in the water. Salvatore came to pommel him in the ear, but Benedick caught it with his free hand.

Sopping, Hortensio emerged from the water. Rather than attack, he glanced over Benedick's shoulder. "She's past. Get him."

Stripped of his weapon, Benedick found himself lifted in the air, a Rakehell on each limb, and repeatedly dunked head-first into the river.

No one mentioned their absent leader.

◆   ◊   ◆

The departure of Giovanna and Paride was done with little fuss. No grand ceremony or feast. In the inner courtyard of the Scaliger palace, amid the heavy retinue of guards and waiting ladies that would accompany them to France, only family gathered to see them off. And not even all of them.

Verde wished her aunt well, both on her own and her sisters' behalf. Mastino and Alberto gave Paride a fine new traveling cloak and some oil for his saddle.

"Be well," said Cangrande as he kissed his wife goodbye. They had been married twenty years, more than half of the Scaliger's life.

"And you. No more Ponte Corbos."

"Ha! No." The Scaliger turned to grasp Paride by the shoulders. "Despite the plethora of women in Paris, I think you should avoid marriage while away. A doubling of your name might bring unfortunate consequences."

Inured to jokes about his name, Paride was looking around, his brow knitted. Cangrande snapped his fingers. "How thoughtless of me! I ordered Cesco to ride to Padua this morning. He was furious, as he wished to see you off. But duty calls. You understand."

Paride nodded, knowing it was a lie, knowing Cesco was somewhere in the city. Just not here. Climbing onto his horse beside the carriage, he smiled. "Tell him not to burn down the city while I'm gone."

◆   ◊   ◆

"A second Rakehell gone," said Poco, watching through the window as the carriage and its escorts passed. "First Rupert, now Paride. Antonia says Thibault is returning to his uncle's. And those two mercenaries are back in their camp with Otto, preparing for

Treviso. Cesco will have to hold recruitment parties, and look back on these as the halcyon days of glory."

"Halcyon days rarely last." Not yet allowed to sit up, Pietro lay propped up on bolsters, a chamber-pot close to hand. "Everyone talks about the great days when Mari and Antony and I were all together. It was hardly six months, yet it lives on in everyone's memory. The same will happen with his merry band. Change is inevitable."

"Well, Paride at least won't be changing for weeks to come. Looks like they're not taking much in way of belongings."

"I imagine Donna Giovanna plans to purchase everything once they arrive. Fortunately she has a bottomless purse," said Pietro, who knew how pricey Paris could be.

"Stop scratching!" snapped Morsicato from across the room. His back was turned.

"I'm only scratching my face," retorted Pietro. Unshaven for the first time in his life, his face was constantly itching.

"I tried growing a beard once," said Poco. "I won't repeat what father said about it." Laughing made Pietro wince. "How are the maggots?"

"Don't! Or I *will* start scratching." Pietro paused. "No sign of Cesco?"

"He was seen this morning, according to Antonia. Stopped off in the kitchens for some bread and water. But no one knows where he's been disappearing to."

It was awful to miss the brawling. Because no one knew what the quiet portended. "Detto's with him?"

"Yes. Has he not been here?"

"Twice since I left the palace. Each time no more than a few minutes. He doesn't want to tire me, he says." Thinking of sleep, Pietro yawned uncontrollably, which his brother took as a sign to exit, closing the door behind him.

For anyone looking, Cesco was in the most unlikely place in all the city – the Basilica of San Zeno. He sat for a long time in the confessional, silent. Then he had crossed down the stairs to the underside, with its ornate tombs. He liked the darkness. He sat with Detto, talking softly of nothing at all, sharing the sweet pine nut brittle that he so liked.

So it had been each day since his return from the other San Zeno's. He had come to sit where Lia had sat, conversing with the empty space in the confessor's seat. Then he had stopped by other places, places of meaning only to him, reviving memories until now buried.

One place he had not been back to was *La Rosa Colta*. Detto wondered if by staying away he was trying to protect that dark-skinned girl. Somehow he didn't think so.

Today when they arrived at the church, the Abbot of San Zeno asked Cesco to have a proper confession. Cesco had offered him only the fig.

"That wasn't smart," observed Detto, watching the fuming abbot storm off.

Cesco spoke in a soft tone. "I'm not interested in finding God. And even if I were, I wouldn't go to him. He doesn't deserve the satisfaction."

Detto did not respond. He spent most of his time in silence. He had already said too much.

Used to his cousin's mercurial swings, he was not foolish enough to mistake Cesco's stillness for calm. For six months he had raged, beating at every target, punching both below him and above with abandon.

This silence was different. As though the wild destructive force, so eager and free, and been turned inward. Against itself.

After their time out, Cesco suggested they dine at home. Passing by the Casa Montecchio, they were waylaid at once by young Romeo. The boy began as usual, with an invitation to wordplay. "Ho, the loverly lover!"

Cesco's head snapped around, the look on his face so raw that Romeo at once began to tremble, his lip to quaver. There was no more hiding behind masques, it seemed. "Why lover?"

Blanching, Romeo shook his head. "I only – I met the lady Rosalia. At the church. She was kind. But sad, as lovers are."

"As lovers are," repeated Cesco. "I envy you, boy. It seems everyone saw her but me."

Romeo was so shocked by the lack of playfulness, the blunt plain-speaking that one never heard in Cesco, that he responded in kind. "My father asked, if I saw you, to carry a message. He would like to see you."

"I will wait while you fetch him."

Romeo darted off in relief. He fretted that he had said or done something to give the lady's secret away. But he hadn't – he knew he hadn't. Finding his father, he chose not to return to the gate, but instead sought his mother.

Outside, Mariotto talked to Cesco for five minutes. Cesco was reticent until Lord Montecchio mentioned that he had planned to ask Count Alaghieri's advice. "You know better than to trouble him," snapped Cesco. "Very well. Tonight after dark. Have him ready. Best apply some colour to his hair. Saffron and sulpher will do."

As they crossed to his own house, Cesco pulled a face. "Detto, best send word to the others to meet. And ask Benedick to supper."

"What reason shall I give? A race?"

"What does it matter?"

Entering his home, Cesco's attentions were immediately claimed by his wife. "Giulietta's cousin is gone!"

Cesco nodded. "Good."

"The one you called the cat," insisted Maddelena. "He's gone."

Though she expected him to tease the absent Thibault again, he merely said, "Everyone goes away."

"The men haven't gone away." She was referring to the guards stationed here since the night of the Palio. "Why?"

Cesco knelt. "Well, Maddelena, you know there are men in the world who wish Verona ill. Bad men, enemies of the Greyhound." She nodded gravely. "Well, these men are guarding you against them."

"Why me? It's the Greyhound they don't like."

"It's impossible to imagine it, but say there was someone who didn't like you."

"My sisters," she said at once.

Cesco almost smiled. "Very well, your sisters. Let's say Sibilia wanted to make you do something for her. What would she do?"

"Hit me," said Maddelena at once.

"But she can't do that, because she can't reach you. Instead she steals something you love. Do you have a favourite toy, or pet?"

"My bunny," said Maddelena reverently.

"What if Sibilia took your bunny, and you had to do everything she said or you wouldn't get it back." Maddelena's face bunched up in concerned indignation. "That's right. Well, some people think you're my bunny. But I'm luckier than you. My bunny is clever and can think and run and yell for help. And you know that, just like if anything happened to your bunny, you'd come to rescue it?"

"Her."

"Her. All I'm saying is, I'd do the same for you. But a clever bunny is one that doesn't get caught. So you need to be my clever bunny and not let anyone you don't know take you away. Understand?"

Bottom lip trembling, Maddelena nodded several times. Dahna rushed forward and scooped her up. "No one is going to take your bunny, sweetheart. My lord, you're scaring her."

"Not as much as she might have been the night of the Palio," snapped Cesco, rising. "Now, my bunny, don't be frightened. These men around our house are here to guard your bunny against your sisters. I gave them special orders to look after her, and you."

Maddelena broke free of her nurse and threw her arms around Cesco's neck. He started, then slowly disengaged from her arms. "Now go and play."

It was the most he had spoken at a single time to anyone actually in the room with him.

Detto returned from playing messenger, and they whiled away the hours until supper with nothing at all. At last Benedick joined them and they set to supper, Vito spoiling them all with delicious fishes and sweet treats. Antonia was there, but the conversation remained harmless in front of the little girl.

After the meal Cesco broke open his supply of pine nut brittle, allowing everyone a piece of the confection made of honey, cinnamon, ginger, and black pepper. His wife ate only a bite before turning up her nose, but Antonia enjoyed it greatly, and Detto had three pieces.

Cesco was genial, if impersonal. He listened to the stories Benedick told, most of which they had all heard before. No one could recall Suor Beatrice laughing so much. She even sang with them, though she was quick to chide any ribaldry. Of which there was little.

Benedick stumbled home, head swimming. He was half-tempted to accept Cesco's offer of a horse to go after Don Pedro's carriage. Preoccupied, he didn't even notice he wore a cloak not his own.

Though he knew the evening plans, Detto had to lie down. He hadn't thought he'd had much wine, but he fell into his bed, heart racing, head spinning, vomit close to churning forth. He wanted to drop into a blessed sleep, but each time he closed his eyes the world seemed to teeter. He stared resolutely at a fixed point on the ceiling. The flickering candlelight didn't help, but it was better than the spinning behind his eyes.

Suddenly Cesco burst into the room, tossing a scabbarded sword down across Detto's legs while buckling on one of his own. "Up, arm, and out."

"Already?" objected Detto, willing his meal back down his esophagus.

"Almost the witching hour." Oddly, Cesco held Benedick's cloak over his arm. "Time for night's black agents to rouse themselves."

Outside, Detto paused a few moments to stick a finger down his throat to purge himself. Feeling marginally better, he mounted one of the waiting horses and followed as Cesco led the way back to the Montecchio stables. "More death-door entrances?"

"Invited this time. Good evening, my lord."

Montecchio appeared, looking furtive. "Thank you for this. With the city guards looking for traitors, you're the only one who won't raise suspicion."

"I wish you had come to me sooner. I could have added him to Paride's retinue, and he could have had an escort all the way to France. Or even departed with Don Pedro. Instead he'll have to take his chances along the lonely road. You have his horse ready?"

"A sturdy palfrey."

"Give him this cloak and have him come out."

In short order Benjamin Montagu appeared, fidgeting and restless, dressed in the stolen cloak. Ludicrously he had red in his retreating hair.

"It itches," said Benjamin.

"Well don't scratch it, or it will all fall out. If the guards stop us, you're Signor Benedick. Just keep your hat forward."

"Thank you, my lord," said Benjamin in halting Italian.

Cesco replied in French. "Come. We'll meet the others by the Ponte Navi."

"Others?"

"Eight men are going riding into the hills. Seven will return. Nothing simpler." Cesco kicked and Abastor started to gallop. Montagu pressed his heels and his palfrey jolted forward.

Thanks to the surprisingly strong wine, Detto was still less than himself. His subconscious registered the sound before his brain acknowledged it. A figure had raced out of the darkness and hauled himself up behind Detto in the saddle.

Sobering, Detto felt a knife press his ribs. "Ride after. Say nothing."

♦   ◊   ♦

Pietro's steward was hesitant at first to admit the latest visitor until the master's brother assured him that Tharwat al-Dhaamin was welcome within these walls.

Taking his ease with hot water and lemon to drink, the Moor asked after the new Count's health, and heard all the tales from the eventful Palio. He then related in just a few short phrases his exchange with Girolamo, and why the crippled diviner had fled.

"Three deaths."

"At least three more deaths," corrected Tharwat. "Verona is heading for an upheaval. What we can say for certain is that three people close to Detto will soon perish."

"For certain," murmured Morsicato dubiously.

Pietro pressed the point. "Two, surely. Petruchio died in January, after the attack on Detto."

"No, these three are all blood-relatives to Detto."

"I can't believe you let him go."

"He is guilty of no crime. He has to choose. I will not force a man to action."

"No, only damn them with their fates," said Morsicato tartly. "And then offer them drugs to keep them in thrall."

Tharwat showed his fatigue in his lack of patience. "If you have something to say, doctor, speak."

"He's worse than ever." Morsicato stroked his beard with both hands. "It's not just the hashish, though I think it's feeding his condition. He seems — defeated. He puts on a brave face for Pietro here, but something's happened. Even the brawling is over. He's like — like an animal who has stopped fighting the whip and is just taking the lashes in silence."

"Like he's been broken," said Tharwat.

Pietro winced as he leaned forward. "I don't believe it. Call him here. Let's have it out. It's time."

♦   ◊   ♦

The guards at the bridge made no objection to the gathering Rakehells. It was dark, the only light coming from the torches high above the sentries guarding the bridge gate. Moreover, there was a fog hanging in the air. Men were distinguished by their cloaks, their horses, and their voices.

Barto and Berto were the first ones to arrive, eager for a night-race. Salvatore was next, coming in the company of his future brothers-in-law. Seeing Cesco's black horse approach, they called to him, and he answered, "Patter patter. Shall we race?"

Salvatore asked, "How is the Count?"

"Mending," said Cesco briefly, nodding to the guards as he cantered under the arch and across the bridge.

"What a relief," breathed Salvatore. "Ho, Benedick!"

Under his cloak, Benjamin Montagu raised a hand. Cesco said, "Don't expect much from him. He can barely sit his saddle. We drank a very healthy dinner."

Grinning, Hortensio rubbed his hands together. "Improves our chances."

"What's the course?" asked Barto, dimpling in the shared excitement.

"Across the Navi, down the road towards Santa Lucia, then at the church we cross overland to San Massimo, and back through the Porta Palio."

"That will take half the night!"

"Daunting," agreed Cesco. "We'd best start."

"No, we won't be starting just yet," said an accented voice. Detto's mount had appeared, and the guards had not even challenged the two riders upon it. "First give me the fugitive Montagu. Then you can go your merry way."

Amid the murmurs of shock, Cesco turned in his saddle. "Monsieur Aiello."

"Forgive me for the theatrics," said Aiello, angling the knife against Detto's ribs so it caught the light through the fog. "But I had to wait until he tried to escape. Once the Scaliger sees him alive, I'm free."

"At least until Lord Nogarola catches up with you." Mirth was absent from Cesco's voice. "State your demands."

"I demand only that Montagu be taken before the Scaliger and hanged."

"Trying to succeed at law where you failed in villainy?" demanded Hortensio. The other Rakehells eased their mounts sideways, cutting off any possible escape.

"I did nothing to him!" snapped the Scot. "He cut the rope himself!"

"You were planning to murder me!" cried Montagu, his voice over-lapping Aiello's.

"He's alive! Proof enough that I didn't murder him!"

"But not proof you didn't try," said Cesco. "Your current bargaining tactic does not purchase you any credit. Detto?"

"I'm fine," replied Detto.

Aiello scowled. He did not like being ignored. "Tell Cangrande I'm innocent, put Montagu in chains, free my men, and I'll release Nogarola and get out of this hellish place!"

"Your aim has always been to see him dead," said Cesco. "Even after you knew he must have relayed his true message to us. Why does it matter that he die?"

"Because his death will send a message to his brother. You cannot trifle with power without getting burned."

"Fire," said Cesco. "You meant 'Trifle with *fire* without getting burned'. Your metaphors are particularly – now!"

Having already slipped his foot from the stirrup, Detto dove to his left as Cesco's hand flashed. Something caught the distant torchlight as it spun through the air to land in the Scot's center. Aiello looked down, frozen in horror. "Gah—buh—wha—you—you—"

Landing on his hands, Detto rolled away from his horse, who backed up in fright and reared. Still gabbling senselessly at the dagger lodged in his flesh, Aiello toppled backwards. His head and right shoulder struck the bridge parapet. For a moment he scrambled, then fell over into darkness. The splash was impressive, but before the ripples stilled the thawed Adige had swept the body away.

Dropping from his saddle, Cesco raced forward. "Detto! Tell me you're not hurt."

Detto felt a warm glow and feared that, like Ser Alaghieri, he'd been injured without knowing it. But the warmth came from the certainty of Cesco's affection. Even now, when things were at their worst. "I'm perfectly well."

Relieved, Cesco turned to Montagu, eyes narrowed thoughtfully. "He wasn't lying, was he? Aiello didn't attack you. You faked it."

"What? No. He was threatening me—"

"And you decided to remove him from play by faking your death, knowing he'd get blamed and possibly executed."

On his borrowed palfrey, Montagu glanced from side to side, then his face broke into that charming toothy smile. "I understand the Scaliger faked his own death once. My inspiration."

Cesco's mouth curled, but only on his sinister side. "You should go."

"You don't approve?" asked Montagu.

"I don't care one way or the other. But I doubt the Capitano will like it. Go."

Benjamin Montagu didn't need telling twice. Turning his horse, he kicked it in the direction of Mantua, and from thence to Pisa or Napoli for a ship.

"So," said Hortensio, watching him ride off. "No race?"

◆　　◇　　◆

Arriving home a few minutes later, Cesco and Detto found Antonia waiting for them. "We've been summoned to my brother's house."

"Is he ailing?" asked Cesco quickly.

"No," answered Antonia. "Tharwat has returned."

"O, excellent. That always presages good news."

Ushered into Pietro's chamber by the Greek steward, Cesco found all the old faces – Pietro and Poco, Morsicato and Tharwat, all waiting. Antonia took a place next to her brothers, though she massaged her temples with vigour. Surprised, Detto waited beside the door.

Cesco glared around suspiciously. "I thought we were going to interrogate the villainous Girolamo."

"He is no villain," said Tharwat. "He saved Detto's life, then fled in fear."

"Where is he, then? Detto can thank him, and so can I, for attempting to murder me as a child. In fact, if I try to kill him, Detto can save him, and all debts will be quit."

"Tharwat found him, but let him go," said Pietro, with a cross glance for the Moor. "We just thought it prudent to talk to you. We've been tip-toeing around it, but it's time."

Cesco groaned. "I thought I was past the age for lectures. Or is this an exorcism?"

"Neither." Pietro had clearly been deputed to do the talking. "We just need to know what you want."

That was startling. Cesco demurred. "Thank you, but I prefer to keep my wants to myself."

"You shouldn't," said Tharwat in his soft, rasping voice. "That's what the Scaliger has always done. He is now a vainglorious drunkard, a shadow of the brilliant man he once was."

"That's hardly fair, is it? He's the Vicar of the Trevisian Mark, Capitano del Popolo, and a dozen other titles. He's a patron to the arts, a builder. A lover. He embraces philosophy and learning, encourages literacy, discourages discrimination, keeps good laws, and is fair and just to all who live under his rule."

"And you hate him," said Pietro.

"Do I? I always wondered what that emotion was. But that is beside the point. As you like to say, Nuncle – no man is just one thing. Cangrande della Scala may be what you say, but that doesn't change what he has done with his life. I doubt the Greyhound could do more." Cesco turned, only to find his path blocked by Detto. "You too?"

"You know what I think," said Detto.

"Yes, you made it quite clear that I am wasting my life. But it's mine to waste."

From his sickbed, Pietro's voice was low but urgent. "We all love you. And we are on your side. But we need to know what you want. Do you even know?"

Cesco dropped his head, clenching his fists. When he turned back to them, his expression was no longer bland. It was full of rage. "You want to play? You can't even see the board."

Pietro blinked. "What do you mean?"

"Fine. I'll give each a piece. Do with it what thou wilt." Hands folded, he turned to the doctor. "Ser Morsicato, we'll start with you. Who benefits from your wife's illness?"

It took a moment for the shock to settle in. "What?"

Though his pupils were large, Cesco's expression remained detached. "Come along, it's obvious."

"Cangrande," answered Pietro. "He wanted to strip you of all support. He sent me to Avignon. Tharwat had to leave because of the riots. He only needed to remove the doctor as well."

Cesco shook his head. "Whatever you think of him, he is uninterested in poison."

"Mastino then," said Tharwat, who had clearly thought of this as well.

"Or Giovanna," offered Antonia.

"It can't have been poison," said Morsicato firmly, looking around at all of them. "I tell you, it can't! Do you imagine I didn't think of it? I changed cooks, I monitored all her food. I hired a nurse from another region who knew nothing of the Scaligeri. It wasn't poison!"

"Truly?" Cesco's condescension was maddening.

"No one had the opportunity," said Morsicato firmly.

"There was one person."

The doctor swelled. "Are you saying it was *me?*"

"Ha! No. It's right before your nose. How many potions are laying about your home? She must have picked up a few tricks from you over the years."

Morsicato's jaw fell slack. "Esta poisoned herself?!"

Cesco tapped the side of his nose. "She lacks you, you see. For years you were running off to war, first after the Emperor, then Bailardino and his family, then me. But those years in Ravenna weren't nearly as bad. She was close to you, and you were close to home. But she couldn't bear returning to Vicenza only to have you running off after me hither and yon. It couldn't have been hard. She might have asked anyone – Fra Lorenzo, perhaps? He knows plants. Even dear Suor Beatrice knows them. What potion did you use to rid yourself of the effects of the rape, Auntie? Was it rue? Do you rue it? Or was it hellebore? I almost died from that, you know. I feel a kinship for your unborn child."

There was an awful, breathless pause. Antonia was too stunned to respond. The doctor was frozen in place. Poco's mouth was fish-like, waiting for a hook. Tharwat was mournful, while Pietro looked as though he'd been hit with a stunning hammer. "What?"

"While you were off looking after your own godliness, God was allowing another to take from Suor Beatrice that which she had promised to Christ alone. Right there in the holy house. I don't wonder that she didn't tell you, but could you truly not see the change? She went from lioness to mistress mouse in the span of a few short months. Did you never wonder? Did you never—?"

"Stop! Just – stop!" Pietro ran a trembling hand over his face, trying to control his breathing. His features expressed a changing landscape – horror, failure, shame, sorrow, rage, disgust, all mingled together and amplified to a thunderous echo.

Cesco had experienced those same emotions three years before. And again last fall. And every moment since. How good it felt to share.

Dazed, Pietro lifted unwilling eyes towards his sister. Through a distended jaw he said one word. "Who?"

She shook her head, so Cesco answered. "You don't have to trouble her over it. He confessed before I killed him."

"Fuchs." The word trembled as Pietro said it, vibrating with menace, hatred, rage.

"Indeed. The great jouster will tilt his foul lance no more."

Cesco was shocked to find himself lifted bodily and thrust hard against the frescoed wall at his back. Ignoring his wound, ignoring the shouts from his doctor and friends, Pietro had bolted from the bed and now his hands threatened to pull Cesco's shoulders apart. "Don't you laugh! Don't! How – how can you laugh?"

"Why not laugh? It's all so mockable."

Tharwat and Morsicato hauled Pietro back to at least sit on the bed. His stitches had torn, but not badly. As the doctor examined them, Pietro said, "You're telling the truth?"

Stretching his bruised shoulders, Cesco folded his arms. "Why lie?"

"To hurt me. To wound me." Pietro's voice was indeed wounded. "To make everyone around you suffer, the way you made to suffer."

"It's true, it seems I am made to suffer. As to your accusation, would that I could. The truth, Nuncle, is that I'm tired of secrets. Of lies. Let us all be men, shall we? Knight to knight. Truth is supposed to be paramount. *'While truth is always bitter, pleasantness waits upon evildoing.'* To Hell with pleasantness, then. If I am embittered, I'll speak the bitter truth. Your sister was raped by Fuchs. More than once."

Pietro flinched. Antonia was sitting with Poco's arms about her as she vibrated with a brittleness he only now comprehended. "O, Antonia!"

She rose and came to take his hand. "Forgive me."

"O God, no! It is for you to forgive me!" Pietro wept hot tears, but her gaze remained clear as she soothed him.

Cesco filled the time by crossing to an empty chair. "I have avenged a part of that indignity. Fuchs is dead. But Mastino must have known, so he has to pay as well."

"That's enough, boy," growled Morsicato. He stopped examining the damage Pietro had done to his healing wound long enough to glower.

"But I thought you all wanted to play. What I cannot learn, try as I might, is if the Capitano had a hand in it. So Imperia can help me after all. Did he say anything?"

Woodenly, Antonia said, "'No quarter.'"

"Equivocal. But it's not as though I lack cause to revenge myself upon him. I should hurt him if only for Uncle Pietro's sake. After all, Cangrande tried to sacrifice him for the Paduan peace. But we got in first, making Ser Alaghieri a hero instead. I think it pleased him – he's not evil. He just knows what he wants. I wish I did."

Tears still flowing, Pietro held his sister while Poco stroked her hair through the caul. It was the younger brother who said, "You're a bastard."

"In every sense, *il veltro*," agreed Cesco, planting his feet on the edge of the table. "Back to the artful way I was stripped of my companions. You mentioned the riots. They were fortuitously timed, weren't they? Because the only one Cangrande couldn't send away was the Arūs. Better than the most faithful dog, determined to stay with me at all costs. Cangrande knew there was no other way but to kill him, and the fall of Bursa was the perfect excuse. Cangrande tried it twice, using agents to stir up resentment among the people. So what if a half-dozen poor Muslims died in a few riots? Tharwat, being Tharwat, was able to defend himself with his skin intact. Next time, I was sure, he'd be so outnumbered he'd fall. So I sent the Moor on a foole's errand. To Avignon."

"Was it a foole's errand?" asked Tharwat.

"Clearly. Look at you. My fault. It saved Cangrande the need of killing you. But is this better than death?" Cesco glanced down at his folded hands. "No matter what I do, people suffer."

"Arrogance," said Tharwat. "Not everything is due to you. I choose my own path."

"No, the stars choose it for you. Isn't that the way?"

Though his head was reeling, Morsicato thought he saw the outline of Cesco's words. "You mean to kill Mastino and Cangrande."

Cesco opened his hands in a helpless gesture. "They are *sanguis meus* – blood of my blood. But I've done it before." It was the first time he'd admitted complicity in Federigo's death. His hands began to shake, and clasped them more tightly. "You mistake me, doctor. Death is too kind. I plan to make their existences a misery worse than any grandfather Dante envisioned. I had plans for Fuchs, but he foiled them by making me kill him. That's one score settled."

Antonia raised her head. "I do not need avenging."

"Ask your brothers, or the doctor, or the Moor. I think they disagree. Dear, dear auntie – you understand why I stayed away?"

Holding her tightly, Pietro looked as though he wanted to unearth Fuchs' body to murder him again. He asked, "How can we help?" and surprised himself by meaning it.

"Choose your game and throw your die. For me, my plans were to ruin Mastino and eclipse Cangrande entirely. It's been his terror all along. He shouldn't have taken such pains to break me, as it only showed me how very much he fears me."

Cesco leaned back. "But last September I finally saw that the whole thing was a pointless joke! A cosmic jape, played on me. You asked me what I want, Nuncle. I want the thing I cannot have. One thing for myself, just for me, and it's denied to me. Ever since then, I've seen the pieces, but refused to play the game. Can you appreciate that, Tharwat? I defy the stars."

"You cannot."

"No? As Nuncle Pietro likes to say, if not my stars, I can control my actions." Cesco crossed to a far table with a bottle and several goblets. He poured for himself. "But things were already in motion. I had a notion that Detto has been helping me carry out."

"And what is that?"

"You should have tumbled to it, Nuncle. You're the one who caught Detto near the Doge's palace. I'm betraying Verona to Venice."

A thunderous silence followed this remark. Cesco filled it by drinking off his wine.

In a remarkably soft voice, Pietro said, "You're doing what?"

"The galling part is that, when I found out about the prophecy, I showed myself to truly be Cangrande's son. All I wanted was to prove the damn thing wrong! That took on a great importance to me," he said, gazing over his goblet at the middle distance. "I am the Greyhound of Verona. What better way to deny the prophecy than to remove all my own power? And in the process, Cangrande's and Mastino's as well. I think you'll find that Venice has been usurping Veronese trades since the wedding. O, the wedding! And Christmas, and the Palio. Such largesse, such extravagance! The coffers are entirely bare. Only the income from all her investments will save her. But when the summer arrives, the money won't be there. The damage won't be clear until autumn, I think, and not even fully appreciated then. But there are some loans, taken through various banks in the Scaliger's name, that will come due soon. Things will be very tight. We might have to start pawning towers."

As stunned as the rest, Morsicato was strangely soft-spoken. "You'd ruin the city? The lives of everyone you know?"

"I'd burn the city to the ground and salt the earth, only I wouldn't get as much satisfaction."

Pietro looked to Detto, who was ashen. "You knew?"

"I – I –"

"He knew he was helping to ruin Mastino. Even Dandolo doesn't know that I plan it as a trap for him as well. Because if he tries to take a bankrupt Verona, he'll find he's not the only claimant. The Holy Roman Empire won't let Verona fall to a neutral party when it could be the Emperor's Italian capitol instead. Rupert and I had many long conversations."

"Rupert? But he attacked Detto!" protested the doctor.

Cesco snorted. "Of course he didn't. You forget, I've known Rupert these last two years. He saved my life at the Emperor's court. Even as I sent him away, I knew he hadn't arranged it."

"Then who did?"

Cesco sipped again. "That's the question, isn't it? I didn't see the pattern at first. I thought it was part of the larger game. But during the Palio I realized there was a new player on the board. At least, one I hadn't counted on. Detto, Benedick, Carrara, me. The attacks were playful, almost. Everyone was offered a chance to survive."

"Not Petruchio," said Morsicato. "And not Pietro – it's a miracle he's alive."

"Those are a case apart," said Cesco. "Each was real, and quite desperate. I thought for a moment the poisoning was Dandolo, but why risk it when I'm ruining Verona for him? And who wants Pietro dead? All of his foes have turned into loving friends. It's a neat trick.

You'll have to teach it me someday." He saw all their faces and held up his hands, palms forward. "Never fear! I am no longer bent on total annihilation. I always left myself a death door to escape through. The pieces were set for three different games. Victory through destruction, victory through strength, victory through indifference. I can easily mislead Dandolo, and thus recoup Verona's losses twofold. Verona will be stronger than ever before. No one will suffer but Verona's enemies."

"You were on the path of destruction," said the Moor. "What changed?"

"You mean why am I telling you all this?" Cesco drank, then looked levelly towards his best friend. "Detto. He's not much of an orator, but what he lacks in rhetoric he makes up in vehemence. He gave an impassioned speech the night of the Palio. And I had a fright, I confess. I realized — something. Then he delivered a letter."

"From Rosalia," said Pietro.

Touching the coin at his throat, Cesco nodded.

"You never speak of her."

"Nor will I now."

Composed again, Antonia rose and drew near him, though she refrained from touching. "You cannot help what you feel, Francesco. There is no sin in that."

Biting down hard on his lip, Cesco almost spat. "The law of contradiction is basic Aristotle. To repent the sin and at the same time want to commit it is a contradiction. And I am full of contradictions. But I'm trying!" He swung a fist and punched the nearest wall hard enough to make his knuckles bleed. Staring down at his hand, he laughed to himself. "Very trying, I'm sure. Bear with me. Youth is a turbulent time, they say." He took in a second ragged breath. "The *Remedia Amoris* says it best — *love yields to busy-ness*. If I cannot cure my liver of this sickness, I can use my mind to make prophecy a reality. That will occupy my every waking moment from now to the grave. Then I can die in peace and look God in the face. I have a few questions for Him."

Mingled with fear and grief, there was relief in Antonia's face. "So you do believe."

He snorted. "What day is it? I believe and don't believe. I want to believe, because then I could blame. Look what He did to you, let alone me. I want to find the stairway to Heaven and climb it armed for war."

"Is that what you want?" said Pietro. "I thought you wanted to ruin Mastino and Cangrande."

"Eclipse, at least," admitted Cesco. "I'm outshining my dogged cousin in every field he ventures into – if he tried to be a tailor, I'd learn to sew. As it is, I can out-joust him in the lists and out-fight him in a battle. Already I've made him a foole, little though he knows it. His tenderest spot is his pride." Cesco took a sip of his wine, still watching the slight rise of blood across his knuckles. "That's an appetizer. For the next course, I could devour the Capitano's authority. I've got the next generation of Verona's lords eating out of my palm. Detto there is going to be Podestà of Vicenza when his father dies or retires. I've also got a whimsical desire to make Signor Benedick da Nobody the next Capitano da Padua – either him, or Signor Salvatore, who will soon wed Bonaventura's daughter. Either one will do, even if it means sticking my hand up his arse and putting words in his mouth. All this is to say that when our beloved Capitano dashes himself on the rocks of his ambition, I'll be there to take the reins."

Poco frowned. "How do you know he'll—"

"Because his ambition is limited by his fear. He is more interested in prophecies than victory. To be sure, he wants his due. But he's fearful he's not due more than he has. Honestly, fourteen years to take Padua? Had he truly believed in himself, he would have swept them away in a single season."

Listening, Pietro could not help thinking back to the night Cangrande had first let victory slip from his grasp. In 1314, instead of chasing the routed Paduan army and taking the defenceless city, Cangrande had set out to receive the child Cesco. *More interested in prophecies than victory. How true.*

Cesco continued. "No, Treviso is about the limit of his daring. After that he will posture and threaten, but make no move."

"What about you?"

"Me? I have a standing invitation to join the imperial court. I am Franz der Hund, remember? The noble heir to a despised vassal lord. But if Ludwig knew how many of his secrets I've gleaned, he would see me dead before I ever arrived. And with good reason. Uneasy is the head that wears the crown."

Antonia gasped. The Moor stood a little straighter. The doctor's mouth hung open. Detto and Poco both stared. It was Pietro who voiced their common thought. "You mean to become Emperor."

"The victory through strength. How else can the Greyhound bring about another age of man?" Cesco gazed at them all in turn. "I am not mad, you know. I could do it."

None of those present doubted him. Morsicato asked, "When

did you scheme all this?"

"During my absence in Padua last Fall. Oh, I saw the framework years ago, long before I knew about the prophecy." He laughed darkly. "Ambition's a ladder, and everyone seems to forget — I'm a Scaliger, too."

Tharwat's voice broke the long silence that followed. "You have said you *could* do this, that this is all possible. But you have not answered the Count's question. Is this what you want?"

Cesco's smile was only a degree more genuine. "I'd have expected the poet's children to focus on my semantics. You've hit it, of course. I *could* do all this. I still don't know if I want to. Spiting Mastino and my father seems a poor reason for all that effort. Sometimes — O, sometimes I just wish to disappear. Travel to Arabia with your friend Battuta. Or go with Montagu to England. Or Don Pedro to Aragon. Somewhere far off, where no one has ever heard of Cangrande, or the Greyhound." His laugh was unamused. "Victory through indifference."

"If that's what you want," said Pietro, "we'll help. We are on your side."

"Provided he chooses the right side," said Morsicato harshly. "Run away? Hide in drink? In hashish? Is that the best you can do?"

"I don't know," said Cesco. "Detto, let's go. I'm too tired for this."

"Yes, go sleep it off," snapped Morsicato. "The ultimate sleep. You'll never be tired again. Want to defy the stars? There's the easy way. Just die. Poof, thwarted."

"Doctor!" snapped Antonia.

"It's the other thing he's been flirting with," said Morsicato. "The brawls, the drinking, the hashish — he wants someone to take the decision away from him. He's pushing us all to make the choice for him. And if we won't, one of his enemies will."

Cesco shook his head angrily. "That's not — I don't—"

"He's right," said Detto. "You have to choose. *'Be what you might be, must be.'*"

Shaking, Cesco leveled an angry finger. "Don't!"

"*'Be your self.'*"

Cesco launched himself at Detto. "You have no right—!"

Catching Cesco's fist in his own grip, Detto held his gaze until the doctor and Poco got between them.

"It's the drug!" snarled Morsicato. "He's numbing himself to death."

Cesco pulled free. "What are you talking about?"

"The hashish," said Tharwat sternly. "You are abusing it."

"I'm not!" cried Cesco.

"Your eyes betray you. And your words."

"He isn't," protested Detto.

"Detto, you may not have noticed it—"

"He gave it all to me," protested Detto. "I burned it up."

"What?" asked several voices at once.

"I threw it in the fire. The night of the Palio, the night Ser Alaghieri was stabbed – he told me to burn it, and I did."

Grasping Cesco's face, Morsicato opened the eyelid. Cesco pulled away, but not before the doctor had seen what he needed to see. "He's definitely been dosed."

"If not by his own hand," said the Moor, seeming to grow in stature, "then by whose?"

Morsicato swiftly crossed to where Detto stood and repeated his examination. "He has it, too. Not so deep. I might not have noticed it."

"Antonia," said Pietro. "Show Morsicato your eyes."

She obeyed, and the doctor reared back in horror. "You've all been dosed!"

Cesco started laughing, laughing so hard his side ached and he had to cough. He now understood why he hadn't needed the wafers all these weeks – the reason there had been so many for Detto to burn. And why his sense of detachment lasted until the night of the Palio, when the need became intense. He had been absent from his home all that day, and into the night. And so he had not partaken of his favourite treat. "Pine nut brittle!"

"O God," said Antonia, her head swimming as she explained. "Pine nut brittle is a treat made by Vito only for Cesco. The cook is very careful to see that no one else eats it. Only tonight we all..."

Pietro felt a fist grasp his heart. "Does Maddelena...?"

"No," said Antonia, recalling the taste of the sweet on her own lips. "She hates the stuff. It made her sick once."

"Smarter than all of us combined," said Detto, feeling wretched and now understanding why.

"The cook? Vito?" asked Poco. "Who could have put him up to it?"

The bottom dropped out of Antonia's stomach. "I may know."

"Not Fra Lorenzo," said Cesco, skin crawling. "He tried to make me cast off the habit."

"No, not Lorenzo." Slowly she explained. It was so much easier, now the rape was out in the open. So much of the past three years could be explained – her timidity, her re-embracing of the Order, her close relationship with the Abbess. And with the friar, who had procured the tea that had rid her of Fuchs' monstrous child. The Bible said that only priests were allowed to perform that act.

"The Abbess knows everything?" asked Pietro, careful not to sound as angry as he felt. He couldn't blame her, not after what she had been through. But why hadn't she come to him? And how had he been so self-absorbed that he hadn't felt the change, even from Avignon?

"Not everything," answered Antonia defensively. "I told her I could not share state secrets, or secrets that did not belong to me. But I did share our fears of Cesco and the hashish."

"There's no telling who she passed that on to," said Poco. "Mastino, maybe?"

Antonia shook her head. "Giovanna has visited the Abbess often these last few months, and always when I am not expected."

"That bitch," said Pietro. "She's fortunate to be on her way to France, and out of reach of my arms."

Morsicato looked to the Moor. "I thought she made a vow not to move against Cesco."

"The promise was contingent upon Paride's elevation. She might feel we did not hold up our end of the bargain. And she was not murdering Cesco. Merely rendering him volatile. She may have hoped he would speed his own destruction."

"No wonder he wasn't falling asleep – he wasn't even taking our mixture." Morsicato straightened himself to face Tharwat. "I apologize."

The Moor shook his head. "I should never have started him on this road. I have given the enemy a weapon."

"No." Head in his hands, Cesco's voice was muffled. "You gave me a tool. My fault I let someone use it against me."

Wincing, Pietro leaned forward. "Cesco – how do you feel?"

"Unclean," came Cesco's muffled answer. "And profoundly stupid."

"What do you want?"

Cesco's head jolted up. Fighting through the haze that had been surrounding him all these weeks, he struggled to find the truth within him.

"I want to win."

THIRTY-FOUR

THE PLAN THEY MADE was a good one. They would spread the story that, to aid Ser Alaghieri's recovery, Cesco was escorting his foster-father south to the seaside, staying with friends at Pisa. They would divert *en route*, and pick a less populous place where Cesco could endure the painful weaning off the drug. Suor Beatrice would remain in Cesco's house to look after his little wife, while Poco, Morsicato, Tharwat, Detto accompanied the traveling pair.

They had to tell Cangrande the truth, but they were sure he would not object. Nor did he — the prospect of his troublesome heir vanishing for weeks or even months meant he could settle the Paduan discontent in Verona. "Just be sure he is ready for Treviso."

"He will be," said Cesco, who did not enjoy being talked about as if he were not present.

Morsicato wrote to inform his wife that he had to journey with Ser Alaghieri, wondering what the reply would be. When it came, he felt a pang of disgust — Esta wrote that she was feeling poorly again, and had taken to her bed. He dashed off a curt reply:

Then you'd best stop dosing yourself. I have real medicine to practice.

Pietro, Poco, and Antonia spent hours alternating between talking, weeping, and staring in uncomfortable silence. Through it all, they were themselves — Pietro solicitous and concerned, Poco indignant and hurt, and Antonia practical and stern. Of them all, she was the least forgiving of herself. Pietro was as understanding as he could be, but could not stop himself asking, "Why didn't you come to me?"

"You were gone," Antonia told him. "And Cesco had no one left. It was the price I was willing to pay."

He took her fingers in his. "Too high, too high. Cesco would never have wanted it paid."

"Which is why I hoped he'd never know. No one was supposed to know," she added bitterly. "But for my weakness, no one would have known, and Cesco would not be suffering—"

"Nonsense. Firstly, he knew without you telling him. Second, Cesco was correct about one thing. Secrets are a disease of their own. You see what they've done to Cangrande, Katerina, Giovanna, all of them. Keeping secrets is the problem, not the solution."

"That's what Abbess Verdiana said." She was feeling particularly bitter towards the Abbess, and was glad to be sleeping elsewhere than the convent.

"She wasn't mistaken. You just chose the wrong person to confide in. Something we've all done from time to time."

Antonia leaned her head into her brother's shoulder. It happened to be his bad side, and he winced but put his arms about her and held her close for a long time.

◆ ◇ ◆

"You're mine!" shouted Maddelena, holding fast to Cesco's legs. "You're mine!"

"So I am," her husband answered. "But as I am yours, Count Pietro is mine, and I must look after him. Just as you must look after Icarus while I'm gone, and Felix and the puppies. And little Giulietta, who is smaller than you and is losing her father soon to the war."

"You're not going to war," sniffed Maddelena. "You're going to sit by a sick man."

"You'd rather I was fighting a battle?"

"Yes!" cried Maddelena. "What can you do for a sick person? You're not a doctor. Stay!"

Trembling, Cesco tried to laugh. "I don't want to go. But I must. And you must be brave. I promise, you will see me again."

She hadn't even considered the possibility that she might not see him again. As she burst into tears and was led away by Antonia and Dahna, Cesco felt the pang of guilt. He had brought her into his life, his world. A world in which there was nothing but pain.

♦   ◊   ♦

"What of us?" asked Signor Benedick, crushed to discover he was not invited on this journey. Salvatore was beside him, less indignant but clearly vexed. The remaining Rakehells, from Thibault to Hortensio, would hear of this departure second-hand.

"I have orders for you," Cesco informed him. "Take the rest of the Rakehells and join Otto's camp. He'll be at the forefront of Treviso, and I want us in the thick of it. Oh, and spend this for me," he added, tossing a bag of golden florins at Benedick's feet.

Benedick's eyes lit up. "As you command."

Cesco pointed at Salvatore. "Don't get married until we return."

"I won't," said the grey-eyed Paduan with a smile.

Benedick ventured a question. "Do you mean to stop at *La Rosa Colta* before you go? The girls have been asking for you."

"One in particular," added Salvatore.

Cesco shook his head. "I have not the stomach for it. Tell her I shall call when I return."

♦   ◊   ♦

They brought none of Cesco's household staff save his cook, who made the very best sweets. During a stop on the carriage ride south, Tharwat drew Vito aside to taste a local nut. They did not return in time to catch the carriage, but Tharwat showed up that night, very calm. "Vito has elected to ply his trade elsewhere. Perhaps in France. But not before he samples his own cooking."

"Did he offer a name?"

"He did. Very readily."

"Too readily?" Seeing the Moor's expression, Cesco's nostrils flared.

They stopped over in Parma, where Cesco's uncle-in-law was currently serving as Vicar of the city, similar to Podestà. The situation here was very like how Padua had once operated – the Correggio family held sway, but elected a foreigner to rule.

Rolando Rossi feasted them, and they spent a pleasant evening in the company of his sons. Late in their talk, he became a little serious. "Can I persuade you all to remain here? There's trouble brewing, I can feel it."

"Trouble?" asked Morsicato, stroking the forks of his beard as he cast a worried glance at Cesco. They had put him back on the little sticky chews, hoping to ease the weaning process. The doctor worried he might think himself cured already, and take up the troubles of his wife's family.

"Florentines have been sniffing about the city," said Rossi. "The Guelphs have Pisa in their power. I believe they mean to snaffle up Parma next and take control of the whole Po Valley. You know what that would mean."

"No siege of Treviso," said Pietro. If Parma was lost, Verona's cause would be worse off than before the fall of Padua. The Guelphs would own the only Ghibelline foothold south of the Po River, leaving Cangrande's flank open, with Mantua ripe for the Guelphs to besiege and win. Instead of besieging Treviso, the Scaliger would have to use his army to defend his own territories.

"Won't you consider staying?" pressed Rossi. "With a famous knight such as Count Alaghieri and the Scaliger's own son here, the Guelphs might think twice before marshalling their forces."

"It might have the reverse effect, making Parma more alluring," offered Cesco. "Florence has no love for our friendly Count. And if the papal forces were able to capture the heir of Verona, they could force all kinds of concessions. No, I think it best we don't stay." He acknowledged Rossi's disappointment by lifting a cup. "Never fear, uncle-in-love. We'll bend our brains to solving your dilemma."

Rossi did not seem comforted. Likely he had heard too many tales of Cesco's high living, brawling, and philandering to take the boy seriously. He was of use for what he represented — a link to the rising power of Verona. All it had cost Rolando's brother was a daughter. It had cost Rolando nothing at all.

♦   ◊   ♦

After Parma they continued on west along the Taro river until it turned south. There they diverted, heading for the seaside town of La Spezia. Built into a crescent bay at the foot of rolling hills, the seaside resort had existed since pre-Romans days. Here, under assumed names, they came to a halt. It was the second week of April, and the promise of Spring was in the air. Rains came and went, scrubbing the countryside clean.

In many ways, the following weeks were reminiscent of their years in Ravenna — a seaside home, anonymity, no pressure to be anywhere. Indeed, their stay would have been idyllic, save for all the screaming.

Cesco's pain was caused by his flat refusal to take another sticky chew. When he was reminded that they also contained the poisons he had been exposed to, growing his immunity, he snarled. "Give me the poisons, then, and be done!"

After just three days he had disappeared behind his eyes. He lost weight, returning to the spindle-thin form of his days being hawked by Cangrande.

Tharwat was with him at all times, ready to soothe or restrain, as the moment required. He had seen this process before, and knew better than anyone how to cope with it. He also had the most guilt, having exposed Cesco to the substance that his body was now craving with such terrifying hunger.

It was hard for them all, forcing them to relive that terrible night four years earlier when poison had left Cesco dangling at the edge of life. This time was less mortal, but it lasted longer.

"Heaven knows what the neighbours think we're doing to him," muttered Morsicato. But their villa was in the hills above the city, with little danger of prying eyes.

Because of his injury, Pietro could not do much more than watch. Any attempt to hold Cesco would aggravate his own wound. But he quickly discovered something he could do. Poco had found a well-stocked library in the city. Pietro asked him to borrow a copy of Virgil, and another of Ovid. Books in hand, he set himself up in a comfortable chair and proceeded to read through the day and into the night until his voice grew hoarse.

The first few days were absorbed by *The Aeneid*. But Cesco seemed better when listening to something he did not know as well, so Pietro switched to *The Metamorphoses*. He began with the primal chaos, moving through the ages towards the flood. Passing swiftly through Jupiter's rape of Io, Pietro did take the time to read Mercury's retelling of the story of Syrinx that so lulled Argus that Mercury could strike off his head.

In Ovid's second Book, Pietro was disconcerted to find another rape on the part of the great god, first of Callisto, then of Europa. He had never noticed how often this violent act was depicted in literature. Worse, it was ever the woman who received punishment – Io transformed into a cow, Callisto into a bear, Semele consumed by fire. *At least Europa became a queen.*

It was remarkable how often Mercury appeared in these tales. And also the stars. Unhappy creatures were constantly being transformed into constellations. *Perhaps that is why they torment us – unhappy in life, they strive to share their despair with the living below.*

Pietro read aloud the story of Actaeon, turned into a stag and killed by his own hounds for spying on the naked Diana. He read of the birth of Bacchus, the judgment of Tiresias, the story of Echo and Narcissus. Coming to the tale of the lovers Pyramus and Thisbe, he told of the wall separating them and their plan to meet in secret. Of the lion that frightened Thisbe away, leaving only her veil behind to be gnawed by the beast's bloody maw.

He related what came next:

Serius egressus vestigia vidit in alto pulvere certa ferae totoque expalluit ore Pyramus; ut vero vestem quoque sanguine tinctam repperit, 'una duos' inquit 'nox perdet amantes, e quibus illa fuit longa dignissima vita; nostra nocens anima est. ego te, miseranda, peremi, in loca plena metus qui iussi nocte venires nec prior huc veni. Nostrum divellite corpus et scelerata fero consumite viscera morsu, o quicumque sub hac habitatis rupe leones!

Having gone out later, Pyramus saw the creature's tracks in the deep sand, and his whole face went pale. When he also found the veil stained with blood, he cried, 'Two lovers will be lost in one night. She was worthy of a long life. I am the guilty spirit. I have killed you, O pitiful girl. I, who told you where to come by night, and did not reach it first. O whatever lions dwell under this rock, tear apart my body and devour my wicked entrails with your fierce jaws!

Sed timidi est optare necem.' velamina Thisbes tollit et ad pactae secum fert arboris umbram, utque dedit notae lacrimas, dedit oscula vesti, 'accipe nunc' inquit 'nostri quoque sanguinis haustus!' quoque erat accinctus, demisit in ilia ferrum, nec mora, ferventi moriens e vulnere traxit.

But it is cowardly to wish for death.' Lifting Thisbe's veil, he carried it with him to the shade of the tree they had chosen. Kissing the token, wetting it with his tears, he said, 'Accept now draughts of my blood too!' Without hesitating, he drove his iron sword into his bowels. Dying, he dragged the sword from his steaming wound.

Cesco sighed. "Idiot."

Pietro paused, unsure if Cesco was responding to the story or lost in his delirium. "What?"

"He's a fool. Make certain she's dead, at least, before opening your veins. I'm thirsty, Nuncle."

Setting the book aside, Pietro winced as he rose to bring Cesco some water. He had to fetch a second and hold it, as Cesco's own hands spilled too much of the first cup from shaking.

Cesco began to improve, if slowly. He vomited up the food he tried, but kept nibbling wafers of bread and slivers of fruit until he was able to hold them down. Prone to blinding headaches now, he forbid light, which left Pietro to read from the next room, or from behind a curtain.

Yet the doctor was pleased. "I'm not sure if it's his youth or the fact that we've been dosing him with poisons for the last three years, but his body is recovering."

"What about his mind?" asked Poco bluntly. "He's been utterly deranged."

Morsicato waved that off. "Delirium. But there may be changes in him. All we can do is watch for the effects, and hope he'll tell us if he feels anything."

"That sounds likely," muttered Poco.

♦   ◊   ♦

At first, it seemed the delirium was here to stay. Waking, Cesco would see them and pose the oddest questions – What time was it under the earth? Where had the singing gone? Did they think he was drowning in an ocean of air? He wondered aloud if there was only one light in the night sky and the blackness was actually dark stars blotting it out. And once, in deadly earnest, he yelled, "Answer me this – did Adam and Eve have belly-buttons?"

He also made strange requests, such as paring his nails in order of left thumb, right thumb, left forefinger, right forefinger, and so on. "Must attain balance," he told them. He refused to sleep on one side longer than the other, and asked to be turned over at every hour. And he asked for oysters. "They have the secret, you see."

Yet he could be lucid. There were moments of banal conversation, though often he seemed amused by random comments. When someone departed the room, he bade them farewell as though he might never see them again, and greeted them on their return with fierce joy. "I was afraid I had forgotten you."

It was the middle of the night when Pietro finally understood. All the others were asleep, but Pietro had remained behind to read, at last drifting into sleep in his chair. He did not know what called him from the depths of slumber, but when he opened his heavy lids he saw Cesco's eyes fixed on him.

"Forgive me," said Cesco.

"You didn't wake me," answered Pietro.

"No," agreed Cesco. "I was wishing you didn't exist."

"Sorry to disoblige." Pietro had endured worse insults these last few weeks.

"No," said Cesco, shaking his head. "You misunderstand. I think it means you're real."

Pietro stared. "Of course I'm real."

Cesco gazed back in interest. "How do you know?"

"Because I'm here. I feel the floor, see you, hear Morsicato's snores."

"The detail is amazing, isn't it?" mused Cesco. "But how do you know? Maybe what you see is not what I see. Maybe what you think is snoring sounds like a choir to me."

"It's loud enough. You're interested in philosophy?"

"In what's real. I always thought I knew. But this has shown me how frail reality is. How do I know you're really here? That I'm really here? How do I know that I'm not really living in the world I call dreams, and that this is the illusion, that the reality?"

"What do your senses tell you?"

"Senses are tricked by any number of things."

"We're talking. Right now, you and I are having a conversation."

"I could be imagining this conversation. I could be imagining you exist at all. That's what I was trying to do – use my mind to make you vanish. I can do that in my dreams, sometimes."

"There's your proof. This is not a dream."

"I could be dreaming you saying that."

"Yes, you could." Instead of frustration, Pietro felt relief. That was what had been going through the young man's mind! Each time someone left, he was afraid he'd never see them again because they were a figment of his imagination.

Pulling his chair closer, Pietro launched into the talk he'd had with his father on this very subject when he had been younger than Cesco. Having read some passages from *L'Inferno*, Pietro had asked if Hell was indeed real.

"It is," Dante had replied. "But not just because God decreed it so. It is real because we believe in it." Seeing his son's perplexed face, Pietro's father had grown grave. "The world around us is an agreement. The details may vary, but most men agree that the sky is blue, that grass is green, that night is dark while day is light."

"Those things are all facts," young Pietro had protested.

"Are they? Or are they the way we perceive them? Reality is not factual. It is based on an agreement between minds. You and I concur that the sky above is blue. So do most men. But say there is a man who says the sky is red, a bleeding red that pressed down on us."

"He's mad," said Pietro at once.

"But what if he's correct, and we're all wrong?"

"That many people couldn't be wrong," Pietro had protested.

"Of course they can," Dante had scoffed. "Groups of people make the worst thinkers. But you see what I mean about perception being an agreement. We all agree that the sky is blue, and therefore we define reality. Just so with Hell. Most men agree that Hell exists."

"The Bible tells us so."

"There was a Hell before there was a Bible. For the Greeks, it was the Underworld. Tartarus, as far below Hades as the Earth is below Heaven. If you had never read the Bible, you would still fear a Hell. It is part of our agreement as living men."

"So a man who denies Hell exists can avoid it?"

"No," Dante had replied. "No more than a man who denies the sky is blue can change its colour. As long as the whole believes, the world remains the same."

Relating this conversation now to Cesco, Pietro was surprised to find those words had stayed with him. "Father said that perception does not actually belong to an individual. Because you're correct, the senses can lie. Only when we pool our perceptions can we define what is real."

Cesco scowled, not in anger but in thought. "So one man, even if he sees a truth, cannot change the world? And here I thought Truth was the ultimate power."

"It is. And you're wrong. One man can make a difference. Not by seeing a Truth, but of convincing others. Christ, of course. But also Plato, Socrates, Aristotle. Your beloved Democritus. They changed the world with their truths, and continue to do so. For centuries Aristotle was lost, only to be found again. The shift is on-going, but as long as one man has the power to change the minds of men—"

"—he can reshape reality." Cesco smiled. "So if enough men believed man could fly, he could fly?"

"I don't think it will ever happen," said Pietro wryly before turning serious. "But I also don't underestimate the power of belief. Which, after all, is another word for faith."

Pulling a face, Cesco sat forward. "What if someone convinces the world of a lie?"

"Then the lie becomes real," said Pietro. "Whether it is factual or no. So long as men agree, the lie will shape their world."

Cesco was silent for a time, brooding. "I'm supposed to bring about a new age."

"That's what a prophecy says. Which will only be true if enough men believe in it. There are plenty of prophecies that have not come true."

Cesco sounded hopeful. "So the future can change."

Pietro opened his palms. "How would we know?"

Falling back into his pillows, Cesco flashed a small smile. "It would be easier if nothing was real."

Pietro reached out a hand and squeezed Cesco's arm. "I know."

◆   ◇   ◆

Easter arrived on the 23rd of April, and Pietro walked carefully beside his brother to the church at the bottom of the hill. It was a rich city, one that had been building of late. New structures made from sandstone absorbed the sun, which was brighter here than in Verona. Even in this remarkably cold winter it had barely snowed, and now banks of flowers showed their shoots as they absorbed the rain and sun, reaching for the sky.

The church was named for the local saint, San Giuseppe. Pietro had come down for Palm Sunday, and again for Maundy Thursday and Good Friday. Now that Cesco was past the worst, Pietro was trying to walk each day. It was amazing to him that a wound in his side could steal strength from his whole body. His limp felt more pronounced than it had in years, and he often had to stop to catch his breath.

The service celebrating the rebirth of Christ was joyful. Most men were wearing new doublets, as was acceptable this time of year. Lent was over, and men could begin thriving again. Husbands could again partake of their marriage beds, though that was one thing few ever gave up for Lent.

Returning to their villa, Pietro was alerted by the tracks outside that they had missed a visitor. Over-cautious, he sent Poco to the side entrance before entering the main door, his hand upon his sword. But he found his three companions well. Tharwat was reading the borrowed Virgil while Morsicato washed a tunic he had spilled wine upon. Cesco was curled in a ball, a bolster over his face, groaning slightly, but no worse than when they had left. "Who was here?"

"Christ," said Cesco from under the bolster. "He came to say He has risen. You just missed him."

"A messenger from the Scaliger," said Morsicato. "He's marshalling his forces and wishes to have an answer before the Ides of June."

Pietro opened the side door and waved his brother in. "What's the question?"

"Will we be ready to fight," replied Cesco. "At the moment, I'd ride into battle just to escape the smell." Valuing privacy, they had not hired anyone to do their cleaning, and focus on Cesco had kept them from more menial chores.

"Truth is truth," said Morsicato, wrinkling his nose. "Too damn close in here." He crossed to the far wall and threw open the shutters.

Having peeked out, Cesco recoiled behind his bolster. "So many doctors forget that patients are people, too."

Pietro asked Morsicato, "What did you tell him?"

Morsicato shrugged. "That we'd send word when there was word to send."

"He means when he's decided if he has to burn just the bed or me with it," offered Cesco.

"I thought your head hurt," snapped the doctor.

"It hurts whether I talk or no."

"Then show some respect for my frayed nerves."

"You? There's not a dragon alive could fray your nerves."

"There's no such things as dragons."

Beneath the bolster, Cesco snorted. "And you call yourself a learned man."

Most of the afternoon was spent discussing the publishing venture that Poco was nominally heading. Cesco was engaged in this purely literary diversion, speaking late into the evening of what manuscripts would be suitable for publication.

The day was marred by sad news, relayed by Antonia. Manuello Giudeo, he of the magic music and wicked tongue, had died on a visit to Fermo.

"I told him not to retire," said Morsicato. "Sixty-eight years old, with nothing to do? I'm surprised he lasted three months."

"I wonder what will happen to his writing," mused Cesco.

"What writing?"

"Love poems. He told me he introduced the sonnet to his tribe, with no small success. And apparently wrote his own version of the *Commedia*, but for Hebrews. I asked him to translate it for me, but he never got around to it. Now he never will." Cesco sighed. "But sixty-eight! That's a race well run."

"We should all be so lucky," agreed Morsicato.

"Truth," said Cesco, "is truth."

♦   ◊   ♦

Cesco woke in the middle of the night. Thirsty, he sat up and reached for the pitcher that was beside him. But his desire was intercepted by Tharwat, who poured and passed him the cup.

"Ironic," murmured Cesco. "Years ago, you gave me hashish to help me recover from poison. Now it's the hashish poisoning me."

Even for the Moor, what followed was an uneasy silence. Cesco cocked his head and demanded in Arabic, "What plagues thee now?"

There was another long pause before Tharwat spoke. "Dost thou forgive me?"

It was a serious question, and Cesco answered it seriously. "For what precisely? The training thou didst give? Thy failure to learn more of my mother? Or the charts?"

"For them all together."

"No. I don't forgive you." Cesco paused maliciously. "Because there is nothing to forgive."

Pouring a second cup of water, Tharwat seemed to accept this. "It has been months. Thou hast not spoken of the charts."

"This humble soul was waiting for an opportune moment. It never arose."

"Doubtless thou wilt have questions."

"Several." Cesco launched the topic with the obvious points, moving on to more abstruse ones. Finally he came to the heart of the matter. "So one chart is removed. Leaving two."

"At least two. There were many portents that night, and none recorded accurately."

"But basically two. Despair, and struggle. Hope is gone."

"Yes. Hope is gone."

Laughing, Cesco switched momentarily to Italian. "The Devil damn thee black! Oh wait, he already did. One final question. Had Donna Katerina asked, wouldst thou have shown the charts to my poor young self?"

"I would have burned them before allowing thee to see them."

"But why? The work is thine."

"May my hands be removed before I do another such. Thou wilt be great, little dancer, but great men should not be aware of their futures."

"Some say fore-warned is fore-armed."

"Some do indeed. Yet it is one thing for a man my age to know the hour of his death. It is quite another for one of thy tender years."

Cesco's voice was strained. "I am married."

"I know."

"Not for love."

"Is that so? Didst thou not marry one to spare another? Was not that love? Do not presume to understand the stars, dancer. They are more deft with words than even thee."

"Dost thou mean to say the stars lie?"

"I do."

"Then thou liest, for they do not! They hang, hang in the sky. And may they hang for the lies they tell. Now shut thy ever-flapping mouth, shadow mine, and let decent people sleep."

"Sleep then, dancer. Tomorrow will be here, will you or no, and we must all face it."

Cesco mimed slapping the sky. "If it comes too early, I'll face it with the back of my hand, thus."

THIRTY-FIVE

IN THE FELTRO, war was in the air. While the forces of Verona sharpened their swords, drilled their horses, and oiled their war machines, the citizens of Treviso girded themselves for the inevitable siege. It had to come. Amazing it had been delayed so long. Cangrande had been anointed Vicar of the Trevisian Mark fifteen years past, and he could not fully claim that title without ownership of Treviso.

In recent years Cangrande had been picking off Trevisian castles, one by one. Last summer, with the bulk of his forces on the Paduan border, a few of Cangrande's ablest commanders had still managed to strip the Trevisians of Ceneda and Cavolano. But even that had not lured the Trevisian army out from behind its walls. He'd tried taking the city by stealth, but his agents had been thwarted and hanged.

The buffer to all-out war had been Padua. Those on-going hostilities had spared Treviso the brunt of Cangrande's wrath. Knowing this, the Trevisians had supplied Verona's enemy with money, arms, and men, helping Padua resist Ghibelline aggression out of pure self-interest.

That war was now over. Worse, it was over without heavy losses for either army. Worser still, those two armies had merged, becoming a force no one in their right mind would chose to engage.

But until the previous April, Cangrande had lacked the all-important legal reason for war, the *cause juste*. Scrupulously correct,

Cangrande never entered into a conflict without some pretext on his side.

In this case, he claimed to represent the true rulers of Treviso. Two years earlier there had been a governmental *coup d'état* when Guecello Tempesta had seized the reins of power and exiled all those who threatened him, turning Treviso into a near-autocracy.

While with the Emperor in Marcaria, a band of those exiled by Tempesta had come to Cangrande begging for aid. Benevolently acceding to their requests, Cangrande had his pretext for all-out war.

Waiting for the moment to strike, Verona's forces trained. The common thought was that it was enough to assemble an impressive body of men, arm them, and point them towards the enemy. But Cangrande had read the works of Vegetius and followed the old Roman's dictates. Under the command of men like Otto the Burgundian, Verona's soldiers trained and trained and trained until they were among the most elite in Europe.

Years ago, when he'd first brought his program of training in line, the majority of his soldiers had balked – mercenaries, they were unwilling to do anything out of the normal line. But he'd raised their pay for their troubles, and after a few years they discovered that their training allowed them to raise their rates wherever they went. That was when they embraced Cangrande's regimen with whole hearts.

Scattered among the foreign *condottieri* were his loyal Veronese commanders. Mastino was in Mantua, practicing with the finest cavalry Verona possessed in hopes of making himself an even better horseman. Alblivious was with him, eager to prove he was good for something more than amusement. Castelbarco was given the garrison at Peschiera. In lieu of the injured Pietro, Bernardo Ervari was given command of San Bonifacio to train his men. Nico da Lozzo was up near Schio. Bailardino, Lord of Vicenza and the oldest and most experienced of them all, remained in his city with the largest of Cangrande's forces.

Surprisingly, Rizardo da Camino, the importunate husband of Cangrande's niece Verde, appeared with a hundred horsemen and a large body of foot. All paid for by his wife's jewels. She was determined to make him a man of substance, a force to be reckoned with. That, at least, Cangrande could respect, even if he could not respect the man himself. But soldiers were never unwelcome – so long as they were in someone else's pay.

For that reason the Scaliger also accepted the young knights of Verona into his plans, despite their wintertime tomfoolery. But in one respect Cangrande had checked Cesco's plans. He had not grouped the Rakehells together for their training. Instead the Scaliger sent them to various outposts in his domains.

Having squired for Lord Nogarola, Hortensio and Petruchio were back with him in Vicenza, in command of troops twice their age. With them was Detto's brother Valentino, knighted before he was a squire and now trying to pick up the training he'd never had. Cangrande's two bastards Barto and Berto were working hard to learn the rudiments of warfare in, of all places, Padua, under Marsilio da Carrara.

Of the original Rakehells, three would not be partaking of the coming war. Paride was in France, and Rupert was again with his uncle, the emperor. The other missing member was Thibault Capulletto, forbidden by his uncle to join the war. Unlike the others, he was not a knight, and also not yet a man. Though he protested, he was kept firmly within doors while Antony himself rode off to prepare the men under his command. Shut up in his uncle's house, Theobaldo Capulletto spent his fourteenth birthday the same way he did every other day – practicing attacks out of his fight-books until the light failed, then curling up and savouring the hot tears of rage for the injustices of the world forced on him.

Since they had explicit instructions, Cangrande allowed the two Paduans to go to Illasi and train with Yuri and Fabio under Otto. The Burgundian put them through their paces, and more than once Benedick was tempted to open his mouth and curse at the short, grizzled warrior. But he was soldier enough to recognize the excellent training he was receiving. His only real resentment was that Cesco and Detto were not undergoing similar trials. But then, they were noble, and rich. They could afford to skive off.

Cangrande himself was everywhere at once, riding from one group of soldiers to another. Cheerful, quick, leaner than he'd been in years, his *allegria* flashed for every man under his command. Trading jests with the lowest foot soldier, his manner was of a man in utter control of his destiny.

May arrived, and the Trevisians expected to see the banners of Verona, Mantua, Padua, and Vicenza come marching over the hill, carried by the largest army seen since the days of the Romans.

But as May crept into June without an attack, they allowed themselves to hope. For they had heard of a snag in the fabric of the Scaliger's plans. As feared, Parma was under siege, Rolando Rossi fighting off the same Guelph forces that had taken Pisa years earlier.

Technically, Parma was not part of Cangrande's domain. But the fact that it was presently ruled by his heir's uncle-in-law made it seem so. And in practical terms, the Scaliger had to rescue Parma or else fear an attack on his southern flank just as he secured his eastern one.

Yet he was unwilling to split his forces. Once, perhaps. But he was no longer the daring young commander who would hazard all upon the throw of a die. His wound and rout at Ponte Corbo had changed his tactics. These days he never entered the field without outnumbering his foes at least three to one. Never again would his life be in danger on the battlefield. He had too much left to prove.

Treviso was an impossibility until Parma was safe. If Rossi lost, Cangrande would need his army to defend his own lands. So he fretted and sought some easy solution. When none came to him, he summoned Marsilio da Carrara from Padua for a conference where he laid out his dilemma in bald terms.

Concluding, he said, "You were a devout and loyal Guelph for years, and are still in good standing with the Church despite your defection to my cause. You know these men, fought beside them. And our mutual relative Rossi is in command of Parma. Surely you can negotiate a peace."

Carrara's eyes reflected his pleasure. This would be a welcome boost to his reputation – if he could pull it off. "I know the Guelph Legate, I can make him come to the table. But winning him – I'd require some aid."

"From whom?"

♦   ◊   ♦

"I'm summoned," said Pietro, reading over the Scaliger's message.

"Treviso?" Cesco was now able to sit at table for meals like a human.

"Pistoia." Pietro passed the letter over.

Cesco barely frowned as he worked out the code. "My uncle-in-law was correct, the Guelphs are knocking at Parma's gates. Poor Cangrande – if he doesn't take Treviso this year, I don't know how he'll bear it. Ah!" said Cesco, arriving at the heart of the message. "You are to meet Marsilio da Carrara and aid him in crafting a peace!"

"Why Pistoia?" asked Poco.

"Symbolic," said Pietro. "Castruccio Castracane won it off Florence, but since his death last Fall they've gotten it back. It gives the Guelphs the advantage. Acknowledging that we are coming from a position of weakness. Which, by conceding, strengthens our cause."

"What reason do the Guelphs have to bargain?" asked Poco.

"A siege is costly for both sides, and the outcome is fairly certain. If it drags on, Cangrande will intervene, and the Guelphs will lose. But it will cost him Treviso. So they strike now in order to gain concessions, without any real hope of taking the city."

"Will they accept you as negotiators?" asked Morsicato.

"Carrara and I are both emissaries of Ghibellines, yes. But I was born in Florence, and am newly restored by the Pope himself. Carrara has fought against the Imperial forces for most his life. We'll be accepted."

Cesco set the letter aside. "How very clever! Since you two implacable foes were able to sit across the table to fashion the *Pax Verona*, you can now sit side by side and make a *Pax Italia*!"

"Nothing so grand," said Pietro. "And I have not agreed to go."

"Of course you're going," said Cesco, ladling up some soup. "We're all going."

"You're not," said Morsicato at once. "Even if you want to help your uncle-in-law."

"Actually I don't," said Cesco. "He forgot Maddelena's birthday, so let him whistle. But nevertheless, I am going."

It was an argument they wanted to lose. Cesco was improving daily, and sunshine, open air, and purpose would do him no end of good. The miracle of youth.

The real question was if Pietro wanted to aid Carrara, and thus ensure the siege of Treviso went forward. Like hummingbirds, the consequences flitted through his mind. Credit among lawyers, if not the general public – Carrara would take the laurels for the peace. But here was a chance to ply his craft on the highest levels, increase his experience, and do some good while he was at it. How many lives would the peace save? And how many more lives would be lost at Treviso? But as Treviso was the key to Verona's dominance of Lombardy, and Cesco was the heir of Verona, the result was never truly in doubt.

The next day they packed and left the house in the hills of La Spezia. It was just over two months since they had arrived, and before they departed they celebrated Cesco's fifteenth birthday. There was no longer any point in keeping it from him. He had seen the charts, and knew what they meant. So they chose to celebrate his day with laughter, music, and good cheer.

It was the 13th of June. The Ides.

No one knew that, just the day before, Rosalia Rienzi had gone into labour. It was painful, lasting far into the night. But she was delivered of her burden just before dawn.

◆   ◊   ◆

In Pistoia, Pietro was greeted by Carrara with amused warmth. "My dear Count. I wasn't certain you'd come."

"Neither was I," admitted Pietro. "Have talks begun?"

"On the morrow. Your timing is, as always, serendipitous. The Scaliger needs equitable conditions for a truce in Parma. But I'm no lawyer."

"You could have brought Bellario. Why choose me? Did the Scaliger suggest it?"

Carrara's eyes narrowed in an ironic smile. "Believe it or not, asking for you was my idea. You've always been honourable, and you thought of everything in Ravenna. Besides, you don't mind letting someone else take the credit."

Almost a compliment, almost an insult, the remark somehow managed to perfectly capture their relationship.

"I did have one idea," said Pietro.

◆   ◊   ◆

The negotiations themselves were friendly and short, concluding on the 17th after just two days. Both sides were eager for the siege to end, and both were willing to make concessions. Parma was forced to pay a sum of gold and to receive back its exiles – there were always exiles, as Pietro well knew. But Parma was not forced to return land confiscated from those exiles, nor to admit them into the higher echelons of government. Prisoners on both sides would be returned, without ransom. Cesco's uncle-in-law would retain some power, and all of his men.

The key provision, Pietro's own invention, was that Parma would become an open city, neither Guelph nor Ghibelline. No army could be quartered within its walls. This satisfied both sides. Cangrande couldn't use the city to launch an attack south, but neither could the Guelphs use it to attack the north. As long as the truce remained unbroken, this new *status quo* would hold both factions in place.

The deciding factor was the approval of the Correggio family, the most powerful force within the city of Parma itself. Fortunately, they gave their heart-whole blessing to the bargain. Caught between the forces of the Emperor and those of the Pope, theirs had ever been a perilous state. Becoming an open city, the first of its kind, was a novel solution that put Parma in thrall to neither party, while allowing it to profit from both.

The only marring element to all this was Pietro's certainty that both sides left the meeting to start planning when and how to break the truce. But that was the nature of diplomacy.

Cheerful, and at last wholly recovered from his wound, Pietro took the air around Pistoia, with Poco, Cesco, and Detto as his companions.

"Congratulations," said Cesco. "The idea of an open city is brilliant. Quite a coup."

"For which Carrara gets the credit."

"So?" asked Cesco. "All the men in the room know who was the brain behind the terms. They won't forget."

Feeling justifiably proud, Pietro nodded as he took in the sights. Pietro knew the city from his half-remembered childhood. Halfway between Lucca and Florence, nestled snugly into the foot of the Apennine mountains, the city had grown rich and prosperous in recent years. There were new walls, with a gate in each of the city's four quarters, and new buildings under construction. Still, some things did not change. There was the Palazzo dei Vescovi, with its mullioned windows and fine frescoes. And there was the Tower of Catilina, which purported to be Roman but was clearly not.

Whereas in Verona the banded marble alternated between cream and rose, here it varied between green and white. This was most prominently seen in the oldest building in the area, the eight hundred year-old Cathedral of San Zeno. Verona also venerated Zeno, and thanks to its doors the Veronese cathedral bearing his name was more famous than this one. But there was a rugged simplicity in this ancient structure. It had been damaged by fire three hundred years ago, and been rebuilt in more modern terms, but keeping the original design.

Cesco was less enamoured, though his frown had nothing to do with the basilica itself. Noting Cesco's peaked appearance, Pietro misinterpreted the cause. "I need to sit down for a bit. Jacopo, I saw some venders in the next street. Do you think you could find us some nuts or fruit to graze on? And some water?"

Appropriately, the cathedral faced the Piazza del Duomo, and there were benches for communing with society. Detto offered to accompany Poco, thus releasing Cesco to sit on the marble bench beside Pietro.

"What do you think of Pistoia?" asked Pietro.

"Pleasant enough. A bit dull. This is high summer – where are the faires, the revels? Perhaps I'm spoiled by Verona."

"That's a safe wager." Pietro was tempted to mention that if Cesco had succeeded, those kinds of revels would have ruined Verona. Pietro was still frightened by how far Cesco had gone down that road before checking himself. But they were staying away from accusing him of anything just now. "We could visit Castruccio Castracani's grave. I hear it bears a bas-relief of a hound."

Cesco pulled a face of mock indignation. "That bastard! Usurping our symbol. Of course, he was a *cani* as well."

"Not as canny as you."

"Wordplay, Nuncle? I didn't know the wound in your side had tickled your brain. Though I note you have yet to find a diversion for us."

"Well, if we stay until the end of July, we can see the *Giostra dell'Orso*." Pietro described the event where twelve mounted knights ran courses at a bear-figure to win an ancient rag.

"Thank heavens it's not a real bear," said Cesco. "Detto wouldn't tolerate it." Just today several stray dogs had started following them, looking to Detto for attention.

They sat for a time on the bench, just enjoying a beautiful day.

"So," said Pietro at last. "Treviso."

"And then the world," mused Cesco. "Or at least enough to create a new age of man. How does the prophecy go again?"

Pietro blinked. "I meant to be more practical. But if that's what's on your mind, let me say this – I'm sorry I never… I mean – I saw what it did to Cangrande. It ruined his life, first thinking he was, then finding out he wasn't. I didn't want that kind of pressure put on you—"

"I thank you for your concern. And, if this is my destiny, I should embrace it, shouldn't I?"

"Does this mean you know what you want?"

"I've had time to think about it. And yes, I think I know."

"So that means—"

"Yes yes," said Cesco, making a face. "Let's not belabour it."

"Fine." They lapsed into silence again. Yet there was something Pietro wanted to say. "You know, you're not only Cangrande's son."

"I know that," said Cesco. "I'm also yours."

Though pleased, Pietro waved that off. "I meant Dante."

Cesco pulled a wry face. "Grandson, perhaps. He was never very fatherly."

"Nevertheless, he saw in you someone to whom he could relate. You proved him right after his death. I think you were the son he always wanted."

Cesco stared at Pietro for a long moment, then shook his head. "Nuncle – your father envied you."

"What? No, he didn't – what?"

"He did, I assure you. You were the man he always wanted to be. The good man. You are correct, in me he recognized something familiar. Restlessness. Dissatisfaction. Despair. Joyful malice, or malicious joy. Call it what you like, but it was in your father as well. So I may be the son he always wanted, but you are the man he wanted to be."

"That's – very kind of you to say. But you're missing my point. I'm talking about the prophecy. You don't have to follow in your father's footsteps, anymore than I followed mine in his. Dante Alighieri proved that a poet can change the world just as much as a soldier or leader." Pietro paused. "I know you're in rebellion against the Church, but there is an important lesson from Christ himself in this."

Cesco was wary. "And that is what, turning the other cheek?"

"Turning the other cheek is not a sign of weakness. It's a show of defiance. But no, the lesson is this – many of Christ's followers expected the Messiah to be a leader in war. All the great heroes before him had led the Jews into battle. But he showed there was another way to lead. Prophecies don't have to mean what people expect them to mean. You will usher in a new age of Man. You might do it in war. But you might also do it in words. You have the skill."

"I might do it by overthrowing the entire Church," said Cesco. "Have you thought of that?"

"I have," admitted Pietro. "And I will fight you in that, and love you all the while. The Church may not be perfect, but God is."

"If He exists at all, He must be," said Cesco, "to have someone as worthy as you following Him."

Pietro placed a hand on Cesco's shoulder. Cesco put his own hand over it, and together they shared a moment of peace and warmth. Then Cesco stood. "Where are they? I'm starved!"

Pietro rose from the bench, only to stop in his tracks and stare across the square. When Cesco realized he was no longer walking in Pietro's shadow, he turned in concern, his hand dropping at once to his sword. But Pietro simply continued to stand like a statue, utterly immobile.

"What is it?" Receiving no reply, Cesco strode to stand directly in front of Pietro, gazing where the older man's eyes were trained.

Across the square a group of young women were passing the time in conversation. All were finely attired in the latest fashion, fitted gowns cinched in close to the waist, with a fair display of décolletage. Panels were a thing of the past, and the fabric of the overdress was bunched at the back, showing a tantalizing hint of the underdress. The sleeves were absurdly long and wide, ending in a definitive point.

Off to one side stood a woman. Her oval face was dominated by two enormous eyes over a snubbed nose and pert rosy cheeks. She was clearly unwed, for her rich black hair was uncovered, falling to the small of her back and shimmering in the summer sun. Her gown was more modest than those of her companions – the broad violet band that stretched from shoulder to shoulder barely dipped below her neckline, displaying none of her chest. Her overdress was ivory with lavender accents, and her under-dress was midnight blue. She looked like the sky.

Ignoring the nearby conversation, this young woman was staring back across the piazza at Pietro, as transfixed as he.

Cesco's tension vanished, replaced by mirth. "You dog. Finally we have an answer to the question, 'What kind of woman is Count Alaghieri attracted to?' Shall we discover her name?"

Pietro hissed, "Don't!" But Cesco had already turned to wave brightly to the young woman. She raised one hand, freeing it from her long sleeves just enough to wave shyly in return.

Cesco clapped Pietro on the back. "That's as much invitation as a man could hope for. Now, if you'll excuse me, I'm off to be violently ill. Let me know when the wedding is." He walked off, whistling.

Mustering more courage than it had taken to ride to Vicenza, or to challenge Carrara to a duel, more than it had taken to face off against Bernardo Gui and the Inquisition, Pietro forced himself to walk, doing his utmost to hide his limp. A dozen introductions flashed through his mind: he could use his father to impress her, he could say he was a knight, or a count, or the foster-father of the heir to Verona. Yet when he reached her all he could say was, "Lady – you are the most beautiful woman I have ever seen. I would like to know you."

Such a smile! Open and welcoming, she showed just the smallest flash of teeth. One of those teeth was imperfectly turned, giving a very human flaw to utter perfection. Knowing his own teeth were a little crooked, he seldom used them to smile. But he could not help himself answering hers in kind.

"*Signore*, I – oh, how do I answer a beginning like that?" she said, flustered.

"By saying you'd like to know me."

There was nothing of challenge or defiance in her laugh. It was a sound of joy, and Pietro joyed in it. "I would like to know you, *signore*."

Pietro could not imagine ever wanting anything more in this life but to hear those words come from this woman's lips. For once all thought of duty, of honour, of God, of Cesco, of Cangrande, of his father – these passed entirely from his mind. His world was reduced to one person, and his heart hammered in thunderous claps for excitement and fear.

By now her friends had noticed their discourse. Thinking to defend her from unwanted advances, they intervened. "Dolce? Who is your friend?"

Dolce! What a sweet name. And she was sweetness personified as she blushed. "We have not yet reached the point of exchanging names."

Forced to introduce himself, he started small. "My name is Pietro," he said into her eyes. Then, for her friends, he bowed and used it all. "Ser Pietro Alaghieri, Count of San Bonifacio, son of the poet Dante, and Knight of the Mastiff of Verona." He took up her hand from the voluminous sleeve and raised it to just below his mouth. "Your servant."

Evidently his name was suitably impressive, as his welcome among the gaggle became noticeably warmer. But Dolce looked less impressed than happy – here was a man with a name no one could besmirch. "We are most pleased to make your acquaintance, Count Pietro. Allow me to introduce my friends." She did so, though the names flew out of Pietro's head the moment they were uttered. At last she arrived at her own name. "I am—"

"Dolce," he supplied.

"Jacopa," she answered over her friends' twittering titters.

"Forgive me," said Pietro. "I thought she said—"

"My father is Dolcetto dei Salerni," she told him. "My name is Jacopa. My friends call me Dolce, for him."

"My brother is called Jacopo," he said.

"Heavens! Then please, call me Dolce."

"So long as you call me Pietro."

Under the gaze of sleek stone lions high above, the conversation continued, mostly revolving around Pietro. He tried to remain modest, but his reason for being in Pistoia was unavoidable. They congratulated him on making the peace, then asked questions about his famous father. After a time Dolce's friends stood back, amused, as she and Pietro launched verbal barrages at each other like flights of arrows. He was eager to learn everything he could, and at the same time desperate to impress her.

When the bells began to ring, the friends reminded Dolce that they had a prior engagement. Pietro could have murdered them all. By now they were all aware of the looks passing in both directions and before departing the group of girls retired a few steps to give these two a moment alone.

Quickly Dolce said, "Ser Alaghieri, are you engaged?"

"Engaged? I – no, I have never—"

As he sputtered, she blushed. "Tonight! Are you engaged tonight?"

He had promised to dine with the ambassador from Florence. "Not at all."

"Then, if I may be so bold, I am certain you would be welcome at my father's table."

"If you will be there, I'll be honoured."

They gazed at each other in surprise and pleasure and hope and fear. Dolce said, "I have to go."

"Go," he said, denying his words by taking her hand. Again he bent low, and this time he kissed her wrist. "As long as I know I'll see you again, I'll survive."

She smiled, then ran to join her friends. Even as they turned the corner out of the piazza she was casting glances back over her shoulder at him.

Pietro stood in the square a long time, feeling an excitement he'd never known. So fast! It couldn't be real. Yet it was! *Forgive me father, Petrarch – everyone who has spoken of this.* Until tonight he'd never believed their stories – love at first sight were for the French romances. But at first glimpse of her, he'd had his breath stolen away.

Cesco sidled up beside him, with Detto and Poco on the other side. "That seemed to go well."

Pietro blushed, and they teased and tormented him all the way back to their lodgings. There, as he dressed in his finest clothes, he instructed Cesco to beg forgiveness from the Florentine ambassador, but he had a pressing engagement he could not afford to miss.

♦　◊　♦

The dinner went far better than Pietro had dared hope. Dolce's father was a kindly businessman who had planned for his daughter to marry some as-yet unidentified suitor from a good local house. But seeing the way this handsome knight-lawyer was staring at his daughter, and the way she stared back at him, he at once changed his plans. By the end of the evening, Pietro and Dolce were unofficially engaged.

"You'll have to wait a year or two," Dolcetto Salerni said. "I promised her grandmother that I wouldn't let her marry until she was twenty, and if I break my word, the old biddy will rise from her grave and hound me to death. But if you two wish, we'll read the banns this year and make the whole thing official. Now, Jacopa, will you see our guest to the door? I think I have something to do in some other room."

Pietro lingered as long as he decently could, and they agreed to see each other the next day. He walked towards his borrowed house on winged feet, the soles of his boots hardly seeming to touch the ground. For the first time in his life, Pietro considered abandoning duty.

Was this the parting that Tharwat had envisioned? Not Cesco abandoning Pietro, but the other way around? Pietro starting his own life, his own family. Cesco was fifteen now, a man. With Treviso secure and Cangrande running Verona, with Cesco no longer bent on destruction but instead on becoming all he was meant to be, could not Pietro choose to pursue his own course for the first time in his life?

He would never have thought it possible until today. But now Pietro wanted to be selfish. He had something he desired more than honour, more than loyalty. *Dolce. Sweet Dolce…*

He was in such a daze that he did not register the number of men outside the house until they had seen him and were approaching. It was the shouting of his brother that wakened him to the threat. "Pietro! Run!"

"Pietro Alighieri?" asked a gruff man with a very full moustache.

"Alaghieri," corrected Pietro automatically. "Yes?"

The mustachioed man held up a large parchment, though it was not light enough to read it. "Pietro Alighieri, we are here to arrest you in the name of the Republic of Florence." With that, they laid hands upon him.

"Wait — what?"

"You are to be returned and tried for your crimes against the Republic."

"Pietro! I've sent for Carrara! Don't let them take you!"

There was little he could do to prevent it, as the men disarmed him and bundled him into a carriage. Inside it sat a man beribboned in a doublet of stuffed and slashed sleeves. He smelled of roses and orange petals. Though Pietro did not at once recognize him, there was something familiar in his posture, which was elegant and refined.

"Ah, Count Pietro. Welcome. I see you chose to honour the summons. A pity. Here I was hoping you would put up more of a struggle." The scented man leaned forward, and the lamplight displayed a wispy moustache, with stronger whiskers along his chin. The perfectly arched eyebrows looked tweezed.

Dominating it all was a nose that had been hideously broken and sat like a squashed turnip in the middle of his face. "Had you fought, you could have uttered the words, 'I am a sore and sorry ass.'"

Cianfa Donati.

THIRTY-SIX

IN SPITE OF HIS PREDICAMENT, Pietro began to laugh. He had no idea how serious the situation might be, nor if he would even survive the night. Perhaps thoughts of Dolce made him impervious, or Cesco's newfound stability, or the suddenly rosy future. Whatever the cause, the laughter burbled right up out of his throat and into Donati's surprised face.

Donati was hardly amused. "I'm afraid this is no laughing matter, my dear Count."

"Of course it is! O Cianfa, you foole. You couldn't steal my father's bones, so you'll take mine?"

"Tch. Such bluntness, and from a poet's son! It is fortunate that your foster-child did not inherit his wit from you."

"That's right, you were a witness to his wit," said Pietro.

"More a victim of it." Donati's hand twitched towards his face. "I confess, I had half-hoped he would be here tonight."

"If you wait, he'll be here. He's dining with the Florentine ambassador."

"Yes." Donati plucked imaginary lint from his hose. "You were supposed to be arrested there. When you did not arrive, the ambassador sent word that you were attempting to flee."

"I had another engagement." Even in his present circumstance, that last word brought a smile to Pietro's face.

"I hope it was pleasant, as it will be your last evening of freedom." Donati thumped the carriage roof. "On, driver!"

The movement of the carriage quashed some of Pietro's joy — he was being taken away from Dolce. At once the lawyer in him took control. "What is the charge?"

"What else? Treason. Your family was exiled, and you are therefore a traitor to the Republic. You are here, close to Florentine power. You are being arrested and returned for trial."

"You realize there's no real charge to answer. I'll pay a fine, give up the house, and go free. Why bother?"

"No charge?" repeated Donati. "Why, as an exile, you've been fomenting sedition. By publishing and reading your father's infernal work, you've been spreading slander against a dozen famous Florentine families, mine included. By siding with the Holy Father's enemies, men such as Occam and Bonagratia, you prove yourself unworthy of your renewed place in God's sight. And by working so closely with the Greyhound, you threaten stability of the region." Donati leaned back comfortably. "I think there are many charges to answer. And you'll find the penalties far more severe than a mere fine."

Now Pietro understood. Florence was using the pretext of his exile to stir up a quarrel with Verona, thereby distracting Cangrande from attacking Treviso. So long as even one city in the north held out against the Scaliger, the allied Guelph states would breathe easy.

All that was nothing to Donati, who was merely looking for a pretext for punishing Pietro and Cesco for the insult to his father — and the insult to his visage. The nose really was squashed almost flat. *And it had been such a fine patrician nose...*

Shouting outside caused the carriage to jerk to a halt. Raised voices, some familiar, all demanding. The door was flung open and Cesco poked his head in. Seeing Donati, his mouth fell open. Then he started to laugh.

It was most unfortunate that Pietro had retained much of his good mood. If he hadn't, he might not have joined his foster-son in doubling over with mirth. They slapped at each other, trying to stop, which only made them howl the harder. Clinging to each other they climbed from the carriage, Donati in their wake. He was shaking with rage, his jaw clamped tighter than the Pope's purse.

They were surrounded by Carrara's men, and Rossi's. Both great men were present, looking on in wonder as these two played the fooles.

Dragging in a breath, Pietro told Cesco the important news. "I'm to be married!"

Eyes streaming, Cesco reared back in shock. "Nuncle, did he

molest you? The handsome Cianfa has a voracious appetite, I know. He once made overtures to me!"

Donati reddened, but his voice was even. "I mistook you for a maid. So small then, and with a girlish temper."

Hearing the man speak set Cesco into fresh paroxysms of laughter – the fine voice was now comically nasal. "Can you not tell the difference between a hart and a hind? Or is it the hind you like? Oh, I see! You cannot smell them out! Your poor patrician proboscis is a little less proud than of yore."

Whatever Donati had been about to say, he was forestalled as Lord Rossi and Lord Carrara both approached and demanded the reason for Count Pietro's arrest. Donati answered by producing the writ from the Florentine Signoria demanding Pietro's appearance before their court. Donati concluded his oration. "So if you will permit me to bring the accused, he will receive his day in court." He gestured for his men.

"Not so hot," said Carrara, interposing his person between Donati and Pietro.

"Quite," said Lord Rossi. "The Count is a guest of this city, and under its protection under a seal of peace, signed by Florence. If the Signoria wish to bring him to account, they must do so in Pistoia's courts, not their own."

Donati seemed to expect that argument. "He is not a citizen of Pistoia, nor even Parma, but of Florence."

"Actually," said Morsicato, elbowing his way forward, "the city of Florence stripped him of his citizenship two decades ago. He's a citizen of Verona now. The Scaliger made him first a knight, then a count."

"He's also an honourary citizen of Padua," declared Carrara at once. "I have the right, and here I declare him a Paduan. So he is under my jurisdiction, not yours."

That engendered a fresh wash of amusement. Carrara had tried to murder him on two battlefields, and again in a duel. Today he was rallying to Pietro's defence. The moment was not lost on Carrara, who winked. Pietro laughed and raised his fist in the air. *"Patavinitas!"* Which in turn had Carrara chuckling.

The laughter made Donati purse his lips so that he looked like a duck. With his ruined nose, it was hardly an improvement. "Ser Alaghieri is charged with treason and sedition."

"And I'm not?" asked Poco. "I'm Dante's son as well."

"You have paid your fine and been forgiven," said Donati coolly. "A pity your brother did not take the time to do the same."

More and more armed guards were arriving, these latest belonging to Lorazzo Cancellieri, a local magistrate. Seeing his crest, Pietro groaned inwardly. Here was another man whose ancestor was languishing in at least a literary Hell, if not the real one. *Well done, Pater! Did you have to insult the whole world?*

Cesco was laughing again, murmuring, "Canto thirty-two. 'Nor yet Foccaccia....'"

"Quiet, you deranged little maniac," murmured Pietro, barely holding his own piece. "You'll get us hanged."

A verbal battle was waged between Donati, Rossi, Carrara, and Cancellieri. There was no question of the Count's arrest — he was here under safe conduct. Donati argued that, his mission concluded, Signor Alighieri was no longer Pistoia's concern.

"I don't know why Donati's complaining," whispered Cesco. "Cancellieri's ancestor occupies a much lower place in Hell than his father, and *he* seems perfectly content."

At last the Florentine ambassador arrived to craft a peace, which had likely been the intent all along. At his insistence, Pietro would remain in Pistoia until a court could be convened that would satisfy Florentine justice. "Florence requires an oath that the Count of San Bonifacio will not be allowed to abscond north until this matter is settled." Cancellieri agreed, turning at once to Pietro and offering to house him in the palace as a guest.

Normally Pietro would have protested. Thinking of Dolce, he instead thanked Cancellieri with such real pleasure that Donati looked quite put out.

Cesco seemed to have finally recovered himself. He stepped forward to face the Florentine ambassador, a member of the Amidei family. A large and gruff man, naturally sour of visage, his ancestor had fared better in Dante's hands, being mentioned in *Paradiso*. "Lord Amidei, when the time comes for the trial, I'd like to proffer counter charges against the wily Cianfa here. Grave-robbing, to be precise. I am a witness. So is Bailardetto."

As Amidei looked on in surprise, Cianfa Donati was scornful. "I have witnesses who will swear I was in my room on the night in question, and nowhere near Dante's tomb."

"Did I say it was Dante's bones you were trying to steal?" replied Cesco politely. "You were always petty, Cianfa. Like your father, giving the fig to your betters instead of owning your faults. Now be gone before someone ends your nosing around by removing it entirely. *Cosa fatta capo ha.*" This was aimed at Amidei, who knew the phrase far too well, being part of his family's lore. *What's done is done.*

Failing to conjure a biting reply, Donati clambered into his carriage and it rumbled away with his armed men riding close behind. Amidei was apologetic, Rossi sympathetic, Carrara amused, Morsicato angry, Poco furious. Cancellieri was solicitous. "Count Pietro, I'm sorry, but I gave my word I would not allow you to leave until this matter is settled…"

Pietro waved this concern aside. "I'll gather my things and come to the palace right now. Please have your men accompany us, so you have no fear I'll 'abscond', as Donati put it."

Rossi was a bold man, and his disgust at this evening's events was manifest. "What a cockroach!"

"Cockhound, more like," said Cesco. "He is always chasing a tail, most often his own. I'll walk with you, Nuncle."

As Carrara and Rossi returned with Cancellieri and Amidei to the palace, Pietro, Cesco, Detto, Poco, and Morsicato trooped along to their lodgings, watched by two of Cancellieri's men.

Checking over his shoulder, Cesco made certain they were out of earshot when he spoke. "How did Donati learn you were here? It was decided in Verona, and the business was finished almost as soon as you arrived. Yet he had time to arrange your arrest?"

Pietro frowned. The note had been signed by the Signoria — not a quick affair. "It doesn't seem possible…"

"More likely another jab from our unknown enemy. Like I said before, malicious but playful. An inconvenience, rather than a serious attempt on your life. Though if you died, I'm certain our foe would not mind."

"Comforting. You know who it is, don't you?"

"I have a suspicion."

"Are you going to tell us?"

"Not without proof." Cesco grinned. "But tell us, how was supper? Is she pregnant yet? *Cosa fatta capo ha.*"

Pietro blushed, thinking of another pregnancy. But he thrust Rosalia from his mind as he related the evening's events. The guards were forced to wait a long time while the close friends of Count Pietro Alaghieri raised cups to his good fortune.

Pressed to describe his love, Pietro did his best, but he was not his father. Words failed him.

♦   ◊   ♦

The peace settled, Carrara had to leave for the north. For the war. Cesco elected to ride with him. "We'll be safe in his company.

We'll stop over in Verona and give Auntie Imperia your happy news. Then we'll travel on to join the army. Now that Parma is safe, the Scaliger will move swiftly."

Pietro felt a pang. He would not see the fall of Treviso. But that pain was balmed by the knowledge that he would be here for the reading of the banns. There was still no rush for the actual wedding. Two years, her father had said. It hurt, but neither Pietro nor Dolce truly minded the wait. Each wanted to give the other time to regret, withdraw their proffered affections, though both were sure nothing of the sort would happen. It was a love match.

Poco elected to remain with his brother, hoping to protect him from their homeland. But Tharwat and Morsicato both mounted — they would travel with Cesco and keep him safe.

With embraces and good wishes, Pietro put his arms about Cangrande's heir, unaware that it was for the last time.

The ride was pleasant and uneventful. Carrara was amusing, though he did have a tendency to scratch his skin. "As I age, I find my skin flaking. My father was much the same. By the time he reached forty if he touched his beard, it looked like it was snowing on his tunic."

"Which is why you shave close," observed Cesco.

Carrara grinned. "A man is not a man who does not like a close shave."

They parted near Padua, angling westwards for Verona. They arrived in Verona the following day, to squeals of delight from Cesco's little wife.

"We are now both a whole year older," he told her, dropping a saddlebag full of presents. "But you are catching up to me. I used to be three times your age. But in two more years, I'll be just twice your age."

Her face fell. "Icarus died."

Antonia had already written, so Cesco was prepared. "But not with an untimely fall. He lived a good life, and died knowing he was loved. What more could anyone want?"

He left Maddelena smiling and thinking that her husband did not look as sad as he had before.

Cangrande happened to be in the city at the moment, signing papers and hearing petitions, clearing his desk before hostilities distracted him. "I'm always astonished how swiftly your hair grows."

Cesco scrubbed his mane. "I think all my growth goes to my hair, defeating my attempts at height."

"Not entirely defeating. You're taller than when you left. Though you look like a dancing girl."

"I have excellent legs. Care to see?"

"I only want to see them running towards Treviso. Is Count Pietro recovered?" It was not Pietro the Scaliger was asking after.

"If he's not, he never will be."

Cangrande grunted. "Very well. Tomorrow you can ride out to join the army. It's mustering around Padua."

Tomorrow suited Cesco to the ground. He had one interview to make before the war. One that he had put off long enough.

♦   ◊   ♦

Cesco sent ahead to *La Rosa Colta* to tell her he was calling. It was the least he could do. He wrote formally, and mentioned an interview, lest she have the wrong idea. He did not want to arrive and have her throw herself into his arms.

One look smote him. She knew. Without knowing why, she knew. It did not make what he had to say easier. If anything, it made this all the worse. It occurred to him that he was under no obligation to say anything. She was a whore, and had been paid. But after all he had put her through, he owed her at least this.

They entered her room, hung with its exotic drapes and smelling of pungent spices. It made him feel ill, as though the walls were seething at him. He remembered all they had done in this room, and wished they were anywhere else in the world.

"Buthayna. Please sit down."

Still she said nothing, simply obeying him by curling herself gracefully down onto a large pillow and gazing up at him with dark eyes full of hurt.

"First, I must apologize that I did not call after the events of the Palio. That was extraordinarily unkind. I was ill. It is not an excuse. It is plain fact." She nodded that she understood. "But I also stayed away because of shame. My shame."

He sat down on a cushion opposite her, at a distance. "Last year, Buthayna, I fell in love. A woman of your years, possessing a beauty quite different from yours. It was the kind of love that burns, that fills your mind. It ended – badly. And when it ended, I missed her. But I missed myself as much. The self that I had been when I loved her."

He drew a ragged breath, knowing it was unfair – he should

show no weakness, invite no pity. Showing his struggle would not absolve him. Nor should it.

"I threw myself into debasing everything that we had shared. Including sex. I came here as often as I could to forget the feel of her flesh. I knew it was a danger, you see. Yet still I fell." He looked at her levelly. "You understand what I am saying? I wanted to be in love. I wanted to burn, to have my mind filled. So I chose you to fill it, to burn me."

He shook his head. "But I did not burn. I did not pine. I did not perish. You are a remarkable woman, Buthayna Warda. You have charm and wit and courage, generosity and grace. You have all the things that, in another life, I should have loved."

He did not say how foolish he felt, falling into such an obvious trap. He had bought her affection, just to be certain it would be his. He had chosen, of all the willing dames in *La Rosa Colta*, the one who was the most foreign, the most *other*. They even had a private tongue. In every way, he had crafted a circumstance in which he would have complete control. He did not say this, because it would diminish her, turn her into an object. More than he already had. He had made her the vessel of his affection, rather than allow her to be the cause of them. His entire affair had been a performance, proof that he could be an excellent lover. Except, of course, that he had not loved.

She did not need telling. She was intelligent, and more worldly than he. If he felt shamed, how must she feel? To have fallen for him, believed his promises. For that is the nature of lover's lies.

Buthayna was silent, but her expression had altered. She was no longer wounded. She was angry. Good. Hate would make it bearable.

Cesco rose. "I have purchased your freedom. And I have here a second purse that will buy you passage to anywhere you care to go. There is enough to take you home, should you wish it."

He held out the bag of gold, but she did not rise, did not take it. He set it gently on the bed.

Finally she spoke. "One final payment for the whore. Should you not take the pleasure you are paying for?"

What had he expected? Understanding? Forgiveness? He shook his head. "I don't think there would be pleasure in it for either of us, Madonna." He bowed to her and departed.

Buthayna remained, reliving his words, his reasons, his terrible, remote civility. If she had clung to the notion that he had stayed away for love of her, those hopes were now utterly demolished. No, her first impression of him had been correct. Here was Trouble personified.

She wished she could say she had no regrets. But she regretted not listening to her wiser self. She regretted having given so much of her self to him – not just her body, but her mind and soul. She regretted that Fortune had put her in a position where he could buy her freedom, for which she was obligated to be grateful.

Most of all she regretted having spoken. There was such power in silence.

♦   ◊   ♦

Cesco departed Verona the next morning, leaving Antonia to explain to his wife why he was departing again so soon. "He has duties. He has to go, because he is a good and responsible soldier."

Maddelena mumbled something about showing him what she'd learned, but it was fairly unintelligible, and they coddled her and distracted her with the pretty gifts Cesco had brought for her.

The good and responsible soldier took the road for Padua, with Detto, the Moor, and the doctor riding beside him. Their path took them to Vicenza, where Morsicato went to finally have a long-postponed conversation with his wife. Detto went off to visit his father and brother in the camp of Vicenza's army. Tharwat accompanied Cesco to the palace, but had no desire to enter. So it was that Cesco knocked and was admitted alone.

He found the lady reading – her left hand did not permit her to sew, and there were few other pursuits a stationary woman could perform. The leather cover bore the title Ὀδύσσεια – *The Odyssey*. Setting her book down in her lap, a finger to mark her place, she gazed at him. "I have just been reading about you."

"I have escaped the isle of the lotus-eaters."

"So do you now face Circe?"

"I do feel a bout of swinishness coming on."

"I do seem to recall that bringing that out in you." She had clearly been working on her speech. There was hardly a slur at all. "Dear me, so many tropes to play upon. Tharwat can be the Cyclops, who has the ear of the god determined to punish you."

Cesco nodded. "We should put on a play for Treviso. Cangrande can be Achilles, Bail Ajax, and Capulletto can be Menelaus. Instead of a giant horse, we'll build a hound and all drop from its balls."

"Hm. In one way you are more fortunate than Odysseus. If you were to stay away for twenty years, your wife would be just blooming when you returned."

Even had he been inclined to laugh, the jest was soured for

him. Penelope had been another guise Lia had employed during their courtship. "You look well enough, lady."

Katerina studied him. "You're thin. I'd have thought that after all your excesses this winter you'd have grown fat and placid."

"Like you?" Ungallant, but true. Her immobility had caused her to weight to increase, making her appear slightly puffy. Yet she remained just as beautiful in the half-light as she must have been in the sun a dozen years before.

"Well, there isn't much to do while you brave cavalieres are off conquering the known world. We graze and bear, because we must, and take what scraps of your precious time we are offered."

"Poor neglected auntie. Such a martial spirit! If the heathens are correct, in your last life you must have been Charlemagne."

"And if they're not? I prefer who I am to who I was."

"Or will be?"

"That, always, is in the stars."

Cesco's eyes were cool. "Not God's Will? But then who punched out those holes in the night? And, if we peer through them, I wonder if will we see God's candle burning bright. Or only oblivion, to which we are beckoned like moths to the flame."

"Donna Maria could answer you, if you only knew how to reach her."

Cesco sat on a stool. "I was sure you'd know by now. Believe it or not, I haven't come to bicker. I came to say one thing to you, then depart."

"Here I was hoping for the bickering – at least I'd have your attention. Or must I force you to strike me again? I promise, Bail will never know."

"Is that how you seduced Nuncle Pietro?"

"I tried, but alas, he was too wise."

"Not that wise. He is betrothed."

"Congratulations to him! It is past time."

"I agree. It is past time to let go of roles we have outgrown – or should never have had in the first place."

The right side of Katerina's face beetled. "How oblique! I pray you, say what you came to say, and be gone. I'm dying to learn how Odysseus survives Sirens."

His brow furrowed for a moment. "Very well. I knew her for five minutes, no more. But Donna Maria was more mother to me than you have ever been, or ever will be." With that, he rose and departed, leaving her in silence.

♦　◊　♦

On the second day of the month named for Julius Caesar, Cangrande gathered his western-most forces in Villanova, parading them for the hundreds of Lombards who had come to see his banners snapping in the wind.

The next day he marched to Vicenza, sweeping up Bailardino's forces in a grand display. But he did not rest there, continuing on to Padua, where he entered the city to a shower of flower petals and paeans of praise. Here, as a sign of his favour and complete trust, he gave command of the foot soldiers to Marsilio da Carrara.

That night, as the army camped outside Padua's walls, Benedick found Cesco and Detto. After an effusive greeting, the red-headed Paduan began telling tales of the weeks of training and waiting. "It got so bad that Salvatore and I began holding races. Our own band of Rakehells."

"Otto did not object?"

"Not in the slightest! He likes contests with a purpose, and encourages competition among the men."

"A commander after my own heart. Where is Salvatore?"

"Here," said the fellow himself, coming forward. "I was off talking with Hortensio. We've set the wedding day."

"I'm sure you and Hortensio will be very happy." The ensuing protests drew in more of their fellow Rakehells – Petruchio and Hortensio, Barto and Berto, even Detto's brother Valentino.

Watching from a small distance, Tharwat was reminded that most of these fellows were mere boys. Technically Cesco had achieved manhood, but he still looked younger than Detto despite the advantage of a year. The twins were thirteen, Valentino was twelve. Berto was the same age as Detto. Of the Rakehells, only Barto and Salvatore were near twenty, with Benedick as the aged mascot in his late twenties.

Only after they had hoisted their cups several times, saluting everyone from Cangrande to the noble Count of San Bonifacio, did Cesco slip away to join the Moor. They had an appointment – not with a person, but with a place.

♦　◊　♦

"So this is the house."

Cesco stared up at the walled casa that had been his first home. Being in Padua, it had been impossible to resist visiting, and Tharwat had dutifully brought his young lord to see it.

Cesco's memories of that time were doubtless too dim to glean anything new. The carved *caduceus* gave him pause, and as he walked through the dusty halls he examined the frescos with interest. They were completely average, without any special meaning he could draw from them other than good taste.

Staring at one that depicted green fields and stone buildings under a blue sky, Cesco said, "I wonder if that's Scotland. Was she homesick? It's sad that she was never able to return."

"We don't know that. She might have gone back many times while you were in Ravenna." In truth, the Moor shared Cesco's doubt. The way she had arrived so swiftly when called, she had likely been nearby, waiting for the moment to reveal herself if needed.

"You've searched the house," said Cesco. "There was nothing?"

"Nothing. No papers, no coin, no seals. No clue as to who Signor d'Amabilio might have been." Tharwat cleared his throat. "I was planning to remain here in the city and resume the hunt."

"If you do," said Cesco, "I'd prefer you start with the woman who hired those kidnappers. I'd like a word with her. And I'd like you to buy this house for me. Do you think that could be arranged?"

"Being under Scaligeri control, the city might just give it to you."

"I'd rather pay," said Cesco. "I want the deed to be uncontestable. It's close to the Rossi clan. And it's easily fortified. This can be Maddelena's home while I'm away."

"Away?" asked Tharwat.

"Once Treviso is dealt with, I imagine I'll be busy for years to come." Cesco paused, looking closely at one of the painted walls. "Bring that lamp here."

The Moor obeyed, squinting. "Is that a ship?"

Indeed, there was a three-masted vessel painted on the wall, sailing into an Italian harbour, but flying an English flag.

They both stopped breathing as they leaned their noses so close they nearly touched the varnished paint. There, just above the captain's cabin on the rear of the ship, was a name. *La Alisceote.*

They were silent for a time, drinking this in. Then Cesco laughed. "Well done, *madre mia!* The answer in plain sight. Hidden in art!"

V

Dreamers Often Lie

THIRTY-SEVEN

Treviso
Tuesday, 4 July 1329

THE WAR BEGAN in broad daylight, in an almost leisurely manner.

Cangrande's army struck camp long before daylight, and the first rays of the sun found the amassed horse and foot of Verona, Padua, Vicenza, and Mantua all idling, wondering at the delay. It was thirty miles overland to Treviso, and they all wanted to be encamped before nightfall.

Before the command tent, their leaders were watching the Scaliger scarf down a boiled egg and some bread. Talking with Carrara, the Scaliger wiped his chin and stared around him. "Sorry — were you waiting for something?"

Carrara was amused. "I believe they're awaiting an order."

"Another egg."

"Not that kind!"

"Then give them one," replied Cangrande. "I can't be bothered."

As the men laughed at his apparent unconcern, Carrara said, "I don't think they'll leave without you."

"O very well!" Standing, Cangrande pulled on the great Houndshelm. "Let's go start a war."

A rousing cheer erupted from every throat as the order was given: "March for Treviso!" Not a light march, which meant speed, sore feet, and horseshoes thrown. Nor a defensive march, slow and heavy. Cangrande called for a parade march, a sharp step with only

basic armour on, no helms, shields shipped to the rear. Almost a holiday parade, far more for show than military sense. But they looked
splendid as they passed through town after town along the road from
Padua to Treviso, and the people admired, cheered, sang, and gave
prizes of food and drink.

While the foot levies from Verona, Padua, and the rest of
the Feltro were under Carrara's command, Bailardino led his loyal
Vicentines. The various *condottieri* answered to Otto the Burgundian,
who rode with Castelbarco by his side. Rizardo del Camino rode at
the head of his own force of men, Trevisians bent on *'liberating'* their
home city.

The rest of the nobility were gathered into one magnificent
force, a multi-coloured column of knights mounted on their finest
riding steeds. Nearly three hundred knights were in attendance, each
with at least one page or squire bringing along his master's *destrier*.
In all it was a show of force and power that would have awed an
emperor.

Cesco rode at the head of this body, alongside the Scaliger
himself. On a purely physical level, they looked nothing alike. One
enormous, one of medium height. One with short chestnut hair
tinged with silver, the other with a long fell of wavy curls streaked
blond by the sun. One set of eyes cornflower blue, the other green
as grass. Yet something in the posture, the attitude of the head, the
easy authority, that spoke volumes. Nothing alike, and yet entirely
the same.

Even in their accoutrement, they were a mismatched pair.
Cangrande rode a white stallion, while Cesco sat astride Abastor,
black as night. Yet they wore identical half-armour, each with a
golden *petta* across his chest, with matching gorget and greaves. The
arciones of their saddles were silver, with acid-etched swirls evoking
the Scaligeri crest. If Cesco's helmet was not as impressive as the
Houndshelm, he did not care — he still thought the thing looked
ridiculous, with its snarling greyhound and spreading wings. He said
so, and Cangrande merely smiled. "Wait until you see an enemy run
from it. You may reassess what is ridiculous."

Detto rode on Cesco's right, looking just as fine in his glitter-
ing half-armour. Detto seemed happy at last — his friend was restored
to a noble purpose, he was at peace with his father, and they were
on their way into war. Cesco was tempted to fart loudly to remove
some of the solemnity.

On Cangrande's far side rode Mastino. Amusingly, Cesco's
cousin had chosen some of the armour Cesco had sent him, finer

even than the Scaliger's. Which did not go unnoticed, especially by Cangrande himself.

During the second hour of their march Cesco started to complain. "I'd rather ride with the light cavalry." Otto was about to send forty light horses ahead to scout and forage. In battle the light cavalry were the quickest of the attackers, and the poorest armed. This meant that they could be either devastating or devastated, determined solely on the skills of their commander.

Cangrande shook his head. "I can't give them to someone who worships chaos."

"Worship implies blind obedience. Chaos is a tool. So is discipline. I can use either."

"Noted. Though you never enjoyed discipline during your hawking. Isn't that a bit hypocritical?"

"Different circumstances, different rules" said Cesco cheerfully. "And if I'm a disappointment to you, it's because I've always aspired to be."

"It's good to dream," said Cangrande.

"Really? I rather think that dreams are our downfall."

Cangrande laughed. "Well, then, don't tell Pietro. I'd hate to disabuse our latest Veronese lover." Ser Alaghieri's new infatuation was the subject of much good-natured jesting. "Is it true they're already engaged? Good for him. He needs a child of his own. If only to stop fathering you."

"Speaking of children," called Mastino from across Cangrande, "how's your wife?"

Cesco gave a lunar-sized roll of his eye. "Off the teat and on to the thumb."

"No doubt your cock will be next."

Detto growled and despite his light answer, Cesco looked angry. "Alas, her teeth have come in. What about Taddea? Is she swelling yet? Word is she can hardly walk."

Mastino smiled blandly. "What, eager for competition?"

"Any competition is welcome. Old rivalries grow stale. The della Scala line needs some new blood."

"In that we agree," said Mastino.

"Ears, lads," said Cangrande, meaning they were where anyone could hear them. "Cesco, ask Otto if he's willing to give you command of the light cavalry. The decision belongs to him."

Cesco looked pleased. "At last, a chance to prove myself."

"I confess I'm interested to see you lead men, not a rabblement of hot-headed boys. Just don't do anything stupid, like dying. I'd miss these little chats."

"So would I, believe me," replied Cesco. "I'm just now growing to like them."

◆   ◊   ◆

As the newly-installed commander of Otto's light company,
Cesco rode with the Burgundian at the head of the mercenary army,
Detto by his side. The men under his command were doubtless
unsure of him. They might have seen him race neck-and-neck with
their beloved Otto, but they had also seen him spewing wine from his
nose that same night. Whatever tales Yuri and Fabio had told would
be little reassurance. But at least they weren't rebelling. Helms fitted,
they spurred out behind their new commander, riding through the
glorious summer countryside at a good clip, not so fast as to blow
their horses, but swifter than any messenger or warning could travel.
They passed through Zero Branco and only tugged their reins at an
inn called Frascata.

The innkeeper came forward, a portly man with a long beard
and hands the size of mallets. Those hands were held wide in a show
of peace. "Are you from the Greyhound?"

"We are," answered Otto.

"Can I offer your men food or drink?"

Otto shook his head. "We'll pay for anything we eat."

The innkeeper gave an ingratiating smile. "Figured I'd offer, as
there's nothing I can do to stop you."

Another man would have put the man at his ease. Not Otto.
"Are the Trevisians within their walls?"

The innkeeper scratched his bearded chin. "Not since last I
heard. They've known it was coming, of course. But it's hard, staying alert for weeks and weeks. I think they hoped you'd all decided
not to come."

"Mm." Signaling his men, Otto led his force forward towards
Treviso itself.

"Can that be true?" marveled Yuri, riding along with Otto.
"Do they not know we're coming?"

"They're fools if they don't have scouts and signals planned,"
said Fabio, at his other side. "But then, they're fools to hold out at
all."

Cresting the final hill, they saw the brownish-red bricks of
the city's southern walls across the narrow water of the river Sile.
Amazingly, the gates were open. Evidently the innkeeper had spoken
true — word had not yet reached the city. There was even a party of

foragers gathering wood and plants from the field, and many citizens out at their daily business.

Seeing the open gates across the wide bridge, Cesco murmured, "If we could reach those gates…"

Detto understood. If they could get inside, they could hold a gate open until Cangrande arrived and the city would fall in a single night. The temptation was enormous.

A decision had to be made, and at once. But would Cesco's men follow him? Or would they see it as the daredevil, hair-brained action of a wild, foolish boy and not follow him. Once Cesco might have thrown all caution to the wind. But this new Cesco glanced sidelong at the commander of the company. "Otto?"

"No question," said the Burgundian. "Give the order."

Cesco drew his sword and waved it, hissing the air over his head. "Charge! Take those gates!"

The light company cheered and spurred to attack en masse. Detto saw the relief in his friend, and the joy. Hesitation was gone. Now it was only death, or glory. Otto rallied his main force into a charge as well, and soon the whole mercenary company was racing full-tilt for the unsuspecting gate.

Citizens and foragers took one look and turned tail. Otto's cavalry was closer to the gates, at an angle to the foragers, with Cesco's force on the far end. It meant that as he raced for the gates, Otto would cut the Trevisians off, leaving Cesco to cut them down. Otto would reach the gates first. But what did it matter, so long as they won?

Sword out, Detto felled one man as his horse trampled another. It was his first kill in war and he wanted to relish the moment, but it was distasteful. The foragers were all running away, their backs to the racing horses. There was no glory to be had here.

But there could be victory so long as the gates remained open. The winches had to be moving by now. Yes, the doors were closing. In moments the portcullis might drop. Only the streaming bodies of citizens and soldiers prevented the Trevisians from cutting that cord.

"Swiftly now!" shouted Cesco. Slashing left and right, Detto glanced ahead. Otto was pressing hard, Yuri and Fabio at his flanks, galloping desperately up the paved road to outpace the men working the fortified gate.

Over the cries of citizens and the thunder of hooves, Detto could hear the whine of huge ropes pulled taut and the thuds of wheels working within wheels. There was a loud snap and something passed over the city like a speeding bird. An instant later the earth shook in a way that had nothing to do with horses. It happened twice more before Detto could put a name to it. "Catapults!"

"Keep going!" Cesco's company wasn't yet within range of the missiles, but Otto's men were and they hadn't stopped. More stones landed around them, some right in front of their horses. The beasts balked but still Verona's mercenary cavalry rode for the gate.

Then there was a scream. It was not a single voice, but a dozen united in a single horrified cry. Detto, far back, twisted around to see what had happened. Otto's men had just stopped, their horses trembling and panting, as they stared at a stone that had just landed in their midst. Under it lay Otto, crushed to a bloody smear by a perfectly launched siege stone. His horse's legs were still twitching, but Otto's splayed hand was entirely still.

Leaving his men to finish dispatching the foragers, Cesco raced Abastor to where Yuri, Fabio, and the rest stood stunned at the sudden loss of their imperturbable leader. He grabbed Yuri and slapped the big man's tear-stained face. "Get them back!"

"The gate—" protested Fabio weakly.

"Too late! Just get them out of range! Retreat! Retreat!"

"He didn't even cry out," said Yuri dully.

"Get back out of range!" Cesco began tugging on reins and kicking horses with his spurs. "You want to end up like him?"

Another stone landed close, startling several of the horses. This, more than Cesco commands, awoke the men to their danger. Under the jeers of the defenders on Treviso's walls, they pulled back, halting just out of range of the catapults.

Upon hearing of Otto's death a half-hour later, Cangrande wept openly. "Treviso has already cost too much!"

"We might still have made the gate," said Cesco as he quietly explained events. "But the men had lost heart."

"Are you sure it was the men?" demanded Cangrande darkly.

Cesco looked him up and down from head to heel and back. "I'll go storm the gate now." He started to leave.

Cangrande caught him by the arm. "That was unworthy. You made a good decision."

"You sound surprised. Now excuse me, I must return to my men."

"Tell them this," said Cangrande, tears still on his cheeks. "Tell them I vow that, should the siege last fifty years, I will not depart without having Treviso in my power!"

◆　◇　◆

Cangrande set up his command tent near the monastery of the Quaranta Santi, the Holy Forty, and set about dividing his army into two parts. One, under Bailardino, would guard the north-east side, while the remainder under Carrara would take the south-west. Since Treviso was a rectangular-shaped city, the Veronese army could watch all the entrances from these two vantage points.

The bulk of the army was put to work creating massive and permanent camps. Tents were raised for soldiers and massive multi-coloured pavillions for their commanders. Trees and branches were felled to build lean-tos, using axes or, in the case of the German mercenaries, their wickedly-sharp curved falchions. By the second day of their occupation it looked as though Verona's army would never leave, as if Cangrande was willing to abandon everything else to follow only this enterprise.

The siege started the next day when, rested and eager, the Veronese army was given their stations and their orders. These last were simple, and issued directly by Cangrande to his commanders. "No one in. Deserters are free to leave. Give them food and drink and anything else they want. We welcome the Trevisians with open arms."

"Not just arms?" asked Cesco. The men of Otto's company had expressed their desire for blood.

"No," said Cangrande firmly. "Warring is very like wooing. Let us take a page from the late Petruchio's book. Let us kill them with kindness."

◆   ◊   ◆

Venice

Tharwat al-Dhaamin clambered heavily from the bottom of the gondola and paid the driver, who was careful not to touch the skin of his passenger's hand. Long inured to such treatment, Tharwat had no room in him for indignation. He was tired, more tired than he would have cared to admit even to himself. A journey that should have taken him two days on horseback had taken four in a carriage, and he had been too exhausted upon arrival to visit the Jewish Quarter then and there. Instead he had taken lodging for the night just outside the city, in the home of some of his fellow Moors who worked the wharves. They asked no questions, and he told them nothing. Normally he would have offered them charts as payment, or produced his pendulum, a more immediate form of comfort to those in search of answers. But none of these men had questions they wanted answered. Their futures were known to them. They wanted no confirmation.

Being in Venice was an enormous personal risk, as Tharwat was still charged on the city books with poison, sorcery, and more. But he doubted that Doge Dandolo wished to cause a rift with Verona at present. Only when Treviso fell would he make his move.

Making the effort to straighten himself this grey morning, Tharwat had donned his finest robes and done his head up in the Eastern style, making himself appear a very fine merchant. Disguise was second nature to him, a fact he had often wondered at. With too many disguises, do you lose the man beneath?

Walking with the aid of a stick, he entered the Yellow Crescent, known as such because of the shape of the swath carved out for Hebrews to inhabit, and for the yellow hats adorned with devils' horns the residents were by law forced to wear. How many humiliations must a people suffer? But then they, like Tharwat, seemed too tired for indignation.

It was a bright morning, the sun so blinding that it was difficult to see more than a dozen steps ahead. But Tharwat had walked this route before. Curious gazes followed him, though when he reached the house he sought, everyone averted their eyes.

Tharwat knocked. When there was no answer, his knocks became louder and more insistent. The man never left his home untended. But perhaps there was no one left to answer the door.

Yet Tharwat heard a voice within, speaking softly. He hammered for a good twenty minutes before a door across the street opened and a man stuck his head out. "The one you seek is not there."

Tharwat knew the intimidating effect his broken voice could have, so he used his lower tone, almost a whisper. "I have come to see Shalakh."

The bulky neighbour nodded. "That is his house, but he is not home."

Tharwat shook his head. "I've heard his voice inside."

The neighbour sighed and came waddling across the street. "Yes, I know. But I did not lie. He is not at home." As he reached the door, the man produced a massive lead key and worked it in the lock until the heavy door swung open.

Tharwat followed him into the dark house. The interior was pitch dark, but the muttering became distinguishable. "...daughter... *ducati*...a Christian, a Christian...ruin..."

The ponderous neighbour lit a taper, then led the way into Shalakh's office where Tharwat saw a shocking sight. Shalakh, the short, precise, bird-like usurer of yesterday now paced across his wood floors, naked, his hand running distractedly through his hair. "…damned judges…daughter, my daughter…oh, *mi ducati*…a Daniel, a Daniel…" Shalakh's mind seemed as broken as the Moor's voice.

"Master Shalakh?" said Tharwat.

"He cannot hear you," said the neighbour. "He may respond, but not in any meaningful way. Too many reverses. He lost his fortune, his daughter, and his faith all at once."

Lowering his voice, Tharwat said, "Is he mad?"

Shalakh reared up. "Mad as Hell! Hell, for I have eaten pork! I am unclean, unclean! Mad as my old God, but I must love – that's what Christians do, they love! They murder with love. So I will love! I love you, Jessica! I love you, Antonio! I love this land, and the Doge, and the judge – I love them all! Let them feel my love!" He paced, his bare feet sliding across the floor in what must have been the work of days, for the varnish was gone from the wood. At one point his eyes seemed to come into focus, for he smiled at Tharwat's companion. "Tubal! Will you come and share some swine with me? I have a curious craving for a pound of pig's flesh."

"Not today, my friend," replied Tubal gently. "Today is a time for rest. Go, go and rest your weary mind."

"Rest? Christians cannot rest until they have loved their enemies…oh, my daughter…the Doge! The Doge will have it, I have no choice…I am ruined…oh, *mi ducati*…"

Once the fit was off him and his ravings were reduced to mere rambling, Tubal put an arm around Shalakh's shoulder and guided him upstairs. When he returned, Tharwat said, "I heard of the trial, but not the aftermath. It drove him mad?"

"Worse. He is a Christian now. His funds are in trust for his daughter. He has no livelihood, and no future. He is left with nothing. Even his house was sold."

"This house?"

"Out of pity I purchased it and allow him to live here until such a time as we may mend his mind."

"Is there nothing to be done?"

The neighbour shook his head. "Time alone can heal this wound. It hasn't killed him, and that's sign enough that he will weather this. Though he must soon leave this house." Tubal showed a sad smile. "Christians are not allowed to live in the Crescent."

"You are kind to look after him." Though disturbed by Shalakh's fate, Tharwat had not forgotten the matter of his visit. "What has happened to his business?"

"What's left of it, I have," said Tubal. "I bought up his debts, and have undertaken to make them good."

"I must see his records."

Tubal was suddenly brisk, guarded. "What right do you have to them?"

"The right of one of his clients. He has done a great deal of business for the Scaligeri of Verona. Some gold passed to the family Amabilio. I have been asked to track down any records pertaining to that name, and a ship called *La Alisceote*."

"I am not certain I have the right. It is not good for a business to reveal its dealings."

Tharwat paused, his mind working. Slowly he said, "If I were to offer a pension for Shalakh's interests, in honour of the good work he has done for the Scaliger's family, would that sway the balance?"

It was Tubal's turn to consider. "I would need an offer in writing."

Tharwat bowed in the manner of his native people. "I shall see to it."

Tubal showed him out. "I shall look into the records. It may take some time."

"Thank you." Giving his name and where he could be reached, Tharwat departed as swiftly as he could manage. It did not behoove him to linger long where madness grew.

◆   ◊   ◆

Pistoia

With nothing to do save await a trial that would likely never occur, Pietro thought he would make time to work again on his commentary on his father's great work. But try as he might, he could not focus upon the writing. His quill would pause for a moment that turned into an hour as he remembered his most recent visit with Dolce, or imagined his next one.

He did force himself to answer letters, even bitter ones. He was now corresponding with Albertino Mussato, the Paduan poet laureate now in eternal exile. Knowing what was coming, he had fled Treviso for Chioggia. Reading, Pietro to empathize with his father's old rival, the man who had penned the play that had so irked the Scaliger.

> I find myself ruminating on the nature of
> Tragedy. I once believed there were only two kinds –

the fall and disaster of great kings and princes, and the trials such men endure on the battlefield. But now I see there is also the personal Tragedy, not at all epic, and yet greater due to its utter humanity. Mine is a Tragic tale. I wrote all these years in the style of Seneca. I neglected to note his history, which was to spend his life trying to instruct evil princes of their duty. He was ordered to take his own life by the very one into which he had poured his heart.

I have poured my heart into Padua. And it has given itself over to the beast. But they do not care enough even to order my death. They simply bid me pack, and forget my name. Ten years ago I was a hero of the Arts. Today I am a traitor. I, who have betrayed no one, least of all myself.

I will remain true to what I have written, and believed. Seneca will show me the way.

Pietro wrote back, but the letter was returned to him. Mussato had died just after writing to Pietro. Those were likely the last thoughts set down by the poet whose true Tragedy was to have his genius overshadowed by one even greater than he. Pietro wondered if, like Seneca, Mussato had died in his bath.

The letter from Tharwat in Venice was a welcome jolt of real and immediate news. After reflecting pityingly on the fate of Shalakh, he came to the heart of the message. Tubal was willing to hunt for the information in exchange for an annuity to cover Shalakh's expenses. As Tharwat wrote:

For obvious reasons, I do not think we should put this to the Scaliger. Would you be willing to undertake the cost? It may lead to no answer at all, but it would be helping a man who has lost his family, his fortune, his faith, and his wits.

Pietro wrote back at once, instructing Tharwat to have Tubal himself draw up the contract. Pietro would sign it happily. Though for the first time he was thinking of spending money on himself — a fine new house here in Pistoia, so they could visit Dolce's family. Gowns and jewels for her to wear, servants and tapestries and horses and every modern convenience. As he often did, Pietro caught himself and laughed when he journeyed too far down this particular road. But he could not help himself. *God help all lovers,* he thought.

♦   ◊   ♦

Treviso

After just two weeks, the besieged city was suffering from an excess of Cangrande's kindness. Though there had been no assault or bombardment, there was also no let. Anyone who wanted to leave was allowed to do so, provided they carried neither arms nor messages. But those who remained within the walls started to breathe air as cloying and suffocating as if they were sealed in a tomb.

Every dawn, soldiers from Verona's army set out into the countryside, cutting down fruit trees and denuding the land of any hope of a summer harvest. The Trevisians began to fear Cangrande meant his oath and would remain through the fall harvest and into winter, when the city's supply of food would be long gone. Farmers saw the fruit of their labours being eaten and tossed about – even burned! – by the army outside the walls and wondered if life would be so much worse under Scaligeri rule. Look at Padua! They had not suffered. Cangrande's earlier clemency and generosity paid dividends within Treviso's walls, as the whispers grew.

The podestà of Treviso, one Ser Gerozzo de' Bardi, made a speech exhorting continued resistance. "In the name of God, my friends, let us not be craven! Let each citizen join to defend our lands! Do not doubt, but remain resolute, fighting like leopards until rescue comes!"

But from where would rescue come? Cangrande had sent a large force under Alblivious to block the alpine passes, blocking any means for Cangrande's longtime adversary, the Duke of Corinthia, to send aid. Verona's own lands surrounded Treviso, cutting off any sympathetic force. The only road Cangrande did not own led to Venice, and Doge Dandolo was not at present inclined to offend the Scaliger. The Capitano da Verona's star was rising, and all Italy feared his displeasure.

Meanwhile more nobles were arriving with their private armies in tow. Count Gherardaccio da Collalto arrived with a host of hardened warriors – a particular insult, as he had sworn to defend Treviso against the Scaliger. Cangrande embraced Collalto like a long-lost brother and gave a great feast in his honour that consumed even more local food.

Rumours of political treachery inside Treviso's walls began to reach the Capitano's ears. Guecello Tempesta dared not leave his house for fear of being rent limb from limb by the citizens. Each day more voices spoke of Cangrande's clemency, and each night more of the garrison slipped over the wall or out the side gates to go over to the enemy. Tempesta knew that if he held out to the bitter end, not only would he lose the city but also his own personal estates, perhaps even his life.

The lack of fighting meant there was little for this massive army to do, a fact especially true for cavalry. Not that soldiers disliked idle time. But the mercenaries had signed up for wealth, and the best way to enrich one's self was by sacking a city. Fortunately, Cangrande had an open hand. Fortunate too that his heir was inventive.

Cesco had taken command of Otto's company, with Bevilaqua as his second. They stationed fifty of their men within an easy reach of each of the city's gates, ready to chase down anyone going in or out. These men spread out at night to intercept any refugees with arms and alms.

For the men not on duty, the goal was to refrain from dying of boredom. Cesco aided in that, devising races and sports that would at once keep them occupied and at the same time dishearten the watchers on the walls. Races, *giostre*, mock duels – all the sports he had given the Rakehells he now brought to bear with the army. Training, disguised as amusement.

Cesco had once read that a Roman general had held chariot races on a course made of the raised shields of his legion. Not wanting to risk their horses, he proposed footraces, and it became a game in itself as different groups of men were told to move their shields, making the track undulate under the racers' feet.

Each morning Cesco appeared before Cangrande's tent to report, and offer suggestions:

"What about digging a trench and undermining the wall?"

"I've always wanted to try building one of those siege towers, like in the Crusades."

"A battering-ram under a tortoise-like shell."

"Water-weapons. What if we start digging to divert the Sile?"

"How about a giant horse? Wait, that's been done. What about a rabbit?"

Cangrande finally snapped. "No attacks! We want to demoralize the defenders. The more of their own they see living well outside the walls, the more their spirits will sink. That's why I'm not bombarding them or setting them on fire. Defiance strengthens a man's spirit. I want them wondering why they're holding out." He smiled. "That, and I want the city in good condition when we take it."

"Then what are the trébuchets for?" The small artillery had been sitting idle since it arrived.

"Only for show, I'm afraid."

Cesco's brow furrowed in thought, but he said nothing as he departed. Not much later, Cangrande was in his pavilion going over Veronese tax complaints when he heard the first trébuchet fire, then the second. By the time the third sent its missile aloft he was out of his tent and running towards the sound. "Who the Devil is firing?!"

Siege weapons had not changed greatly since the days of Caesar. There were only three methods of sending large missiles over a distance – tension, torsion, counterweight. The trébuchet was of the third kind, with a long arm bearing a sling on one end, and heavy weights on the other. The sling-arm was hauled down, the sling filled with projectiles, then released. The counter-weight on the other end came crashing down, sending the arm up to hurl the contents of the sling at the target. The triangular wooden structures had wheels attached for easy movement, and when not in use the long arm stood upright.

Verona's trébuchets were not where they had been stationed, nor were the arms upright. They had been moved within reach of the city, and the arms were hauled in close to the ground, the slings being refilled for firing.

Cesco stood by the tall launch trough for the long sling, directing the engine-master's aim. Then he stepped back behind the machine, holding the trigger lanyard in his hand.

"Cesco! Stop this instant!" An angry Cangrande made all men step clear of their instruments.

Cesco just smiled. "I was showing initiative."

The insolence goaded Cangrande to berate his heir in public. "I said no damage, no bombarding! Are you deaf, or deliberately insubordinate? Whichever, you aren't fit to command an army of lepers off a cliff, let alone real soldiers. Pack up, you're going back to Verona this instant!"

Cesco nodded. Dropping the lanyard, he turned to the ashen-faced men around him. "You heard the Capitano. Put the food away." He stepped forward, wrists outstretched. "Shall I be clapped in irons for my return?"

"Food?" Cangrande's head snapped to the contents of the nearest sling. It was indeed filled with food – bread, apples, oranges, figs, and the like. "What's the meaning of this? Do you want the siege to last longer?"

"I was hoping to shorten it. It was your idea, actually."

"Mine?"

"You said you wanted to demoralize them. What could be

more demoralizing than your foe giving you food? Once they figure out it isn't poisoned, they'll realize what it means – that you're here for as long as it takes. You're so confident, you'll even give them food. That's how sure you are you're going to win."

Looking around, Cangrande saw Otto's men standing in clumps beside each trébuchet, their arms full of food. Cesco said softly, "They needed to do something. This was the best I could come up with and remain within the spirit of your orders."

"I note you didn't tell me first. You made me into a foole."

"No one thinks the Greyhound is a foole, my lord," said Cesco.

If there was a tensing in the Scaliger's arms, only Cesco saw it. Then Cangrande threw back his head and laughed. In his usual battlefield voice he cried, "I love it! Carry on, boys! Make them despair. Just put a note in each bundle bearing Otto's name. Let them know it's his final gift to them!"

Cangrande walked off, waving merrily at the cheering soldiers. Then he went into his tent, where he stayed for hours, not receiving visitors. He did, however, call for wine. It was brought by his brother-in-law, Rizardo da Camino. "I confiscated some local vintages."

Cangrande accepted the offered bottle warily. "Is it any good?"

"I haven't tried it," replied Rizardo.

"Then take a chair and help me find out," said Cangrande, waving Verde's husband to a seat as he poured.

♦   ◊   ♦

Cesco was taking his role of commander seriously, diligently riding from group to group, checking their readiness. Detto was with him at sunset when they came to the camp by the north walls that contained Benedick and Salvatore. "Haven't you Paduans betrayed us yet?"

"We'll wait until your back is turned," said Salvatore. "Do you come bearing orders?"

"Alas, no," said Cesco. "Just looking for rust on your weapons."

"There's no rust," said Benedick, "but we have supper ready. Care to join us?"

"Stomach, some ache. I wonder you are not fatter, Signor Benedick. You are continually thinking of your appetites." Nevertheless Cesco and Detto took stools around the fire and accepted meat, sopping up the juices with good bread brought by villagers eager to ingratiate themselves with their soon-to-be masters.

Seeing Benedick's frown, Cesco punched the Paduan in the shoulder. "What ails you? Triumph is the name of the hour! Wake up!"

"Was I asleep?" Benedick slapped his own face comically, then shook his head. "I just don't enjoy not doing! How does a soldier prove himself without battles?"

Cesco laughed. "The world is broad and wide. A witty man with a quick blade can always find amusing employment. Even if this were Verona's last war – which it most certainly is not – I can think of half a hundred kings looking for good swordsmen. Even a couple in Sicily," he added carelessly.

Benedick sat up straight. "I wasn't thinking of her!"

"Of course you weren't. I mention Sicily, you protest at once."

"Speaking of love," said Salvatore, "is it true that Ser Alaghieri means to wed?"

"If you mean the Count of San Bonifacio, then the answer is yes."

Salvatore waved a hand. "Forgive me, I forget. But if he's to marry, he'll have his countess and a brood of budding nobility in no time."

Benedick snorted. "He never struck me as a foole. I swear, a good bachelor hears the bells of thirty years ringing and he thinks they're wedding bells."

"You'll be thirty in a couple years," teased Detto.

"And the only bells I hear are those of Florence, that call a man to do what he will repent."

"That's not how the saying goes," said Cesco. "Besides, Salvatore here is not yet twenty, and yet he plans to wed. To Vittoria!"

"Vittoria!" everyone echoed, raising their cups.

Never perturbed, Salvatore took his mockery in stride. "Perhaps the good Count and I should imitate you and hold a double wedding. How is the lovestruck Count faring? Wasn't there some trouble with Florence?"

"There might have been, but for his nature. Another man would not have so many friends willing to stand between him and the axe. But he is trapped in Pistoia for the time being – a hardship he is happy to endure, as it keeps him close to his love. He sees her daily, and they plan for the future." Cesco's gaze became distracted by something in the middle distance. But there was nothing there.

"They should ask your Moorish friend," offered Benedick. "Is he with them?"

"No, we left him in Padua, hunting."

"Hunting whom?" asked Salvatore from across the fire. "The one behind the attack on Detto? Or the one who kidnapped your great love from the brothel? Whoever it was, we owe him a few inches of steel."

"My great love..." said Cesco, frowning.

The silence that followed became awkward, so Detto filled it. "Evidently they were hired by a woman."

"A woman?" said Salvatore. "Do you know her name?"

"No, but never fear." Cesco was suddenly bright. "Tharwat has ways of loosening tongues. Not all of his time with the Inquisition was wasted. And it only cost him an eye."

"An eye for an eye," said Salvatore. "My kind of justice."

"Yes, if only justice were as just as that," mused Cesco, biting into a sausage that burst, sending liquid down his front. Kneeling forward, he cursed. "Hot! Hot! Detto, do you have a spare tunic?"

They retreated to Detto's horse for a moment, then Cesco returned and hung his grease-stained one on a branch over the fire. "Fan the flames, let the Trevisians smell it!"

Salvatore returned to the earlier discussion. "So the Moor is in Padua?"

"Perhaps." Cesco's eyes narrowed, thinking of the ship called *La Alisceote*. "When we departed, he was following a most promising clue."

Salvatore raised a cup. "Here's to success! His and ours!"

"Success!" echoed Detto.

"Love and health to all!" cried Benedick.

Standing, Cesco raised his own cup. "To Otto. Would he were here. A friend when we needed one most."

"To Otto." Every man present said the name reverently. Then Cesco and Detto took it in turns to tell the tale of how Cesco and Otto had met three years before, when Cangrande was thought dead and Mastino had seized Verona's throne. "It was Otto joining our ranks that helped seal the coup, removing Mastino from power. Of course, then Cangrande arrived, not dead after all."

Salvatore said, "I hear you tweaked your father's nose a little."

Cesco was all innocence. "I don't know what you mean."

The wine flowed, and soon it was time for the changing of the watch, which meant that Cesco and Detto had to inspect the placement of their men. Rising unsteadily, Detto almost fell over. "Someone kept filling my cup..."

"Let him sleep here," said Salvatore. "I'll ride along with you."

"By all means," said Cesco, adding testily, "Detto, sleep it off."

"No, I can go," protested Detto, trying to climb into his saddle. His foot missed the stirrup, and Benedick led him off, protesting feebly.

Cesco mounted Abastor, and Salvatore leapt up atop his own mount, a dappled gray stallion. They rode together in silence to the first band of Cesco's men, led by Yuri, whom he approached from the rear at a slow pace. Alert, they whirled about to challenge him. Identified, Cesco asking if any more Trevisians had slipped out to surrender.

"Half a dozen so far," reported Yuri. "Two women and four children. They're fed and off to the next town. Bound to be more before dawn."

"Treat them all well, but see they're not armed and are put nowhere near the siege engines." Cesco spurred past them, towards a treeline, Salvatore in his wake.

The Paduan asked, "Where are we going?"

"I want to surprise each division," explained Cesco. "We'll come at them from behind, out of the trees, and see how ready they are."

Their horses maneuvered easily through the arbour — it wasn't a real wood, just several clumps of trees and bushes that happened to grow near each other. To keep them out of view, Cesco let Abastor take the easier path to the lower ground behind a rise.

"Do you hear that?" asked Salvatore.

Cesco checked his reins and was just turning his head to listen when something burst alongside his skull. Feeling flushed and sick all at once, he barely registered hitting the soft earth. Training made him roll, just as training had him draw his weapon. Luckily he had kept his sword attached to his hip instead of his saddle. The blade was longer than his arm and had a grip that allowed him to use one or two hands. It was called a bastard grip. The name as well as the practicality appealed to him.

He didn't touch his scalp — he knew it was bleeding, touching it wouldn't do a thing. He wished he'd been wearing his helmet. They were at the bottom of a gulley that had once probably been a shallow stream. Nothing grew around Cesco's feet but a few creeping roots covered in silt. Both sides of the gulley were lined with trees, hiding them from view of the camp.

Head ringing, Cesco said, "Salvatore?"

"I'm here," said the Paduan.

It was the tone that said it all. No hurry, no fear. It was icy calm. Cesco lowered his sword to squint at the dismounting figure. "Was it something I said?"

"I just thought we should conduct our affairs without prying eyes."

Cesco offered a weak laugh. "As I told Signor Benedick, I am no one's *bardasso*."

Salvatore shook his head. "Always coarse. Like a toddler obsessed with scatological humour. They say you have a great mind, but I have yet to see it."

"Was that the cause of the blow? You wanted to see my brains?"

"You forced my hand. I must leave tonight. I have business in Padua."

"Padua," repeated Cesco, connecting the stars into a sensible constellation.

"Aye. But before I go, I have to finish splitting your skull in twain."

"May the condemned man ask why?"

"Of course," said Salvatore, relishing the words. "Because it is the will of the Count of San Bonifacio."

With that dire pronouncement, Salvatore charged.

THIRTY-EIGHT

Sword flashing in the starlight, Salvatore flicked his blade left and right in a series of feints. Cesco didn't watch him coming, but rather lunged low. Salvatore beat the thrust aside then leapt as Cesco's leg came arcing around. Instead of catching his foe's ankle, Cesco's kick met only air. He rolled and desperately parried a hard downward stroke that would have ended him had it met his flesh.

"I've spent months watching you fight," said Salvatore, pushing down hard. "Always so eager to show off all your tricks."

Flat on his back, Cesco's right hand held his sword's grip while his left was on the blade itself, reinforcing the parry to hold off Salvatore's pressure. A wise move would have him twist left, sliding his opponent's blade down his. Cesco rolled his shoulders right, ignoring the other's man's blade as he stabbed his own upwards.

Salvatore was quick, spinning lightly away. Before Cesco could rise further than his knees the blade was back, angling towards Cesco's ribs. Still dazed, Cesco parried it but stumbled. The stumble saved him, as Salvatore used the momentum of his checked blow to bring his sword around his head and hiss the air where Cesco had been.

Reversing his grip, Cesco used his sword's tip to push off the ground and regain his feet. His sword was still upside-down when he caught Salvatore's point, warding it away from first his shoulder, then his knee, then his head. Using the crossguard to beat away this final blow, Cesco slashed with all his reach, forcing Salvatore back.

Only now did he have time to wonder. *The Count of San Bonifacio.* This was clearly not Pietro's doing. Of all the betrayals, that one was unimaginable.

Blinking to clear his head, Cesco purchased time with words. "It's about damn time."

"That I reveal myself? Well, you weren't going to figure it out."

Cesco let that pass. "Once you've killed me, will you run back to Padua? Is this all for *patavinitas*?"

Salvatore circled slowly around Cesco, enjoying words before blows. "The hell with that. But yes, first to Padua to finish the Moor, then Pistoia where I'll prevent a wedding. Poor Pietro di Dante, to die so soon after finding his heart's desire."

"Forgive me, I thought it was Nuncle Pietro who sent you."

Salvatore shook his head. "Not that pretender. The *true* Count of San Bonifacio."

Cesco thought he knew, but still he asked, "And where is he?"

Salvatore spread his arms wide. "He stands before you."

Though there were more questions to ask, the opening was too inviting. Cesco stabbed, but checked and windmilled his blade up past his own shoulder to descend on Salvatore's head. Ready for the attack, the Paduan was just enough fooled by the feint to make him dodge sideways, desperately slapping aside Cesco's blade with the flat of his hand. He swung his own blade and Cesco leaned back, feeling the steel pass just an inch from his throat. He lunged again, and so they danced for the next minute, Cesco pressing his attack and Salvatore giving ground.

At last Cesco stumbled, and Salvatore laughed. "Head hurting? Wanted to finish this fast, did you? I rather thought I'd let you wear yourself out. No one's coming to help."

Cesco sank to one knee, his blade ready to parry should Salvatore attack again. But his foe leaned his back against a tree. "Go on, catch your breath. If you tell me what the clue was, I'll even let you try again."

"Clue?"

"The promising clue Alaghieri and the Moor are hunting. What is it? I thought we left no trace."

"What are you talking about?"

"At supper you said they were following a clue that would lead them to the people who hired the swords to attack your little bride. I want to know what we missed."

"We?"

"Stop fishing," said Salvatore with obvious amusement. "You're here to give answers, not get them."

Cesco thought his mind might be bursting, and not just from the blow. How was Salvatore possibly connected to the ship that brought Cesco's mother to Italy?

He wasn't. Slowly he began fitting pieces together. When caught, what had Pathino told Pietro? *'The Count of San Bonifacio isn't done with you, boy!'* He and the old Count had once been partners, unlikely allies in the attempt to unseat the Scaliger. No one had ever answered the question of what brought them together...

"A woman hired the kidnappers," said Cesco. "An older woman. Your mother, I presume."

"Yes," said Salvatore, listening intently.

There it was. "Allow me to hazard a guess at her surname. Is it Pathino?"

Salvatore's grin did not reach his eyes. "This is like watching a blind man discover fire. No light, but at least some heat. Go on."

"Another Scaligeri bastard. There are so many of us. But this one's a girl. Alberto della Scala kept on seeing your grandmother, even after she was hidden from view." That was something Abbess Verdiana had kept from them all. "She was Pathino's full sister?"

"Was and is," said Salvatore, enjoying himself.

"So your mother was the link between Bonifacio and Pathino. Was she Vinciguerra's wife? Or are you yet another link in the chain of bastardy?"

"They met during my father's exile, and were wed in secret," said Salvatore. "I imagine father was amused at taking a Scaligeri to wife, even one born out of wedlock. In her veins ran old Alberto's blood. In time, he meant to introduce his family to Verona. What better way to seal the title and power of two warring families than by uniting them into a single line?" Salvatore's smile dimmed. "He died before he ever got the chance. Your dear Nuncle impersonated him at Vicenza, causing Carrara to murder him for his seeming betrayal. I was barely five years old when my father was taken from me."

"Pity you didn't say something before. We could have traded – my lost mother for your lost father. Is your name even Salvatore?"

Salvatore came off the tree, holding himself proudly in the starlight. "I am Salvatore da San Bonifacio, the legitimate son and heir to Count Vinciguerra da San Bonifacio. That title belongs to *me.* How foolish you must feel, having shared your table and your friendship with the son of your father's greatest foe, the nephew of the man your beloved Nuncle Pietro murdered."

"And how proud you must be, following in his murderous

footsteps. You hired the men who attacked Detto, and had Rupert blamed. Detto I understand, his father fought yours, but what had Rupert done?"

"A proxy for the Emperor, whose predecessor chose the della Scala clan over ours. Besides, Rupert was close to you, almost as close as Detto. My aim was to remove all your allies, so I might take their place."

"The better to usurp me when the time came. Is that why you cut the cord during the goose-pull? To kill Benedick?"

Salvatore sounded hurt. "Do you think so little of me? If I wanted him dead, there are surer ways. Death is too easy. Benedick stole my father's horse, so I dragged him from his saddle."

"And the attack on Carrara before the Palio—"

"—was me as well, yes. He murdered my father. He must die. But not too soon! Marsilio will be losing his hair with paranoia before he falls. My father lingered in his death, ranting and raving with fever. The suffering of those responsible must last in direct proportion to their crime."

"Then why try to poison Cangrande? I take it you're the one who doctored his drink? That must have hurt, missing the target and removing your fiancée's father instead."

"Ah, Vittoria," said Salvatore with a sigh. "What a shame we weren't wed before this came to light. At least I was able to taste the peach. No decent man will have her once that becomes known. But I was so looking to turn her whole family against you, in time."

"The Bonaventura clan?" Cesco shook his head. "It wouldn't have happened."

"It would if they thought you'd killed their beloved lout of a father. You've been a great help – your antics these last months undermined both you and the Greyhound. You went from daring darling to unstable liability, while proving your father both arrogant and ineffectual. How easy it would have been to turn the city against you both. Especially when they found out about your filthy secret habit. No, I don't mean your Arab whore. The hashish."

Feeling his cheeks flushing, Cesco hoped his head wouldn't bleed faster. "You knew?"

"Of course. In fact it was Rupert who told me. He knew of it from your time with the Emperor. So your cook was paid to make your hunger for it grow. I was sad to hear he had been dismissed. But he thought he was working for the Scaliger's wife, though the money came from my mother, in Giovanna's name. I had no fear of discovery."

"Giovanna's innocent? I don't think I can forgive you for that. I hate owing apologies."

"Your good fortune, then, that you won't have to tender it." Salvatore drew a regretful breath. "I do wish you hadn't forced my hand. I hadn't planned on killing you for months and months. Not until everything was in place."

There was a crackling of some brush in the middle distance. Salvatore turned to listen intently. But the sound was not repeated, and was most likely an animal lurking in the trees.

Rather than call out, Cesco returned to his earlier question. "So why try to kill Cangrande?"

Salvatore grimaced. "Poison? A woman's weapon. I want the Greyhound to know who brought him low. I'll certainly enjoy telling him how I murdered his heir."

"Your mother was Scaligeri. Which makes us kinsmen. Didn't dear uncle Gregorio ever tell you about grandfather's curse?"

"His great mistake, believing in it. Which is why he didn't kill you when he had the chance."

Salvatore was about to lift his blade. Cesco said quickly, "Detto, Benedick, Carrara. And then your mother hired men to kidnap both me and Buthayna."

Salvatore relaxed, enjoying himself. "Your great love. I listened, you know. The walls are not so thick. I made sure I was in the next room each time you dipped your quill in that dark ink. I heard you profess your love."

"Then why bring Barto and Berto to rescue her?" Salvatore made a pitying noise. "Ah, I see. You were the hero who defended my love. You brought my brothers in case it looked too suspicious, you just appearing from nowhere. But did she live or die, I would owe you a debt for trying. "

"Oh, I wanted her to live. Your link to her was another stain in the gloss of your reputation. In love with an infidel whore? It was too perfect. By the way, speaking of apologies, I feel I owe you one. I meant to be there far earlier, especially with the heavy rain." Salvatore frowned. "What I did not anticipate was Cangrande giving your beloved Nuncle Pietro my title that very night. The man who had caused my father's death and chopped off my uncle's head, usurping what was mine by rights? I'm afraid passion got the better of me. I played drunk, and in the darkness no one could see the knife I slid into his ribs. Then I raced around to meet him at the palace door. Such a pity he survived. But I'll remedy that as soon as I've dealt with you. Unless Florence does it for me. Was Cianfa Donati not persuasive enough? From Detto's tale of your meeting I thought he'd be more competent. But at least he inconvenienced the imposter Count. Now, before you die, tell me – what clue is the Moor following? How did we give ourselves away?"

Cesco's lips narrowed as he began to laugh, murmuring softly to himself, "This family. This family. No one else can touch us. It's always from within." He laughed harder. "And you! You're such a foole!"

"What do you mean?" demanded Salvatore sharply.

"The clue had nothing to do with you!" Cesco's laugh became more real with each second, and there were tears in his eyes. "All those pretty plans spoiled. I'm so sorry, Salvatore – you were barely important enough for us to bother with. Frankly, I thought it was Benedick."

"What?"

"His tales of being raised by his uncle, of needing to prove himself. I thought he was the one related to Pathino." Salvatore was silent, and Cesco went doggedly on. "See, I knew these attacks were linked, but I thought they were from a different corner. But the night of the Palio you made two errors. Your mother couldn't resist boasting to the men she hired that they were working for the Count of San Bonifacio. So we at least suspected someone from Padua. And then you made an enormous blunder. You chose the wrong love."

"What do you mean?"

"Whatever you heard me say, Buthayna is not my true love. I came racing only to find my foe doesn't know me as well as he thinks. It spoke volumes, eliminating a host of suspects. It could really be only one of the Rakehells. Not any of the ones whose parents we knew. Which really left only four. Yuri and Fabio were easy enough to clear. Being Paduan, suspicion fell on you and Signor Benedick. He was my first choice. He has red hair, as did the late Count, or so I hear. He is ambidextrous, and based on the angle of the wound, whoever stabbed Pietro used their left hand. And he was so conveniently bedding his Beatrice when all the trouble happened. I thought he was creating an alibi. But no, he truly does love her, poor sod. Instead it's you. And rather than making me force the issue, here you've confessed everything. I repeat, you're a foole. Detto!"

Another crackling of brush as the familiar voice called back, "We're here!"

"You suspected me?" demanded Benedick from the darkness.

"You'd be more hurt if I didn't," answered Cesco. "Are the rest close by?"

"Yuri's company is just behind the hill!"

"You see, my dear Salvatore, you slipped again tonight when you called Buthayna my great love. I soiled my shirt so I could draw Detto aside and told him to play drunk. You did very well, by the way!"

"I've had months to watch you!" called Detto. "Shall we come and arrest him now?"

"I think friend Salvatore would prefer the court of swords. Since we are not in Verona, dueling is permitted. What do you say, Count of Nothing?"

Salvatore didn't snarl or curse. Instead he came forward in silence, his blade speaking for him. Letting the blow slide off a hanging parry, Cesco rolled across the silted earth and found his feet, easing himself into a loose fighting stance. "Come, shall we dance?"

They engaged, hacking, stabbing, shoving, kicking. Cesco caught the flat of Salvatore's blade against his foot, trapping it on the ground. But Salvatore used his free forearm to block Cesco's next stroke at the wrist and bashed his head against Cesco's shoulder, sending him back. Blade free, Salvatore came whirling at Cesco, who dodged around a feeble tree and lunged. Stopping the blade against his own, Salvatore snaked his foot out and hooked Cesco's extended leg at the knee. Instead of falling, Cesco dived in the same direction, rolling and just missing the steel that buried itself in the soft earth.

They clashed again and again in the moonlight. Salvatore was older and stronger. To play up his advantages, Salvatore began striking harder, each blow shocking Cesco's wrists and elbows. In answer, Cesco slipped more of them, allowing them to slide off his blade to left and right while he danced around Salvatore, looking for an opening.

Cesco's head had cleared somewhat, though he knew that the moment his pulse stopped pounding he would be a wreck. His head was a mess as well, but he ignored the pain in favour of survival. Salvatore pressed his attack again and again, and Cesco found himself backed towards their horses, standing uncertain and skittish.

Salvatore launched himself forward. Cesco parried and stepped sideways to avoid the swipe that followed. Quick as lightning, Salvatore pulled his blade back and lunged beneath Cesco's guard towards his breast. Cesco dodged, but Salvatore's sword managed to slice the flesh along Cesco's left shoulder, cutting deep.

Cesco rolled away and rose, knocking away the follow-up strike with all his strength. He glanced at the wound and spit at the Paduan's feet. "Second blood to you, you posturing Paduan ponce."

Salvatore's smile creased his face. "Third's the charm."

"Come and show me, you botched poseur."

By now Detto and Benedick had lit torches, the better to see by. Cesco had barely noticed the brands until he was half-blinded by the reflection on Salvatore's sword. He stepped back and to the side, that the torches were not directly behind him. Both were on their guard, both looking for an opening. Salvatore favoured the German style, sword held high, right hand tight below the crossguard, left hand guiding the pommel at the end. This was the *ochs*, the ox guard. Cesco held his own sword low in the *porta di ferro*, the iron gate, leaving his chest open.

Salvatore accepted the invitation to attack, thrusting forward and down, aiming for Cesco's wounded shoulder. Cesco's blade whipped up and over as he side-stepped right, beating Salvatore's sword away in an arc. His left foot kicked out at his enemy's knee, but Salvatore was already clear, dragging his blade to give Cesco a ringing backswing that sent shocks up and down Cesco's parrying arm.

"Not enough, you dull-witted gruel-monger!" Cesco's arm was in an awkward position, his tip pointed at the ground and his right wrist over his head. Ducking low, he pivoted, turning to his right and leaping forward as he slashed at Salvatore's belly. Salvatore evaded, beating the point aside to be certain, then brought his sword around and down to cleave Cesco's skull. On his knees Cesco caught the blow on the true edge of his sword, his arm twisted so his right hand was by his left ear.

Salvatore didn't withdraw, pressuring the blade to hold Cesco in place. Cesco jabbed the pommel of his blade forward, crunching Salvatore's nose, which exploded in a spray of blood. "Third's the charm."

Salvatore staggered back, but Cesco was too desperate for air to press the attack. They both retreated, gasping. They'd been fighting for ten minutes, an exhausting exercise.

"Bastard," said Salvatore, voice muffled from the blood clogging his nose.

"Truth is truth," Cesco huffed. "I am a bastard in more ways than you could possibly know. You make very free with your title. But you don't know mine. I am *Il Veltro*. The true Greyhound. My life is foretold by the stars, a destiny full of prophecy. And I don't die at your hand!"

Salvatore was utterly unprepared for the wild attack that came at him. Cesco's blade moved like a snake, attacking high and low, whipping left and right in moves too fast to see. The traitorous

Rakehell gave ground, trying desperately to keep up, choked by the blood running down his face and into his throat. In desperation, his hand fell to his belt and he drew his dagger, parrying Cesco's spinning, seething attack with steel in both hands. He swung the dagger at Cesco's neck, barely missing. "Ha!"

Dodging the next dagger stab with a snarling laugh of his own, Cesco brought his sword up so fast he nearly took Salvatore's arm off. The Paduan pulled it back in the nick of time and stabbed again.

Cesco started to spin away but caught his foot on a buried root and fell sprawling on his face. Hearing Salvatore's cry of triumph, Cesco let go of his sword, took two handfuls of earth and rolled, throwing them up. Half-blind, Salvatore didn't check his downward blow. But Cesco hadn't rolled away. Instead he pushed forward off his feet, throwing his body into his attacker's.

Over onto his back, and suddenly Salvatore's face was being smashed by Cesco's left fist. Salvatore's dagger was caught in Cesco's right hand, but his sword arm was still free. His nose being thoroughly pulped, his eyes starting to close, Salvatore did the only thing he could – he brought the round metal pommel of his sword to crack Cesco's already-bleeding skull.

Cesco saw it coming and rolled away, taking nothing more than a glancing blow off his chin. Still it felt as if his jaw had been broken. Salvatore's dagger lunged out, but Cesco was three feet away, scrambling for his sword. His fingers found it and he turned just as Salvatore rose.

They stood, legs shaking, blinking the sweat, blood, and dirt out of their eyes, their weapons still raised. Moving his aching jaw, Cesco tried to spit blood, but it just ran down his chin.

Rushing forward, Cesco seemed to fall. But just as the dagger flashed towards his throat, Cesco turned sideways, his left arm falling while his left knee came up. Knocked free, the dagger landed in the dirt.

Salvatore put his whole weight behind his sword's next swing. Cesco parried, the shock of Salvatore's blow radiating up his tired arms. Salvatore spun and lunged. Cesco pulled back, only to find the sword still coming for him. Salvatore had opened his grip on his sword, letting the handle slide forward through his gloved fingers. Salvatore's hand snapped closed on the very end of the sword, gripping the pommel only. This gave his thrust a precious extra three inches.

The point entered Cesco's ribs at the level of his sternum on his right side. It was the slightest penetration, but both men felt the blade enter Cesco's body. Salvatore's left hand grasped Cesco's outstretched sword arm and readied to press his right shoulder forward and ram the blade straight through Cesco's chest.

"The stars were wrong," taunted Salvatore.

"I wish," said Cesco thickly. His sword arm still caught in Salvatore's grip, Cesco twisted to his left. The blade scored his chest all the way to the armpit. But the force of Salvatore's attack brought him into Cesco's extended arm, catching him just below the chin. Choking, he pulled Cesco down to the earth where they fought with every weapon they had remaining to them, fending off blows with knees, elbows, and hips, twisting, and wrenching, biting and tearing.

Shoving Cesco off him, Salvatore dragged his blade free and swung it down once more on Cesco's head, sure that this time he had won.

Cesco's blade met it, the ringing clash echoing all around them. Both were on their knees, staring at each other, muscling their blades with both hands. Grasping Salvatore's right forearm with his left hand, Cesco suddenly leaned forward and lifted both swords up and over his foe's head. For a moment the startled Salvatore felt the steel of Cesco's blade against the back of his neck.

Lips against Salvatore's ear, Cesco spoke in a fierce whisper. "Tell your father the Greyhound sends his regards." Cesco heaved, intending to sever Salvatore's spine.

Salvatore ducked, and the drag of the blade ripped open the flesh along the back of his skull. Releasing his grip on his blade, Salvatore shoved Cesco down. Hand clasped to his bleeding head, he ran in silence for the nearest horse. Mounting, he kicked and the horse bolted. Benedick and Detto were shouting as the Paduan tried to trample Cesco, but the horse leapt just as Cesco threw himself down into the silt.

Detto and Benedick hurried forward, shouting loudly. Cesco was on his knees, breathing hard, two swords in his grip. Just as they reached him, he leaned over and vomited in the dirt.

"Are you hurt?" demanded Detto. "Should I go get Fracastoro? Morsicato?"

"No," said Cesco between pants. "No. No one. Bastard. Is Yuri—?"

"Chasing him now," assured Detto.

"You thought it was me?" demanded Benedick, half mocking, half injured.

"Forgive me," said Cesco, standing shakily. "Remember – *tutti matti*."

Benedick shook his head. "Truth is truth."

"In the face," added Detto. Laughter was cleansing.

◆   ◊   ◆

Cangrande was summoned. In the torchlight, he looked at the ground, then at Cesco. "Quite a duel."

"We're not in Verona," said Cesco at once.

"Not what I meant. Salvatore? Who is he really?"

"Veronese, by way of Padua." In short gasps, Cesco explained, only leaving out the detail of the ship. That didn't matter.

Cangrande gazed at him. "In all our private battles, it's good to be reminded there are others who don't respect the game. Come. Rizardo has sent a case of wine to my tents. What say we drink until it's gone?"

"Sounds perfect. I hope I didn't take you away from anything important."

"Only victory." Cangrande was grinning his perfect *allegria*. "Tempesta has sent a party to treat. I thought you'd want to be there."

"You'll have to find me a mount," answered Cesco. "That son of a bitch took mine."

Cangrande peered into the dark night after the stolen horse. "We'll find him. And Salvatore. Poor Vittoria."

"Lucky, you mean," said Cesco. "She escaped a cad. We both know what a poor marriage can lead to. Did you say there was wine?"

"Aye. Come along." Together the two princes of Verona climbed the ridge and headed back to the camp, followed by their various retainers. But they chose this night to be alone together, not reveling in company, but rather basking in something shared. In short order they were in the Scaliger's tent, Cesco's wounds tended while they both drank deeply, ordering bread, beef, and mustard to sop up the wine that continued to flow uninterrupted.

Morsicato was present for the tending of wounds, but departed when they began singing lines of Cino da Pistoia as a drinking song:

Io fu' 'n su l'alto e 'n sul beato monte,	*I was on the high and blessed mound,*
ch'i' adorai baciando 'l santo sasso;	*Where I worshipped, kissing the sacred stone,*
e caddi 'n su quella petra, di lasso,	*On that rock, in weariness, bowed down,*
ove l'onesta pose la sua fronte,	*Where Purity laid her forehead in the ground,*
e ch'ella chiuse d'ogni vertù il fonte	*Sealing there the fount of every virtue,*
quel giorno che di morte acerbo passo	*When the woman of my heart, alas,*
fece la donna de lo mio cor, lasso,	*Travelled through Death's most bitter pass,*
già piena tutta d'adornezze cònte.	*She who was already in her gracious life renown'd.*

Quivi chiamai a questa guisa Amore:	*So there I called to Love, in words again:*
"Dolce mio iddio, fa che qui mi traggia	*'Sweet Lord, let Death take me for his own,*
la morte a sé, ché qui giace 'l mio core".	*Now, since in this place my heart was slain.'*
Ma poi che non m'intese 'l mio signore,	*But when my Lord showed only his disdain,*
mi diparti' pur chiamando Selvaggia;	*Still calling on my Selvaggia, I passed down:*
l'alpe passai con voce di dolore.	*Travelling the mountain with my moan of pain.*

They were still at it as the sun rose and Tempesta's messengers arrived.

♦   ◊   ♦

"I regret it took this long," said Tubal to the Moor as they met just outside the Yellow Crescent. "I had to be certain I was not betraying a confidence."

"You are satisfied?"

Tubal nodded. "The ship in question was employed on several occasions. I have copies here of every reference."

Tharwat thanked the Hebrew and returned to his lodging. Within minutes, he had seen all there was. The year Cesco was born, *La Alisceote* had landed in Genoa. Which would be the Moor's next port of call.

♦   ◊   ♦

Gueccello Tempesta of Treviso arrived at the monastery of the Quaranta Santi, there to treat with the Vicar of the Trevisian Mark — a title Treviso had never respected until now.

Considering his position, the terms Tempesta sent were outrageous. He was to retain his personal castle at Noale, and be granted the title of Capitano da Treviso. He would get a personal salary of one thousand Venetian *ducati* a month, and be granted the right to choose the podestà of the city. His mercenary army would be paid out of Cangrande's own funds. For all this, he agreed that most the exiles could return to the city, excepting his personal enemies, whose banishment Cangrande was to declare perpetual. For the protection of the citizens under his care, he made no provision at all.

Cangrande agreed at once.

Messengers were sent haring off in every direction, and celebrations erupted all over the Feltro. The Lombard wars were over. Foes abounded, of course, annoying pockets of resistance. Venice remained, an autonomous entity at their eastern edge. To the west, Bergamo still fulminated and caused minor troubles. To the north were the Alps and the Germanic states. But since the nearest was ruled by a distant relative, called Escalus, it was no concern. To the south, Pisa and Florence shivered in anticipation of Cangrande's next move.

Verona now ruled from Feltro to Feltro, as the saying went. Give him five more years, everyone thought, and Cangrande would own all Italy. After that, well, already rumours were flying, rumours that spoke of greater ambition, rumours that would give Emperor Ludwig many uneasy nights.

The following morning Cangrande would enter and take the city, much as he had done the previous fall in Padua. So on this, the eve of the final capitulation, the Scaliger ordered a celebratory feast for all his men. Then he retired to his pavilion to vomit.

"Christ, I wish we hadn't drunk so much last night," murmured Cangrande, waxen-faced and sweating.

Guarding the tent-flap lest someone enter, Cesco was little better. "My stomach was churning all through the negotiations. Did we agree to those terms because you wanted the siege over, or the talking?"

"Both," admitted Cangrande with a wan smile as he leaned over the basin. "I hope history sees it as evidence of my magnanimous nature." The last word was lost as the Scaliger heaved again.

A waft of hot summer air brought the smell of vomit to Cesco's nose, which had him swallowing his own breakfast a second time. "No more local wine."

"Agreed," gasped Cangrande, laughing. He forced himself to heave twice more, removing all the contents from his stomach, then wiped his mouth and stood. "Give me some mint to chew, and let's go celebrate."

"So long as we can do it without eating, drinking, or even smelling food."

It was a forlorn hope. A massive clearing had been prepared for the festivities, full of tables and benches and spits of meat, kegs of ale and barrels of wine. "I hope somebody's still on guard duty," said Cangrande loudly. "It would be terrible if they came and slaughtered us while we were too drunk to raise a sword!"

"All hail the conquering scalawag!" cried Bailardino, overjoyed.

"Hail!" cried Nico da Lozzo, raising his tin cup of ale.

"Imperator!" shouted Castelbarco, mimicking the Roman salute. Several men picked it up, and soon the whole army was shouting, *"Im-per-a-tor! Im-per-a-tor!"*

Cangrande waved them off, but couldn't help mirroring the salute as he did so. "Oh, that won't feed the rumours," observed

Cesco with a grin.

Cangrande flashed him a wolfish smile. "Why do I owe Ludwig assurance? A crown is not a relief from cares, but rather a bringer of them."

"A wonder that you should long for one, then."

"What I long for is food I can keep down. Do you think we might try a little bread?"

Cesco was more successful than the Scaliger at keeping his meal down. Cangrande had to escape twice to vomit again, and when he returned in fresh hose, Cesco correctly deduced that the stomach had turned in both directions. Cesco's own buttocks were firmly clenched against any sudden movement of his liquefied bowels.

Watching the proceedings, the Trevisian guests observed how their foe was beloved. If there were a few flashes of Scaligeri temper, or long looks at someone's wife, or a little too much pleasure in flattery, it was drowned by the voices calling out his name in genuine admiration. And what wasn't there to admire? Caesar had owned a temper, and a body, and a pride. No, each decided silently, there was no shame in submitting to this man. Though they had feared the sun, they couldn't be faulted for not preventing its rise.

In the whirlwind of the day's events, there had been little time to digest the previous night's betrayal and revelation. Calling all the remaining Rakehells together, they discussed Salvatore's betrayal. Berto, and Barto were astonished, mouths hanging open in slack-jawed shock. Petruchio and Hortensio were enraged, demanding they find the treacherous bastard who had toyed with their sister's emotions. But he had eluded Yuri and the rest. He was gone.

"She's well out of it," said Cesco, choosing not to repeat what Salvatore had said of their sister's virtue. "Besides, it's not like he got away with her. Whereas I miss Abastor like I'd miss my own legs."

"Have you sent to Ser Alaghieri?" asked Detto.

"The Count, you mean," corrected Cesco. "We must all remember to call him so, and blot out any hope that Salvatore has of claiming that title. Nuncle Pietro must hold a festival this fall for all the people of San Bonifacio, and live there with his new bride. They'll love him. They won't be able to help themselves."

"But you did send," repeated Detto urgently.

"I did, and so did the Scaliger. If Salvatore is foolish enough to seek out Pietro or Tharwat, they will at least be warned. Ooh." He put a hand to his stomach.

"Is it the wound?" asked Benedick.

Cesco shook his injured head. "The wine." He caught a concerned glance from Detto and laughed weakly. "Truly! The Capitano was aiding me in lubricating my wounds, and as a result we've both been spewing all day."

Through the night the remaining Rakehells cavorted together. Benedick, Petruchio, Hortensio, Berto and Barto were all having the time of their lives. Astonishingly, Mastino joined the festivities, bringing his brother Alblivious and the younger Castelbarco with him. In short, the whole of youthful Veronese chivalry were present, singing, eating, drinking, boasting and challenging each other to mock duels and contests of strength and skill.

For a while the sport was knife-throwing, the target being a butt of wine placed on the edge of a high wagon. Each knife that penetrated the wood created a trickle of liquid that men eagerly vied to be beneath. The aim was to plant the knife in such a way to make a spout before the butt was empty. Cesco's throw was the best, opening a hole at the very bottom of the barrel. Accepting the acclaim, he said, "I just pretended it was my own back."

After the knife-throwing, Detto arm-wrestled all comers, and at fourteen years he beat men twice his age. Benedick engaged in bouts of wordplay, besting anyone who dared to challenge him to a duel of insults. Berto invented songs from his own pure brain, while his brother showed an unsuspected skill at art, sketching in coal the faces around him.

Looking at a drawing of himself, Cesco was bemused. "Is this what I look like?"

"Aye," said Barto, sucking in his cheeks and raising his chin in mockery. "Your left profile is better than your right."

"What you mean is that I look better from a sinister point of view."

Barto grinned. "That's exactly what I mean."

Cesco continued to wander among friendly faces. For a time he joined the badinage with Benedick, letting fly with barbed missiles from his own pure brain. Then Cangrande called him over, and they sat close together the rest of the night, amazing old courtiers and new adherents with their wit, their talents, and their daring. So very alike. Frighteningly so. A dynasty in the making. There had been four other Scaligeri rulers over only two generations, and none so great as these. Here sat the future, and it promised to outshine its forebears as the sun outshines the moon.

♦   ◊   ♦

On July 18th, 1339, Cangrande della Scala made his official entry into the conquered city of Treviso. Citizens poured into the streets to cheer him as they had no one else in their history. Bugles blared, trumpets sounded, drums and castanets, bagpipes, flutes, lutes, and every kind of noise-maker was employed, as if men wanted to pierce the sky with sound. Not since the days of Caesar or Charlemagne had a single frame so embodied all that a man was meant to be. Having been relieved of their defiance, they now embraced him with the fervor only a new convert can possess.

Children preceded him, some holding up his banner, others bearing simple ladders stolen from shops. The people cried their acclaim for the Capitano di Verona, their new lord, the man who would at last bring them honour, fame, and victory. It was his crowning triumph — literally, as someone had made him a chaplet of oak-leaves. They hailed him another Caesar. At long last the whole of the Mark lay at his feet.

The procession was filled with famous men, most of whose faces until now were unfamiliar to Trevisians: Carrara, Nogarola, Camino, Aldrighetto, Castelbarco, Novello, Bonaventura, Montecchio, Capulletto. The once and future Capitano da Treviso, Tempesta, rode near the front of the huge body of knights, as did his friend Avogaro.

The head of the parade was reserved for the Scaligeri. The bastards Barto and Berto were young and handsome. Alblivious was his genial self, free and open and guileless. Mastino was bedecked in his finest armour, almost richer than Cangrande's own. But he lacked the Houndshelm, the most fearsome mantle in Italy.

Dressed in golden armour that blinded onlookers in the bright summer sun, Cangrande carried the Houndshelm in his lap for all to see. His horse was tall and, draped with the caparison of his house and offices, so full of honours that it was almost indecipherable. But the ladder was clear, the eagle was embroidered in gold, and the silver hound seemed to be racing as it flapped with the movements of the horse's legs. He carried no sword, no spear, but instead the staff of lordship, marking him as Treviso's new master. Over the staff, as upon his head, was a chaplet, signifying peace.

But where was that famous smile? Those not dazzled by the reflected light saw Cangrande looking grave and austere in his saddle, and they worried at the absence of his renowned *allegria*. They fretted that they had held out too long, angered him too much. How much would their defiance cost them?

His heir, too, looked grim. Riding at the Scaliger's side, he was dressed in plainer style than either Cangrande or Mastino, though

still in armour that would cost the average nobleman three years'
rent. He waved from time to time, and sent the occasional wan smile
into the thronging crowd. But his face was closed, his eyes turned
inwards, unwelcoming, ungracious.

In reality, it was all Cesco could do to stay in his saddle without vomiting. His stomach roiled, his bowls churned, his esophagus worked to swallow the heavy saliva filling his cheeks, drowning
his tongue. Taut as a hunting hound, his stomach, jaw, and buttocks
clenched lest one should revolt and lead to a complete overthrow.
Waxen-skinned and sweating, only the strongest effort of will kept
him upright.

Smile! He forced himself to wave. There was nothing to be
done at the moment. He'd already asked Morsicato to find him after
the parade. Until then, there was naught to do but smile.

The parade ended at the palace of the Bishop of Treviso, where
Cangrande was to stay. The Scaliger dismounted, climbed the steps,
and turned to face the crowd.

And there it was! The smile that was now as famous as Caesar's
luck, as Hercules' strength, as Odysseus' cunning. The Scaliger had
entered the city grave and reserved, only to reveal now, like a master
showman, what they all longed to see. His perfect teeth shone as
bright as his armour, and his eyes danced like angels before the fall.

Feeling his stomach turn over, Cesco willed the moment to
end so he could get inside and find a chamber pot.

Waving the cheering crowd to silence, Cangrande made a show
of piety. "O King of Heaven, you who are worthy of glory, I praise
and thank you, because you have sated my mind, which has so long
yearned to unite Treviso with her sisters! Together we shall form a
new constellation in your Heaven, one that will outshine the stars of
old, and write a new destiny for all Mankind!"

He stood there, under the cheers from thousands of voices.
Women on balconies, children on their fathers' shoulders, tradesmen,
nobles, clergy, peasants, merchants – all shouted the praise of this, the
greatest of his line. "Sca-*la!* Sca-*la!* Sca-*la!*"

Cangrande offered a final wave to the people before turning
and entering the bishop's door. In the shade of the cool interior, he
pitched forward onto the floor.

THIRTY-NINE

CESCO QUICKLY SHUT the doors, locking out the rest of the procession. Cangrande lay shivering and shaking on the tiled floor. Suddenly he retched, and vomit flew forth as if shot from a trebuchet. Cesco took a step back, but the smell caught him and he turned to spew forth the contents of his own stomach on the other side of the entrance hall.

Under the eyes of horrified servants, Cangrande and Cesco glanced at each other. They both flashed the weakest of grins. "Apologies," said Cangrande.

Cesco groaned. "You owe me new hose."

Cangrande started to laugh, but the tightening of his stomach muscles caused him to begin retching again. Still in his armour, he knelt on all fours, heaving and heaving long past the time when there was anything left to heave.

"Who closed that damn door?" demanded Bailardino, bursting in from a side entrance. His annoyance turned to concern as he saw his best friend's armour covered in bile, while Cesco sat with his back against the wall, breathing shallowly. Throwing aside his gauntlets, he raced forward and knelt. "Are you injured?"

"No," said Cangrande with a weak grimace. "Too much mixing of wines and ales, and perhaps some bad beef. There was a lot of celebrating last night." He was clearly speaking for the benefit of the frightened servants. This was not the work of bad food.

Morsicato appeared, his eyes quickly taking in the scene.

Practical in a crisis, he asked Cesco, "Can you walk?" Cesco waved his assent, so the doctor knelt on Cangrande's other side. Using a knife he made fast work of the ties and straps holding the outer armour in place. Then, with Bail's help, he got Cangrande upright and asked the way to the Scaliger's room. Cesco followed, with Detto appearing to steady his arm.

With the aid of both his doctors, Cangrande slept all that day, and all the next. When he did wake, he woke puking and excreting torrents of liquid. His bowels seemed to have become water, and he had to be cleaned again and again. Despite candles and burning herbs, the room smelled like a latrine.

The first rumour that was spread said Cangrande was busy at work setting the city aright. The second, the one given to the Trevisian, Veronese, and Paduan nobility, was that he was dead drunk. Thus no one questioned when Fracastoro and Morsicato entered his room with buckets of water, or when they heard retching noises from within.

Cesco's own room was not far away. Morsicato checked on him throughout the night, but was far less concerned. The young man slept soundly without aid, whimpering only occasionally as his stomach contracted. He awoke thirsty, and craving food. An excellent sign.

At noon the second day, Cesco rose from his sickbed, looking stronger. He bathed and dressed himself, and was steady on his legs as he entered the Scaliger's sickroom. There he saw Fracastoro and Morsicato, the first fluttering, the other sitting still and watching.

Drawing close, Cesco looked down on the Lord of Verona, shivering and twisting under the blankets. "What is it?"

"It could be dysentery," said Fracastoro.

"No," said the other doctor, his voice flat. "This is poison."

"Are you certain?" asked Cesco.

"No," said Fracastoro.

"Dead certain," said Morsicato.

The tone spoke as much as the choice of words. "But my symptoms were just the same, and I recovered."

Morsicato lowered his voice. "And you have eaten a steady diet of poison these last three years. Your body has a tolerance his does not."

Cesco crossed to the unoccupied side of the bed and sat on a stool. Reaching out, he took the large hand into his own and began to rub. He looked at Morsicato. "That's right, isn't it? It's what you told Detto to do."

"That's right," said Morsicato slowly. "But not necessary – not now."

Still Cesco did not stop caressing the Scaliger's hand. "Who knows?"

"Bailardino. Castelbarco. A couple of his personal servants – we called Tullio from Verona. Fracastoro. Me. And now you."

"What about the Count of San Bonifacio? Tharwat?"

"I sent a letter to Venice, in code. But it won't reach him. After it had gone, I received word from al-Dhaamin that he's on his way to Genoa to look at ship manifests." He spoke obliquely, but Cesco understood that Tharwat had uncovered a promising lead. "I sent another letter after him."

"Well then, who's been managing the public? The transition?"

"Bailardino, Carrara – and Mastino."

"I should go, then," said Cesco.

"I suppose you should. After all, you're his heir."

There was a strangeness in the doctor's tone that brought Cesco's chin up. "You think I did this."

Morsicato flushed. "Did I say–?"

"No, but you wondered. You're just shy of accusing me."

Morsicato started gnawing his beard with his upper teeth. "I just – I wonder what people would say. You're both poisoned, but you recover? It will be suspicious."

"A cobbler should not judge above his last. I am, alas, innocent," said Cesco, squeezing Cangrande's hand once more before rising to his feet. "There is nothing I want less than this. Our race hasn't finished yet, his and mine. So keep him alive, doctor. No excuses. Death is not an option."

As the door closed behind Cesco, Morsicato shook his head. "Death is always an option."

◆   ◇   ◆

Tharwat reached Genoa without incident. It took only hours to track down the ship's history. It had sunk ten years ago, but that was of little interest. It was an earlier voyage that had all the Moor's attention. What he found made his hands tremble.

◆   ◇   ◆

At noon on the Twenty-First of July, Cangrande della Scala awakened clear-eyed. His first words were, "Is it poison?"

Fracastoro rushed to his master's side as Morsicato offered a cup of water to the cracked lips. "We fear so."

Cangrande drank, some of the water running past his lips and down his face. Swallowing, his stomach clenched again. "Is there hope?"

"There is always hope," answered Fracastoro, in a tone whose true meaning all patients know.

"What is the date?" Remarkably, when they told him, he smiled. "An auspicious day. My stomach has a thousand butterflies in it." He groaned. "Or scorpions. May I sit up?"

Fracastoro aided him. Upright and bolstered with pillows, Cangrande saw Cesco sitting at the foot of his bed. "The wages of sin." His voice was thready.

"Let love be without dissimulation," said Cesco. "What do you need?"

"You, last of all. No, not an insult." He licked his lips and accepted more water. "Give me – a moment to think."

Cesco waited in silence as Cangrande collected his thoughts, then received his instructions. As he departed he pulled Morsicato aside. "This bodes well, doesn't it? That he can speak?"

Morsicato shook his head. "It is the last moment of clarity before the end. When you return, choose your words with care."

Cesco vanished at a run down the hall. In short order he returned, bearing with him Tullio, Castelbarco, Bailardino, Mastino, and Carrara. The last three were asked to remain outside for a moment, while Cesco ushered Castelbarco and the Grand Butler into the chamber.

By now word had spread that the Scaliger was ill. No hangover lasted two days, and the concern emanating from the room was as pungent as the smell. Standing outside the chamber, Bailardino and Mastino pressed Cesco for information, and he repeated what the doctors had said.

After a few minutes, Tullio d'Isola emerged from the chamber, weeping openly. His fingers were stained with ink, and in his hand he held the seal of Verona.

Castelbarco came behind him, looking old. "Bail. Mastino. Marsilio. He wants you all."

They entered the chamber, whose windows had been thrown open to the air. They had visited before, but were now shocked by the wrecked frame of a man who had been so large – larger than life. He was now shriveled, a shadow of the great man who had, three days before, achieved his highest honour yet. They understood that today would be his last.

"O Francesco!" cried Bail, kneeling beside the freshly-changed bed and taking his hand gingerly in his own. Bail had practically raised Cangrande. Child to page, squire to knight, Bail had been Cangrande's guiding hand in the world of men, while Katerina had spent her powers on other parts in the Scaliger's shaping. Together for thirty-two years, more than half Bail's own life, Cangrande's passing would at once strip him of both a brother and a son.

Cangrande patted his old friend's hand with a smile. "Bail. I owe you more than I can — say now. There is no time left. Soon I will evanesce, and there are — matters to be concluded. Some after-math, a final reckoning. Marsilio?"

Breathless, Carrara knelt beside Bailardino. "Lord."

"You are the two greatest men in the Feltro. You rule — two of her greatest cities. I must ask you — to carry on in my name."

"Of course, Lord," said Carrara.

"No," protested Bail. "Not without you—"

Cangrande smiled. "The alternative is — not possible. Look after my people — and my bloodline. See that no evil comes to either."

"Of course, Lord," said Carrara.

Bail just sat staring at the gaunt face, holding himself still lest the sob in his chest escaped.

"Good. Now, listen." He gave instructions for the disposition of his soldiers, the best way to keep their loyalty in the face of this reversal. He then produced a letter sealed with the ladder crest. "Treviso must be ruled by one of my loyal generals, but Padua — I have a loyal man in Padua." He pressed the crest into Carrara's grip. "I release you from bondage. Padua is yours."

Looking at the letter in his hand, Carrara pushed it back into Cangrande's fingers. "I've tried to be my own master and I failed."

Cangrande pressed it back. "Take it. With Cesco and Bail behind you, you cannot fail."

"In your name," said Carrara. "I will be Lord of Padua in your name." He glanced at Cesco, who was leaning against the far door. "And in the name of your heir."

"Good. That's good. Now go. I have to talk to my family." Carrara departed, looking shaken, trying to imagine the world they were about to enter.

Cesco shut the portal behind him as Cangrande gestured Mastino forward. "I have two — natural sons that must be trained — to bring honour to me."

When Bail did not answer, Mastino said, "We will take care of them. I swear it."

"Bail?"

Bailardino nodded.

"Now Bail, I need you to go home. Kat. Kat cannot hear of this from anyone but you. Tell her—" He paused, searching for the words. "Tell her I go contented. Tell her that. I am content. And that I love her. Go. And God bless you."

Bail was a long time going, lingering at the door, drinking in the last sight of the best friend he would ever have. The guiding star of his life was about to be snuffed out, leaving him without direction.

When Bail had gone, Cangrande asked for a private moment with Mastino. The doctors withdrew, and Cesco stepped outside, his face wary. When Mastino emerged, just a few moments later, he beckoned everyone in. "Tullio, Guglielmo. Cesco. He needs us all."

Given water, Cangrande began to murmur softly to his steward. Over the next hour Cangrande conducted his business, making his dispositions through a weeping Tullio d'Isola, who never imagined out-living this Scaligeri the way he'd outlived Alberto's other sons. Rapidly but with characteristic precision, Cangrande dictated the documents that were needed. He signed the order confirming Tempesta's possession of Noale, thus completing his agreement for the ownership of Treviso. Similar documents were made naming Nogarola and Carrara the perpetual rulers of Vicenza and Padua, respectively. Many more deeds and decrees were made, all with Cesco, Mastino, Tullio, Morsicato, Fracastoro, and Castelbarco as witnesses.

They had to pause for another bout of vomiting.

The last paper reaffirmed his will, declaring his natural son Francesco della Scala as the sole heir to the captainship of Verona. Everyone signed it, including both Mastino and Cesco. Shivering, Cangrande affixed his seal, then slumped back with a sigh. That last burst of energy had taken with it almost all his light. "Now, find me a priest. Then, Cesco – you alone."

They filed out of the chamber while the Scaliger retched over the side of his bed. Summoned, the Bishop of Treviso entered and Cesco closed the door after him, staying outside while Cangrande confessed.

When it was over and the Bishop gone, Cesco entered the room one last time, and alone. He shut the door and leaned against it. "Have you prayed?"

"I have," said Cangrande, breathing shallowly. "*Extra ecclesiam nulla salus.* I have. All my sins – are confessed. Save one."

"And that is?"

Cangrande wagged a trembling finger. "A secret."

Despite himself, Cesco released a short laugh. "I detest your secrets."

"You should. They're always – about you."

Cesco walked slowly forward. "There's quite a gathering outside the palace."

"I'm sure. Don't let anyone – defile me. I want a – proper burial."

Cesco sat on the stool closest the bed, on the Scaliger's left. "You'll get it. With palm fronds and frankincense and myrrh, and a coronet of fire."

Cangrande offered a wisp of his famous smile. "A shame I am not – a pelican."

"True!" Cesco laughed more easily. "So – at the last, here I am. Would you like me to sing?"

Cangrande shook his head, a barely noticeable gesture. "Something I must say."

"About Lia?"

Cangrande shook his head. "Maria."

"My mother?"

"Yes," gasped Cangrande. "Stop looking. If you love Verona – if you want your destiny, and mine – stop now."

Cesco felt the urgency in the plea as Cangrande gripped his wrist with all the strength left to him. "Very well. I'll call off the hunt. But I want something in return."

Cangrande closed his eyes. "You are – my heir. What more – do you want?"

"A different kind of acknowledgement. Less public, and worthless on the market. But priceless to me."

"What?"

"You know."

There was a silence between them. At last Cangrande shook his head. "I have acknowledged you – in every way I am able."

The Scaliger slipped into sleep. Cesco sat for the next few hours, very still, very quiet, listening to Cangrande's laboured breath.

Suddenly the Scaliger opened his eyes. "Cesco!"

"I'm here."

Cangrande relaxed. "You know who did this."

"Yes," said Cesco. "Petruchio, too."

"Can't punish. Ruin the family."

"You don't want justice?"

"I already have it. I die today. Do you see?" Cangrande stiffened and, through sheer force of will, rose to sit upright. "Three days! Three days – three after –"

Cesco put his hand on Cangrande's shoulder, trying to ease

him back down. "Shh. Easy."

Choking, face purple, the Scaliger raised a finger. "You – are not – you – not you! Not –"

It was the last of his air. Fear of dying this instant forced him to calm himself and concentrate on breathing. Cesco fetched water, but the Scaliger couldn't swallow until he'd heaved again. There came a foul stench as he soiled the bed.

Cangrande fell back, exhausted from the effort. When at last he felt able, he said, "Indignity. Puking and shitting myself to death. No way for a man to die."

"You don't have to die today."

Cangrande's eyes shot open. "I must! The prophecy says – three days after –"

"I know what it says," snapped Cesco. "Was Treviso your greatest deed? Will it bring about a new age of man?"

Cangrande smiled. His perfect teeth looked strange in his mouth, as the gums were receding. No more *allegria*. "For want of a nail – the empire fell."

"I wish you were right," Cesco whispered to him.

"I am. I am." From behind closed eyes, Cangrande drank in shallow sips of air. "Dante – had his Hell. I've had mine. You have – yours."

"What is your Hell?" asked Cesco.

"Not being – what I would."

"While mine is being what I would not."

Cangrande was once again passing into unconsciousness. Behind his closed eyes the room was fading. But he managed four final words.

"I am *Il Veltro*."

♦   ◊   ♦

As bidden, Bail rode straight for his own palace at Vicenza. As it was forty miles overland from Treviso to Vicenza, he rode with no armour and only a light escort. If he hurried, he might return with some word from his wife, some final offering to balm the hurts of a lifetime.

With him rode Detto. Val had wanted to come, protesting loudly. But at twelve years old, he would not be able to keep up on the thunderous overland ride.

They changed horses twice en route, gulping water and snatching bites of bread while the fresh mounts were saddled, but otherwise they did not stop. There was no conversation beyond directions.

It was hard riding, and under the rumble of the hoofs Detto could pretend not to hear his father's sobs. He understood well enough. The father was thinking of losing his friend, while the son was fearing what such a loss would do to his own friend. Having just rediscovered himself, would Cesco descend again? Or would he rise to the challenge?

It was late when they entered Vicenza's walls, long after dark, in the middle of the night. Recognized, the master of the city raced to his palace. There he met long faces. Had they already heard?

Antonio Nogarola came forth to meet them on the palace steps. He used his one arm to grip his brother's shoulder. "We did not think the messengers would reach you so swiftly. Bail, Detto — I'm so sorry."

Detto was still confused, even as his father drew a long breath. "When?"

"Two hours ago. Another stroke."

Now it was Detto's turn to draw in that breath of understanding. His mouth remained open, his limbs frozen, his mind locked. "Mother?"

Bail said, "Tell me she was not alone."

"Her niece Verde came to call the day before. They were together. The lady is within now, making the necessary arrangements."

Bail reached out and wrapped his arms about his numbed son, squeezing him tight. "Fitting. It was only fitting. She loved him so much. And she was spared his passing."

It was cold comfort. For Katerina had also been deprived of the only honest declaration of love her brother had ever offered her.

♦   ◊   ♦

Somewhere in the dark hours of the night Cangrande stirred once more, wakened by a final spasm that had him violently vomiting and churning his bowels. Cesco called in Morsicato and Fracastoro, who brought with them a bevy of servants. Cesco retreated to the wall to watch as they tried to delay the inevitable.

In the midst of the terrible contractions and purges, as his body fought to expel the poison that had wasted his system, he stiffened with one prodigious lurch, sickness and excrement and vomit all spewing forth at once. In that moment his heart erupted and he collapsed, racked no more.

In the silence that followed, Cesco heard the bells of the nearby Santa Maria Maggiore, known to locals as La Madonna Granda. They rang, marking the Benedictine hour of Lauds. Which meant it was three o'clock in the morning of July Twenty-Second.

Cangrande's final triumph had taken place four days earlier.

FORTY

In Treviso the sun refused to rise, as if unwilling to usher in this wretched day. Morsicato came from the death-chamber, his hands washed clean of the touch of corruption.

Those few in the know had gone home for some fitful sleep. They would need it.

Mastino and Alberto appeared at the door, summoned by Cesco.

"There's no doubt?" asked Alberto. "He's done this before. I've heard of drugs that mimic death. Is he truly..?"

"Dead," said Morsicato. "I held a mirror to his lips and pierced his nose with a needle. His blood is settled and his joints are stiff."

Mastino sighed, not with relief but with a kind of assurance. "Where's the boy?"

Morsicato gestured. "In the chamber. What's been decided?"

"Castelbarco will inform Montecchio, Capulletto, and the others. But we'll keep it a secret from the Trevisians for another day or so. They might still rise up."

"And the body?"

"He must be buried in Verona. But how do we get him back without drawing attention?"

Drawn by their voices, Cesco emerged from the chamber. He kicked the door closed behind him. "I'll need a wagon. Four horses. Some empty crates – no, better, fill them with chickens. Or swine, whatever. Something awkward to steal. I'll set out at first light."

"A team of horsemen," said Morsicato. "We must preserve his body for burial."

"At the expense of anonymity," replied Cesco. "Armed men will invite questions and worse."

"What's worse than questions?"

"Rumours."

Mastino saw the sense in that. "Fine. You, me, and three men, with clubs visible and swords hidden."

"Just the wrong side of right," said Cesco. "Too weak to defend us from a real attack, strong enough to invite speculation. Give me a cart, a straw hat, and a sword, and I'll see you in Verona by tomorrow night."

"You're not going alone," said Mastino.

"Heaven forefend," said Cesco. "I'll take my father with me."

It was an argument none of the adults expected to lose, but Cesco prevailed by saying simply, "It was his wish."

♦   ◊   ♦

Servants carried a crate out of the Bishop's palace and down to the nearby stable, with no notion as to the true nature of their burden. Inside the stable were Nico da Lozzo, Antonio Capulletto, and Mariotto Montecchio. Anyone who saw them thought they were servants, for they worked in their shirts. Castelbarco appeared in his own attire, presumably to give orders.

When the servants had gone, all four men took the corners of the crate and strapped it carefully to the wagonbed. Then, feeling insanely awkward, they began loading the wagon with crates of snorting, snuffling pigs.

For once, Mari and Antony held off from any bickering. They worked side by side, united by tragedy.

"Too soon," murmured Nico, pushing the last crate into place. "Too soon."

Cesco appeared, dressed in peasant clothes. Climbing into the diver's seat of the wagon, he thanked them all. "Remember, let no word of this out until tonight. I'll see you all at the rendezvous. Oh, and Guglielmo – bring Signor Benedick along, will you?" Pulling a borrowed straw hat down over his eyes, Cesco urged the four horses out of the sheltered stable and, without any sign of hurry, started towards the south gate.

To the four men watching in the stables, and the others looking down from the palace windows, this was a prosaic and uneasy moment. Their lord was dead, and they had a new lord, young and vivacious. What kind of prince would he be? Already he was as strange and daring as his forebear. Would he be as successful? Only time would answer.

Separately they returned to their various lodgings to bathe and dress and prepare to journey back to Verona for the state funeral. It would take a week, they had figured, to prepare things. The coffin had been filled with herbs, and Morsicato had wrapped the body in a manner that would preserve it for as long as necessary. For, of course, the first tomb would not be the final resting place. This great man would be laid to rest under the floor of Santa Maria Antica until a suitable monument was ready.

Being so young, Cangrande hadn't even begun thinking of his tomb. It was perhaps the only thing for which he had never had foresight.

◆   ◊   ◆

Pietro had again dined with Dolce and her family, and was weightless as he strolled back through the streets of Pistoia. He had heard by now of the victory at Treviso, and also of the perfidy of Salvatore. Pathino's nephew, Bonifacio's son! Astonishing. But wonderful to have it explained. There was nothing so terrible once the danger was identified, and could be fought.

He had barely entered the palace when he sensed something was wrong. The servants explained that his friend, the Moorish astrologer, had arrived, and was waiting for a private interview with the Count.

Behind closed doors, Pietro smiled at his old friend. Then he saw Tharwat's face. "What's the matter?"

Tharwat produced several papers. "Read these."

The news was shocking, entirely erasing all of Pietro's equanimity. "Dear God."

"We must tell him. At once."

It meant Pietro breaking his vow to remain in Pistoia. But it could not be helped. This was too important.

Just as they were deciding how best to slip out of the city unseen, a messenger arrived carrying a note from Morsicato. The grave news it bore made their journey even more urgent.

◆   ◊   ◆

Cesco took the ride easily, conversing with passers-by, sharing the road with a convoy carrying strawberries until they turned off for Padua. The rest of the day he spent in silence. If he was tempted to converse with the spirit still lingering around the body in the wagon, he must have decided they had already said enough.

At nightfall he pulled up to a little country church, La Pecchiena. Explaining he was bearing a humble soldier's body home, he paid the rector and gained the man's help in removing the anonymous coffin from the wagon and placing it inside the chapel. They covered it in a silken pall and surrounded it with candles. Then, with the holy man's permission, Cesco knelt beside the plain wooden box and prayed through the night. He spoke to God, though the discussion was one-sided. As his cross, he held the hereditary sword of the Scaligeri. Once Cangrande's sword, now his own. The grip was bound with iron wire and the crossguard was gold, and both reflected the light from the candles, making the weapon shine in the near darkness.

He was up before dawn, breaking his fast with the rector, whose eyes grew wide as Cesco rose to greet the great men of Verona, Vicenza, and Padua. Word had begun to spread now. Carrara had brought the news back to Padua. Bernardo Evari, one of Cangrande's closest advisors and the current podestà of Padua, had arranged a more royal conveyance, gilt and beautiful.

Looking at the plain wooden box that held his lord, Ervari said, "Death, you've shot a bolt to pierce my heart."

The Rakehells were all present save Yuri and Fabio, still commanding Otto's men. And Detto was missing, a gap explained by the news of Katerina della Scala's death. Already portentous, Cangrande's demise now took on mythic proportions. The loss of whatever had driven that remarkable pair in life had snuffed out both their candles at once.

Cesco fretted, wondering if they should take the body to Vicenza. But Benedick shook his head. "They're burying her today. Detto went back for his brother, and they're all together now. Besides—" the red-headed Paduan paused. "Lord Nogarola is upset. He says if you had not caused her stroke in November, she would not have died."

"And if he had tamed her of her wildness, she would be living to old age in comfort. Figs. No, it's fine. It's only that I should be there too. She helped to raise me. I owe her something."

"You are where you should be," stated Benedick with certainty. Cesco was forced to agree.

While the other nobles transferred the humble crate into the new conveyance, Cesco dressed in richer, if somber, clothes. Then he took his place at the head of the procession to escort the body the rest of the way.

They approached Verona from the east, just as the sun was at its zenith. They had removed the roof from the golden carriage, displaying the box whose shape was barely visible under the layers and layers of ornately embroidered cloth.

The bier was preceded by a dozen knights: Mastino, Alberto, Rizardo, Carrara, Castelbarco, Lozzo, Montecchio, Capulletto, Ervari, Spinetto, Villafranca, and the desolate Tullio d'Isola, an honourary knight this day, taking the place of the absent Bailardino.

Leading them all was Cesco, dressed in the white of mourning. In his white tunic, white doublet, white cape, black hose, and black boots, he seemed to float above the horse. In his right hand he held Cangrande's naked sword. On the saddle before him was the Houndshelm, as bright as it had been when last the Scaliger had donned it. Behind him, Mastino carried the Scaliger's plainer war helm. The rest of the procession bore the ladder, on banners, on shields, on their chests.

Cesco set a measured, stately pace, and it was not until noon that they entered Verona itself. Word had spread, but of course most refused to believe it. The citizens of Verona had heard Cangrande's death tolled so many times, it was impossible to credit it now. He would appear in a day or two, as large in mirth as ever he was, laughing at their gullible natures.

Sight of the solemn parade of knights dashed those thoughts to shards. Yet there was no weeping or wailing, no gnashing of teeth or tearing of hair. As if ruled by a single mind, the people of Verona thronged the streets, roofs, and windows, parting only to clear a path for the body.

They arrived at Santa Maria Antica, the family chapel. Castelbarco made a short speech, with Cesco, Mastino, and Alberto standing close at hand for all to see, with Berto and Barto not far off. Though their greatest scion had fallen, the Scaligeri line still flourished.

Castelbarco declared three days of mourning, during which time market activities would be halted, law courts adjourned, business suspended. Tomorrow he would read out Cangrande's will. Until then, they should go home to their families and pray for the soul of Verona's greatest son.

They obeyed Castelbarco's injunction, willingly offering prayers for Cangrande's soul. All knew the contents of the will, having heard it before. Thinking of the earthquake and how their new prince had taken care of them, some were heartened. Thinking of the months of pointless squabbles and vain quarrels, some were uneasy.

As arranged, Cangrande was buried under the tiles of Santa Maria Antica, where outside his forebears lay at peace. His uncle, the first della Scala to rule the city. His father, the great Alberto. His beloved brother Bartolomeo. Now there would be another monument engraved with a ladder. At last Cangrande della Scala, the greatest man in all of Italy, was at rest.

As everyone departed for their homes or guest houses, Cesco drew near Mastino. With two gentle fingers, he tapped the stiff leather of his cousin's sleeve and murmured in his ear, "Shall we talk?"

"By all means." They set off together in what to every eye appeared perfect amity.

♦   ◊   ♦

Tharwat was not the active man he once had been, and the ride to Verona was slowed by necessity. Pietro himself found he winded easily these days. Too much easy living.

But the urgency of the matter drove them on. Cesco was in mortal peril.

♦   ◊   ♦

Cesco accompanied Mastino into the new palace, the Palazzo Cangrande, on the southern side of the Piazza dei Signori. After passing a few consoling words with Taddea, Mastino sent his wife to find her uncle, lodged in his own house in the city. Then he and Cesco entered Mastino's study, a room with few books but a great number of weapons.

On the center table was set a tray of food and a bottle of wine. Mastino waved a casual hand as he unstrung his cape and tossed it aside. "Help yourself. I ordered enough for two."

Cesco removed his own cape, then dragged a chair far back from the table, but did not sit. "Ah, you Cassandra, you. You were expecting me. Brave of you to stay."

"I have nothing to fear from you." Sitting, Mastino removed a knife and speared a hunk of meat. "Eat, if you're hungry."

"Alas, while your meal is probably the only safe food in the Feltro tonight, my stomach is still uneasy." Though he had handed off the Houndshelm to Tullio, Cangrande's sword was still on Cesco's hip. Unbuckling the belt, he propped the sheathed weapon against the chair. Then, from a satchel at his waist, he withdrew a bottle of wine. "Still, I thought you might like a celebratory drink. I brought one of Cangrande's own bottles."

Mastino eyed the bottle with a gimlet eye. "I see. You believe I poisoned him."

"Didn't you?" asked Cesco brightly.

"No," said Mastino.

"Of course not," agreed Cesco. "Poison is a woman's weapon."

Mastino bit into the meat on the end of his knife. "Or a coward's."

"Another word for womanish. Though we don't know many cowardly women, do we? Certainly not inside the family. Who will ever take the place of Katerina? So strong, so fierce. Braver than a hundred knights, smarter than a thousand men. And sister to a great prince. I wonder if anyone is ambitious enough to replace her. Of course, she was not alone at the end, was she?"

Swallowing, Mastino was silent.

"How is cousin Verde? Rizardo certainly looked upset. Will she comfort him? Console him? Did he truly not know what was in the bottles she gave him?"

In a stoic tone, Mastino said, "I don't know what you mean."

"Oh dear. I thought we were going to talk. If that's not the case, I'll take this bottle to Castelbarco and try feeding it to some of those pigs that followed us home and watch what happens." Picking up the bottle and the sword, Cesco turned to go.

Mastino said, "Sit down." Cesco arched an eyebrow. "Please."

Smiling, Cesco replaced the items and sat. "Shall we send for Verde? Must I listen to her denials?"

"There's no need," said Mastino. "I know it was her hand behind this. I knew it the moment Bonaventura fell dead. I saw her doctor my uncle's drink."

"Dear me. She has no fear of the family curse?"

"Something you two have in common," said Mastino.

"Shouldn't you rush to condemn her? Does not the curse fall on you if you stay silent?"

"Why? I knew nothing, and did nothing."

"Truer words were never uttered."

Mastino banished his flicker of irritation. This was too important. "If you know, and have such proof, why stay your hand?"

"For the family. It was my father's will. That's not to say I am afraid to act. But I'd like to avoid more scandal. Right now, the blame falls very neatly at the feet of Salvatore. My friends are already speculating that he poisoned both Cangrande and myself before he fled. I could be willing to leave it there."

"But there are conditions."

"There are," said Cesco. "First, Rizardo will go to England, as my ambassador. We'll give Mariotto's cousin the help he requires. And Rizardo will naturally take his beloved wife with him – she's the brains, and will hopefully carry off any needed subterfuge with grace and cunning."

"And second?"

"I think the campaigning season is done for the year, don't you? With the death of our beloved Cangrande, Verona must spend the coming months solidifying our base and fortifying our defences."

"And that's what I'll be doing?"

"No no! Such dull work for such a glorious knight, internationally renowned for his skill at the *giostre*! I thought you would much rather travel. You have so many foreign admirers. What could be more natural than to join the tournament circuit?"

"Exile," said Mastino.

"Hardly. Verona will pay every expense, and rejoice in your every victory. You can see the world, bringing the glory of Verona to foreign shores. With my connections at the imperial court, you will have entrée everywhere."

"A life of leisure," said Mastino.

"Of sport and fame," replied Cesco.

"Of no significance."

"None whatsoever," agreed Cesco.

Mastino nodded. "I'd like some of that wine – my bottle, not yours."

Cesco slid the open bottle across the table, and Mastino poured into his cup. He drank deeply, licking his lips. "And if my sister and I decide to remain in Verona?"

"It will come out. Rizardo will receive the full weight of law for the murder of Cangrande, and though we have no evidence of Verde's complicity, she'll be damned by association. Especially for the death of Petruchio. For some, that crime will be even greater. And she was with Detto's mother, Donna Katerina, at the hour of her passing. Too many coincidences. The question will be asked, why? Why murder Cangrande? What would she gain? Why, nothing – unless I were to drop dead as well. Since we both drank the doctored wine, it will be seen as an attempt to remove us both, paving the way for you, her beloved brother, to seize the reins of power. Innocent or no, you'll be damned for it. The doctors will come forward and remind the people of our first meeting, and then tell them the truth – that I was poisoned that day. You had nothing to do with it, but I doubt Doge Dandolo will pipe up to claim his own culpability. In fact, to gain Verona's favour, he may even offer to swear you came to him with the plan. Venetians have such a loose relationship with truth. You will be accused of poisoning me. *Then* it will come out that all those rich gifts did not originate from kings and princes, but from a private city fund with your name on it." Mastino started, and Cesco laughed. "Oh yes! All those pretty baubles, those wonderful clothes, that magnificent armour – it all came from your own coffers. Or so it shall appear. How will the masses take that? Spending Verona's wealth for your own aggrandizement? You'll be chased from the city – *hounded*, even – and forced to live that exile you mentioned without the benefit of Verona's purse to support you." Cesco offered a friendly smile. "Leave, and you may have honour and wealth. Stay, and you will leave anyway, but with neither."

Mastino was silent for a long time, turning the goblet in his hands around and around as he examined the lip. He drank again. "It's very good. Very good. I'm impressed."

"Thank you," said Cesco.

Mastino set the goblet down and leaned his elbows on the table. "I would accept the former offer, obviously."

"I thought you might."

Cesco started to rise, but was checked by Mastino's voice. "Still – there is a third option."

Resuming his seat, Cesco cocked his head in amusement. "Oh? And what, pray tell, is that?"

"The same one you offered Fuchs a year ago." Pushing the tray and bottle aside, Mastino leaned forward on his elbows and pointed both forefingers at Cesco's chest. "You run. You take all the blame and run today, this very hour. Run for your life."

FORTY-ONE

Cesco STARED, a smile twitching the corners of his mouth. "Cos, you are fearsome indeed. But there is nothing on this earth that could make me run from you."

Unperturbed, Mastino steepled his fingers. "Not from me, no. But you'll run. In fact, there's a horse waiting at the stable, saddled. A replacement for the one that Paduan stole. My gift to you."

"I'll have to examine its mouth carefully. Are you well, cos? Or are you demented? I'm not leaving. I'm the heir, not you. The armies, the people, the nobles – they'll all follow me."

"Not when they see you run."

Cesco gave a puzzled laugh. "Are you trying to frighten me? I thought you knew me better than that."

"I know you, Francesco the Greyhound, Savior of Mankind," said Mastino mockingly. Cesco's eyebrows went up. "O yes! I know more about you than you do. Fortune put the opportunity in my lap, the means to destroy you. It couldn't have worked while Cangrande was alive. But now the way is clear."

"If you're talking of Rosalia, no one will believe you."

"Ha! No. Not her. Another woman. Didn't you wonder what Cangrande and I talked of, alone, on the eve of his death? It wasn't his daughter. Not even his son. It was of your mother."

Cesco was silent, his face mild as he gestured for Mastino to continue.

"Four years ago this very week. Do you remember? Your grand

entrance into Cangrande's court. The feast thrown by Capulletto, the night his little Giulietta was born. Your thieving of Cangrande's horse. Our little joust that left me in the mud. Well, while you went off to celebrate, I retired to the palace to change and nurse my injured pride. It so happened that your mother arrived in the company of our late, lamented aunt Katerina. Donna Maria d'Amabilio. Such a remarkable lady, with those dark features and that lovely lilt to her voice. Naturally I slipped behind a tapestry to listen. What a chance Fortune was giving me! I overheard Ser Alaghieri talking with your mother, sharing so many secrets. Apparently we have you to thank for the grand ending of Dante's epic poem. Well done, cousin. I applaud you." He clapped his hands together in soft mockery.

Cesco inclined his head, a polite smile across his face. "Go on, please."

"You remember she departed the next day. Cangrande wanted her gone as swiftly as possible, lest her maternal instinct prove impossible to overcome. Well, I had more questions for her. If Cangrande wanted her gone, I had to know why. Fuchs caught her on the road, and – pressed her for information."

Cesco was no longer smiling. "I know how he pressed her."

Mastino opened his hands. "He employed the methods of the Church. She fought, he told me. He asked her in every way, and she kept back the truth as long as she could. But at last she revealed what was hidden."

Cesco was thinking of his mother, but also of Antonia, who had suffered similarly at the hand of Fuchs. And Mastino had known it all.

Mastino, who was now grinning at him. "You're thinking that you'll ruin me no matter what."

"Yes," agreed Cesco.

Standing and crossing to the window at his back, Mastino glanced down at the quiet square below. "You would have done, anyway. Your clemency is like your moods – too mercurial. One day you would remember the debt you owe me for spoiling your marriage to your beloved Rosalia, and send men to murder me in my bed, or in the lists. I'd rather be certain of your enmity."

"You have it," said Cesco. "The horse that's waiting – you'd best get on it. I'll give you tonight."

"Then that's what I'll give *you*," retorted Mastino. "Just this one night to run. And the best part? You'll want to. You'll even want to thank me, though your pride won't let you say it."

Cesco's hand dropped casually to the hilt of Cangrande's sword. "Can I offer my thanks with steel?"

Mastino turned and opened his arms wide. "Be my guest. I am unarmed. Kill me. Strike me down and put my head on the battlements. Just know that if you do, you'll be losing the thing you want most."

"Killing you will save Verona."

"At the cost of the girl."

Cesco frowned. "You said this wasn't about Rosalia."

"No. I said the secret isn't about her. And it isn't. Cangrande's last secret. The one that he begged me to keep from you at all costs. That's what we talked about. Ever since Fuchs confessed to killing your mother, Cangrande suspected I knew the truth. But only as he lay dying did he voice his fear. He knew what a powerful weapon I held. I swore to him that I would never make public what I knew. That was not enough, though. He demanded an oath to never tell you."

"And you're about to break that oath," said Cesco.

"How little you know me, cousin," said Mastino. "I am the keeper of oaths. *I* didn't call down the family curse on my head by murdering a member of the family, as you did with Federigo."

"As did your sister with Cangrande."

"True. But she can hang for all I care. I have no interest in her pathetic schemes, save for how they affect me."

"So why are you taunting me with this secret that you won't reveal to me?"

"Because I've given you all the pieces already. Based on what we learned from your Scottish mother, I had Fuchs buy the house in Padua. I even made sure the name of the ship was plainly visible on the fresco. I have to say, it took you long enough to find it. I've been waiting for months. You've been so disappointing, caught up in your malaise over your lost love, punishing everyone and everything around you. Where was the Cesco I knew and feared? The child who loved puzzles so much he obsessed over the pieces – where had he gone? Now, when I needed him most, he'd vanished! I was counting on you, and you let me down. Even when Aiello inadvertently offered up the huge clue of your mother's nationality, still you did nothing! Then you vanished after the Palio. I heard you were ill."

"Another plot, from another corner of the family," said Cesco. "So many ambushes, they all collided."

"It doesn't matter," said Mastino. "Things have worked out for the best. Now the field is clear. It's just you and I. So, in return for your generous offer earlier, I have an offer for you. You leave tonight on the horse I have waiting. There's a bag of gold, some food, a change of clothes, and a sword. Everything a clever man requires. Tomorrow, I will take that bottle there and declare that *you* poisoned Cangrande. I'll reveal that your tame Moor has been slipping you poison for years to build up your immunity for just this moment. It has led to your instability, which all have bourne witness to. *You* slipped the poison into Cangrande's drink in January, and when your shaft missed its target, you waited until Treviso was won to strike again. At this point, Capulletto's groom will come forward and say it was *you* who murdered Federigo just months after your arrival in Verona, proving you already have a taste for picking off members of the family."

"And why did I do all this," asked Cesco, "when it all would have been mine someday?"

"Because of your plots with foreign powers. It will be let known that you have been leaving your house to scheme with your Moor, using a certain whore in *La Rosa Colta*, an Arab girl, as your emissary. When she was kidnapped, you risked all to save her, which will speak to your devotion to the infidel. She has vanished, but I'm sure the Abbot of San Zeno will have no trouble denouncing you without her testimony. You are already a pariah with the churchmen here. Only your station has protected you. But when your absence in the Spring is attributed not to illness, but rather with meeting your foreign masters, I think your last buckler will be ripped away."

"And at what price have I sold Verona?"

"To the East, you have promised the infidels, whose tongue you speak so well, that you will remove Venice as a threat to their shores. After all, you've shown no love for God, and have publically questioned the tenets of our faith. Is it any wonder, if you've fallen under the spell of the Mohammedans? At the same time you have taken a vow to the Holy Roman Emperor, whose favourite catamite you are rumoured to be, to prevent any Veronese threat to his throne. Thus you murdered Cangrande to keep him off the imperial throne, and mean to thrust Verona into a costly war with Venice to aid your true masters, the infidels."

At the end of this impressive diatribe, Cesco blinked several times, then burst out laughing! "O, cousin! O, my dear fellow – I had no idea! That's marvelous! Absolutely splendid. Truly, it is. So complete. Using every trick of my own history against me, and so well! I presume that Signor Benedick will be indicted, too. But what about the rest of my merry band? You can't murder all of them."

"No," agreed Mastino. "They'll all be innocent dupes. Save for Bailardetto. He's far too much your friend to ever denounce you. I admit, I had some hopes for him early in the year, when you two seemed to be quarreling. But he disappointed me as well."

Cesco was smiling in deep appreciation. "It's really so good." He slapped his knee. "*So* good. I had no idea you could play at this level! My God, it almost makes me like you."

Mastino refilled his goblet. "I'm glad you approve."

"Still, there's one rather obvious flaw in your plan."

"Is there?" asked Mastino, still grinning.

"Yes. I have no reason to take that horse you've so kindly outfitted. And if I am here to denounce you and Verde, your accusations will seem so far-fetched, so ludicrous, they'll never be believed."

"Ah, but that's the stick. You haven't yet tasted the carrot."

"I don't care much for carrots," said Cesco.

"You'll like this one," said Mastino. "I think this particular carrot would make you climb to Heaven and drag Cangrande back down to earth so you could indeed murder him."

Cesco's smile dimmed as his eyes narrowed. "This highly-vaunted secret."

"Yes. The one I promised I wouldn't tell you. But it's no fault of mine if you figure it out for yourself. You found the ship's name. I imagine Ser Alaghieri, the new Count of San Bonifacio, will have the truth by now."

"So we wait for him?"

"We *could*," said Mastino, pulling a pained expression. "But I want to see your face when you figure it out. As it happens, I have all the needed records here." Walking to a chest by the wall, Mastino withdrew a bundle of papers, bound and sealed. "You can thank the Templars. They began the banking trend, and with it they started keeping lists of everything. Shipping records. Passenger manifests." Drawing near the table, he waved the bundle about in the air. "I have here the passenger manifest and port calls for *La Alisceote*. It is a copy, true. But by now your Nuncle Pietro will have seen the original, and hopefully talked to members of the crew. It's also witnessed by the captain. So you can trust it to be true." He held it out. "As I said, I promised Cangrande I would never *tell* you. I said nothing about showing."

Recalling Cangrande's insistence that he stop looking into *La Alisceote*, Cesco knew this was the ultimate secret. The reason for keeping him from his mother, perhaps even the key to the cryptic code she had carved into the wood of the shack where Fuchs had tortured her. *Beware the Prince called Mastino.* More than Mastino's boasting, it was Cangrande's fear that made Cesco certain this was the answer to the questions that had plagued him all his life. Not star-charts, not prophecies. *This.*

He could turn it away, toss it in the fire, deny Mastino the victory he was anticipating. Reading it would jeopardize all the Scaliger had tried to do. Mastino felt certain that, whatever it contained, it would make Cesco run from his rightful title as master of Verona. What could be so terrible? What secret was so awful that it would drive him mad with fear?

Reaching out, Cesco took the papers, broke the seal, and began to read.

◆　◊　◆

Pietro and Tharwat arrived in Verona at dusk. Quickly they heard all the events of the day. They sent an urgent message to Cesco's house, but the master had not returned home after they had interred the Scaliger's body. Only Antonia and Morsicato were there, waiting with the tearful Maddelena for Cesco to appear.

Summoned to Pietro's house, where the walls did not have ears, the doctor and the novice were brought directly to his study, where they found Pietro laying out the originals of the documents Mastino had copied so long ago.

Exhausted from days of tending to a dying man, Morsicato saw Pietro's face and misinterpreted the look. "Pietro, it's true. He's gone. I had hoped our message would find you—"

But Antonia knew her brother's face. This was not just grief. It was anger. Anger, and fear. Even Tharwat looked ashen. "What's the matter?"

Seeing the door closed behind them, Pietro spoke rapidly. "We found the manifest for *La Alisceote*. There are two passengers – Donna Maria d'Amabilio and a Signor Leonardino d'Amabilio, traveling from Scotland to Genoa."

"The lady and her cuckolded husband," said Morsicato. "Do we know who he was?"

"It says here only that he was a gentleman of Verona."

"Verona?" asked Antonia. "Not Padua."

"Verona. He was Veronese. Beyond that, we don't know."

Morsicato stroked his forked beard. "Then what's got you in such a lather?"

"The dates. Look. The ship sailed in from a port called Perth on November 27th, 1313. It called at London the following week, and departed there on December 5th." His finger traced the dates, one after the next. "It sailed to Lisbon, where it landed on December

26th, and they stayed through Christmas. From there it sailed to Barcelona, but they hit bad weather and had to stop twice on the way. They didn't reach Barcelona until January 23rd."

"So?" asked Morsicato, looking back and forth between Pietro and the book.

But Antonia saw it. Wide-eyed, she placed her hand to her mouth. "O lord."

Pietro nodded. "Yes. They departed Barcelona on January 29th, 1314, called at Marseilles, and arrived at Genoa on the 15th of February."

"So?" repeated Morsicato, glancing back and forth between them.

It was Tharwat who answered. "Cesco was born on the 13th of June, 1314."

Morsicato frowned, counting. Then the blood drained from his face. "And where was—?"

"Here the whole time," said Pietro, "starting the war against Padua."

At last the doctor saw it. "Dear God. That's means they couldn't have — that he wasn't—"

"Yes," said Pietro, feeling a terrible satisfaction at sharing the thought that had been making him sick for the whole journey. "Even if they raced home, Maria couldn't have been in the Feltro before March."

Antonia was shaking her head. "But why? *Why?*"

Tharwat's voice almost inaudible. "We do not know."

"But there is one thing we do know for certain." Pietro drew a ragged breath. "Cangrande wasn't Cesco's father."

FORTY-TWO

WATCHING LIKE THE HOUND he was named for, Mastino prepared himself. This young man was always one for the unexpected. Standing, he leaned against the wall between two windows, intent in his search for even the slightest flicker in Cesco's expression. He had dreamed of this day for years, and wanted to relish every second.

To Mastino's vast disappointment. Cesco didn't deny it, didn't demand more proof, didn't even laugh disbelievingly. His expression was curiously blank. After a time he pushed the papers aside. "Then who?"

"You don't seem surprised."

"It's a piece to a puzzle. Not one I had considered, but it makes sense of some things. It confuses others. If not his, then whose son am I? It has to be a Scaliger — I'm too obviously part of the family. Why such a massive deception?"

"How well do you know the family history?" asked Mastino, pressing on without waiting for an answer. "Mastino, Alberto, Bartolomeo, Alboino, Cangrande. Five rulers of Verona."

"I make six."

Ignoring that, Mastino pressed on. "Those five names, they're the only ones anyone remembers. But there were offshoots from those branches. My namesake and grandfather Alberto were broth-ers. But they had another brother, Bocca, who was killed in their rise to power. The first Mastino had a son, Niccolo. When his father died, Niccolo tried to seize power from his uncle, whom he called usurper. He even accused Alberto of joining the plot against his father, Alberto's own brother. That's when the curse was laid down – Alberto swore an oath to God, demanding damnation for any member of his family lifting a hand against another. Now, Niccolo was put down, but his sons and daughters survived. They're relations of the late Bonaccolsi. So much intermarrying."

"So I'm from that stock?"

Mastino lifted his brows. "I'm just making a point – there are lots of Scaligeri out there. Barto, Berto. The Abbot of San Zeno. Rosalia. So why you? Why did both Cangrande and Katerina focus on you? What makes you special?"

"The prophecy," said Cesco.

"That's true for Katerina," said Mastino. "But what about Cangrande? Why would he draw to his bosom the one person he thinks is destined to supplant him? Why make a child not his own heir?"

"I hope you'll tell me. I'm all aflutter."

Mastino refused to allow Cesco's sarcasm to prick his pleasure. "It was love. Pure love. The love only a brother can give."

"You don't mean Katerina."

"Of course not. I mean love for his brother."

Cesco frowned deeply. "I hope you're not saying Alboino. I would hate to have you for a sibling."

Mastino barked a laugh. "Ha! Yes, that would be terrible. Alboino – it's just a name to me. He died when I was three. I hardly knew him, and don't remember him except through my mother's stories. According to her, Cangrande was never overfond of my father. They shared the captainship, but there was never any real feeling between them. Father was married by the time Cangrande was seven, and can't imagine he appreciated sharing his power with a thirteen year-old. How these things do repeat. But it was clear to everyone that our late lamented Capitano was a prodigy, which was why Bartolomeo made it clear in his will that after he was gone, he was leaving the power to both his brothers jointly. And thanks to the lack of brotherly feeling between them, when Alboino died, Cangrande felt no particular compunction about cutting me out of my rights."

"In favour of me."

"Yes. Why do that? Why claim you as his son?" Mastino paused, relishing the moment. He had anticipated it so long, practiced it in his mind time and again. To have it here, he knew he must memorize every sand dropping, every mote in the air, so he could revisit this triumph in all his days to come. "Because there was someone he loved, loved even more than Bailardino. Lord Nogarola was foster-father and brother-in-law to Cangrande. But Cangrande had an actual brother, old enough to be his father. Alberto died when Cangrande was ten, leaving him in the care of Bartolomeo della Scala, whom Cangrande loved more than the world."

Cesco saw it now. But there was an objection. "Bartolomeo had a son. Paride's father, Cecchino."

"Yes," agreed Mastino, pleased to see the links of the chain forming. "If he had lived, neither of us would be having this conversation. In 1290, Bartolomeo took a wife — none other than the elder sister of Cangrande's own future wife, Giovanna. But before he married, when he was just fifteen years old, Bartolomeo fell in love with a girl who had a natural son. They called him Leonardino."

Cesco pointed at the papers before him. "The man in the passenger manifest."

"Yes," said Mastino with real pleasure. "This Leonardino was part of the same *compagnia di ventura* as Aiello's father, sent to Scotland to fight for the rebels. It was his service that caused the Scots leader Wallace to send his thanks. And like Aiello's father, he stayed. When Bartolomeo died suddenly in 1304, there was nothing for him in Italy. He married a local woman and taught her his language. But when she became pregnant, he decided to bring his budding family home." Mastino waved at the papers. "As you see."

"Where is he now?"

"Dead. Your mother said he died before they could reach Verona. Heavily pregnant, she could not turn around. So she purchased the house in Padua and bore you."

"So not *il veltro*," mused Cesco.

"Not a bastard at all, but the son of a bastard," said Mastino mockingly. "Never fear. You'll always be a bastard to me."

Cesco did not rise to the bait. So far his questions were proving maddeningly practical. "Where did the name Amabilio come from? I've never heard of it. Is it a town?"

"I don't know," said Mastino honestly. "It wasn't the name of the family, or I'd have traced it."

Cesco sat under Mastino's thrilling gaze, ignoring his enemy's excitement while he grappled with the tale he'd been told. At last he said, "There are gaps in your story. When Leonardino died, why did my mother buy a house in Padua, Verona's sworn adversary? And why come back at all — as a bastard, he had no legal claim. And how did he die?"

Mastino spread his hands. "I have no answers. But a few guesses. I think your father was murdered on his way to Verona, and your mother took refuge in the one place where Veronese fingers could not reach. Once there, she contacted Katerina, hoping to find sympathy for herself and her newborn son. Katerina offered to take you, in order to fulfill her place in the prophecy. But your admirable mother refused to give you up until there was an attempt on your life. Hired by Katerina or no, your mother knew you would never be safe so long as she remained with you. So she did the only thing she could – gave in, and gave you away. On the condition that you were made Cangrande's heir."

Cesco leaned forward so suddenly that Mastino tensed, expecting the table to be overturned and blades come into play. But the hellion was just straining forward like a hound after a scent. "Why would Cangrande agree to that? What did he gain?"

Mastino shrugged. "I have no idea. Perhaps he was just protecting the grandson of the brother he loved."

"Or perhaps shaping the future in order to deny fate," said Cesco softly.

Mastino frowned. "What's that?"

But Cesco shook his head. "If I was born in Padua, I must have been baptized there."

"I imagine so," said Mastino.

"What name was I given?"

Mastino shrugged. "If Fuchs asked, he never told me."

At the mention of Fuchs, Cesco's eyes narrowed. "A pity you and Fuchs didn't just put her in a room with me."

Now the threat was palpable. Mastino pointed a finger. "Before you consider revenge, think about what this means."

Rising, Cesco tapped two fingers on the pommel of the sword leaning against his chair. "If I decide you have to die, a little forethought won't save you."

"I was hoping your gratitude would overwhelm your anger."

"I'm still weighing the extent of my gratitude."

"You can have her now," said Mastino eagerly. "Rosalia. She is not your sister. A second cousin at most."

Cesco nodded. "My abounding joy is tempered by the fact that you didn't mention this in September."

"No," agreed Mastino. "I didn't."

"At least you don't deny your venality. If I attack, will you fight? Or call for your faithful followers, who are doubtless just outside, waiting."

Mastino's eyes flickered to his own sword. "Draw and see."

"I might."

"We are all meant to die."

"Not me. I will evanesce."

"I'm surprised you haven't evaporated from the room."

"Figs. You expect that, now there are no impediments, I'll go running to her side, leaving everything to you. The tale of poison and betrayal, of Mohammedans and Emperors."

"If you attack me, all the more proof."

"If I stay and denounce you," continued Cesco, "you'll publish my lack of blood-link to our dearly departed Capitano. You can call Ser Alaghieri as a witness. He's so damned honourable, he might not lie for me. You've done very well, cos – I may still call you cousin, yes? Downright brilliant. I've spent years quarrelling with him, shaming him. The night before his great victory, he's poisoned. Who benefits? Me, the disgruntled Heir. Was it blackmail? Was it a trick played by the Paduans? I was born in Padua. Suspicious." Cesco clicked his tongue. "It's excellent. The whole city will have doubts about me."

"Even if Verona doesn't, Padua might."

A heartbeat of a pause. "You and Carrara."

"Me and Carrara. We've had many long and friendly talks during this campaign."

"Long may you live in bliss. So, you've positioned me to leave. If I go freely, I get the girl. If I stay, I'll be hounded out of the city. It's genius – but you've missed one factor." Mastino raised his eyebrows. "Revenge."

"For spoiling your little romance?"

"For Antonia. Suor Beatrice. Fuchs raped her repeatedly, on your orders. How will the Church react to hearing you're a nun-raper? That's a little more serious than bastard or murderer."

Mastino blanched. "That was Fuchs. On his own."

Cesco started edging around the table, the scabbarded sword in his hand. "When did he ever do anything on his own? You clearly knew about it."

"After the fact," said Mastino quickly. "I'll make restitution."

Cesco scoffed. "How? Do you have sway with the goddess Hymen?"

"Payment. A new abbey. A statue to her father. I'll honour the whole family – even Pietro. He can keep his title, lands, and pension. Jacopo too. They'll want for nothing!"

"Your word is worthless."

"But yours isn't," countered Mastino. "If you give me your word to keep my name spotless with the Church, I'll take care of the Alaghieri family."

It was a breathless pause, with Mastino waiting to lunge for his own blade should Cesco even begin to draw steel.

At last Cesco nodded. "Here are the conditions. Pietro, Antonia, Morsicato, all the Rakehells — they must be left alone."

"The locals I'll need," said Mastino. "But your friend Benedick will hang. The crowd needs an execution."

"No, you'll see him safely to a ship — to Sicily," added Cesco. "You must likewise give Tharwat al-Dhaamin a safe conduct out of your territories before you slander his name. Morsicato must maintain his rank and position. And send my wife back to her family so I can have the marriage annulled. Do you agree to these terms?"

Mastino considered. "If you go right now, tonight, and never come back — then yes, I agree. But I have a condition of my own," he added maliciously. "You must write a letter confessing your crime, and my magnanimity. Address it to your beloved Nuncle. And cousin — be convincing."

Cesco did not hesitate. Taking up paper, ink, and a quill from a side table, he leaned over and penned the required note, then handed it over. "It won't be witnessed."

Mastino read it over. "This will do."

"Then there's only one matter left." With lightning speed Cesco drew Cangrande's sword. Mastino lunged for his own, his mouth open to shout for his guards.

But Cesco didn't attack. Reversing the sword in his grip, he held it hilt forward and laid Cangrande's sword on the table between them. "When his real tomb is finished, bury him with it. It doesn't belong to either of us."

"It's the Scaliger's sword," said Mastino. "The Capitano's sword. And I am now both."

Heading for the door, Cesco smiled over his shoulder. "Keep it, then. Nothing tempts fate like hubris." Hand on the door, Cesco paused, looking back. "You think that if I leave, you win. But you're wrong. The victory is mine. I marry for love after all."

And then he was gone.

Mastino stood staring at the open door, listening to Cesco's steps echo on the stair until they faded away. Prepared as he had been, that was as tense as any gambit in his life. But he had known fear alone would never have dislodged Cesco. He had to have the promise of something forbidden. So Mastino had given him the best incentive possible. He offered love.

It could still go terribly wrong. There were so many threads that could unravel, and Mastino wondered which Cesco would resent most – the many lies Mastino had told, or the awful truth he had omitted.

He heard a horse bolting down the street. So it was time to prepare. He took the bottle of wine Cesco had left behind, ready to add it to the litany of proofs. He would have a day or two, at most, to make the initial charges stick. Then he would dole out more and more damning pieces of evidence until he had the whole city screaming for Cesco's blood.

First he had to deliver this letter to Count Alaghieri, or his representatives. For he would keep his word to Cesco. That's what a great lord did. And though no one yet knew it, from this moment on, Mastino was lord of this city and all its lands. Twenty-one years old, and the master of Verona. Just like Cangrande.

But the Greyhound was dead.

Long live the Mastiff.

FORTY-THREE

WITHIN MINUTES the prince's flight was known, and like an infernal fire the news reached every corner of the city. Cangrande was dead, and the Rakehell had fled. What did it mean?

Having just come from laying his mother in state, Detto arrived in Verona to find it roiling with rumours. After calling at the *via Pigna*, where he found an anxious Signor Benedick, they went together to Pietro's house.

Pietro was sitting stunned as everyone else passed from hand to hand a letter just delivered from the palace. Detto took it and read, Benedick craning over his shoulder:

> To Ser Pietro Alaghieri, Knight of the Mastiff, Count of San Bonifacio, from Francesco della Scala, Knight of the Mastiff, bastard heir to Cangrande della Scala, the Greyhound,
>
> I murdered Cangrande. I did this for personal gain, and for revenge for the many wrongs my father had done me. Under the influence of foreign powers, I conspired with Tharwat al-Dhaamin and Signor Benedick of Padua, along with a whore called Arabia, to gain control of this fair city. I poisoned my father's drink the night before Treviso surrendered. I am also responsible for the death of Lord Petruchio da Bonaventura, who intercepted the drink meant for my father.

> I confess my crimes to you and to God, praying to Him above to forgive what I now see are terrible sins. I have opened my soul to my holy cousin, the noble and just Mastino della Scala, who has offered Christian clemency. But I do not deserve charity or pity. To my shame, I will always do whatever I must to gain my heart's desire. Therefore, for the love I bear in my heart, I fly from Verona.
>
> I thank you for your years of kindness, ask your forgiveness, and beg you to follow Mastino in all his just and wise commands. Please see my marriage annulled. For yourself, live, wive, thrive, and forget I ever existed. It seems I never did.
>
> *Francesco della Scala*

Detto was thunderstruck. "It's not true."

"Isn't it?" asked Morsicato.

"Of course it's not!" snapped Pietro.

Detto was turning the letter over, looking for hidden marks or code. "What's he thinking, writing this?"

"That's what we've been discussing," said Antonia.

The blood had fled Benedick's face. "What does he mean, conspired with *me*?"

Tharwat spoke, his rasping voice sawing the air of the hot chamber. "We believe it is a warning. With the note came letters of safe passage for you and I. Yours directs you to Sicily. They are valid until the final day of this month."

"Cesco must have cut a deal," said Pietro. "Our lives in exchange for his confession of guilt. Mastino plans to include you two in his list of charges against Cesco, so you are allowed to flee."

"But where has he gone?" demanded Detto, who was more hurt than pleased that there was no mention of him. "And what could make him sign this? He's the Prince of Verona now! He could have Mastino executed!"

Morsicato pointed. "Just what I was saying! Why run? Running removes all his power."

"Because he knows what you learned tonight," said Tharwat. "Mastino has known all along that Cesco is not Cangrande's son."

"What?!" cried both Detto and Benedick.

In the most cursory fashion, Pietro explained. "Mastino's waited for years to reveal this. Cesco's handing the city over to him."

"Why?" demanded Benedick. "Even if it's true, even if he's not

Cangrande's blood son, he's as good as. No one would believe this, not after Cangrande acknowledged him as his heir, named him in his will. Verona is his for the taking. Why leave it?"

"Because he doesn't want it," said Pietro.

"Or rather," said Antonia, "he wants something else more."

"The girl," sighed Tharwat. "He's gone for the girl."

"I think so," said Pietro. "If he's not Cangrande's son, then she's not his sister. He'll rush to her and head across the Alps before anyone can stop him."

While Benedick looked even more confused, Antonia raised an objection. "But he's married! So is she!"

"His marriage has not been consummated. Nor, I doubt, has hers." Though Pietro had promised not to tell, the situation had altered. "When she married Tiberio, she was already pregnant."

"You knew?" said Detto.

"*You* knew?" countered Pietro.

"I saw her the night of the Palio. She gave me a letter for him."

"So that's how he got the coin back," mused Pietro. "I had wondered."

Morsicato slapped his hands together. "All of this is neither here nor there! If he's gone to get the girl, we must ride and bring him back."

"Must we?" asked Tharwat. "His letter does not say so."

"But it's a letter filled with double-intentions," said Pietro, taking it back from Detto. "He identifies himself as heir to Cangrande, the Greyhound. Does he mean Cangrande was the Greyhound, or that he means to be? He explicitly and repeatedly calls Cangrande his father – something he's never done before. Cangrande wouldn't let him."

"It's a sign that he knows," said Antonia.

"I think so," agreed Pietro. "He also invokes God, something he isn't prone to do. Then he basically says he's getting his heart's desire."

"He also orders you to follow Mastino," said the doctor. "That can't be real."

"But the very next line he asks to have his marriage annulled. If he's going to run off with Rosalia, it's a very practical request."

"This will crush Maddelena," said Antonia sadly.

"She's young, she'll forget him."

"No one will ever forget him," said Antonia.

"But that's just what he asks us to do!" said Pietro. "No code, no hidden meaning that I can see. Is he serious? Does he truly want us to let him go? It has to mean something more!"

Antonia put a hand on Pietro's shoulder. "He also enjoins you to be happy, to marry, and live. Maybe he means just that."

Pietro turned to Tharwat. "You said there was going to be a separation."

The astrologer nodded. "This is it. But we have not yet endured the third death Girolamo predicted. Cangrande. Katerina. One more close blood relative to Detto will die."

"What?" demanded Detto.

As the Moor explained, Pietro squeezed his eyes shut, biting his lip so hard he nearly drew blood. *I want to fight! I want to reach up into the sky and tear the stars apart with my own two hands. I understand Cangrande at last...!*

But no. It was Cangrande who had set all this in motion. So many lies, so many deceits, postures, falsehoods, traps, and schemes – all to defy the stars. While Katerina fought just as hard to ensure they came true. Was there no way to avoid their damning influence?

Pietro had once read a pithy piece of writing in the journals of an obscure Roman his father had found in a library in France. '*When you see Fate, Fate sees you as well.*' Even drawing the stars' attention was to draw their ire. It did not do to meddle with them. The best thing was to ignore they even existed. Look at the road ahead, and find the straightest path.

Pietro stood. "Tharwat – pack. You and Benedick must be gone within the day. Antonia, go to Cesco's house and prepare Maddelena and the staff to leave at dawn, heading to..."

"Padua," answered Tharwat. "He had me buy his mother's house. It will be safe for her there."

Pietro nodded, puzzling. How had Cesco foreseen the need of a safe place for his wife?

Detto asked the only question that mattered to him. "What about Cesco?"

Pietro tried to show a calm he did not feel. "We know where he'll be. In the morning we can send after him. But Detto – he may not want to come back."

Detto nodded, but his mind was far away. As soon as he left the room, he went to join it.

◆　◇　◆

At dawn, the people gathered in the Piazza dei Signori for the reading of Cangrande's will. Pietro stood alongside the bereaved Bailardino, as well as Castelbarco, Nico da Lozzo, Carrara, Montecchio,

Capulletto, Ervari, and so many other famous faces. Of Cangrande's family, Mastino and Alberto were there, and Rizardo and Verde. So were Berto and Barto. Just one person was absent. Noticeably missing was the Heir, which fed the rumours that had begun in the night.

"Where is Francesco della Scala?" demanded Castelbarco in his best public voice. "We cannot read out the will without the Heir!" His eyes were on Mastino, but that man was not speaking at all.

After much confusion, a groom said the Prince had taken a horse in the wee hours of the night and ridden like the Devil was after him. That was when the most dangerous rumours started to fly.

"Come!" cried Mastino, beckoning the whole Anziani towards the Domus Nova. "Let us discuss this matter in private."

As Pietro followed he looked all around him, hoping Cesco would appear as he always did, looking cocky and assured and in complete control of the chaos he had caused.

But Cesco did not appear.

♦   ◊   ♦

By mid-morning Detto's horse was lathered with sweat. He'd departed Verona in darkness, making sure he wasn't seen. Riding all night towards the Alps, at first light he'd started searching for some-one to direct him to Tiberio's holdings.

The night had been warm, and he was in his shirtsleeves, his doublet hanging from a knot in his saddle. But he was clean and fit, sitting atop a fine horse, with a sword strapped to his side.

Seeing men out picking grapes in a vineyard, Detto called to them. Most pretended they didn't hear him, but one had looked up. Reluctantly he answered Detto's calls. "Can you tell me the way to the Tiberio estate?"

The man said nothing but pointed.

"Has another fellow come this way? About my age, a little shorter, curly brown hair. Seen him?"

The man shrugged, and after a few moments Detto allowed him to return to work. Riding on, he took the sloping rise that Pietro had ridden in December. The wind was not so desperate now, offering only a welcome breeze to cool the sweat gathering along his spine.

Dismounting, Detto climbed the hill on foot, leading his tired mount. After a bend in the road, he spied the fortress-like estate, intimidating and forbidding. As he drew near it, he resumed his doublet, lacing the hard leather closed at his chest and sleeves. He put his feathered cap back on his head and fixed his cape bearing the

Nogarola crest across one shoulder. Mounting, he cantered up to the open gates.

He had been seen, for there were two men standing at the gate to demand his name. He offered it, wondering what he was walking into. Had Cesco come and gone already? Had he spirited the girl away? Or was he in hiding in the grounds, waiting for nightfall? *He'll murder me if I spoil his plans.*

Summoned, the hulking form of Bramo Tiberio stalked from the house and across the yard. "What do you want?"

Detto tried to think of an oblique phrasing, but Tiberio didn't seem to be a man to answer oblique questions. "I'm looking for the Scaliger's heir."

Grinding his teeth, Tiberio pointed back down the hill to the church Detto had passed on foot ten minutes earlier. "Down there, greeting my wife."

Not knowing what to say, Detto offered a very formal "Thank you," then turned his steed around and walked it down the hill again. He could feel Old Bramo's eyes scorching his back.

There was already a horse here, hobbled at a post near a gate. Hitching his own horse, Detto removed his hat and crossed onto holy ground, listening for their voices. All was silence. Before him was the door to the small church, ajar. Entering the dark confines, he could feel the emptiness of the building, the lifelessness. He saw a statue, and recognized it at once. San Zeno.

There was a side door, through which the slanting sun sent a beam that looked almost solid in the gloomy nothingness. Detto passed through it squinting, lifting his hat to block the rays. Under the glare, Detto could see several rude and old stone monuments, roughly but lovingly carved into angels, urns, or crosses.

Even before he heard it, Detto was chilled to his core, his mind rebelling, feeling the blood draining from his knees. From somewhere on his left, around the corner of the church, there came a whimper like a dog that's been beaten. Unwilling, Detto set one foot in front of the other and turned the corner.

Cesco's arms were wrapped around a fresh, massive stone cross, his face pressed against the monument.

The first time he tried to speak, Detto's voice failed him. Swallowing, he was able to offer a single word, more breath than sound. "Cesco."

Cesco did not move, did not open his eyes. "She was waiting. My fault. Odysseus never had the sense of a sundial. I'm late. And now, so is she."

Detto knelt on the other side of the headstone. On it was an inscription, new and stark:

Rosalia Rienzi in Tiberio
Daughter, Wife, and Mother
Died June 12th, 1329

Mother—

"She couldn't wait," said Cesco in a dreamy voice. "I'm always late, you see. Late. I will soon be the late one." His head nestled against the stone, scraping the skin of his forehead. "The late Francesco. Better never than late." And he began to recite:

Animula vagula blandula,	*Little soul, you charming little wanderer,*
Hospes comesque corporis,	*my body's guest and partner,*
Quae nunc abibis in loca,	*where are you off to now?*
Pallidula rigida nudula,	*Somewhere without colour, savage and bare;*
Nec ut soles dabis iocosi.	*You'll crack no more jokes once you're there.*

Detto noticed a smear on the stone under Cesco's grip. Brow furrowing, he reached out to grasp Cesco's arms, twisting the palms towards him. They were covered in blood.

Cesco wrenched his hands free and turned, pressing his back against the headstone, his life spilling from his wrists. "Leave me be!"

Detto scrambled around the stone. "Don't be a foole! Let me help you!"

"Help me see her!" shouted Cesco. "Help me explain!"

Struggling out of his leather farsetto, Detto began ripping at his shirt to make bandages. "She's gone!"

"No! I can still see her! She's innocent, we both are! We're not damned to Hell—"

"There's no such thing as Heaven or Hell!" Holding strips of cloth, Detto reached for the bleeding wounds, but before he could wrap either wrist, Cesco punched him in the mouth. It was a weak blow, and Detto rolled with it, then grabbed a handful of Cesco's hair. With a shout he slammed Cesco's skull into the headstone. Cesco fell sideways atop Lia's grave, blissfully still.

Breath coming in gasps, tears on his cheeks, Detto knelt and began the desperate work to stop the flow of blood. With heartfelt curses, he bound the long gashes on Cesco's wrists. "You don't get to give up, damn you! It's not your choice!" Finished at last, he sagged to the ground, weeping.

A while later he carried his friend's limp form to the gate. He was about to heft Cesco up across the saddle of Mastino's horse when he felt a presence. Turning, he saw Tiberio gazing beadily at him from the shade of a tree. "So he wants to die for her. How poetic. Why didn't you let him?"

Panting, Detto lowered Cesco to the ground. "He's my friend."

"Then, friend, I'll give you one chance to take him from here. Take him, and swear you'll never let him return. If you don't, I'll grant his wish and kill him now."

"I swear," said Detto. "For us both."

Tiberio nodded curtly. "This is a more fitting punishment anyway. Let the little cad live out his days knowing he killed her."

Detto couldn't let his friend go undefended. "He loved her!"

"Yes. And then he left her."

Swallowing back a thousand angry retorts, Detto shook his head and bent down to lift Cesco once more. Suddenly he paused. "The grave said mother. She died in childbed?"

The grizzled hulk of a man seemed to debate answering. "Yes. Tell him that was his only gift to her. Death."

"And the child?"

"Born airless. Now get out of here."

Feeling the weight of every step, Detto obeyed. He secured Cesco over one saddle, then mounted the other horse and led both away at a slow walk, back down the hill.

But not towards Verona.

♦   ◊   ♦

Pietro returned home from the Domus Nova, head low. Asked what had occurred, he shook his head. "He is condemned. A sentence of exile. Some demanded death, but Mastino himself argued for mercy. He swayed them. He'll be installed as Capitano next week."

"You didn't challenge him?"

"In private. He was surprisingly plain-spoken. Yes, it was a bargain twixt him and Cesco. He says he knows Cesco had no hand in the poisoning. He also offered to swear on anything I liked that he had no hand in it. He said that if Cesco had remained, his true parentage would have come out, and accusations of being under the control of foreign powers. Then he told me he didn't need to threaten Cesco. He just offered him escape, and a chance for happiness."

"And Cesco took it," said Morsicato. "I'm almost proud of him. Even if it lands us in the shit."

"What proof do the Anziani have?" asked Antonia.

"All they need," said Pietro. "They called on me to produce this note."

"You should have destroyed it," said Morsicato at once.

"Even if I did, Mastino knew it had been written. I'd have been called to testify to its contents."

"Then lie, dammit!" Pietro shot the doctor a withering look that made Morsicato scowl. "Sometimes your damned ethics are a noose around all our necks."

"I told the council I believed Cesco was acting under duress, and that I did not believe the accusations. Cunningly, Mastino said the same."

"Why not tell them everything?" demanded Antonia.

"Because everything won't save him. He's *not* Cangrande's son. Tharwat and the doctor *have* been feeding him poison to build his immunity. He *did* have an Arab girl for a lover. It all looks so very bad." He looked around. "Where's Detto? His father is looking for him."

"Why?"

Pietro dragged in a long breath. "Bail believes the poisoning story. It's not rational, and he'll come around in time. For the moment, if Detto is with Cesco, he'll be disowned. For real, this time."

"If Cesco returns, how do we counter this?"

"We cannot," said Tharwat. "The man who possesses the field wins the battle."

The doctor slapped his hands together. "Then we have to get him back. If we move fast—" Morsicato stopped in mid-speech as the Moor shook his head.

"Try if you wish. But his path is clear. He goes."

"The parting," said Pietro. "Which just goes to show that these damn charts can be wrong. If he's not coming back, then I'm going after him. There's nothing for me here."

Antonia's voice was soft. "What about Dolce?"

Pietro felt a wrench in his chest at the very idea of leaving his beloved. He had already put his wedding in jeopardy by fleeing Pistoia after having given his word. What he should do is return and throw himself on the mercy of Amidei. Yet he shook his head. "It's Cesco. I have to go after him. I *have* to."

"Do as you like," replied the Moor. "It makes no difference. Everything is written."

"No," said Pietro. "Some things are not in the stars. Some things we write ourselves."

FORTY-FOUR

C ESCO WOKE TO FIND himself in an empty wing of the Scaligeri palace at Rivoli. His head throbbed. His forearms itched. He felt sleepy and weak, and unwillingly alive.

There was an open window, with a wall of red flowers just outside, overflowing the unshuttered sill. He didn't know their name, and didn't care. He heard birdsong, and the rustle of leaves in a breeze, and all the hundreds of sounds that live in the background of a summer's day, unnoticed except in moments of dire stillness.

Detto was sitting beside him. He lifted a cup and poured a little water into Cesco's mouth. "Don't worry. We're safe for a day or two. The servants think you were attacked, and I'm hiding you from your enemies."

But Cesco wasn't interested in lies, in schemes, in plots or puzzles. "You son of a bitch."

"Cesco..."

"I mean that. Your mother was a conniving cunt."

"Cesco, don't. Just don't."

"Don't what, speak the truth?"

"Pick a fight. Not now." Detto drew a breath. "I'm sorry, Cesco. About Lia."

"Go be somebody else's martyr. I don't want you as mine."

They sat for a time in silence. Then Detto pulled a knife from his belt. "I can't stop you. I know it. One way or another, you'll make it happen. So I'm going to give you this, then leave the room."

"But first you're going to talk at me."

"No." From a pouch he withdrew Lia's note, carefully preserved. He laid it carefully on the table beside the bed. "I just want to remind you that she loved you."

Detto laid the dagger atop the note and left the room.

In the bed, Cesco tried the impossible. He tried to forget how to think. Because if he thought one thought, another would follow. Like what a foole he had been. An unmitigated foole. Had he honestly thought he had known suffering, the depths of despair? Had he mistaken reversal for true loss? Had he been so arrogant as to believe he knew the worst of what life could dish him? *O no. There's a bottom below...*

Thinking was better than staring at the letter. The words were seared into his mind, etched in acid, carved in fire. But the temptation to once more see her writing, perhaps even catch a trace of her scent, was too much. Stretching his bandaged arm, he pulled the note from under the dagger, unfolded the paper, and held it to the light:

Francesco, my Odysseus, dearest Castor,

Penelope waited, I could not. But she had hope. I have none.

All is well with me. My husband is a good man I have known my whole life. He will take me, damaged as I am. In many ways he is like my father — or, rather, the man I thought was my father. Which means he is nothing like you. That makes it easier.

I think of you and I think of lilacs. Amongst all the superficial pleasantries of life, lilacs are the sweetly scented words of truth. They are scattered about where most aren't apt to look. Inside the lines of the lilac's poems are three ideas — Love, Life, and Beauty. They aren't easily detected, only easily faked by the charlatans throughout existence. We must sit, surrounded by humanity and nature, until we collect a bouquet of lilacs. To lead us. To secure us.

I heard of your marriage with a joy-filled heart, broken. She will grow, your wife, and you must not hate her when she does. She is your wife, and always will be. I am not, and never could be.

I tell myself I'm writing this because of the attempt to murder the lord of Verona. But that is the excuse, not the cause. Much of what I hear of you frightens me. Lacking me does not mean you must lack purpose. Do not let your brilliant mind be overthrown. You shine brighter than any star. Do not use your light to trick those that would follow you by leading them astray.

We played many tricks together, you and I. Why should not the stars play tricks on us? But you cannot punish the stars. They will win, by virtue of not caring. We care, you and I. That is why we suffer.

I would hate to be the ruin of all you can be. Do not make that my legacy. When I cancel out existence, leave only my heart to explain to God, Fate, and the stars why I will not release what I have felt, regardless of consequence. I felt it, to the smallest atom of my being. I cannot honour it. You can. Be better. Be what you might be, must be. Be your self.

Make me proud, my love. My brother. My life.

Sic ego nec sine te nec tecum vivere possum.
Rosalia / *Penelope* / *Death*

He had forgotten that the note bore the mark of her tears.

Gently, as though it were likely to shatter or crumble, Cesco brought the letter to his heart and closed his eyes.

Then he reached for the knife.

♦   ◊   ♦

In Verona, mistrust and fear were thick in the air. At the Montecchio house, several voices were raised at once.

"I won't believe it!" cried young Romeo. "He's not a traitor!"

"Me either!" chorused his cousin.

"Benvolio, son, be silent." Having come to town for the reading of the will, Benvenito was as stunned as the rest.

"We won't!" shouted Romeo.

Mariotto turned to his wife for help. "Gianozza, will you quiet them! We have some serious business to discuss."

"Can you blame him for being worried?" demanded a fluttery Gianozza. "They've been seen together often – our son is branded as the friend of a traitor!"

Romeo balled up his fists. "Cesco's not a traitor!"

"Perhaps not," said Mariotto to his son. "But this is none of your concern. When you're older, you'll have worries enough. Now, please, take your cousin and go upstairs."

"I want to see Cesco!"

"If we could find him, none of this would be happening. Besides, the streets aren't safe tonight. Please, son – go upstairs."

Romeo left the room, sullenly dragging his feet. Benvolio followed, but Gianozza remained. "Have you heard from Suor Beatrice's brother?"

"After that all-day session in the Domus Nova, he disappeared as well. And that letter he read – I half-believe him when he says it isn't true. But then why did Cesco write it? Why not stay and fight?"

Benvenito said, "There must be something else. Something bad."

"Pietro would never be a part of something dishonest – not knowingly. But if Cesco *did* have a hand in Cangrande's death..."

Gianozza paced nervously. "What will we do? We're so tied to them!"

"The only thing we can do. When the Anziani convenes in two days, we'll support Mastino." The words were bitter in Mari's mouth. Throwing his hands into the air, he cried, "If only he hadn't run!"

◆   ◊   ◆

On the other side of the Piazza dei Signori, a little girl was crying. Giulietta had been promised a holiday in the Capulletto summer castle. She was still mourning the loss of this latest little brother, whom she had loved for the few weeks he'd been in the nursery. To ease her mind, it had been decided that the whole family would go away once Treviso had been won. But just now her father had declared they weren't going.

Giulietta wasn't a child who cried for no reason, for which both her parents and her nurse were grateful. She took the news as stoically as an almost-four year-old could. But it was still a disappointment. It was her birthday in four days, and she had looked forward to a holiday with her family. She wanted to see the fish in the Lago di Garda. Andriolo had promised to teach her how to swim.

When she thought no one was looking, she slipped into her room and climbed up onto her bed, burying her face in her pillows. Not only was she not going to fish, but her best friend Maddelena was leaving the city as well! It was as if everyone was trying to ruin her life!

"Stop crying. It never fixes anything."

Giulietta looked up to see her cousin Thibault frowning at her. Turning her face away and scrubbing her palms over her cheeks, she said, "But it's not fair!"

"Life's not fair. It's flawed and unrelenting."

Giulietta perked up at a new word. "What?"

"Nothing," said Thibault.

"Why aren't we going?" she demanded.

"Your father's scared," said her cousin with a derisive sneer. If he'd been honest with himself, he'd have to admit that the fear was justified. If anyone left the city now, they would be suspected of joining the traitors.

"Papa's not scared of anything," said Giulietta fiercely, hopping down from her bed to punch Thibault on the thigh.

Thibault took her hand and spun her in a circle several times. "He should be scared of me."

"Why? I'm not," said Giulietta, pulling free to hug her cousin. "You're my only brother now."

Thibault patted her awkwardly, thinking of her dead brothers, his uncle's lost heirs. He suspected what had happened to them, and was as frightened as he was pleased.

His thoughts turned to Cesco, exiled and fled forever. He expected to feel – something. He had lived in Cesco's house, after all. Rivals, they had almost become friends. Almost, but not quite. Now Cesco was gone, and Thibault felt himself relieved. Without the Greyhound's heir, he would have no competition worth the name.

♦   ◊   ♦

Across the street from Cesco's house, Signor Benedick of Padua packed up all the belongings he could manage (not all of them strictly speaking his), and donned his plainest clothes. Unlike the nobles he'd been rubbing elbows with all these months, he had neither property nor wealth here in the city. Thus he had nothing to insulate himself against reprisals as one of Cesco's closest adherents. Cesco had named him in the letter, a complete betrayal. With no sign of either Cesco or Detto, there was only one practical course left to him – flight.

Leaving his bill unsettled, he slipped away into the night. Count Alaghieri had offered him a horse. Climbing onto its back, his safe-conduct clutched in his hand, he rode straight for the southeast gate and onto the road to Genoa. As the safe conduct specified, he was going to Sicily. Cesco's last bit of wry humour. But Don Pedro *had* offered him a post, if only in jest.

Benedick was only going because he had to. He was definitely not going to see that termagant Beatrice – though the thought of baiting her again made him quite forget the strife and turmoil he was leaving behind in Verona.

♦ ◊ ♦

Under Antonia's instruction, the nurse Dahna packed up all her mistress' belongings and hired a coach to take them both to Padua. They only encountered resistance when they informed the little lady herself. Maddelena stubbornly refused to leave the house, saying her husband would come for her. She had to be carried to the coach, and on the way she bit two men.

♦ ◊ ♦

The wait seemed to last an eternity. Several times during those tortuous hours Detto stood and made for the door. Each time he stopped just short of it, feet pulling in two directions until he reluctantly returned to his seat.

He was sitting when at last the door opened and Cesco emerged, deathly pale but upright. He gazed malevolently at Detto. "God damn you."

"He already has. He made us friends."

FORTY-FIVE

Pietro rode first to Tiberio's lands. There, under the beetling gaze of the bearded Bramo, he learned of her fate.

Rosalia had been Detto's close cousin. *The third death. This is the third death.*

And Mastino must have known, realized Pietro, astonished at the malice that lived in the world. But there was no time to think of anything but finding Cesco, a task all the more serious now. With Rosalia dead, there was nothing left in this life for Cesco save revenge.

Pietro tried every inn, tavern, and private house in the area. Only when he considered Cesco's bold nature did he think of visiting the palace at Rivole.

It was empty. But Pietro was astonished to learn that Cesco had been here, ill, just the day before. This morning young lord Nogarola had put him on a boat and sailed away down the river. Towards Verona.

♦　◊　♦

In near darkness, Cesco awoke aching. "What did you hit me with at the graveyard? My skull feels shattered."

Detto didn't want to say he'd struck Cesco with Lia's headstone. "I had to calm you down."

They were in a small cabin. From the rocking of the floor, Cesco knew they were on some kind of boat. "Where are we?"

"Sailing down the Adige. We'll reach Verona in a few hours."

Detto saw the expression. "You chose to live."

Cesco took several breaths before looking up, eyes unclouded. "Without her, I can never truly live."

"But you can go on."

"Fine. So what do I do now, oh mighty sage? How do I do it?"

Detto made a fearsome face. "We get off in Verona and kick Mastino in the teeth."

"What day is it?" Detto told him. "Two days? Too late. By now he must have the backing of everyone – yes, everyone. Can you blame them? And he has Carrara, and through him, Padua. Venice, too, will support him. He's much less frightening than I am. If I show my face, Mastino will have me executed, either as a poisoner or an imposter." His voice held no anger, only fatigue.

"You'll think of something. You always do."

Cesco shook his head. "I'm too tired. Can't manage, lost, used up."

"I'll do both our thinking, then." Detto stood and began to pace, thoughts racing. "My father won't help us, not if he thinks you killed Cangrande. He already blames you for my mother's death."

"He's right. I didn't denounce Verde when I suspected her. I thought I was protecting my family. Little did I know."

"Be glad you're not one of us. Do you know who your father was? Pietro could not discover that."

Cesco almost smiled. "Zeus. Though I was wrong. Leda is not my mother, egg-friend. Like Athena, I was born of a thought." The smile faded. "A by-blow of Cangrande's eldest brother. I am close kin to Paride."

Though intrigued, Detto was anxious to keep formulating a plan. "We have your troops. Otto's men. Yuri and Fabio will follow us."

"Will they? Or will they think themselves used, wooed to be my arm. And enough of the men will think I killed the source of their funds and hate me for it."

"We can ask the Bonaventura twins or da Lozzo," said Detto.

"By now the twins will have heard my confession to killing their father. Nico will swear vengeance, too."

"Castelbarco might join us."

"His son is tied to Mastino. That's too much to ask anyone."

"Figs," said Detto. "Ser Alaghieri will never believe you're guilty. He can tell them everything."

"Ser Alaghieri doesn't have a faction. Just an ancient Moor, a broken-down doctor, a half-disgraced novice – and us. Against

Mastino, who holds a united Verona, Padua, Mantua, and Treviso. I marvel we haven't won already."

Detto stopped his pacing to plant his feet in front of Cesco. "So we disappear. We go and never look back. We vanish."

"Evanesce," murmured Cesco. "You'd do that? Leave your family, lands, title — just disappear?"

"Yes."

Cesco nodded absently, his gaze drifting off into the distance. "Mastino will outlaw us both. He can't not — it's too good. We'll never be allowed to return."

Detto tried to grin. "No temptation, then."

Cesco returned a ghost of a smile. Then he closed his eyes as the pain returned. All kinds.

"Where do you want to go?" asked Detto.

"It doesn't matter. You decide."

Detto frowned. "My mother. She gave me a message for you."

"I seem to remember you mentioning it," said Cesco, a little of his natural wryness slipping into his tone.

"She said, 'It is hidden where he kept his other amusing puzzles.' What does that mean? What is hidden there? And where?"

Cesco looked a blank. "I have no idea." He closed his eyes. "It doesn't matter. We won't have a chance to go looking, and I truly don't care. Forgive me, but I am finished with your mother and her riddles. I am finished."

An hour later they opened the cabin's little window to gaze out at the twilight. Passing one by one under Verona's bridges, they saw the walls, the crenellated rooftops, the fabled forty-eight towers. Once the tower had been the symbol of Verona. Before ambition's ladder had taken root.

Detto quelled the impulse to cry out, to rouse the city to action. Instead he sat beside his friend and took a final look at the city they both had called home. What had almost become the capitol of the world, had the stars allowed it.

The people of Verona were uninterested in the stars. They plied their trades and went about their lives, loving their families, greeting their neighbors, embracing the simple pleasures of existence. Never knowing that the man who could have changed their lives was instead slowly sailing away from them.

The bells began to toll the hour of Sext. Cesco watched until the last tower was out of sight, and then looked away, towards their unknown future.

Verona was past.

◆　　◊　　◆

Having seen Maddelena safely on her way, Cesco's last adherents traveled east in a carriage. It wasn't as fast as single horses, but between Pietro's leg, Tharwat's ankles, and Antonia's gender, it was the best they could manage.

They had decided to go first to Vicenza, and from there split their numbers, some to Venice, some to Rome, some to the imperial court, wherever it happened to be at present. The doctor could not stop swearing, stroking his beard for comfort. Poco was more excited than frightened, so he was allowed to ride up top with the driver.

At one point Pietro caught the Moor smiling. "What?"

Over his throaty rasp, Tharwat's voice contained grim humour. "I was just wondering if Cesco ever got around to reversing the spying he did for Dandolo. If not—"

"—Mastino's in for a nasty surprise. Verona is about to be utterly without funds." Pietro couldn't help grinning too.

His smile vanished as he felt the carriage slow. They all gazed about in apprehension. Had Mastino broken his vow? Were they being attacked?

"I don't believe it," said Jacopo from over their heads. "Lamo."

It was indeed Girolamo. Pietro stepped out to find the road blocked by the cripple, leaning on a stick. No need to ask how he had found them. But the why mattered.

"The deaths have all occurred," said the cripple through his near-impenetrable accent.

Taking the lead of the interview, Tharwat was glacial. "And with the lady Katerina dead, you are in no more danger."

Girolamo shook his head. "I understand what you meant. About taking an active part. I should have. But I was afraid."

"Conscience makes cowards of us all," said the Moor.

They conferred. No one particularly wanted to add this bunch-backed diviner to their midst. But he had saved Detto's life once. And, more importantly, they needed his skill. Accepting him into their party, they immediately demanded that he produce his map and the stone teardrop, to ply his art. The answer was surprising. They immediately changed their course towards Venice.

The city where anything could be forgiven, if it was done for love.

◆　　◊　　◆

As Cesco had predicted, support for his faction evaporated on the wind. The nobles of the city acted swiftly to assure their positions. The Anziani – including Castelbarco, Montecchio, Capulletto, Lozzo, Ervari – all did the prudent thing and swore allegiance to the new heir apparent. Antonio da Nogarola appeared in the city to kneel before the Mastiff, pledging himself and his brother, who was absent for obvious reasons. Mastino accepted the oath graciously, with understanding and forgiveness in his voice and face. Of Cesco, Mastino made no comment.

The general consensus was that, having reached manhood and not in accord with his father, Cesco had resorted to patricide. Some whispers said it was over a girl, some over money, some over power. The Abbot of San Zeno was righteous in his vindication, loudly declaiming about pacts with Satan and plans with the infidel. No one was told the truth of Cesco's parentage. There was no need to complicate the story.

Mastino was made but joint-captain with his brother. But everyone knew that Alberto's appointment was for show. Mastino held the reins.

As they saw Alberto and Mastino invested, marveling at the past week, the people decided this was for the best. Prince Cesco had been too wild. No telling how far he would go. They had never trusted him anyway. Wasn't Mastino more stable? And handsome, too. Yes, he was a far more fit Capitano than that unpredictable young scoundrel.

The Greyhound was dead.

Long live the Mastiff.

◆   ◊   ◆

Arriving long after decent men had taken to their beds, Pietro ignored propriety and leapt into a gondola, ordering the driver to take him to the Rialto. Poco joined him, and after alighting they made their way through the streets to the Yellow Crescent. Hammering upon the door Tharwat had described, he made enough noise to be certain it opened at once. Ordering the servant to fetch his master, Pietro saw the man already approaching. Without preamble he said, "Have you seen a young man? Thin, brown hair, green eyes – have you seen him?"

Tubal regarded Pietro by the light of the taper. "I have. I'm afraid I did not have as much money as he requested. My resources aren't enough to cover all of poor Shalakh's debts at once. But I was able to give him enough for his voyage."

Pietro's heart skipped a beat. "Voyage?"

"Yes. He said he was taking a trip. For his health. I cannot blame him. He didn't look at all well. He said he would be sought, and left this for whomever came looking."

Tubal placed something in Pietro's hand. It was a letter. Breaking the seal, Pietro read it over. Finished, he lowered the letter to his side. "One more question, then I'll stop imposing on your hospitality. When did he leave?"

♦ ◊ ♦

By the time Pietro returned to the Rialto, the others had gathered. Antonia took a step in his direction, saying, "What's...?"

"Girolamo was correct. We missed him, but only just! If we hurry, we might catch him at the docks!"

Commandeering a gondola, they traveled to where the larger ships were putting out into the Mediterranean. Pietro had promised the driver a princely sum if they arrived in time.

Antonia huddled low in the gondola, wrapped in a shawl against the chill wet air of the night. In the light of a passing lamp she glimpsed something held tight in Pietro's hand. "What's that?"

"Cesco's valediction." He handed it over. She had to wait until they were near enough another lamp to make out the hand she knew so well:

> Dante was wrong. Love cannot move the stars. They move on their own, beating us cruelly before them like the whipped curs we are.
>
> But I defy them. I am not theirs to rule. I refuse my fate. I resign. I withdraw. If I do not trouble them, perhaps they will leave me be. Cosa fatta capo ha.

What's done is done.

The rest was an answer to the final lines of *Paradiso*:

Ma già volgeva il mio disio e 'l velle,	*Now my will and my desire, like wheels revolving*
si come rota ch'igualmente è mossa,	*with an even motion, were turning with*
l'amor che move il sole e l'altre stelle.	*the Love that moves the sun and all the other stars.*

Cesco himself had chosen those words to end the epic. It would have been ironic, had it not been tragic.

Though the gondola driver strained his pole, they reached the dock too late. Upon inquiring, an obliging seaman with an itching palm pointed to a ship just disappearing. Girolamo had his pendulum out, and it almost tore itself from his finger as it swung again and again in that ship's direction.

The sun was just rising behind Pietro and he had to strain his eyes into the darkness before him to see the triple sail. Try as he might, he could find no hirable ship capable of catching it, and without knowing its destination, the ship was impossible to track. Even the pendulum could not predict its course. For the ship was heading into an uncharted sea. It had no foreknowledge.

It only followed the stars.

Epilogue

The captain approached the young knight standing by the taffrail, watching the water slide by. "Your friend, he is below," he said, tugging his forelock. Gold made him uncommonly deferential. "He's unwell."

"He's never been properly to sea." Though wan from some recent illness, the knight showed no sign of sea-sickness. "Neither have I, for that matter. It's – remarkable."

"You bear it well." Long hair streaming across his face, the young knight made no reply. "Have you decided on a destination, master?"

"Wherever we can lose ourselves. What's your favourite port?"

"Brindisi," was the captain's ready answer. "Crusaders and pilgrims use it as their portal to the East. It's a short trip to Greece, or you can go down to Africa, or around to Spain. All the world is open in Brindisi," he finished, repeating a common claim.

"As you please. Just see that the men are recompensed for their trouble."

"I will, master, and they will pray for you. What name should I give them?"

The knight shook his head. "No name."

The captain strode off, leaving the young knight leaning on the rail, eyes upon the water. For once his mind was locked. He was unable to see possibilities, only the doors closed on his past – a past he now saw had been nothing but lies. He carried nothing, owed no one, served no one. Only his body and his brain were left to him. Not even a name. No possessions, no family – just Detto, faithful Detto. *A far better man than I am.*

That doesn't answer the question. Where am I going? How do I survive?

His words to Benedick floated back to him. *It is a wide world. A witty man with a quick blade can always find amusing employment. Even one without a name.*

Unasked, a poem, penned anonymously, flitted through his mind:

I will go, but not in exile.
In your guise you will accompany me so I feel safe,
Hoping to go and return whole.
I am certain to not go badly,
But in many places I will be stopped:
I will pray for those who have prayed for me,
Until I arrive at the Fountain of Learning, your sovereign Lady.
I don't know if I'll be gone a week or a month
Or if my path shall be contested:
I will go for your pleasure near and far;
But I would love to already be there
Because I would commend you to Love...

Damn poetry. Damn it to Hell.

Thoughts of Hell naturally led to Dante. On the subject of exile, the master poet had once written, *'In whatever corner of the world I find myself, can I not look at the sun and the stars?'*

A cool tapping on his chest reminded him that he was not entirely without possessions. In addition to the sword at his hip, he wore the silver coin on the thong about his throat. Reaching for it, he began rubbing the worn Roman disc between finger and thumb.

No name? Nay. That's not so.

Slowly, his lips curved into a lop-sided smile as they formed the single word.

"Mercutio."

FIN

Afterword

Historical Apologies and Addendums

At long last, the moment of crisis. Cangrande is dead. There is a new Prince of Verona. Our hero has fled Italy, taking a new name as he steps onto a wider, wilder stage.

Like him, we are finally departing Verona's walls. As I mentioned in the notes of FORTUNE'S FOOL, this volume is the conclusion to a story I started writing 12 years ago, part three in a single narrative of Cesco's life in Verona. To me, VOICE OF THE FALCONER, FORTUNE'S FOOL, and THE PRINCE'S DOOM are all one book, simply titled IL FALCO. (THE MASTER OF VERONA is mentally dubbed IL VELTRO. To me, these novels have Italian animal names). The original version started with the fake death of Cangrande, and ended with his actual death. There is something very appealing to that structure. Hence my statement that these three novels are one story, told in installments. On their own, they're rollicking good tales. Together, they are something more. It isn't just the rise of Mercutio. It's the fall of Cangrande. So much promise, cut off. Imagine if Julius Caesar had never reached 40. No Gallic war, no Civil war, no Pharsalus, no Cleopatra, no Ides of March, no Augustus, no Empire. That's what, to me, the death of Cangrande was — the cutting off of possibility. A tragedy that changed the course of history.

But then, the same can be said of every living being cut off in their prime. And as this is a tale inspired by Shakespeare's play wherein an entire generation of Verona's youth is cut down, it seems a fitting theme to explore.

◆　◊　◆

These major sources are worth citing again: A.M. Allen's A HISTORY OF VERONA; PADUA UNDER THE CARRARA by Benjamin J. Kohl; Emanuele Carli's DANTE E GLI ALLIGHIERI A VERONA; GLI SCALIGERI, edited by Arnaldo Mondadori; DANTE:

THE POET, THE POLITICAL THINKER, THE MAN by Barbara Reynolds; Frances Stonor Saunders' THE DEVIL'S BROKER. As always, the Dante verses come from the translation by Bob and Jean Hollander.

I was blessed to be gifted with even more books from my Veronese friends, including IL LATINO DEI PRIMI SECOLI E L'ETRUSCO by Giovanni Rapelli, L'IPOGEO DI SANTA MARIA IN STELLE by Luigi Antolini, and IL CORPO DEL PRINCIPE, edited by Ettore Napione.

The Friar's history is borrowed from THE YELLOW CROSS by René Weis. Verona's roots in Etruscan culture I got from talking to Giovanni Rapelli, whose book IL LATINO DEI PRIMI SECOLI E L'ETRUSCO is now well-thumbed by me.

I have used a couple dirty poems directly from the translation of THE FABLIAUX by Nathaniel E. Dubin. The Catullus I cobbled together from other translations, and for the other Latin I nod my head to Professor John Lobur.

Most of my songs are Shakespearean, not Italian, taken from SHAKESPEARE'S SONGBOOK by Ross W. Duffin. Yet the song Manuel sings for Pietro at the wedding feast is clearly Italian, but of unknown origin. Thus I am more than happy to attribute it to Manuello Giudeo, already famous for his song about Verona, to say nothing of his own love poems. Though I do, in fact, give the lyrics to Cangrande himself, as a gesture of genuine affection for a much-wronged knight.

It is also my own gesture to the man who should have been so much more, had he not been saddled with expectations of mythic proportions. Cangrande is a man much maligned by me – countless Veronese are dismayed by my portrayal of him. I can honestly say it came from a place of too much admiration – I found myself in awe of him, and decided to give him feet of clay. If my readers find his end is as tragic as it is ignominious, I will consider myself successful.

◆   ◇   ◆

Lots of short notes:

- The tale of Veronese soldiers aiding the rebellion of William Wallace is a fiction, but a not-impossible one. There are certainly examples of English soldiers working as mercenaries in Italy (John Hawkwood being the most famous). So why not the reverse?

- There is in fact such a thing as an Italian-Scots, though their emigration is far more recent than 1300. Most Scots of Italian-descent arrived in the 19th century, escaping a famine in their home-land.

— Goose pulls were, alas, real, practiced all the way up through the 19th Century. Appalling, I know. But the job of the historical fiction writer is not to impose modern values upon their subjects. Animal rights awareness is a *very* recent sea-change. For hundreds, nay, thousands of years, animal sports were considered great enter-tainment. The persistence of dog-fighting and cock-fighting today says that humanity has still not entirely transcended this particular barbarity. And for young men in a time before Playstations, testing one's prowess against nature was a valued part of entering manhood.

Just as I am adamant about not putting blatant modern values in historical figures' heads, I am certain there were men and women who abhorred such practices. I give those feelings to Antonia, and to Detto, who of course has an affinity for animals.

— A note about Pietro d'Abano, the late 13th Century doctor and philosopher who studied blood-loss. Morsicato is technically incorrect, he wasn't executed by the Inquisition. He died while he was on trial. But he was convicted posthumously, unearthed, and his corpse was burned. So in essence, rather than strict fact, Morsicato got it right.

— The ship called *La Alisceote* was quite real. There's a record of it sailing into Dartmouth in 1315 and 1316. Since there were no records for the year 1314, I have appropriated it, deciding that the 1315 date was its return from a voyage to Italy.

— Benjamin Montagu is a fictional character, though his brother breathed the true air. And there is a real Ben Montague living today, a gifted actor, writer, film-maker, musician, and friend. Ben, Breon Bliss, my wife Jan and I were the co-founders of A Crew Of Patches Theatre Company, a repertory Shakespeare troupe in Chicago. We all acted, directed, and produced, and I have no idea how many times we've performed together. The character of Benjamin is very much based on the real Ben, right down to those cute little ears. You'll see him again someday, where I hope to give him more to do. But of all people, Ben would understand being a plot-point.

— Scott Aiello is real as well. Now a Julliard acting grad and Audible star, when I met him he was part of the same circle of actors doing Shakespeare for little money and less respect, and he was the most cheerfully belligerent, scenery-chewing fellow in the bunch. I cast him as Friar Lawrence, as Peter Quince, and as Mark Antony, and while the performances were great, the stories that came out of those rehearsals were even greater. He and Ben are friends, and it was a delight to pit them against each other, if only for my own amusement.

   - Yet another friend, Brian Amidei, is descended from the Amidei mentioned in *Paradiso*. So I decided to toss in a mention, with an eye towards both the past and the future.

   - The by-now-obligatory Shakespearean anagrams are here, though I've changed it up a little. One is for William Shakespeare, but the other now belongs to the feuding families. Happy hunting.

♦   ◊   ♦

When I started this series, I could not find a death-date for Katerina della Scala. I've found it since — it was around 1305, long before my story began. Records say that in 1306, Bailardino da Nogarola married the Countess da Fogliano, sister to the woman who would marry Cangrande's brother, Alboino, and aunt to Mastino, Alberto, Verde, and the rest.

Had I been armed with this information at the outset, doubtless I would have changed my story. But Katerina is so much at the heart of the tale, I cannot regret keeping her alive. So I have doubled-down on the choice I made then — I have given Bail's wife to his brother Alberto. That keeps the Countess in the family, though only as a minor player, and allows us to hold on to dear Katerina until 1329, when it seems her world was coming to an end.

That is hardly my only historical inaccuracy. With Don Laurito, I am anticipating history by about 150 years. In the late 15th century, Naples came under the influence of the kingdom of Aragon, which led Shakespeare to address Proteus' father as Don rather than Signor — anyone from Naples was called Don, because of the heavy Spanish influence. Of course, in the 1320s there was no direct bond between Aragon and Napoli, just the regular links of trade. But to lay the groundwork for *Two Gentlemen Of Verona* portion of the tale, I bring them all together.

Had Shakespeare given Proteus' sire a name other than Antonio, I would not have needed to twist myself into this tortuous knot. Nor, had I been thinking fourteen years ago, would I have given that name to Lord Capulet. As one of Shakespeare's favourite go-to names, there are far too many Antonios in his plays to keep track of — *2 Gents* (Proteus' father), *Twelfth Night* (Antonio the pirate), *Merchant of Venice* (the titular merchant), *Shrew* (Petruchio's late father), *All's Well* (the Duke's eldest son, mentioned in passing), and *Tempest* (Prospero's usurping brother). And that's without invoking Mark Antony, who has two plays. Given the chance to give Lord

Capulet a first name, what on earth possessed me to use that one? (It was actually a nod to Luigi da Porto, who wrote the first story with lovers named Romeo and Giulietta. He gave the girl's father the name Antonio). Four novels on, I am thoroughly stuck with it, and so must do whatever I can to differentiate one Antonio from another. Hence Don Laurito, when it should be Don Antonio.

By the bye, it is worth noting that, while I touch on many of Shakespeare's Italian plays, it has never been my intention to retell them. That will change when we reach the ultimate volume in this series, but thus far I am wary of attempting to recreate Shakespeare's plots. However, I take great delight in linking certain scenes from the plays to these books. In MoV, it was the tailor scene from Shrew. In FALCONER, we get a retelling of Borachio's ill-fated love affair – one that he will someday duplicate to cause a rift between the lovers Claudio and Hero the night before their wedding. In FOOL, I presented the first Antonio/Shylock scene, and it was the hunt for Shylock's wayward daughter that saved Cesco's life.

Here we have the trial scene from *The Merchant Of Venice,* something I never meant to write. It just happened, with the sidebar of Pietro's interview with Antonio (Antonio the Merchant, not Antonio Capulletto! Argh!) the night before the trial. I was so inspired watching Mike Nussbaum's breakdown as Shylock, I had to play out the consequences of that terrible verdict.

Here too we have the first meeting between Beatrice and Benedick, perhaps my favourite of Shakespeare's couples. Her line in *Much Ado* is 'I know you of old.' There is far too much life in those five words to leave them alone. And the chance to have a discussion between *Shrew's* Kate and *Much Ado's* Beatrice was just too tempting to resist.

There is one thing I would do over, if I could go back and tweak all of my books. Benedick would be named Benedetto, just to be a little less ham-fisted about things. But alas, while I changed many names in MoV, I started with Benedick there, so he remains proudly Benedick here.

Speaking of *Much Ado*, there is a lengthy section in here dealing with Don Pedro's courting of Portia from *Merchant*. Like most people, I'm intrigued by Don Pedro's backward proposal to Beatrice in *Much Ado*: "Will you have me, lady?" And at the end, Benedick's mocking: "You are sad, Prince. Get thee a wife. Get thee a wife!" Since Shakespeare had used the Prince of Aragon as one of the suitors for Portia in *Merchant*, the chance to tie the bit with the caskets to his reluctance/unwillingness to marry was irresistible. He took an oath! Because, seriously, why isn't Don Pedro married? He's pretty great (except that part where he denounces Hero on her wedding day. That was pretty shameful – yet ties nicely into the pride he shows in the scene with Portia. He's clearly grown up a great deal in the interim, but not enough).

The cumulative effect is an awful lot of Shakespeare. This novel has more of his characters running around than ever before. I can only say that this volume was intended to bring together all the threads I had tugged before, weaving them to one ultimate moment. Verona was poised to take over the world, and it's important that all of Will's Italian characters be there to witness its fall.

♦   ◊   ♦

Speaking of falls...

As most of my readers know, I met my wife playing Petruchio to her Kate, lo these many years ago. There is a sequel play by John Fletcher called *The Tamer Tamed*, which starts with Kate dead and Petruchio remarrying a woman named Maria. Seemingly mild until the wedding, Maria vows not to have sex with her new husband until she can *'turn him and bend him as I list, and mold him into a babe again.'*

The hell with that. Dismissing Kate is unthinkable. Perhaps personal reasons make me overfond, but Kate and Petruchio have ever been my ideal couple for this series. I've given them four children and a happy life together. We know from *R&J* that they had a son, as the Nurse points to "young Petruchio" at the Capulet ball (at that same party Capulet mentions Lucentio's wedding, we know it can't be Petruchio himself).

Petruchio is the quintessential Veronese – witty, loud, brave, eager, brash, devoted, humourous, and loyal. There was no greater signal I could give that Verona is falling than to remove Petruchio from the stage. Happiness is gone. Joy tempered with grief was one of Shakespeare's best devices, and I've stolen it here.

After I wrote his death, the community I am blessed to be a part of lost someone precious. Stolen from us far too early, Molly Glynn was a soul so large and giving that none of us can imagine her being gone. In October of 2014 we gathered to mourn her. While the outpouring of grief that night inspired the memorial scene in this book, I could never adequately capture what happened. Those who were there will understand. Love hard, people.

♦   ◊   ♦

Love...

When I was sixteen, I fell in love for the first time. I had dated before, but this was like being trampled by a horse while drinking nitroglycerin. She filled my mind and my heart, my days and my nights. My first love, in all the ways that matter. If she is not the basis for Lia, she is certainly the model for how Cesco feels for her.

Then, after a wild two months, it was over. She went back to her boyfriend before me, a poet. I have hated poets ever since.

I missed being in love, missed it so much that when a very nice young woman showed interest in me, I took all that feeling and heaped it on her unsuspecting head. A few weeks later, I realized I was not actually in love again, just desperate to be. So I did the worst thing possible and jumped out of that relationship just as fast as I'd jumped into it, without any explanation at all. That poor young lady never knew what hit her, or why. Even worse, I was still chasing love, so she saw me flirting and romancing others.

By the time I was collected enough to explain my actions, almost a year later, it was far too late. Of all the people in my life who have wished me ill, that woman was among the fiercest, and had the most cause. And while again she is in no way the basis for Buthayna, Cesco's actions in regard to her are. While railing against love, Cesco has fallen into Gianozza's trap, the one that will ensnare Romeo in years to come. He's in love with Love. The only cure for which is actually falling in love.

As for the fate of Rosalia, a character I love nearly as much as Cesco does, alas, her destiny was clear to me when I was 17 years old and playing Mercutio for the first time. Performing the Queen Mab speech, with Shakespeare's words in my mouth, it was painfully clear to me that, more than talk of war or sex, it is the thought of childbirth that brings Mercutio to his most fevered pitch, his most lost and violent state. When talking of Queen Mab, he says, *"This is the hag, that when maids lie upon their backs, presses them and learns them first to bear, making them women of good carriage. This is she that—"* Romeo has to cut him off, crying, *"Peace, Mercutio, peace. Thou talkst of nothing."*

It's Mercutio's next lines that are his most heartfelt: *"True. I talk of dreams, which are the children of an idle brain, begot of nothing but vain fantasy."* There was a moment, once, when he'd dared to dream. But then the woman was brought to childbed, and the dream died. Rosalia was doomed years before I first set word to page.

And now? Cesco leaves Verona's Arena for an even grander stage. Where is he headed? England? Arabia? Spain? Germany? While

his choices are as boundless as the sea, there's a hint in the title of
the next book. And as for what he's leaving behind, there are several
clues written in the play itself, waiting to reveal themselves to eagle-
eyed readers and open-eared theatre-goers.

It's not just Cesco leaving Verona. It's me as well. After 15
years of living with a single place in my head, I'm off to explore the
world outside Verona's walls. For me, it's a chance to research new
places, introduce new faces, and bring Cesco through the experiences of a changing world – and give him the opportunity to change
it even more.

Cesco is Cesco no more. He is Mercutio. But he is also the
Greyhound. What is his greatest deed? What happens three days
before his stabbing in a street-brawl that will usher in a new age of
Man? The play begins on a Sunday, he's stabbed on a Monday. What
did Mercutio do on Friday? It will take both Shakespeare and history
to answer.

But all that is still far off. There remain untold adventures,
dreadful triumphs, and wonderful disasters – though I hope nothing
as dark as this book until the final volume, when he must return to
play out his destiny. Until then, anything is possible.

Anything but love.

♦   ◊   ♦

Like my cast, the number of people I need to thank has grown
with each succeeding novel. Unlike my cast, I am not trying to bump
any of them off.

First and foremost among them is my friend Anna Lerario,
Veronese film-maker and soul of creativity and perseverance. Along
with her husband Antonio Bulbarelli, Anna contacted me in 2013,
having just completed her documentary about Cangrande. Wisely,
she had refrained from reading my work until after her film was
complete. But once she did read THE MASTER OF VERONA, she
reached out to ask if she could use the title for the English language
version of her film. Seeing the film, I agreed at once. I did a little
work on the English translation for the film, and she reciprocated
by making a book trailer from the footage of her Veronese films.
Suddenly we were thick as thieves, releasing a joint book/dvd edition
of our works.

Then Anna contacted Gianni La Corte at *La Corte Editore*,
asking on my behalf if he'd be interested in publishing an Italian
version of MoV. Gianni was enthusiastic from the start, and turned
it around in record time. At the same time, Anna arranged for the

city of Verona to pay my passage, so for the first time since my son was born Jan and I headed to Verona to see old friends and make new ones as we promoted the Italian release of my first novel. It was a dream come true.

Through Anna and Antonio I met dignitaries and scholars, like the real Giovanni Rapelli, who went with us on our tour of Santa Maria in Stelle, curated by the charming Luigi Antolini. I met the cook Gioco, as well as the very real Yuri and Fabio – Yuri actually played Cangrande in Anna's film, so it was fun for me to put him into this book as one of Cesco's Rakehells. Certainly our nights out in Verona were memorable – or would be, if I hadn't drunk so deeply.

Through Anna I also met Joyce Stewart, an American journalist and ex-pat living in the best apartment I have ever seen, a stone's throw from the Arena. We were lucky enough to be welcomed into her home for most of our stay.

The exception was our night at *La Foresteria*, the apartments on the estate of the Serego-Alighieri family – an estate bought by Pietro in 1353. After a gap of twelve years, Jan and I were again able to interview the Count, this time for pleasure, not work. He told us marvelous stories of his father, and I was able to give him copies of all the novels I had written about his ancestor, including the newly-published Italian version of THE MASTER OF VERONA, rechristened IL CAVALIERE DELLA PROFEZIA DI DANTE.

Other Veronese friends remain constant: Marina Bonomi, Antonella Leonardo, Rita Severi, and David Osborne. Closer to home, I have to thank Tara Sullivan, Rick Sordelet, my parents Al & Jill Blixt, Sharon Kay Penman, C.W. Gortner, M.J. Rose, Constance Cedras, Judith Testa, Alexandra LaCombe, Michael Denneny, and the redoubtable Joe Foust, the bravest man I know.

Between the MSF company and the Patches, theatre continues to feed my soul, while giving me an endless supply of inside jokes. Truth is truth. In the face.

My children inspire me, and bits of them have snuck into this book. Dash, Evie, forgive me.

As ever, I could not have done this without my loving wife, Janice Lee. I have forgotten all their names, because they are not you.

The next novel is entitled *Captive Colours*.

Ave,
DB

MORE DAVID BLIXT
FROM SORDELET INK

The Star-Cross'd Series
THE MASTER OF VERONA
VOICE OF THE FALCONER
FORTUNE'S FOOL
THE PRINCE'S DOOM
VARNISH'D FACES & OTHER SHORT STORIES

The Colossus Series
COLOSSUS: STONE & STEEL
COLOSSUS: THE FOUR EMPERORS
and coming 2016
COLOSSUS: WAIL OF THE FALLEN

HER MAJESTY'S WILL
a novel of Wit & Kit

EVE OF IDES
a play of Caesar & Brutus

Visit
WWW.DAVIDBLIXT.COM
for more information